THE CROSSROADS AT MIDNIGHT

ABBY HOWARD

THE CROSSROADS AT MIDNIGHT

ABBY HOWARD

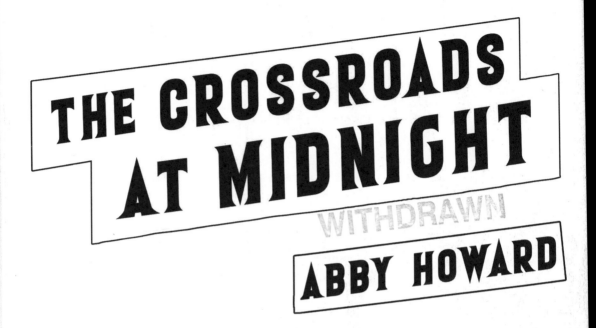

IRON
CIRCUS
COMICS

strange and amazing

inquiry@ironcircus.com   www.ironcircus.com

WRITER & ARTIST
Abby Howard

PUBLISHER
C. Spike Trotman

EDITORS
Kel McDonald & Andrea Purcell

ART DIRECTOR & COVER DESIGN
Matt Sheridan

BOOK DESIGN & PRINT TECHNICIAN
Beth Scorzato

PROOFREADER
Abby Lehrke

PUBLISHED BY
Iron Circus Comics
329 West 18th Street, Suite 604
Chicago, IL 60616
ironcircus.com

FIRST EDITION: October 2020

ISBN: 978-1-945820-68-7

10 9 8 7 6 5 4 3 2 1

Printed in China

THE CROSSROADS AT MIDNIGHT

Publisher's Cataloging-In-Publication Data
(Prepared by The Donohue Group, Inc.)

Names: Howard, Abby (Comic artist), author, illustrator.
Title: The crossroads at midnight / by Abby Howard.
Description: First Edition. | Chicago, IL : Iron Circus Comics, 2020. | Summary: "In this collection of literary slice-of-life horror, five stories explore what happens when one is desperate enough to seek solace and connection in the world of monsters and darkness"– Provided by publisher.
Identifiers: ISBN 9781945820687
Subjects: LCSH: Monsters–Comic books, strips, etc. | CYAC: Monsters–Fiction. | LCGFT: Graphic novels. | Horror comic books, strips, etc. | Horror comics.
Classification: LCC PZ7.7.H73 Cr 2020 | DDC 741.5973 [Fic]–dc23

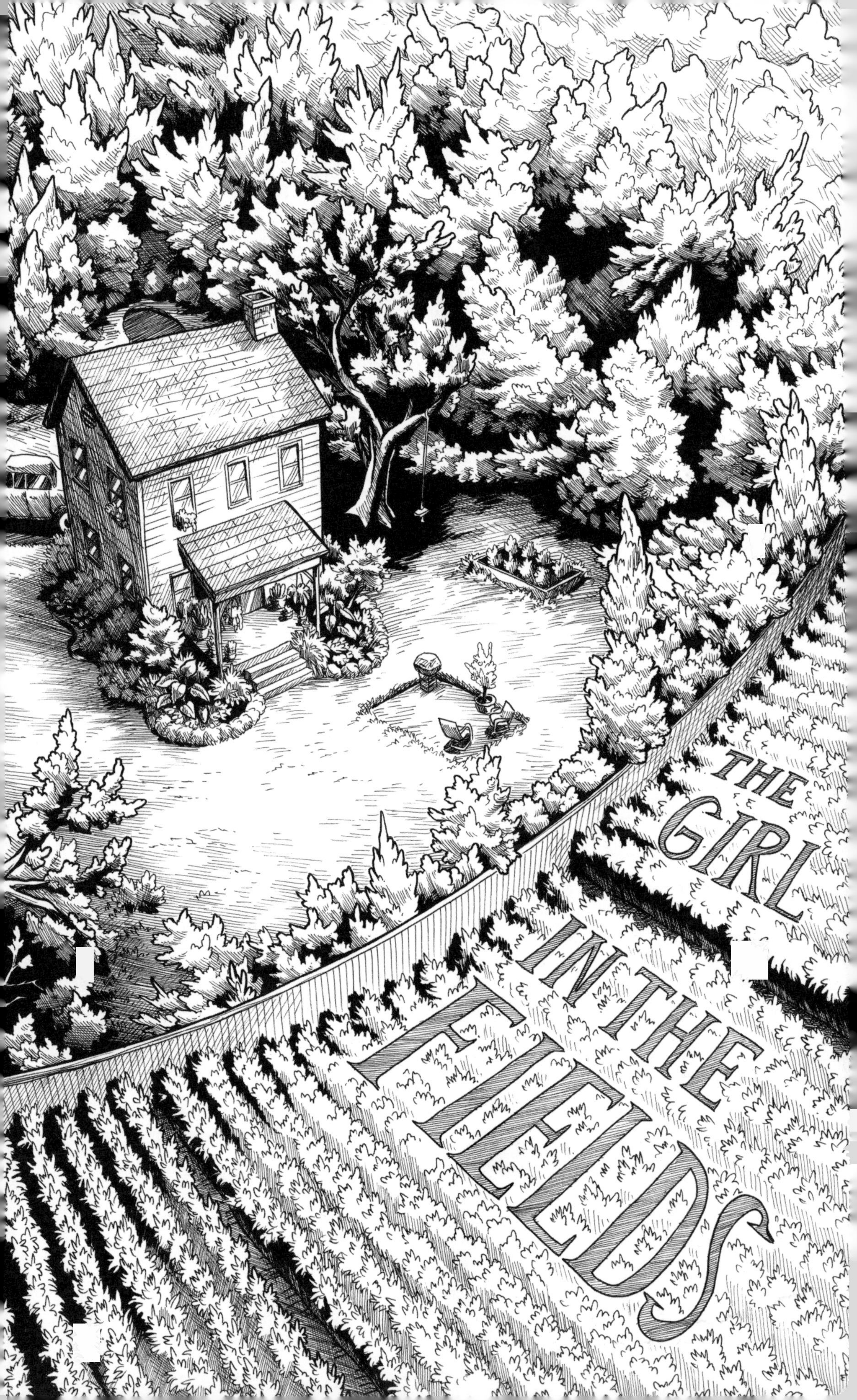
THE GIRL
IN THE
FIELDS

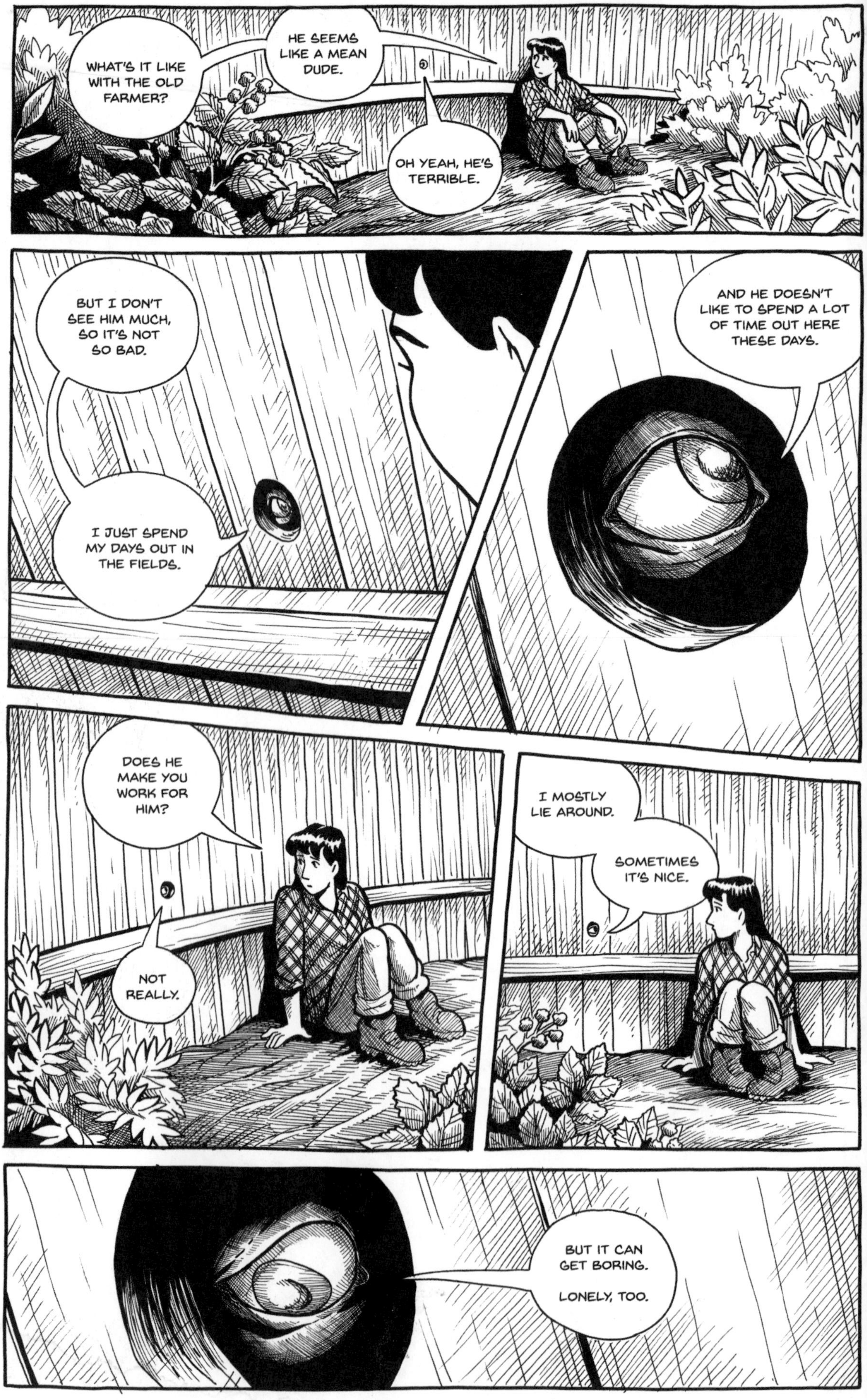
WHAT'S IT LIKE WITH THE OLD FARMER?
HE SEEMS LIKE A MEAN DUDE.
OH YEAH, HE'S TERRIBLE.
BUT I DON'T SEE HIM MUCH, SO IT'S NOT SO BAD.
I JUST SPEND MY DAYS OUT IN THE FIELDS.
AND HE DOESN'T LIKE TO SPEND A LOT OF TIME OUT HERE THESE DAYS.
DOES HE MAKE YOU WORK FOR HIM?
NOT REALLY.
I MOSTLY LIE AROUND.
SOMETIMES IT'S NICE.
BUT IT CAN GET BORING.
LONELY, TOO.

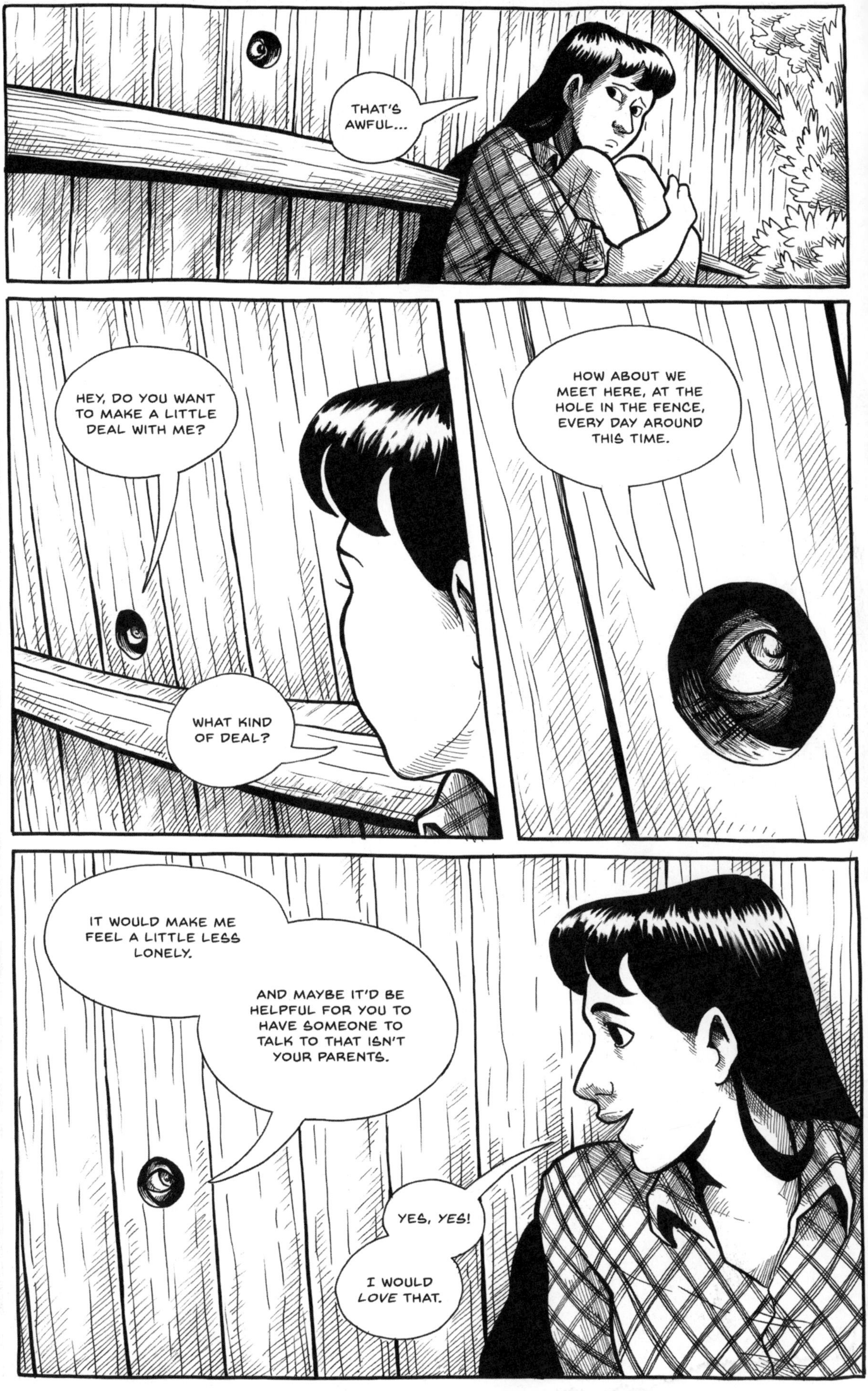
THAT'S AWFUL...
HEY, DO YOU WANT TO MAKE A LITTLE DEAL WITH ME?
WHAT KIND OF DEAL?
HOW ABOUT WE MEET HERE, AT THE HOLE IN THE FENCE, EVERY DAY AROUND THIS TIME.
IT WOULD MAKE ME FEEL A LITTLE LESS LONELY.
AND MAYBE IT'D BE HELPFUL FOR YOU TO HAVE SOMEONE TO TALK TO THAT ISN'T YOUR PARENTS.
YES, *YES!*
I WOULD *LOVE* THAT.

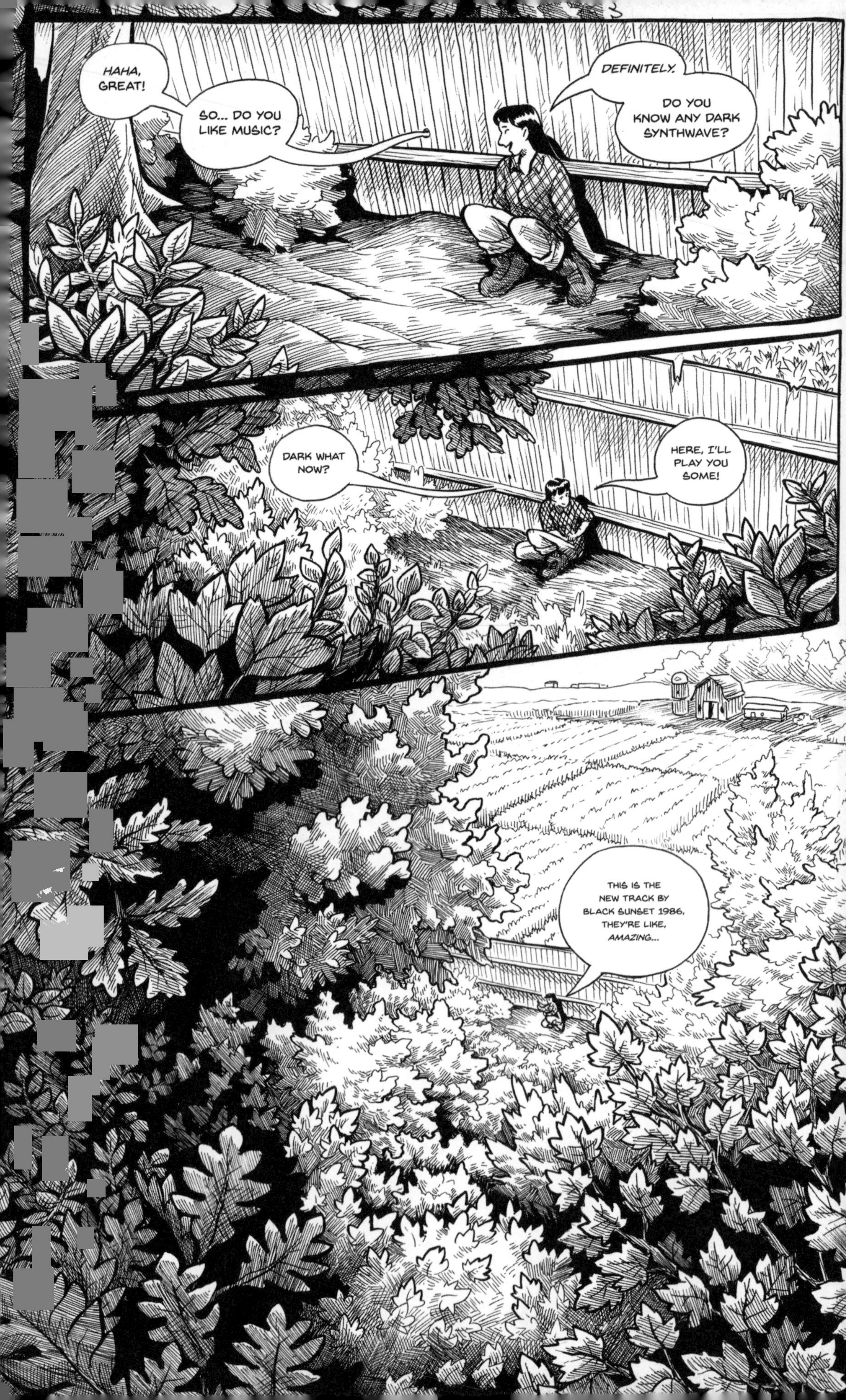
HAHA, GREAT!
SO... DO YOU LIKE MUSIC?
DEFINITELY.
DO YOU KNOW ANY DARK SYNTHWAVE?
DARK WHAT NOW?
HERE, I'LL PLAY YOU SOME!
THIS IS THE NEW TRACK BY BLACK SUNSET 1986, THEY'RE LIKE, AMAZING...

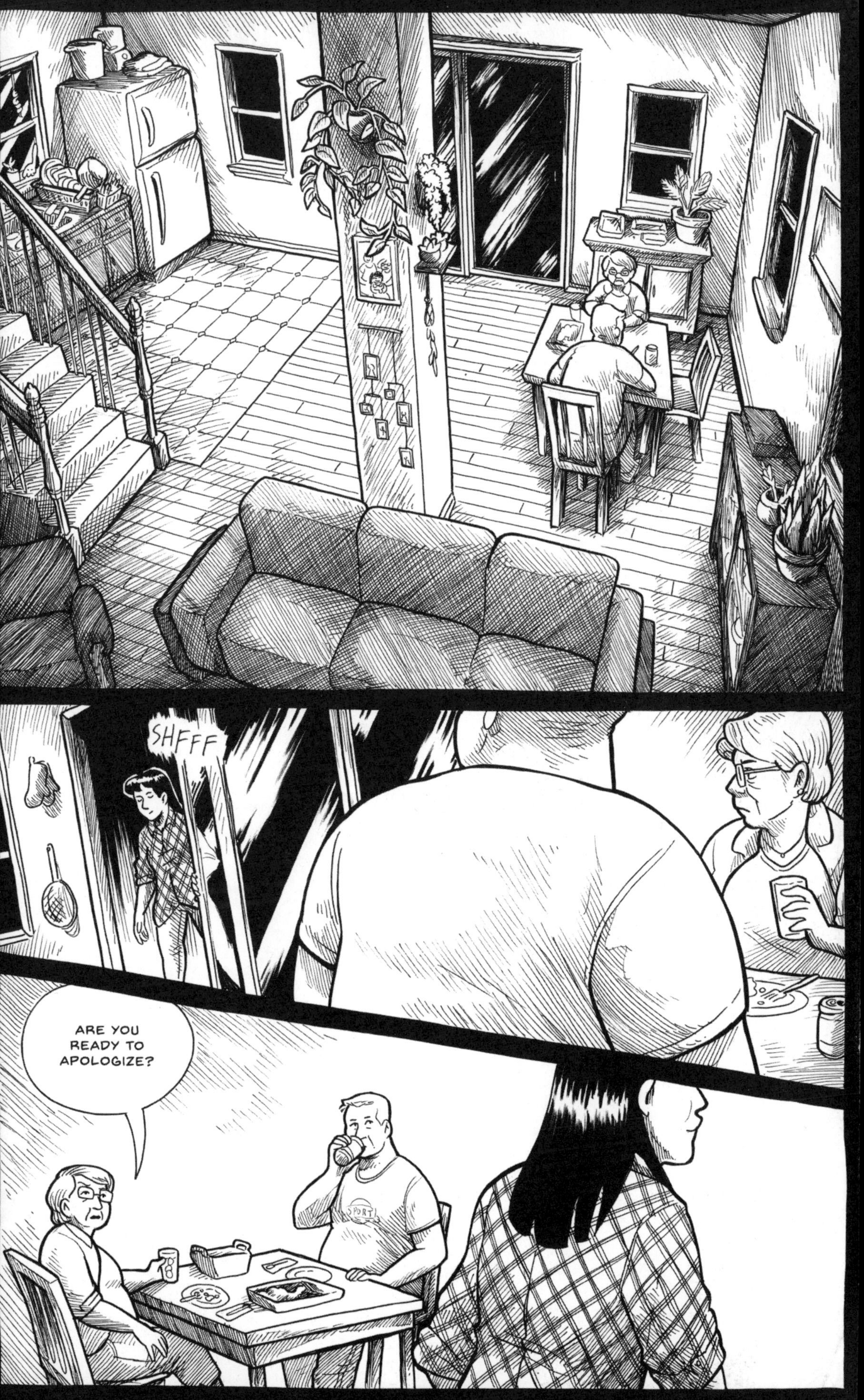
SHFFF
ARE YOU READY TO APOLOGIZE?
SPORT

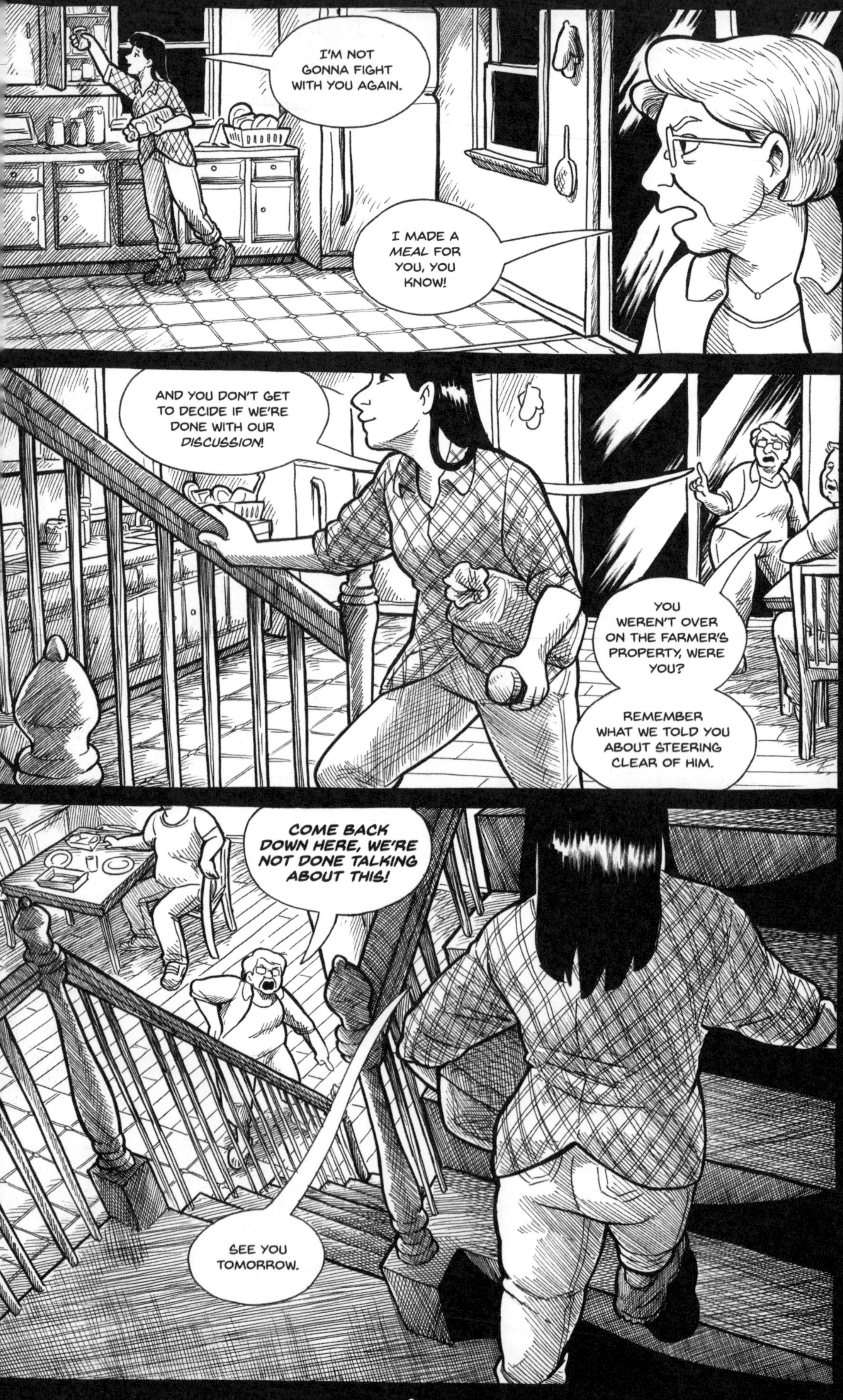
I'M NOT GONNA FIGHT WITH YOU AGAIN.
I MADE A *MEAL* FOR YOU, YOU KNOW!
AND YOU DON'T GET TO DECIDE IF WE'RE DONE WITH OUR *DISCUSSION*!
YOU WEREN'T OVER ON THE FARMER'S PROPERTY, WERE YOU?
REMEMBER WHAT WE TOLD YOU ABOUT STEERING CLEAR OF HIM.
COME BACK DOWN HERE, WE'RE NOT DONE TALKING ABOUT THIS!
SEE YOU TOMORROW.

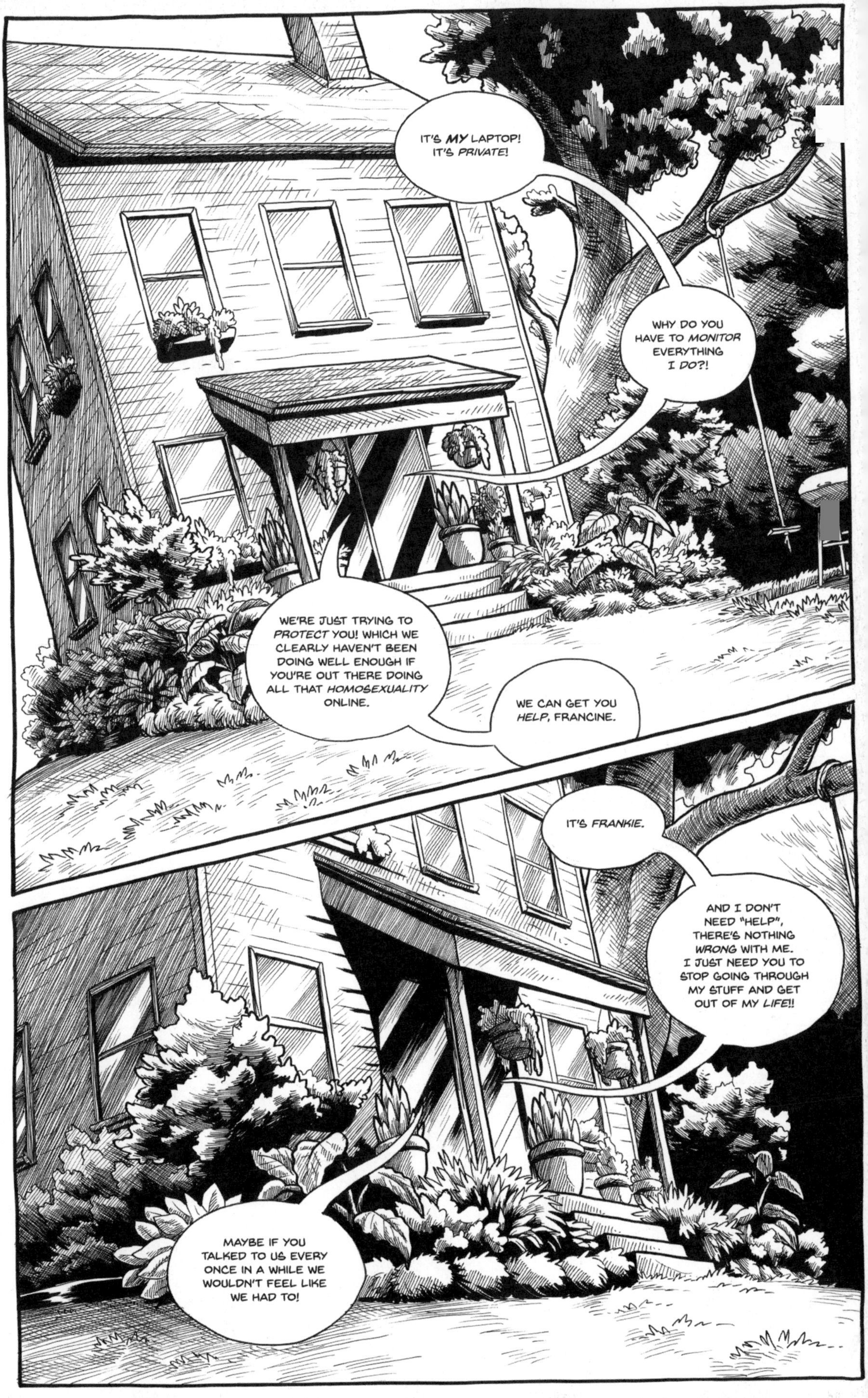
IT'S MY LAPTOP! IT'S PRIVATE!
WHY DO YOU HAVE TO MONITOR EVERYTHING I DO?!
WE'RE JUST TRYING TO PROTECT YOU! WHICH WE CLEARLY HAVEN'T BEEN DOING WELL ENOUGH IF YOU'RE OUT THERE DOING ALL THAT HOMOSEXUALITY ONLINE.
WE CAN GET YOU HELP, FRANCINE.
IT'S FRANKIE.
AND I DON'T NEED "HELP", THERE'S NOTHING WRONG WITH ME. I JUST NEED YOU TO STOP GOING THROUGH MY STUFF AND GET OUT OF MY LIFE!!
MAYBE IF YOU TALKED TO US EVERY ONCE IN A WHILE WE WOULDN'T FEEL LIKE WE HAD TO!

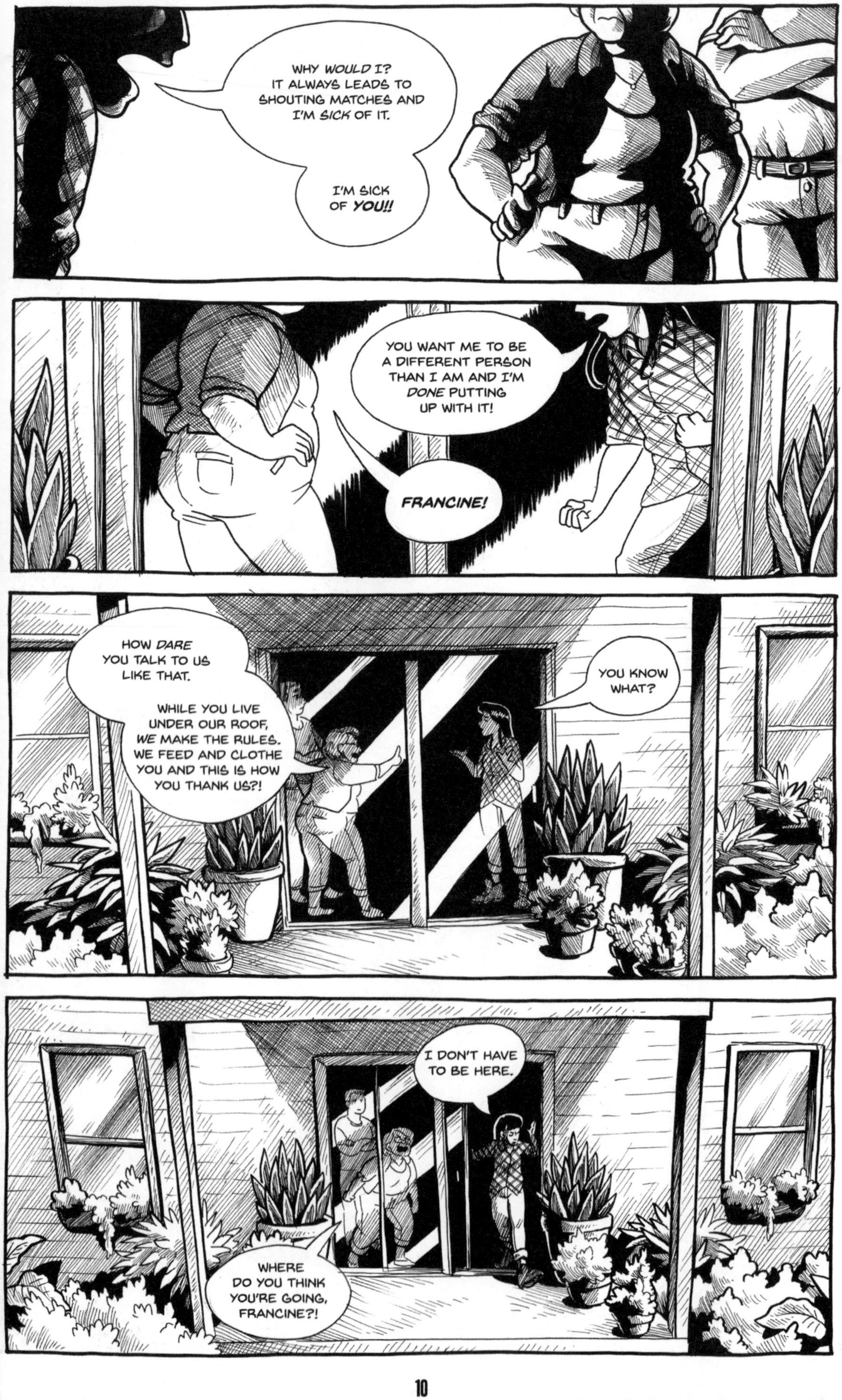
WHY *WOULD* I? IT ALWAYS LEADS TO SHOUTING MATCHES AND I'M *SICK* OF IT.
I'M SICK OF ***YOU!!***
YOU WANT ME TO BE A DIFFERENT PERSON THAN I AM AND I'M *DONE* PUTTING UP WITH IT!
FRANCINE!
HOW *DARE* YOU TALK TO US LIKE THAT.
WHILE YOU LIVE UNDER OUR ROOF, *WE* MAKE THE RULES. WE FEED AND CLOTHE YOU AND THIS IS HOW YOU THANK US?!
YOU KNOW WHAT?
I DON'T HAVE TO BE HERE.
WHERE DO YOU THINK YOU'RE GOING, FRANCINE?!

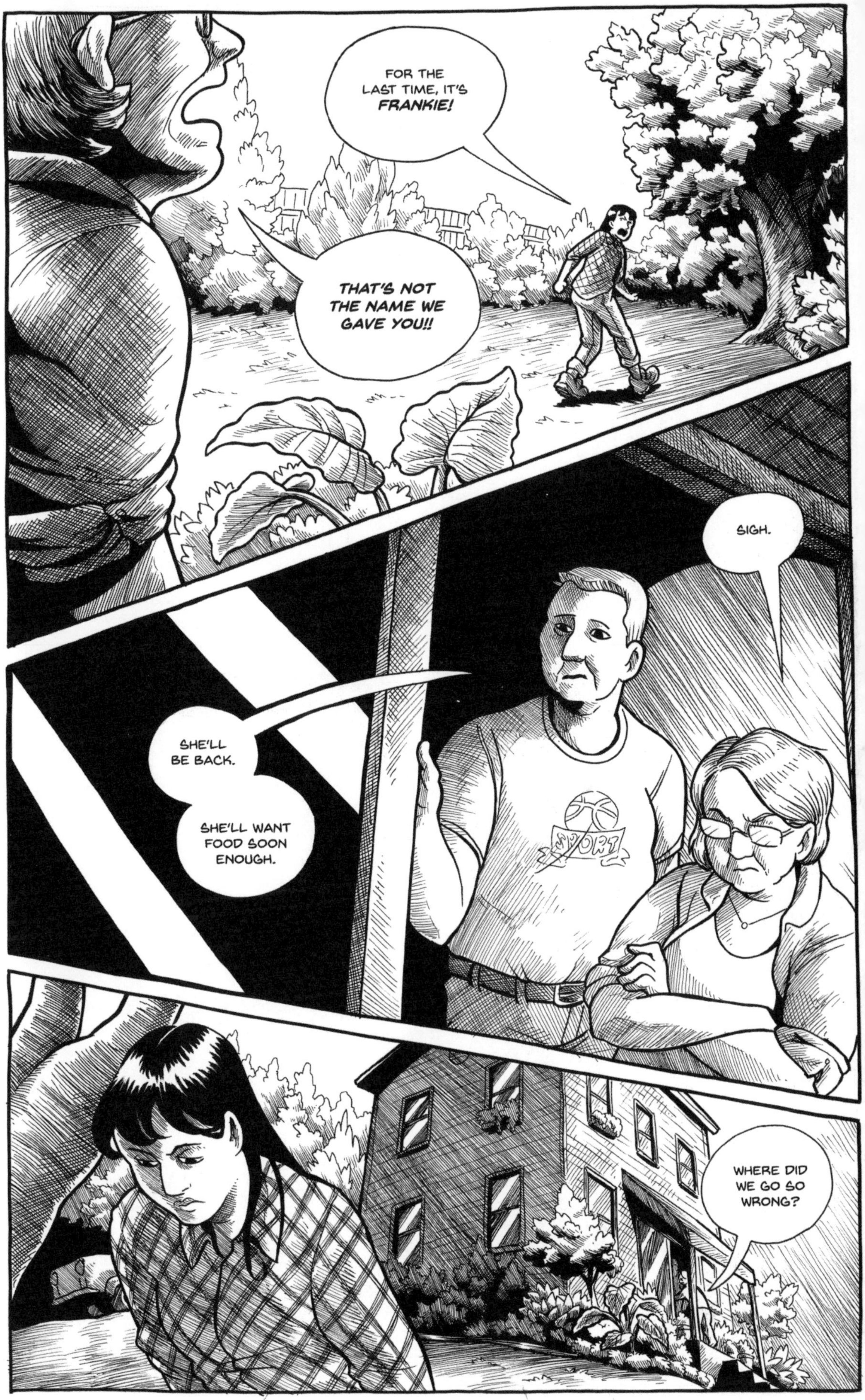
FOR THE LAST TIME, IT'S FRANKIE!
THAT'S NOT THE NAME WE GAVE YOU!!
SIGH.
SHE'LL BE BACK.
SHE'LL WANT FOOD SOON ENOUGH.
WHERE DID WE GO SO WRONG?

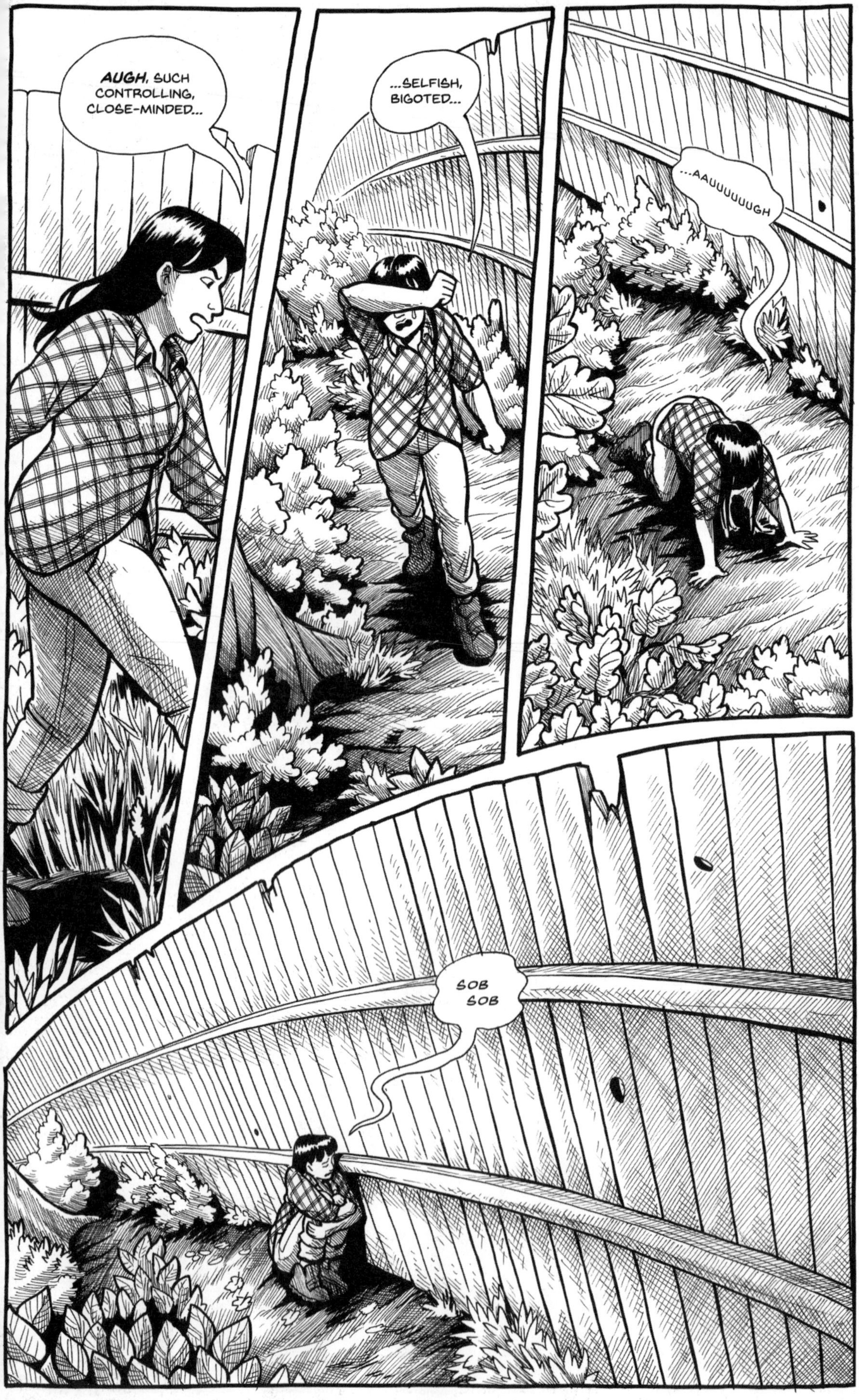
AUGH, SUCH CONTROLLING, CLOSE-MINDED...
...SELFISH, BIGOTED...
...AAUUUUUUGH
SOB SOB

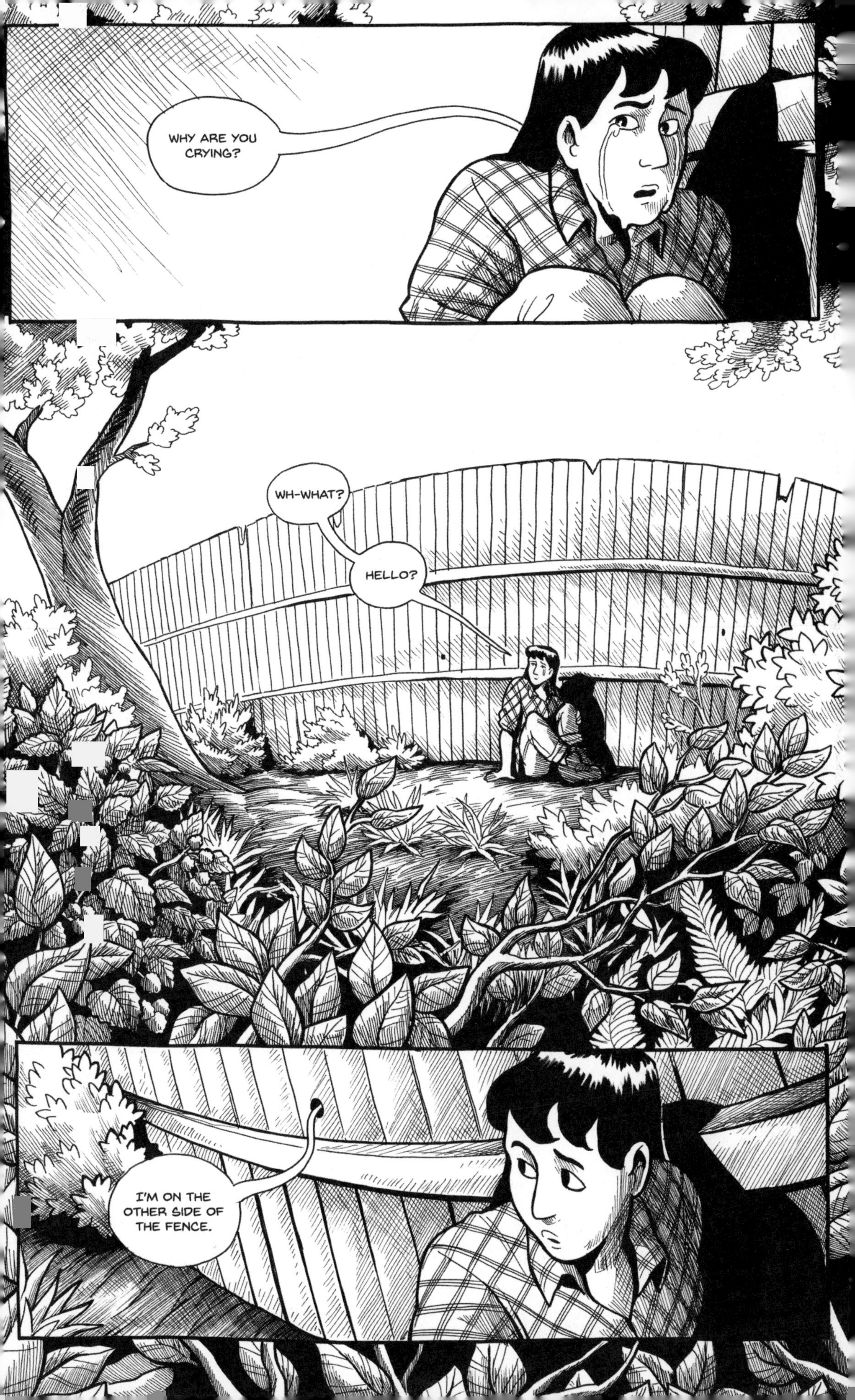
WHY ARE YOU CRYING?
WH-WHAT?
HELLO?
I'M ON THE OTHER SIDE OF THE FENCE.

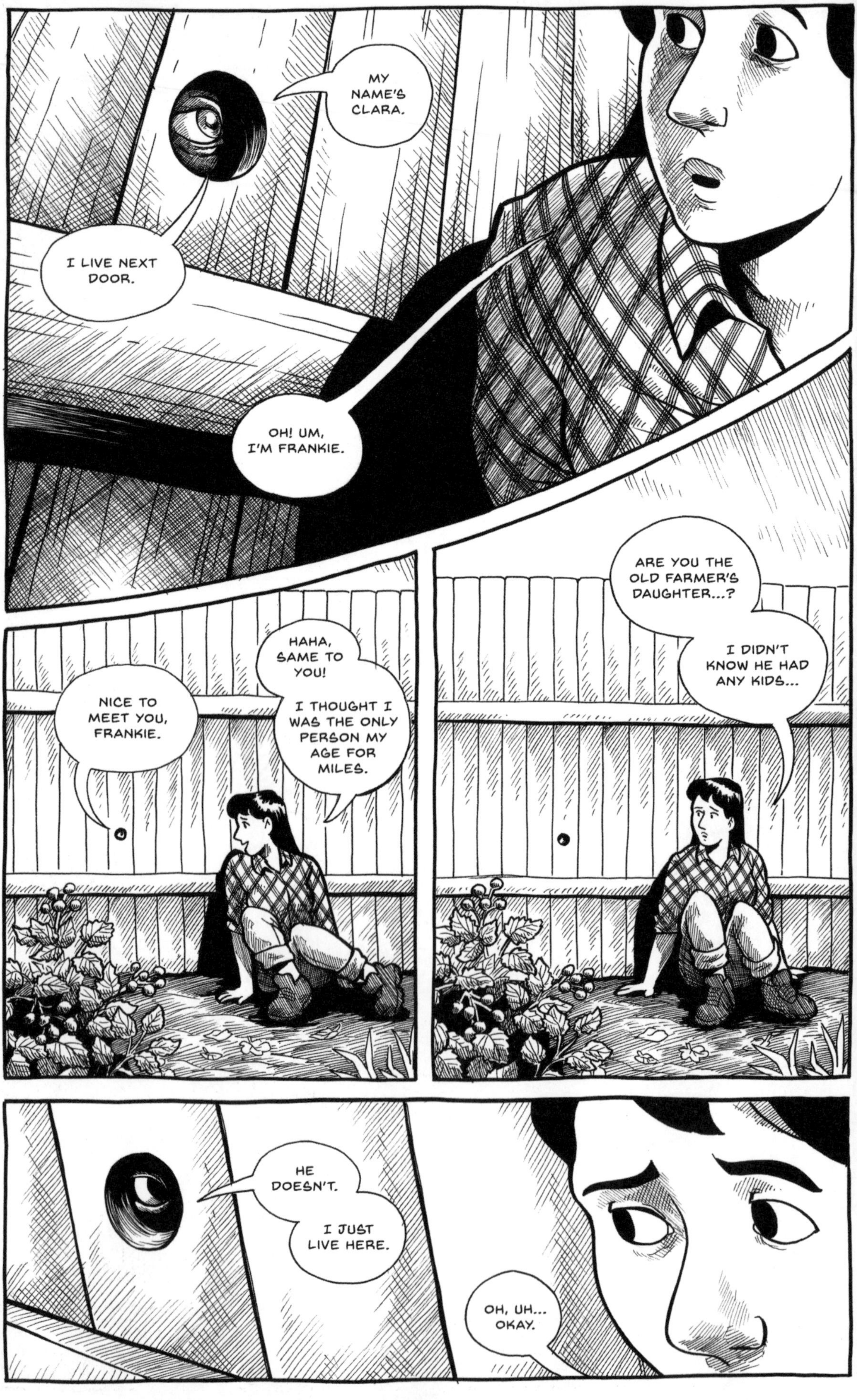
MY NAME'S CLARA.
I LIVE NEXT DOOR.
OH! UM, I'M FRANKIE.
NICE TO MEET YOU, FRANKIE.
HAHA, SAME TO YOU!
I THOUGHT I WAS THE ONLY PERSON MY AGE FOR MILES.
ARE YOU THE OLD FARMER'S DAUGHTER...?
I DIDN'T KNOW HE HAD ANY KIDS...
HE DOESN'T.
I JUST LIVE HERE.
OH, UH... OKAY.

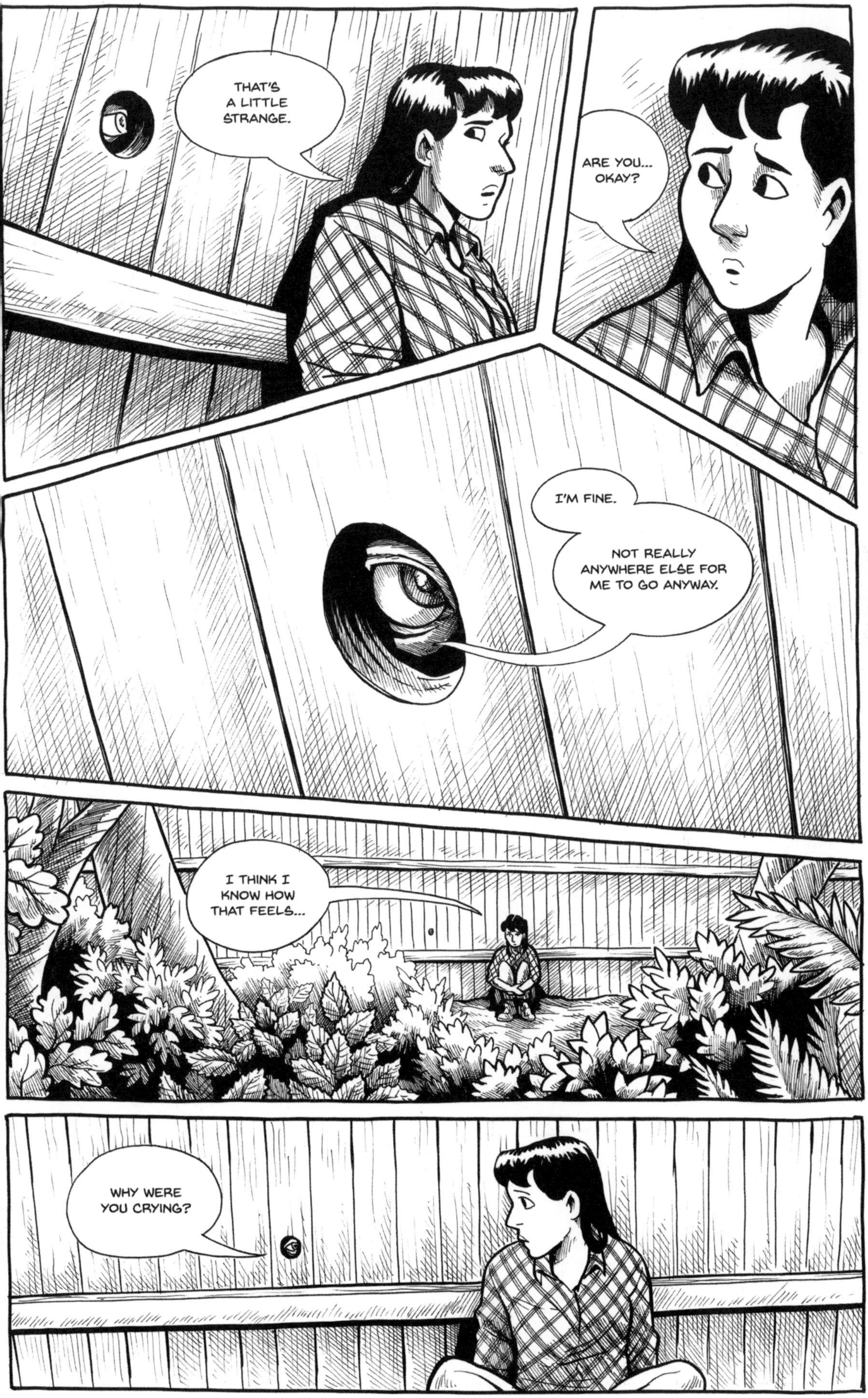
THAT'S A LITTLE STRANGE.
ARE YOU... OKAY?
I'M FINE.
NOT REALLY ANYWHERE ELSE FOR ME TO GO ANYWAY.
I THINK I KNOW HOW THAT FEELS...
WHY WERE YOU CRYING?

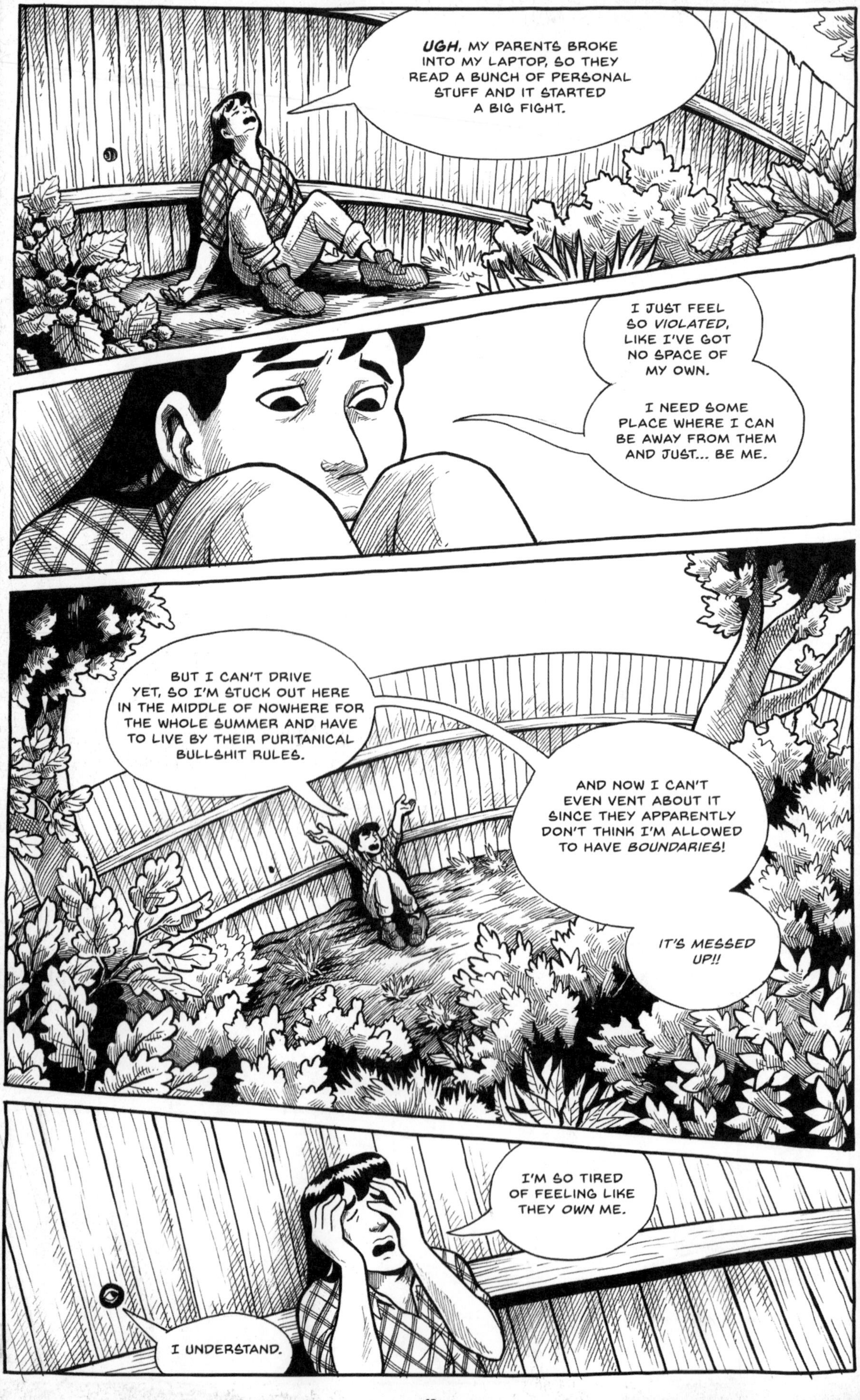
UGH, MY PARENTS BROKE INTO MY LAPTOP, SO THEY READ A BUNCH OF PERSONAL STUFF AND IT STARTED A BIG FIGHT.
I JUST FEEL SO VIOLATED, LIKE I'VE GOT NO SPACE OF MY OWN.
I NEED SOME PLACE WHERE I CAN BE AWAY FROM THEM AND JUST... BE ME.
BUT I CAN'T DRIVE YET, SO I'M STUCK OUT HERE IN THE MIDDLE OF NOWHERE FOR THE WHOLE SUMMER AND HAVE TO LIVE BY THEIR PURITANICAL BULLSHIT RULES.
AND NOW I CAN'T EVEN VENT ABOUT IT SINCE THEY APPARENTLY DON'T THINK I'M ALLOWED TO HAVE BOUNDARIES!
IT'S MESSED UP!!
I'M SO TIRED OF FEELING LIKE THEY OWN ME.
I UNDERSTAND.

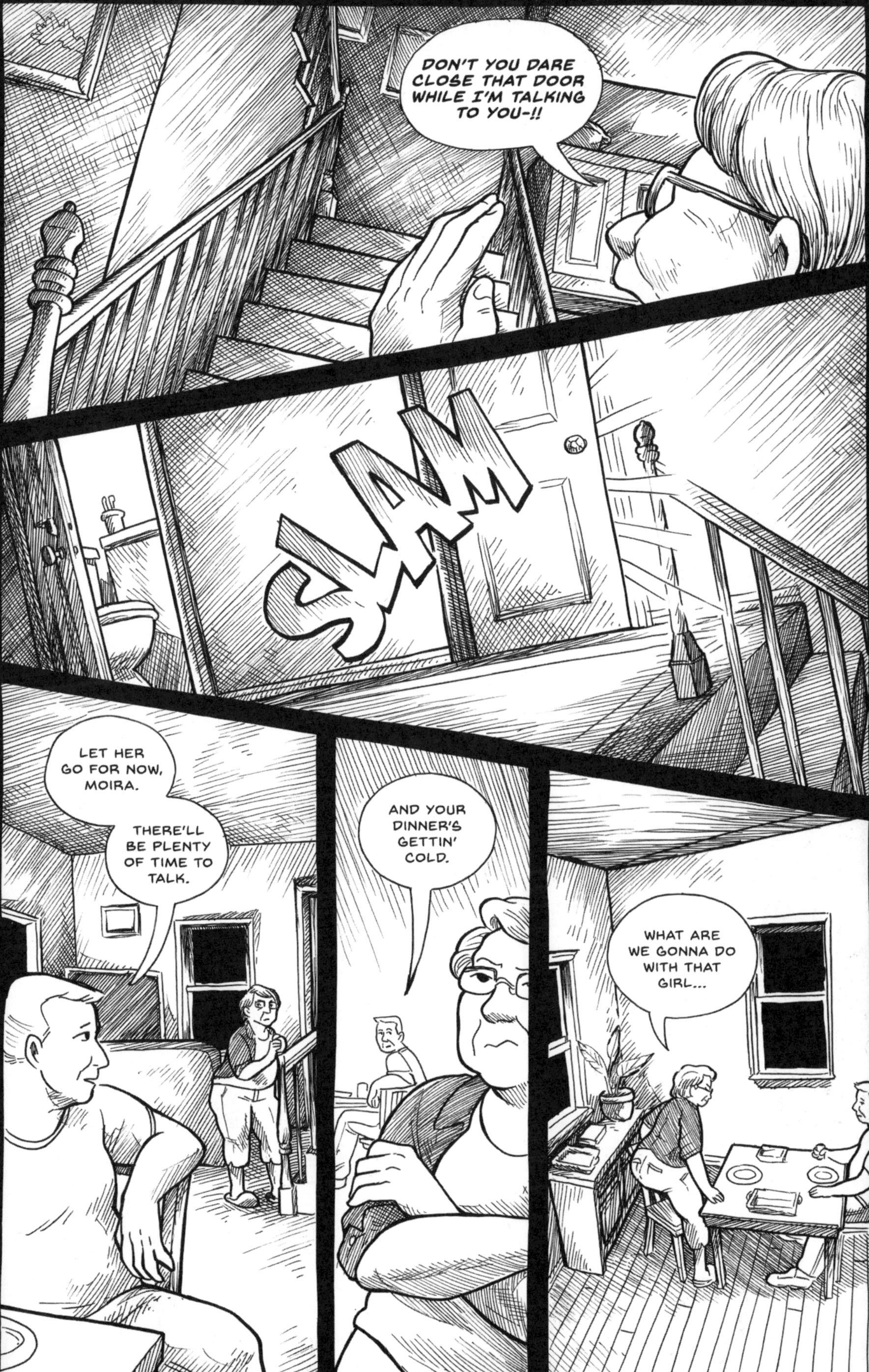
DON'T YOU DARE CLOSE THAT DOOR WHILE I'M TALKING TO YOU-!!
SLAM
LET HER GO FOR NOW, MOIRA.
THERE'LL BE PLENTY OF TIME TO TALK.
AND YOUR DINNER'S GETTIN' COLD.
WHAT ARE WE GONNA DO WITH THAT GIRL...

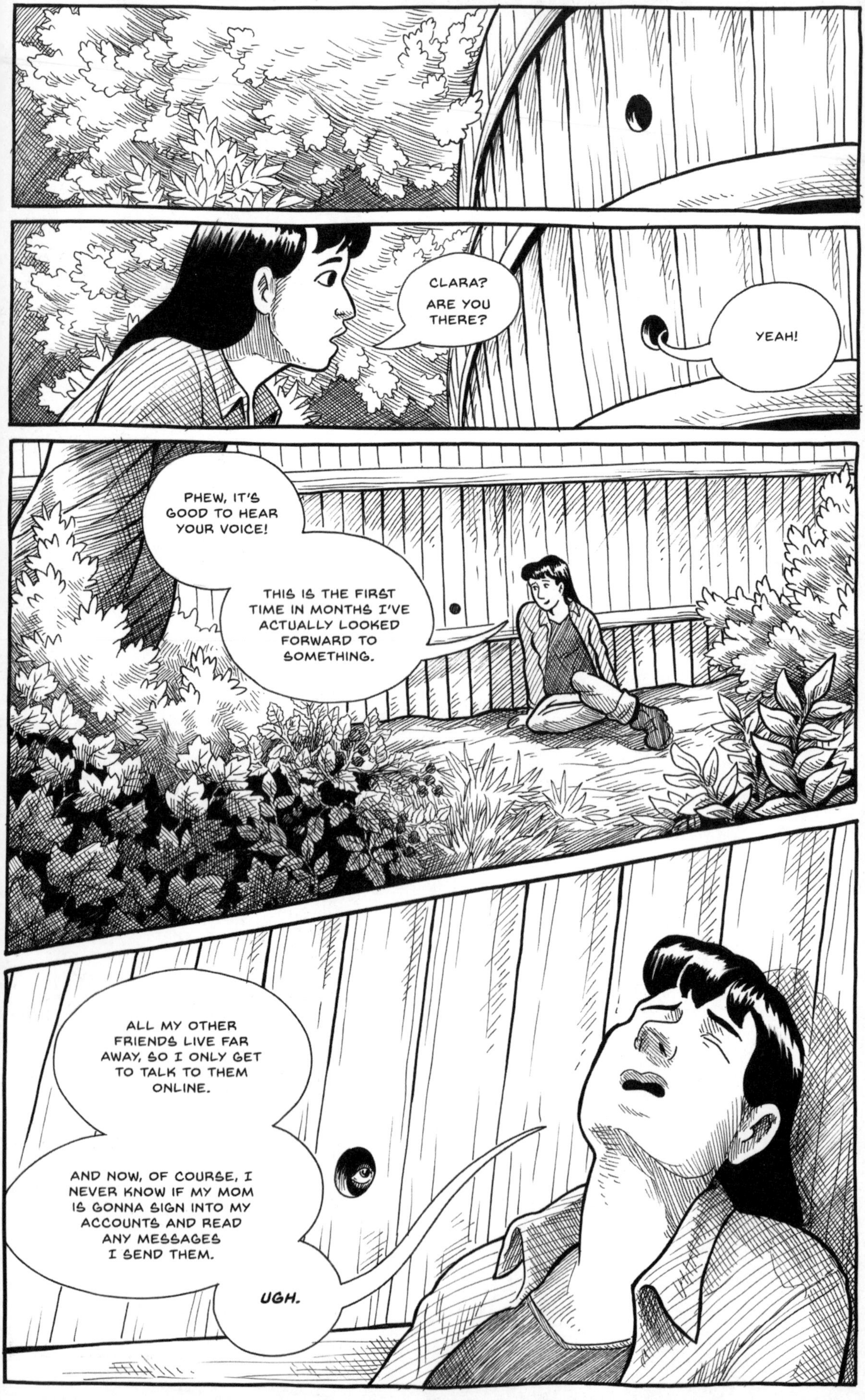
CLARA?
ARE YOU THERE?
YEAH!
PHEW, IT'S GOOD TO HEAR YOUR VOICE!
THIS IS THE FIRST TIME IN MONTHS I'VE ACTUALLY LOOKED FORWARD TO SOMETHING.
ALL MY OTHER FRIENDS LIVE FAR AWAY, SO I ONLY GET TO TALK TO THEM ONLINE.
AND NOW, OF COURSE, I NEVER KNOW IF MY MOM IS GONNA SIGN INTO MY ACCOUNTS AND READ ANY MESSAGES I SEND THEM.
UGH.

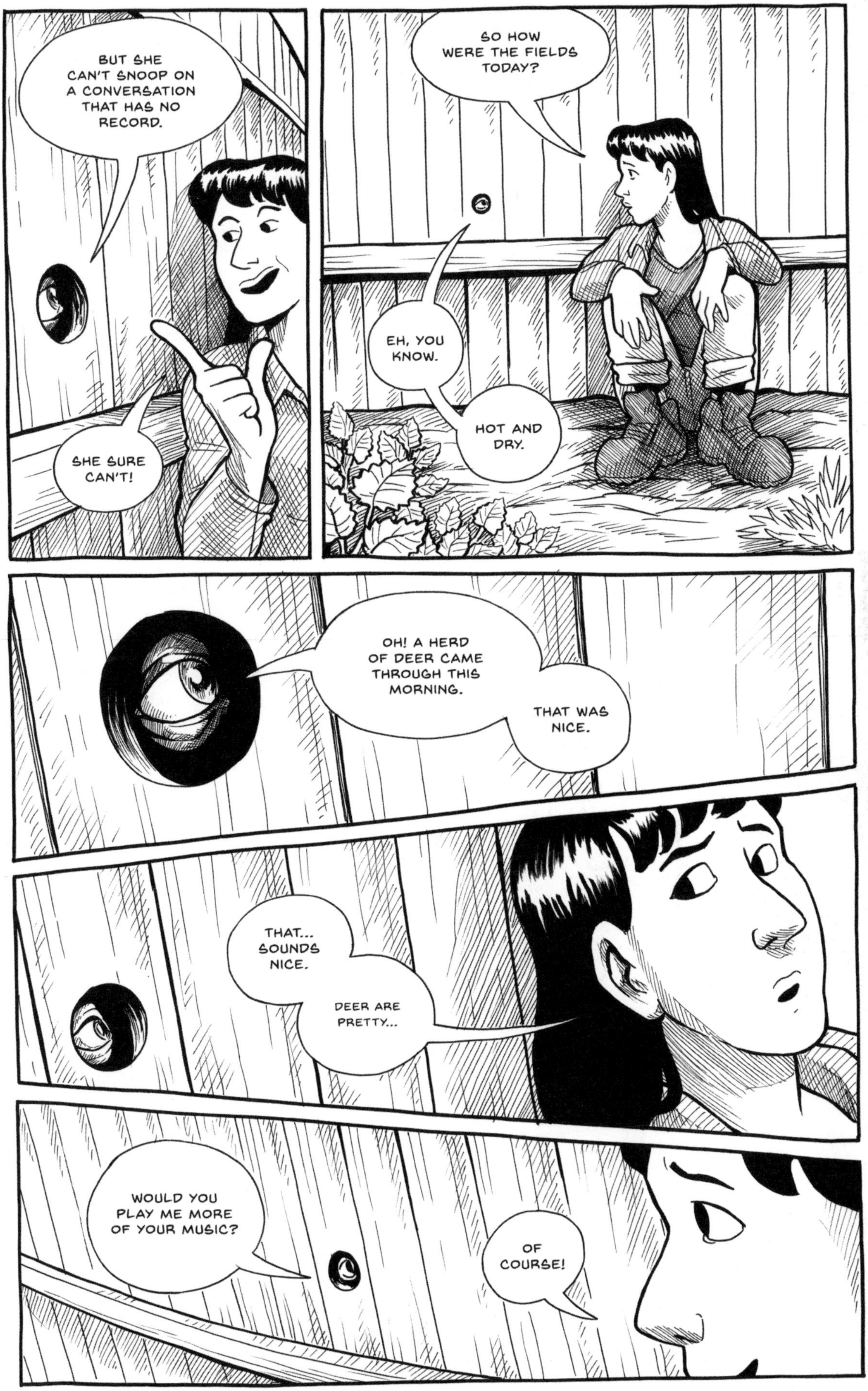
BUT SHE CAN'T SNOOP ON A CONVERSATION THAT HAS NO RECORD.
SHE SURE CAN'T!
SO HOW WERE THE FIELDS TODAY?
EH, YOU KNOW.
HOT AND DRY.
OH! A HERD OF DEER CAME THROUGH THIS MORNING.
THAT WAS NICE.
THAT... SOUNDS NICE.
DEER ARE PRETTY...
WOULD YOU PLAY ME MORE OF YOUR MUSIC?
OF COURSE!

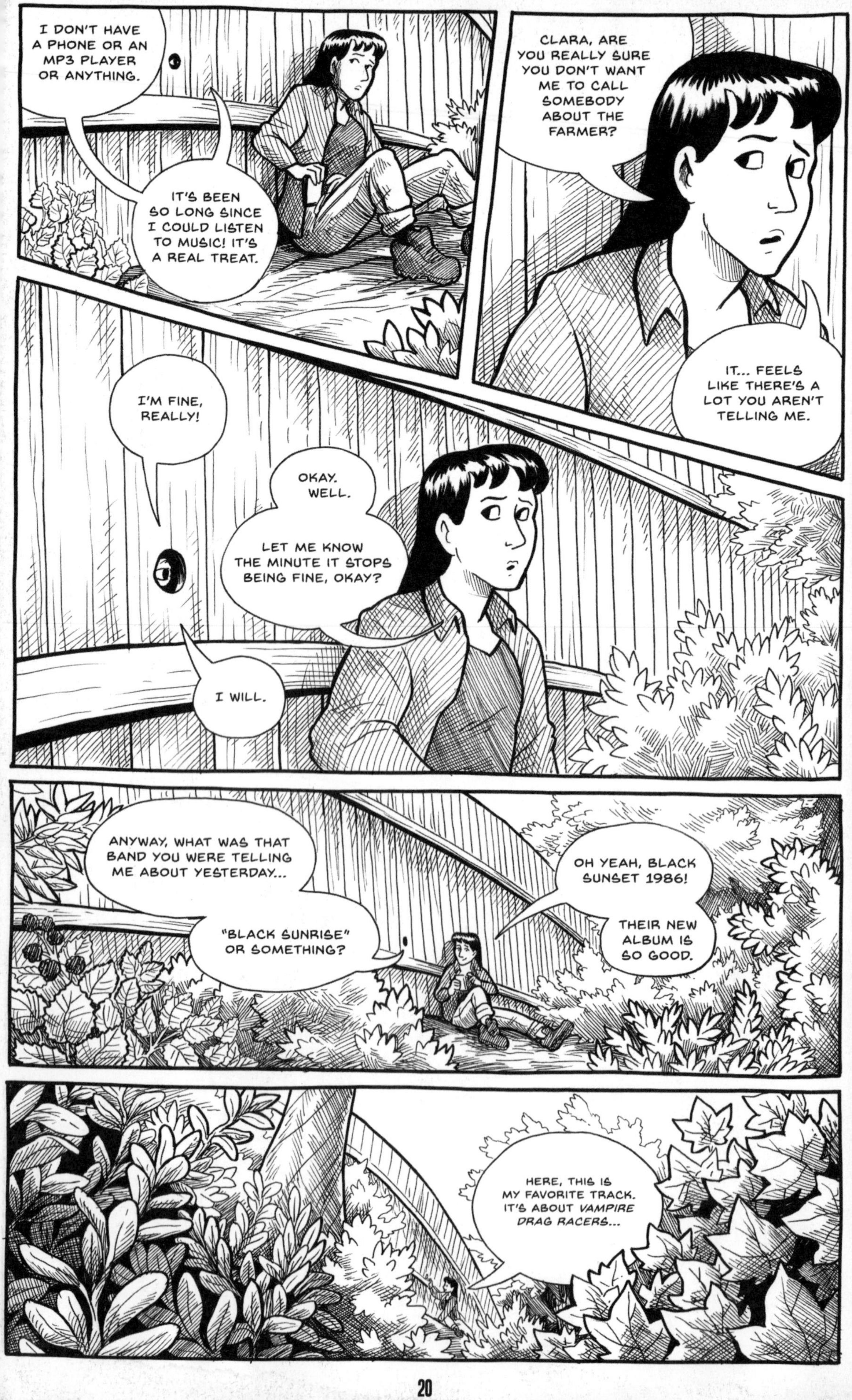
I DON'T HAVE A PHONE OR AN MP3 PLAYER OR ANYTHING.
IT'S BEEN SO LONG SINCE I COULD LISTEN TO MUSIC! IT'S A REAL TREAT.
CLARA, ARE YOU REALLY SURE YOU DON'T WANT ME TO CALL SOMEBODY ABOUT THE FARMER?
IT... FEELS LIKE THERE'S A LOT YOU AREN'T TELLING ME.
I'M FINE, REALLY!
OKAY. WELL.
LET ME KNOW THE MINUTE IT STOPS BEING FINE, OKAY?
I WILL.
ANYWAY, WHAT WAS THAT BAND YOU WERE TELLING ME ABOUT YESTERDAY...
"BLACK SUNRISE" OR SOMETHING?
OH YEAH, BLACK SUNSET 1986!
THEIR NEW ALBUM IS SO GOOD.
HERE, THIS IS MY FAVORITE TRACK. IT'S ABOUT *VAMPIRE DRAG RACERS*...

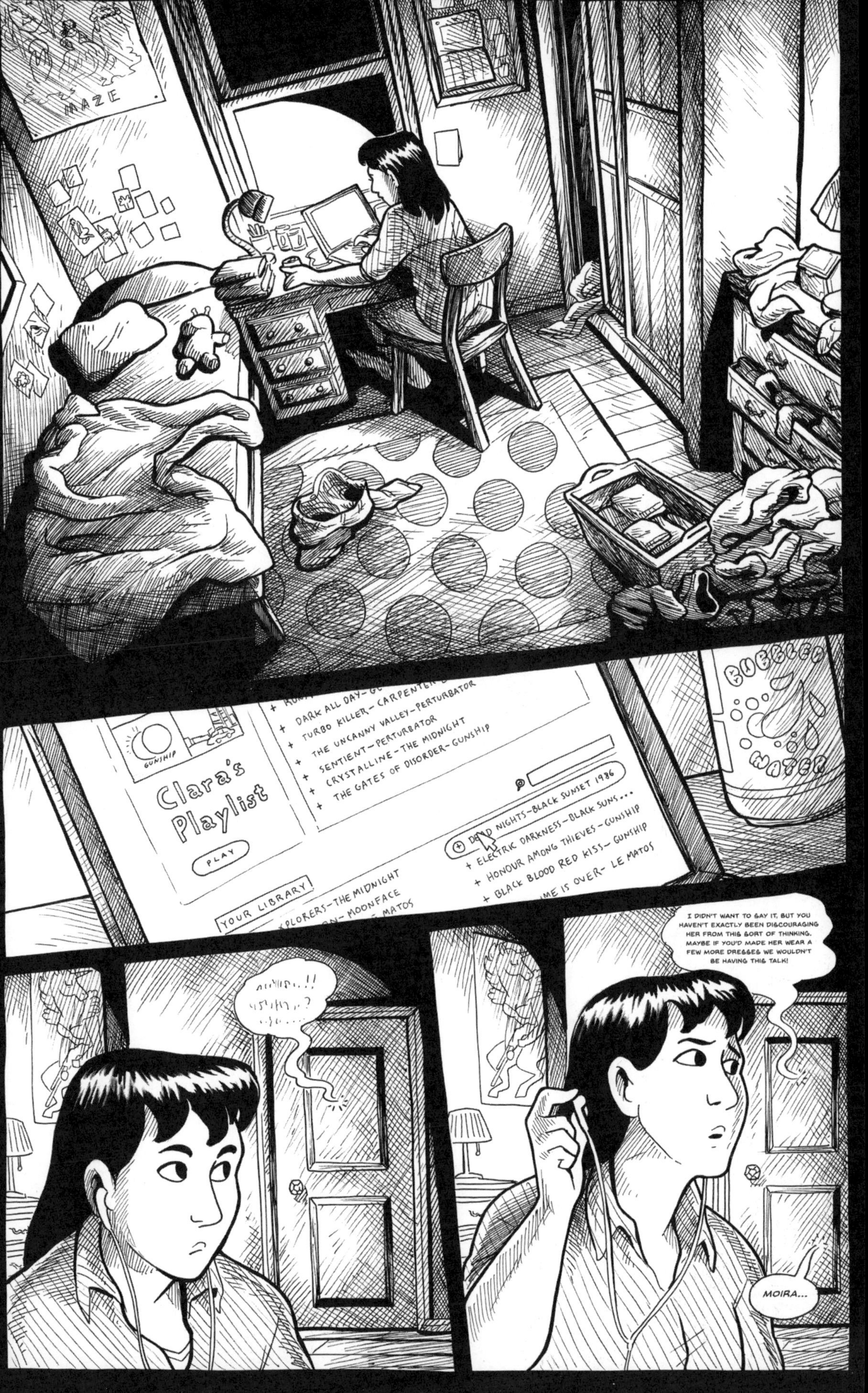
MAZE
DARK ALL DAY-
TURBO KILLER-CARPENTER
THE UNCANNY VALLEY-PERTURBATOR
SENTIENT-PERTURBATOR
CRYSTALLINE-THE MIDNIGHT
THE GATES OF DISORDER-GUNSHIP
GUNSHIP
Clara's Playlist
PLAY
NIGHTS-BLACK SUNSET 1986
ELECTRIC DARKNESS-BLACK SUNS...
HONOUR AMONG THIEVES-GUNSHIP
BLACK BLOOD RED KISS-GUNSHIP
YOUR LIBRARY
THE MIDNIGHT
MOONFACE
I DIDN'T WANT TO SAY IT, BUT YOU HAVEN'T EXACTLY BEEN DISCOURAGING HER FROM THIS SORT OF THINKING. MAYBE IF YOU'D MADE HER WEAR A FEW MORE DRESSES WE WOULDN'T BE HAVING THIS TALK!
MOIRA...

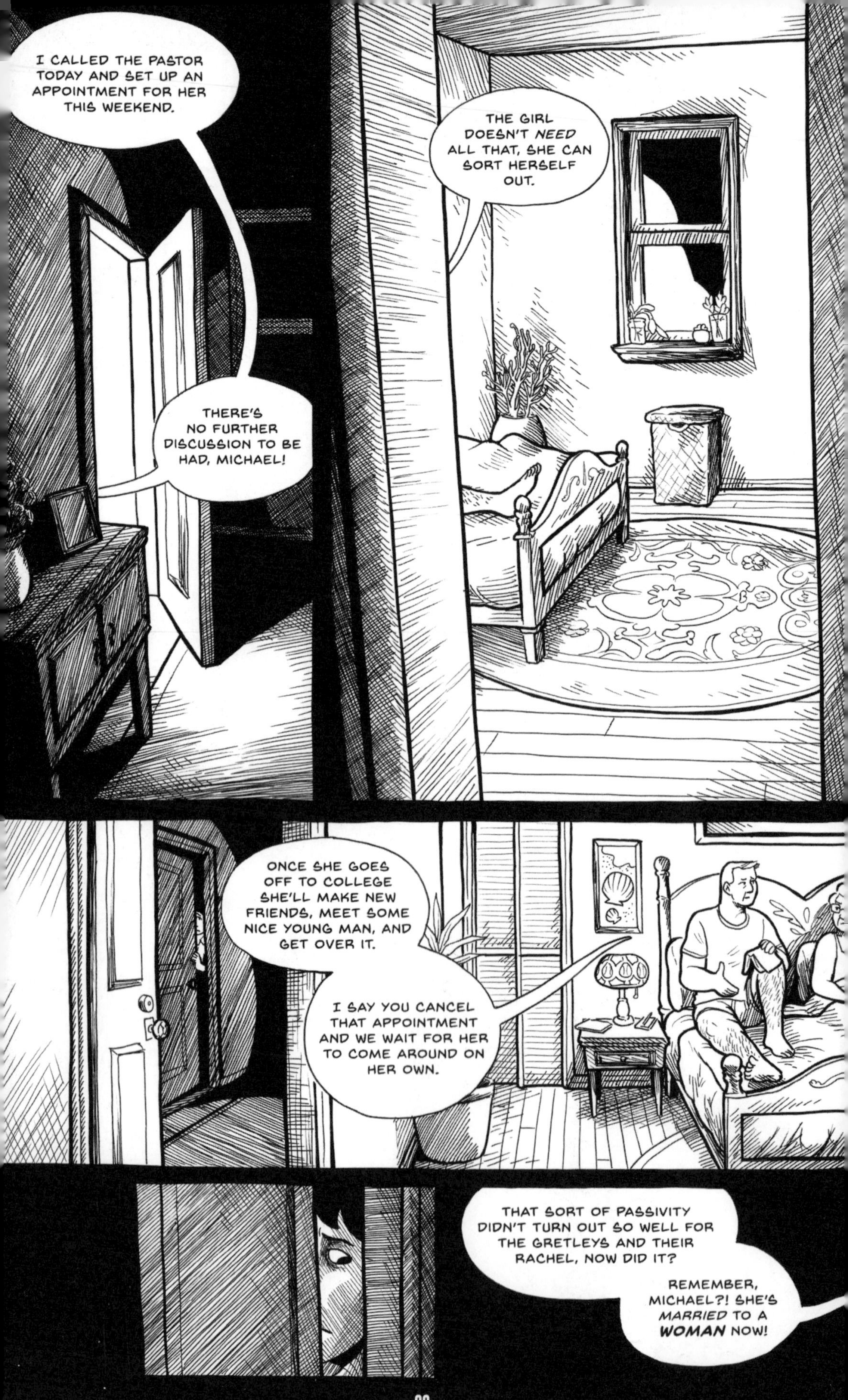
I CALLED THE PASTOR TODAY AND SET UP AN APPOINTMENT FOR HER THIS WEEKEND.
THERE'S NO FURTHER DISCUSSION TO BE HAD, MICHAEL!
THE GIRL DOESN'T *NEED* ALL THAT, SHE CAN SORT HERSELF OUT.
ONCE SHE GOES OFF TO COLLEGE SHE'LL MAKE NEW FRIENDS, MEET SOME NICE YOUNG MAN, AND GET OVER IT.
I SAY YOU CANCEL THAT APPOINTMENT AND WE WAIT FOR HER TO COME AROUND ON HER OWN.
THAT SORT OF PASSIVITY DIDN'T TURN OUT SO WELL FOR THE GRETLEYS AND THEIR RACHEL, NOW DID IT?
REMEMBER, MICHAEL?! SHE'S *MARRIED* TO A ***WOMAN*** NOW!

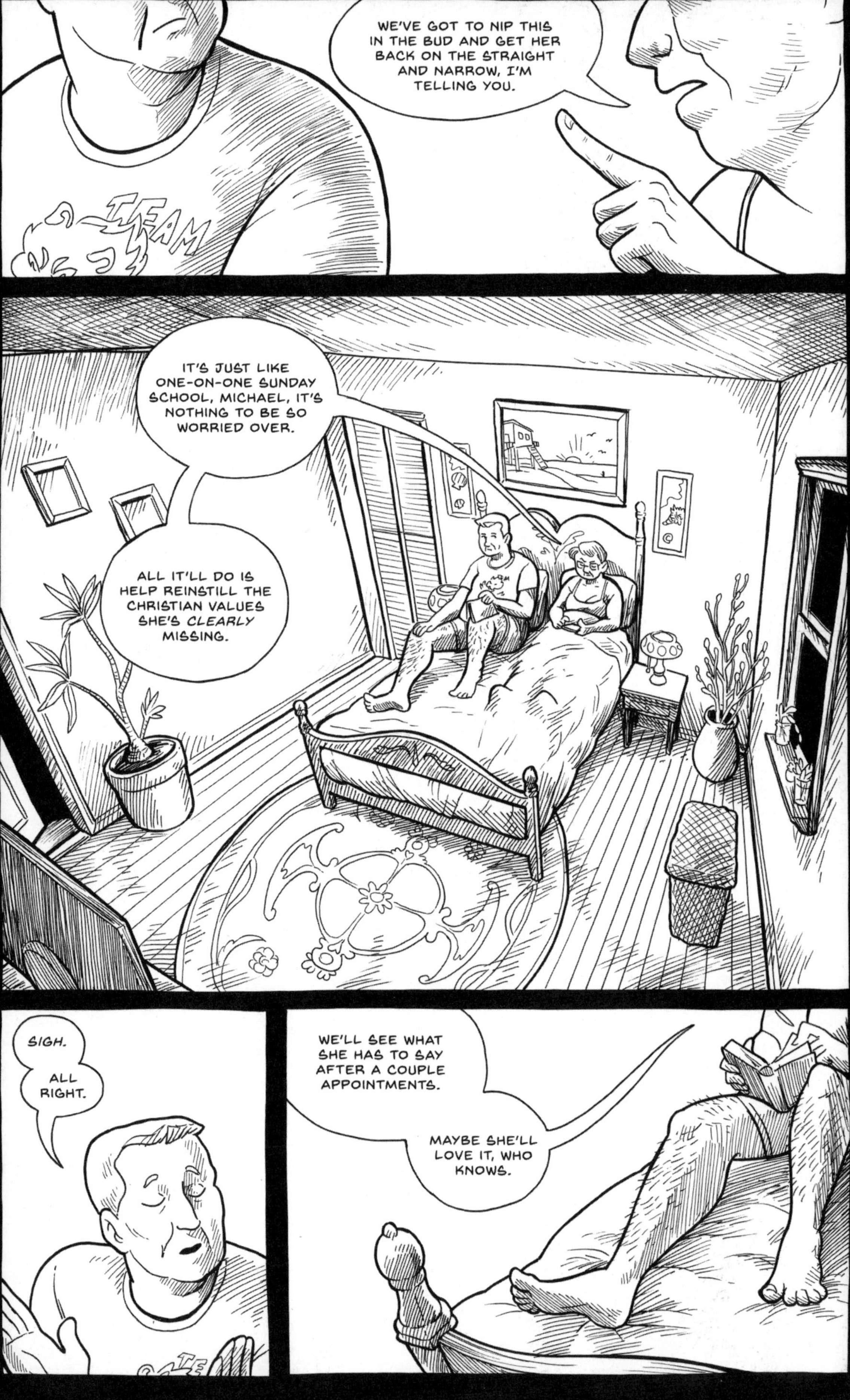
WE'VE GOT TO NIP THIS IN THE BUD AND GET HER BACK ON THE STRAIGHT AND NARROW, I'M TELLING YOU.
IT'S JUST LIKE ONE-ON-ONE SUNDAY SCHOOL, MICHAEL, IT'S NOTHING TO BE SO WORRIED OVER.
ALL IT'LL DO IS HELP REINSTILL THE CHRISTIAN VALUES SHE'S *CLEARLY* MISSING.
SIGH.
ALL RIGHT.
WE'LL SEE WHAT SHE HAS TO SAY AFTER A COUPLE APPOINTMENTS.
MAYBE SHE'LL LOVE IT, WHO KNOWS.

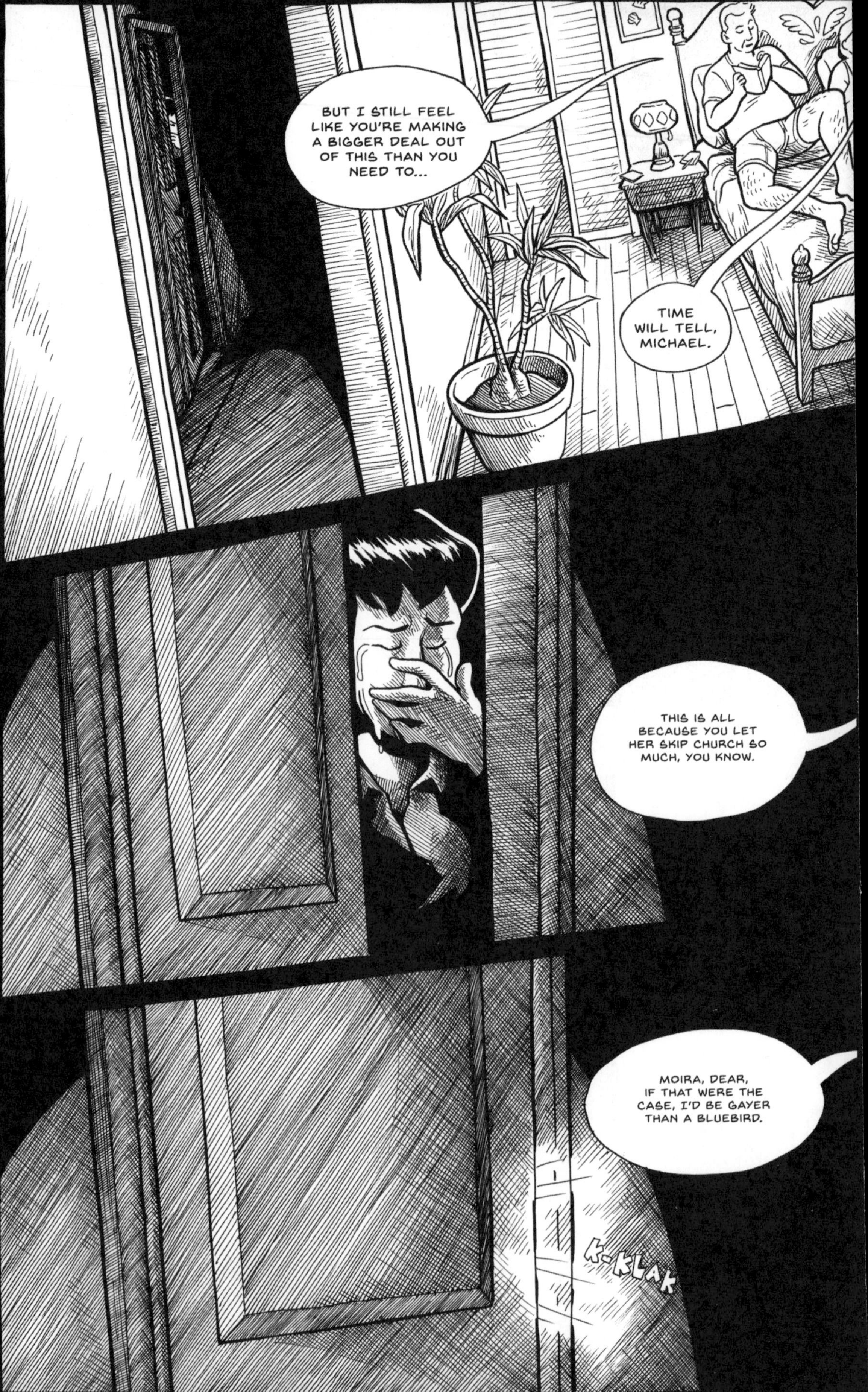
BUT I STILL FEEL LIKE YOU'RE MAKING A BIGGER DEAL OUT OF THIS THAN YOU NEED TO...
TIME WILL TELL, MICHAEL.
THIS IS ALL BECAUSE YOU LET HER SKIP CHURCH SO MUCH, YOU KNOW.
MOIRA, DEAR, IF THAT WERE THE CASE, I'D BE GAYER THAN A BLUEBIRD.
K-KLAK

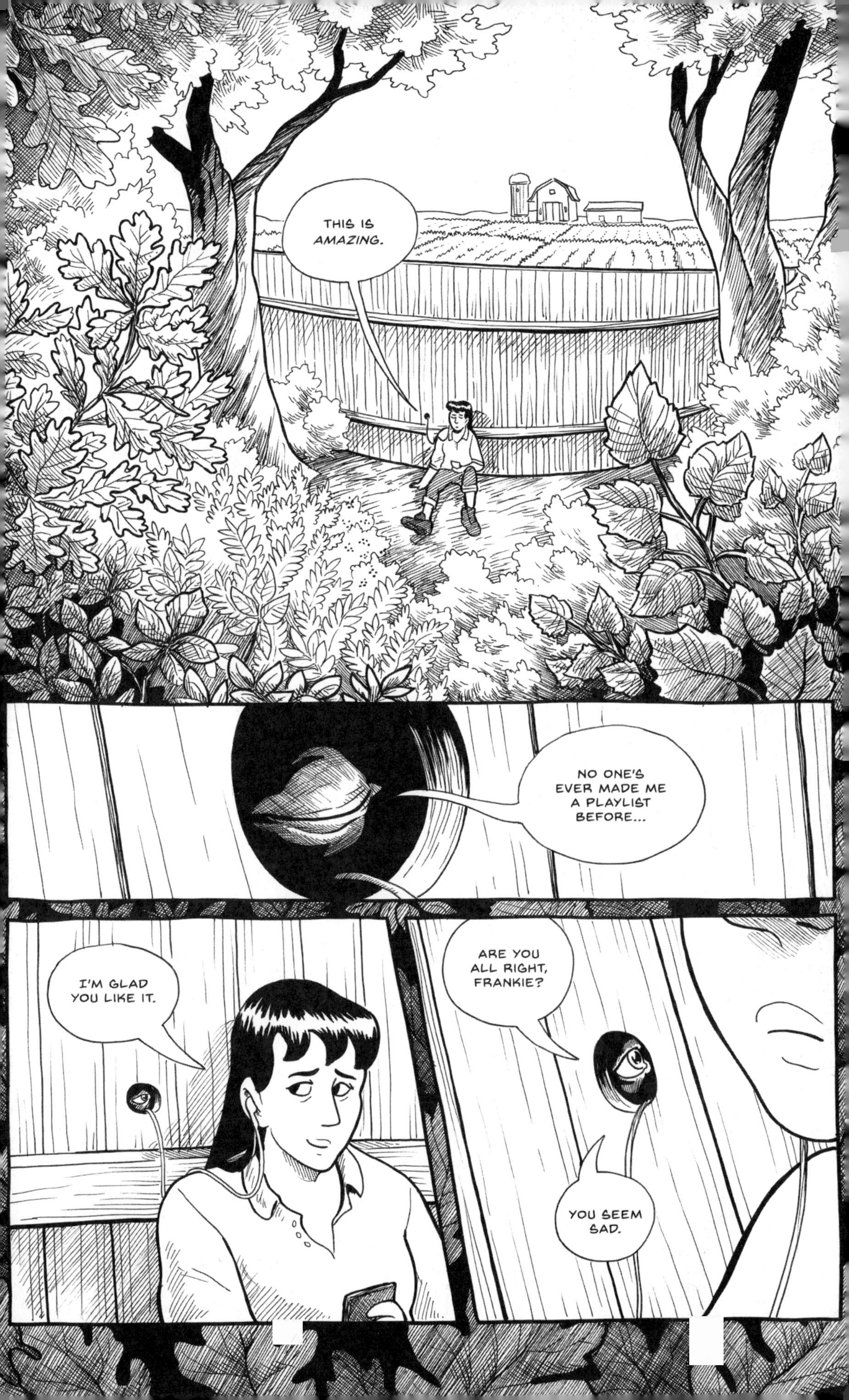
THIS IS AMAZING.
NO ONE'S EVER MADE ME A PLAYLIST BEFORE...
I'M GLAD YOU LIKE IT.
ARE YOU ALL RIGHT, FRANKIE?
YOU SEEM SAD.

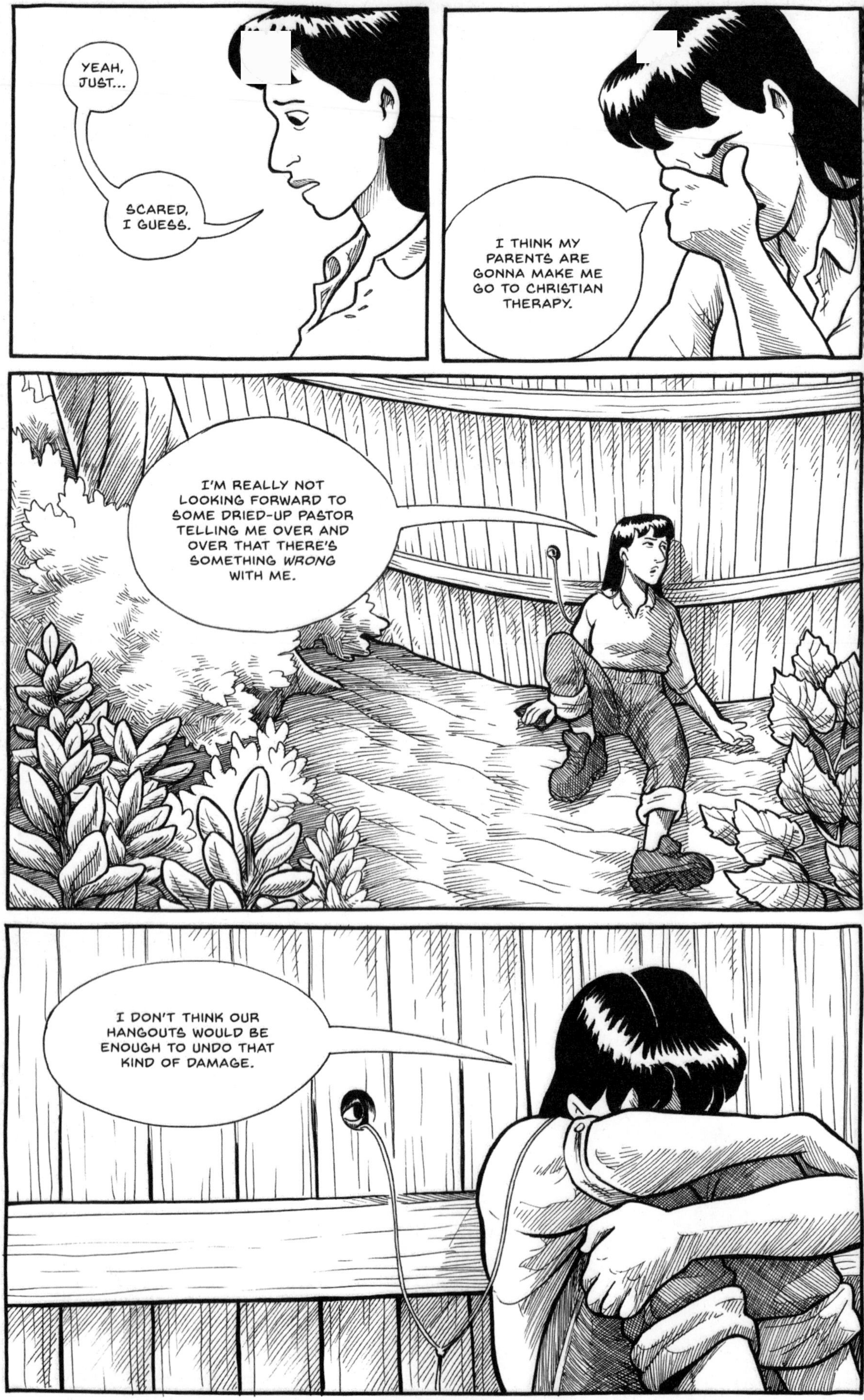
YEAH, JUST...
SCARED, I GUESS.
I THINK MY PARENTS ARE GONNA MAKE ME GO TO CHRISTIAN THERAPY.
I'M REALLY NOT LOOKING FORWARD TO SOME DRIED-UP PASTOR TELLING ME OVER AND OVER THAT THERE'S SOMETHING *WRONG* WITH ME.
I DON'T THINK OUR HANGOUTS WOULD BE ENOUGH TO UNDO THAT KIND OF DAMAGE.

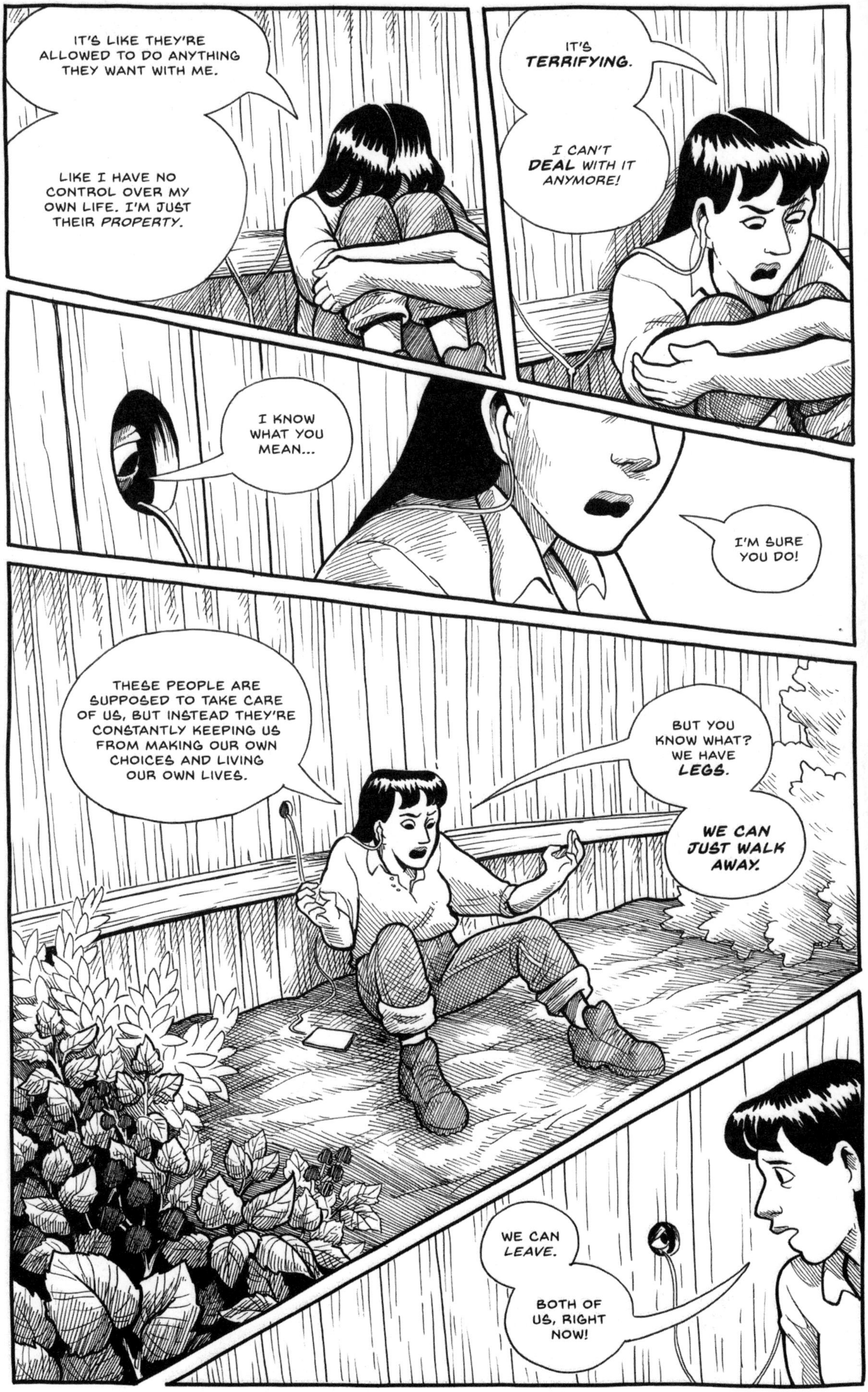
IT'S LIKE THEY'RE ALLOWED TO DO ANYTHING THEY WANT WITH ME.
LIKE I HAVE NO CONTROL OVER MY OWN LIFE. I'M JUST THEIR *PROPERTY*.
IT'S ***TERRIFYING***.
I CAN'T **DEAL** WITH IT ANYMORE!
I KNOW WHAT YOU MEAN...
I'M SURE YOU DO!
THESE PEOPLE ARE SUPPOSED TO TAKE CARE OF US, BUT INSTEAD THEY'RE CONSTANTLY KEEPING US FROM MAKING OUR OWN CHOICES AND LIVING OUR OWN LIVES.
BUT YOU KNOW WHAT? WE HAVE ***LEGS***.
WE CAN JUST WALK AWAY.
WE CAN *LEAVE*.
BOTH OF US, RIGHT NOW!

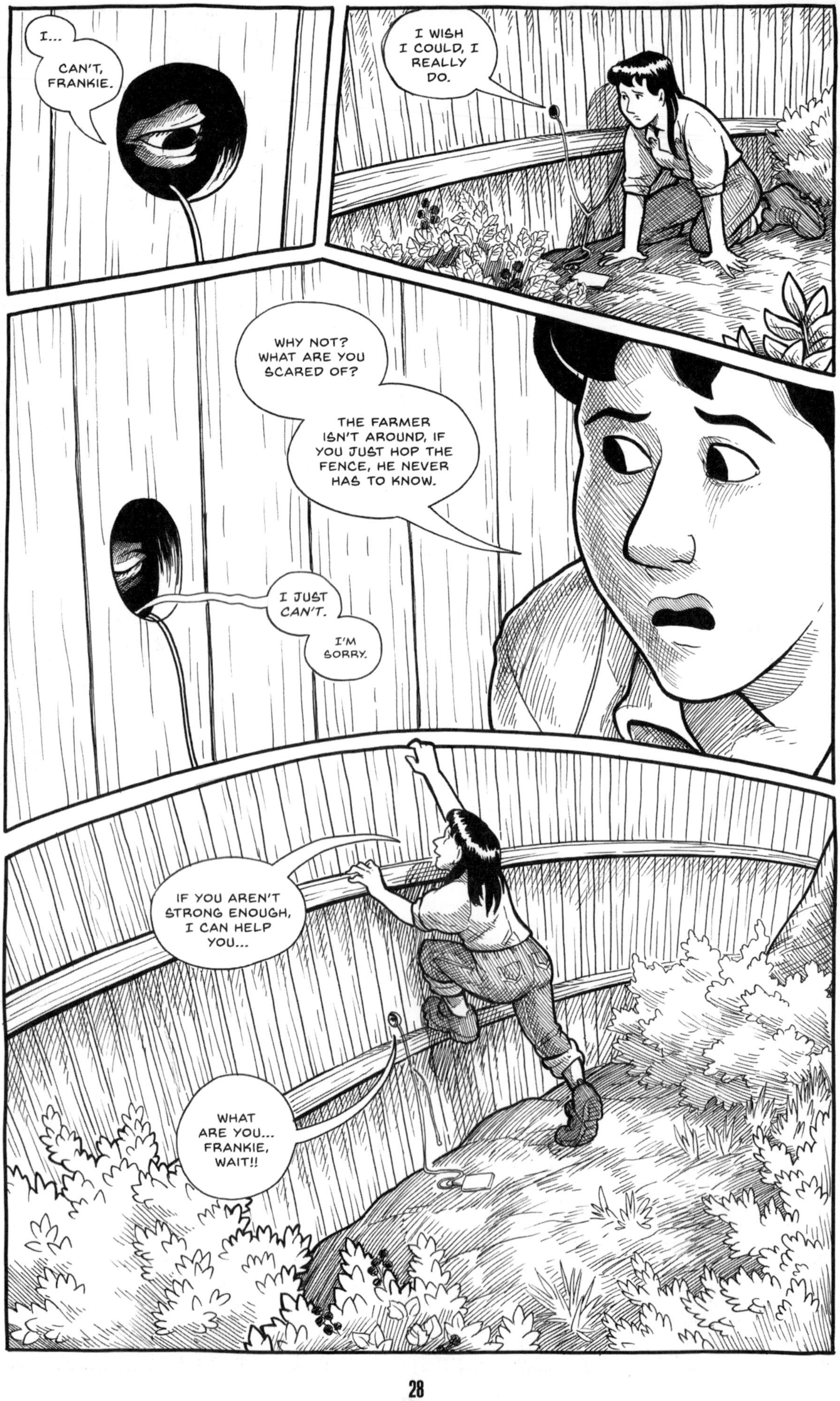
I...
CAN'T, FRANKIE.
I WISH I COULD, I REALLY DO.
WHY NOT? WHAT ARE YOU SCARED OF?
THE FARMER ISN'T AROUND, IF YOU JUST HOP THE FENCE, HE NEVER HAS TO KNOW.
I JUST CAN'T.
I'M SORRY.
IF YOU AREN'T STRONG ENOUGH, I CAN HELP YOU...
WHAT ARE YOU... FRANKIE, WAIT!!

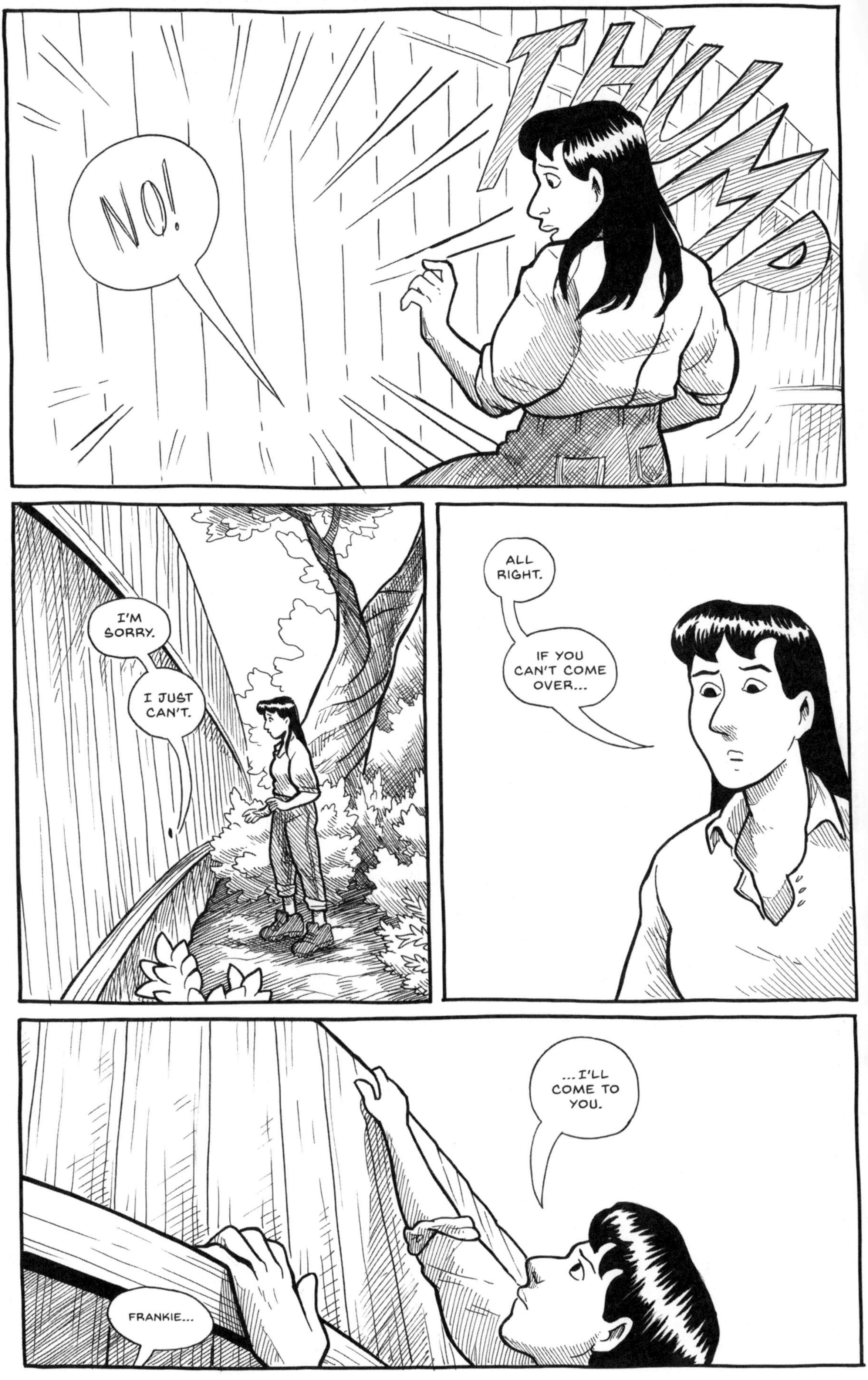
THUMP
NO!
I'M SORRY.
I JUST CAN'T.
ALL RIGHT.
IF YOU CAN'T COME OVER...
...I'LL COME TO YOU.
FRANKIE...

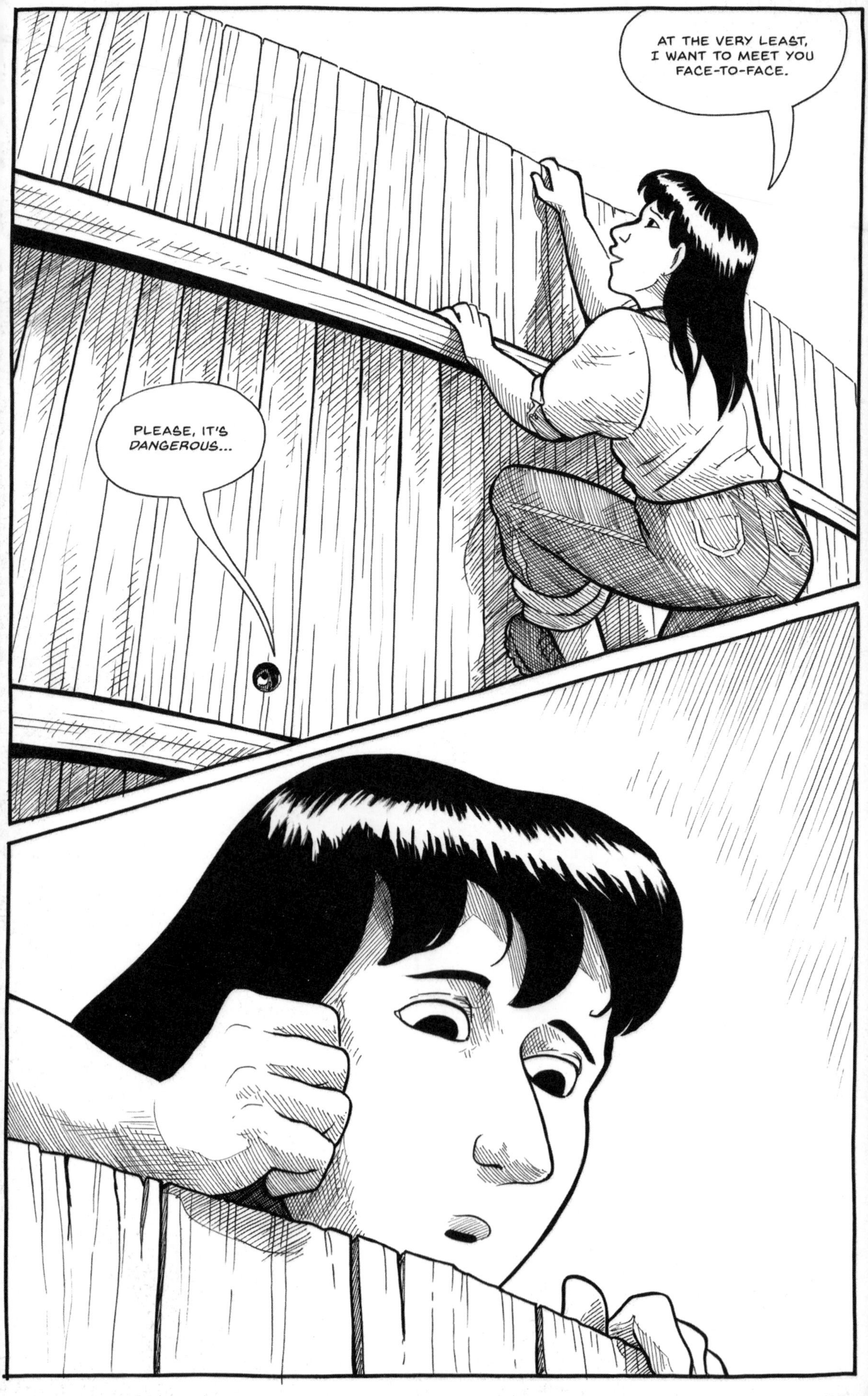
AT THE VERY LEAST, I WANT TO MEET YOU FACE-TO-FACE.
PLEASE, IT'S *DANGEROUS*...

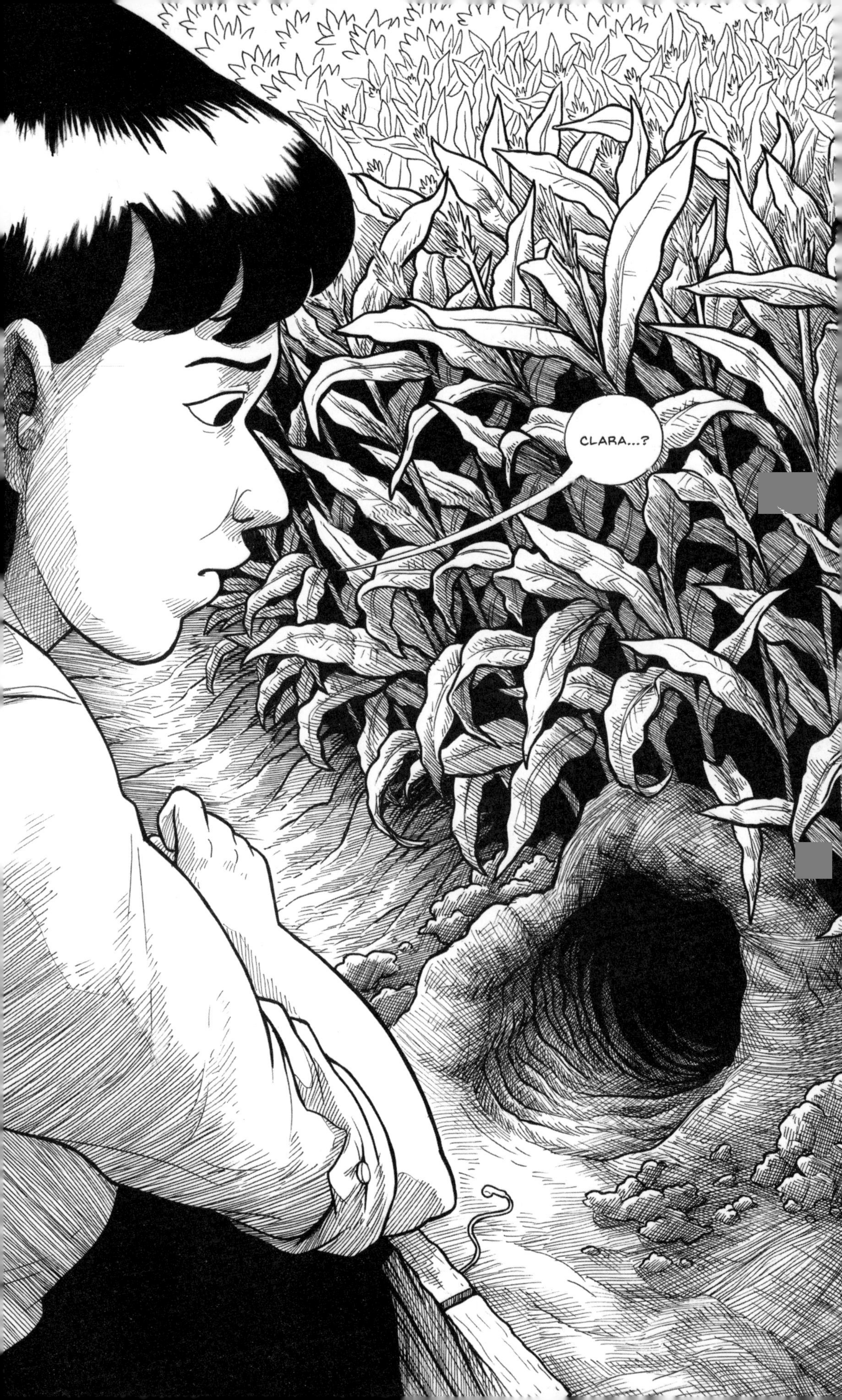
CLARA...?

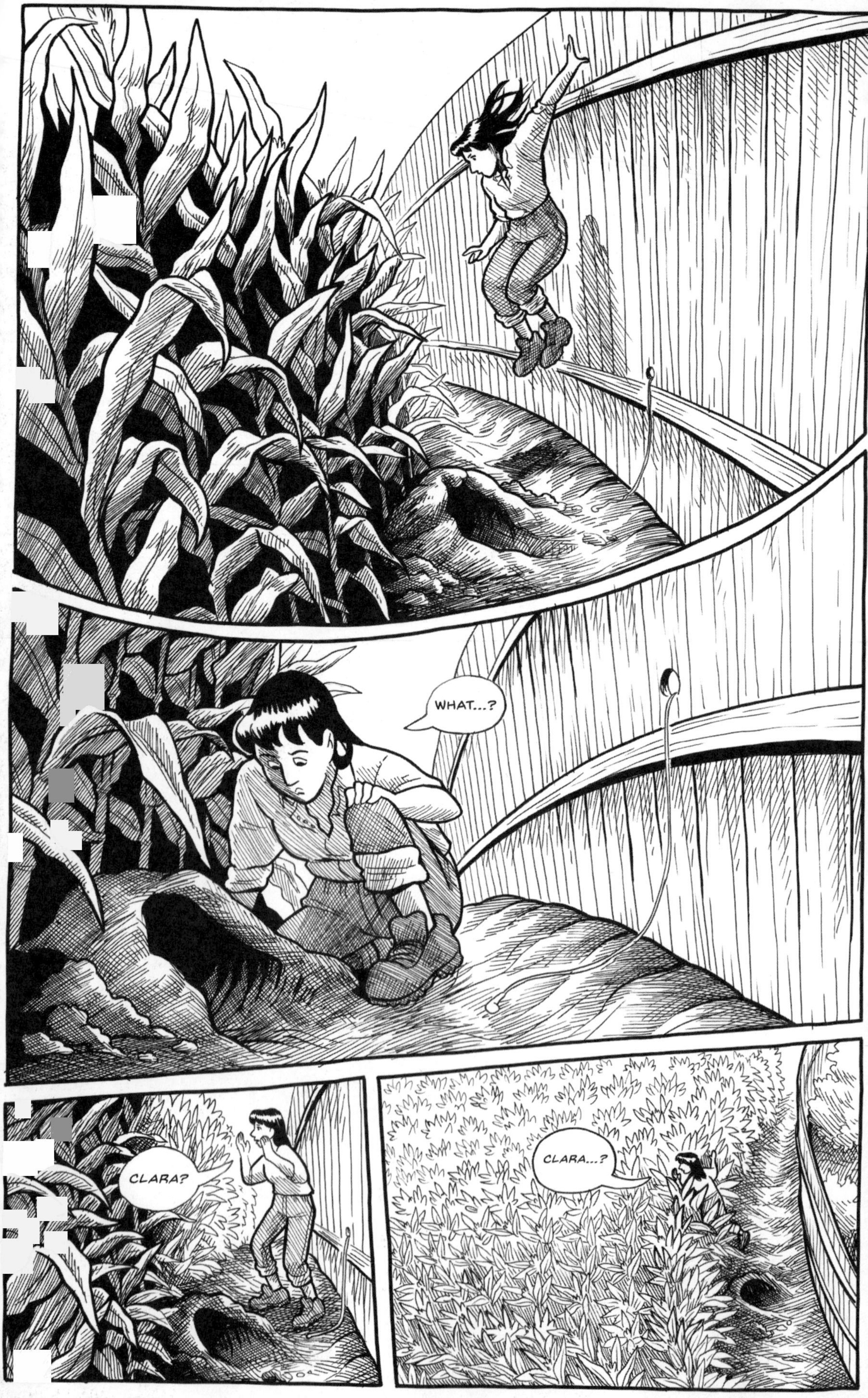
WHAT...?
CLARA?
CLARA...?

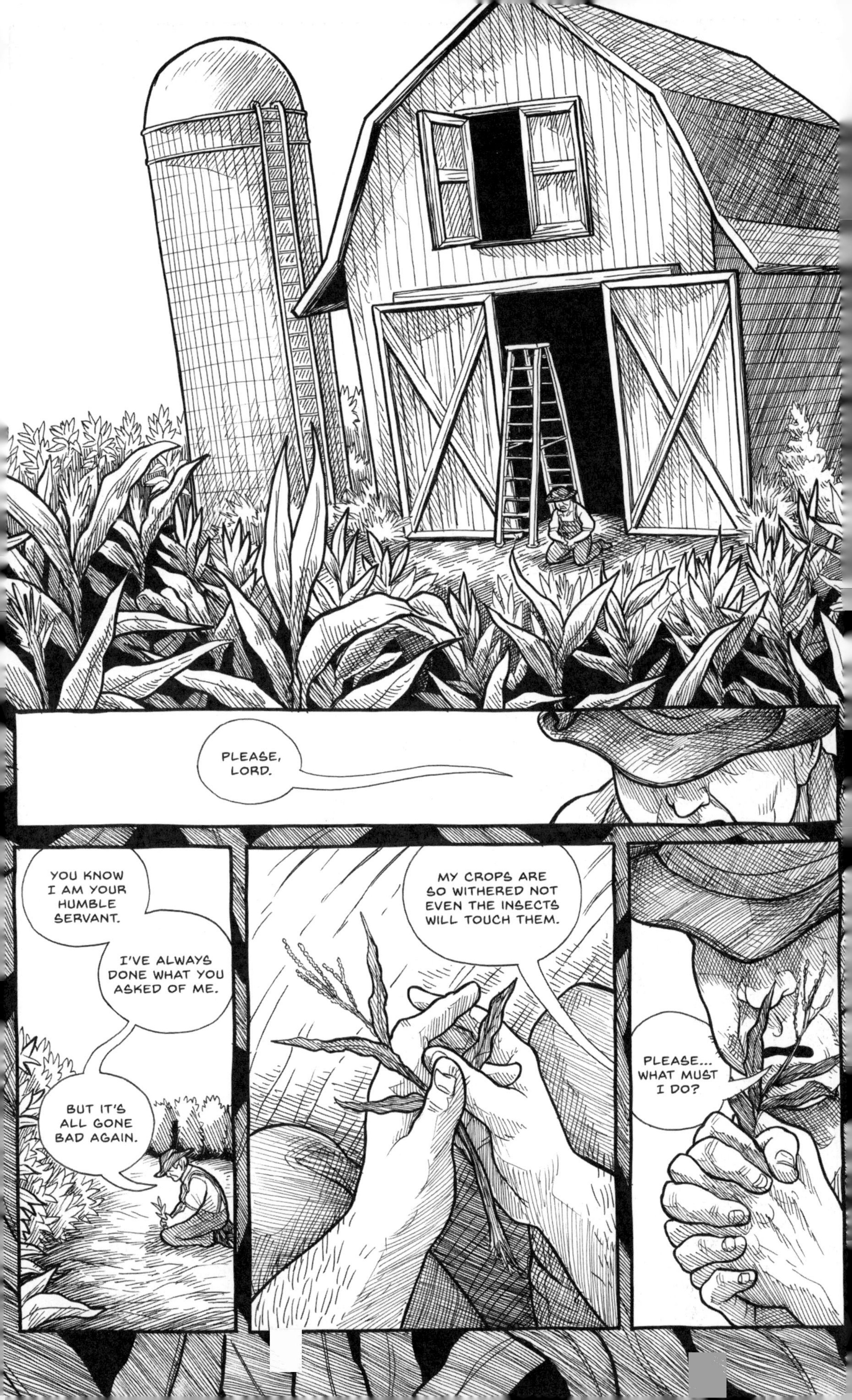
PLEASE, LORD.
YOU KNOW I AM YOUR HUMBLE SERVANT.
I'VE ALWAYS DONE WHAT YOU ASKED OF ME.
BUT IT'S ALL GONE BAD AGAIN.
MY CROPS ARE SO WITHERED NOT EVEN THE INSECTS WILL TOUCH THEM.
PLEASE... WHAT MUST I DO?

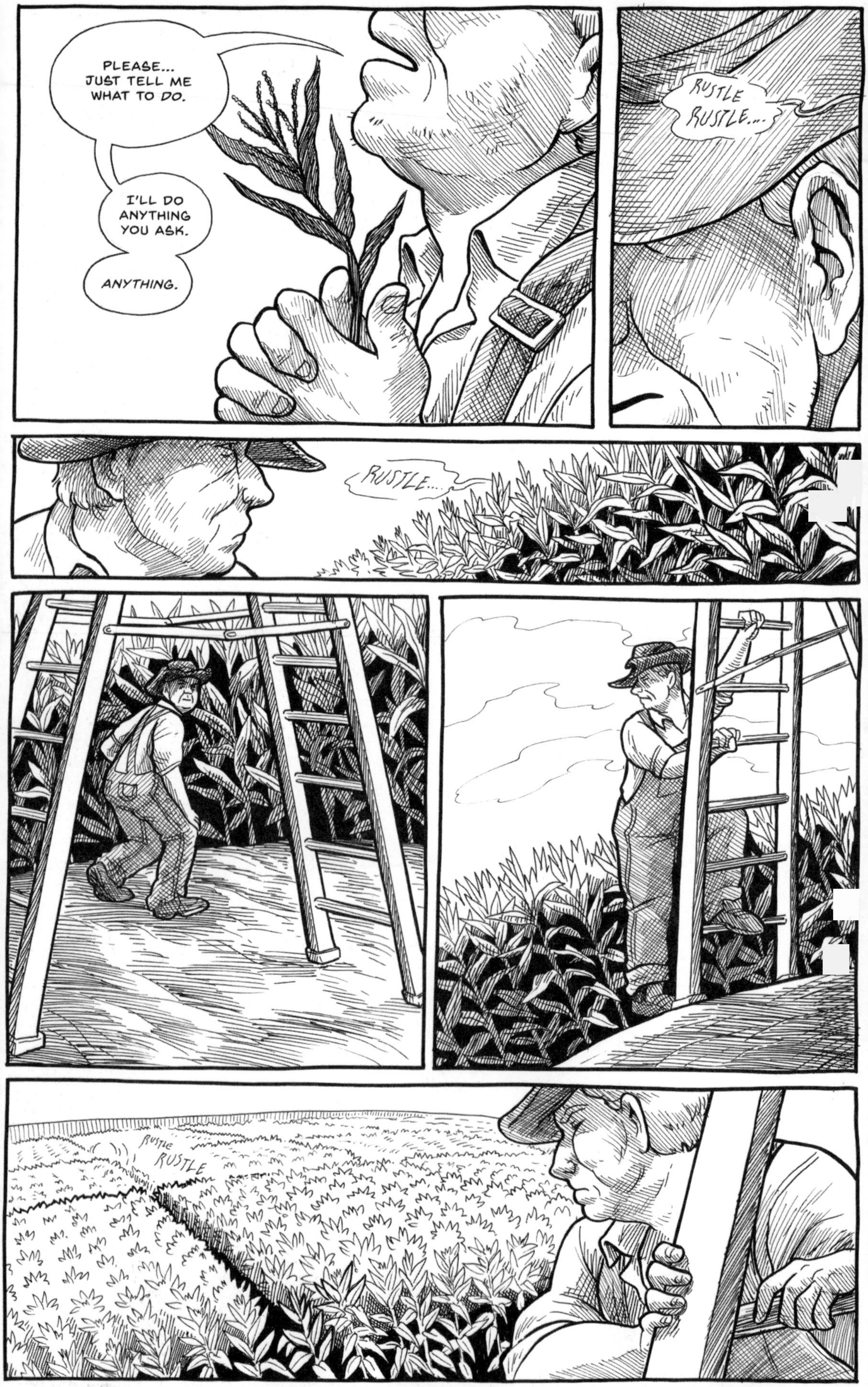
PLEASE... JUST TELL ME WHAT TO DO.
I'LL DO ANYTHING YOU ASK.
ANYTHING.
RUSTLE RUSTLE...
RUSTLE...
RUSTLE RUSTLE

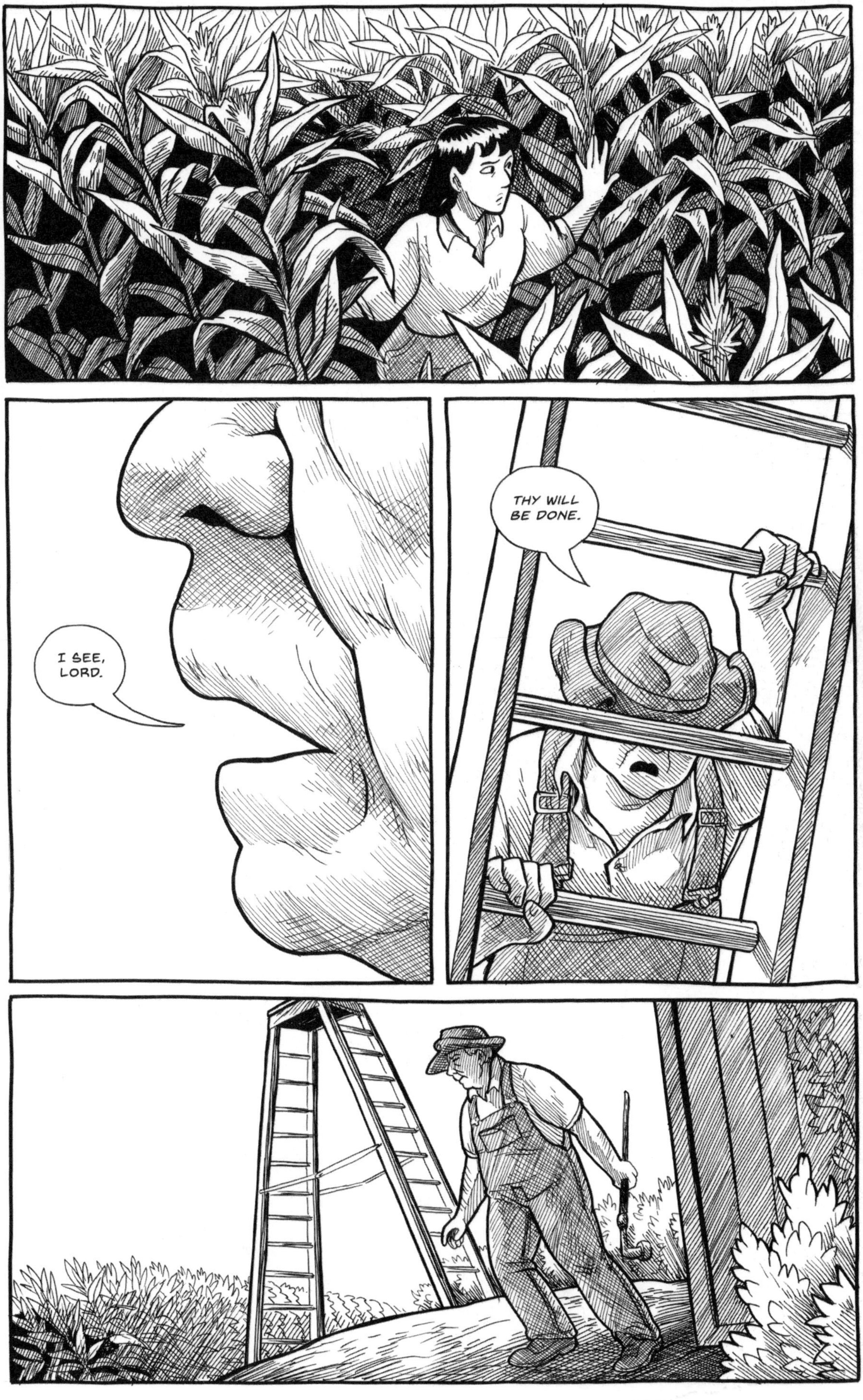
I SEE, LORD.
THY WILL BE DONE.

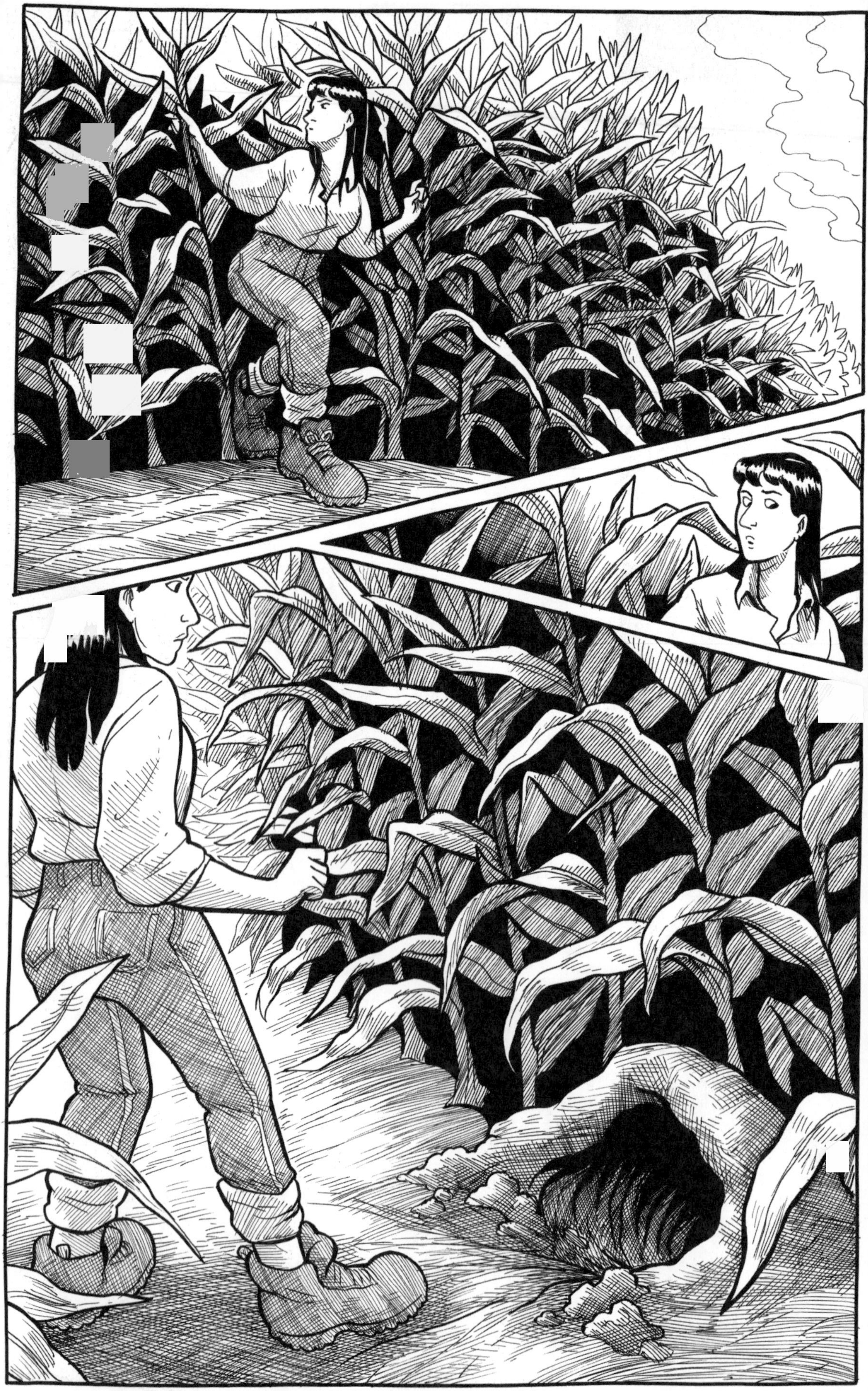

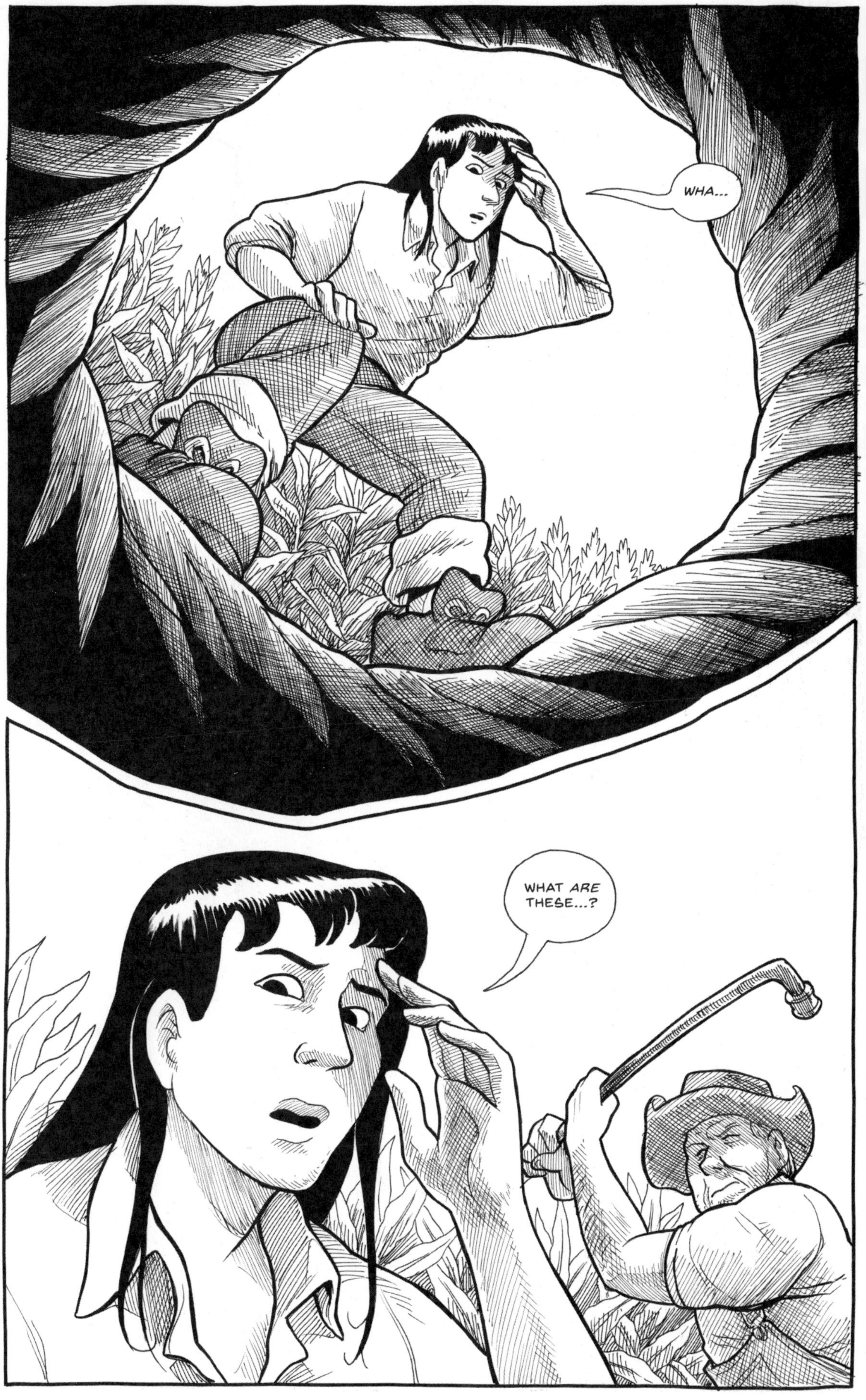
WHA...
WHAT ARE THESE...?

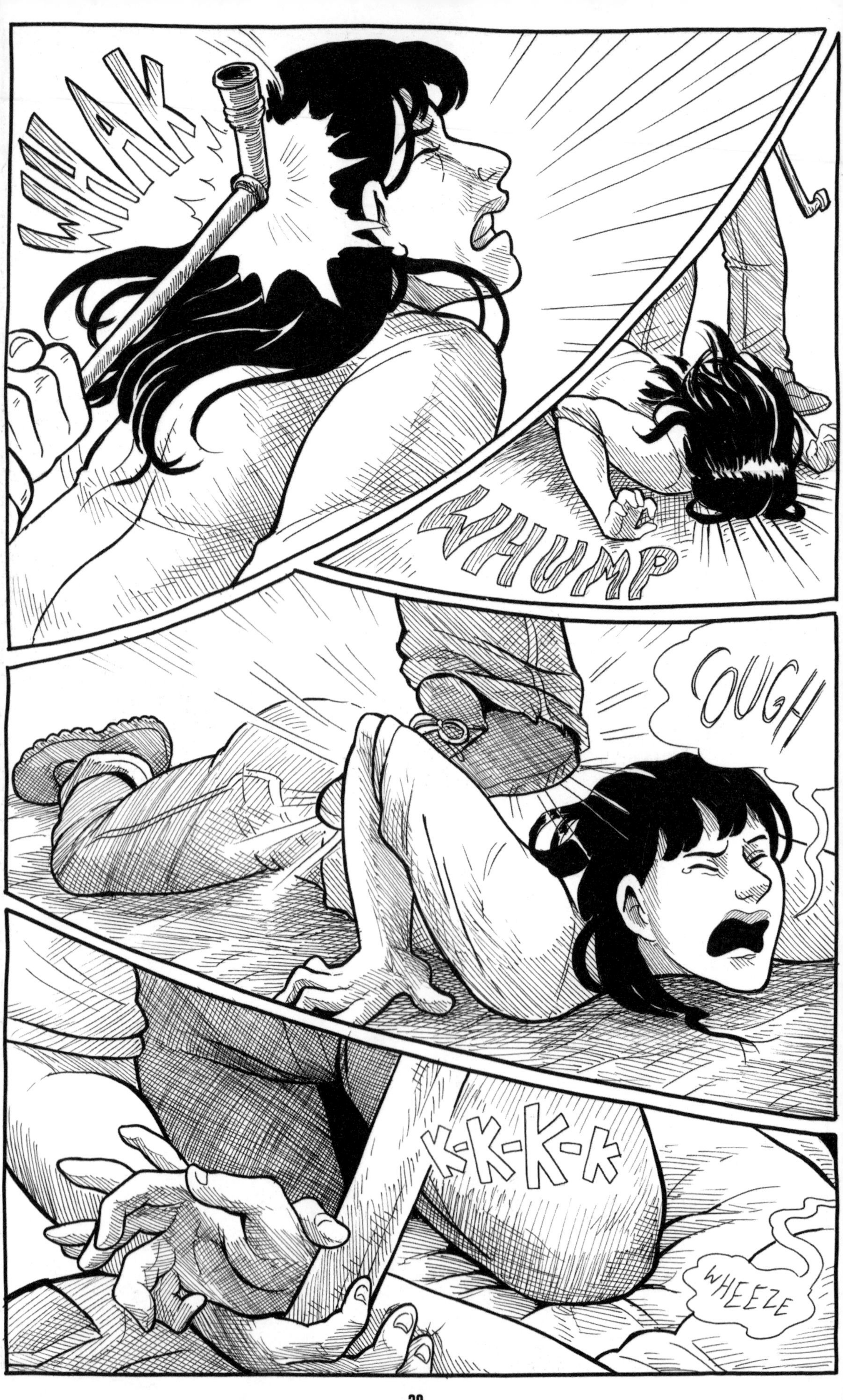
WHAK
WHUMP
COUGH
K-K-K-K
WHEEZE

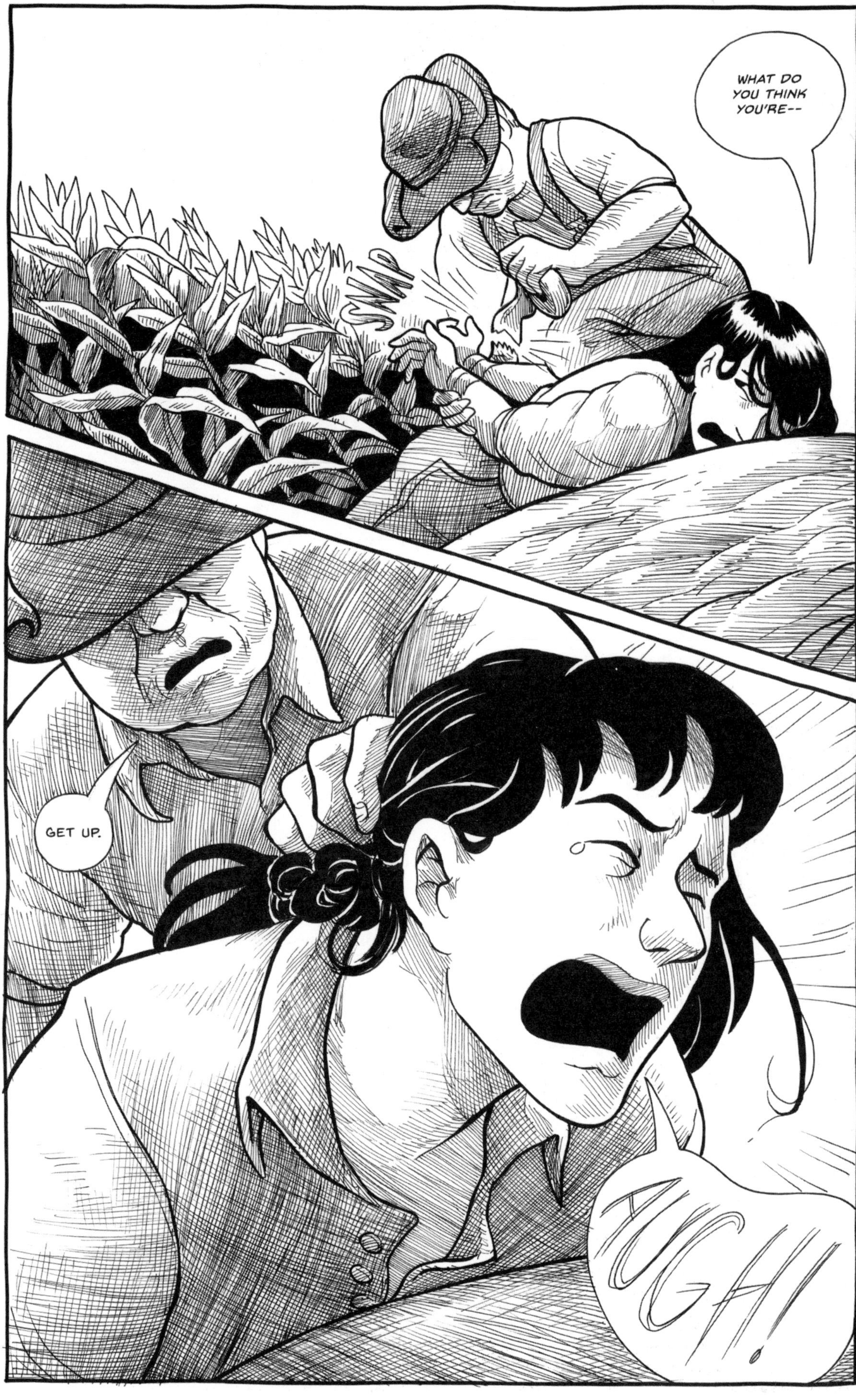
WHAT DO YOU THINK YOU'RE--
SWIP
GET UP.
AUGH!

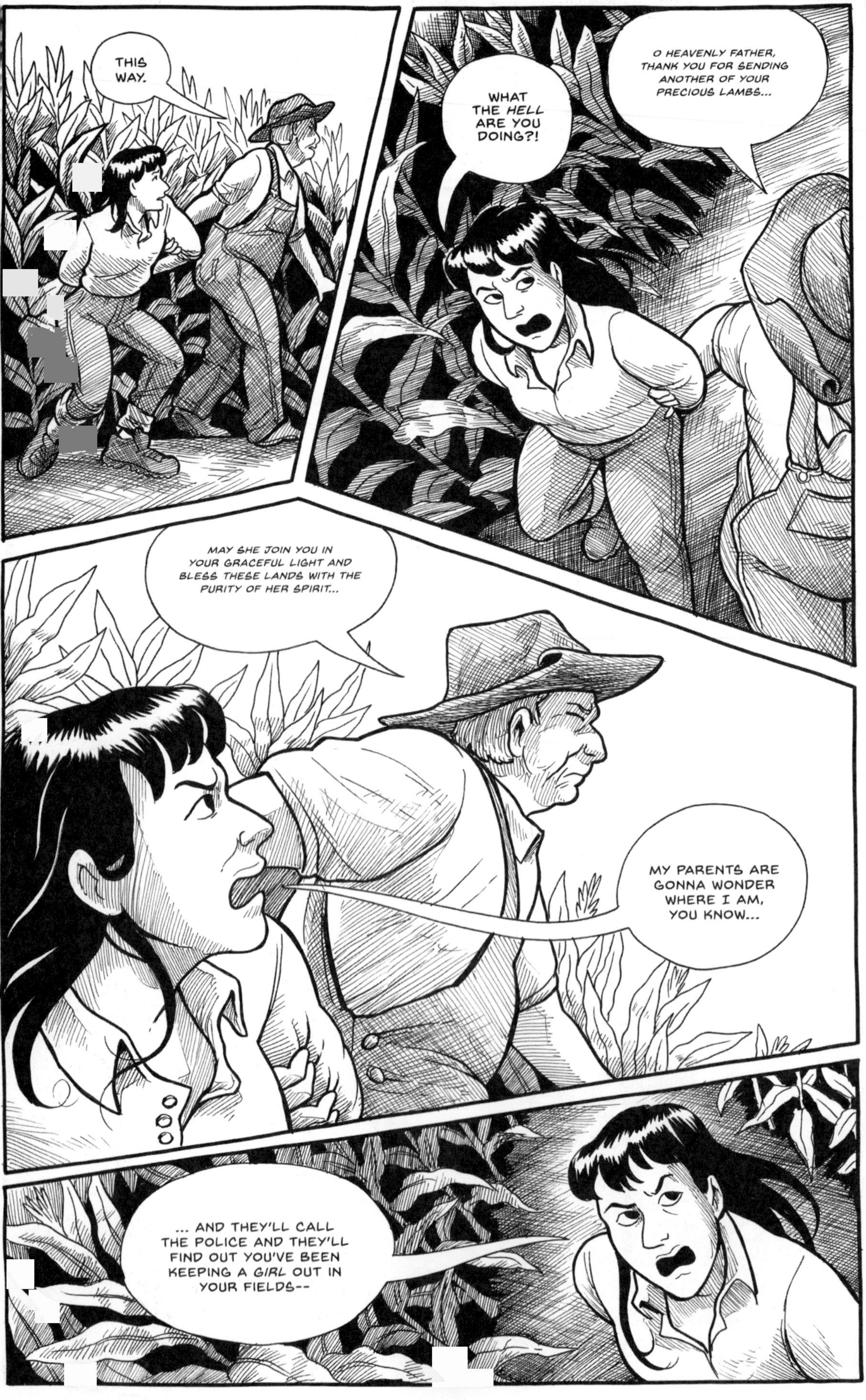
THIS WAY.
WHAT THE HELL ARE YOU DOING?!
O HEAVENLY FATHER, THANK YOU FOR SENDING ANOTHER OF YOUR PRECIOUS LAMBS...
MAY SHE JOIN YOU IN YOUR GRACEFUL LIGHT AND BLESS THESE LANDS WITH THE PURITY OF HER SPIRIT...
MY PARENTS ARE GONNA WONDER WHERE I AM, YOU KNOW...
... AND THEY'LL CALL THE POLICE AND THEY'LL FIND OUT YOU'VE BEEN KEEPING A GIRL OUT IN YOUR FIELDS--

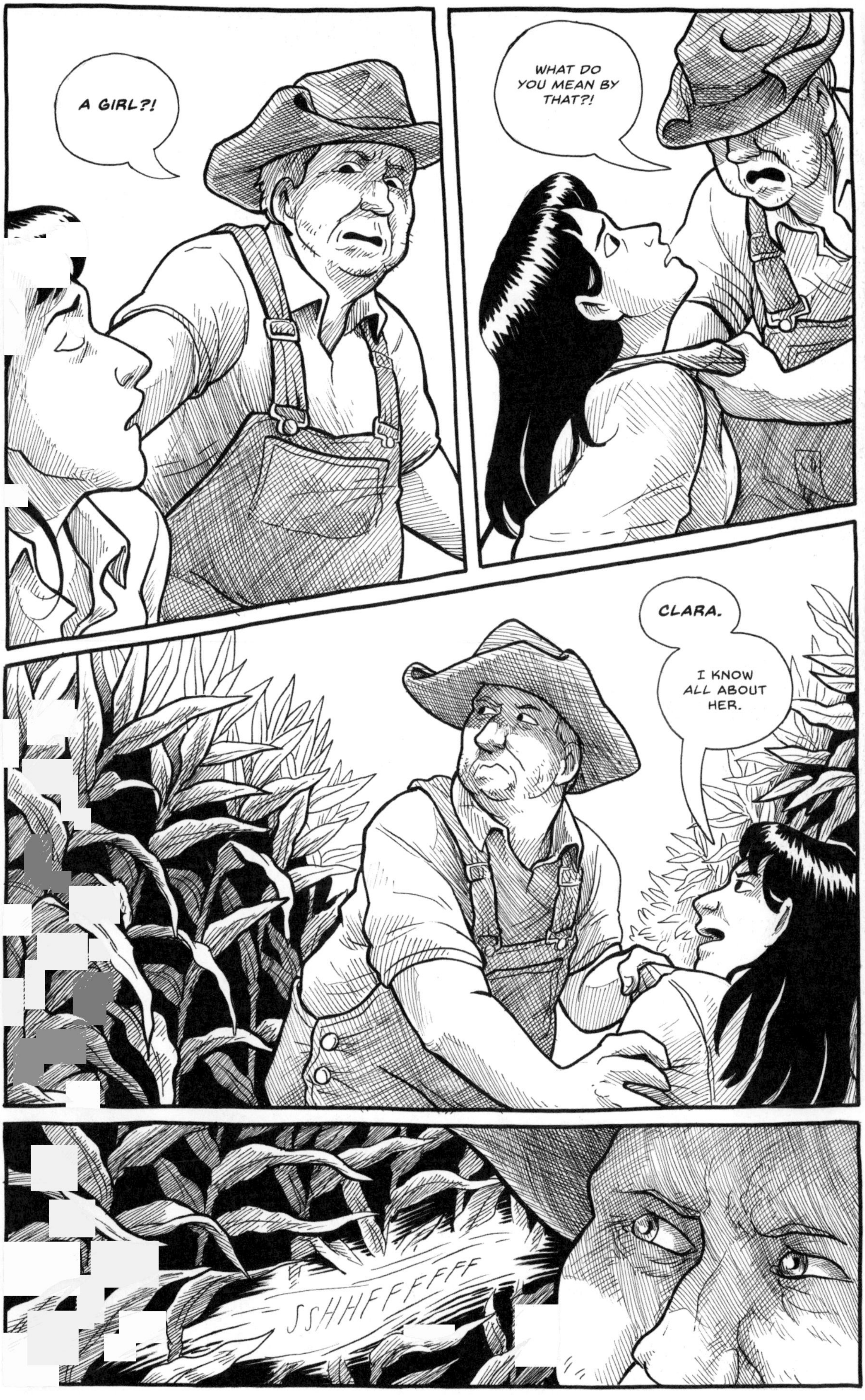
A GIRL?!
WHAT DO YOU MEAN BY THAT?!
CLARA.
I KNOW ALL ABOUT HER.
SSHHFFFFFFF

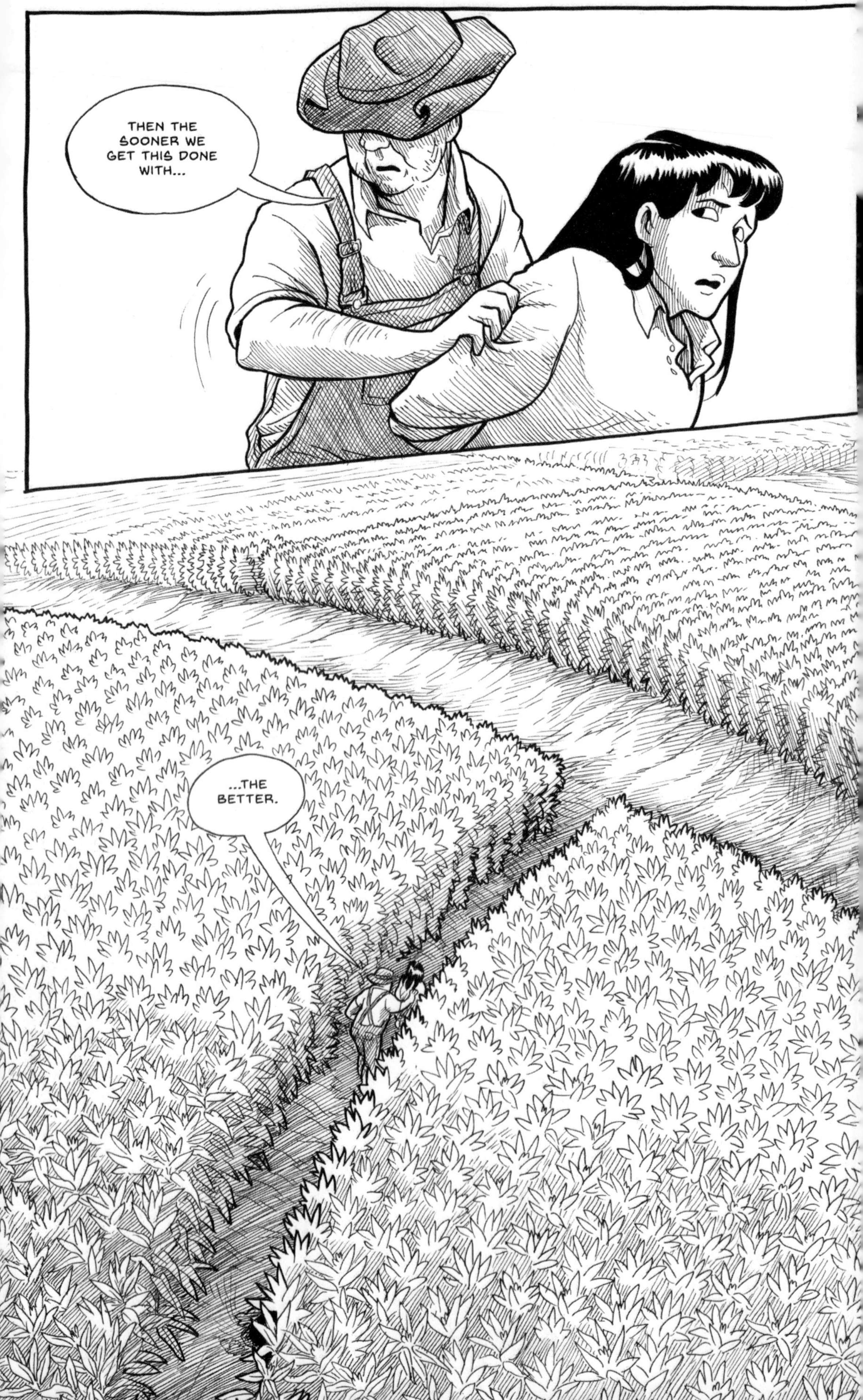
THEN THE SOONER WE GET THIS DONE WITH...
...THE BETTER.

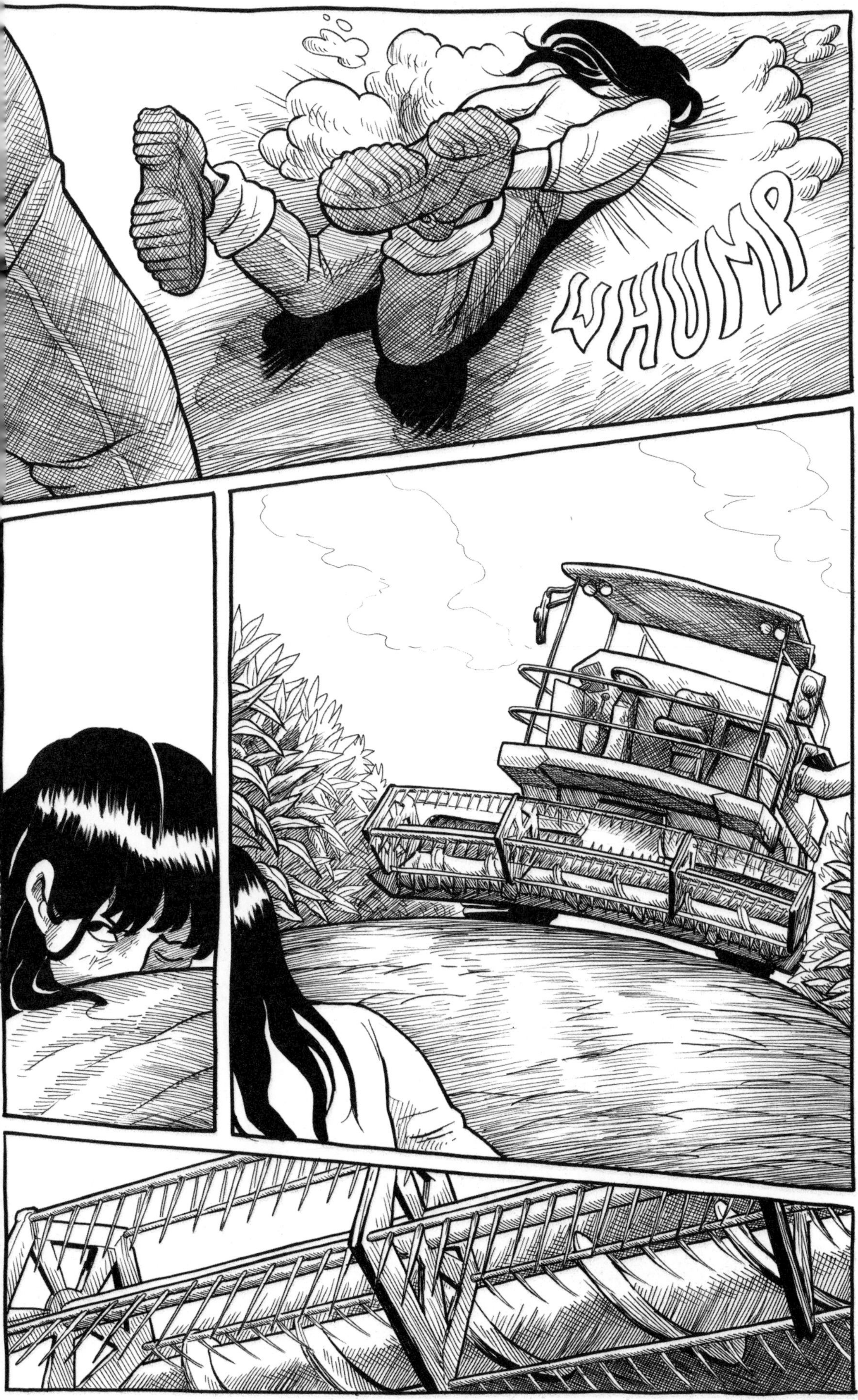
WHUMP

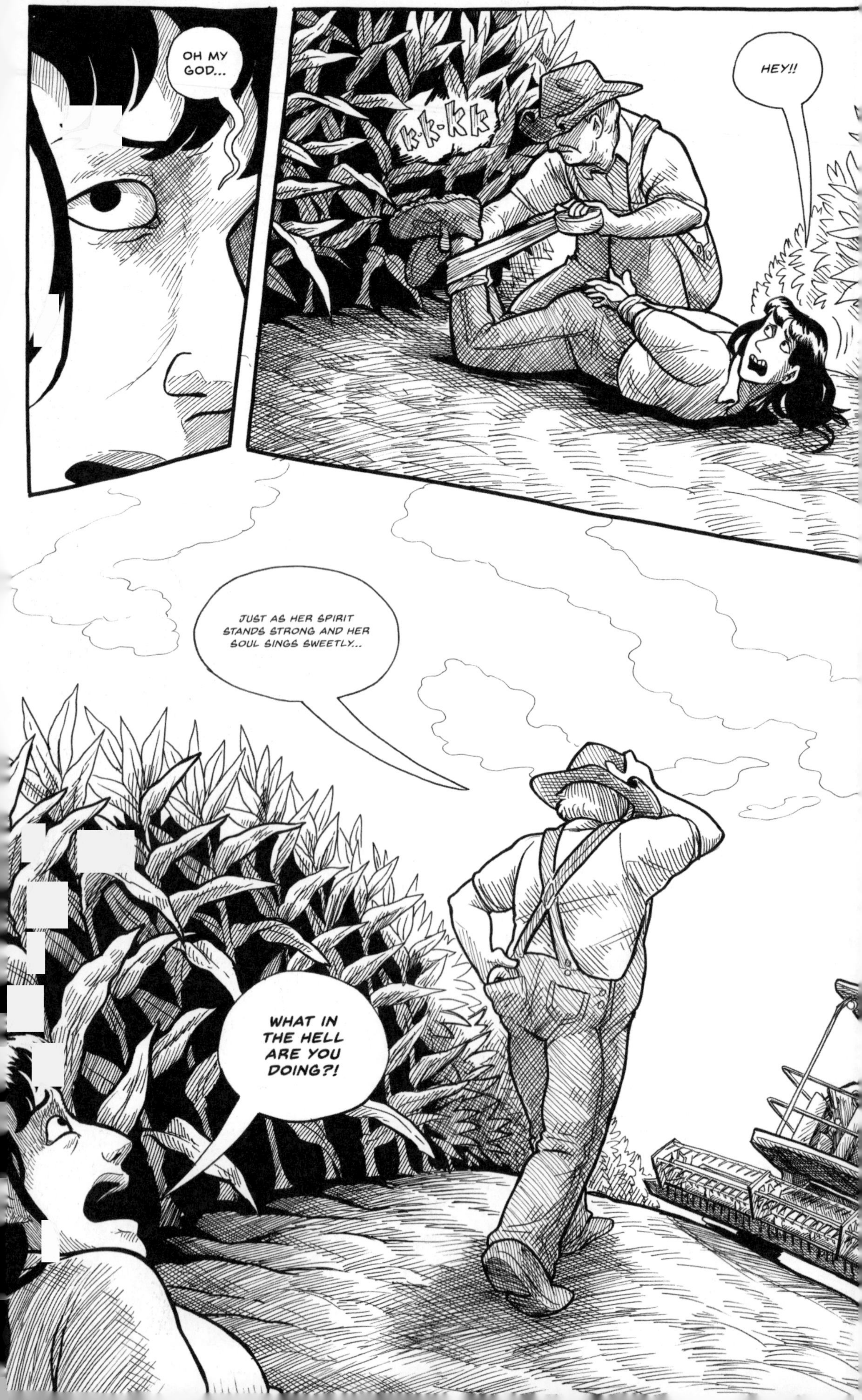
OH MY GOD...
HEY!!
JUST AS HER SPIRIT STANDS STRONG AND HER SOUL SINGS SWEETLY...
WHAT IN THE HELL ARE YOU DOING?!

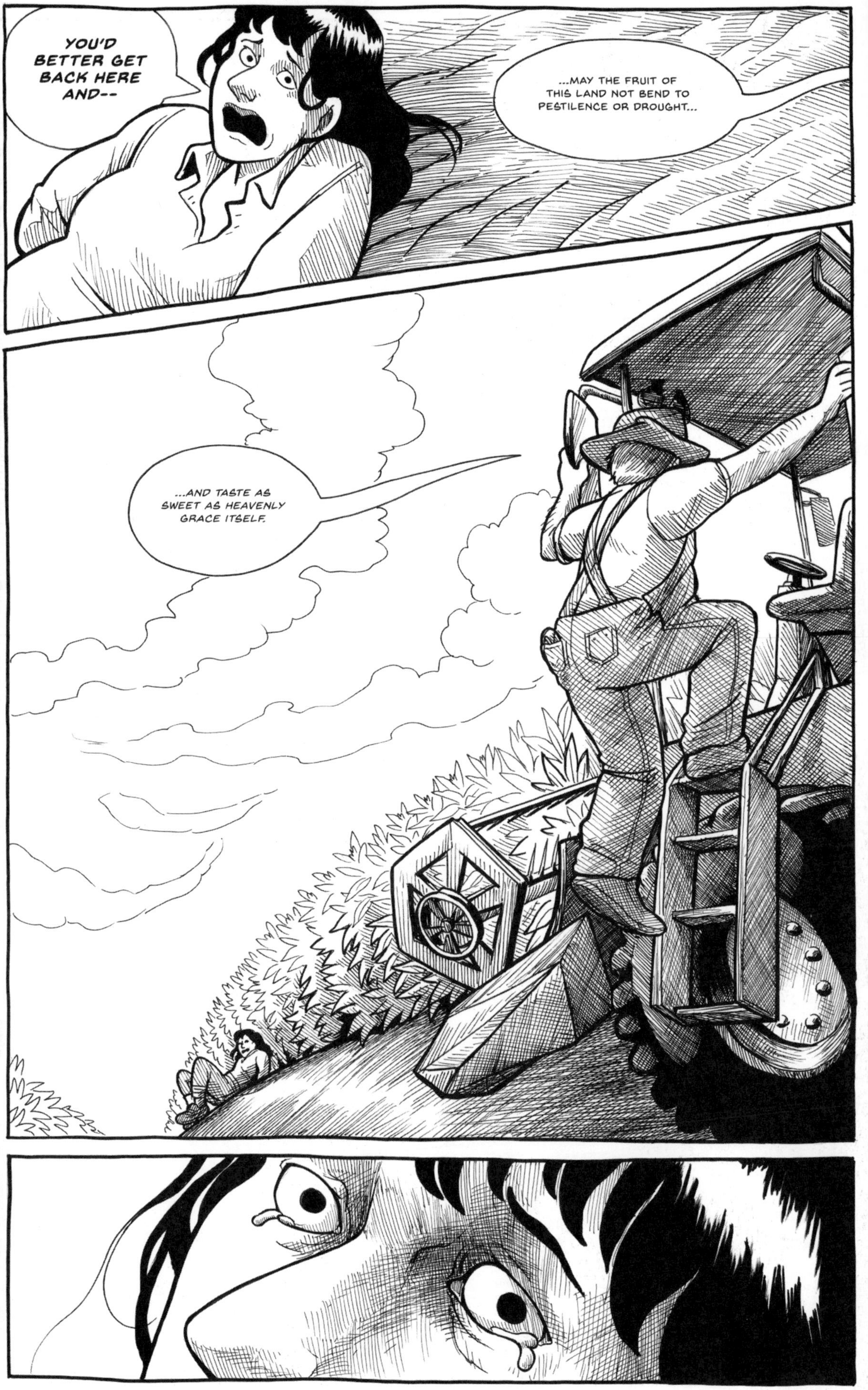
YOU'D BETTER GET BACK HERE AND--
...MAY THE FRUIT OF THIS LAND NOT BEND TO PESTILENCE OR DROUGHT...
...AND TASTE AS SWEET AS HEAVENLY GRACE ITSELF.

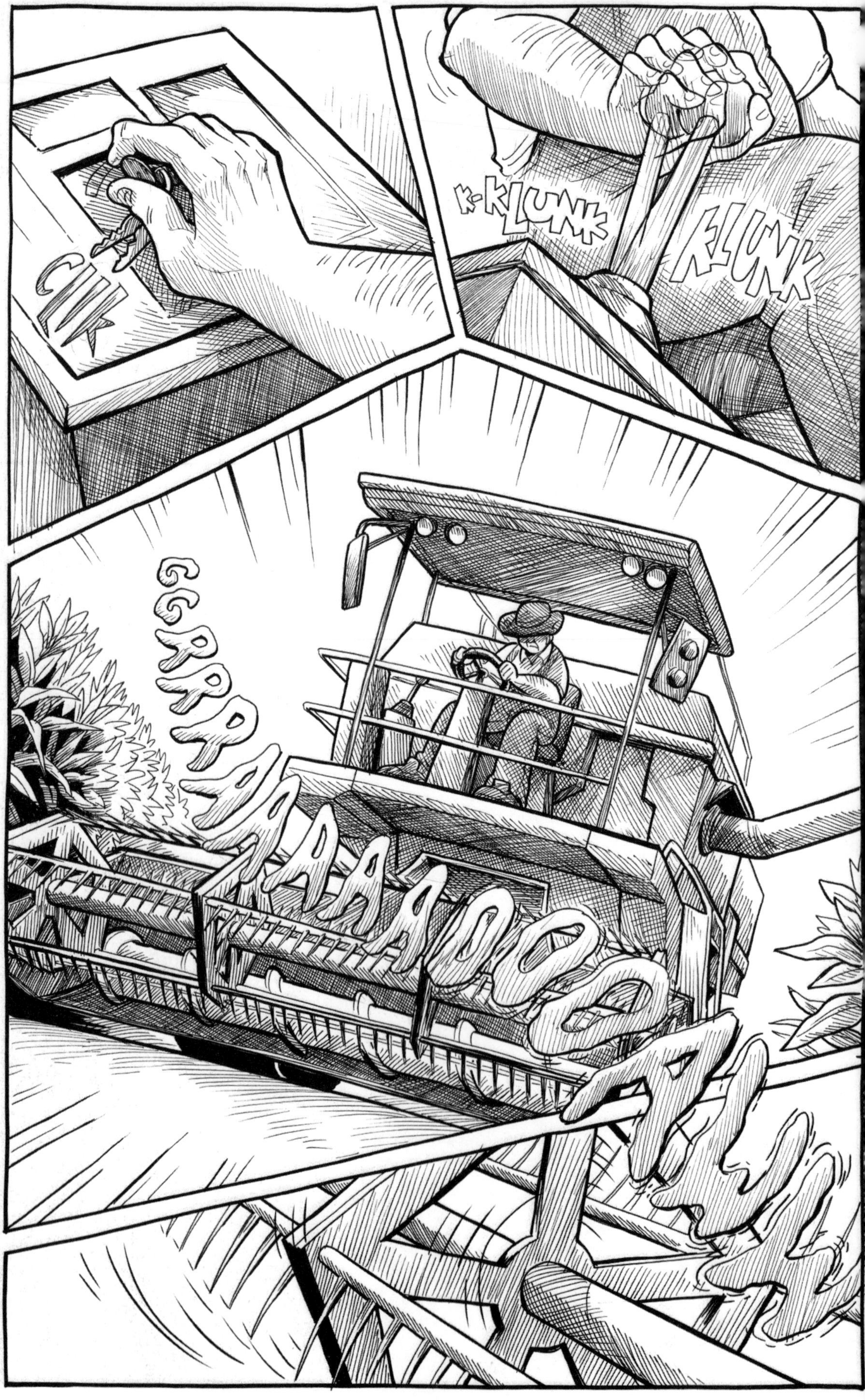
CLIK
K-KLUNK
KLUNK
GGRRRAAAAAOOOAAA

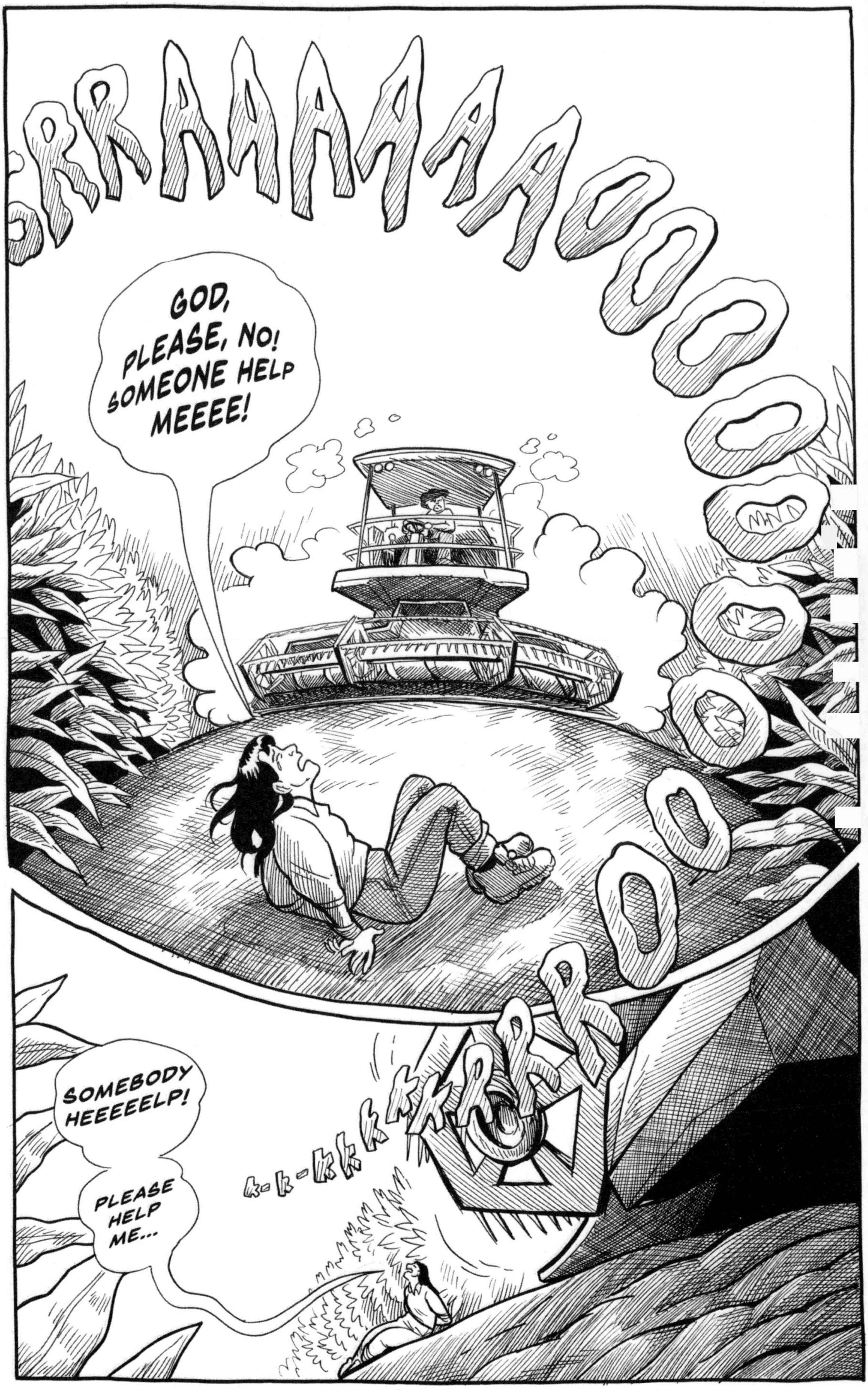
GRRAAAAAAOOOOOOOOOOROOO
GOD, PLEASE, NO! SOMEONE HELP MEEEE!
KRRR
K-K-KKKKK
SOMEBODY HEEEEELP!
PLEASE HELP ME...

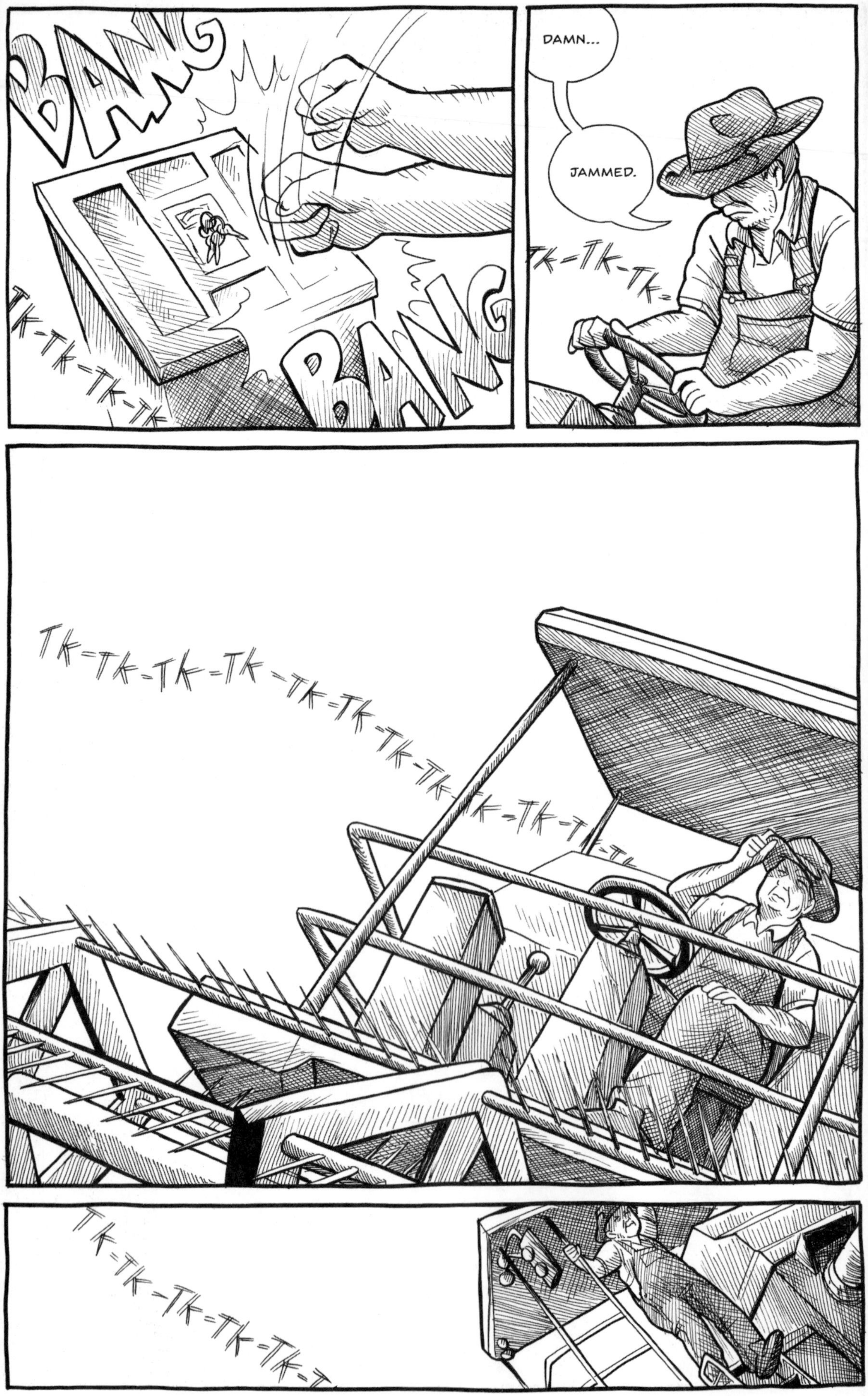
BANG
TK-TK-TK-TK-TK
BANG
DAMN...
JAMMED.
TK-TK-TK-TK=
TK-TK-TK-TK-TK-TK-TK-TK-TK-TK-TK-TK-TK
TK-TK-TK-TK-TK-TK-T

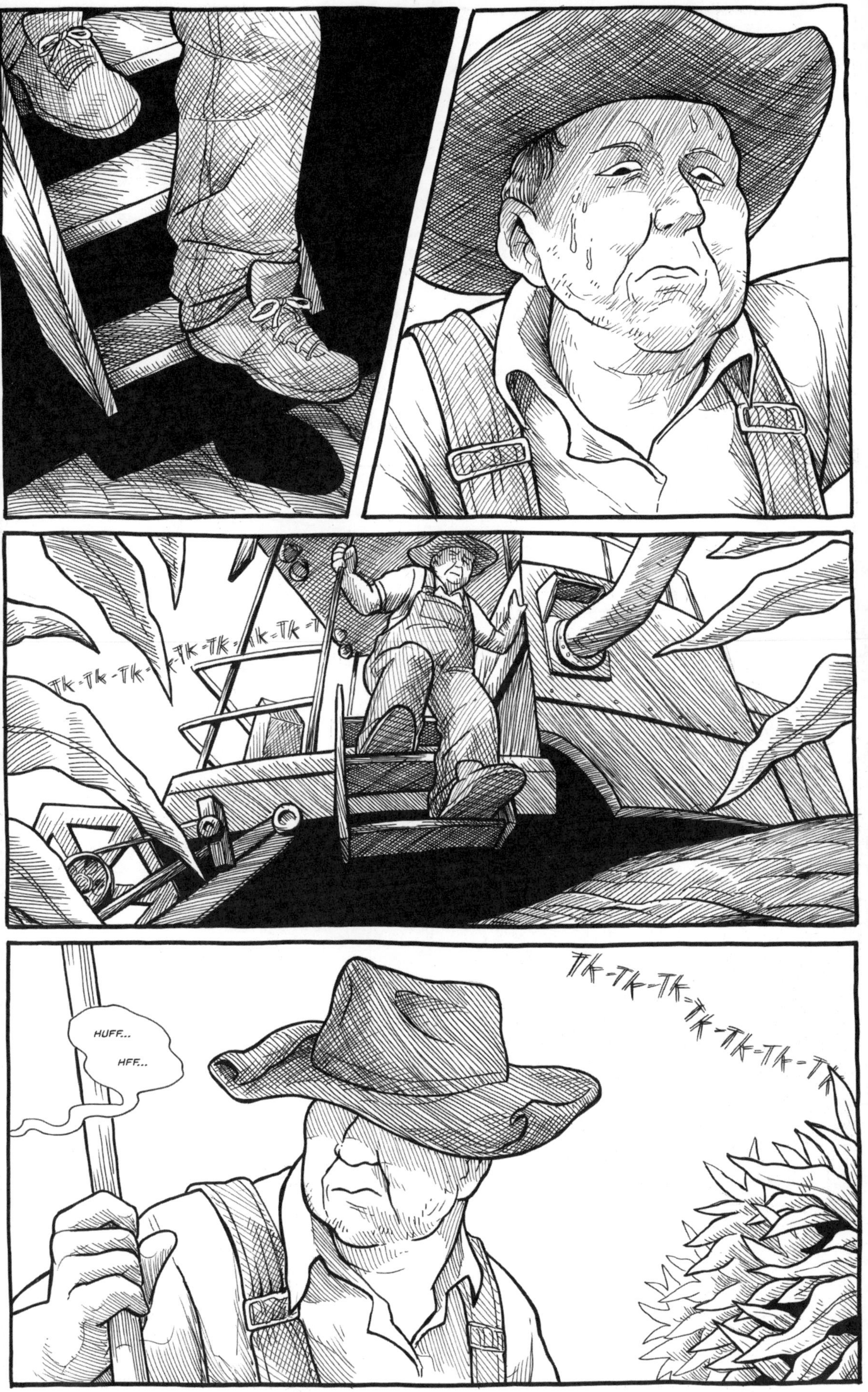
TK-TK-TK-TK-TK-TK-TK-TK-TK
HUFF...
HFF...
TK-TK-TK-TK-TK-TK-TK-TK-TK

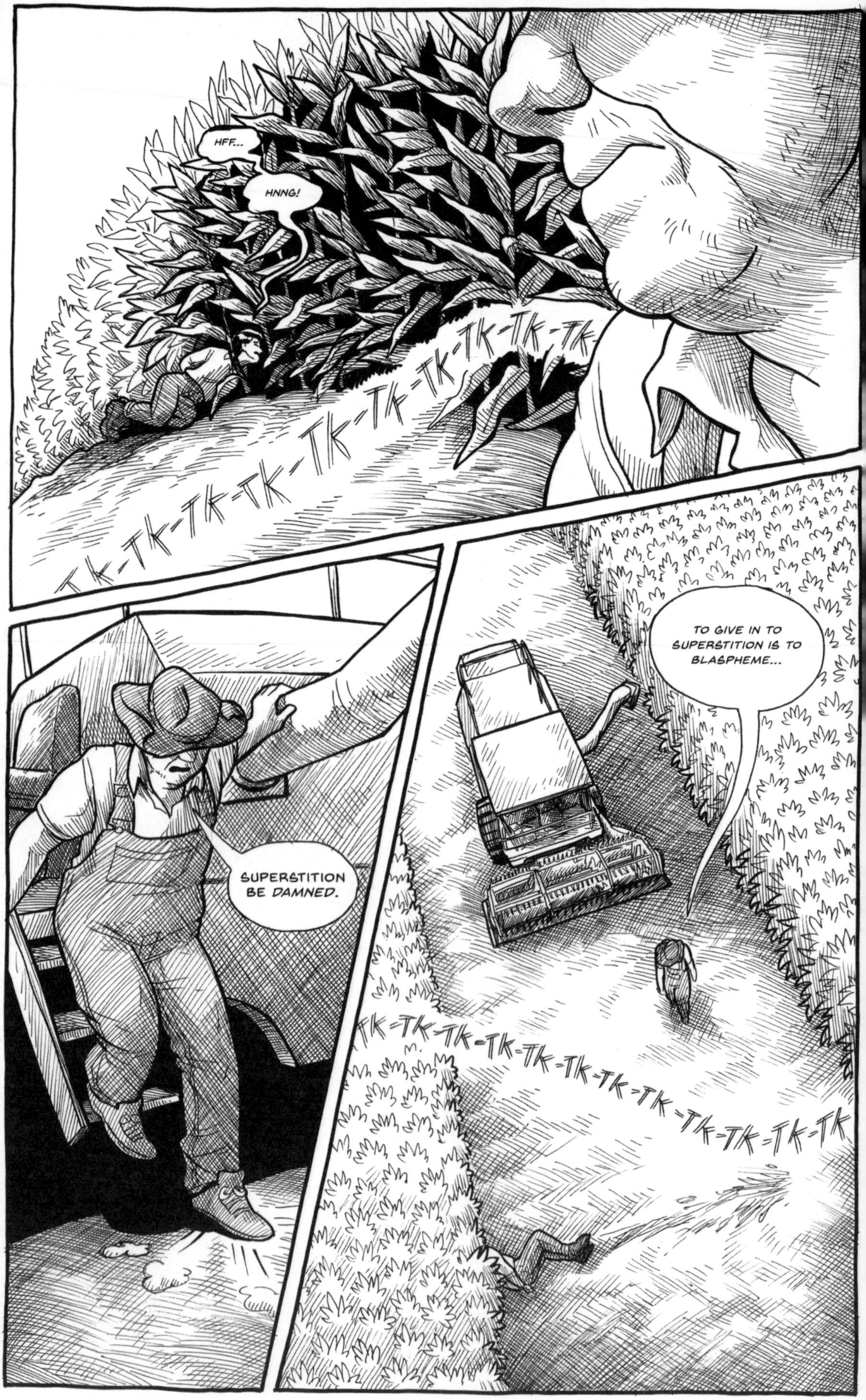
HFF...
HNNG!
TK-TK-TK-TK-TK-TK-TK-TK-TK-TK-TK-TK-TK
SUPERSTITION BE DAMNED.
TO GIVE IN TO SUPERSTITION IS TO BLASPHEME...
TK-TK-TK-TK-TK-TK-TK-TK-TK-TK-TK-TK

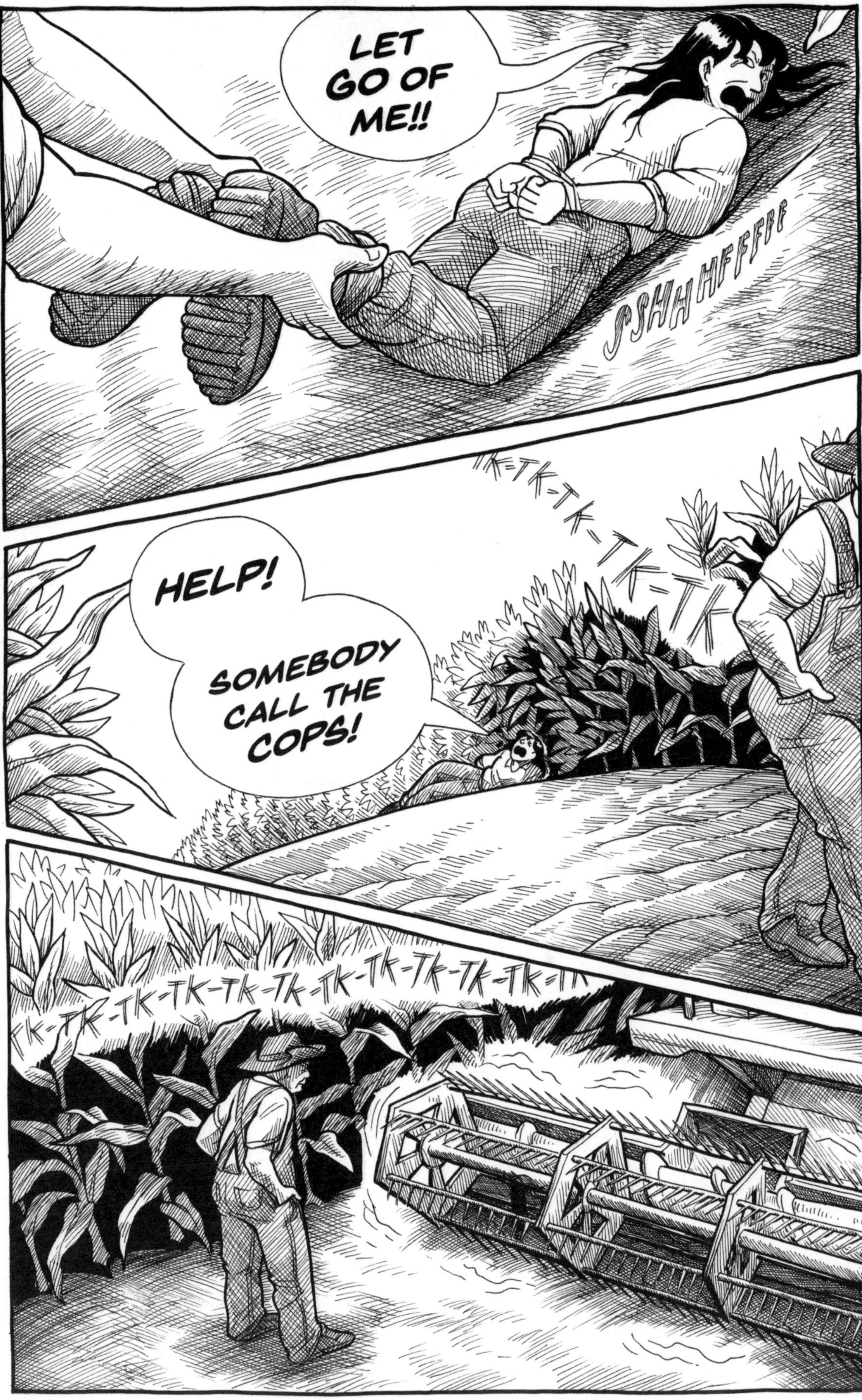
LET GO OF ME!!
SHHHFFFFF
TK-TK-TK-TK-TK-TK
HELP!
SOMEBODY CALL THE COPS!
TK-TK-TK-TK-TK-TK-TK-TK-TK-TK-TK-TK-TK

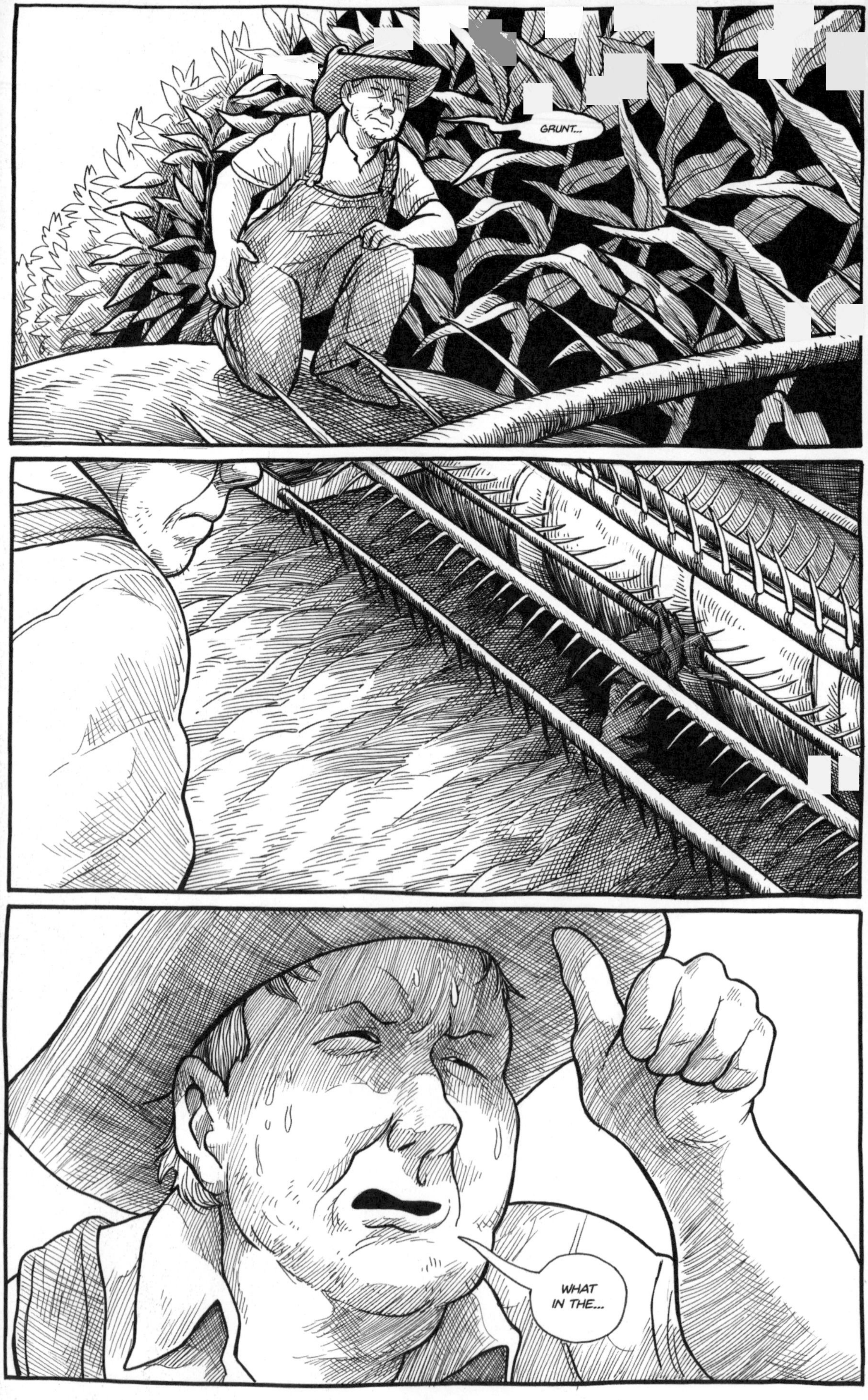
GRUNT...
WHAT IN THE...

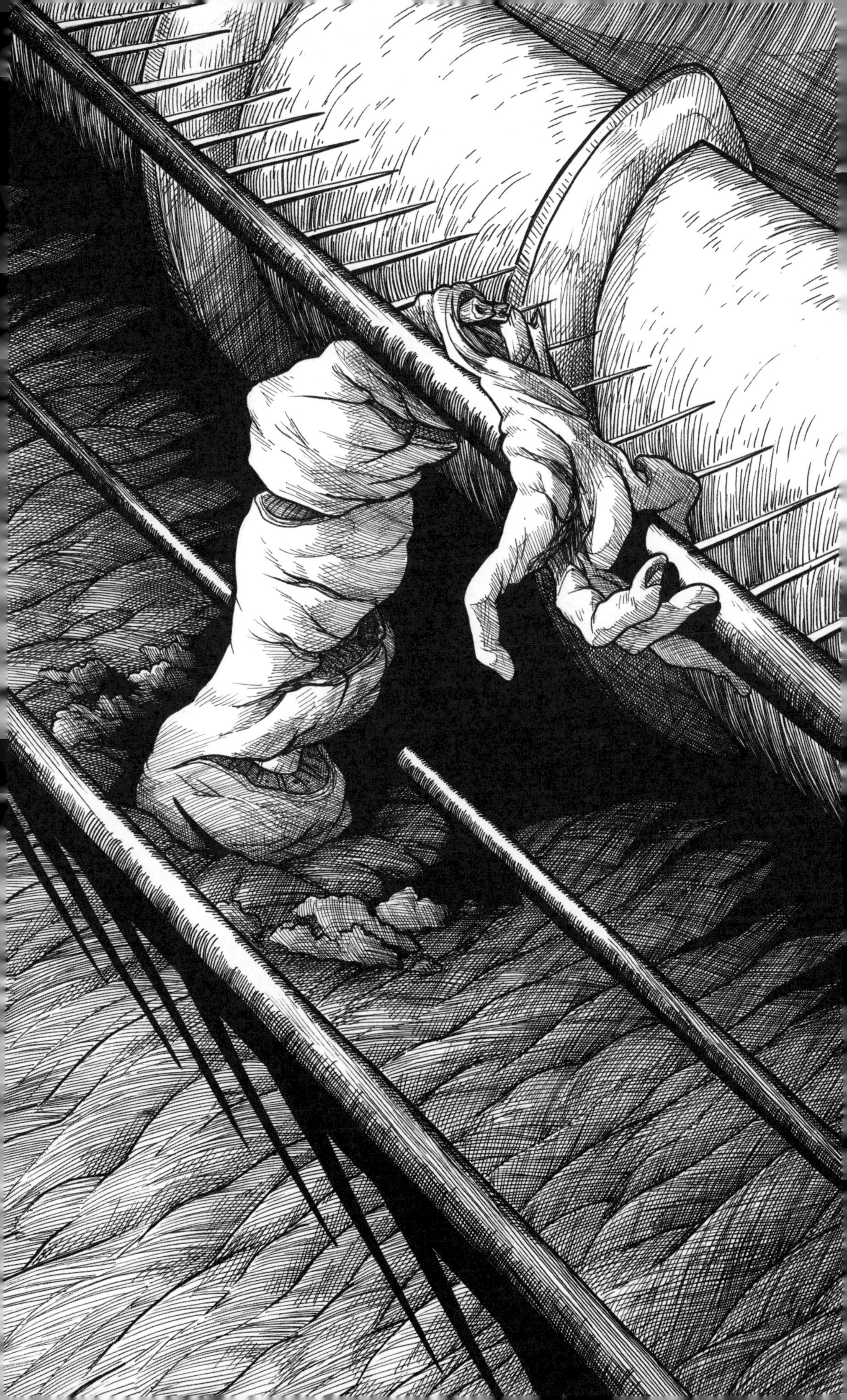

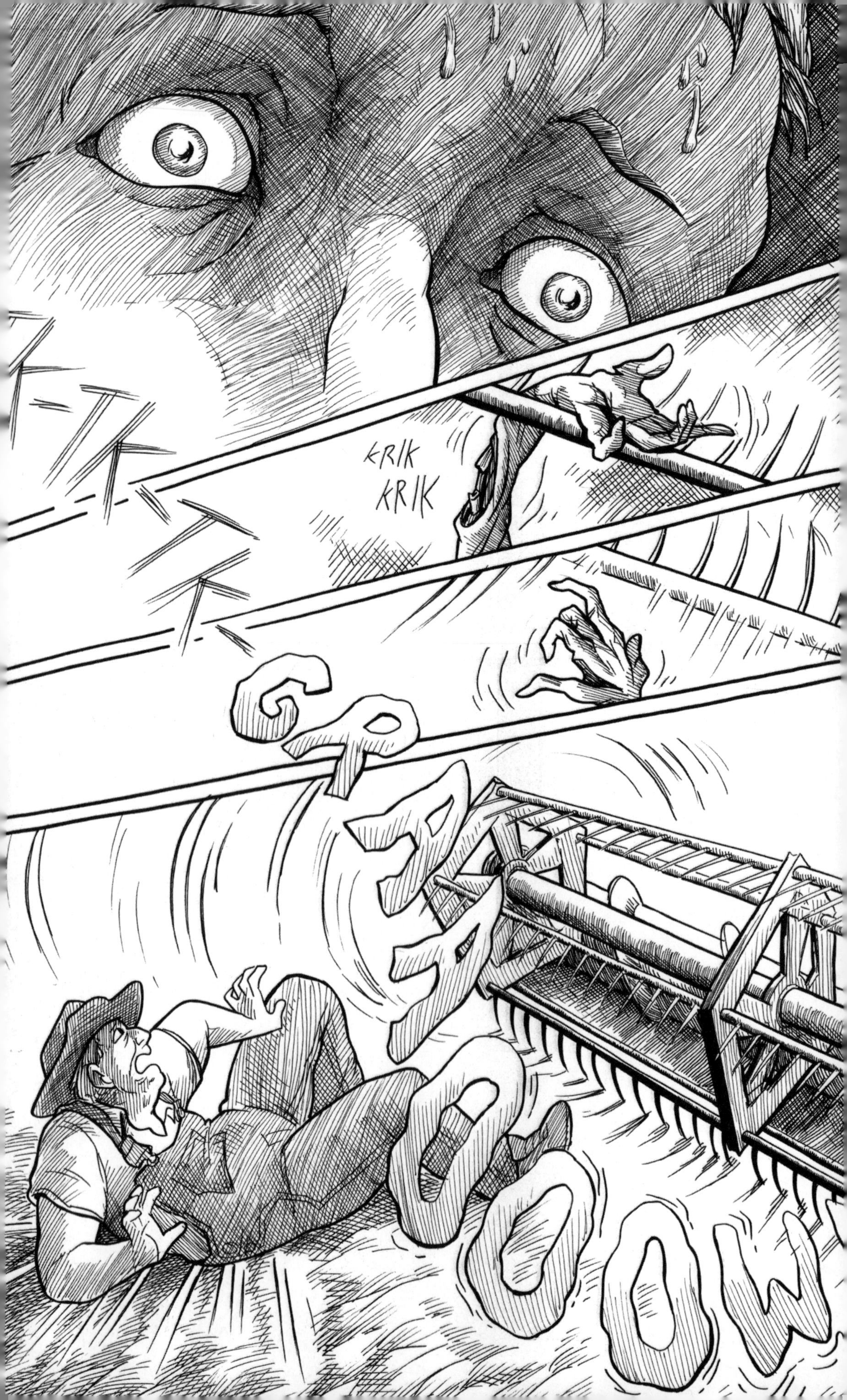
KRIK
KRIK

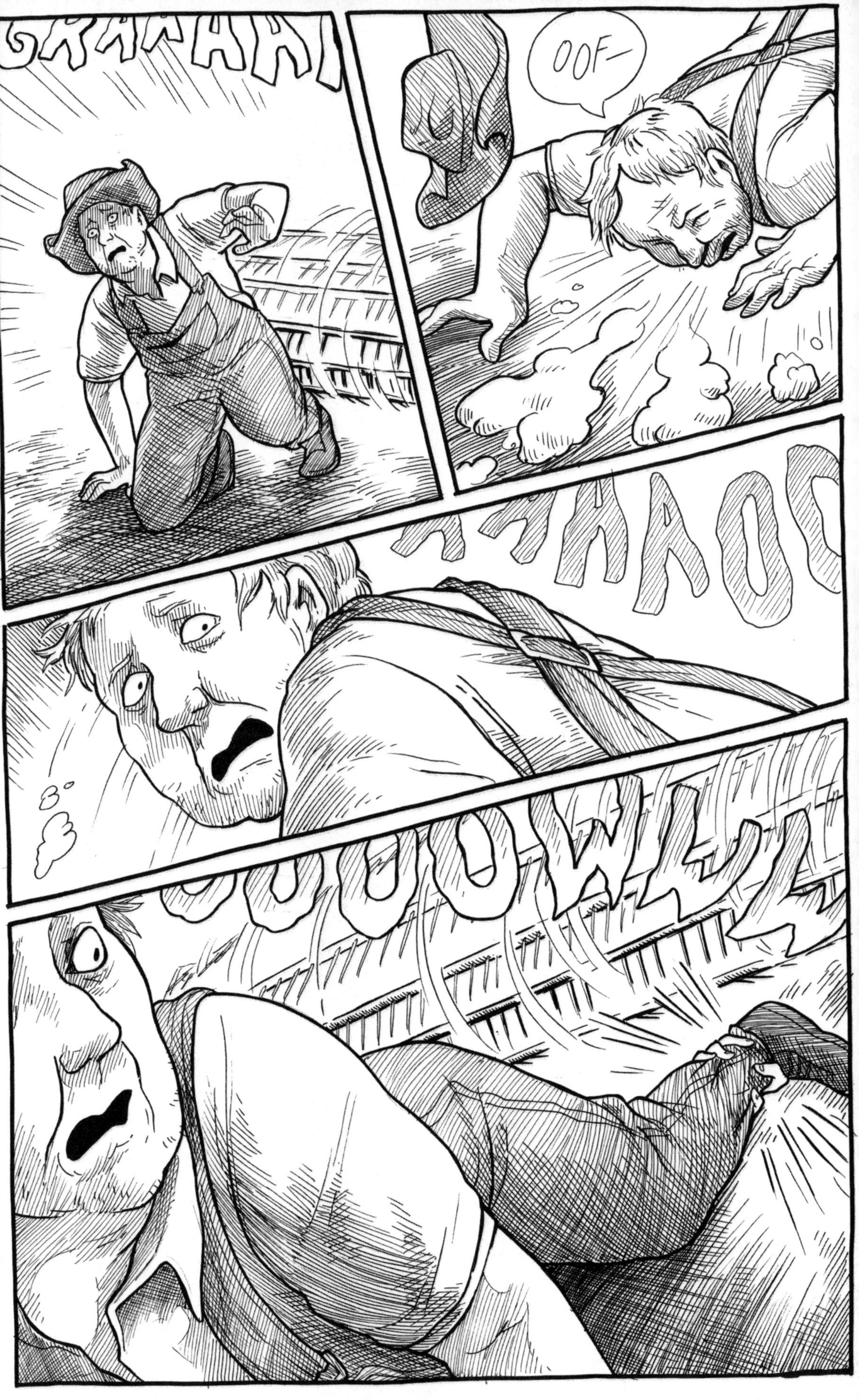
OOF—

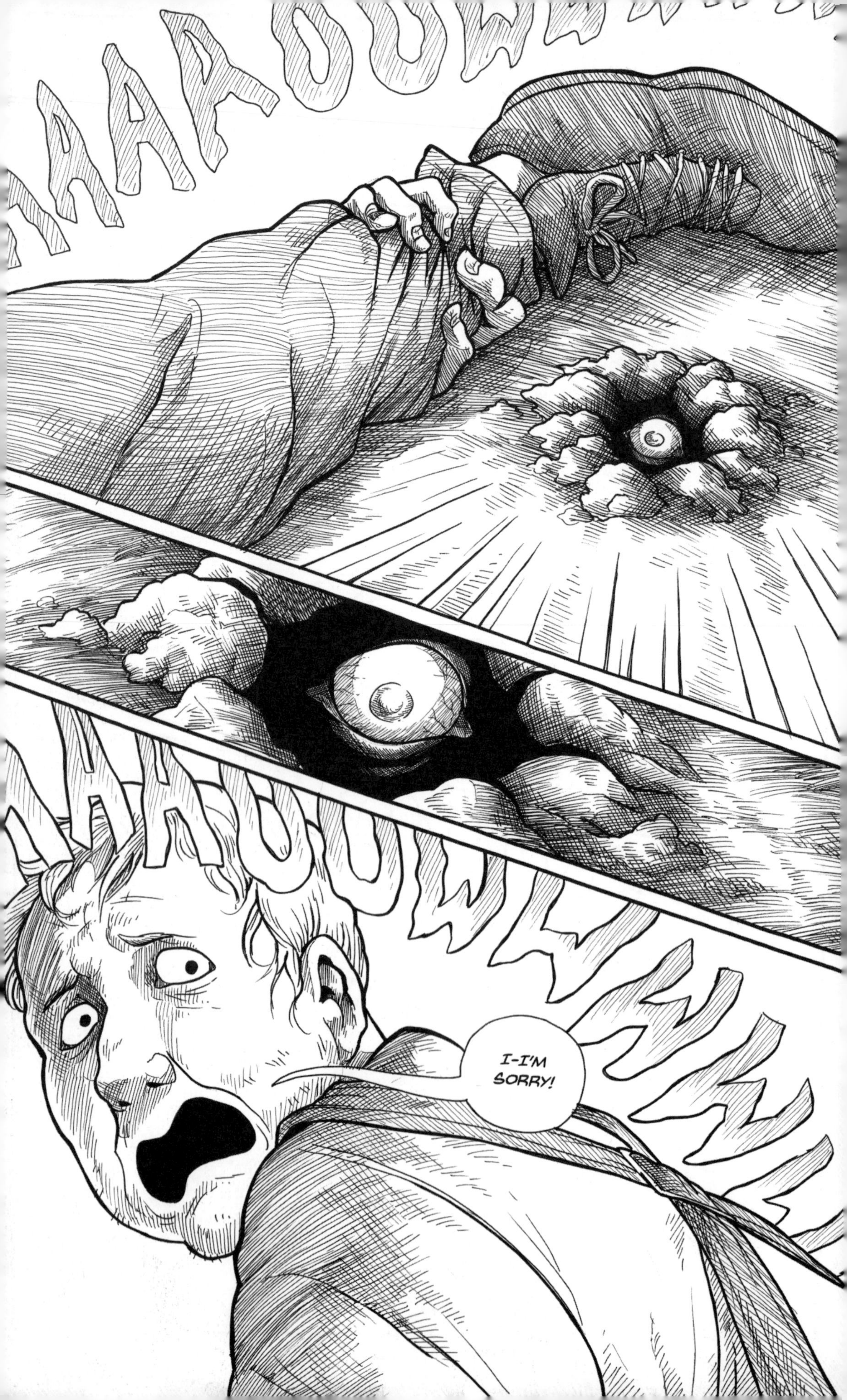
I-I'M SORRY!

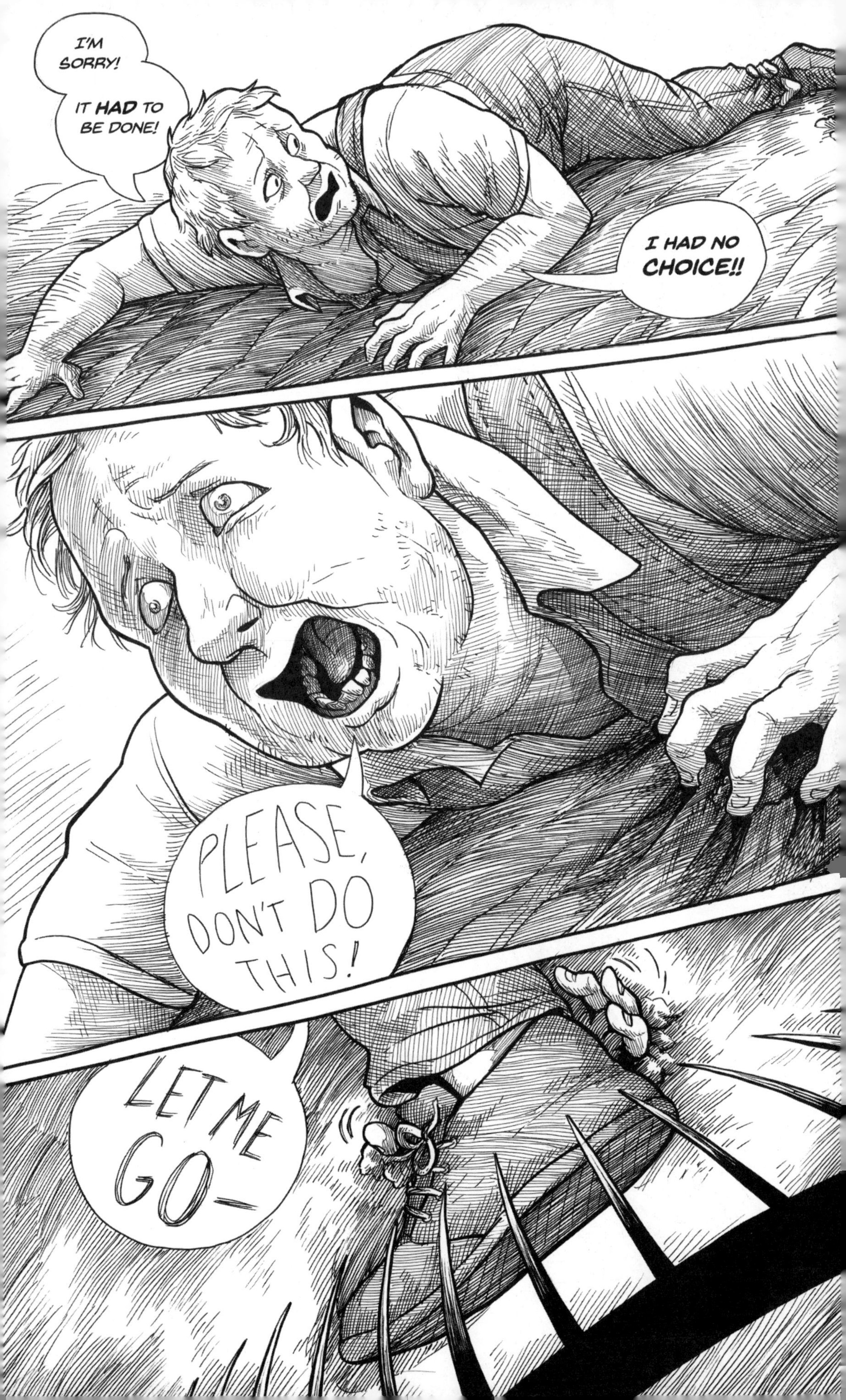
I'M SORRY!
IT HAD TO BE DONE!
I HAD NO CHOICE!!
PLEASE, DON'T DO THIS!
LET ME GO—

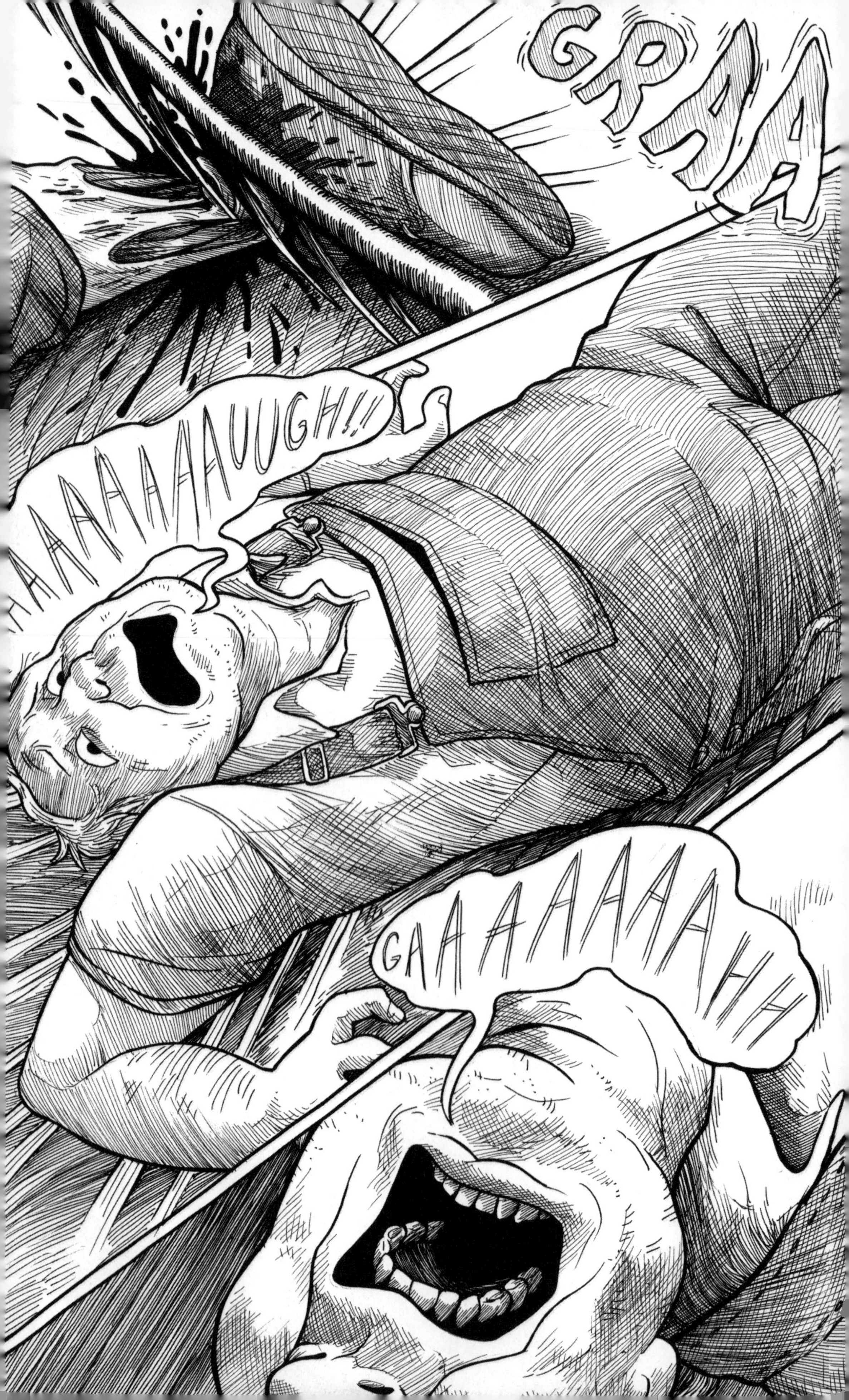
GRAAA
AAAAAAAAAUUGH!!!
GAAAAAAAAHH

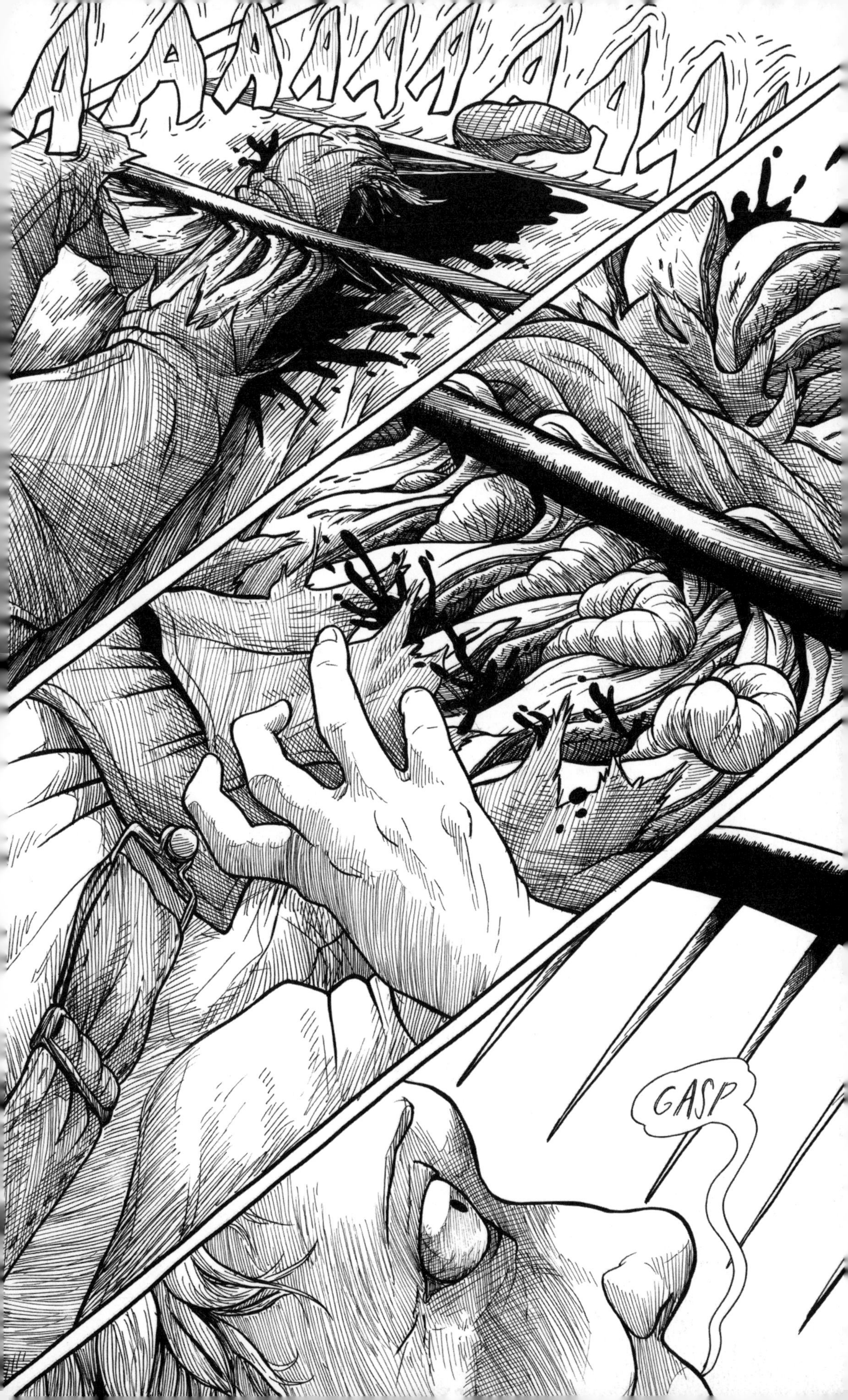
AAAAAAAAAAAA
GASP

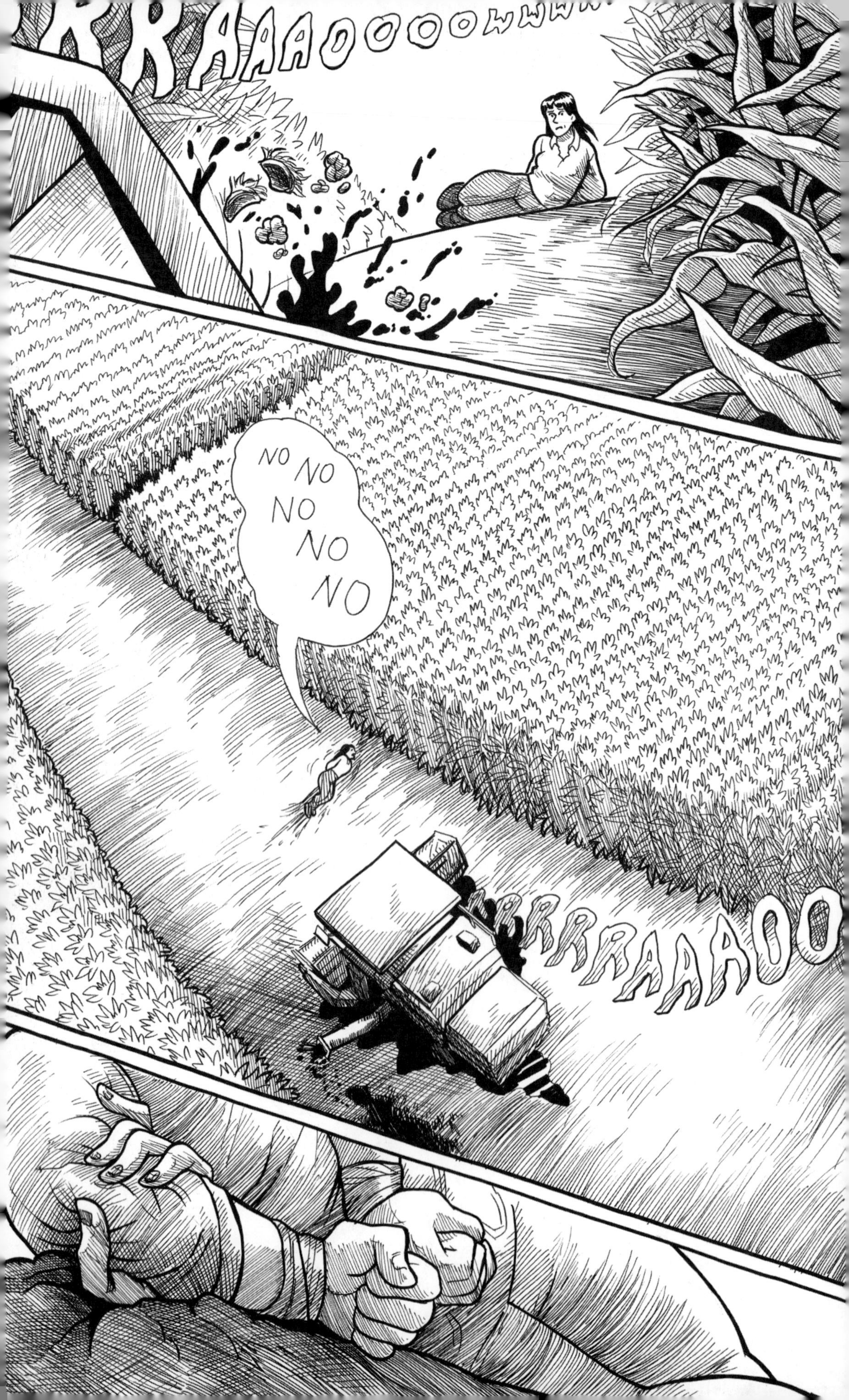
RRAAAOOOOOWWW
NO NO NO NO NO
RRRAAAOO

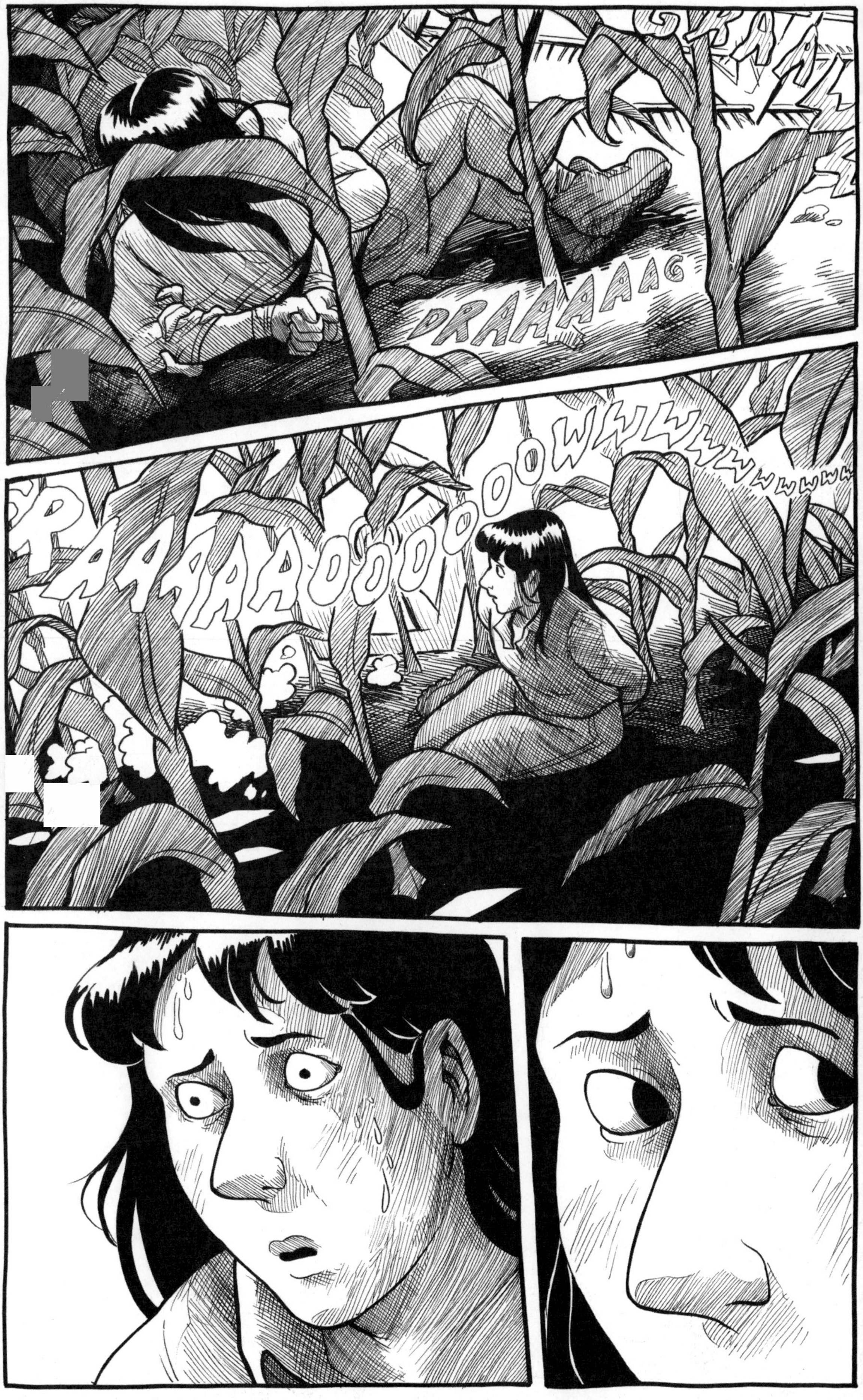
DRAAAAAG
PAAAAAOOOOOOOWNWWWWWWWWWW

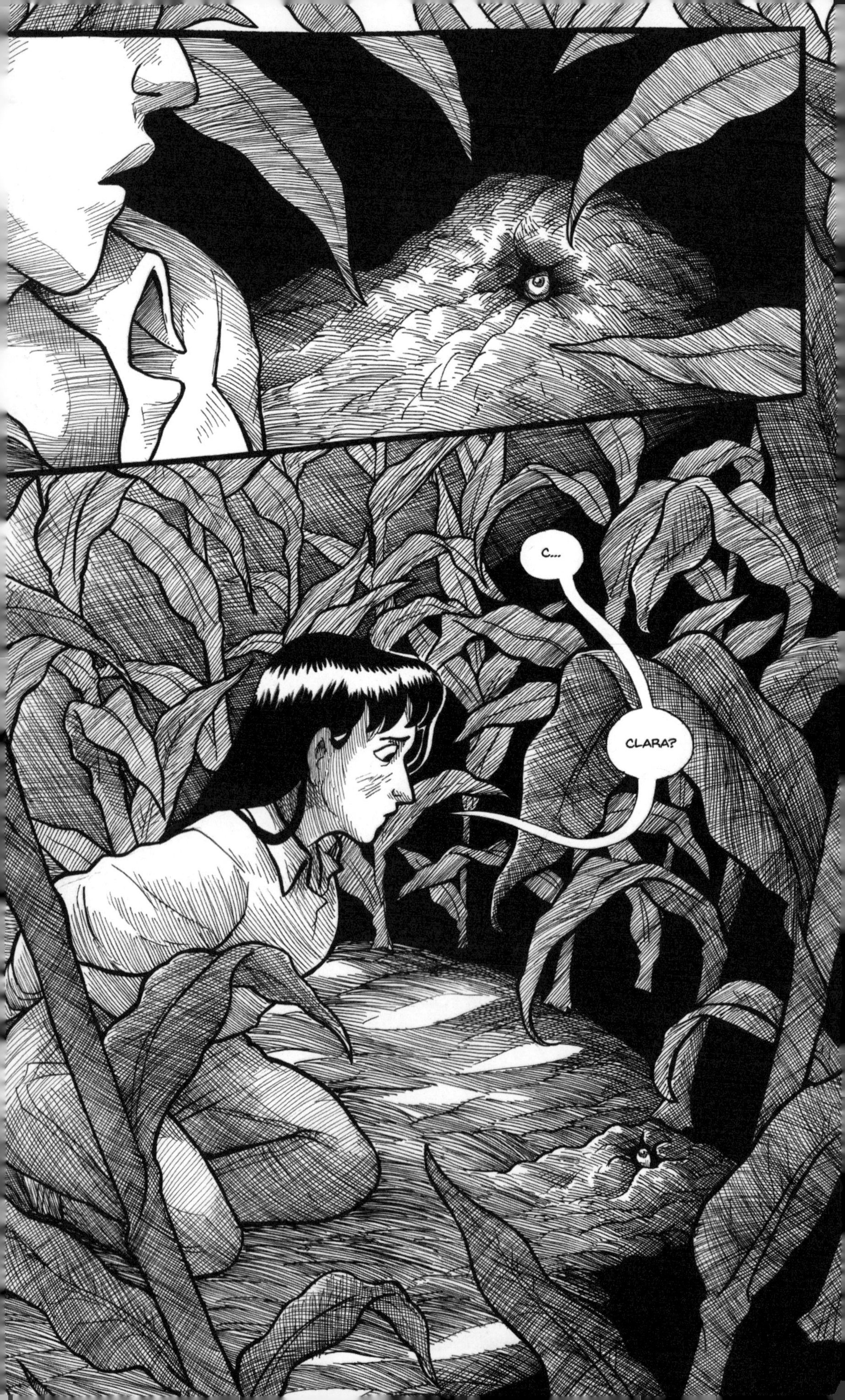
C...
CLARA?

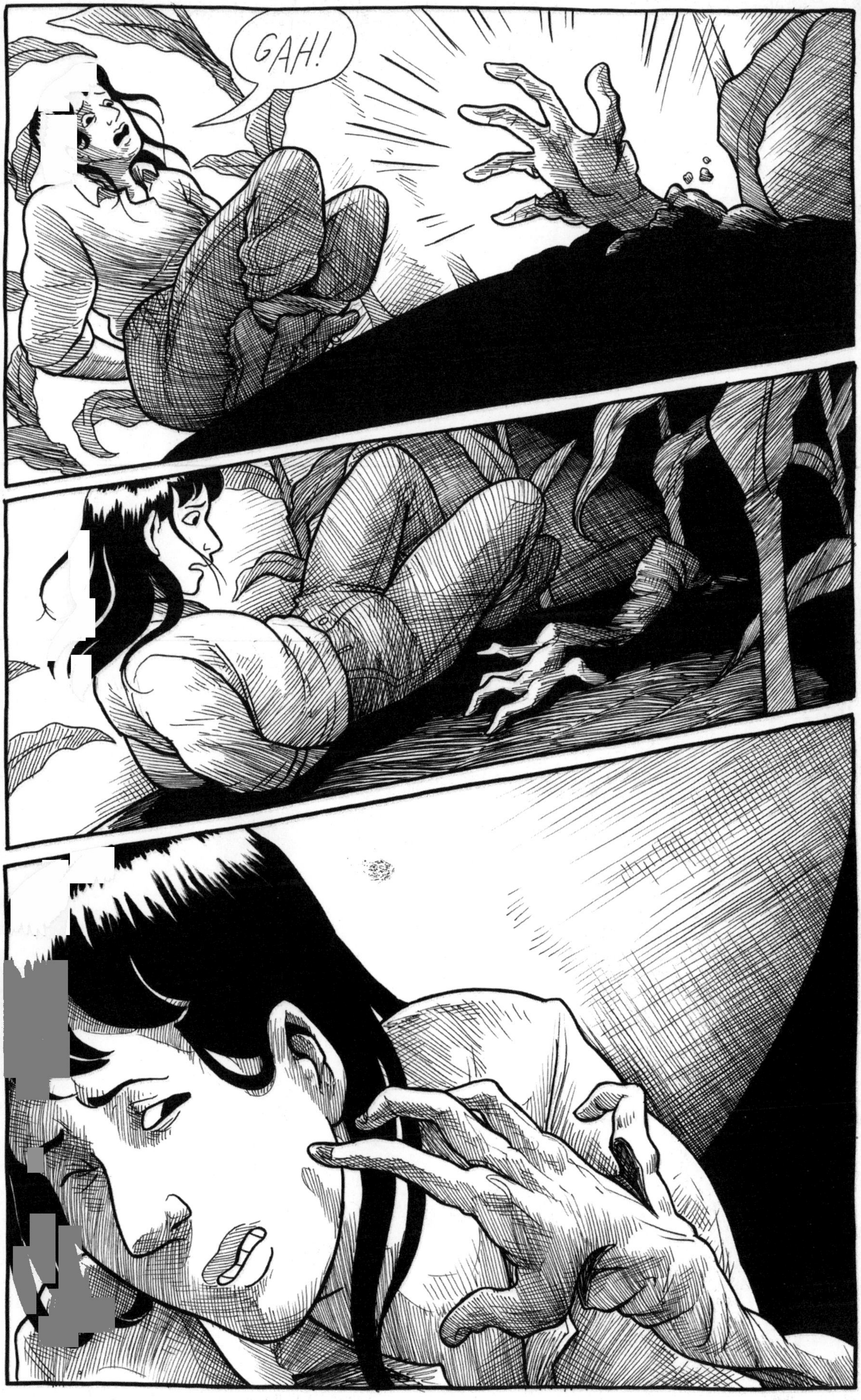
GAH!

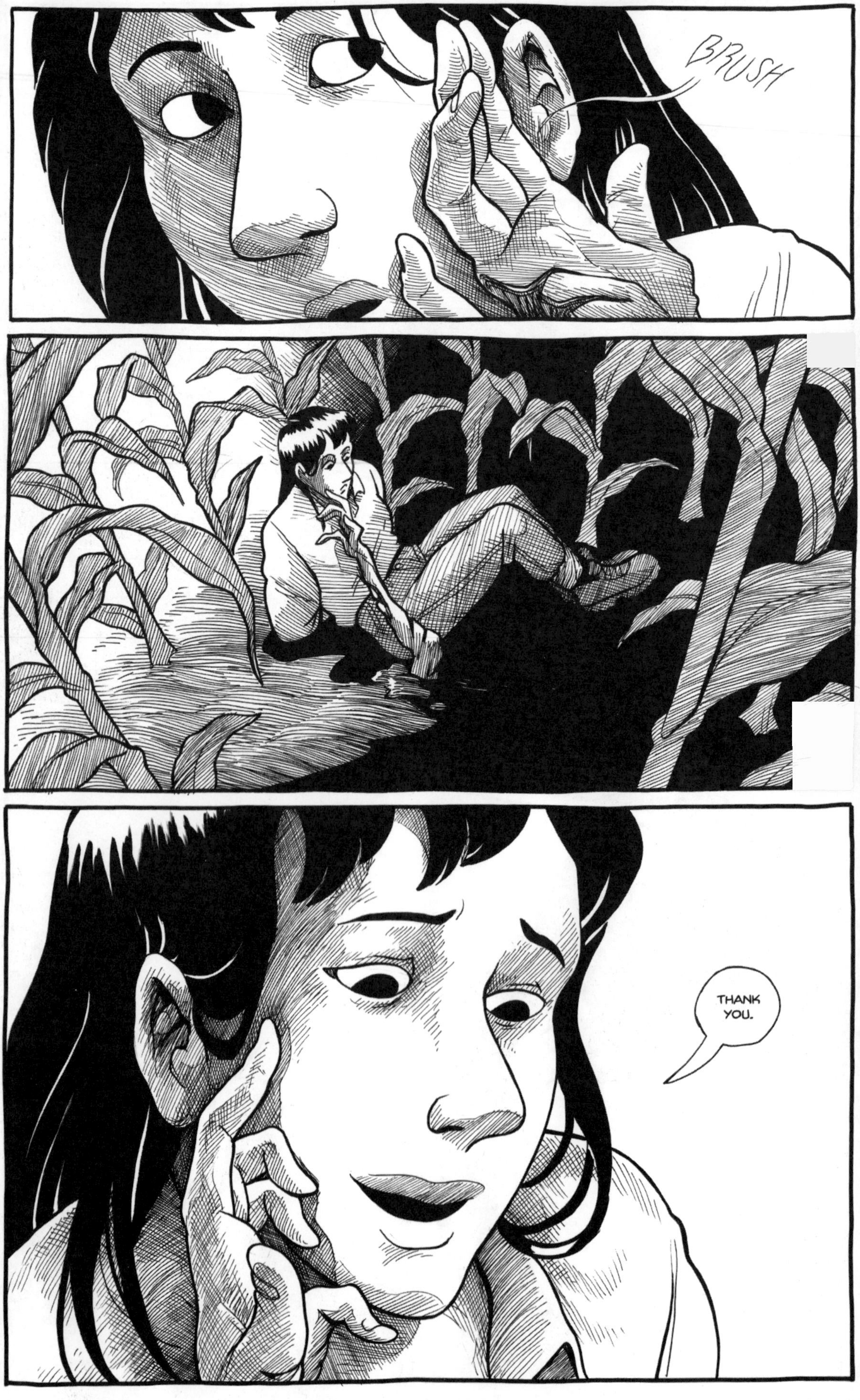
BRUSH
THANK YOU.

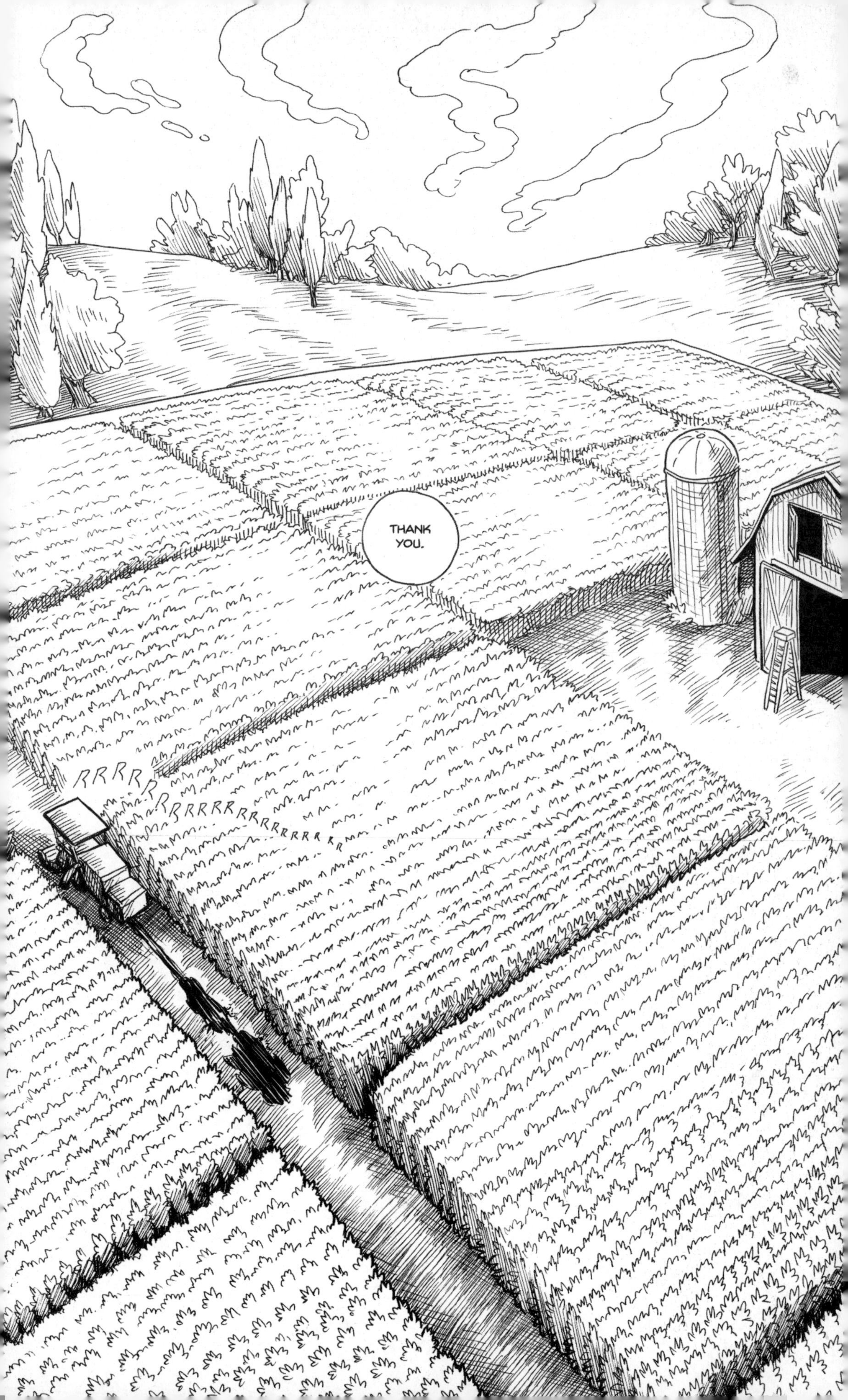
THANK YOU.
RRRRRRRRRRRRRRRRRRRRRRR

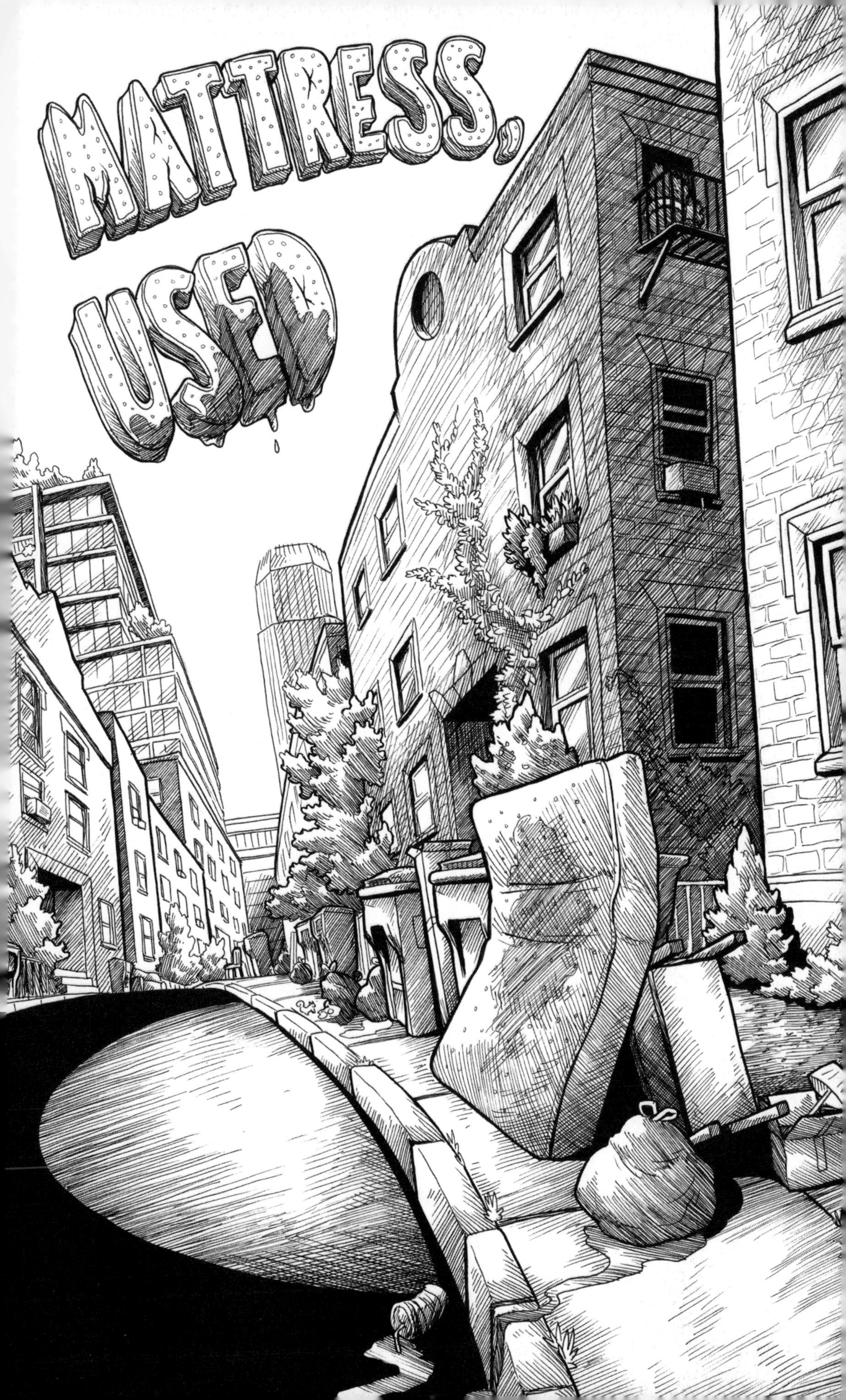
MATTRESS,
USED

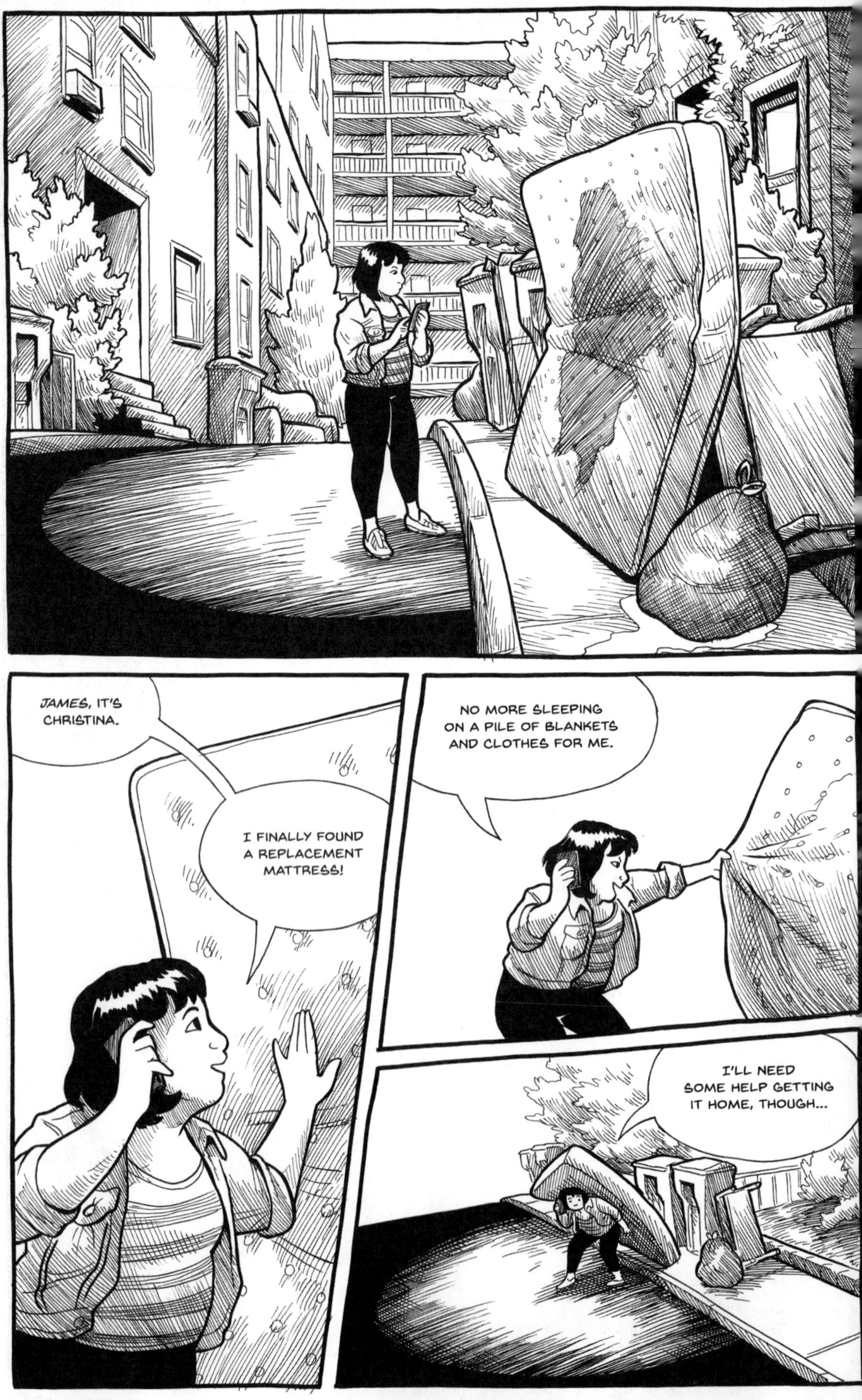
JAMES, IT'S CHRISTINA.
I FINALLY FOUND A REPLACEMENT MATTRESS!
NO MORE SLEEPING ON A PILE OF BLANKETS AND CLOTHES FOR ME.
I'LL NEED SOME HELP GETTING IT HOME, THOUGH...

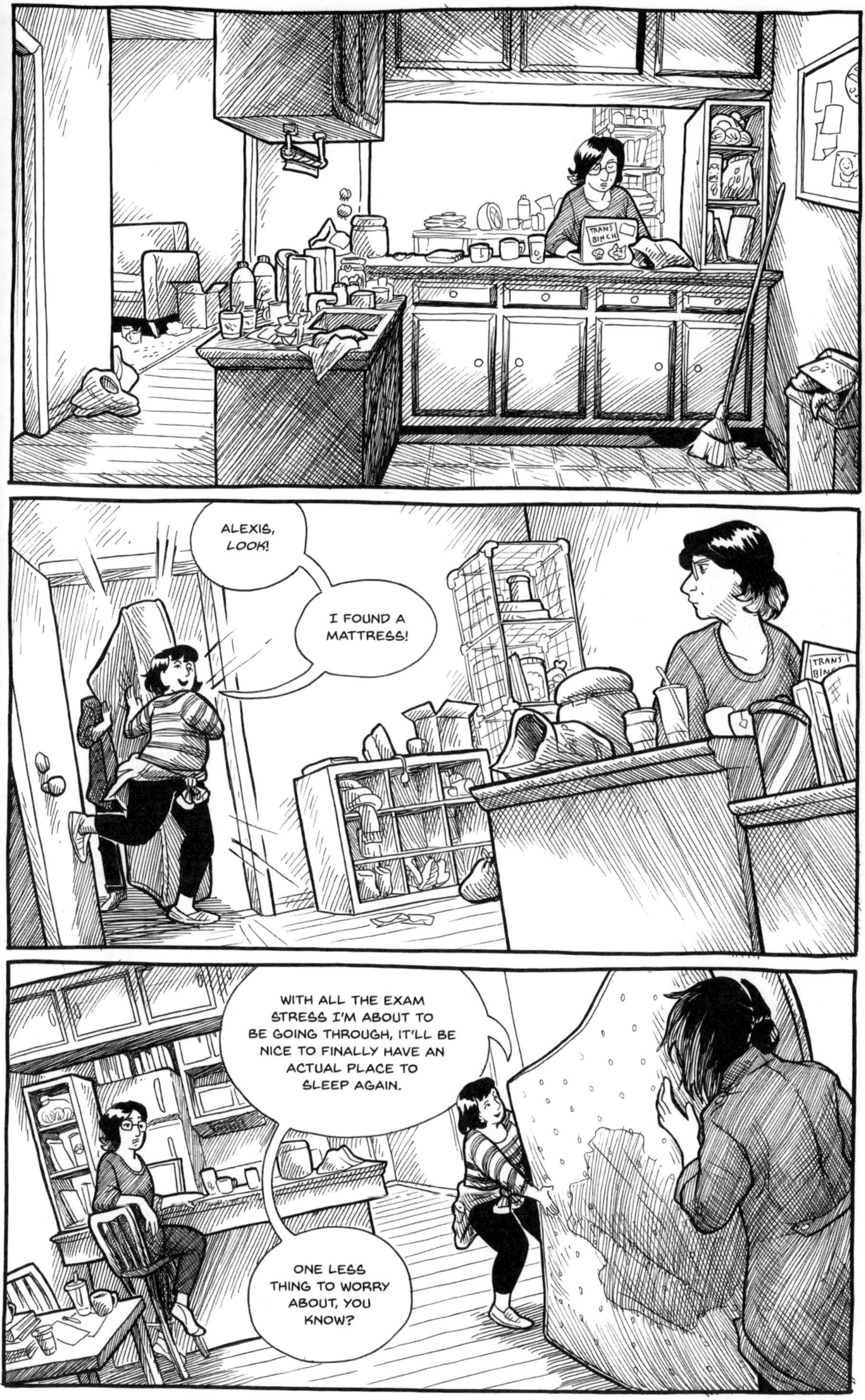
TRANS BINCH
ALEXIS, LOOK!
I FOUND A MATTRESS!
WITH ALL THE EXAM STRESS I'M ABOUT TO BE GOING THROUGH, IT'LL BE NICE TO FINALLY HAVE AN ACTUAL PLACE TO SLEEP AGAIN.
ONE LESS THING TO WORRY ABOUT, YOU KNOW?

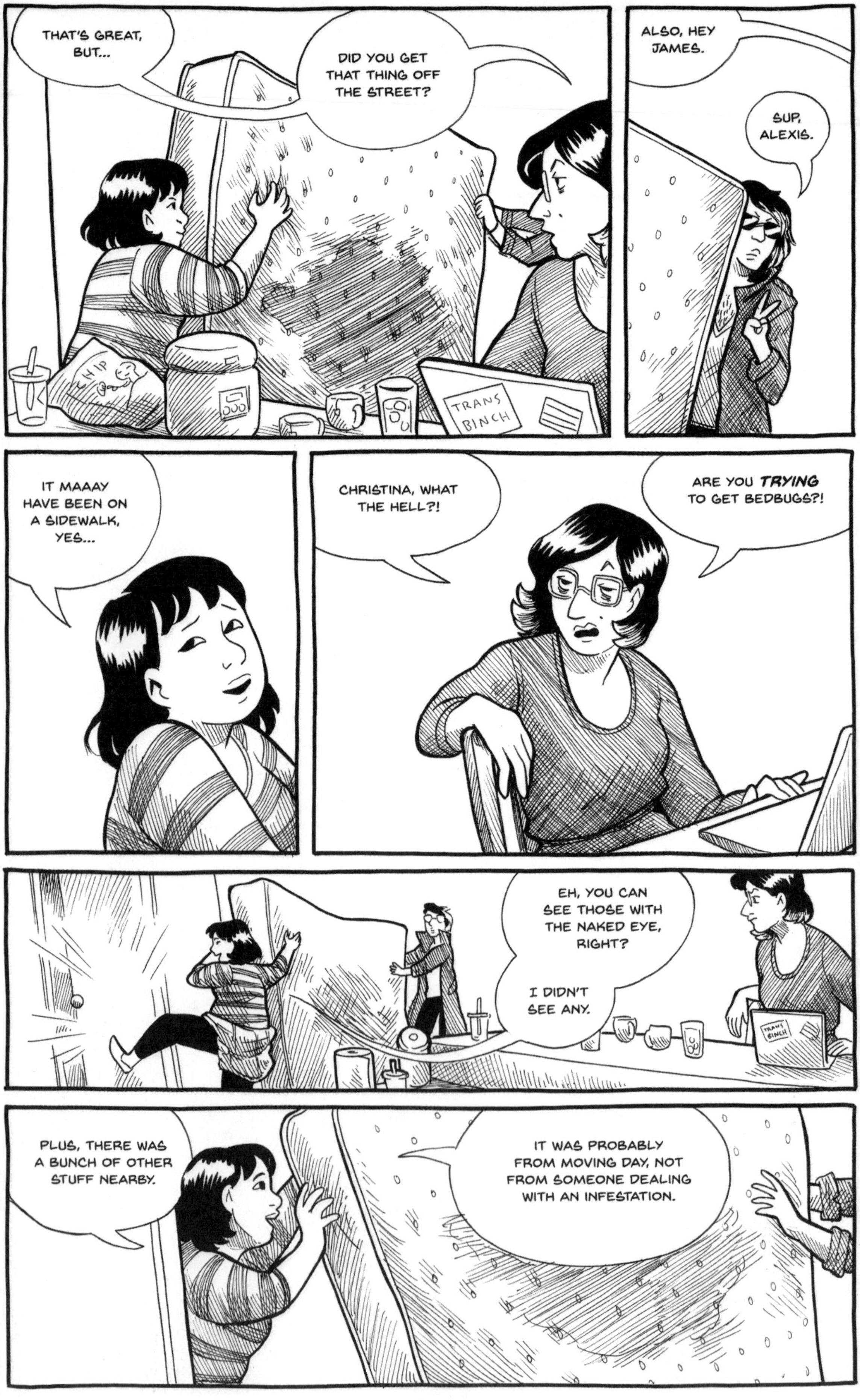
THAT'S GREAT, BUT...
DID YOU GET THAT THING OFF THE STREET?
TRANS BINCH
ALSO, HEY JAMES.
SUP, ALEXIS.
IT MAAAY HAVE BEEN ON A SIDEWALK, YES...
CHRISTINA, WHAT THE HELL?!
ARE YOU *TRYING* TO GET BEDBUGS?!
EH, YOU CAN SEE THOSE WITH THE NAKED EYE, RIGHT?
I DIDN'T SEE ANY.
TRANS BINCH
PLUS, THERE WAS A BUNCH OF OTHER STUFF NEARBY.
IT WAS PROBABLY FROM MOVING DAY, NOT FROM SOMEONE DEALING WITH AN INFESTATION.

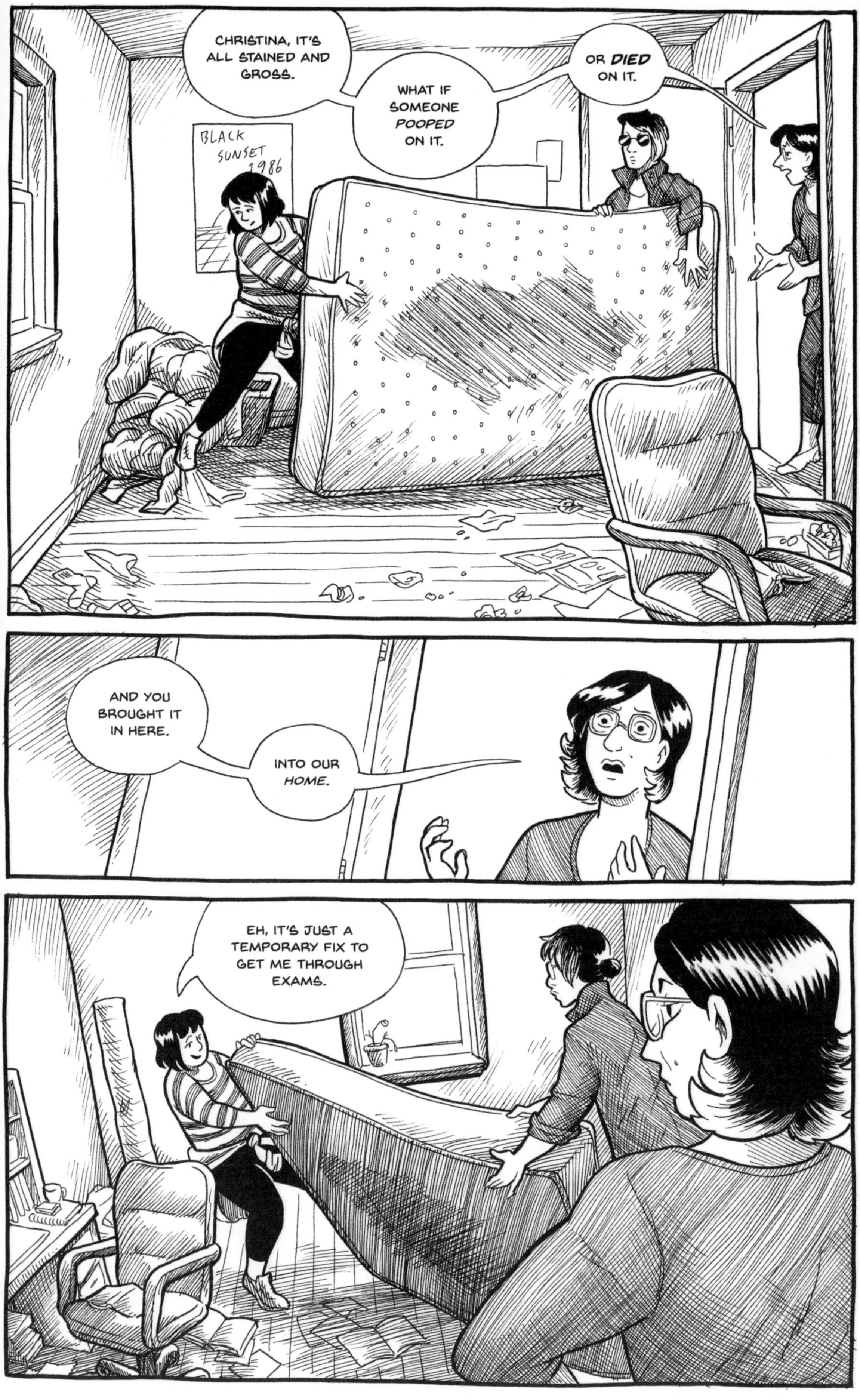
CHRISTINA, IT'S ALL STAINED AND GROSS.
WHAT IF SOMEONE *POOPED* ON IT.
OR ***DIED*** ON IT.
BLACK SUNSET 1986
AND YOU BROUGHT IT IN HERE.
INTO OUR *HOME*.
EH, IT'S JUST A TEMPORARY FIX TO GET ME THROUGH EXAMS.

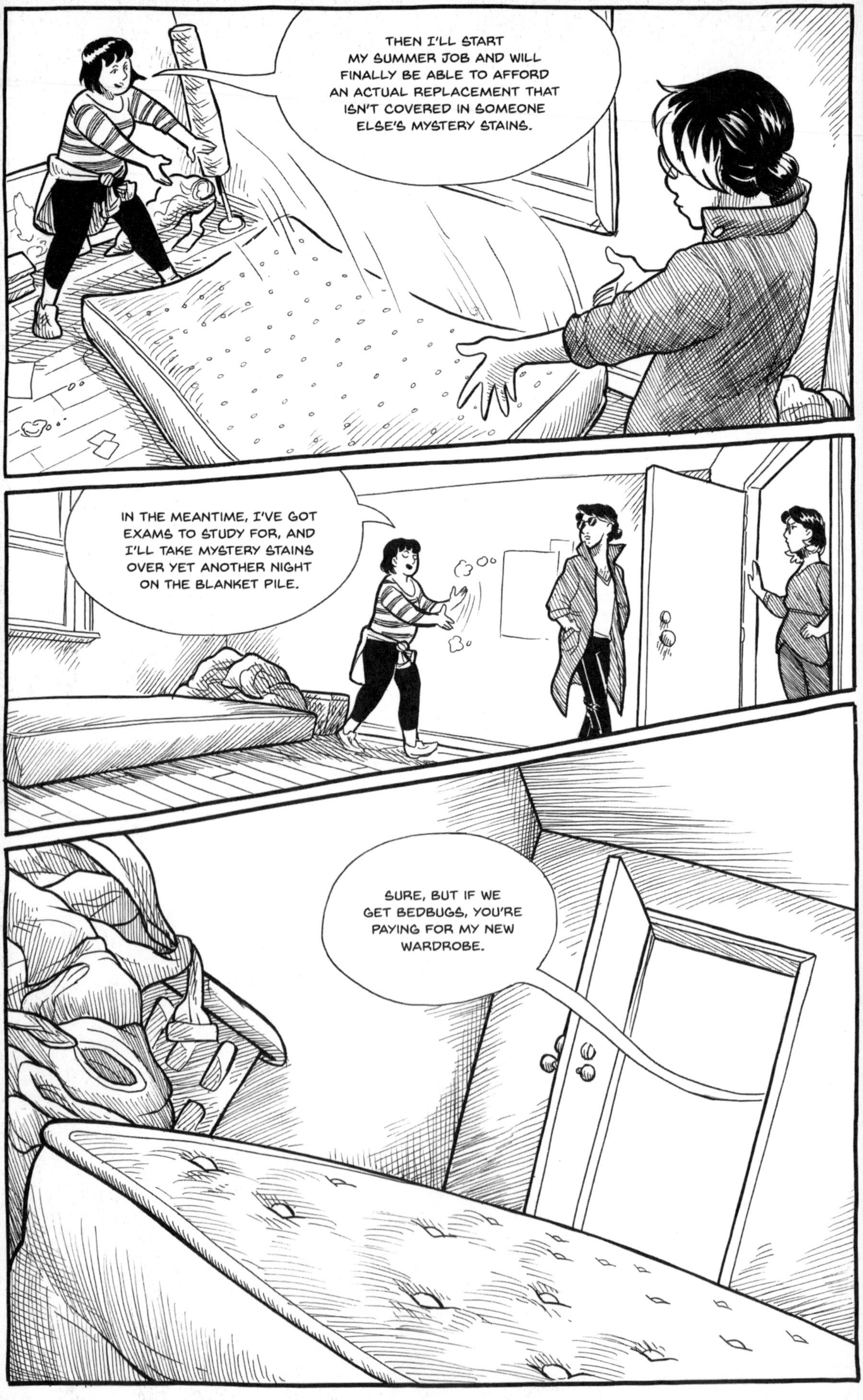
THEN I'LL START MY SUMMER JOB AND WILL FINALLY BE ABLE TO AFFORD AN ACTUAL REPLACEMENT THAT ISN'T COVERED IN SOMEONE ELSE'S MYSTERY STAINS.
IN THE MEANTIME, I'VE GOT EXAMS TO STUDY FOR, AND I'LL TAKE MYSTERY STAINS OVER YET ANOTHER NIGHT ON THE BLANKET PILE.
SURE, BUT IF WE GET BEDBUGS, YOU'RE PAYING FOR MY NEW WARDROBE.

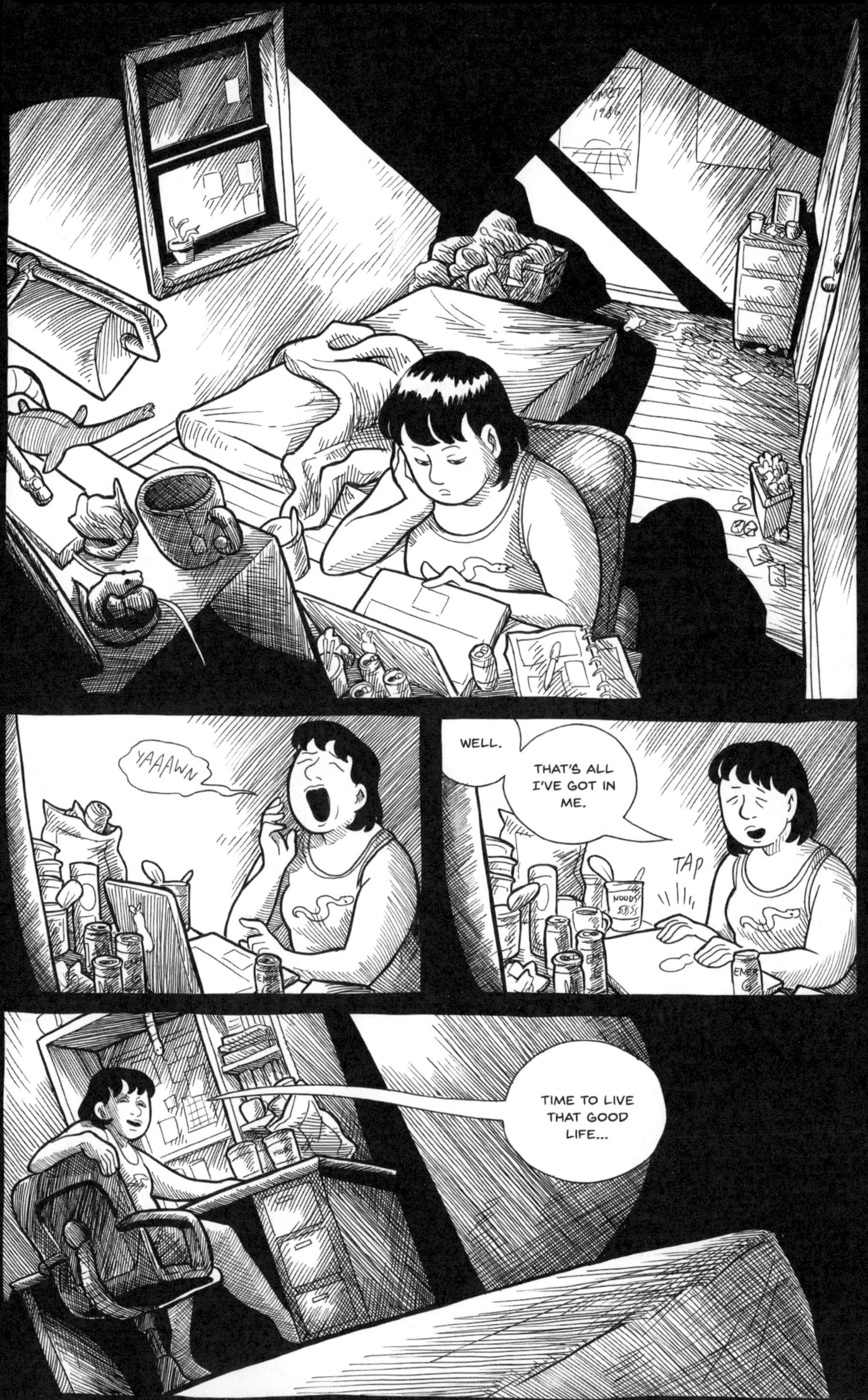
YAAAWN
WELL.
THAT'S ALL I'VE GOT IN ME.
TAP
TIME TO LIVE THAT GOOD LIFE...

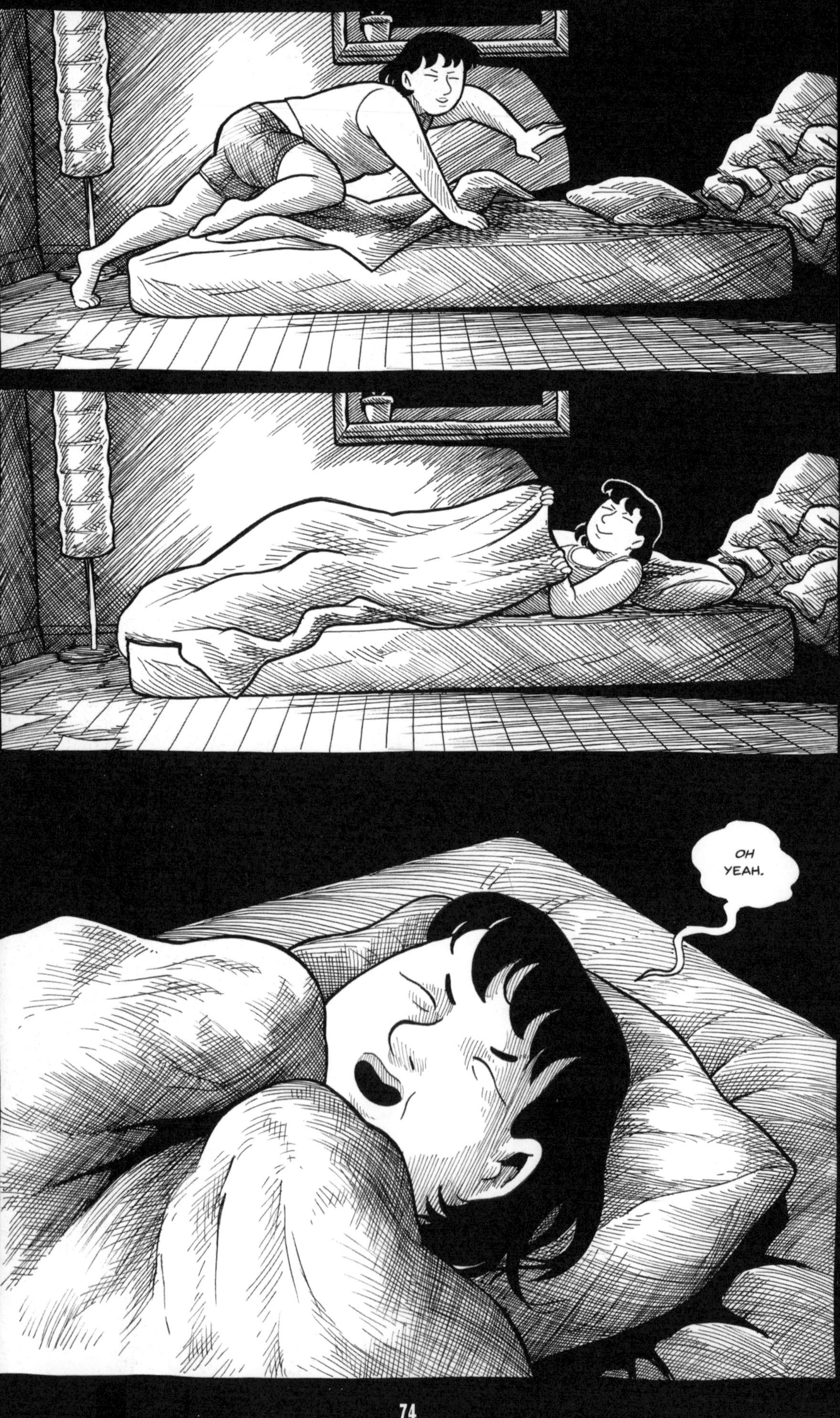
OH
YEAH.

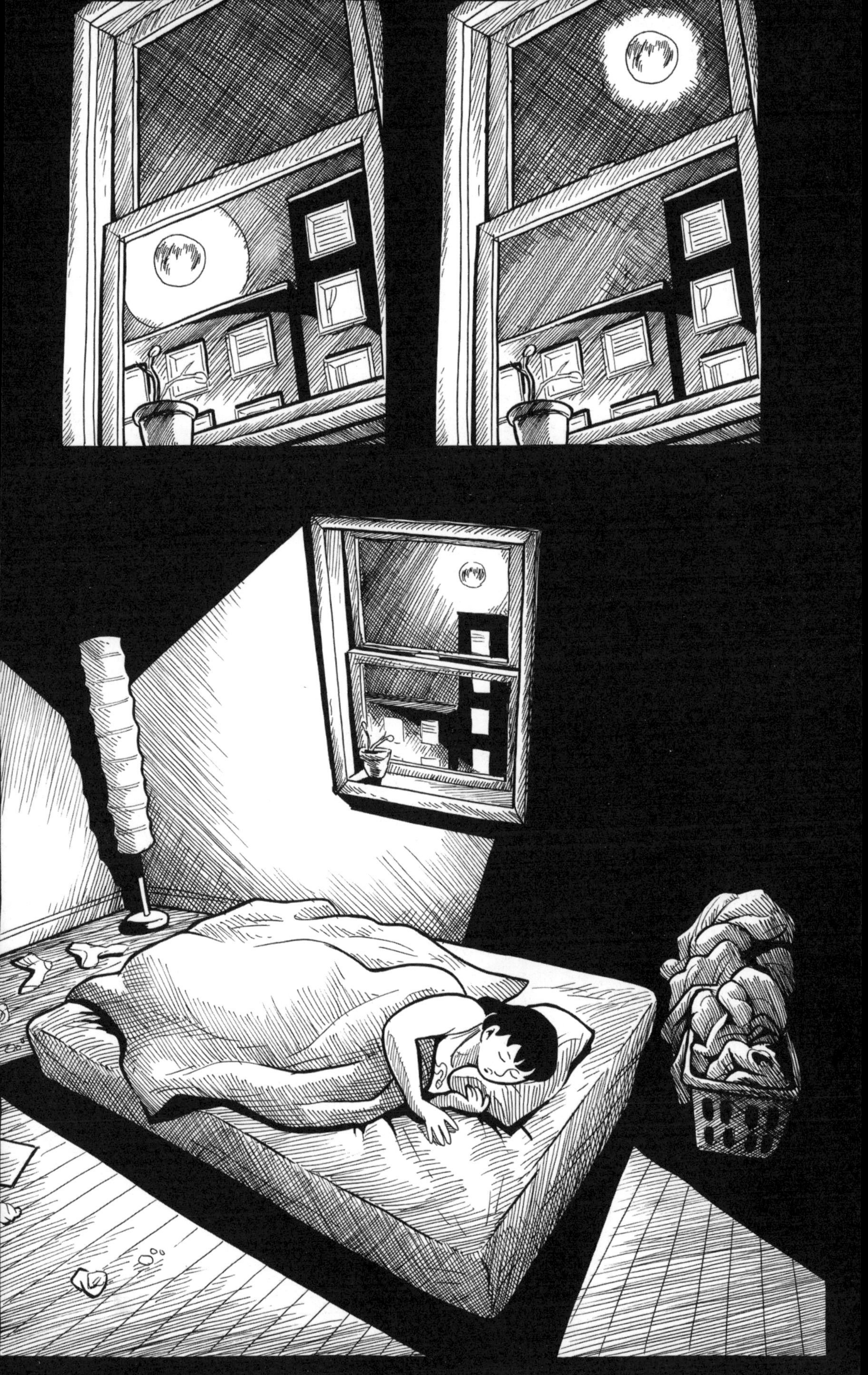

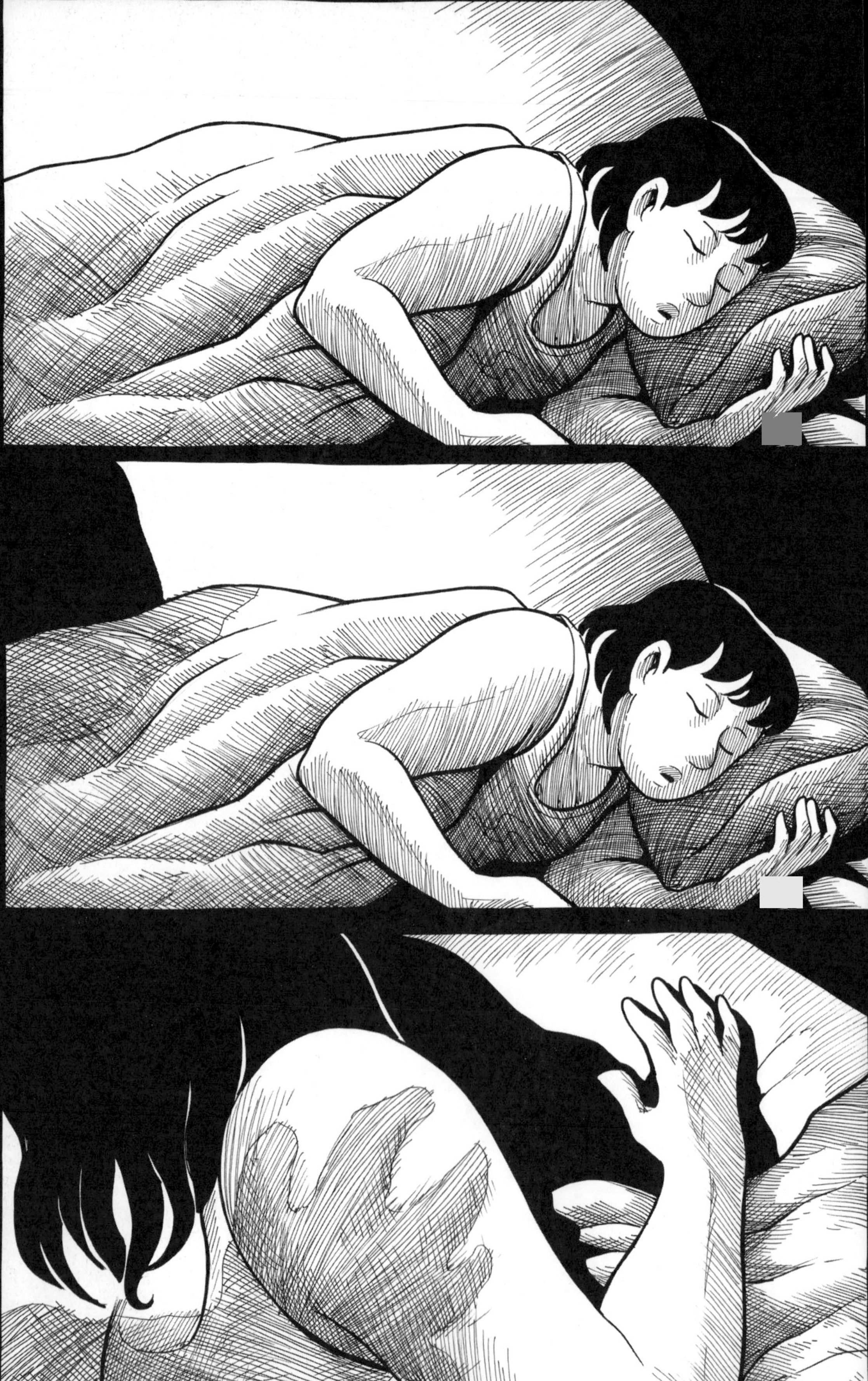

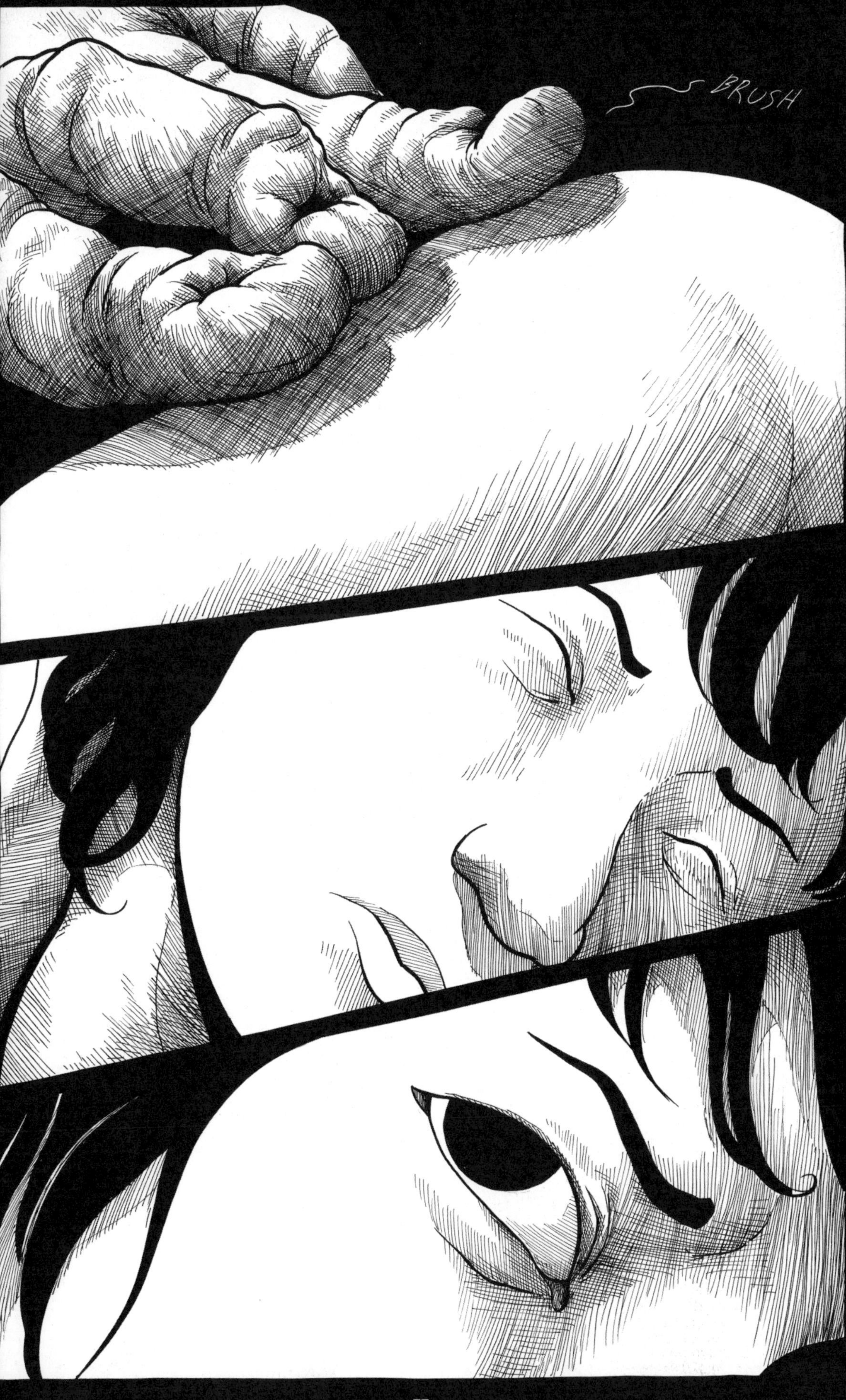
BRUSH

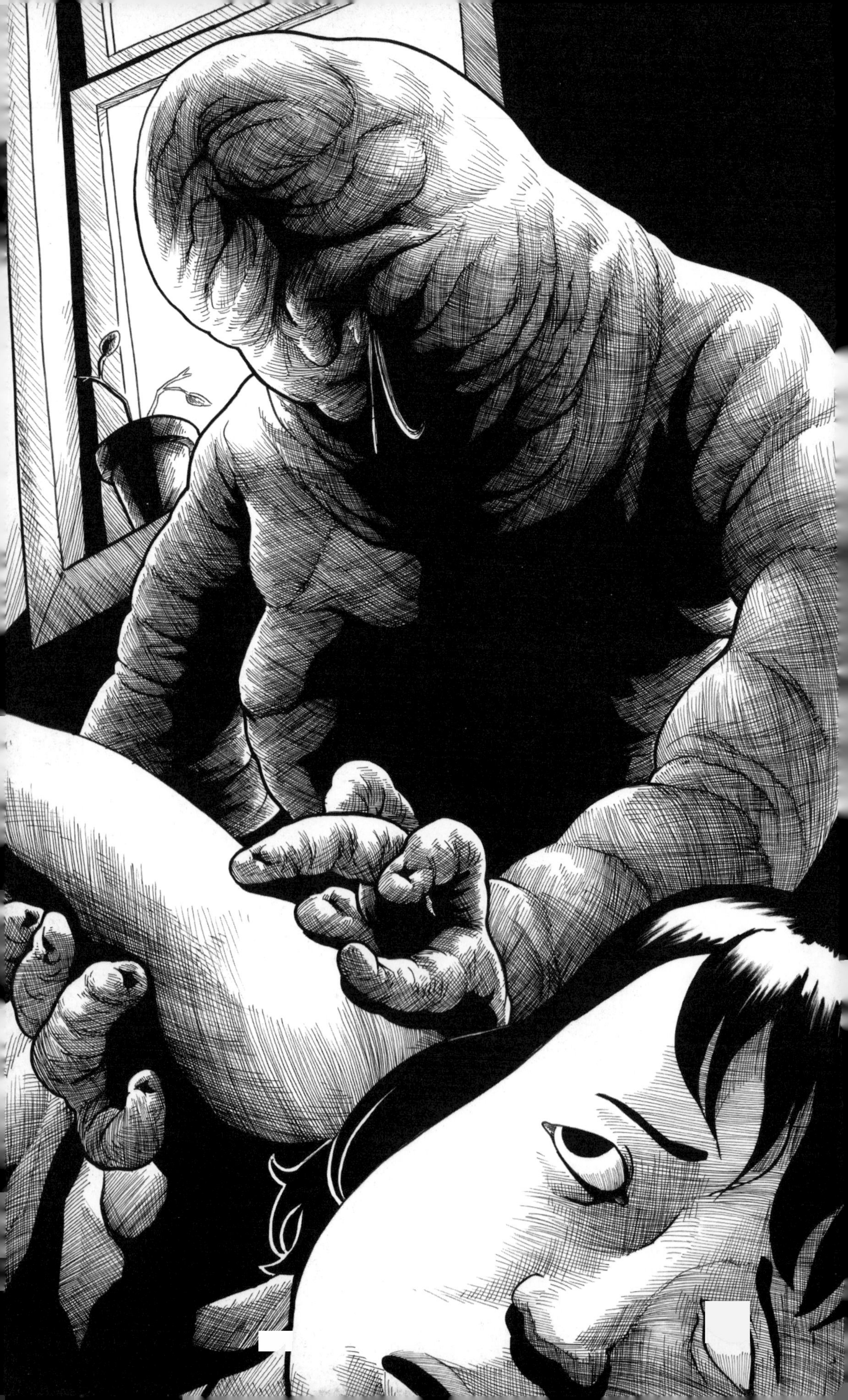

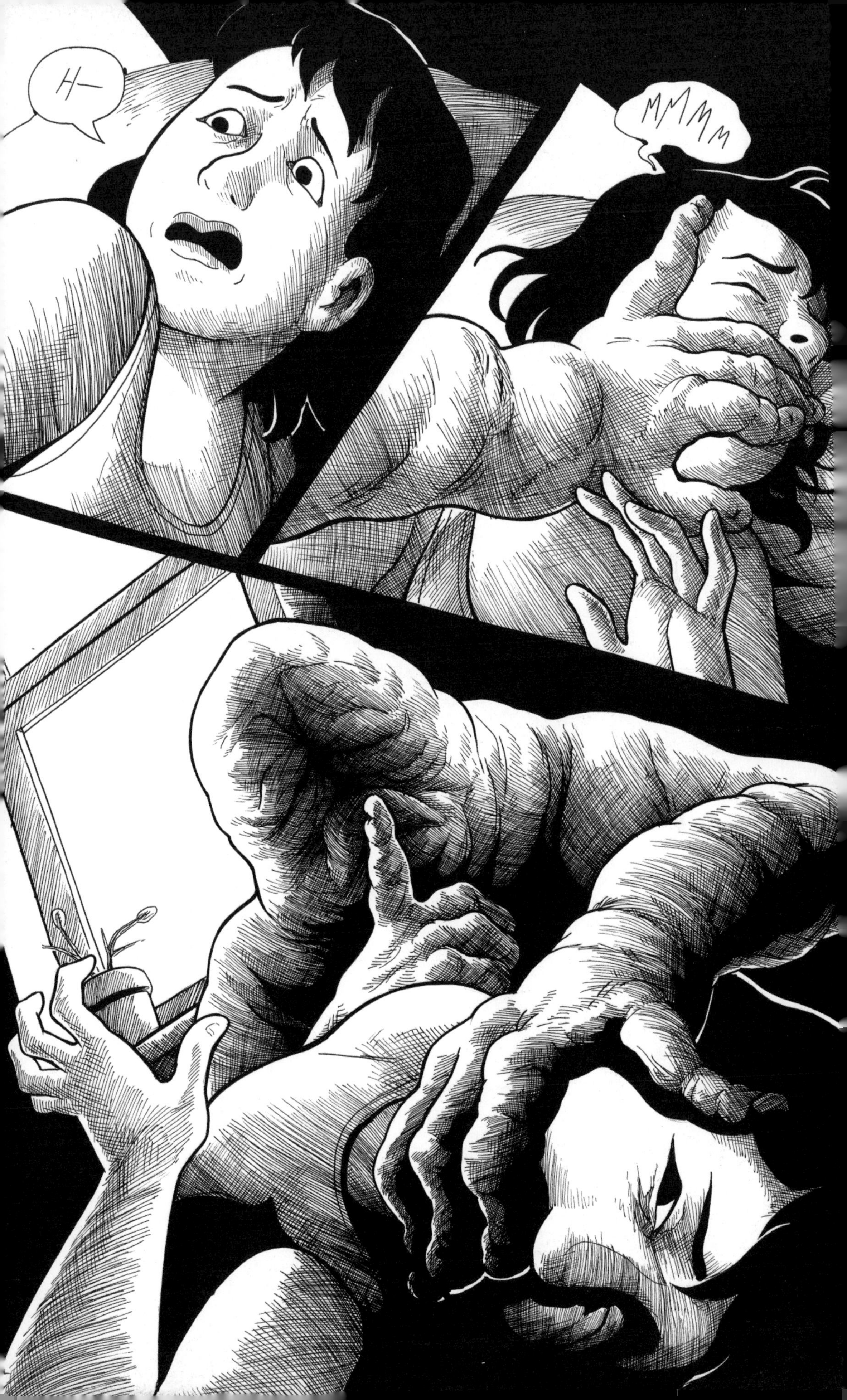
H—
MMMM

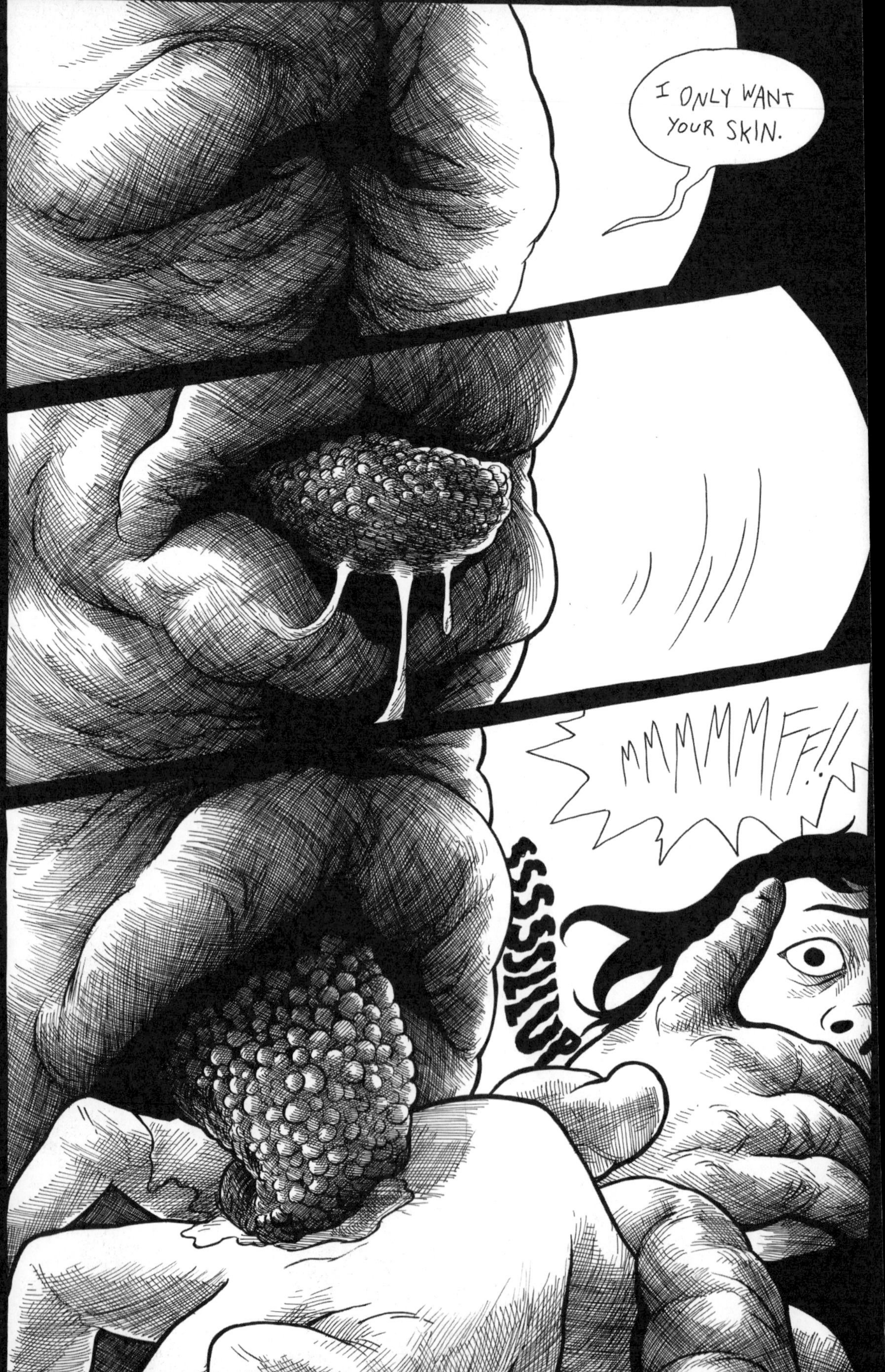
I ONLY WANT YOUR SKIN.
MMMMMFF!!
SSSSLLLUP!

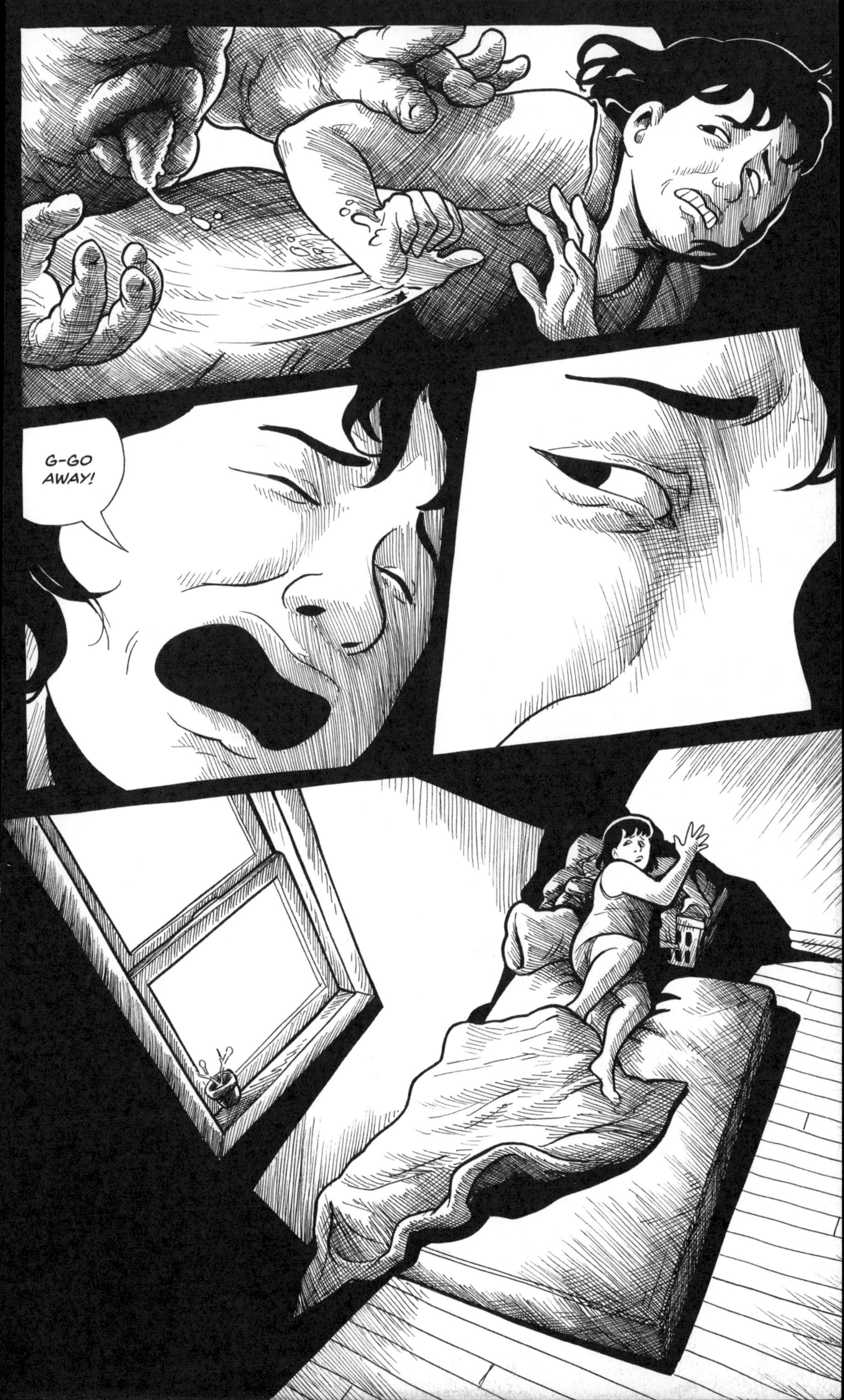
G-GO AWAY!

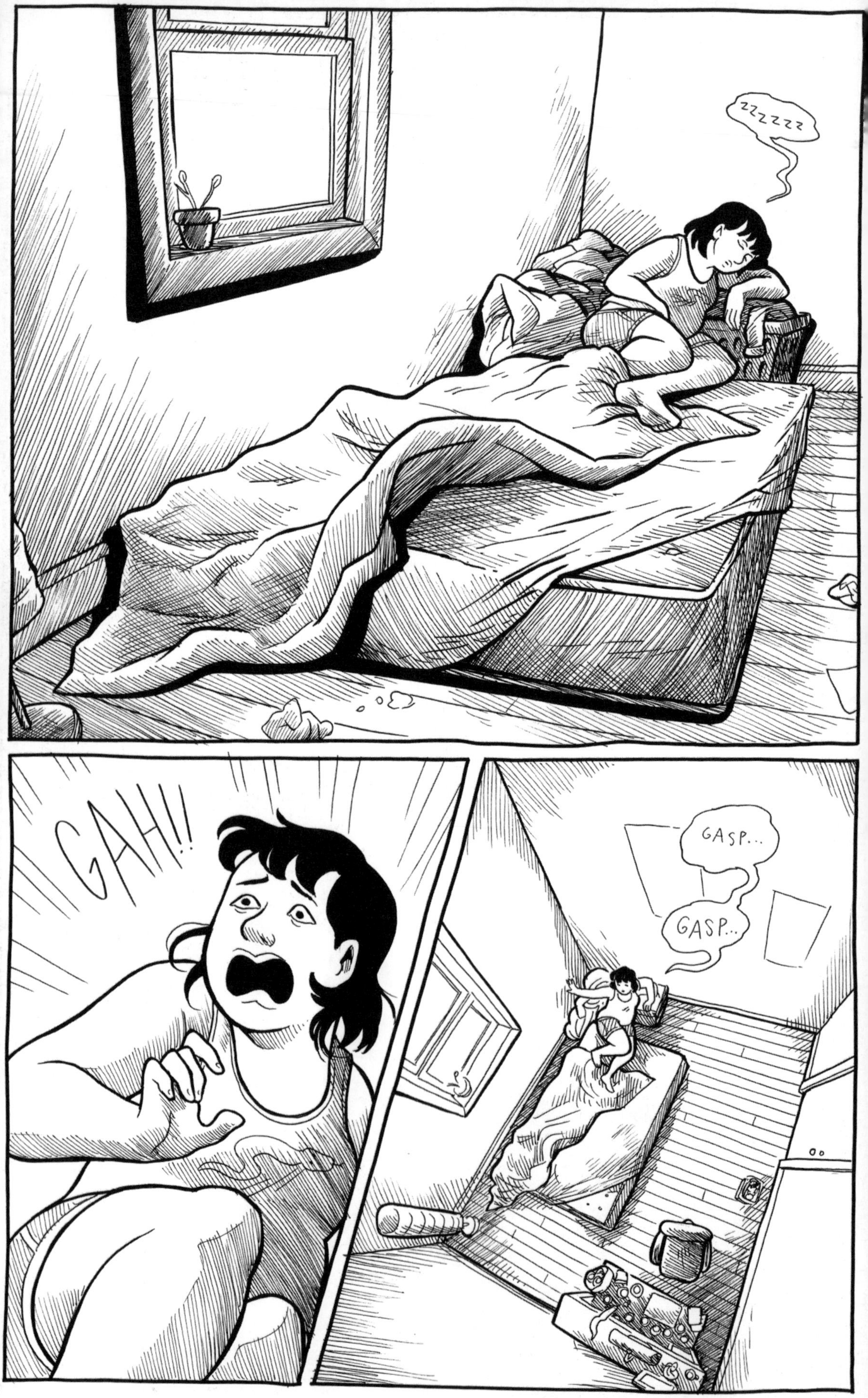
ZZZZZZ
GAH!!
GASP...
GASP...

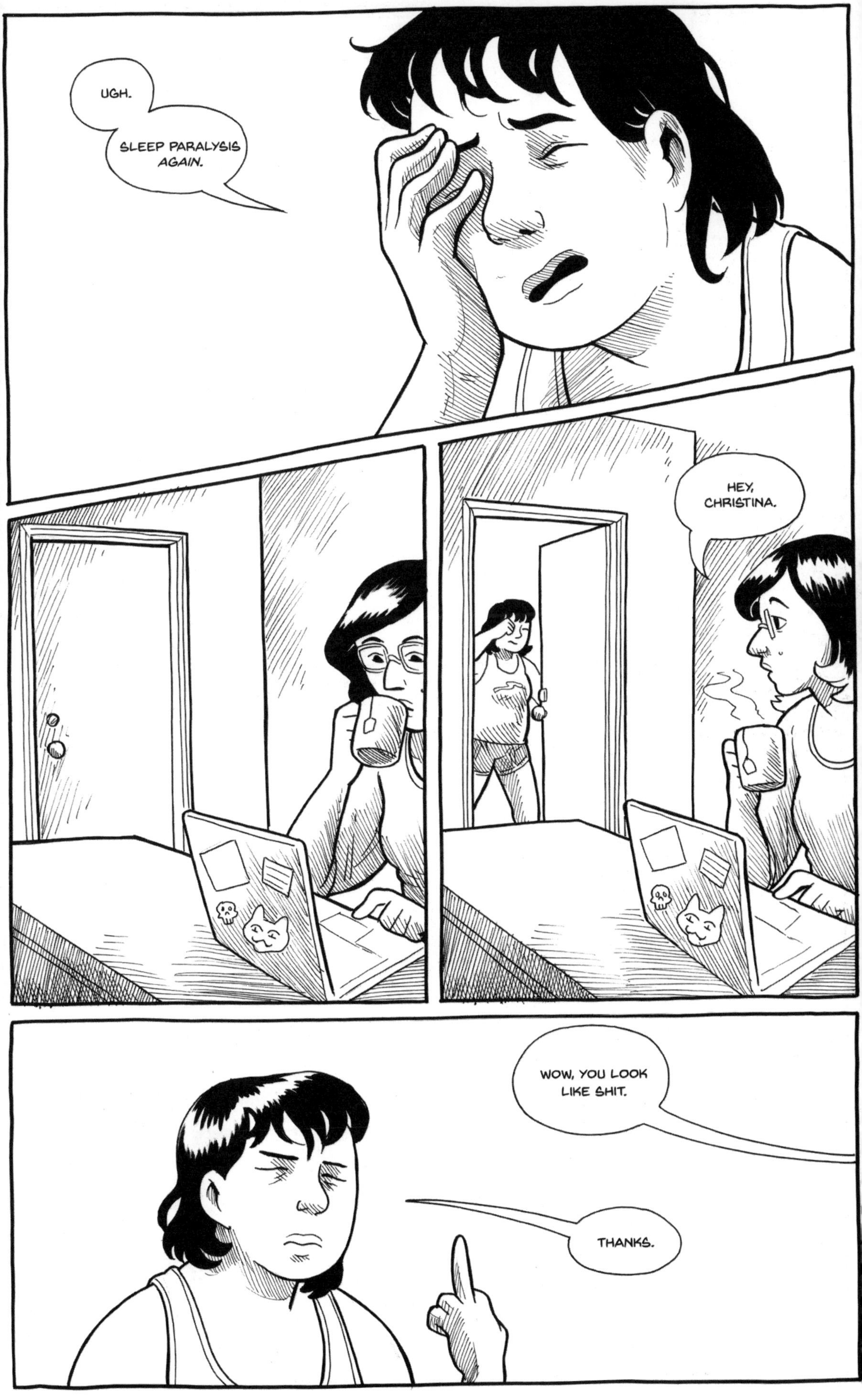
UGH.
SLEEP PARALYSIS AGAIN.
HEY, CHRISTINA.
WOW, YOU LOOK LIKE SHIT.
THANKS.

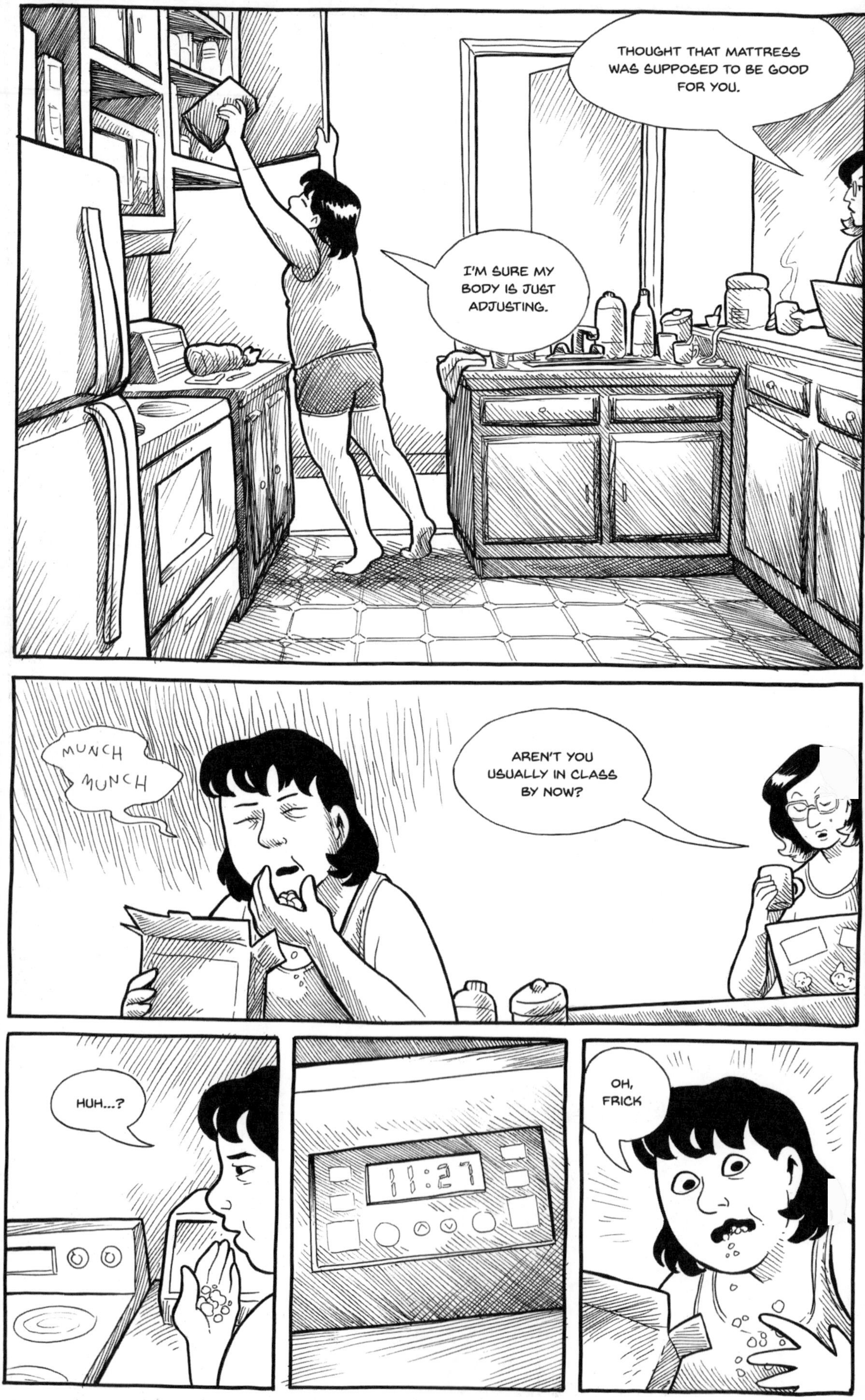

THOUGHT THAT MATTRESS WAS SUPPOSED TO BE GOOD FOR YOU.
I'M SURE MY BODY IS JUST ADJUSTING.
MUNCH MUNCH
AREN'T YOU USUALLY IN CLASS BY NOW?
HUH...?
11:27
OH, FRICK

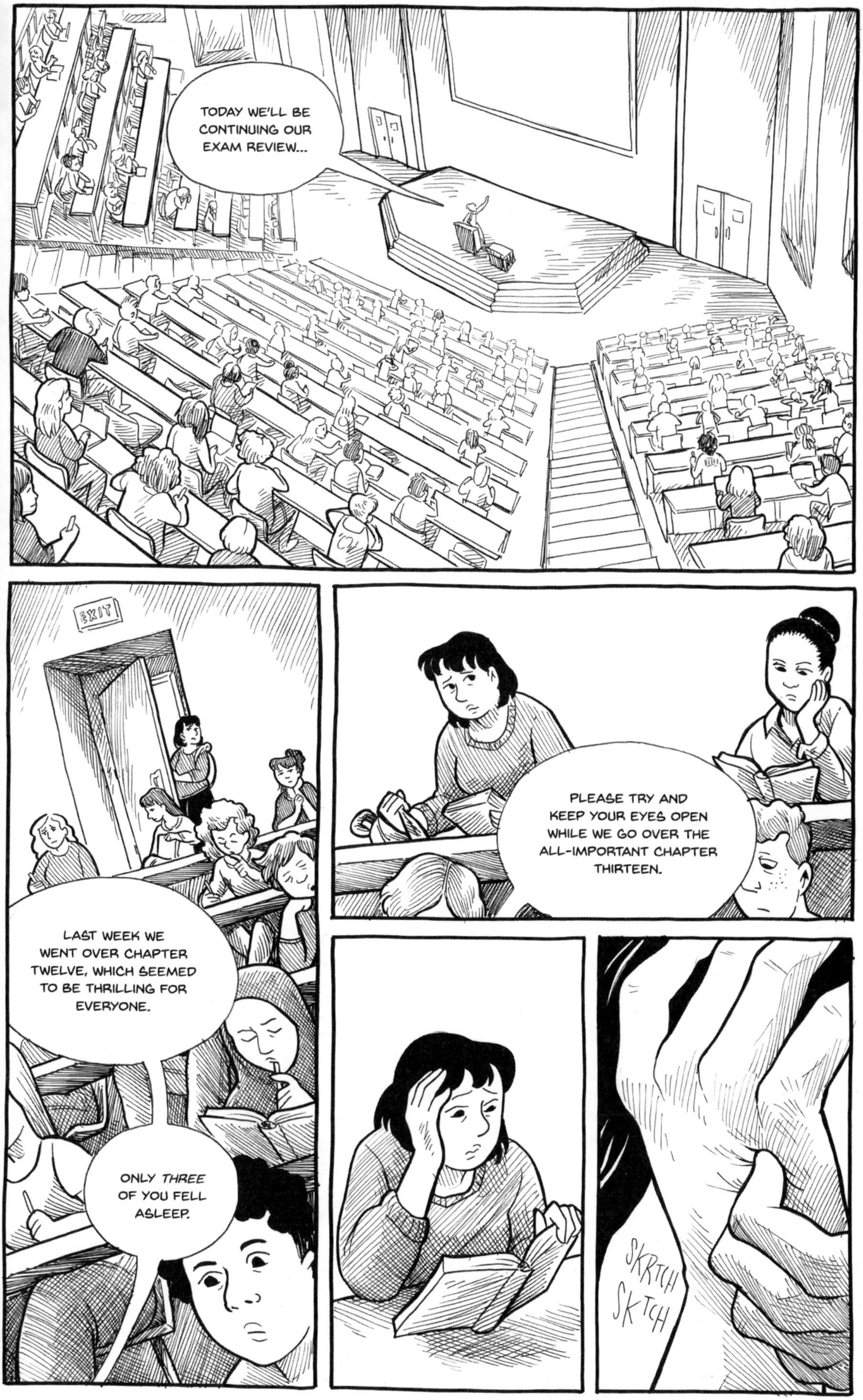

TODAY WE'LL BE CONTINUING OUR EXAM REVIEW...
EXIT
LAST WEEK WE WENT OVER CHAPTER TWELVE, WHICH SEEMED TO BE THRILLING FOR EVERYONE.
ONLY *THREE* OF YOU FELL ASLEEP.
PLEASE TRY AND KEEP YOUR EYES OPEN WHILE WE GO OVER THE ALL-IMPORTANT CHAPTER THIRTEEN.
SKRTCH
SKTCH

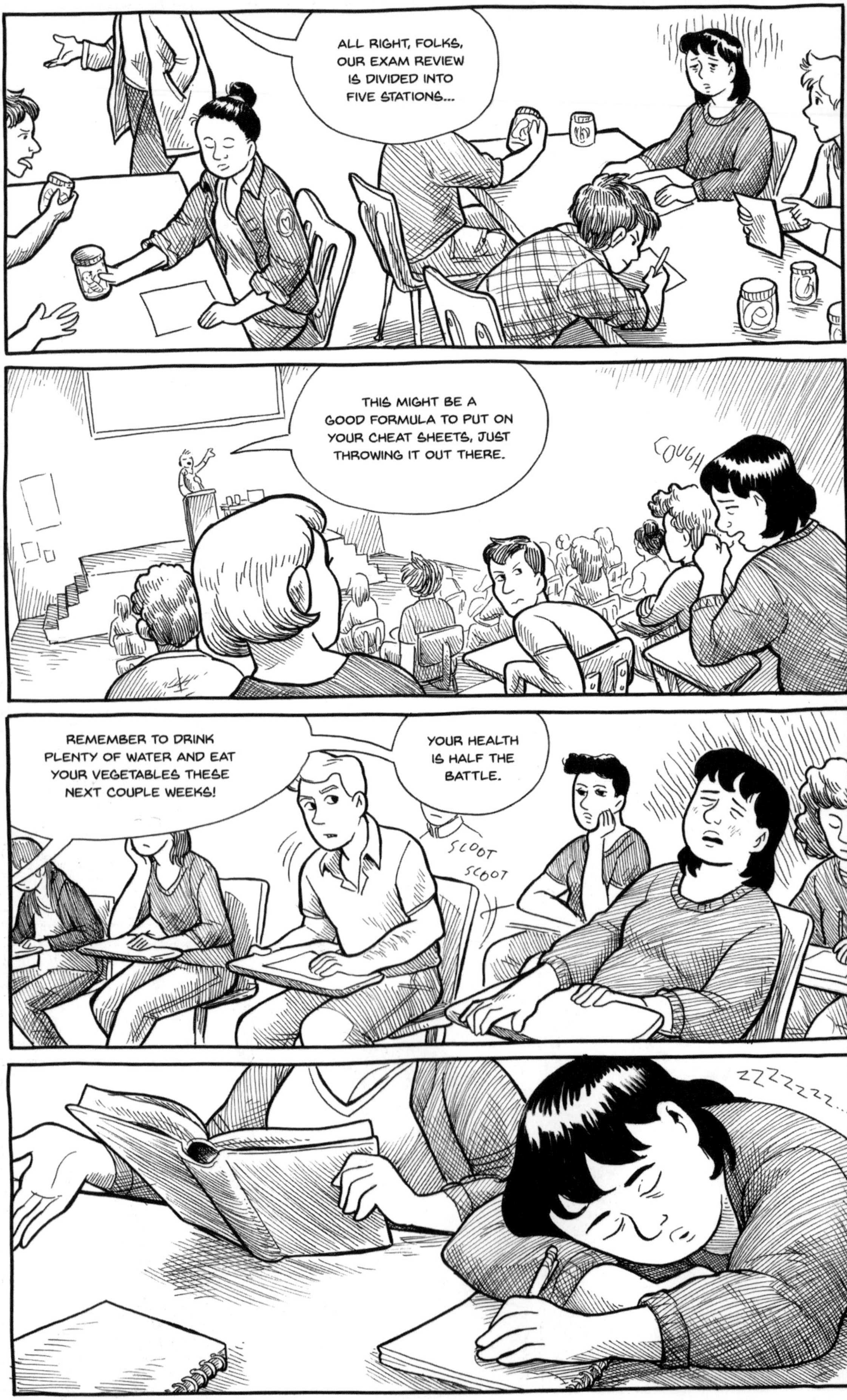
ALL RIGHT, FOLKS, OUR EXAM REVIEW IS DIVIDED INTO FIVE STATIONS...
THIS MIGHT BE A GOOD FORMULA TO PUT ON YOUR CHEAT SHEETS, JUST THROWING IT OUT THERE.
COUGH
REMEMBER TO DRINK PLENTY OF WATER AND EAT YOUR VEGETABLES THESE NEXT COUPLE WEEKS!
YOUR HEALTH IS HALF THE BATTLE.
SCOOT
SCOOT
ZZZZZZZ...

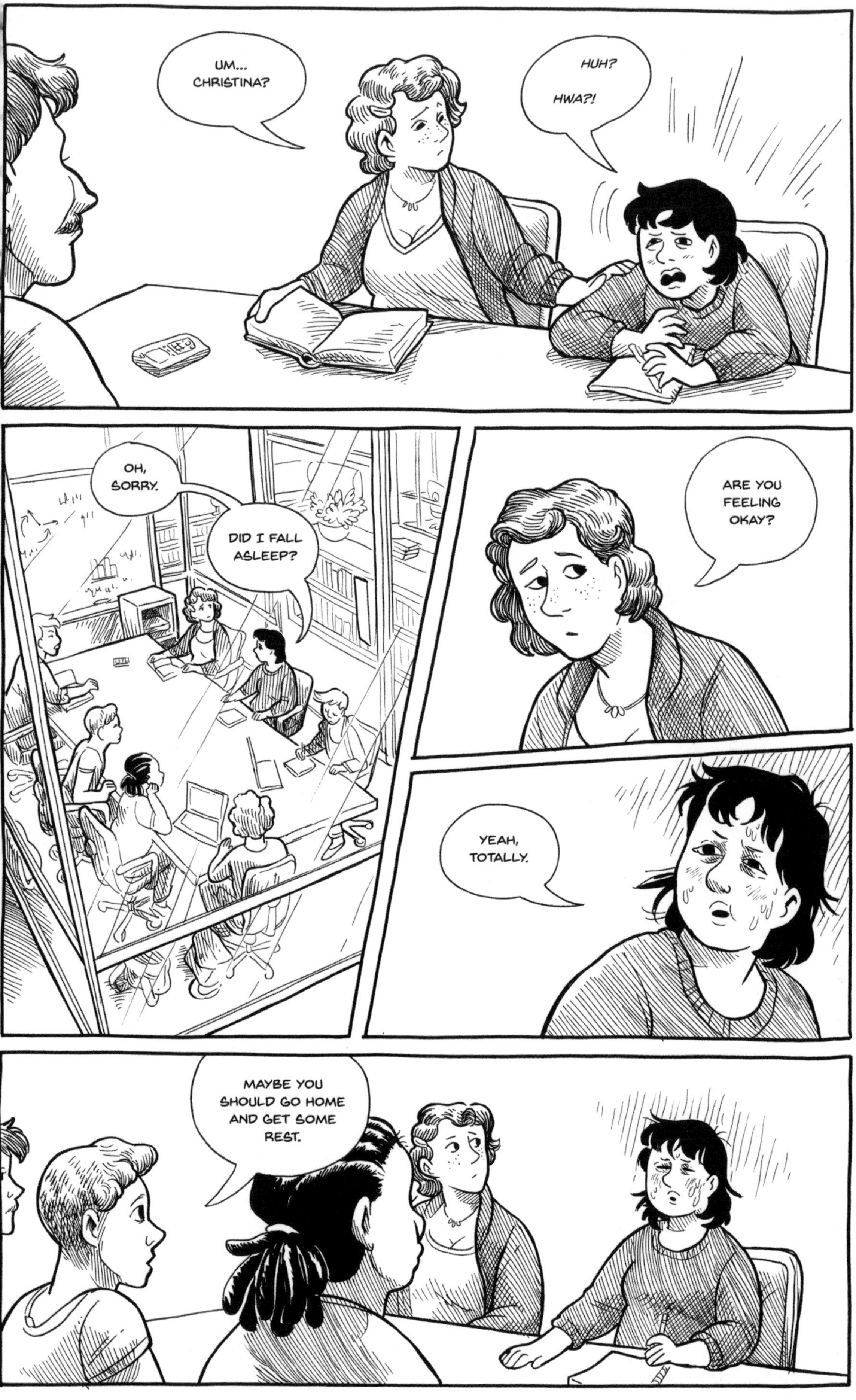
UM... CHRISTINA?
HUH?
HWA?!
OH, SORRY.
DID I FALL ASLEEP?
ARE YOU FEELING OKAY?
YEAH, TOTALLY.
MAYBE YOU SHOULD GO HOME AND GET SOME REST.

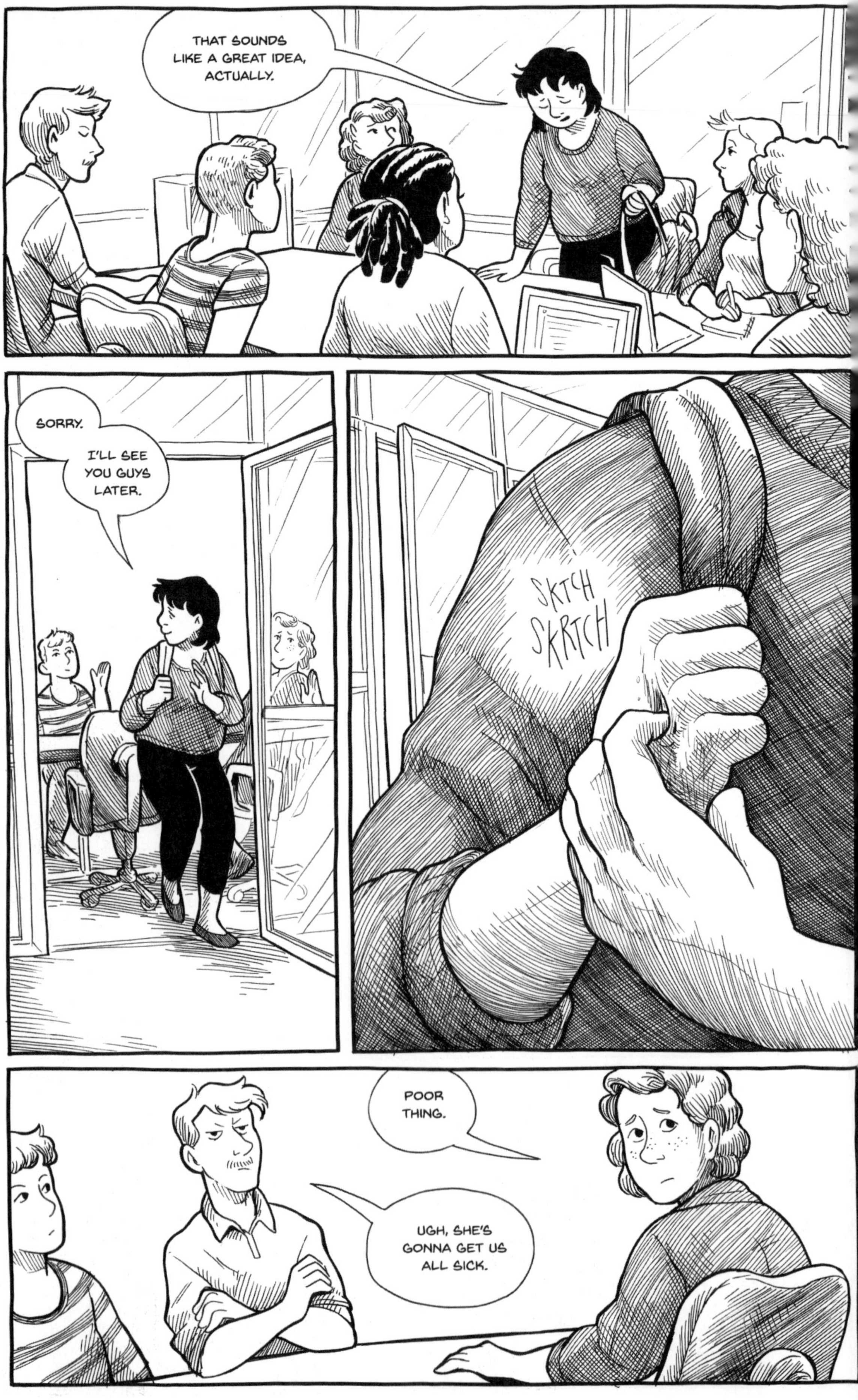
THAT SOUNDS LIKE A GREAT IDEA, ACTUALLY.
SORRY.
I'LL SEE YOU GUYS LATER.
SKTCH SKRTCH
POOR THING.
UGH, SHE'S GONNA GET US ALL SICK.

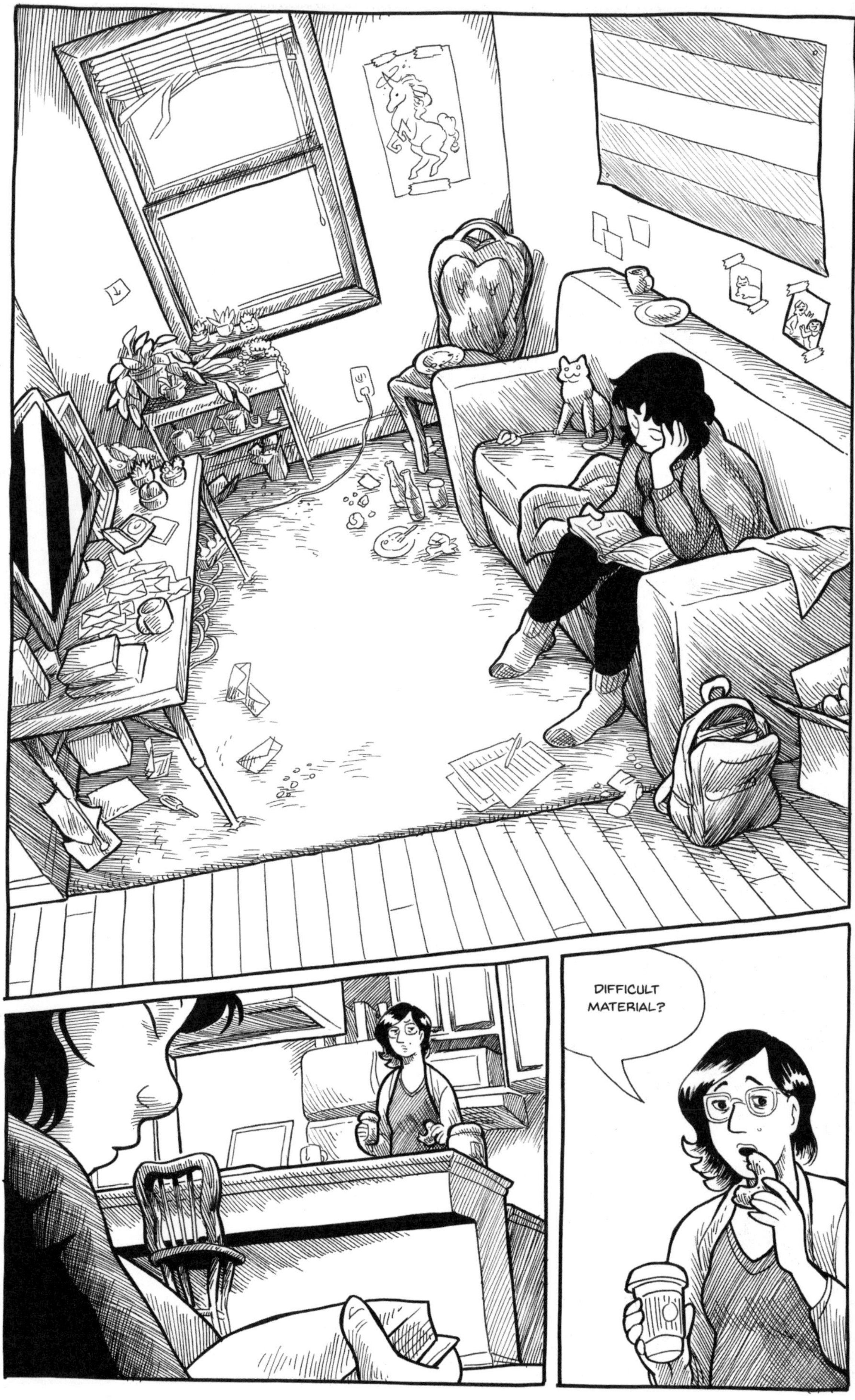
DIFFICULT MATERIAL?

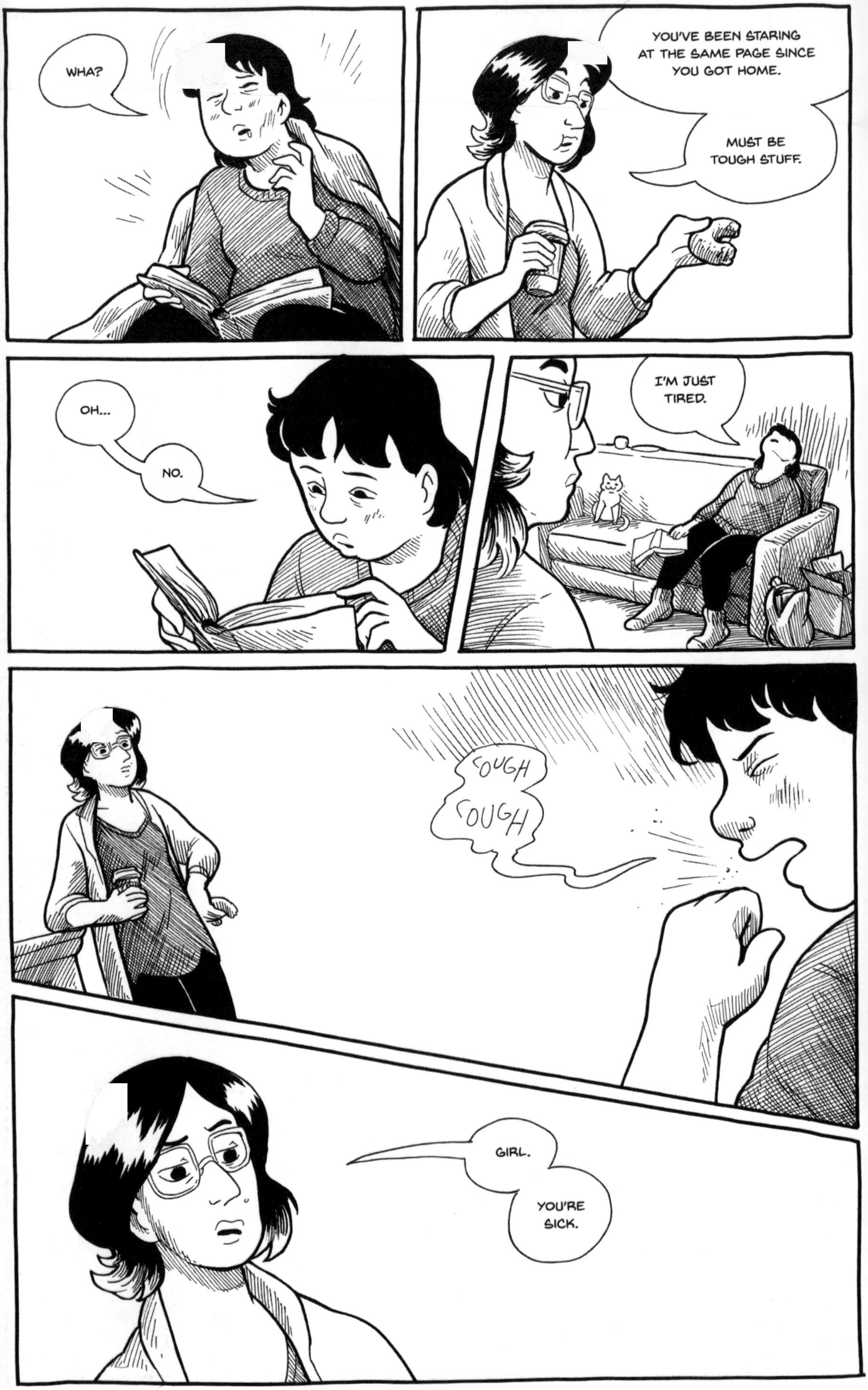
WHA?
YOU'VE BEEN STARING AT THE SAME PAGE SINCE YOU GOT HOME.
MUST BE TOUGH STUFF.
OH...
NO.
I'M JUST TIRED.
COUGH
COUGH
GIRL.
YOU'RE SICK.

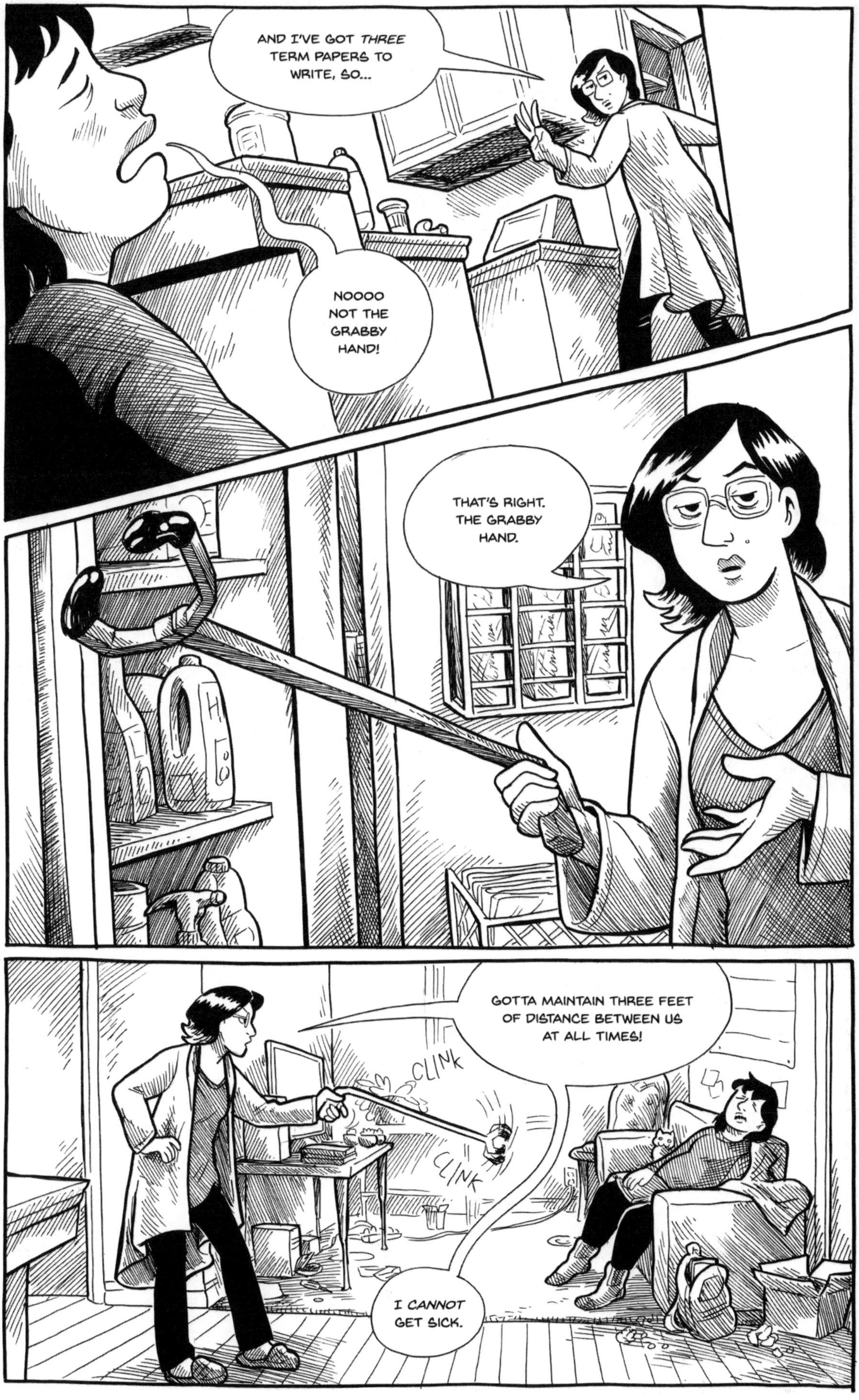
AND I'VE GOT THREE TERM PAPERS TO WRITE, SO...
NOOOO NOT THE GRABBY HAND!
THAT'S RIGHT. THE GRABBY HAND.
GOTTA MAINTAIN THREE FEET OF DISTANCE BETWEEN US AT ALL TIMES!
CLINK
CLINK
I CANNOT GET SICK.

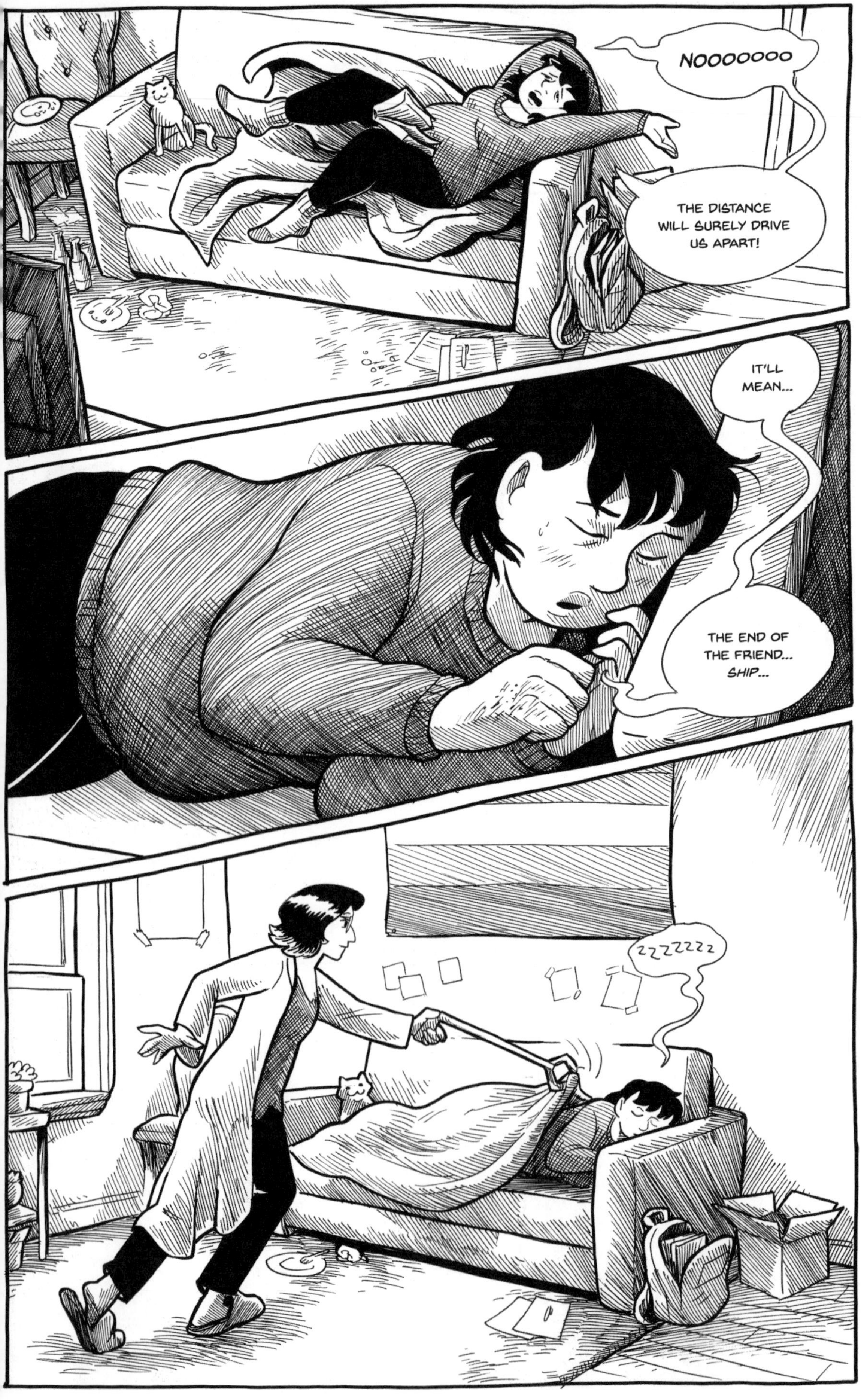
NOOOOOOO
THE DISTANCE WILL SURELY DRIVE US APART!
IT'LL MEAN...
THE END OF THE FRIEND... SHIP...
ZZZZZZZ

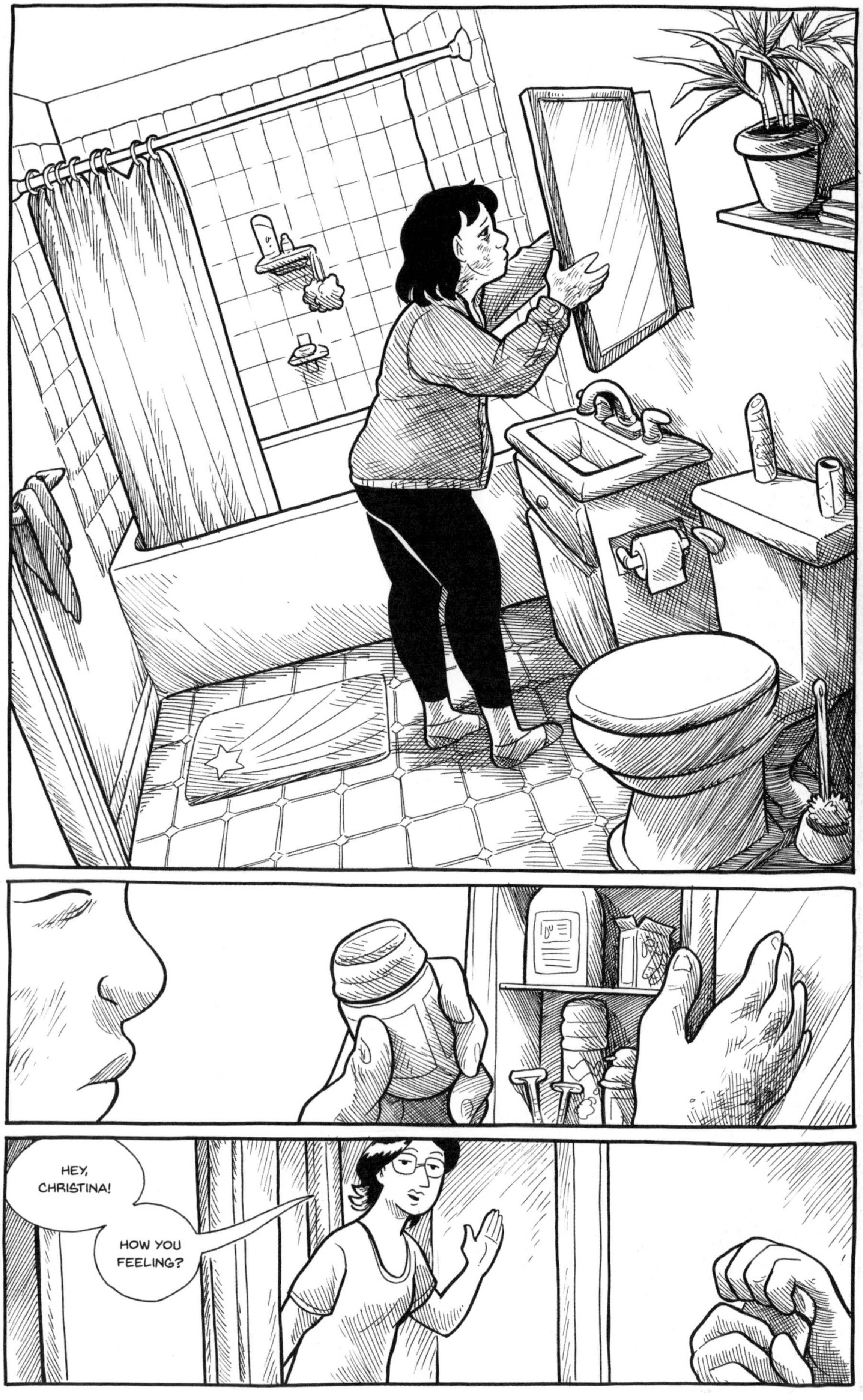
HEY, CHRISTINA!
HOW YOU FEELING?

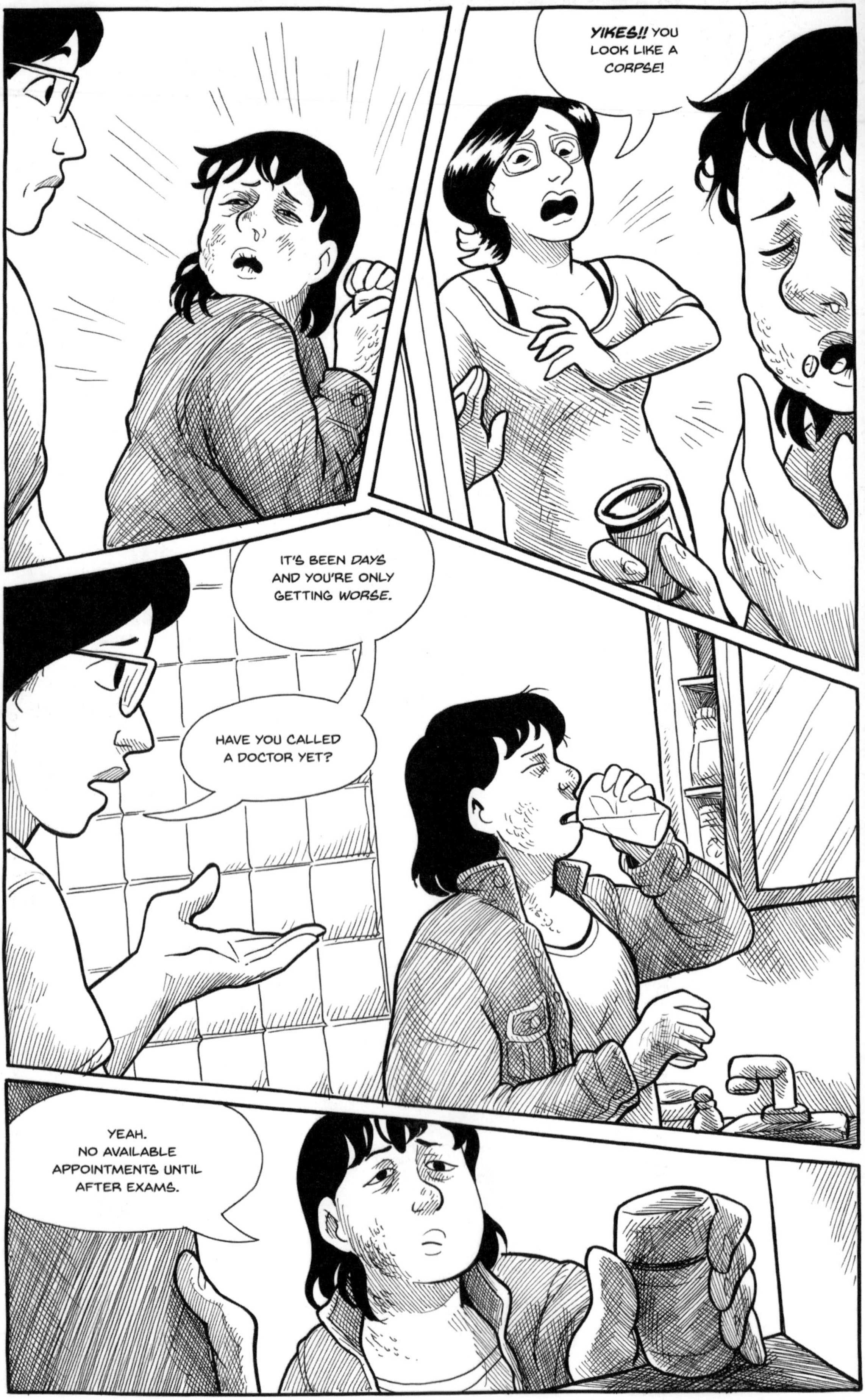
YIKES!! YOU LOOK LIKE A CORPSE!
IT'S BEEN DAYS AND YOU'RE ONLY GETTING WORSE.
HAVE YOU CALLED A DOCTOR YET?
YEAH. NO AVAILABLE APPOINTMENTS UNTIL AFTER EXAMS.

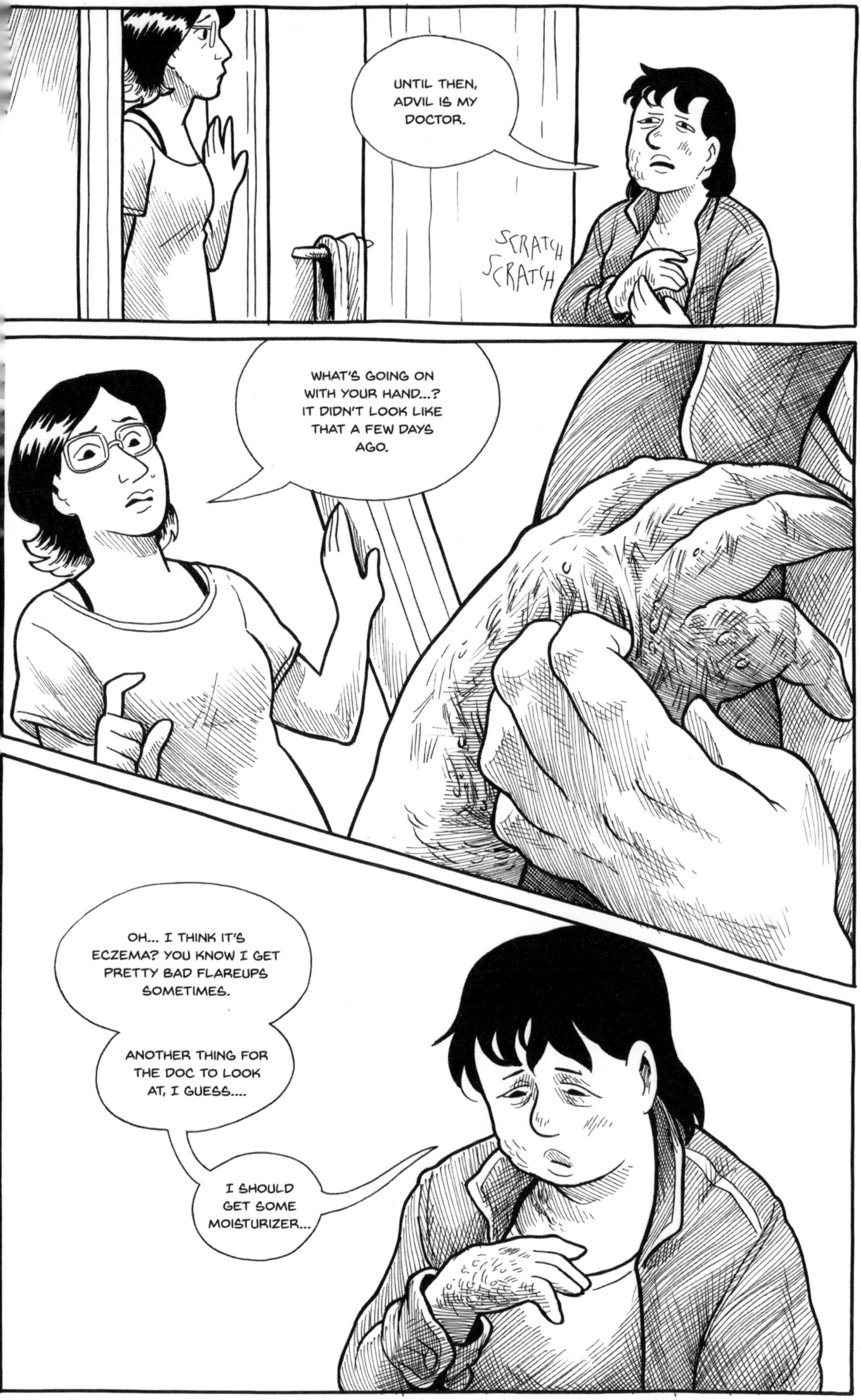
UNTIL THEN, ADVIL IS MY DOCTOR.
SCRATCH SCRATCH
WHAT'S GOING ON WITH YOUR HAND...? IT DIDN'T LOOK LIKE THAT A FEW DAYS AGO.
OH... I THINK IT'S ECZEMA? YOU KNOW I GET PRETTY BAD FLAREUPS SOMETIMES.
ANOTHER THING FOR THE DOC TO LOOK AT, I GUESS....
I SHOULD GET SOME MOISTURIZER...

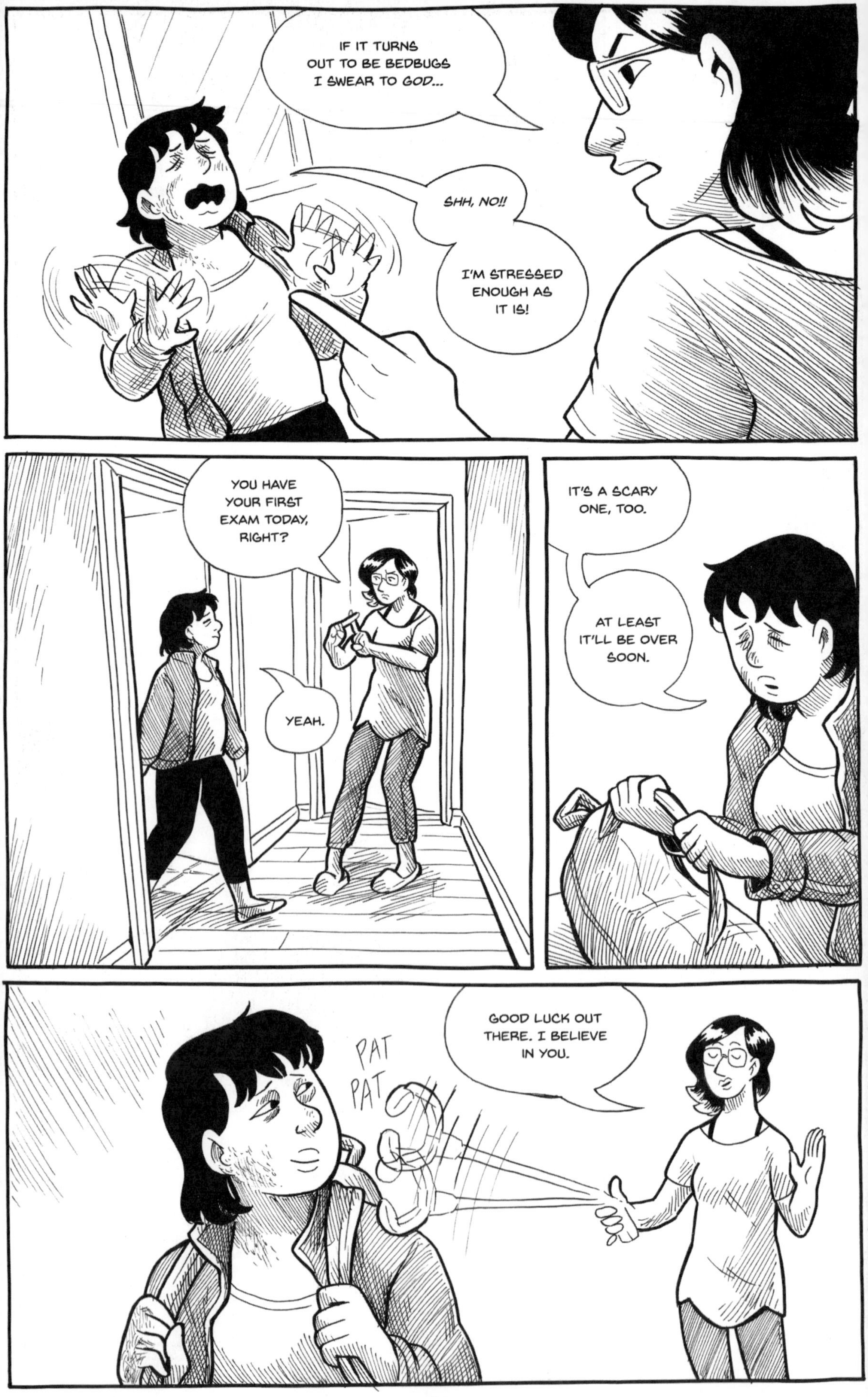
IF IT TURNS OUT TO BE BEDBUGS I SWEAR TO GOD...
SHH, NO!!
I'M STRESSED ENOUGH AS IT IS!
YOU HAVE YOUR FIRST EXAM TODAY, RIGHT?
YEAH.
IT'S A SCARY ONE, TOO.
AT LEAST IT'LL BE OVER SOON.
PAT PAT
GOOD LUCK OUT THERE. I BELIEVE IN YOU.

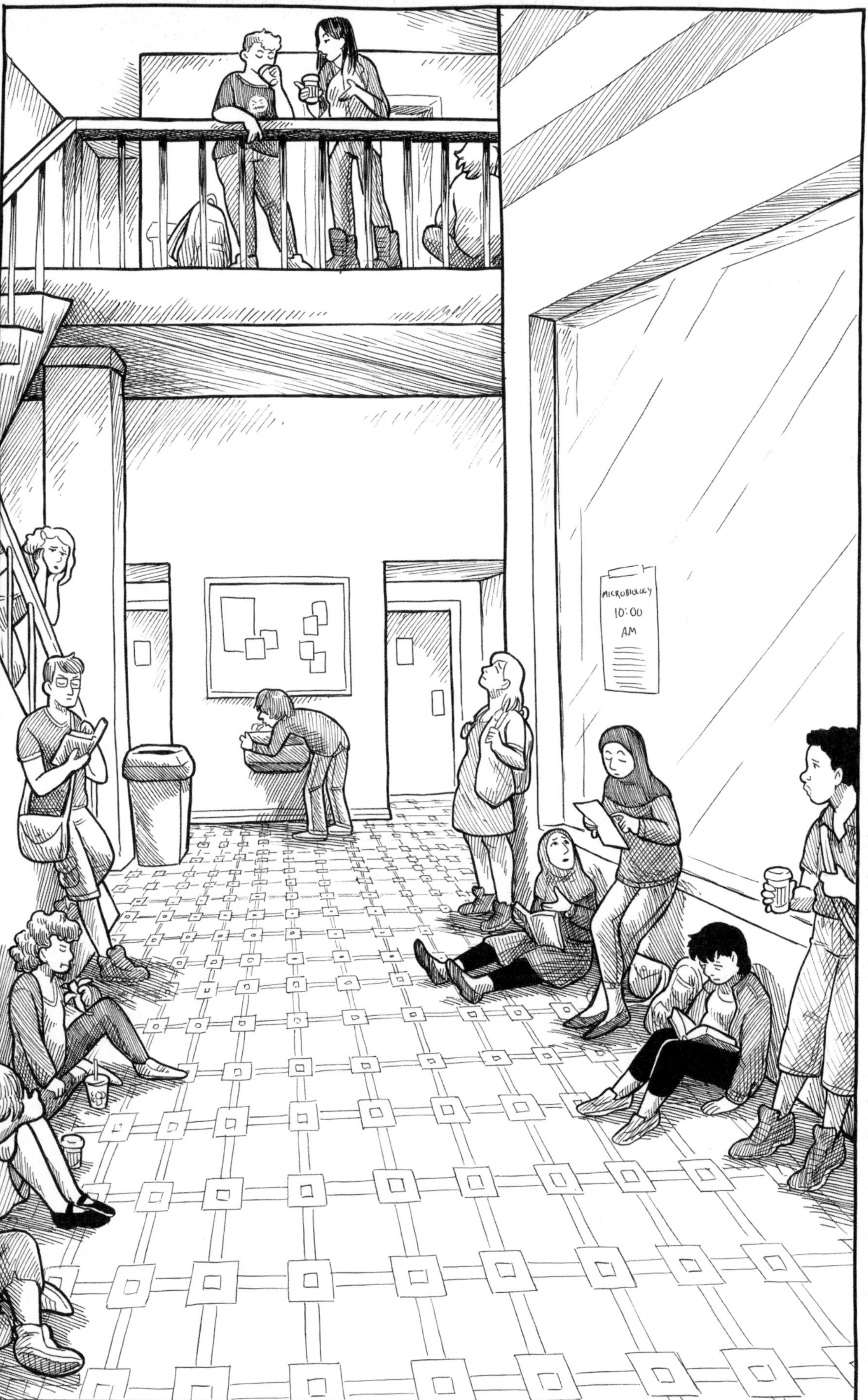
MICROBIOLOGY
10:00
AM

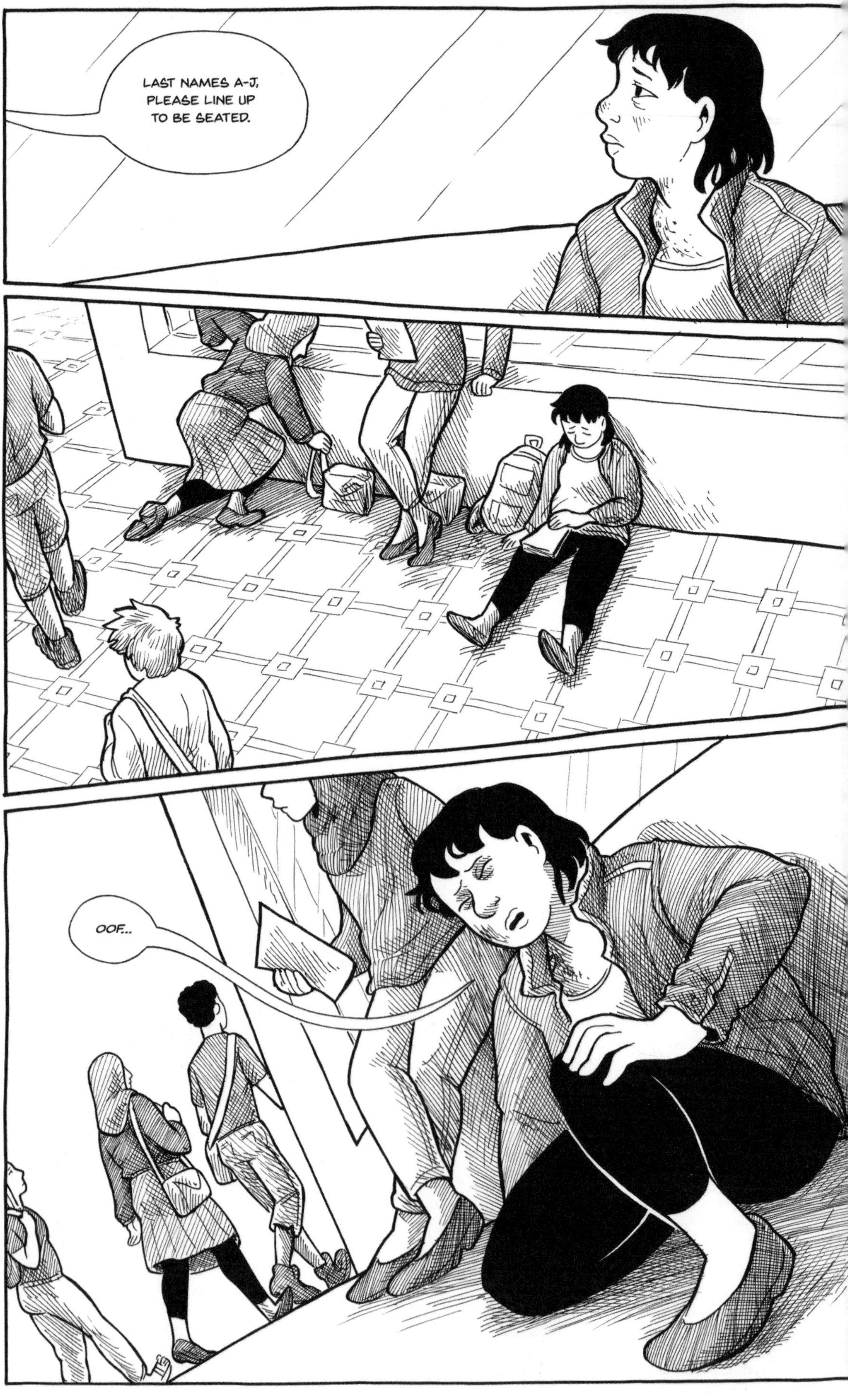
LAST NAMES A-J, PLEASE LINE UP TO BE SEATED.
OOF..

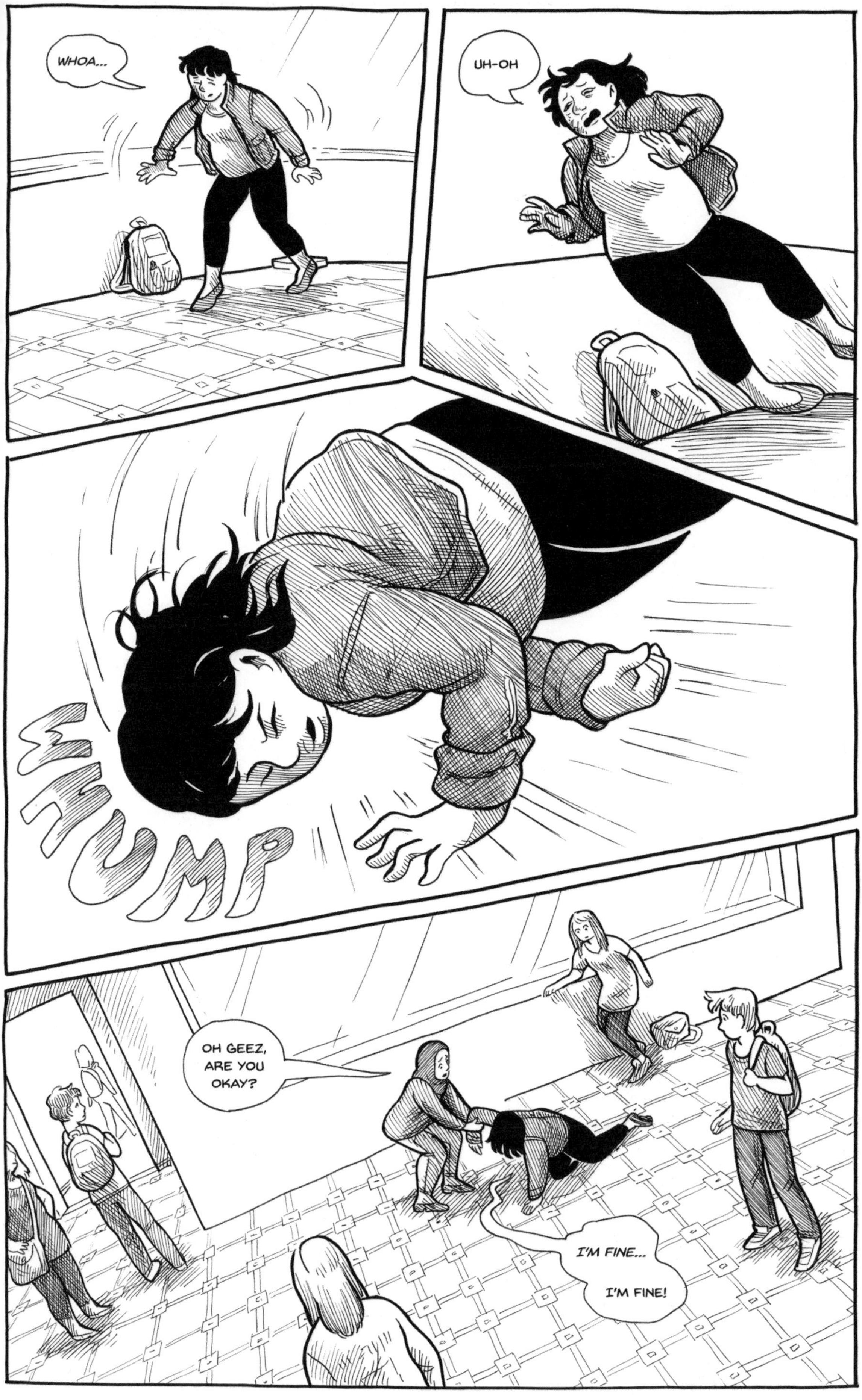
WHOA...
UH-OH
WHUMP
OH GEEZ, ARE YOU OKAY?
I'M FINE...
I'M FINE!

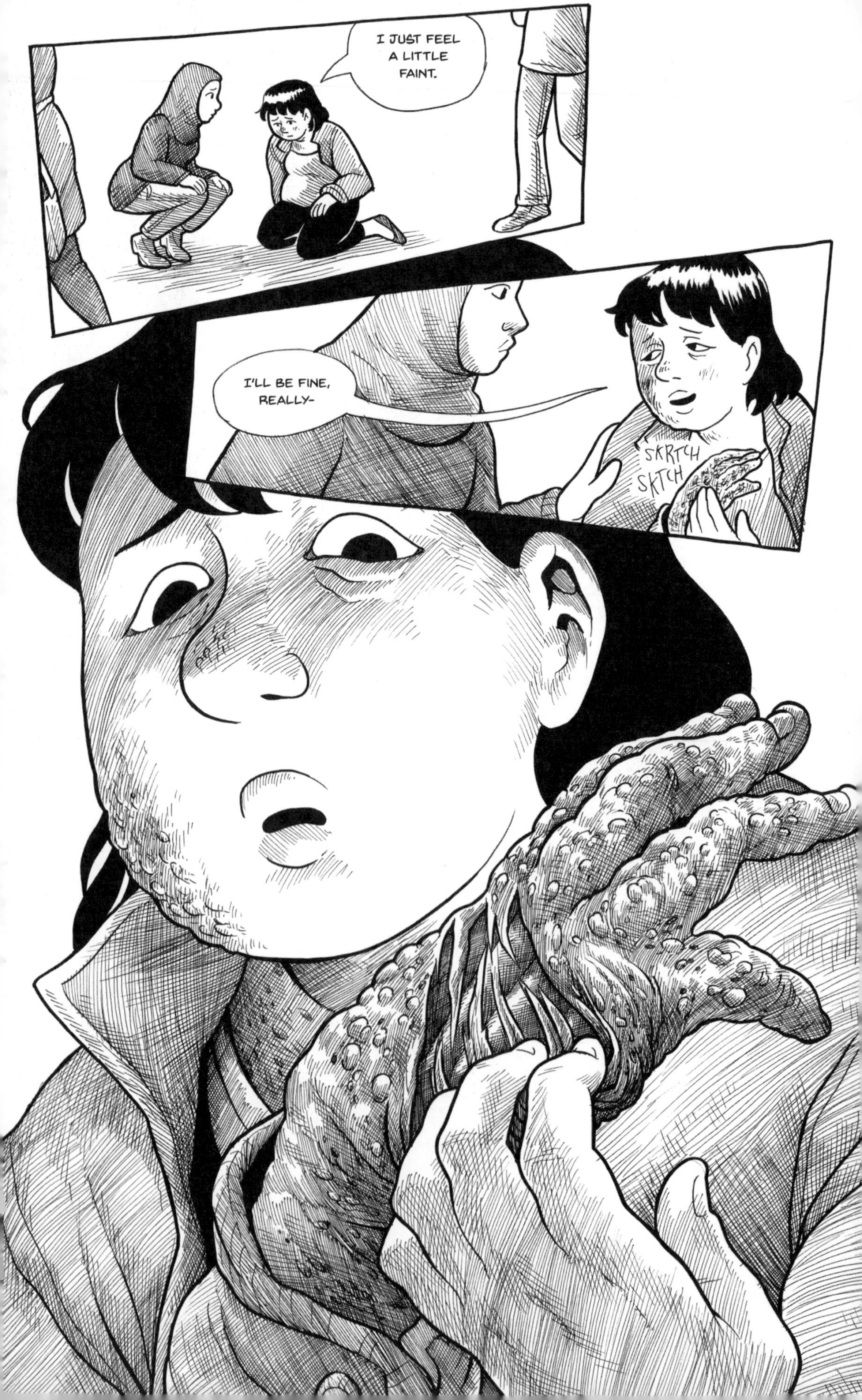
I JUST FEEL A LITTLE FAINT.
I'LL BE FINE, REALLY-
SKRTCH
SKTCH

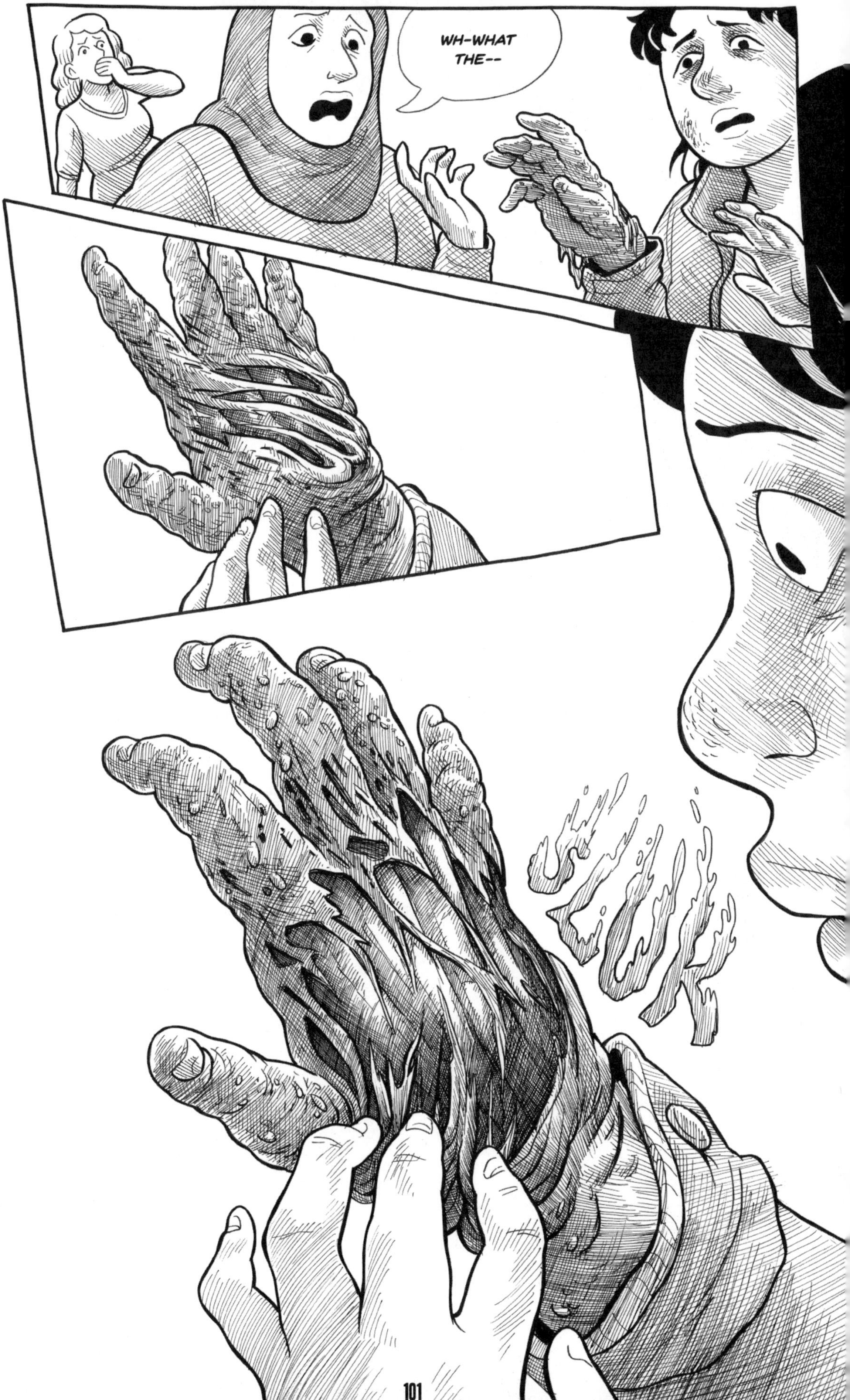
WH-WHAT THE--

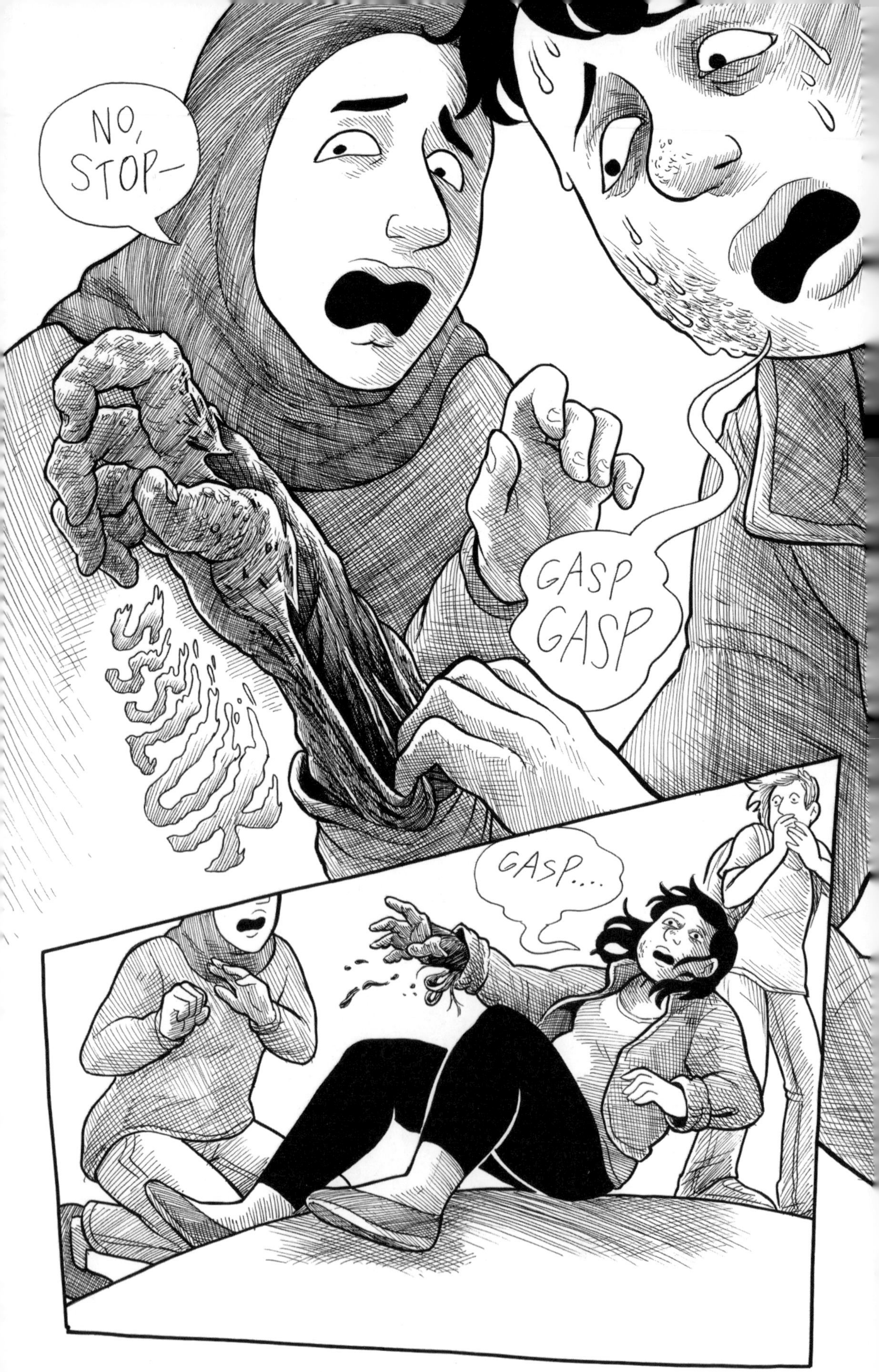
NO, STOP—
GASP GASP
GASP...

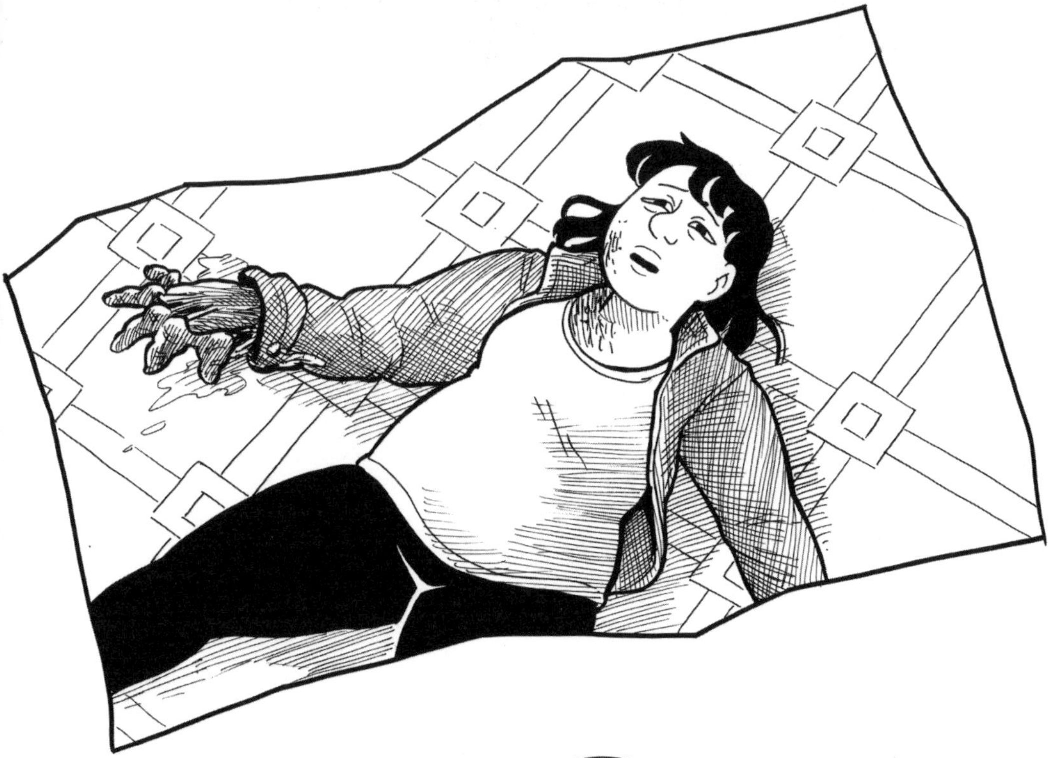

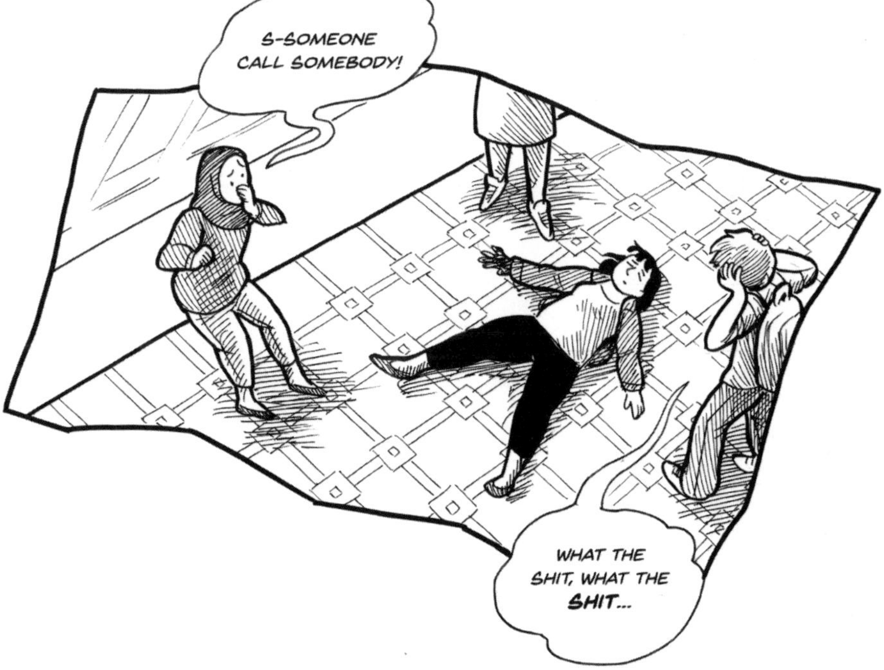
S-SOMEONE CALL SOMEBODY!
WHAT THE SHIT, WHAT THE SHIT...

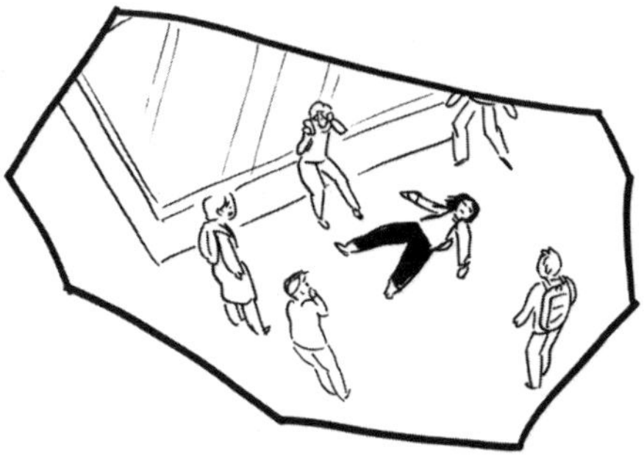

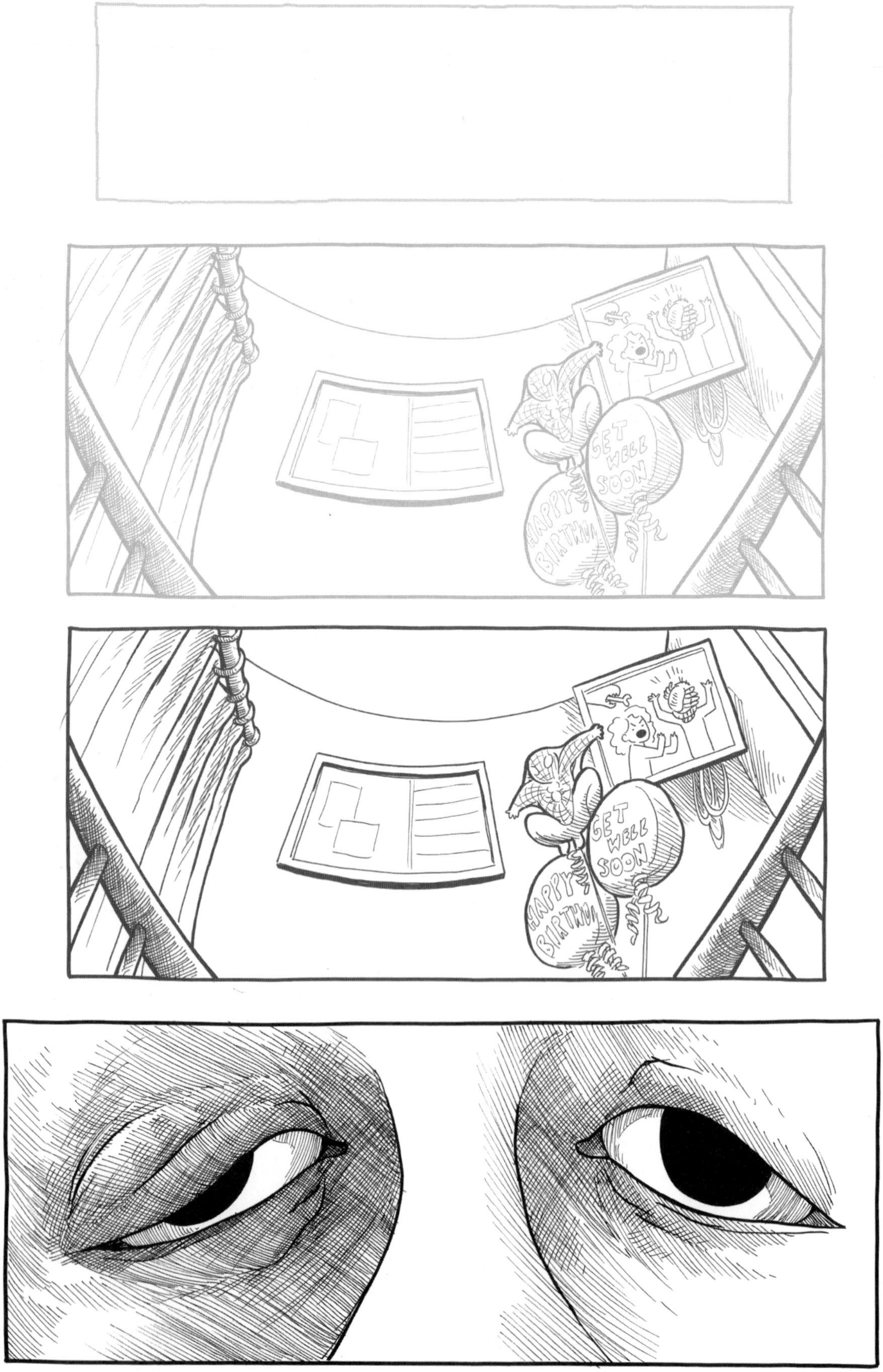
GET WELL SOON
HAPPY BIRTHDA

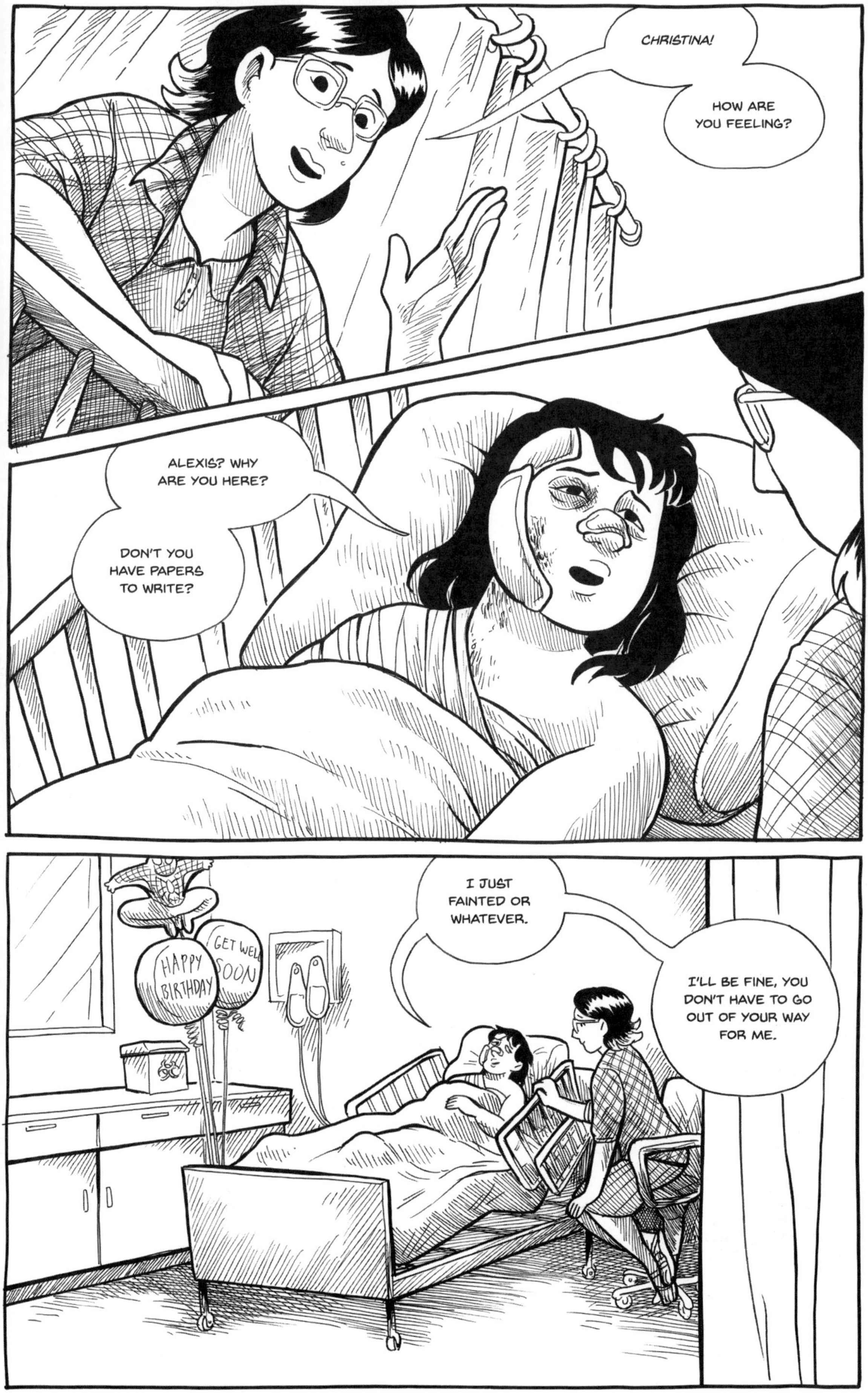
CHRISTINA!
HOW ARE YOU FEELING?
ALEXIS? WHY ARE YOU HERE?
DON'T YOU HAVE PAPERS TO WRITE?
HAPPY BIRTHDAY
GET WELL SOON
I JUST FAINTED OR WHATEVER.
I'LL BE FINE, YOU DON'T HAVE TO GO OUT OF YOUR WAY FOR ME.

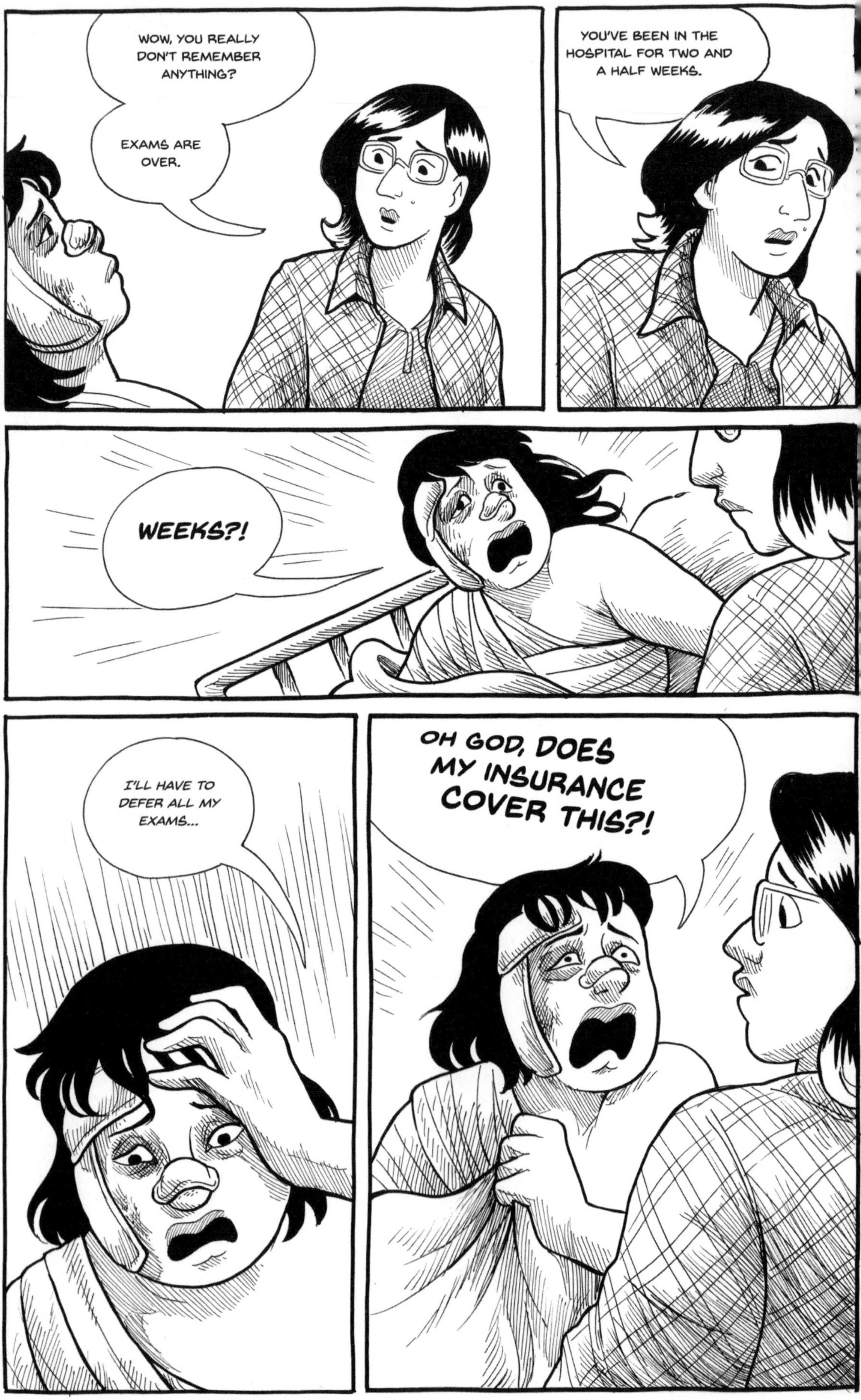
WOW, YOU REALLY DON'T REMEMBER ANYTHING?
EXAMS ARE OVER.
YOU'VE BEEN IN THE HOSPITAL FOR TWO AND A HALF WEEKS.
WEEKS?!
I'LL HAVE TO DEFER ALL MY EXAMS...
OH GOD, DOES MY INSURANCE COVER THIS?!

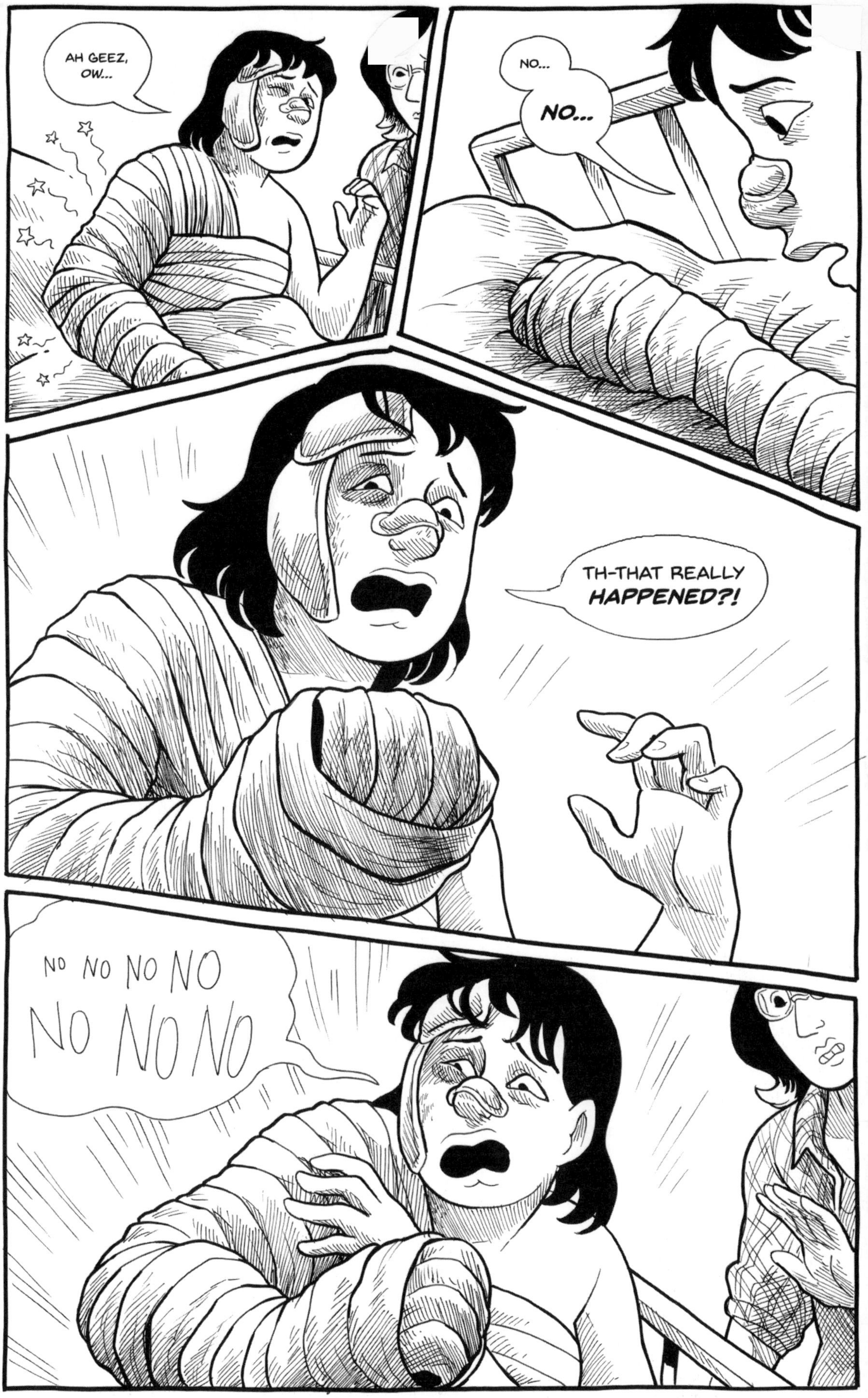
AH GEEZ, OW...
NO...
NO...
TH-THAT REALLY HAPPENED?!
NO NO NO NO
NO NO NO

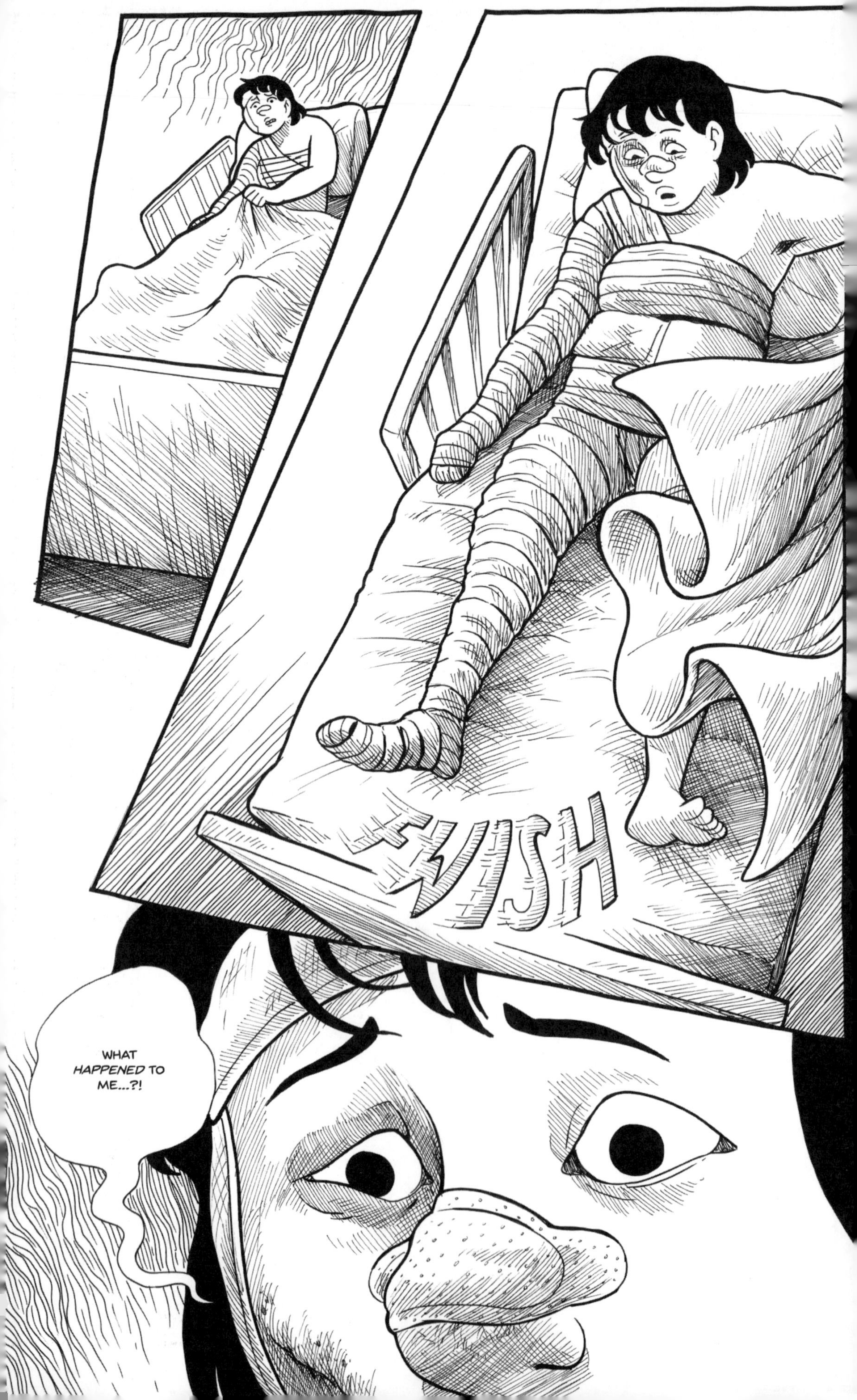

FWISH
WHAT HAPPENED TO ME...?!

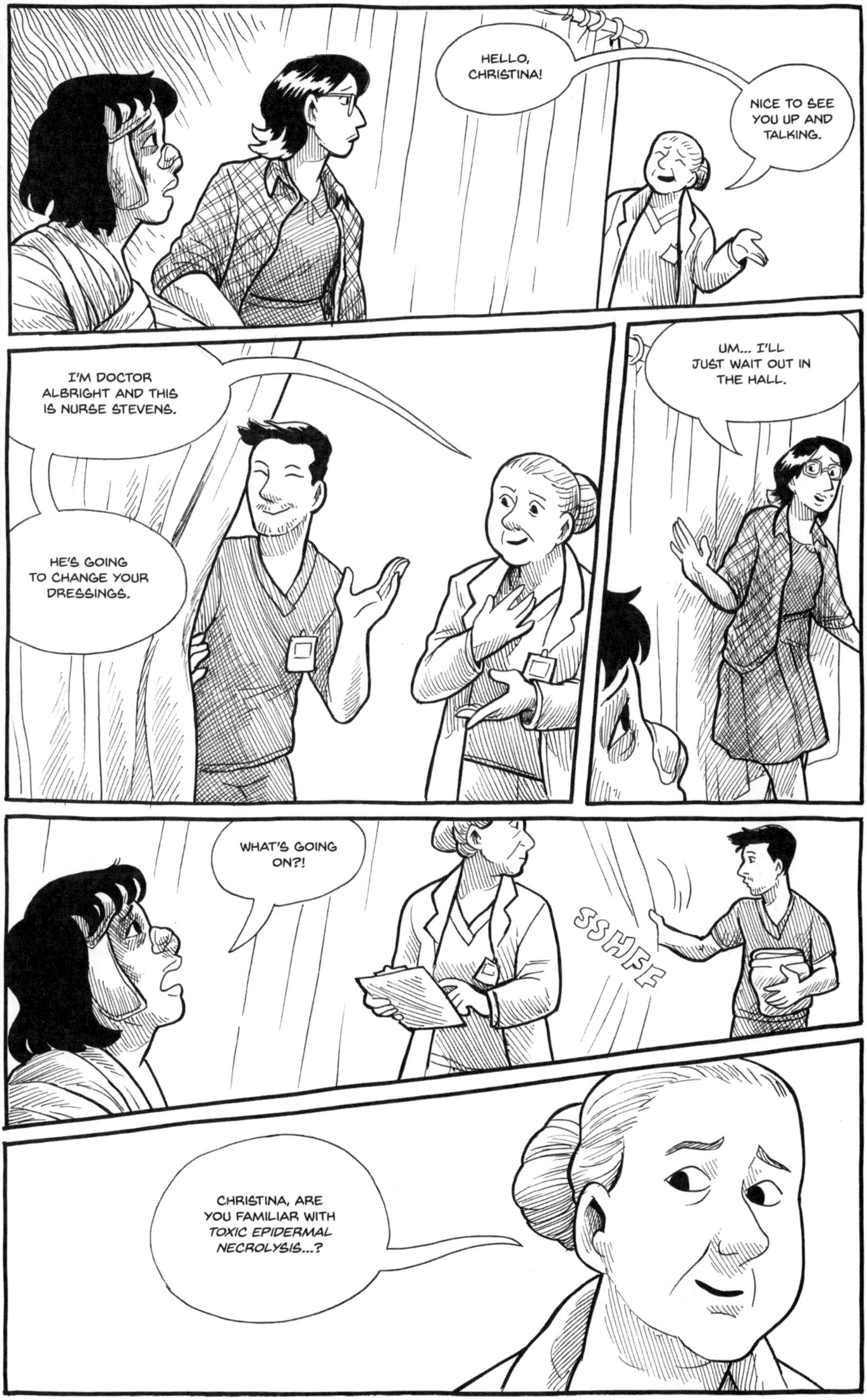
HELLO, CHRISTINA!
NICE TO SEE YOU UP AND TALKING.
I'M DOCTOR ALBRIGHT AND THIS IS NURSE STEVENS.
HE'S GOING TO CHANGE YOUR DRESSINGS.
UM... I'LL JUST WAIT OUT IN THE HALL.
WHAT'S GOING ON?!
SSHFF
CHRISTINA, ARE YOU FAMILIAR WITH *TOXIC EPIDERMAL NECROLYSIS*...?

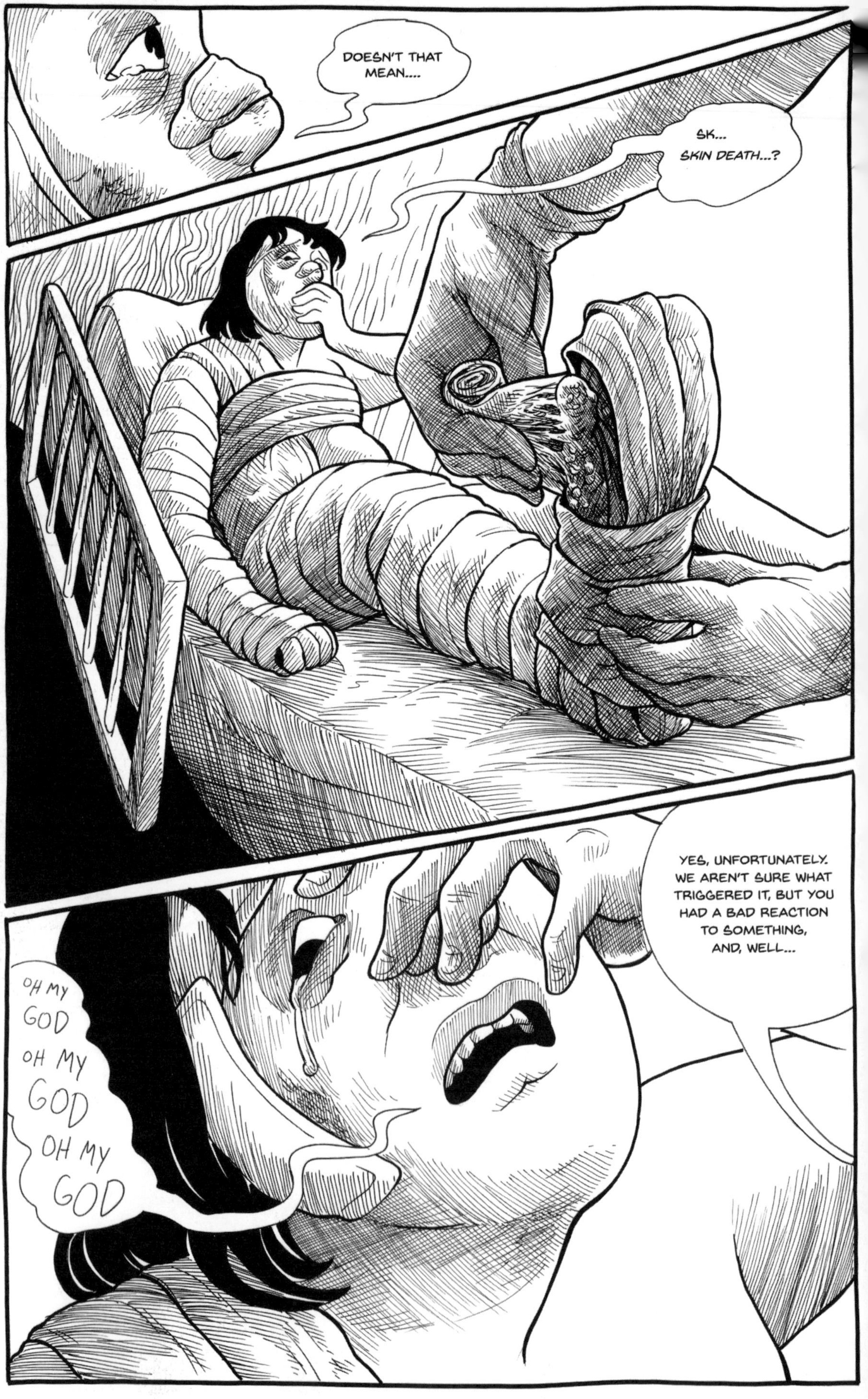
DOESN'T THAT MEAN....
SK... SKIN DEATH...?
YES, UNFORTUNATELY. WE AREN'T SURE WHAT TRIGGERED IT, BUT YOU HAD A BAD REACTION TO SOMETHING, AND, WELL...
OH MY GOD OH MY GOD OH MY GOD

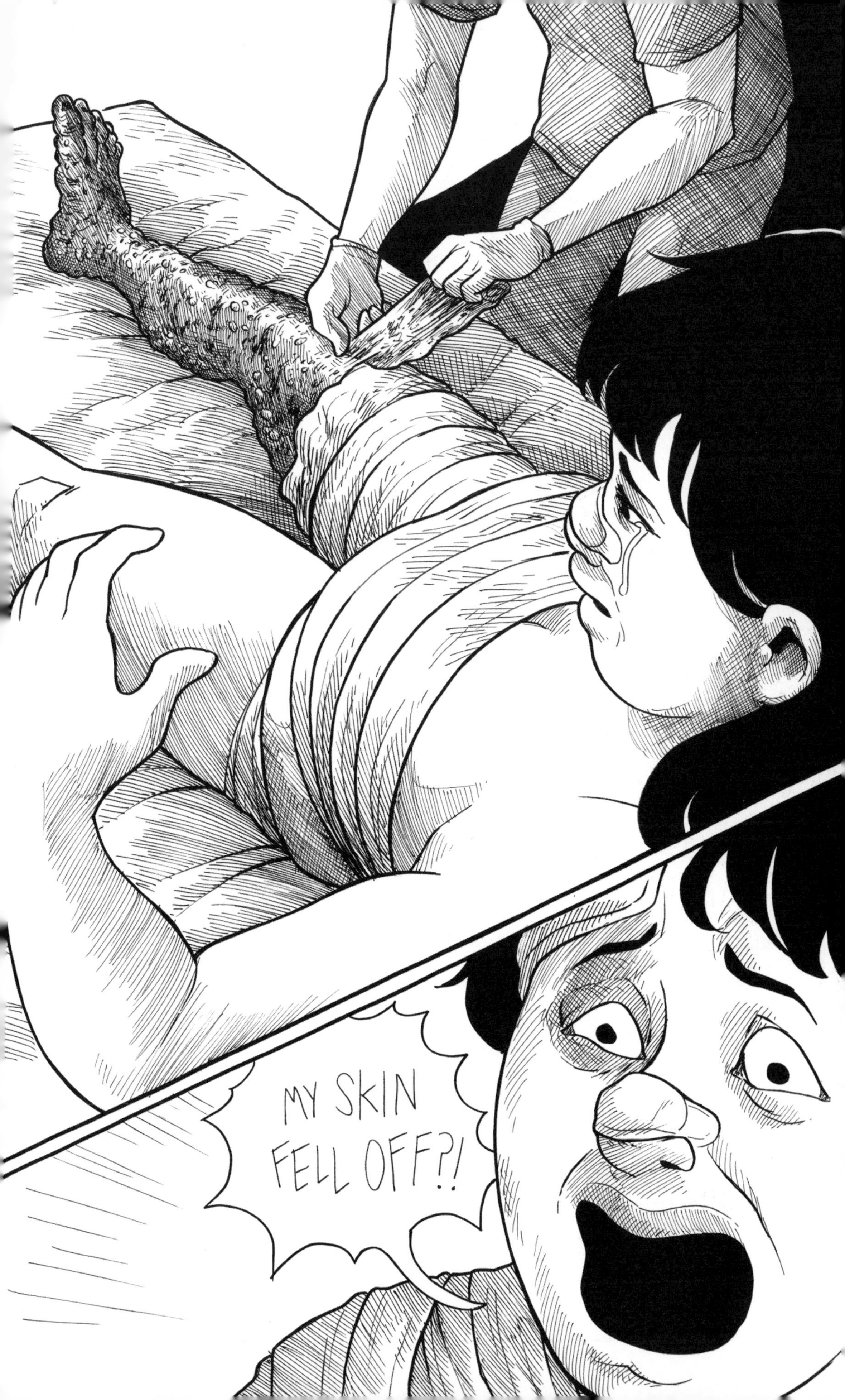
MY SKIN FELL OFF?!

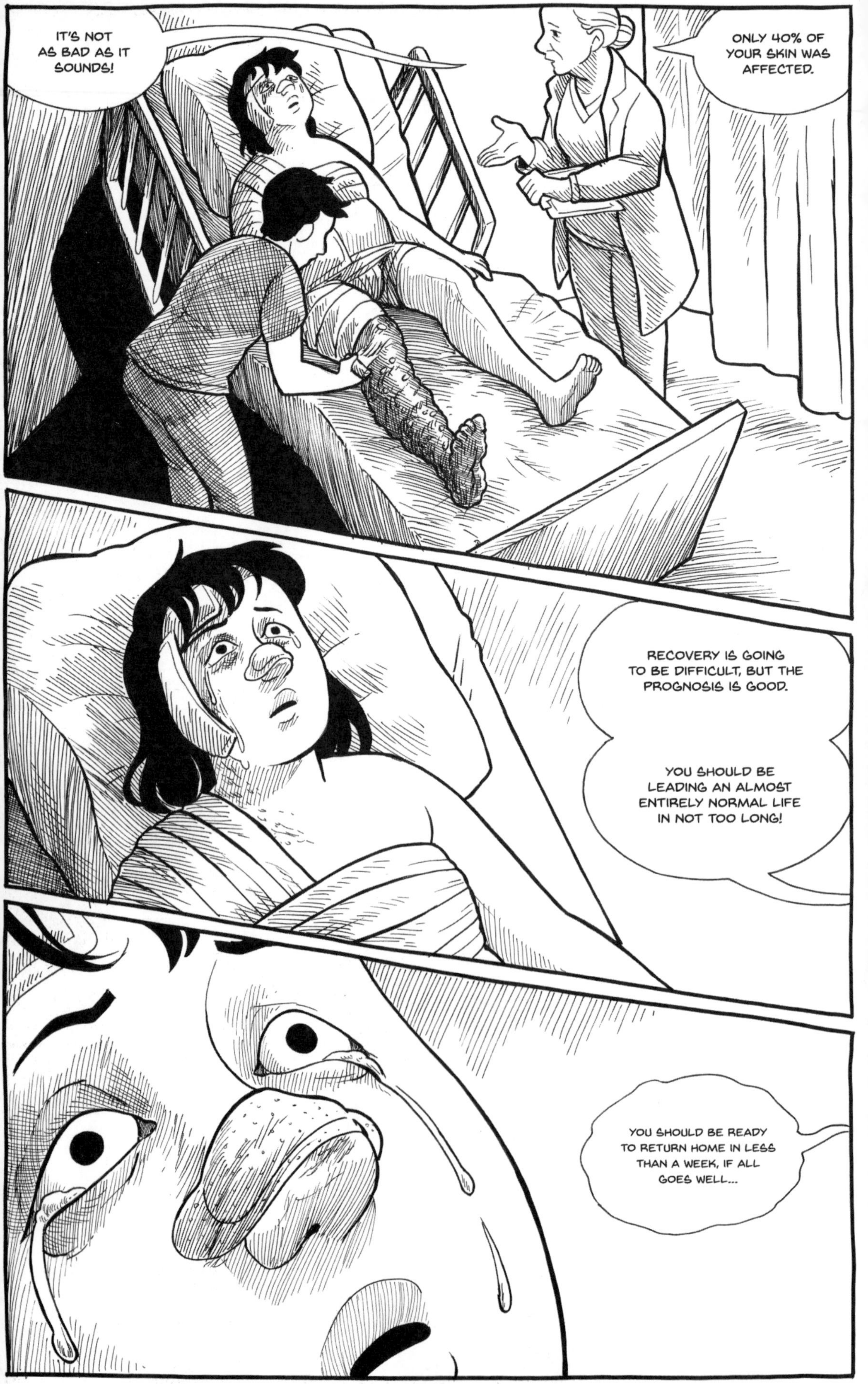
IT'S NOT AS BAD AS IT SOUNDS!
ONLY 40% OF YOUR SKIN WAS AFFECTED.
RECOVERY IS GOING TO BE DIFFICULT, BUT THE PROGNOSIS IS GOOD.
YOU SHOULD BE LEADING AN ALMOST ENTIRELY NORMAL LIFE IN NOT TOO LONG!
YOU SHOULD BE READY TO RETURN HOME IN LESS THAN A WEEK, IF ALL GOES WELL...

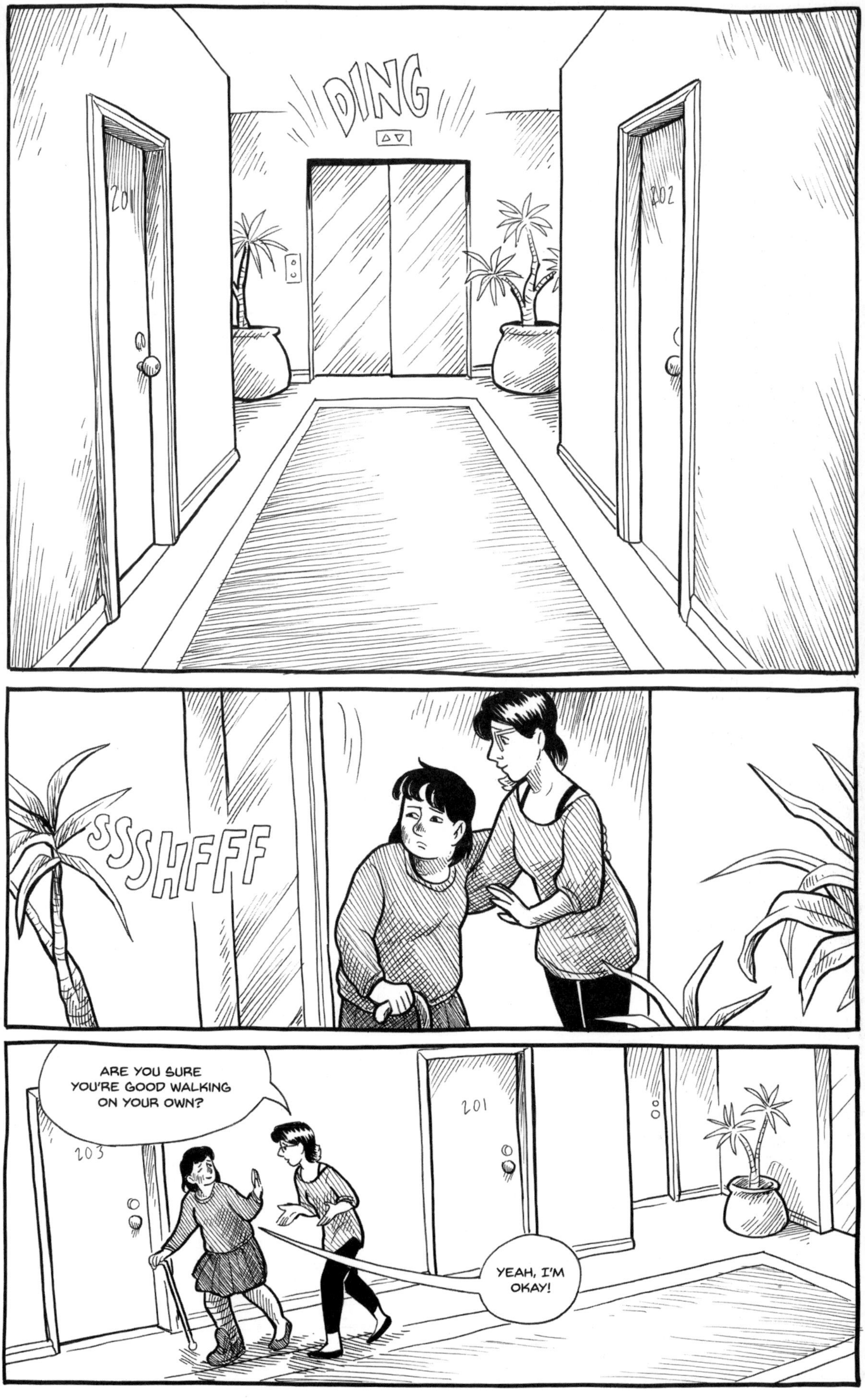
DING
SSSHFFF
ARE YOU SURE YOU'RE GOOD WALKING ON YOUR OWN?
YEAH, I'M OKAY!

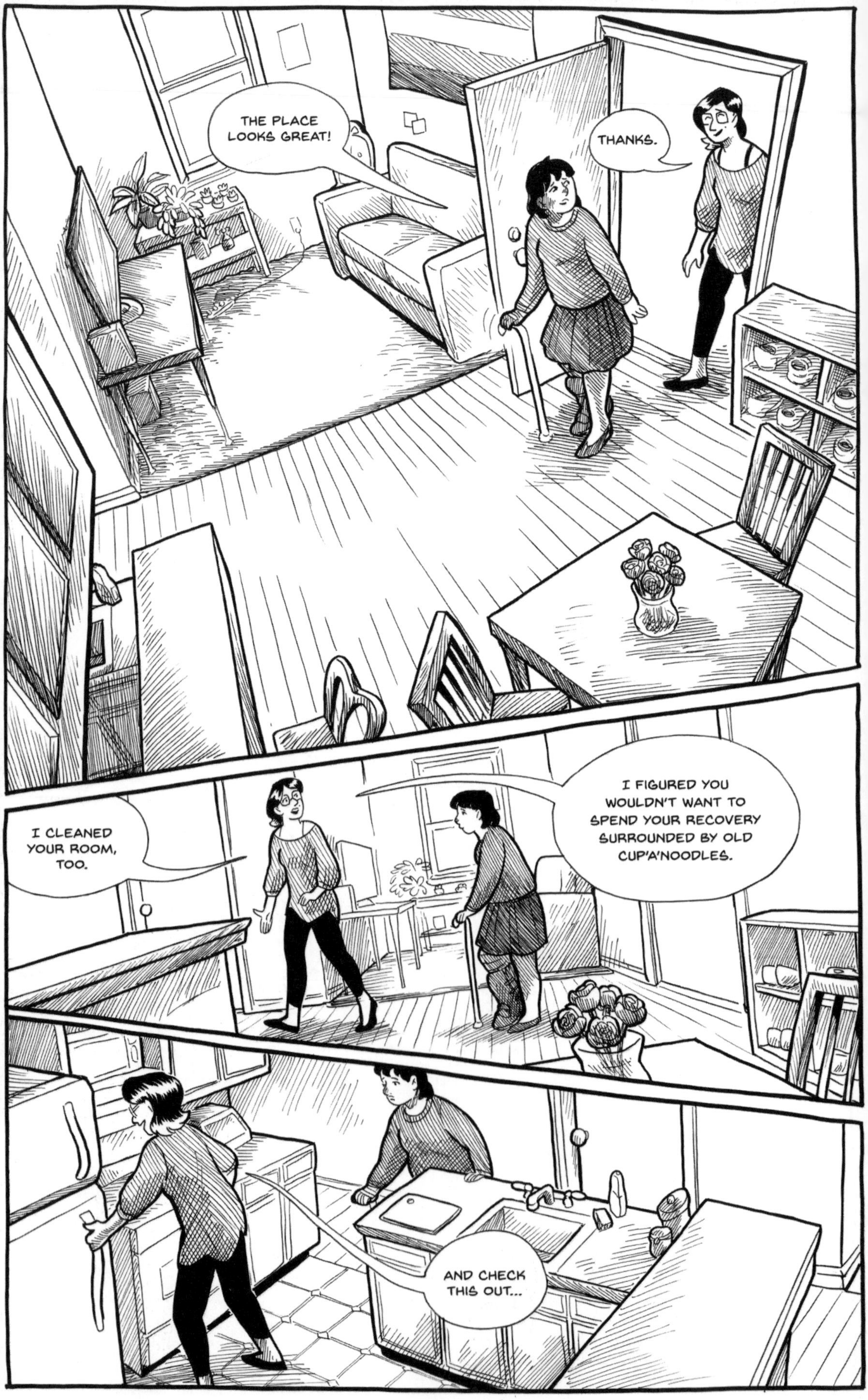
THE PLACE LOOKS GREAT!
THANKS.
I CLEANED YOUR ROOM, TOO.
I FIGURED YOU WOULDN'T WANT TO SPEND YOUR RECOVERY SURROUNDED BY OLD CUP'A'NOODLES.
AND CHECK THIS OUT...

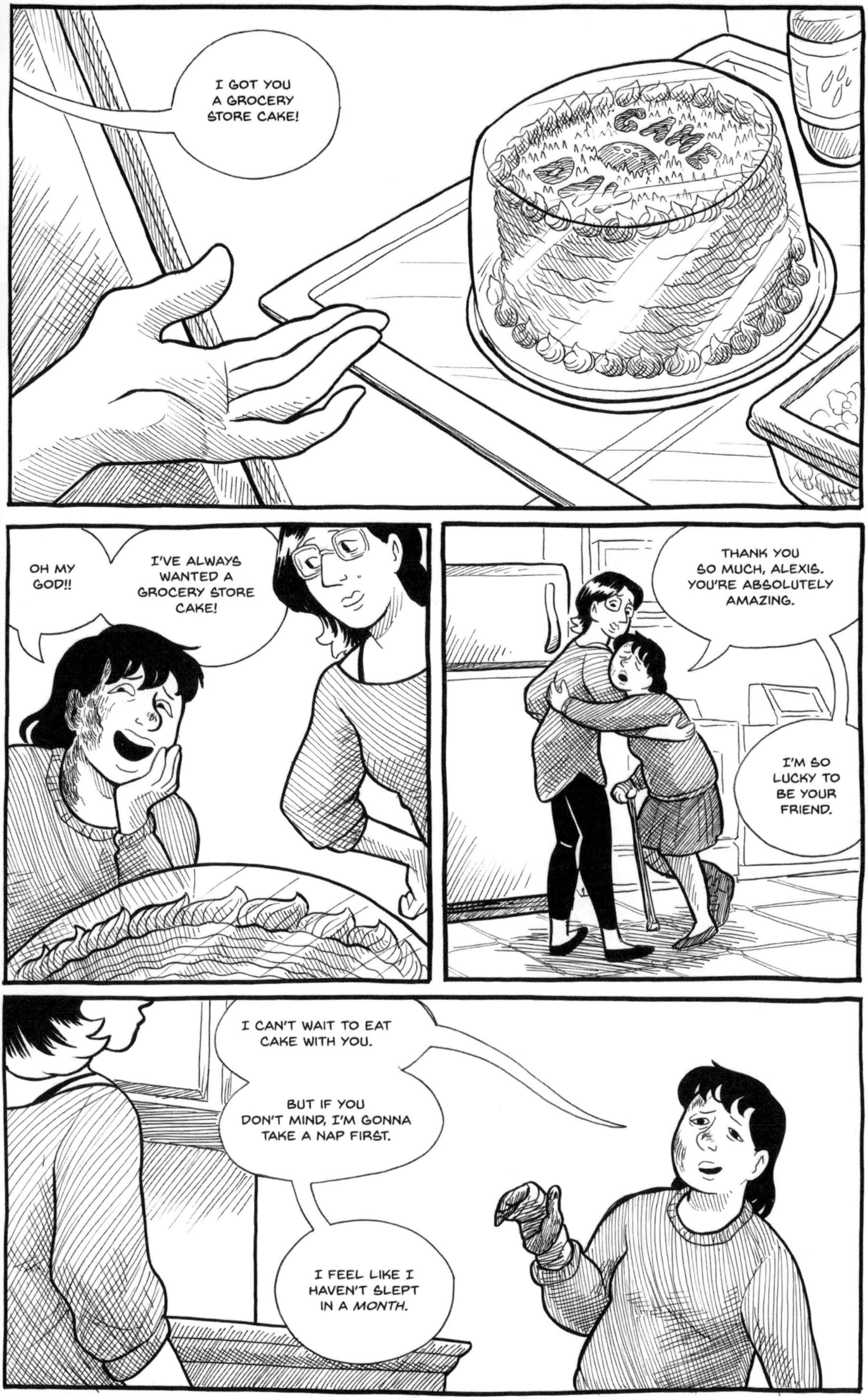
I GOT YOU A GROCERY STORE CAKE!
OH MY GOD!!
I'VE ALWAYS WANTED A GROCERY STORE CAKE!
THANK YOU SO MUCH, ALEXIS. YOU'RE ABSOLUTELY AMAZING.
I'M SO LUCKY TO BE YOUR FRIEND.
I CAN'T WAIT TO EAT CAKE WITH YOU.
BUT IF YOU DON'T MIND, I'M GONNA TAKE A NAP FIRST.
I FEEL LIKE I HAVEN'T SLEPT IN A *MONTH*.

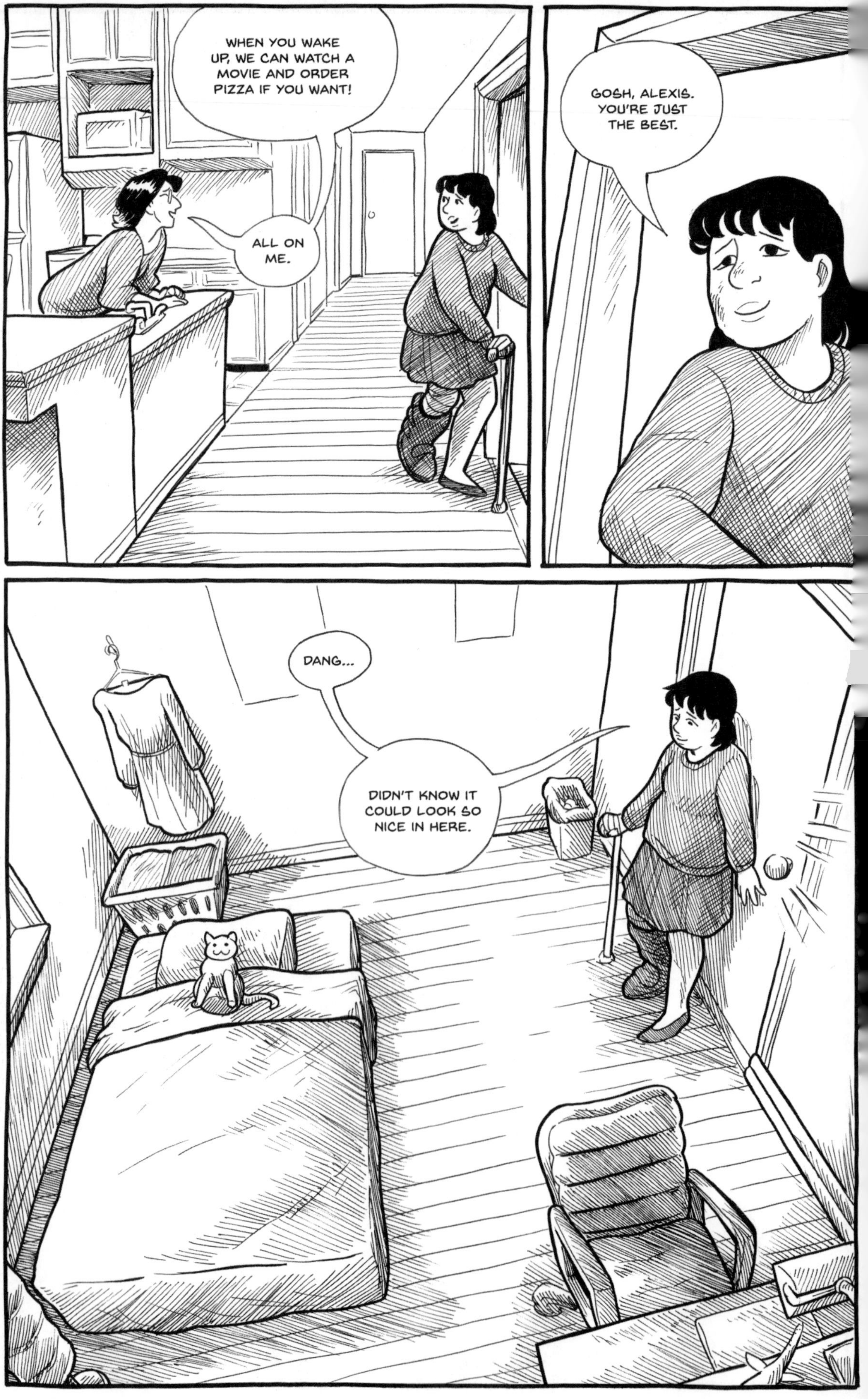
WHEN YOU WAKE UP, WE CAN WATCH A MOVIE AND ORDER PIZZA IF YOU WANT!
ALL ON ME.
GOSH, ALEXIS. YOU'RE JUST THE BEST.
DANG...
DIDN'T KNOW IT COULD LOOK SO NICE IN HERE.

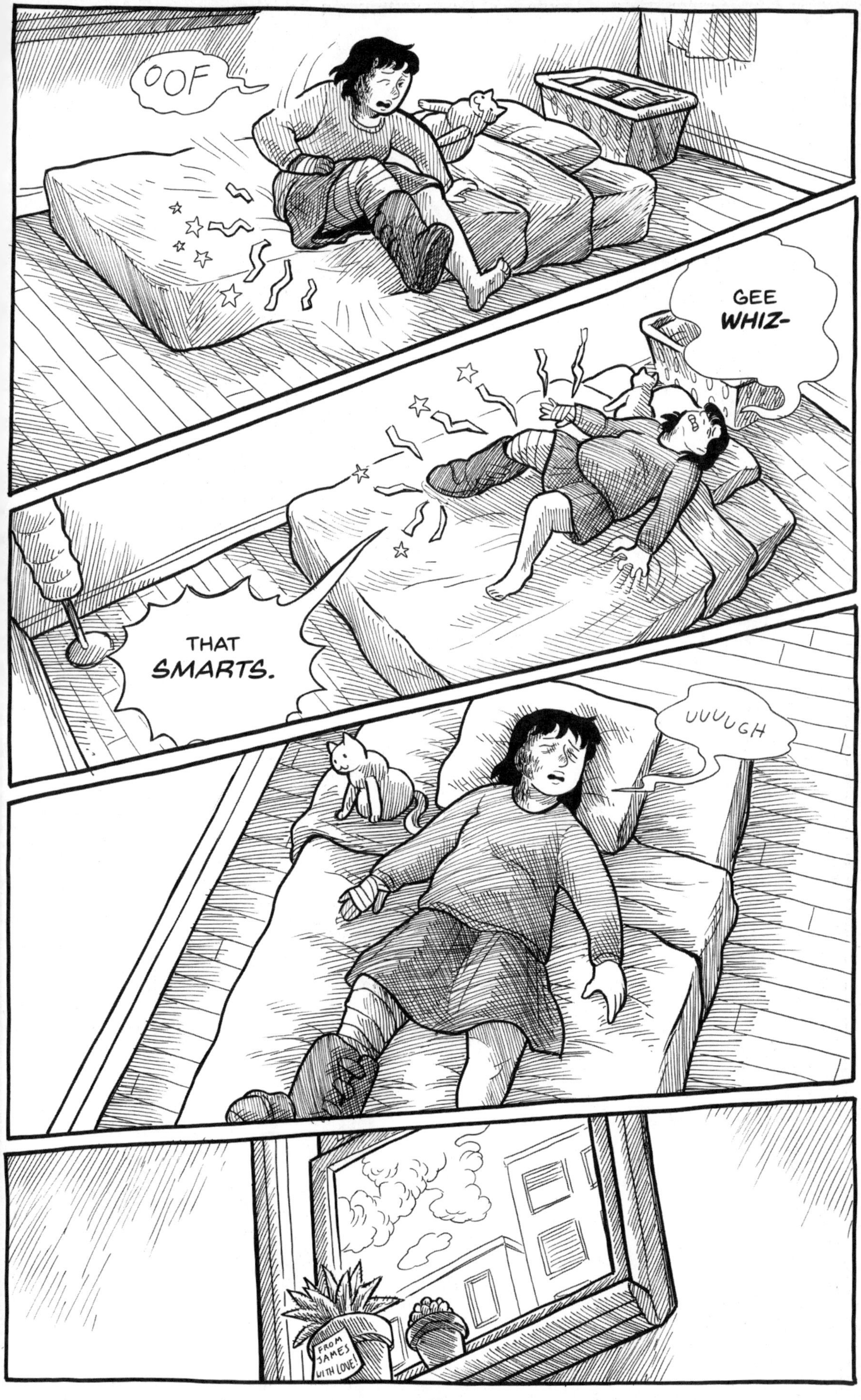
OOF
GEE WHIZ-
THAT SMARTS.
UUUUGH
FROM JAMES WITH LOVE!

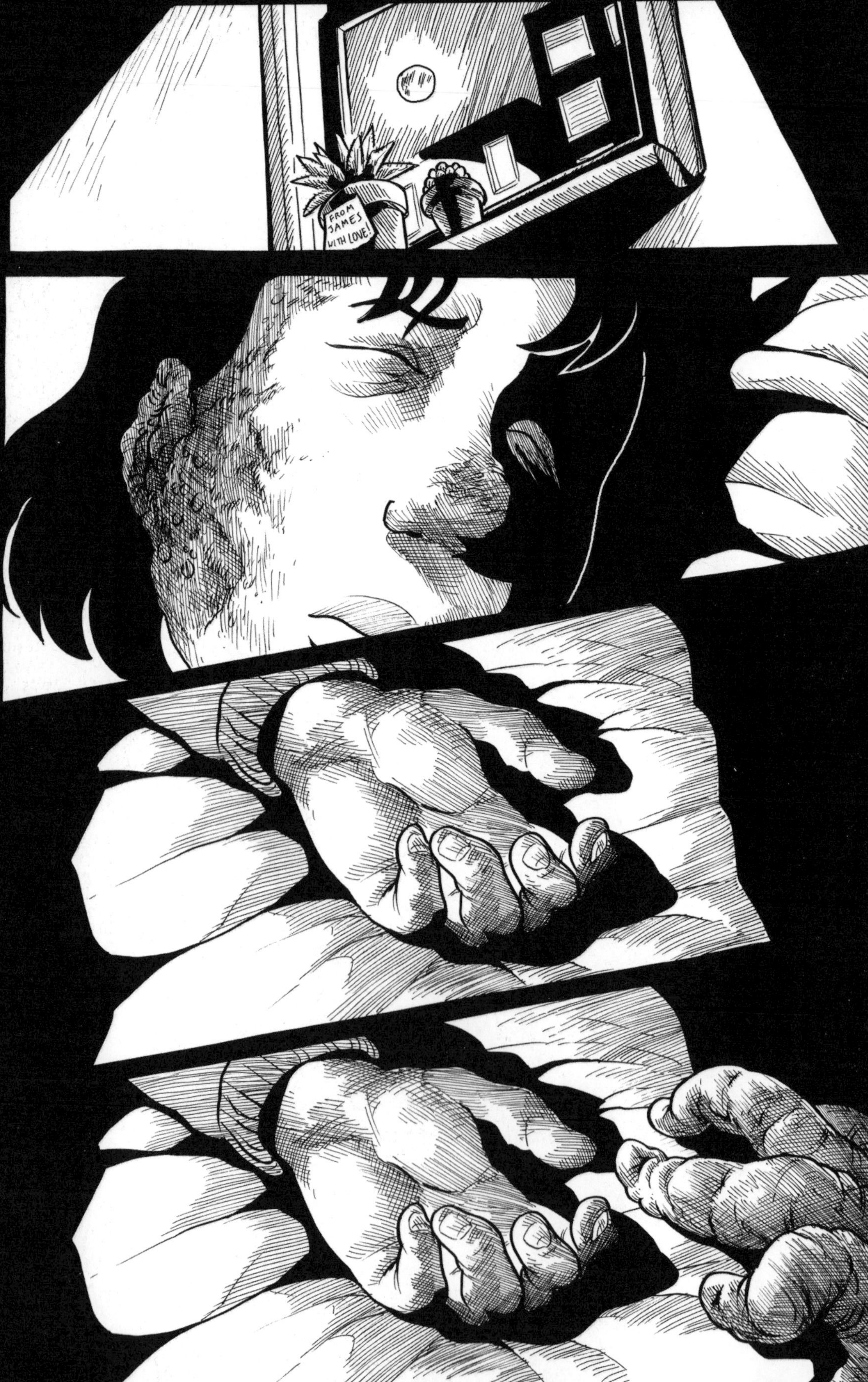
FROM JAMES WITH LOVE!

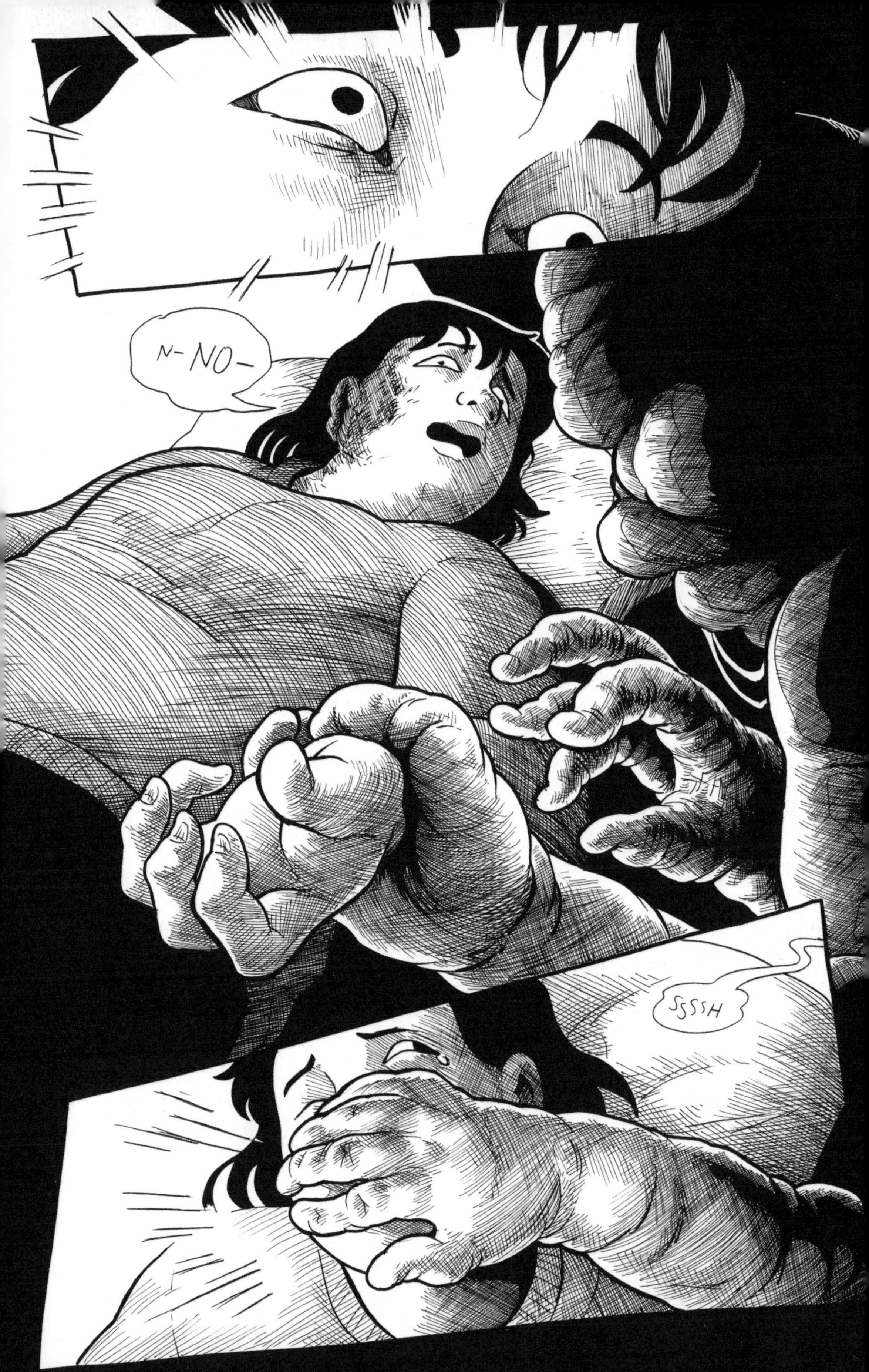
N-NO-
SSSSH

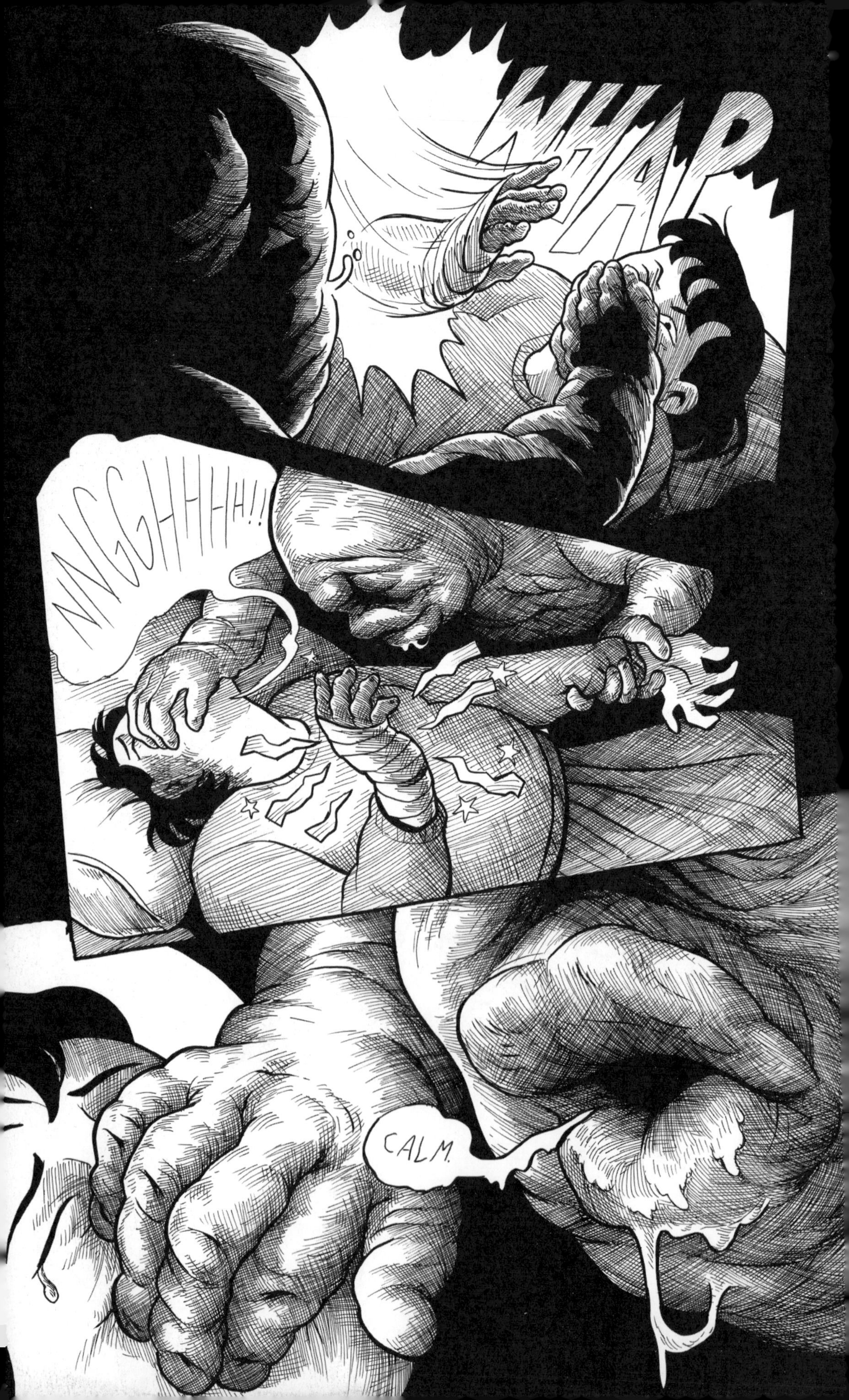
WHAP
NNGGHHHHH!!
CALM.

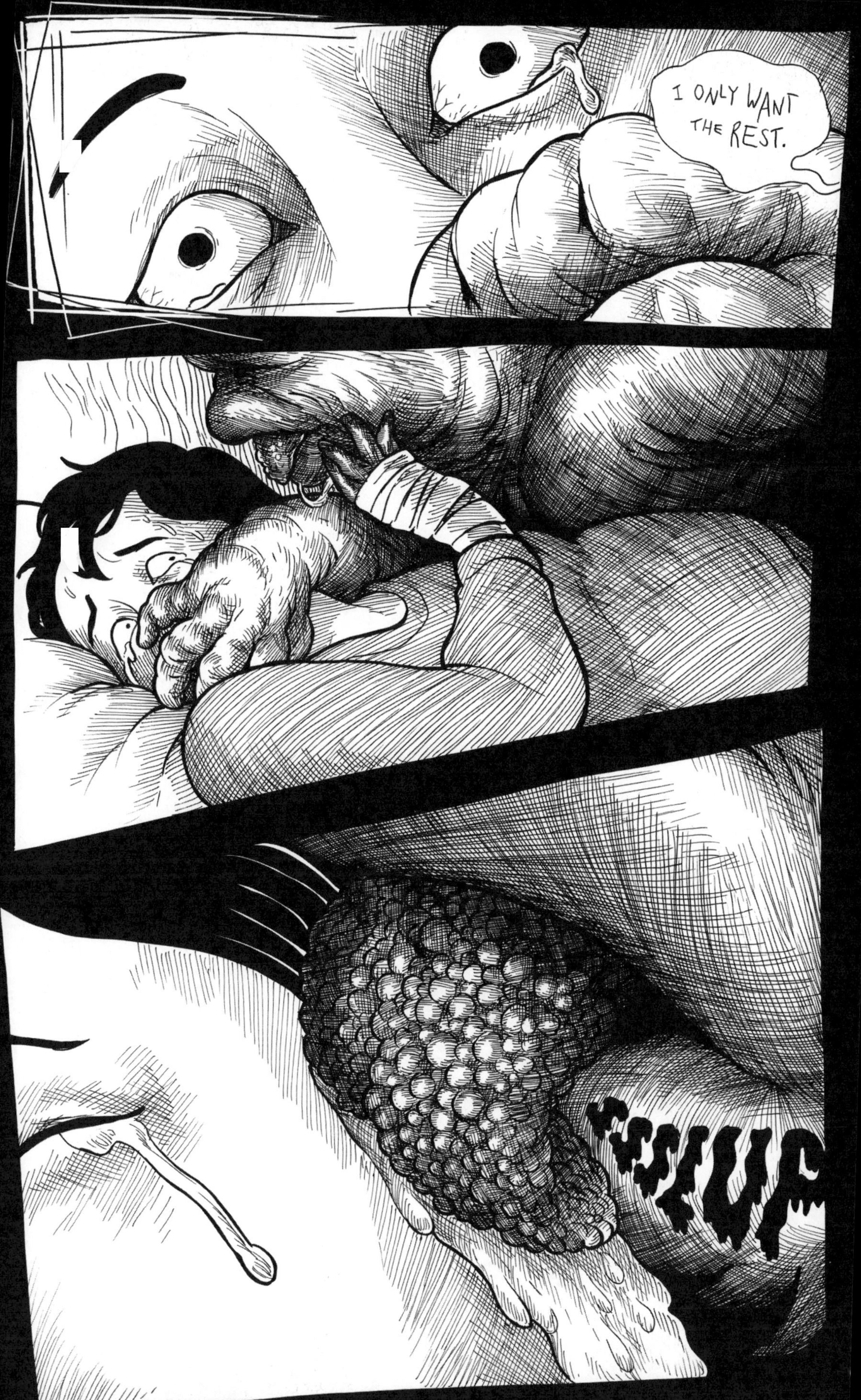
I ONLY WANT THE REST.

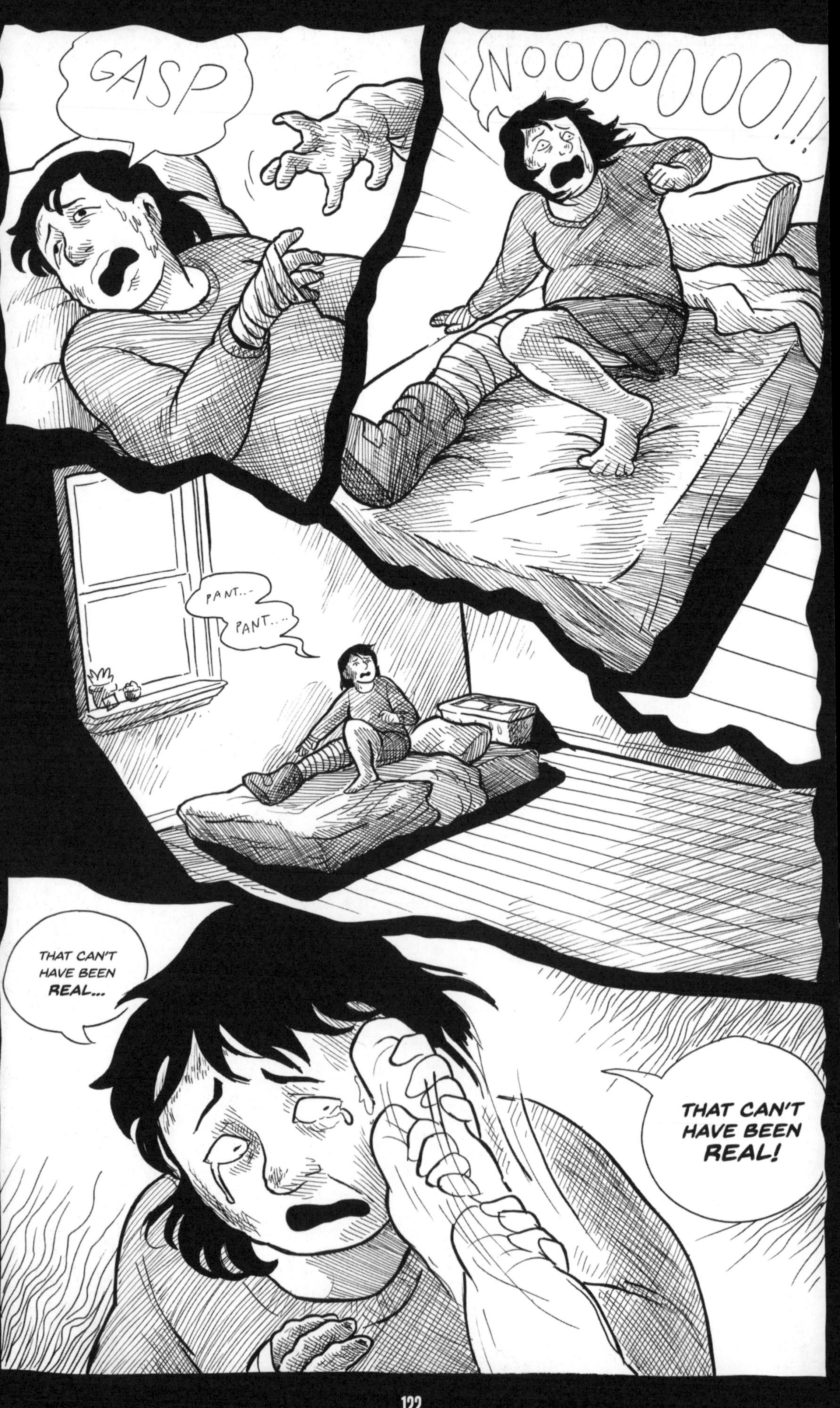
GASP
NOOOOOOO!!!
PANT...
PANT...
THAT CAN'T HAVE BEEN REAL...
THAT CAN'T HAVE BEEN REAL!

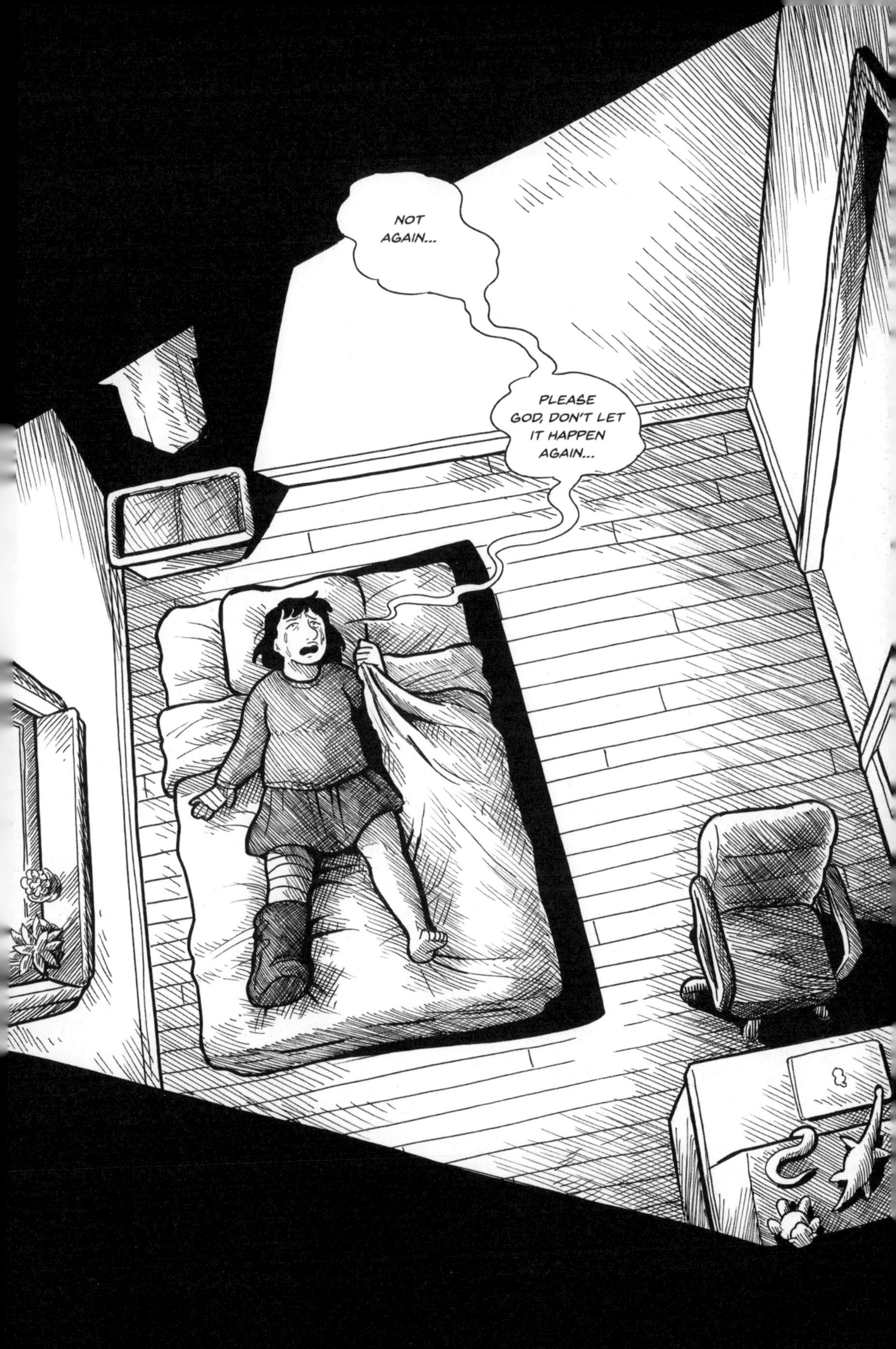
NOT AGAIN...
PLEASE GOD, DON'T LET IT HAPPEN AGAIN...

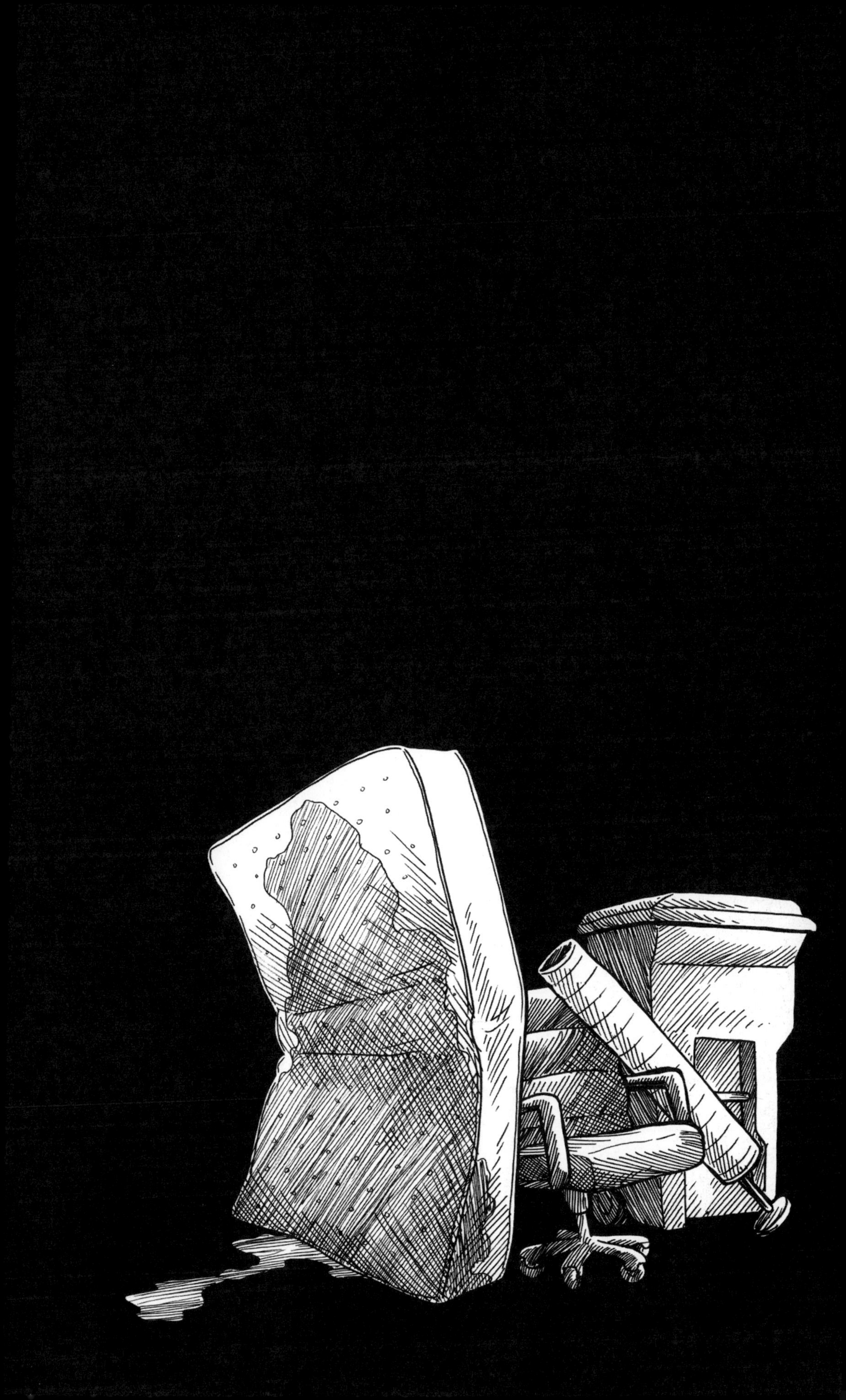

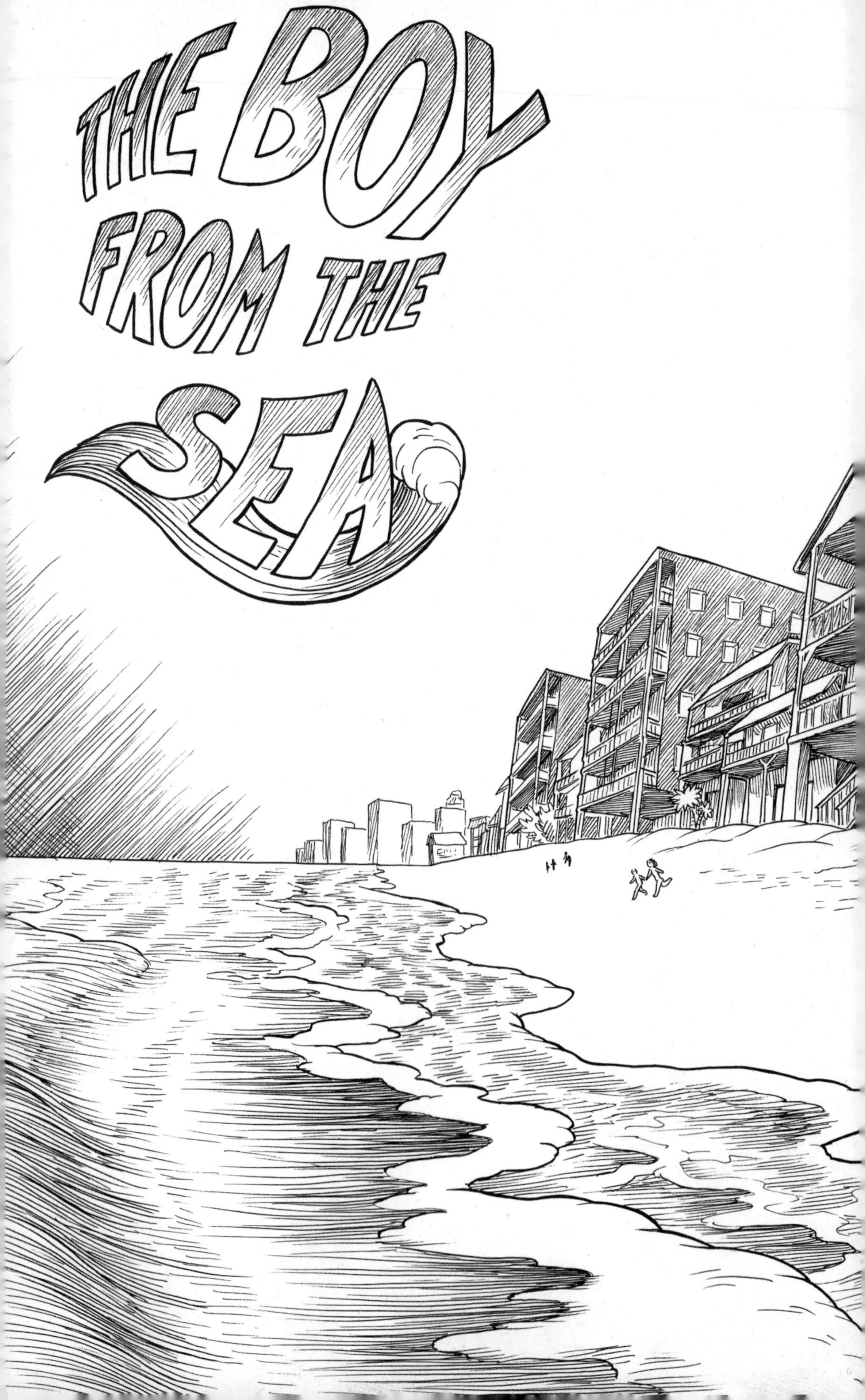
THE BOY FROM THE SEA

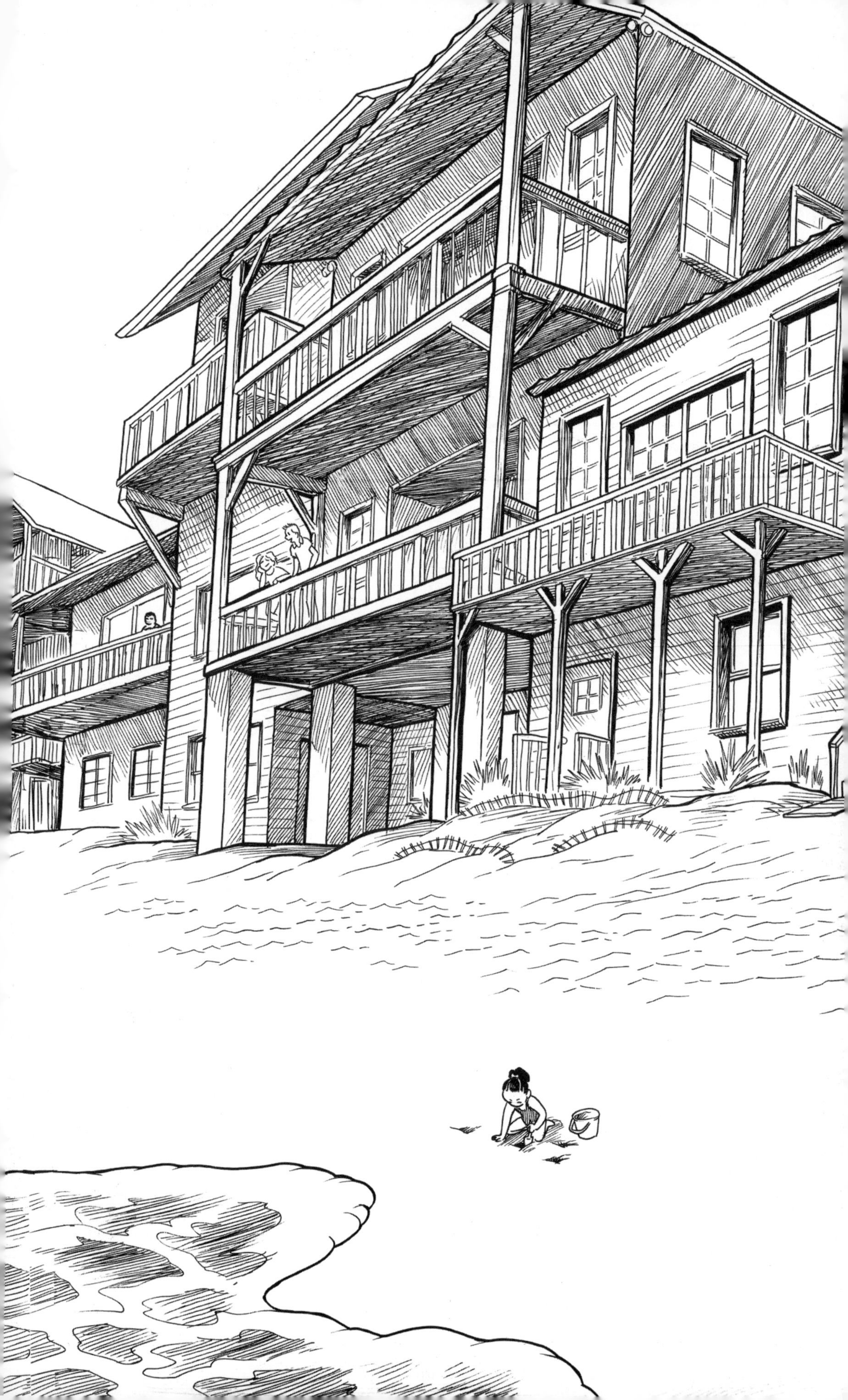

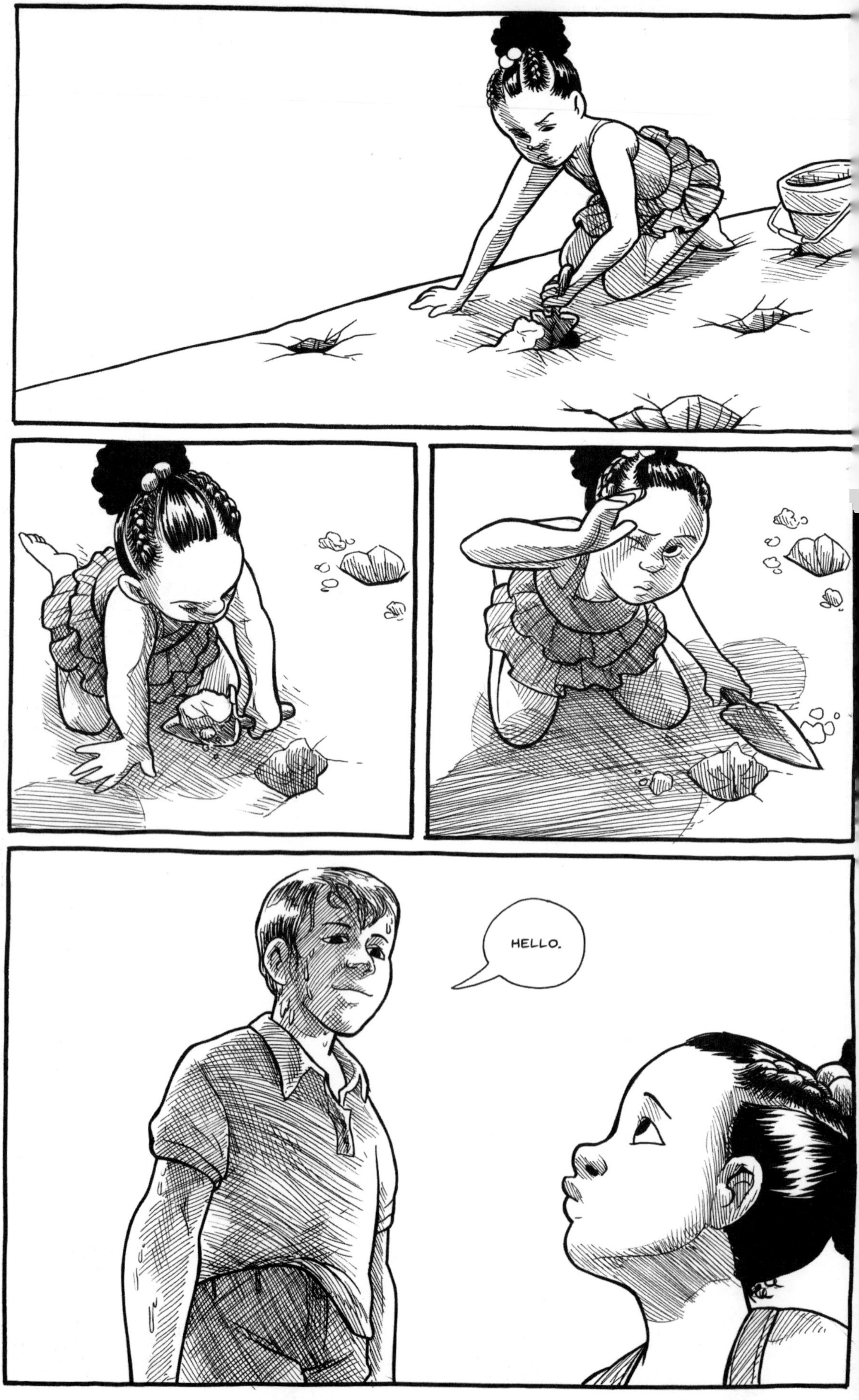
HELLO.

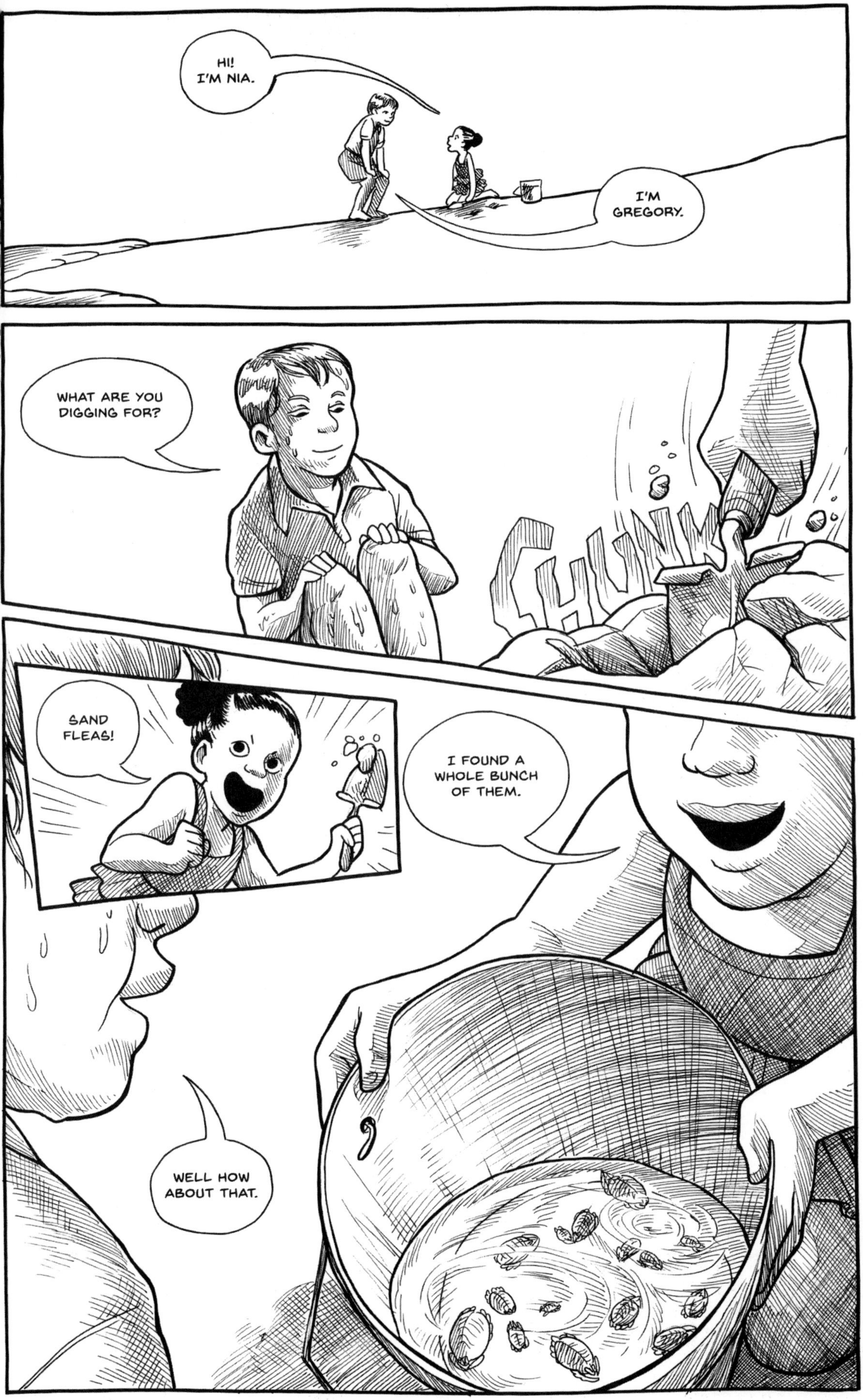
HI! I'M NIA.
I'M GREGORY.
WHAT ARE YOU DIGGING FOR?
SAND FLEAS!
I FOUND A WHOLE BUNCH OF THEM.
WELL HOW ABOUT THAT.

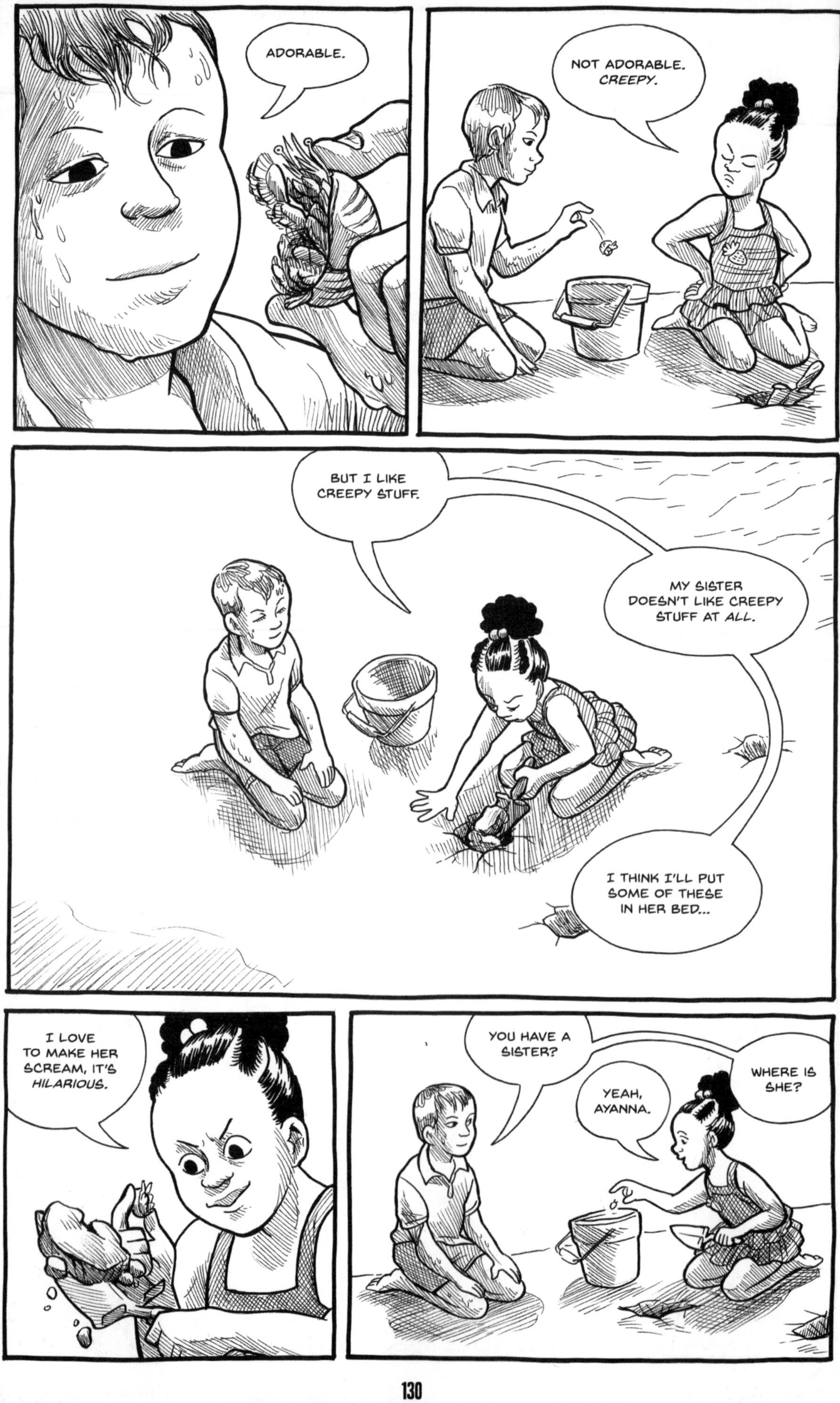
ADORABLE.
NOT ADORABLE. *CREEPY.*
BUT I LIKE CREEPY STUFF.
MY SISTER DOESN'T LIKE CREEPY STUFF AT *ALL.*
I THINK I'LL PUT SOME OF THESE IN HER BED...
I LOVE TO MAKE HER SCREAM, IT'S *HILARIOUS.*
YOU HAVE A SISTER?
YEAH, AYANNA.
WHERE IS SHE?

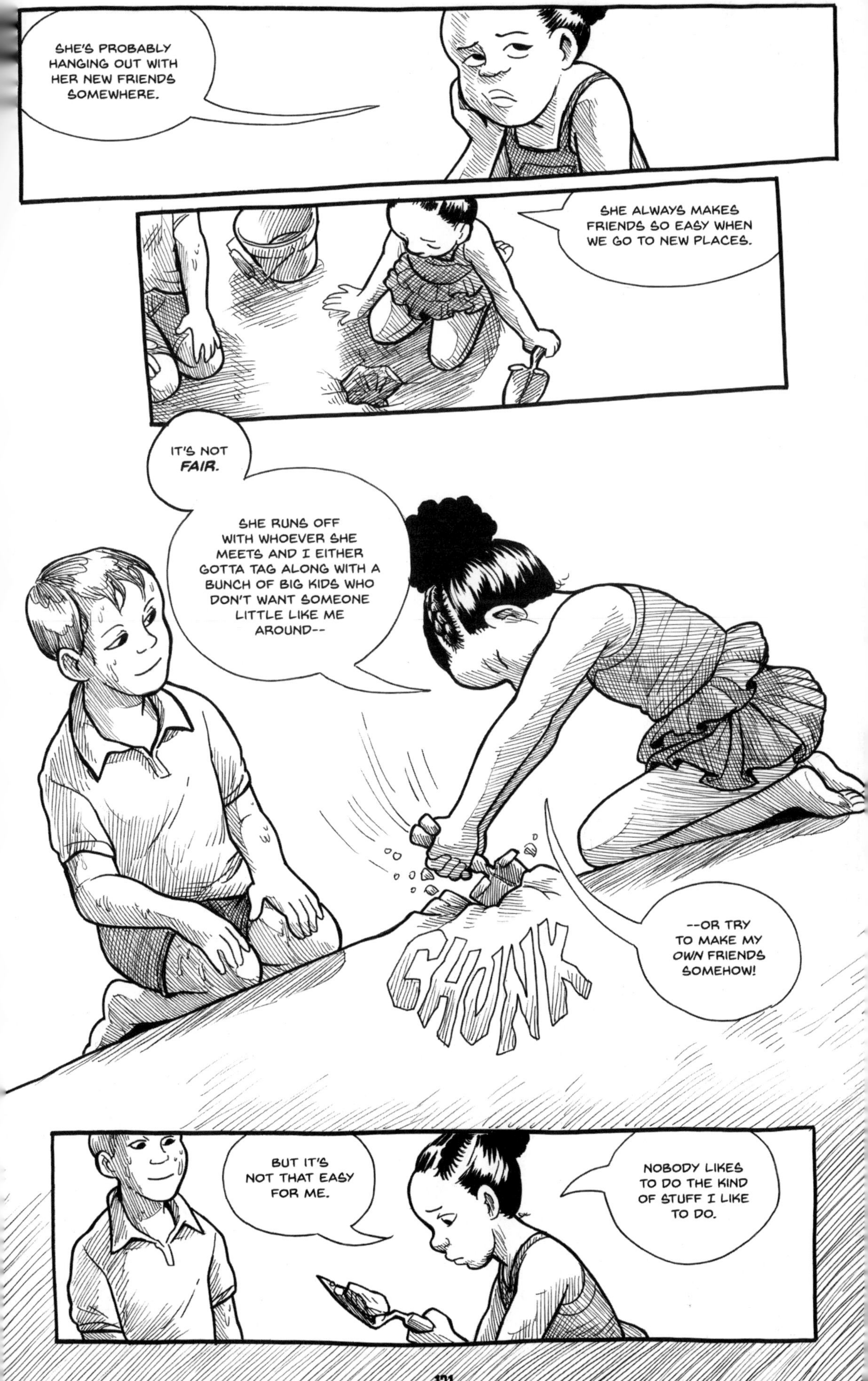
SHE'S PROBABLY HANGING OUT WITH HER NEW FRIENDS SOMEWHERE.
SHE ALWAYS MAKES FRIENDS SO EASY WHEN WE GO TO NEW PLACES.
IT'S NOT FAIR.
SHE RUNS OFF WITH WHOEVER SHE MEETS AND I EITHER GOTTA TAG ALONG WITH A BUNCH OF BIG KIDS WHO DON'T WANT SOMEONE LITTLE LIKE ME AROUND--
CHUNK
--OR TRY TO MAKE MY OWN FRIENDS SOMEHOW!
BUT IT'S NOT THAT EASY FOR ME.
NOBODY LIKES TO DO THE KIND OF STUFF I LIKE TO DO.

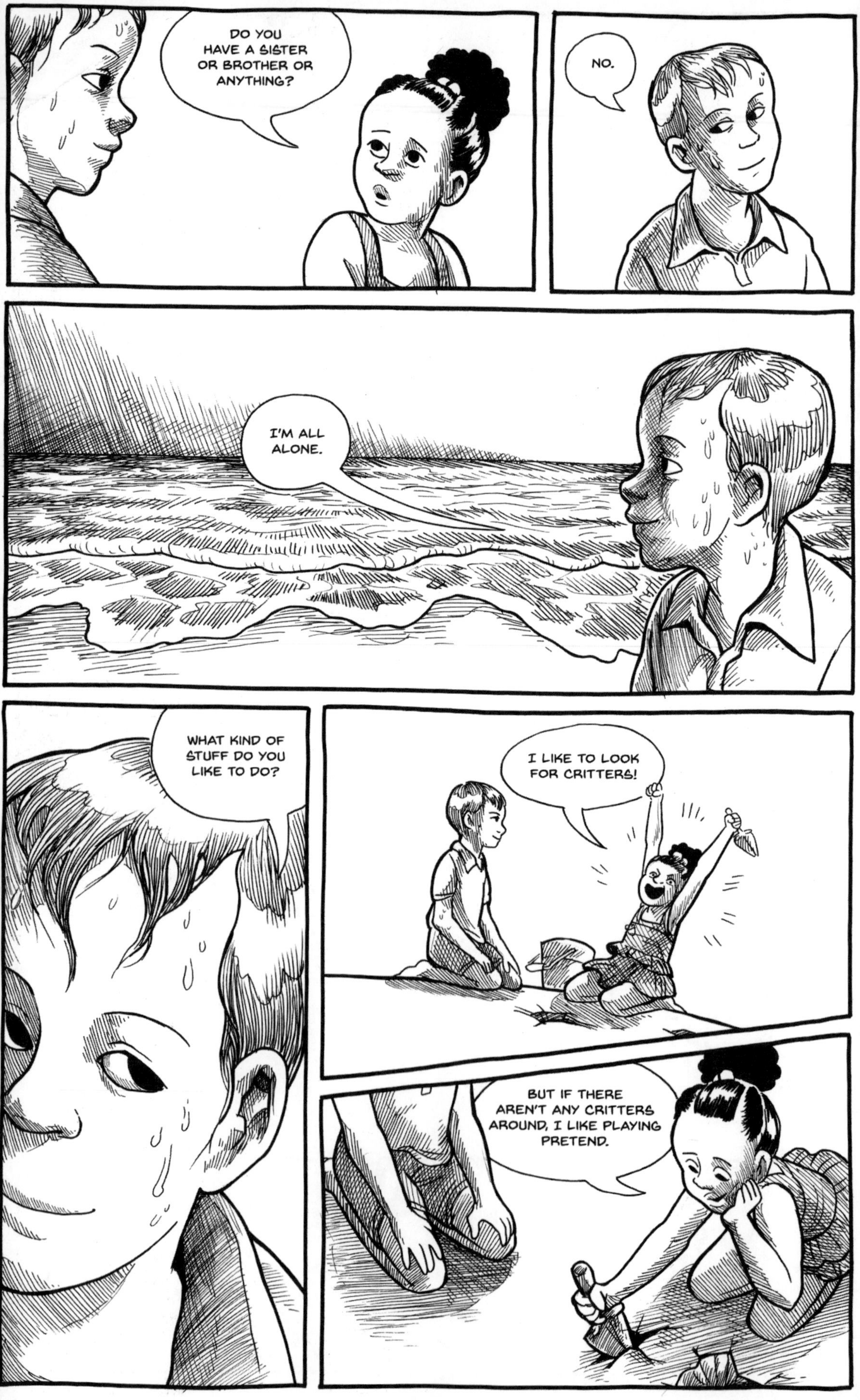
DO YOU HAVE A SISTER OR BROTHER OR ANYTHING?
NO.
I'M ALL ALONE.
WHAT KIND OF STUFF DO YOU LIKE TO DO?
I LIKE TO LOOK FOR CRITTERS!
BUT IF THERE AREN'T ANY CRITTERS AROUND, I LIKE PLAYING PRETEND.

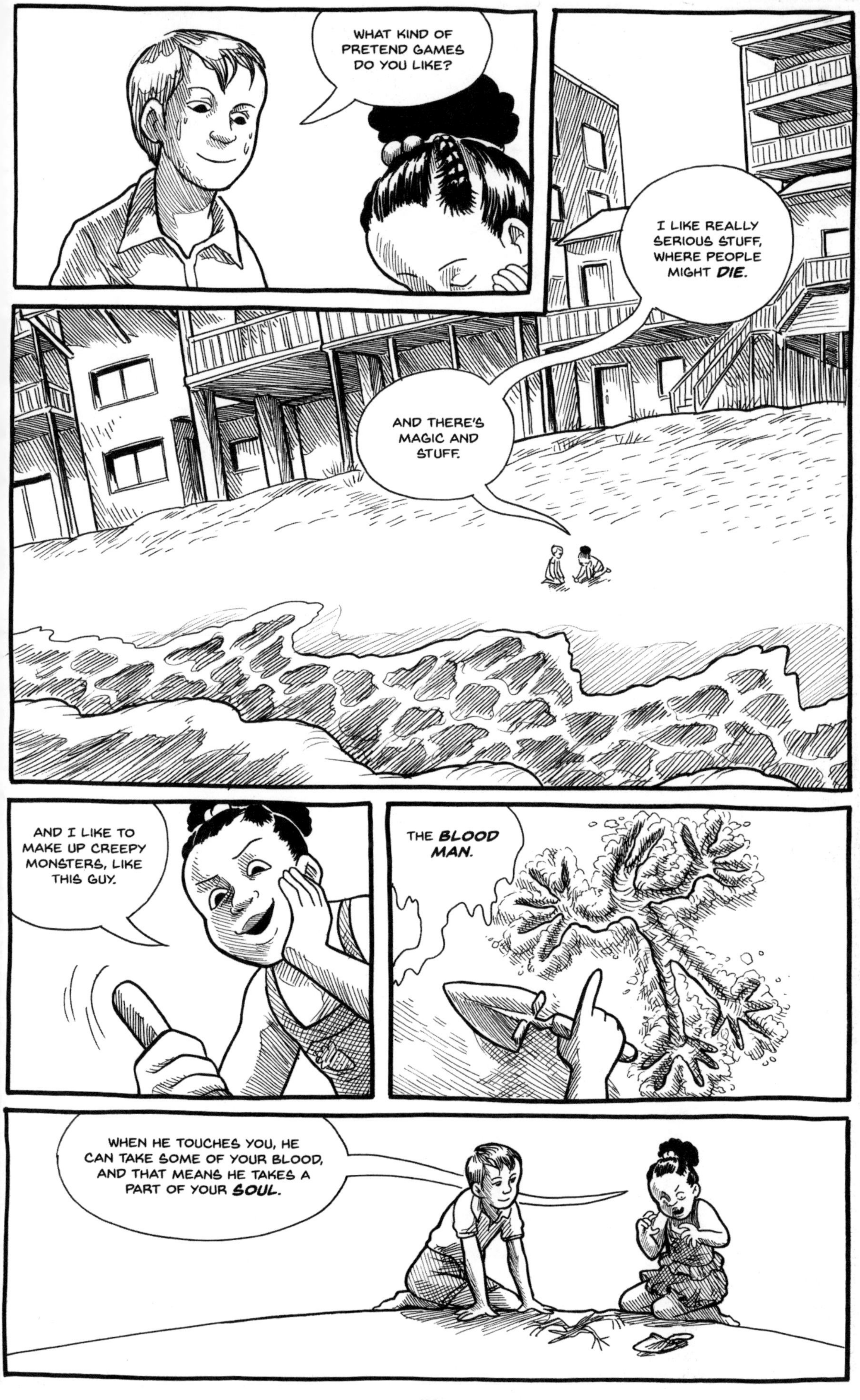

WHAT KIND OF PRETEND GAMES DO YOU LIKE?
I LIKE REALLY SERIOUS STUFF, WHERE PEOPLE MIGHT DIE.
AND THERE'S MAGIC AND STUFF.
AND I LIKE TO MAKE UP CREEPY MONSTERS, LIKE THIS GUY.
THE BLOOD MAN.
WHEN HE TOUCHES YOU, HE CAN TAKE SOME OF YOUR BLOOD, AND THAT MEANS HE TAKES A PART OF YOUR SOUL.

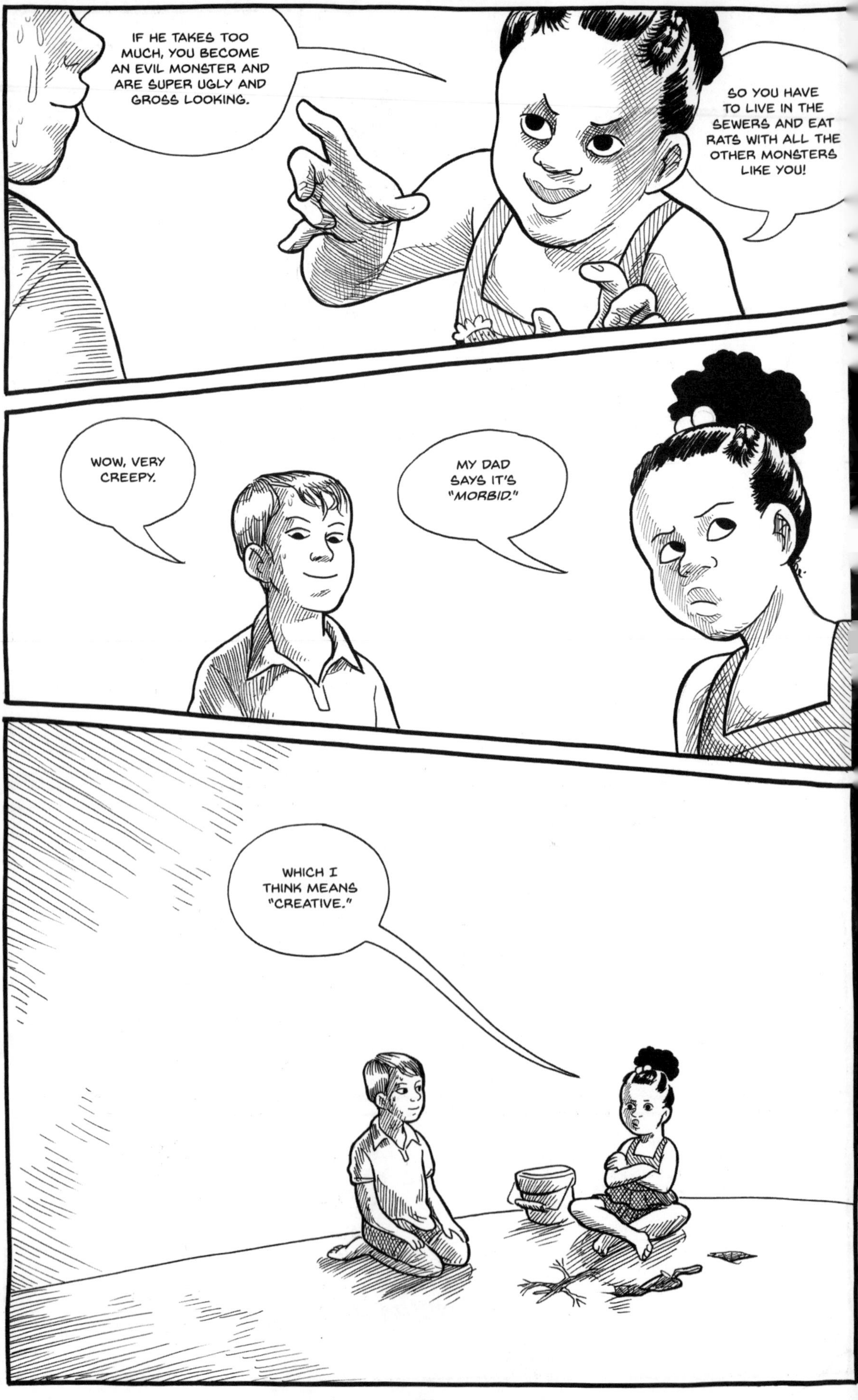
IF HE TAKES TOO MUCH, YOU BECOME AN EVIL MONSTER AND ARE SUPER UGLY AND GROSS LOOKING.
SO YOU HAVE TO LIVE IN THE SEWERS AND EAT RATS WITH ALL THE OTHER MONSTERS LIKE YOU!
WOW, VERY CREEPY.
MY DAD SAYS IT'S "*MORBID*."
WHICH I THINK MEANS "CREATIVE."

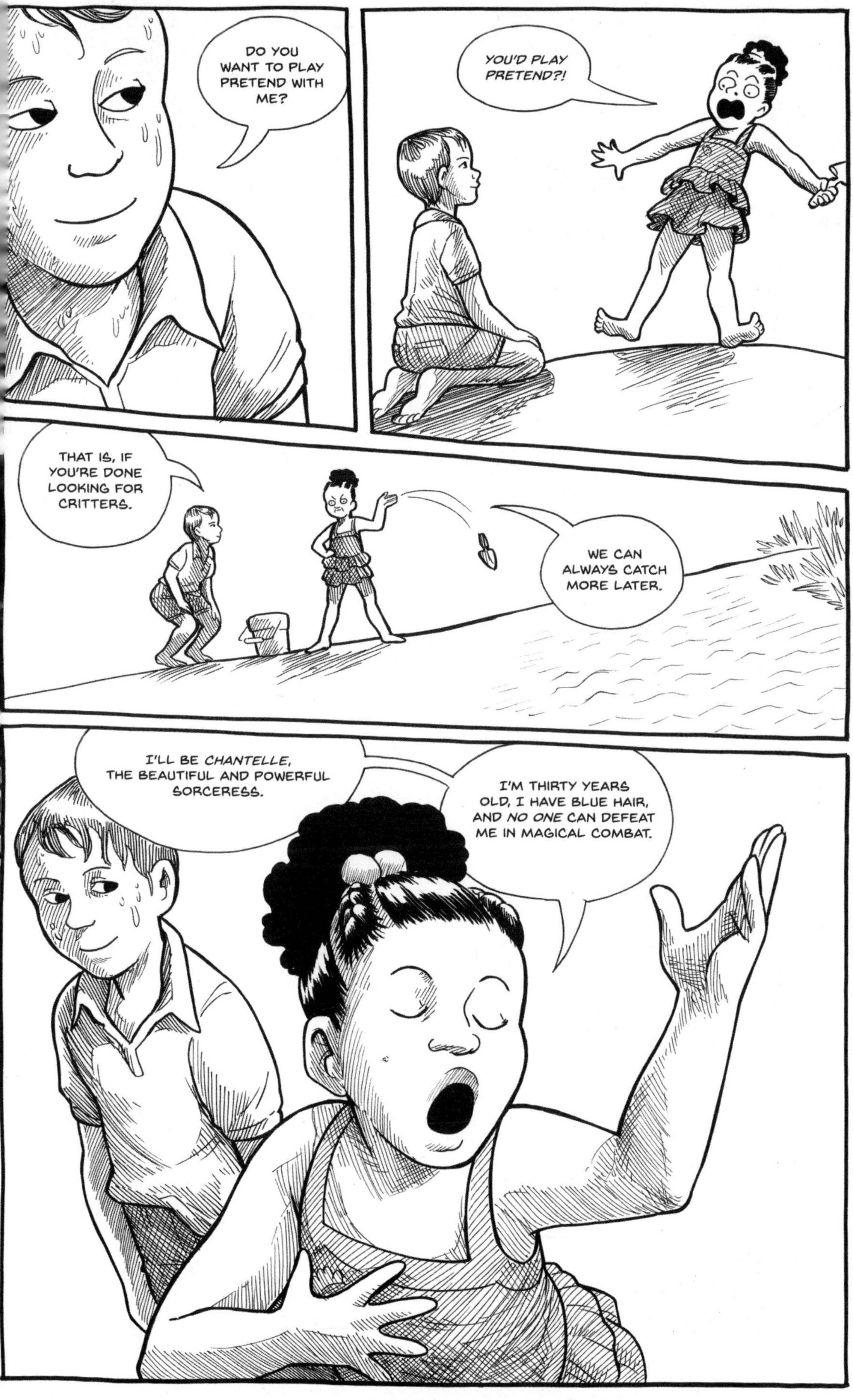
DO YOU WANT TO PLAY PRETEND WITH ME?
YOU'D PLAY PRETEND?!
THAT IS, IF YOU'RE DONE LOOKING FOR CRITTERS.
WE CAN ALWAYS CATCH MORE LATER.
I'LL BE *CHANTELLE*, THE BEAUTIFUL AND POWERFUL SORCERESS.
I'M THIRTY YEARS OLD, I HAVE BLUE HAIR, AND *NO ONE* CAN DEFEAT ME IN MAGICAL COMBAT.

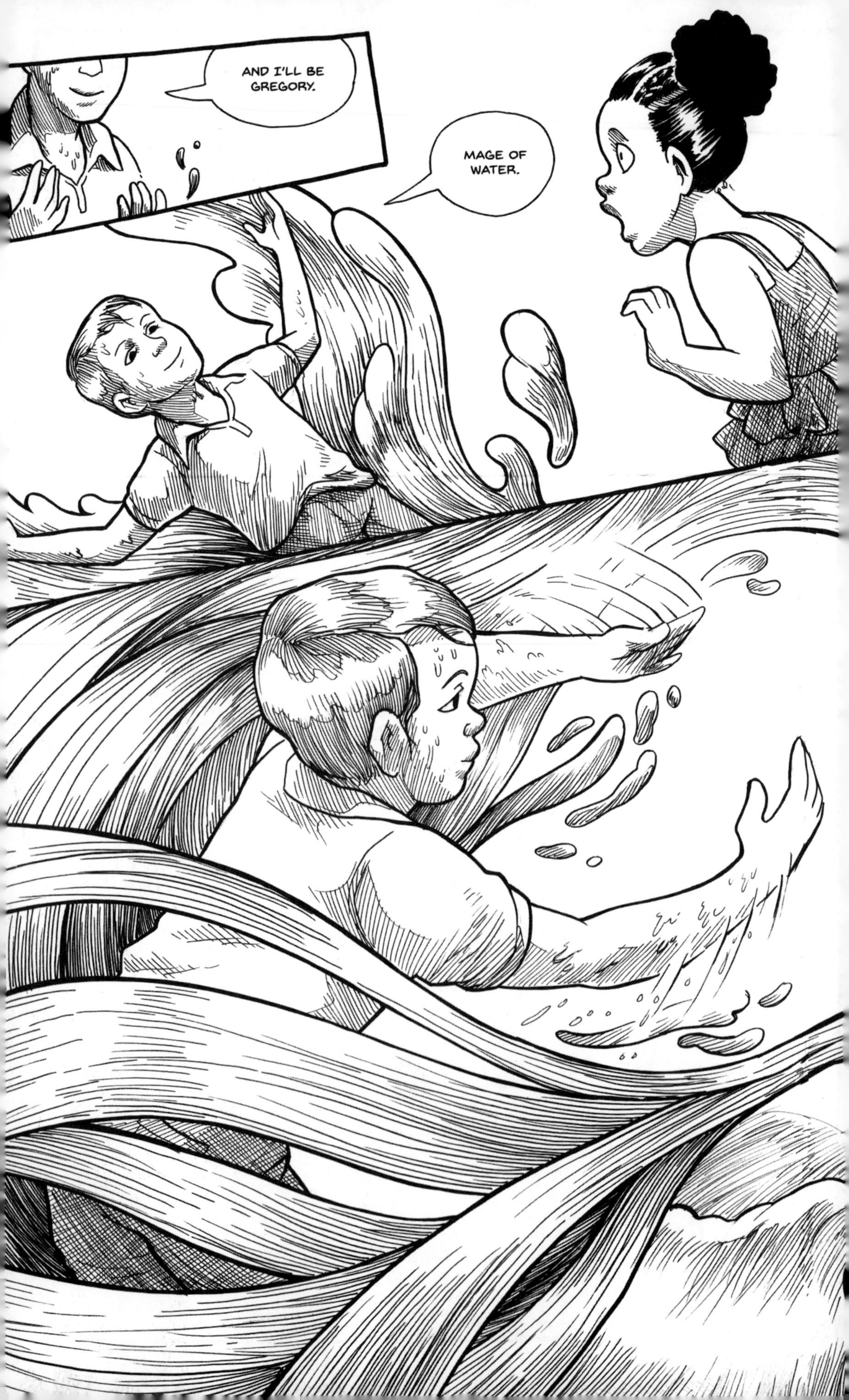
AND I'LL BE GREGORY.
MAGE OF WATER.

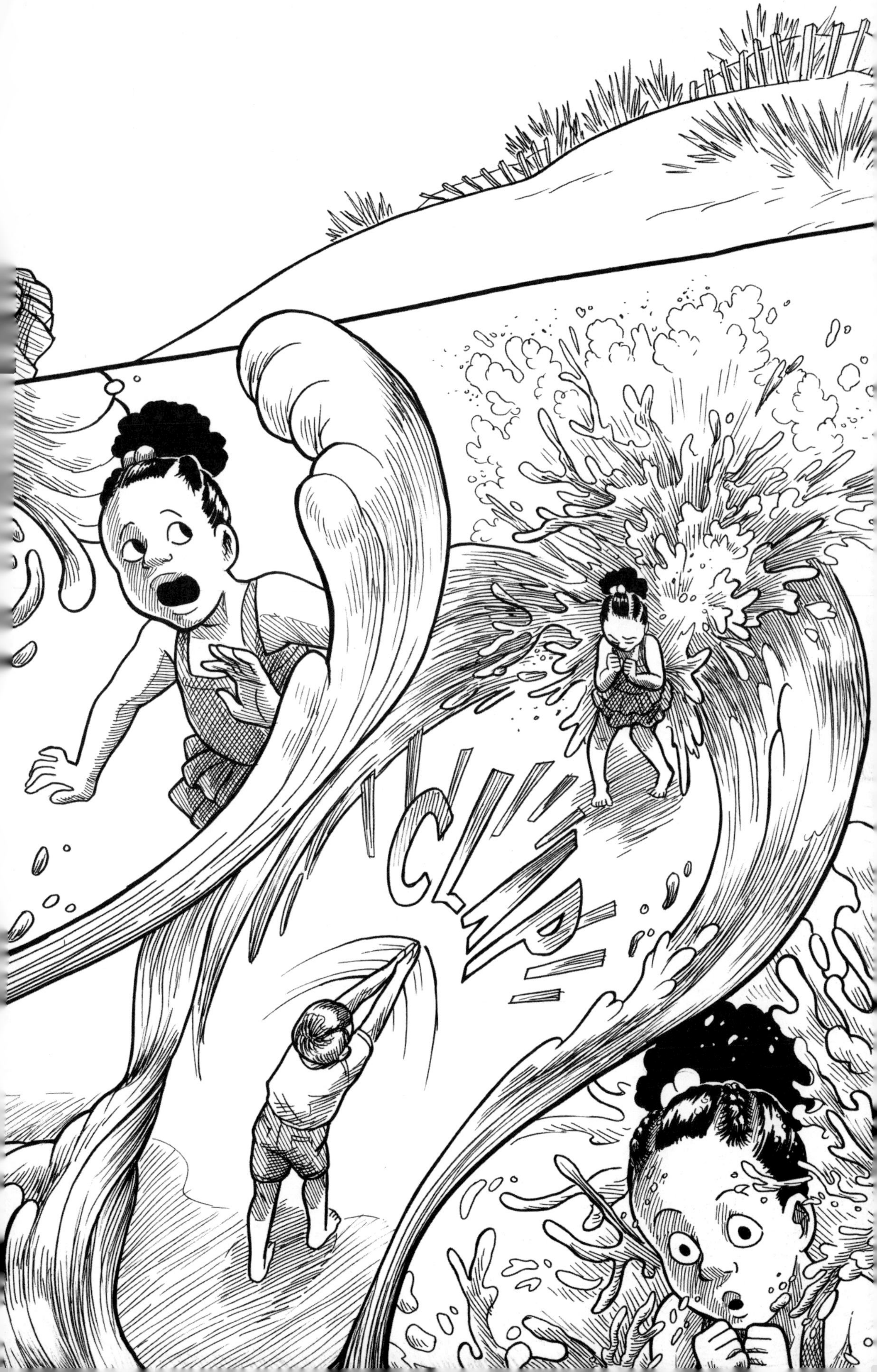
CLAP!

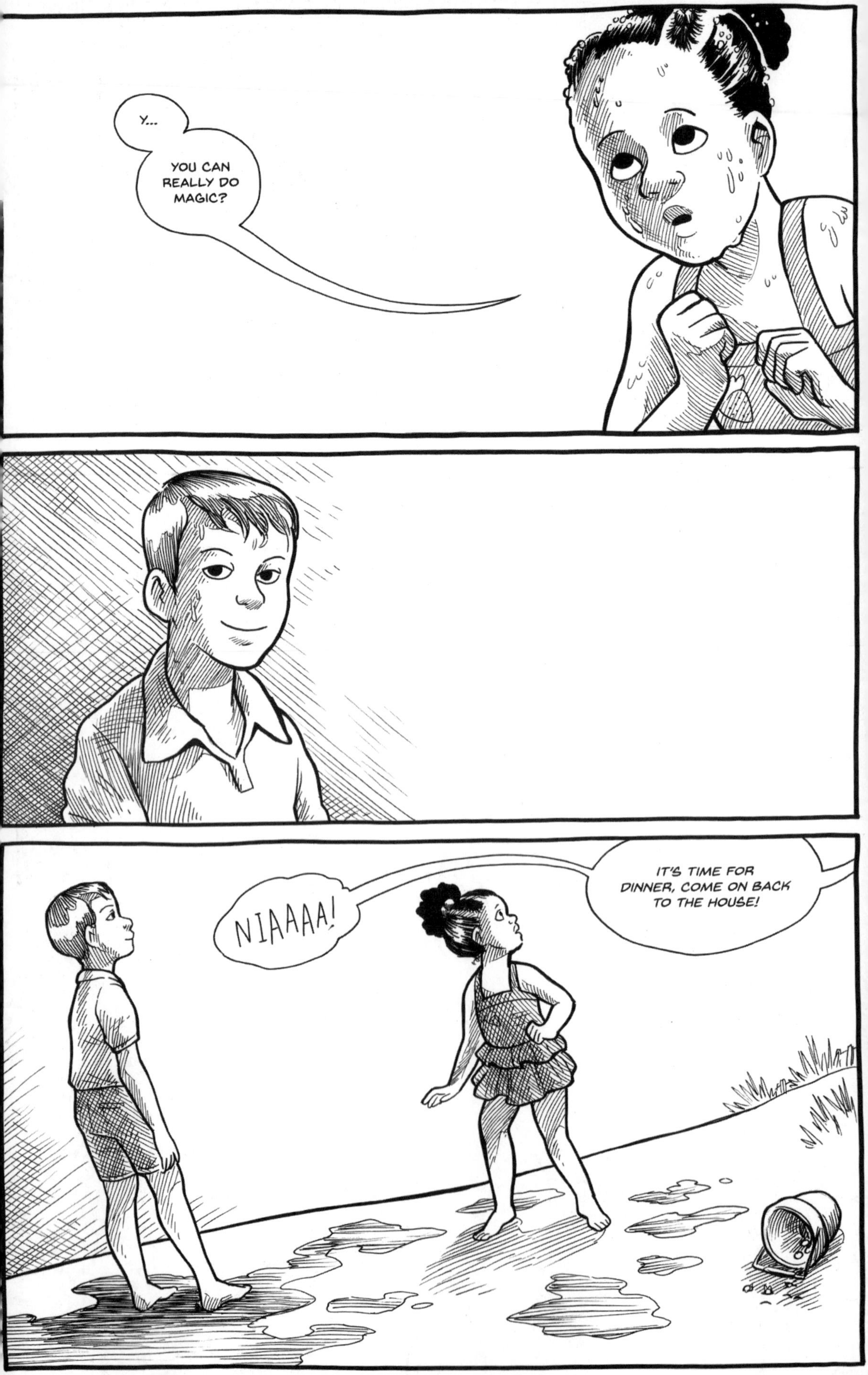
Y...
YOU CAN REALLY DO MAGIC?
NIAAAA!
IT'S TIME FOR DINNER, COME ON BACK TO THE HOUSE!

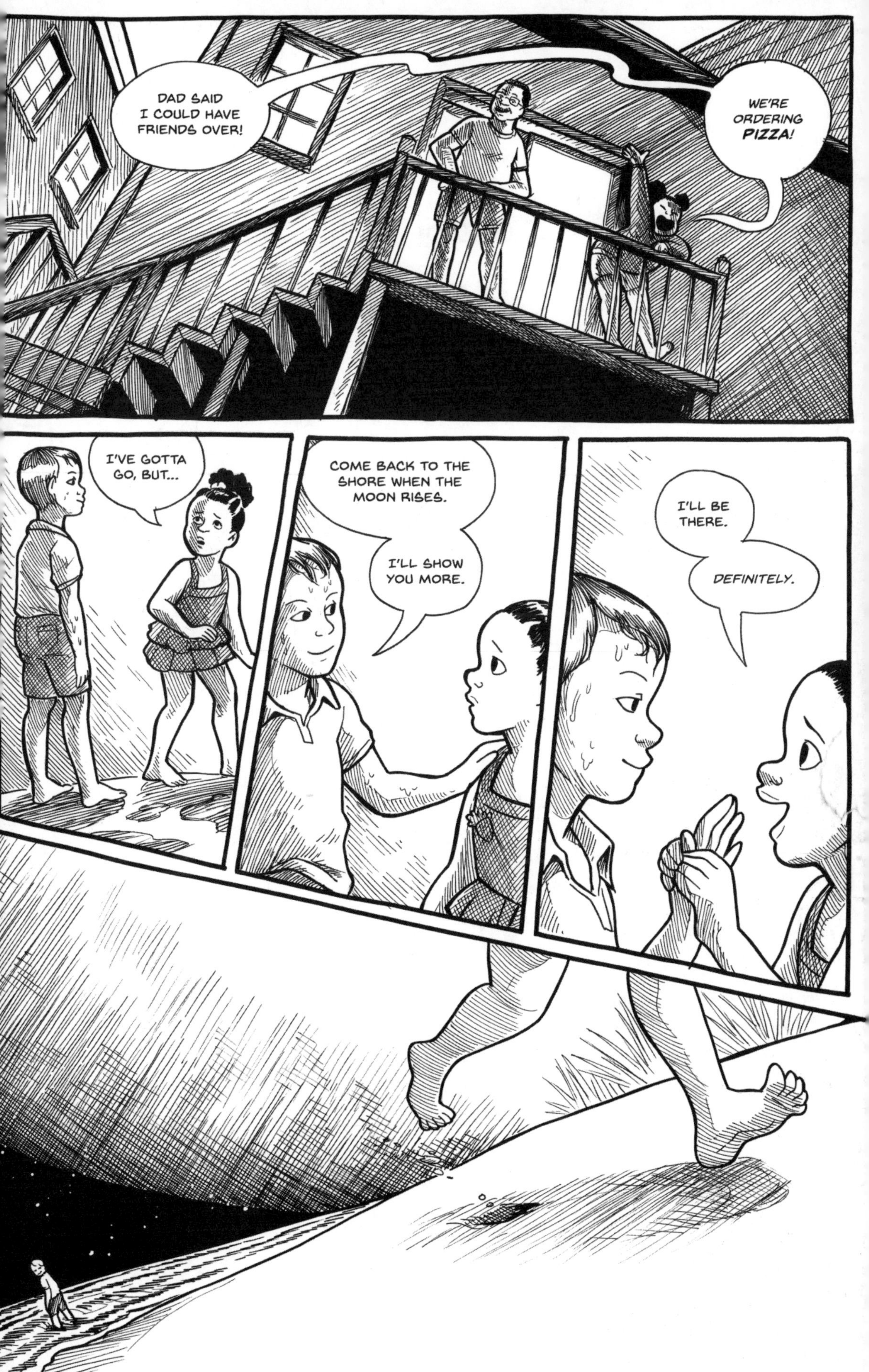
DAD SAID I COULD HAVE FRIENDS OVER!
WE'RE ORDERING PIZZA!
I'VE GOTTA GO, BUT...
COME BACK TO THE SHORE WHEN THE MOON RISES.
I'LL SHOW YOU MORE.
I'LL BE THERE.
DEFINITELY.

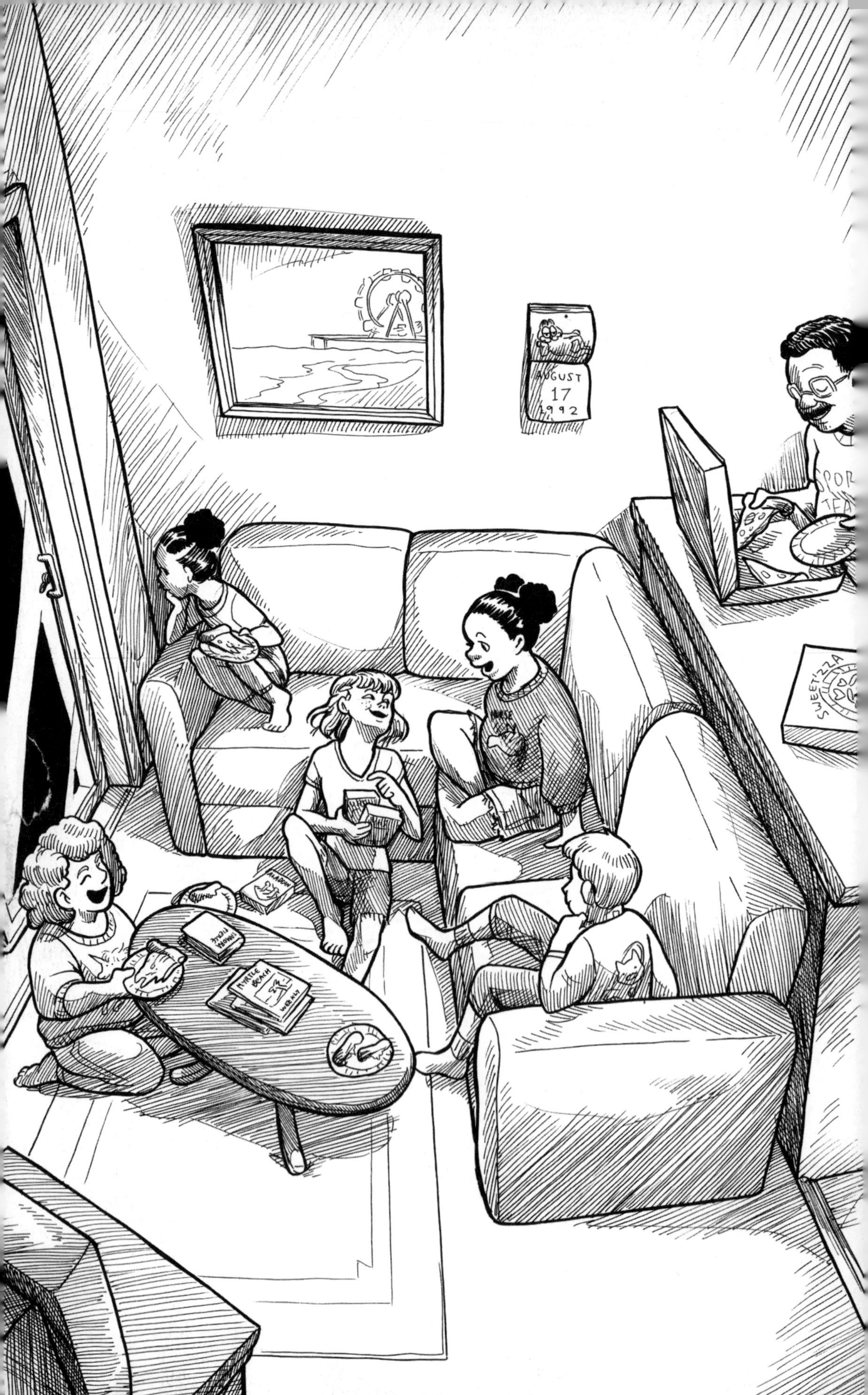
AUGUST
17
1992
SWEETIZZA
MYRTLE BEACH

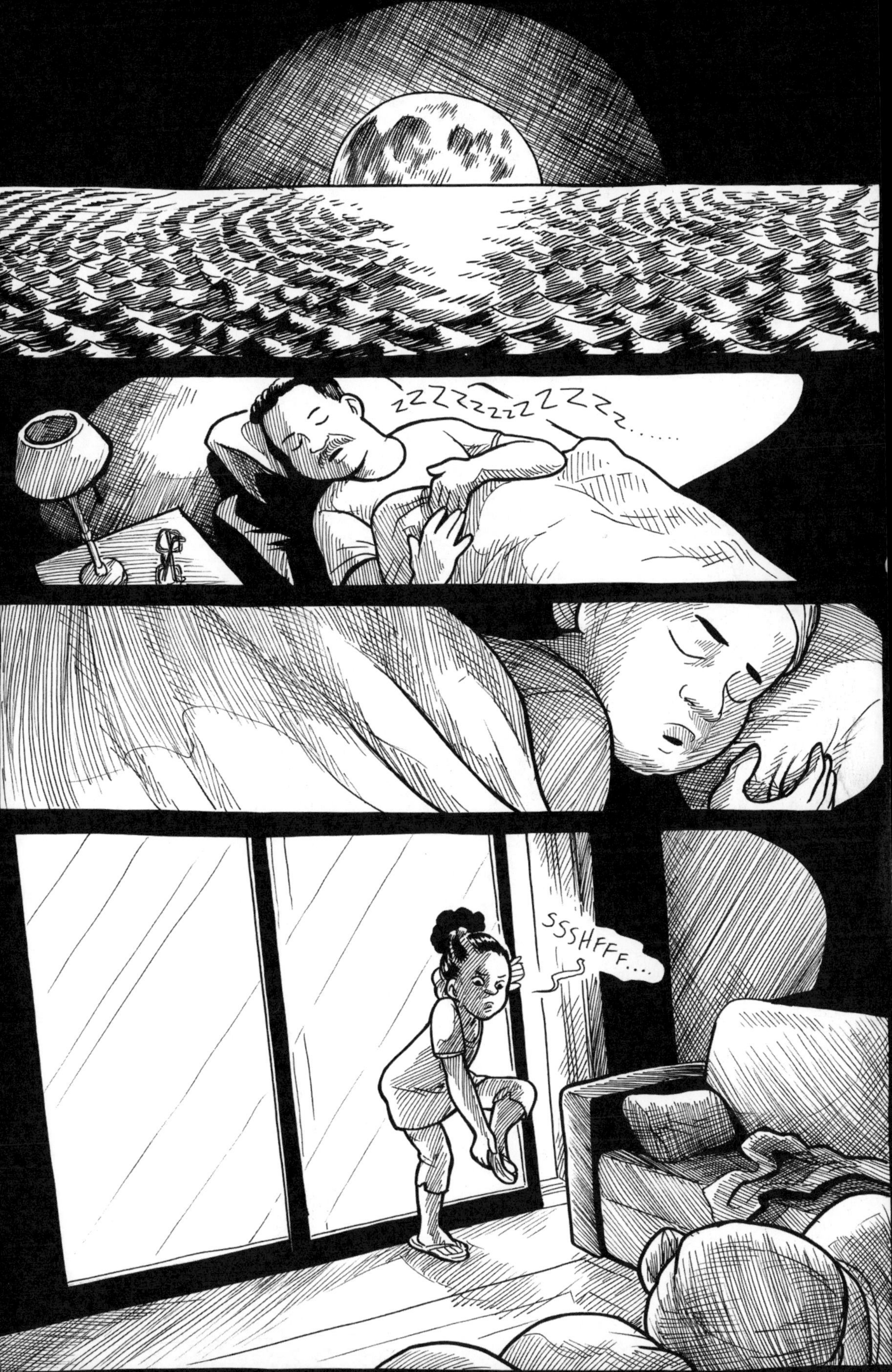
zzZZZzzzzZZZZzz.....
SSSHFFF....

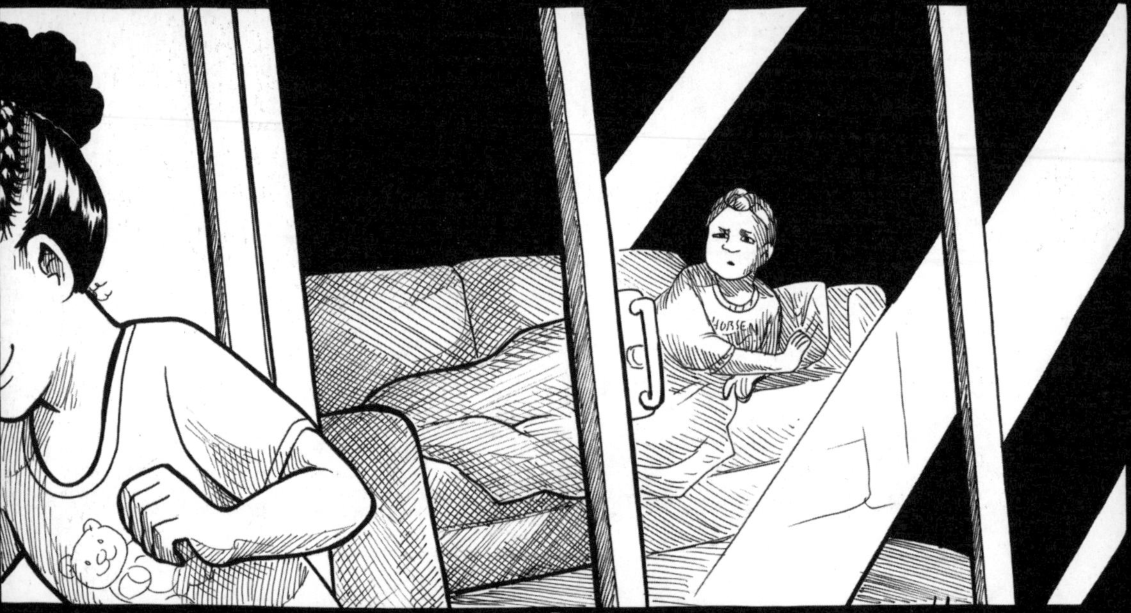

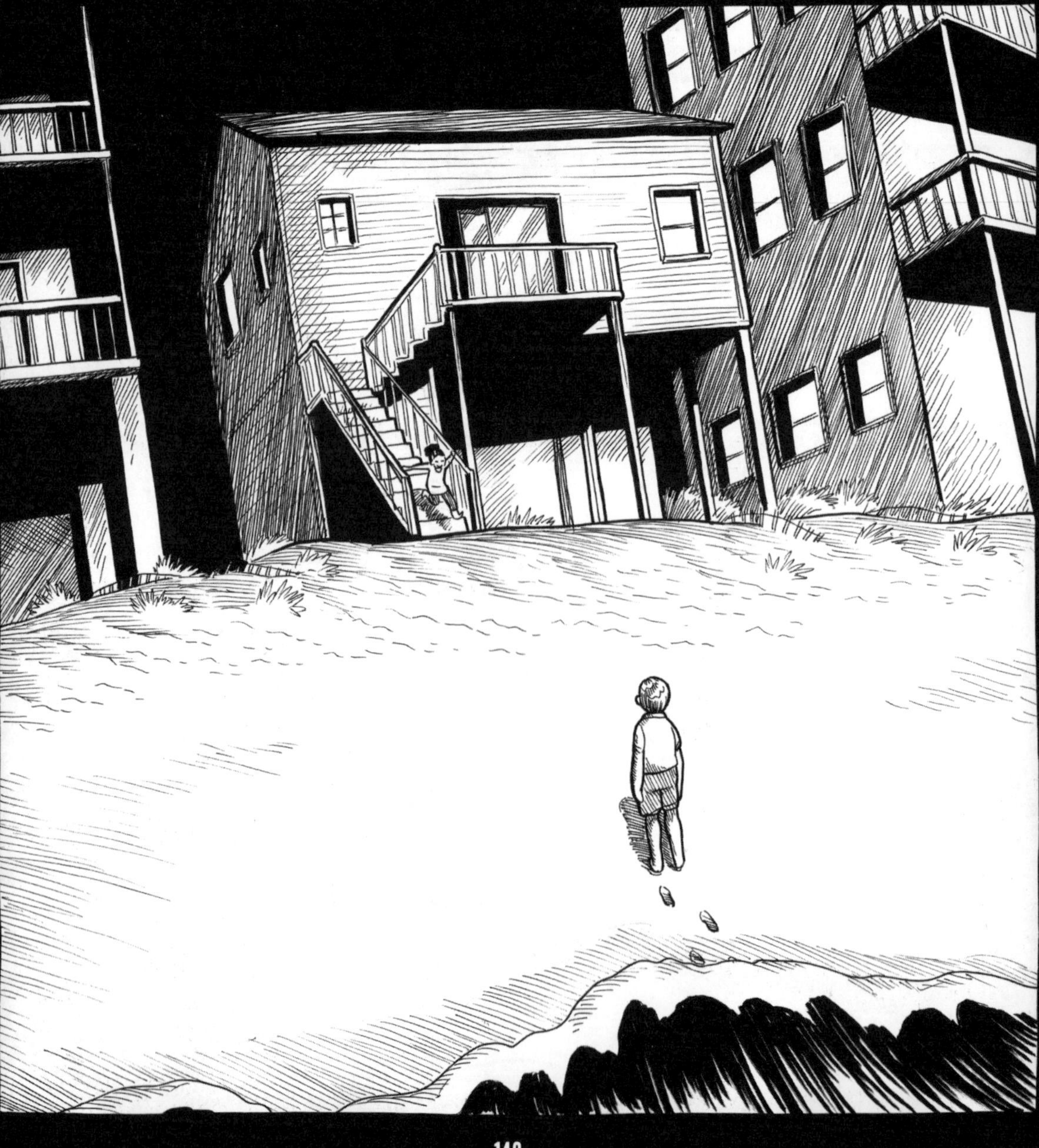

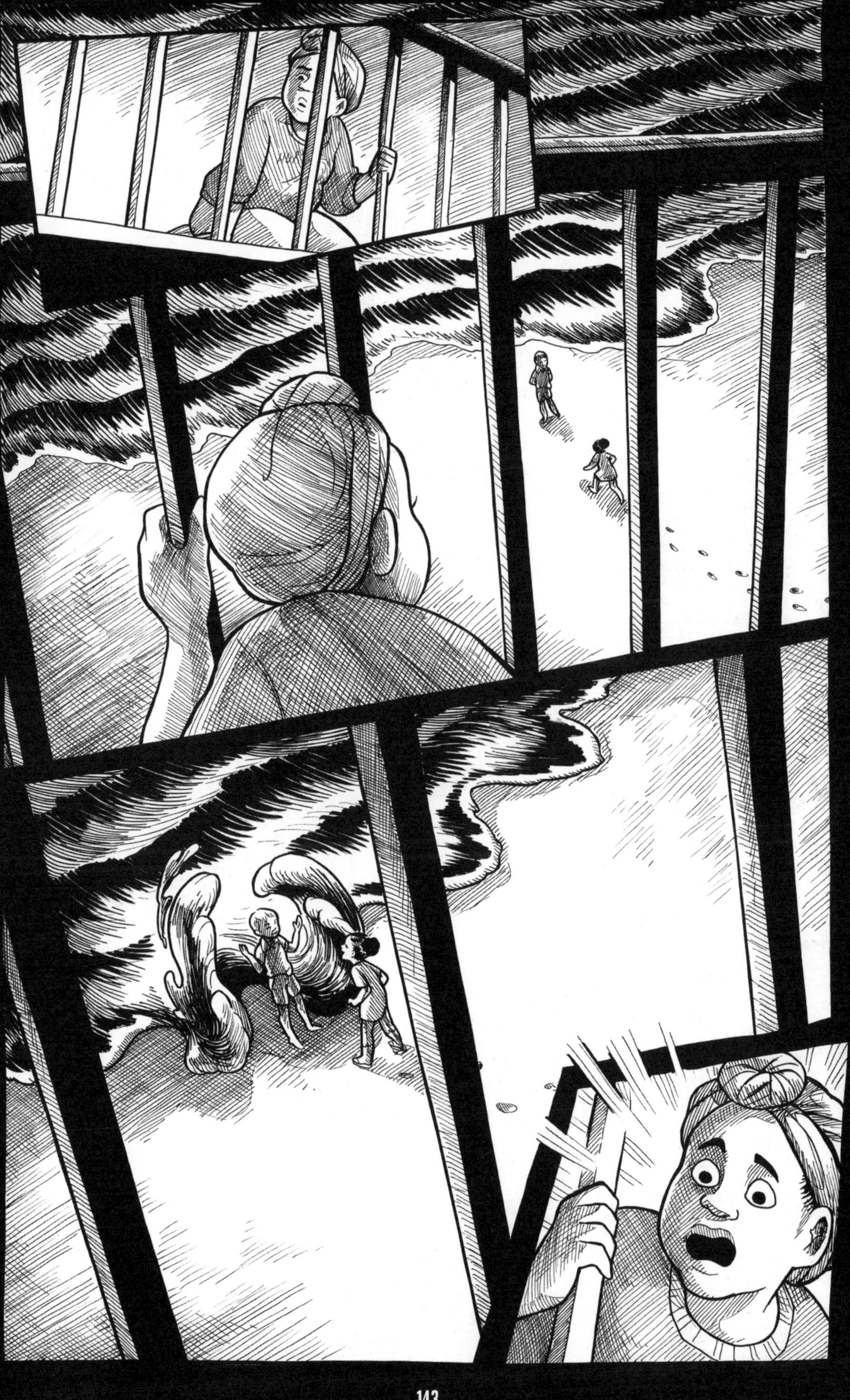

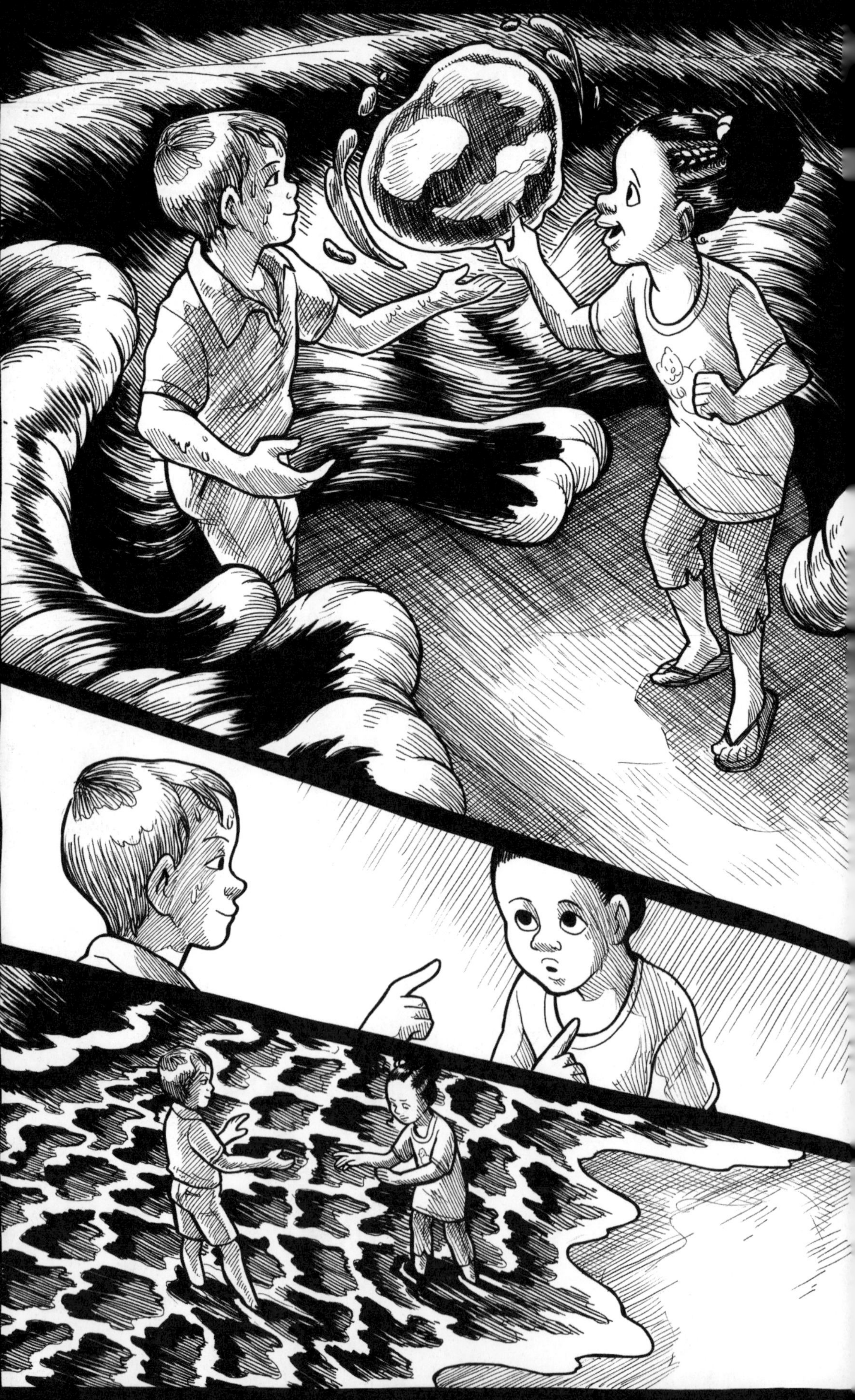

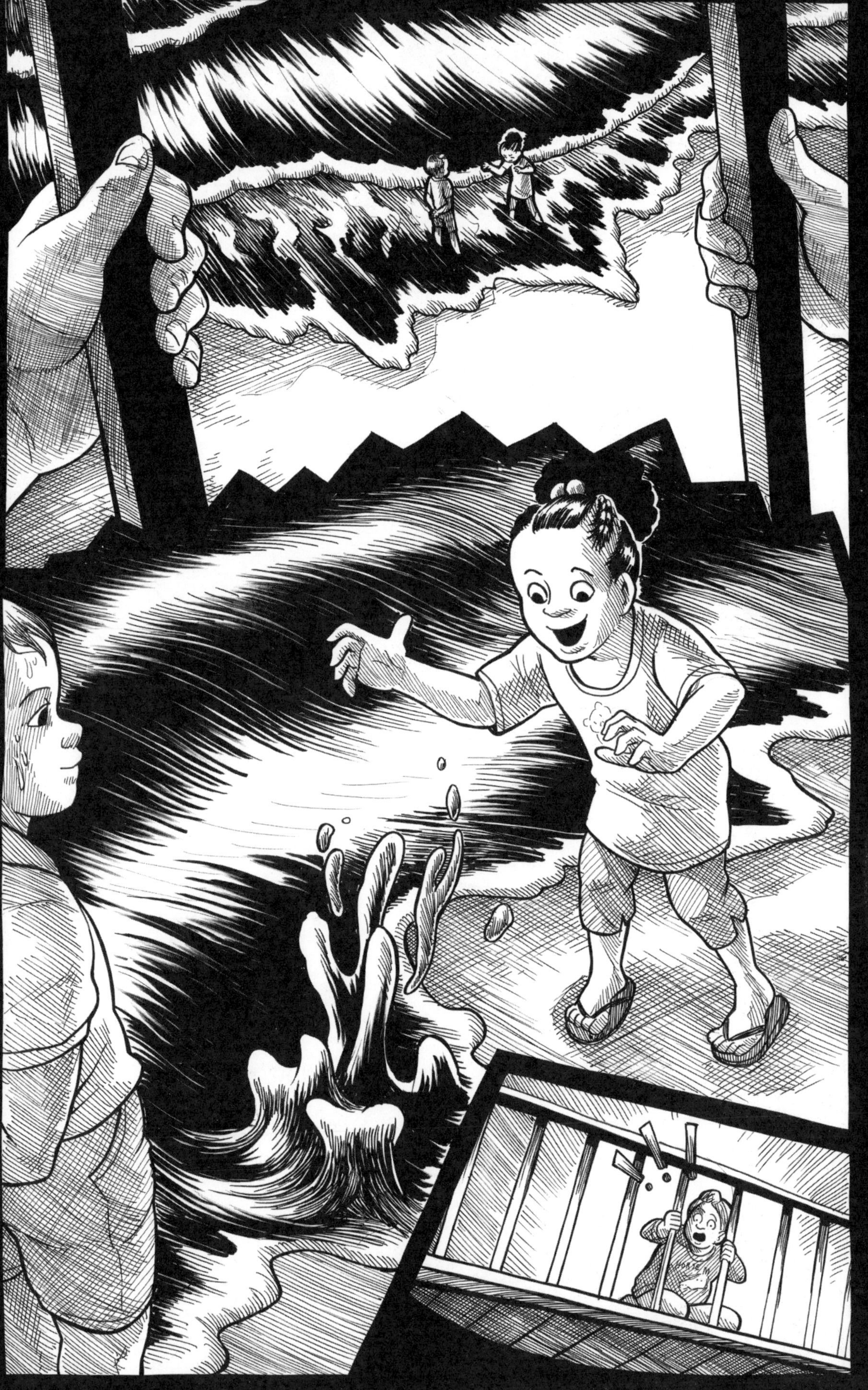

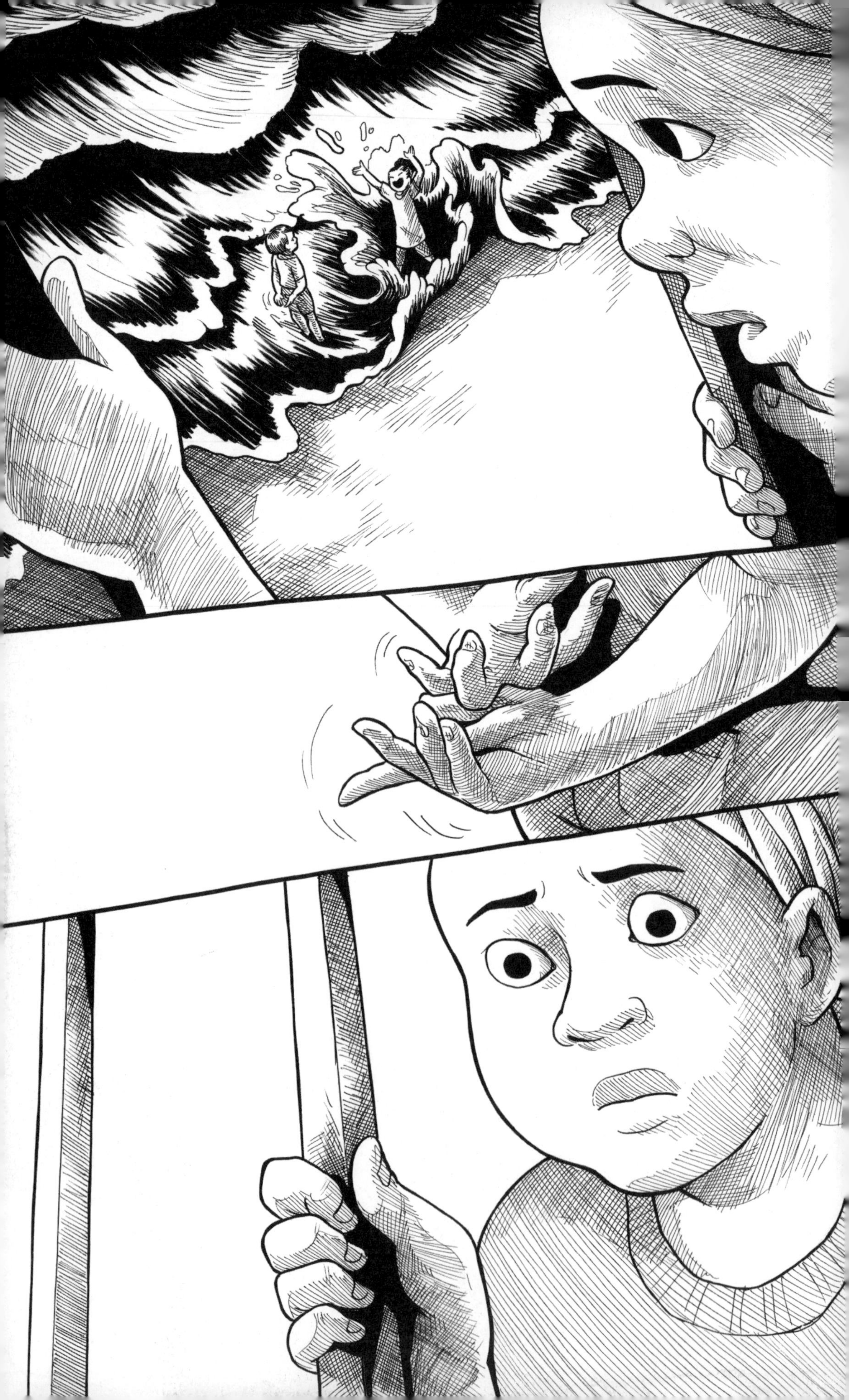

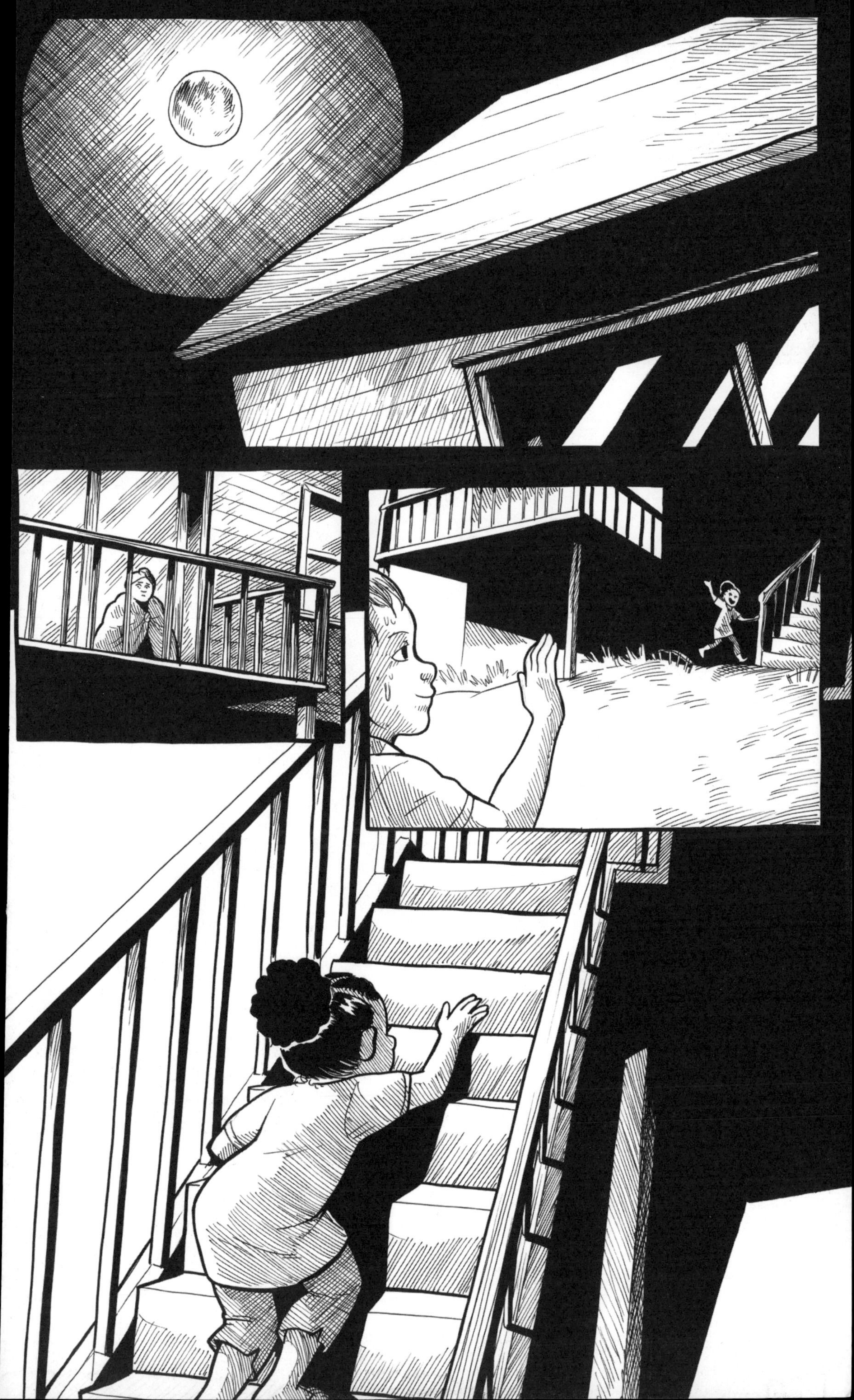

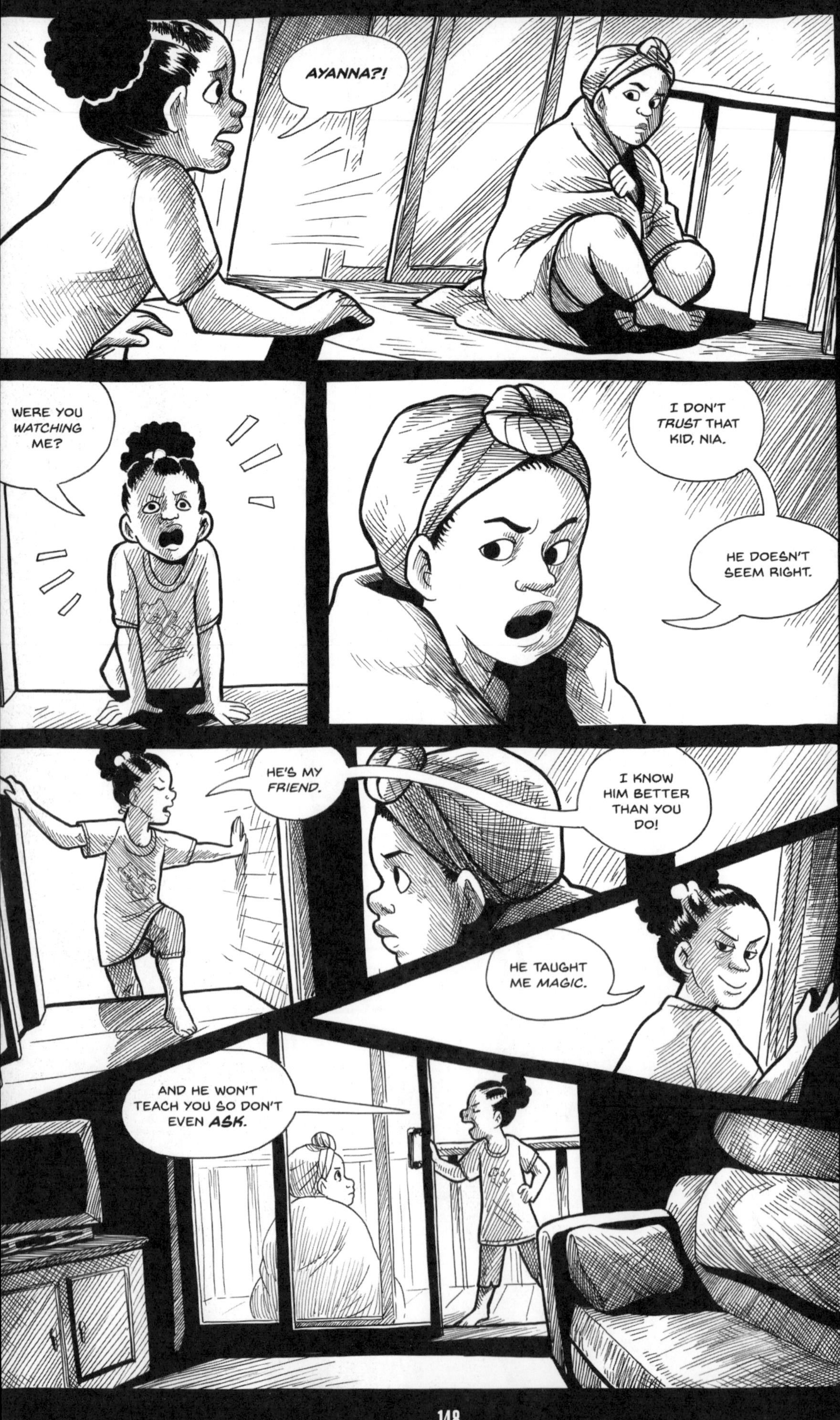
AYANNA?!
WERE YOU *WATCHING* ME?
I DON'T *TRUST* THAT KID, NIA.
HE DOESN'T SEEM RIGHT.
HE'S MY *FRIEND*.
I KNOW HIM BETTER THAN YOU DO!
HE TAUGHT ME *MAGIC*.
AND HE WON'T TEACH YOU SO DON'T EVEN ***ASK***.

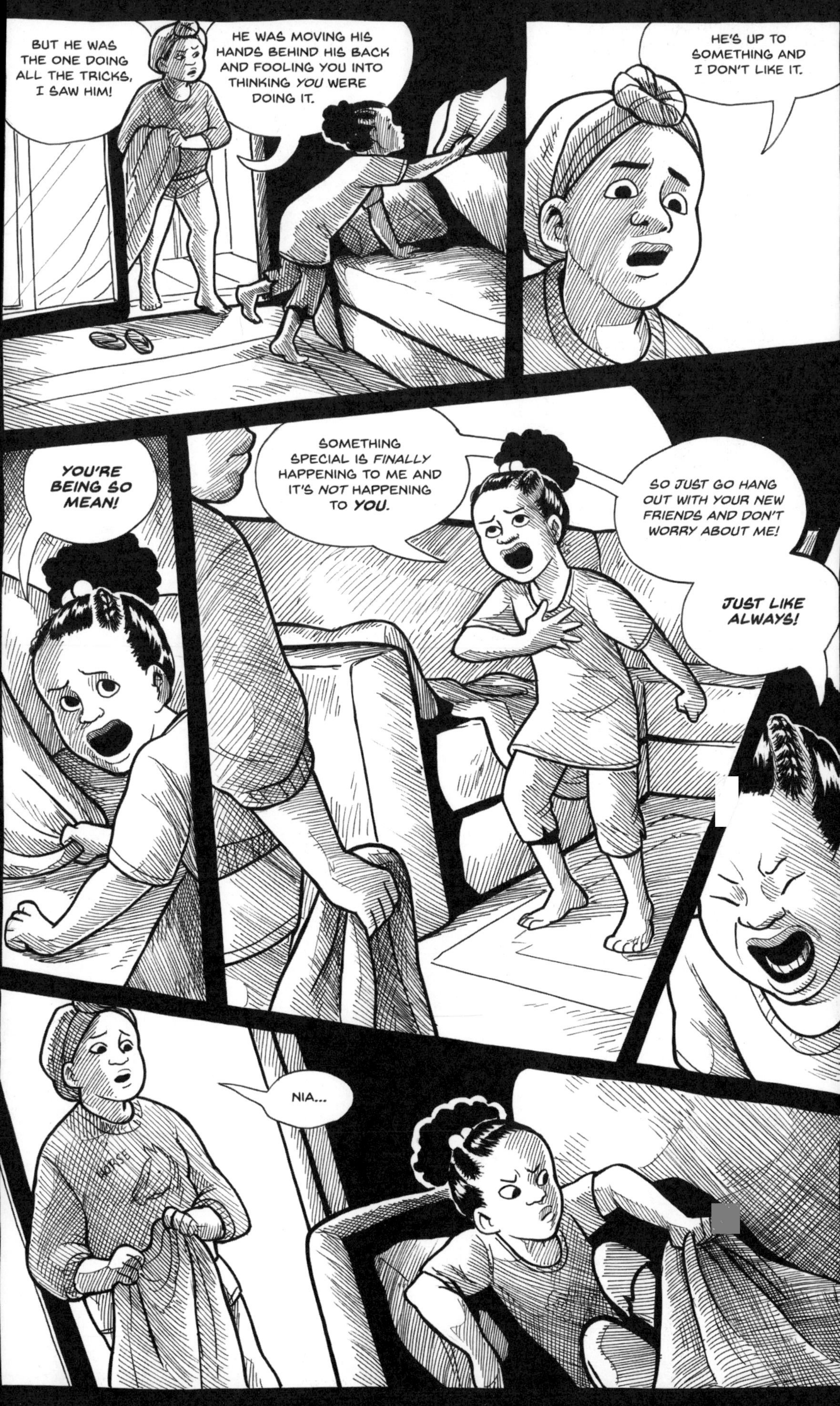
BUT HE WAS THE ONE DOING ALL THE TRICKS, I SAW HIM!
HE WAS MOVING HIS HANDS BEHIND HIS BACK AND FOOLING YOU INTO THINKING *YOU* WERE DOING IT.
HE'S UP TO SOMETHING AND I DON'T LIKE IT.
YOU'RE BEING SO MEAN!
SOMETHING SPECIAL IS *FINALLY* HAPPENING TO ME AND IT'S *NOT* HAPPENING TO ***YOU.***
SO JUST GO HANG OUT WITH YOUR NEW FRIENDS AND DON'T WORRY ABOUT ME!
JUST LIKE ALWAYS!
NIA...

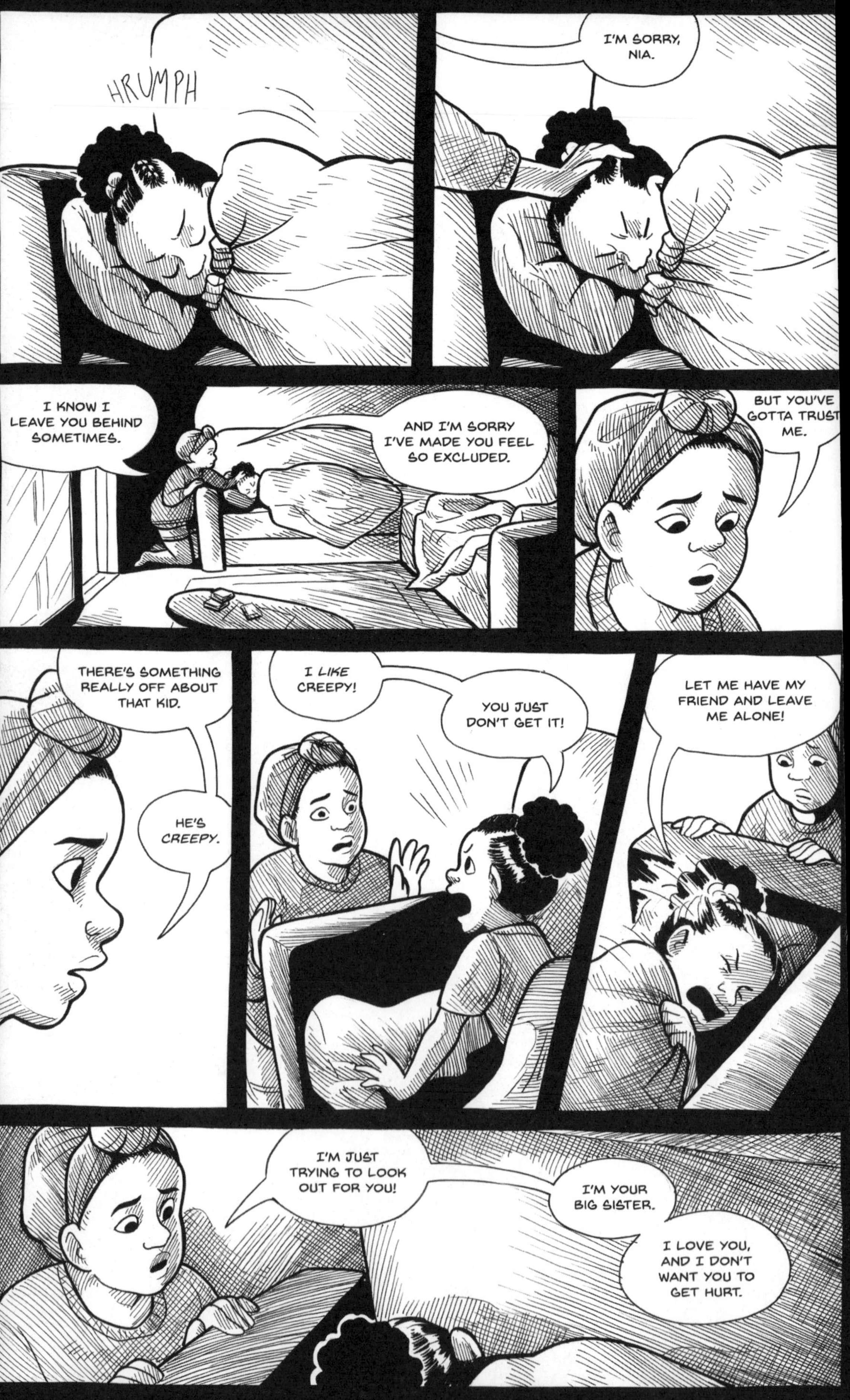

HRUMPH
I'M SORRY, NIA.
I KNOW I LEAVE YOU BEHIND SOMETIMES.
AND I'M SORRY I'VE MADE YOU FEEL SO EXCLUDED.
BUT YOU'VE GOTTA TRUST ME.
THERE'S SOMETHING REALLY OFF ABOUT THAT KID.
HE'S CREEPY.
I LIKE CREEPY!
YOU JUST DON'T GET IT!
LET ME HAVE MY FRIEND AND LEAVE ME ALONE!
I'M JUST TRYING TO LOOK OUT FOR YOU!
I'M YOUR BIG SISTER.
I LOVE YOU, AND I DON'T WANT YOU TO GET HURT.

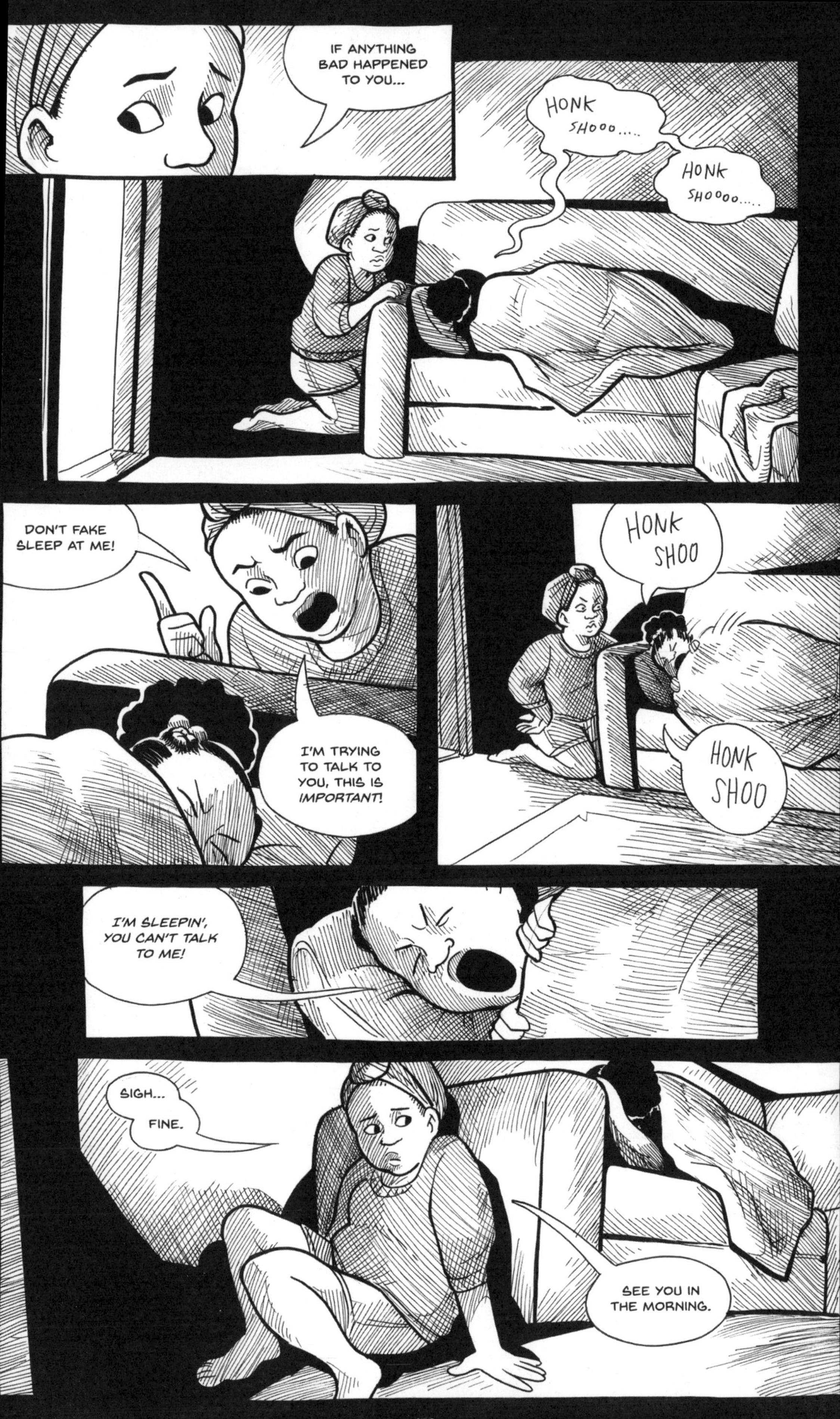
IF ANYTHING BAD HAPPENED TO YOU...
HONK SHOOO.....
HONK SHOOOO.....
DON'T FAKE SLEEP AT ME!
I'M TRYING TO TALK TO YOU, THIS IS *IMPORTANT!*
HONK SHOO
HONK SHOO
I'M SLEEPIN', YOU CAN'T TALK TO ME!
SIGH...
FINE.
SEE YOU IN THE MORNING.

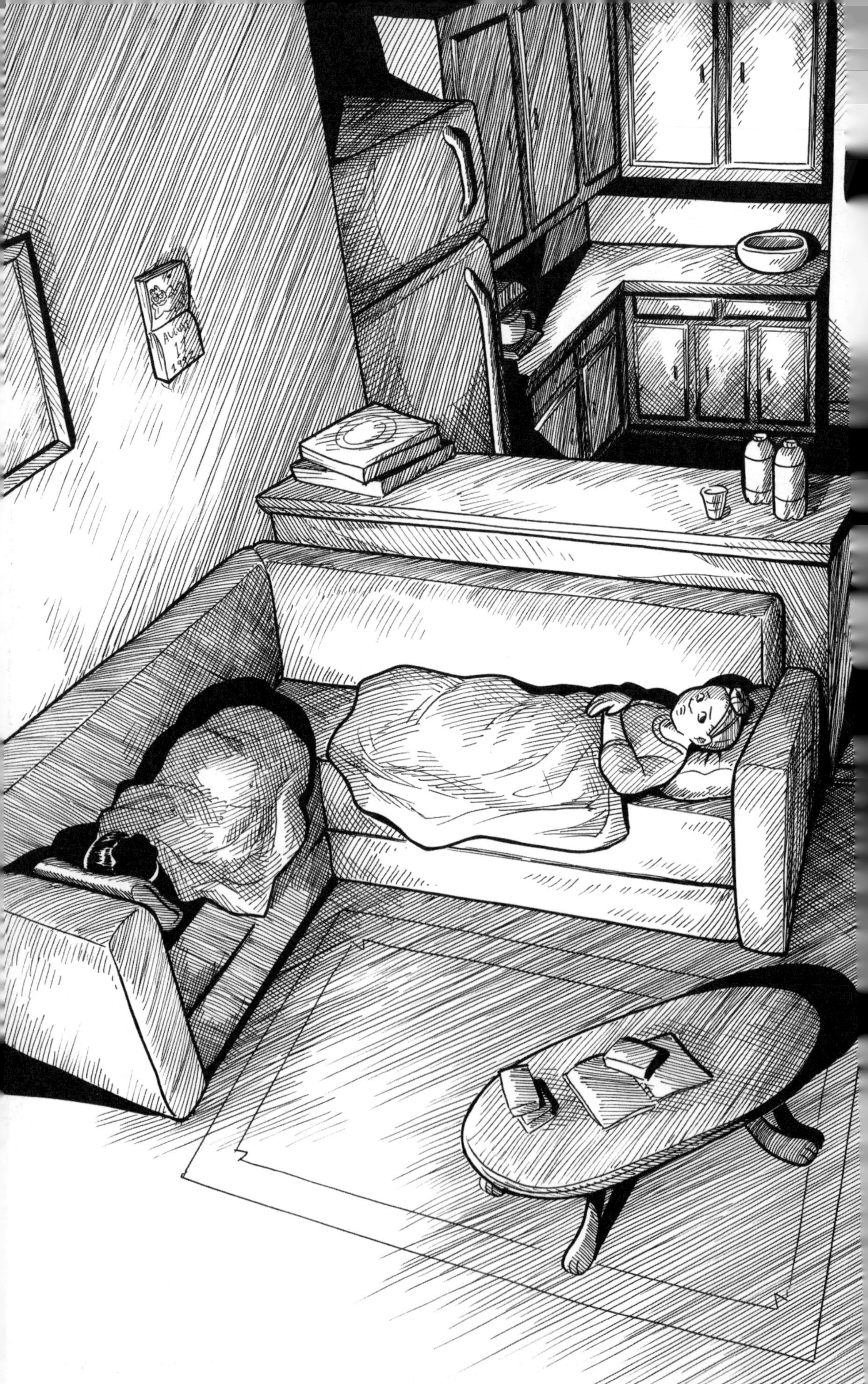

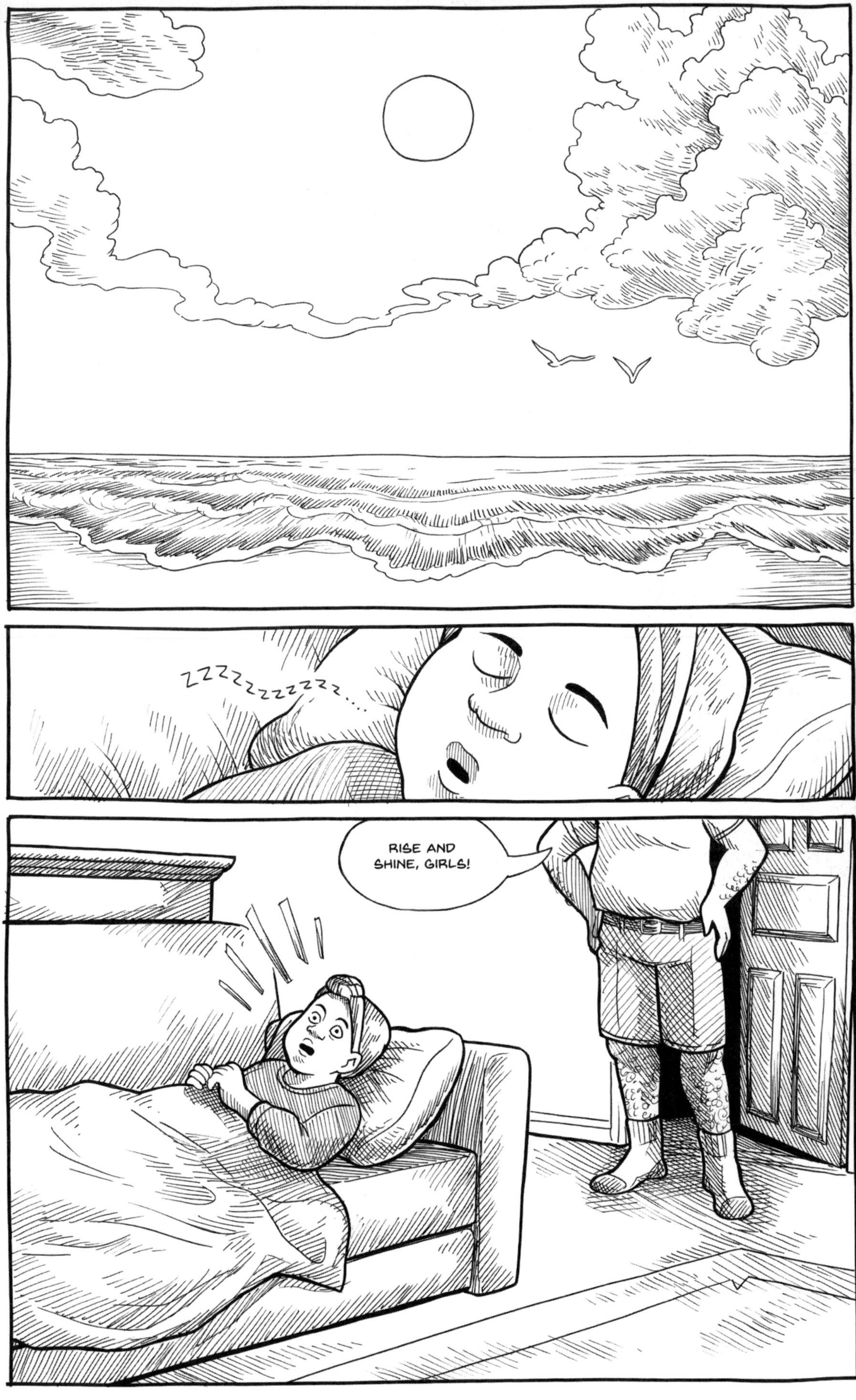
ZZZZZZZZZZZZ...
RISE AND SHINE, GIRLS!

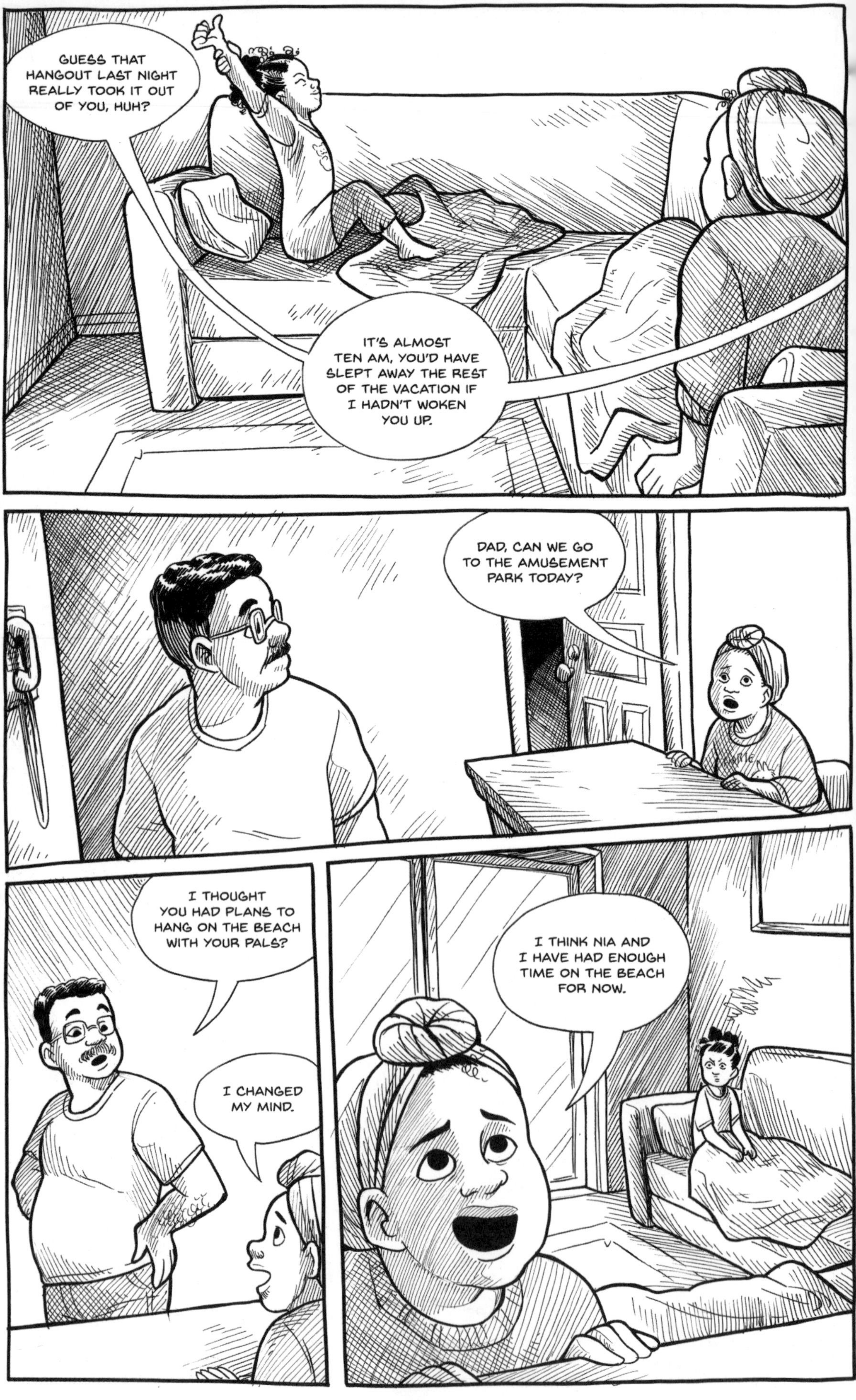
GUESS THAT HANGOUT LAST NIGHT REALLY TOOK IT OUT OF YOU, HUH?
IT'S ALMOST TEN AM, YOU'D HAVE SLEPT AWAY THE REST OF THE VACATION IF I HADN'T WOKEN YOU UP.
DAD, CAN WE GO TO THE AMUSEMENT PARK TODAY?
I THOUGHT YOU HAD PLANS TO HANG ON THE BEACH WITH YOUR PALS?
I CHANGED MY MIND.
I THINK NIA AND I HAVE HAD ENOUGH TIME ON THE BEACH FOR NOW.

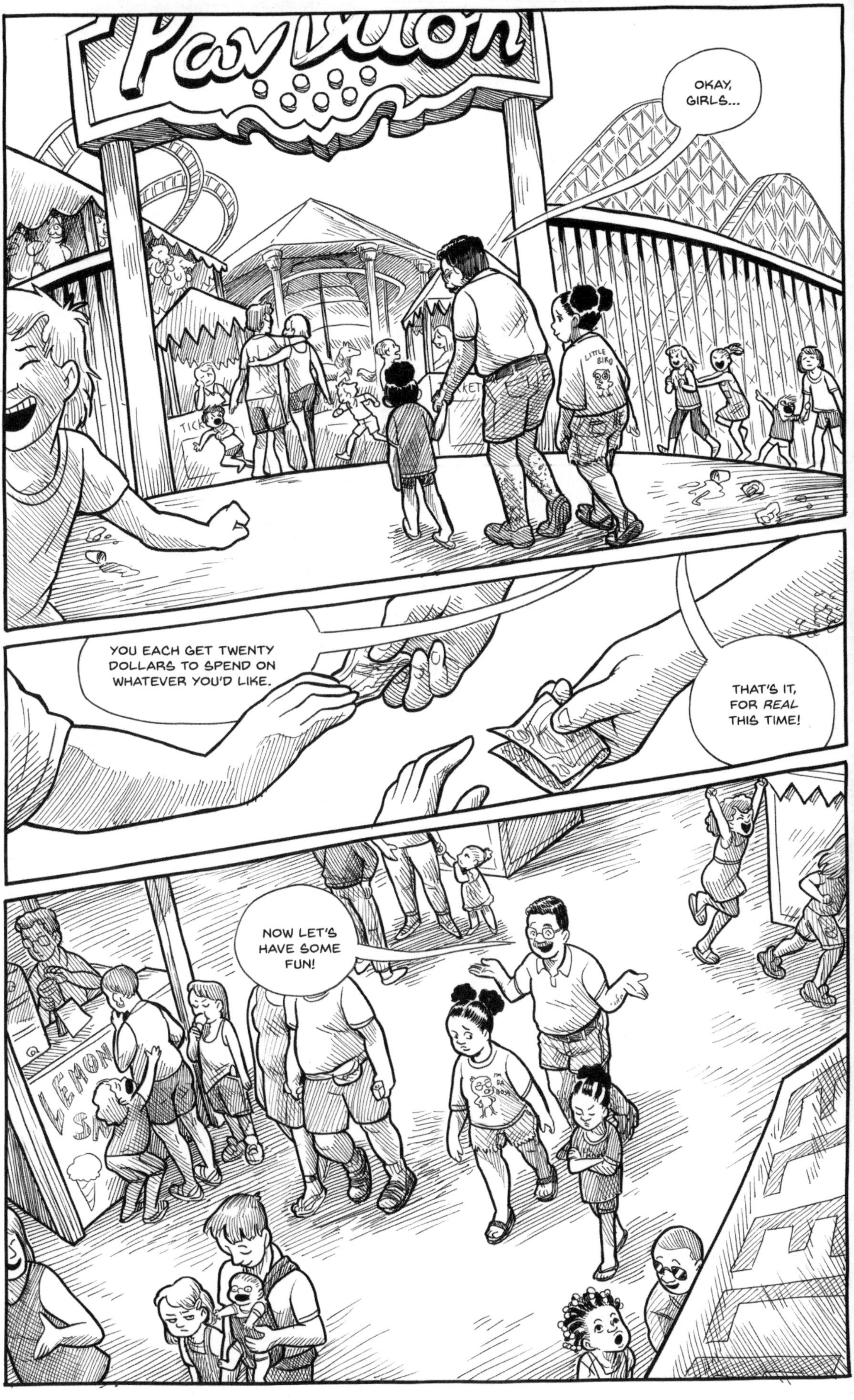
Pavilion
OKAY, GIRLS...
YOU EACH GET TWENTY DOLLARS TO SPEND ON WHATEVER YOU'D LIKE.
THAT'S IT, FOR *REAL* THIS TIME!
NOW LET'S HAVE SOME FUN!
LEMON

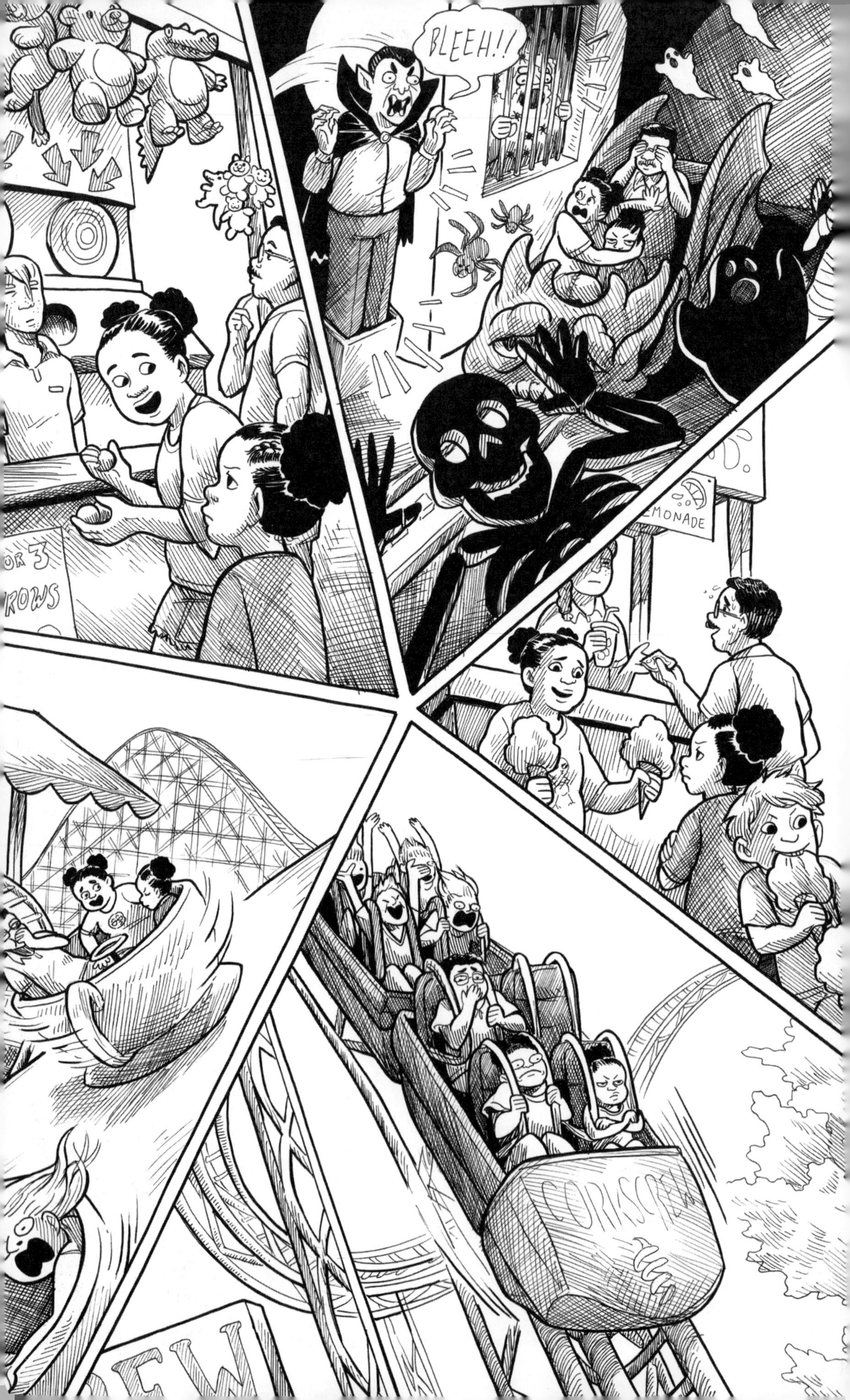
BLEEH!!
CORKSCREW

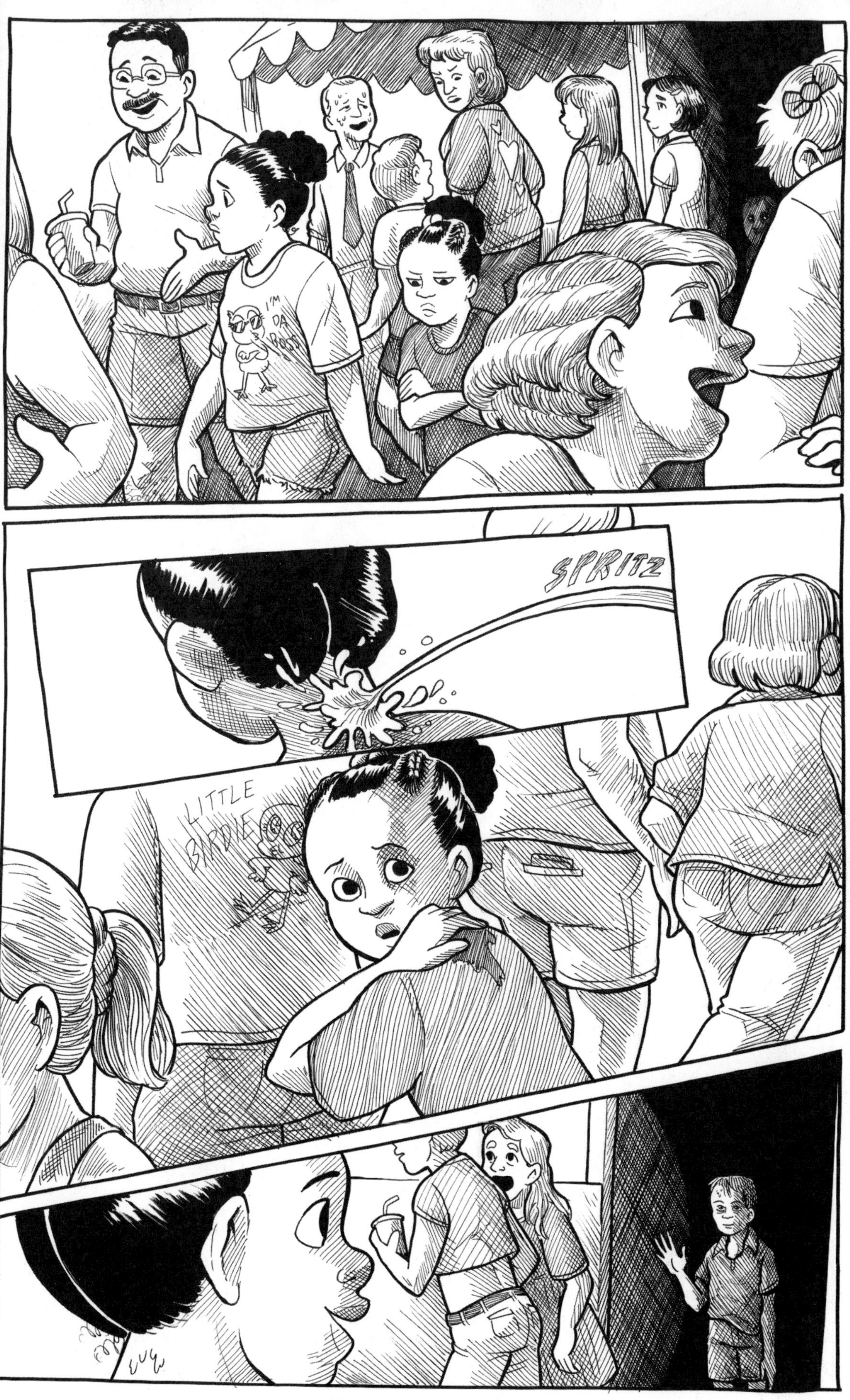
I'M DA BOSS
SPRITZ
LITTLE BIRDIE

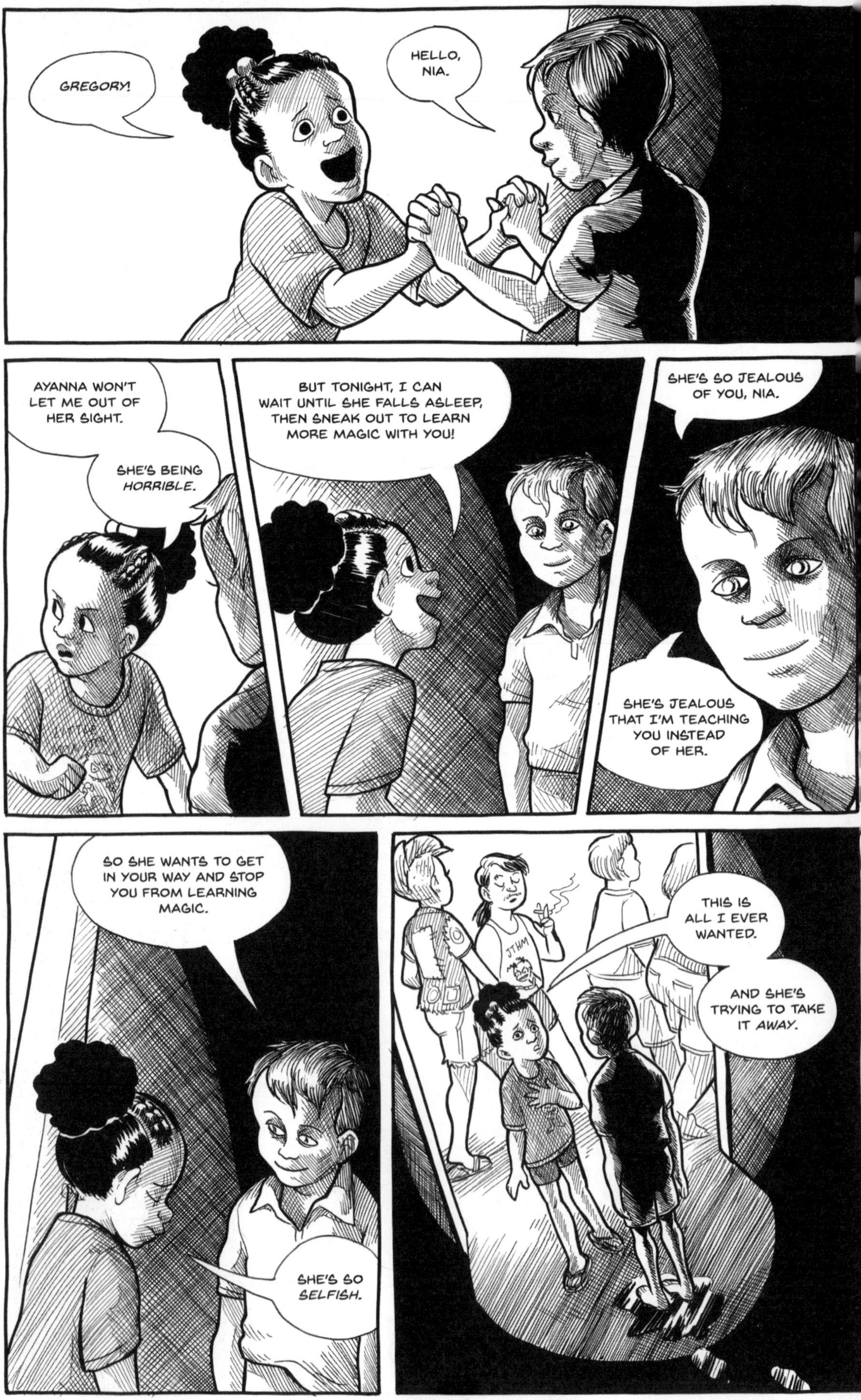
GREGORY!
HELLO, NIA.
AYANNA WON'T LET ME OUT OF HER SIGHT.
SHE'S BEING HORRIBLE.
BUT TONIGHT, I CAN WAIT UNTIL SHE FALLS ASLEEP, THEN SNEAK OUT TO LEARN MORE MAGIC WITH YOU!
SHE'S SO JEALOUS OF YOU, NIA.
SHE'S JEALOUS THAT I'M TEACHING YOU INSTEAD OF HER.
SO SHE WANTS TO GET IN YOUR WAY AND STOP YOU FROM LEARNING MAGIC.
SHE'S SO SELFISH.
THIS IS ALL I EVER WANTED.
AND SHE'S TRYING TO TAKE IT AWAY.

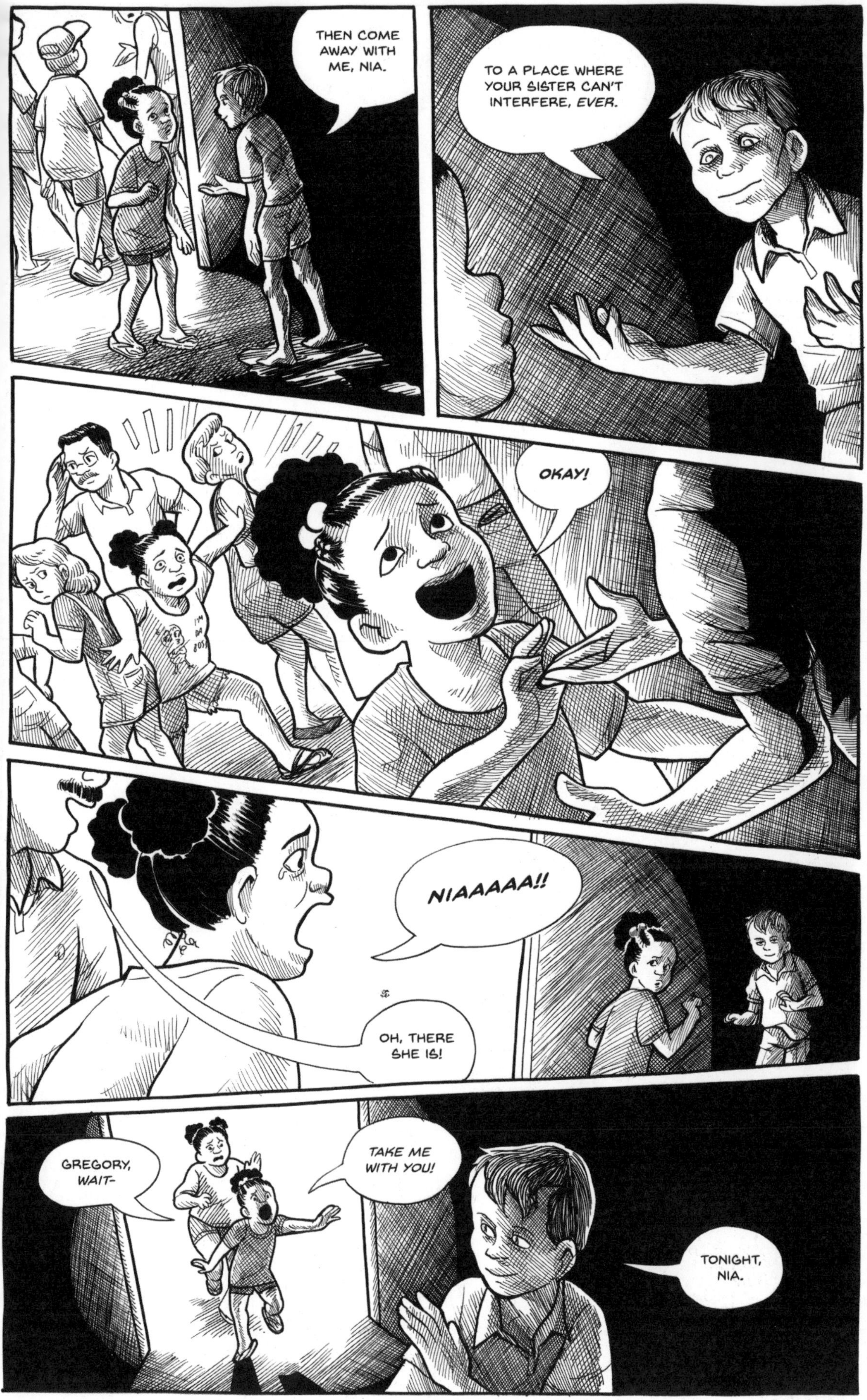
THEN COME AWAY WITH ME, NIA.
TO A PLACE WHERE YOUR SISTER CAN'T INTERFERE, *EVER*.
OKAY!
NIAAAAA!!
OH, THERE SHE IS!
GREGORY, *WAIT-*
TAKE ME WITH YOU!
TONIGHT, NIA.

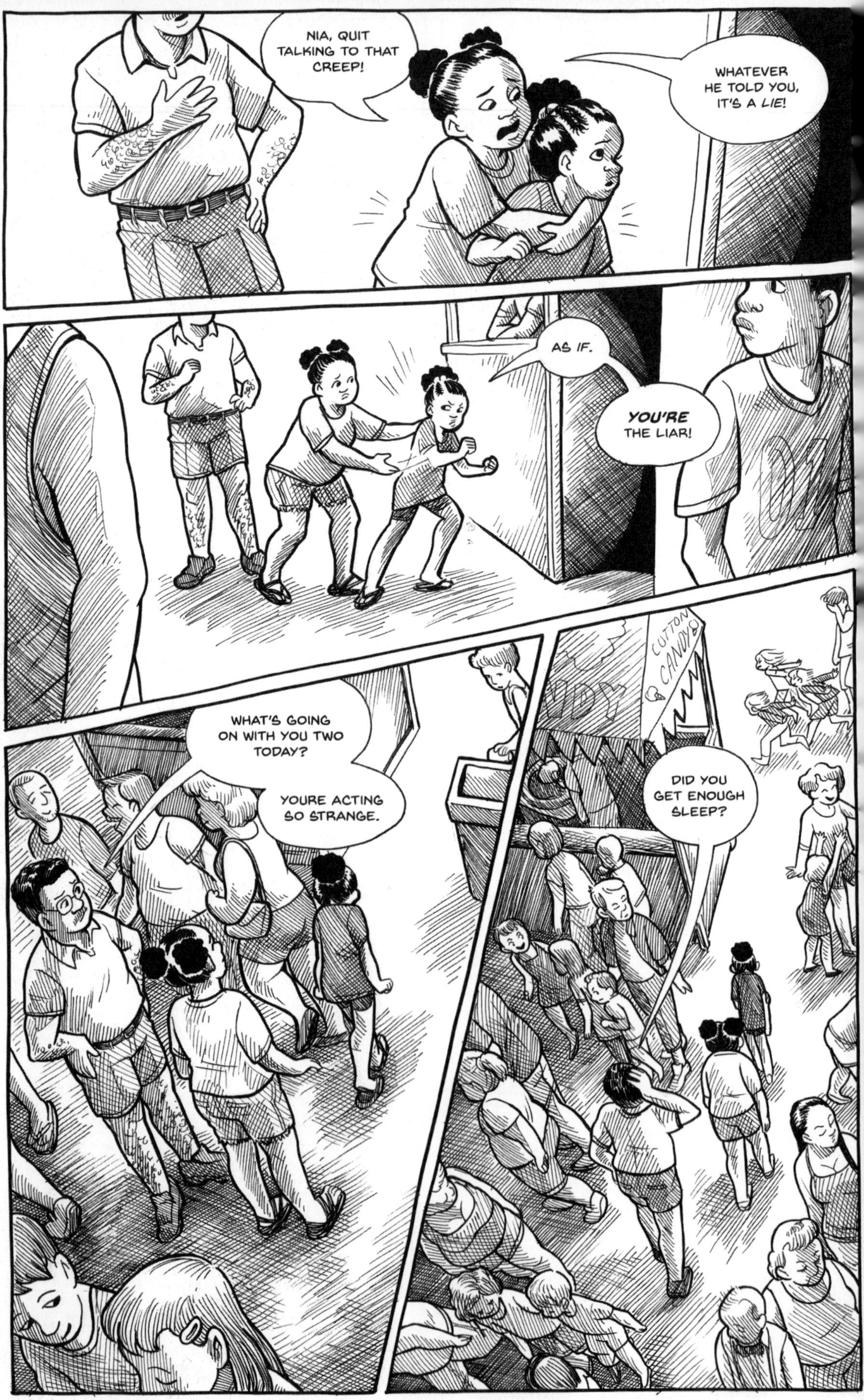
NIA, QUIT TALKING TO THAT CREEP!
WHATEVER HE TOLD YOU, IT'S A *LIE*!
AS IF.
YOU'RE THE LIAR!
WHAT'S GOING ON WITH YOU TWO TODAY?
YOURE ACTING SO STRANGE.
DID YOU GET ENOUGH SLEEP?
COTTON CANDY

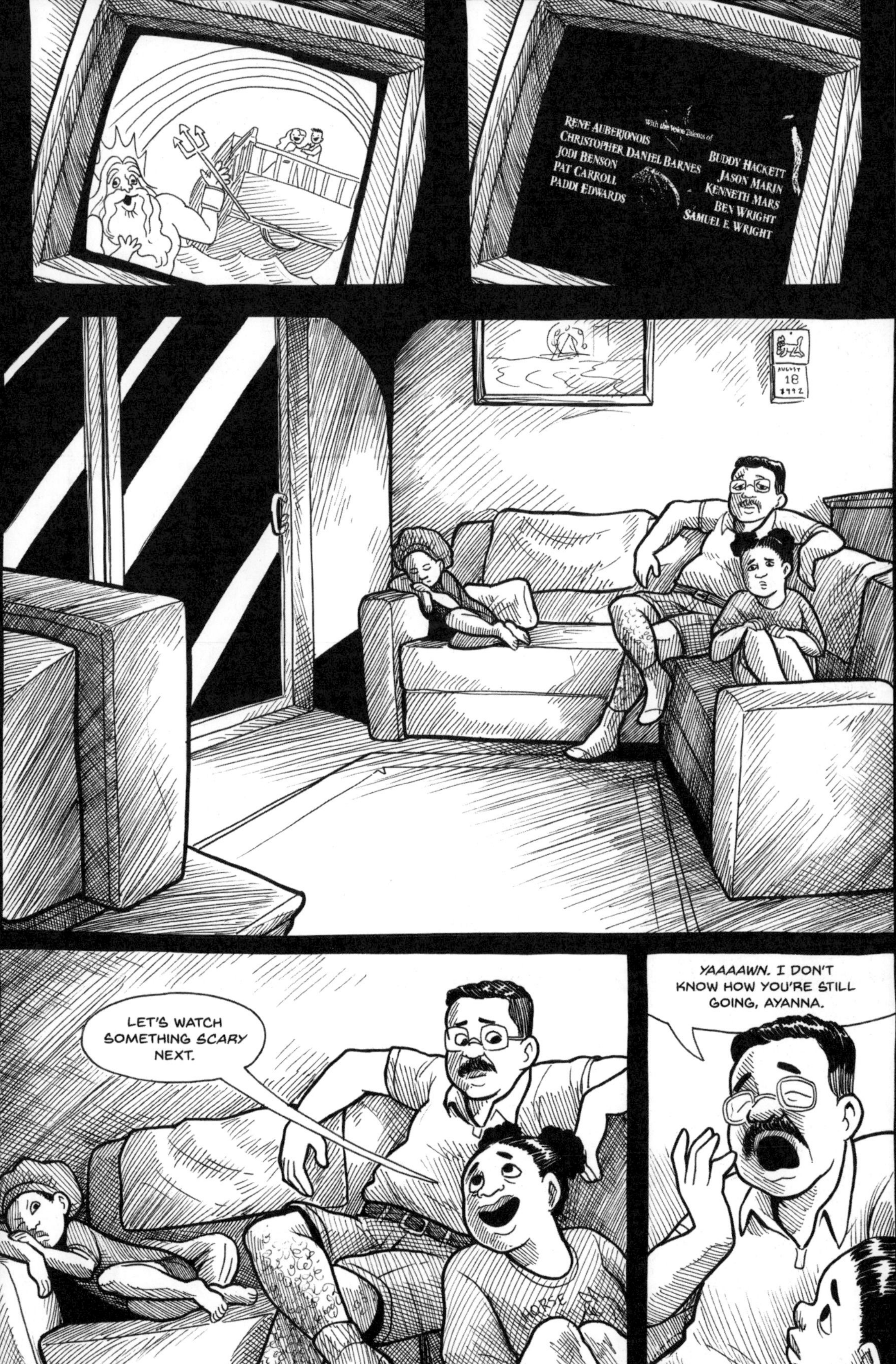
With the Voice Talents of
RENE AUBERJONOIS
CHRISTOPHER DANIEL BARNES
JODI BENSON
PAT CARROLL
PADDI EDWARDS
BUDDY HACKETT
JASON MARIN
KENNETH MARS
BEN WRIGHT
SAMUEL E. WRIGHT
AUGUST
18
LET'S WATCH SOMETHING SCARY NEXT.
YAAAAWN. I DON'T KNOW HOW YOU'RE STILL GOING, AYANNA.

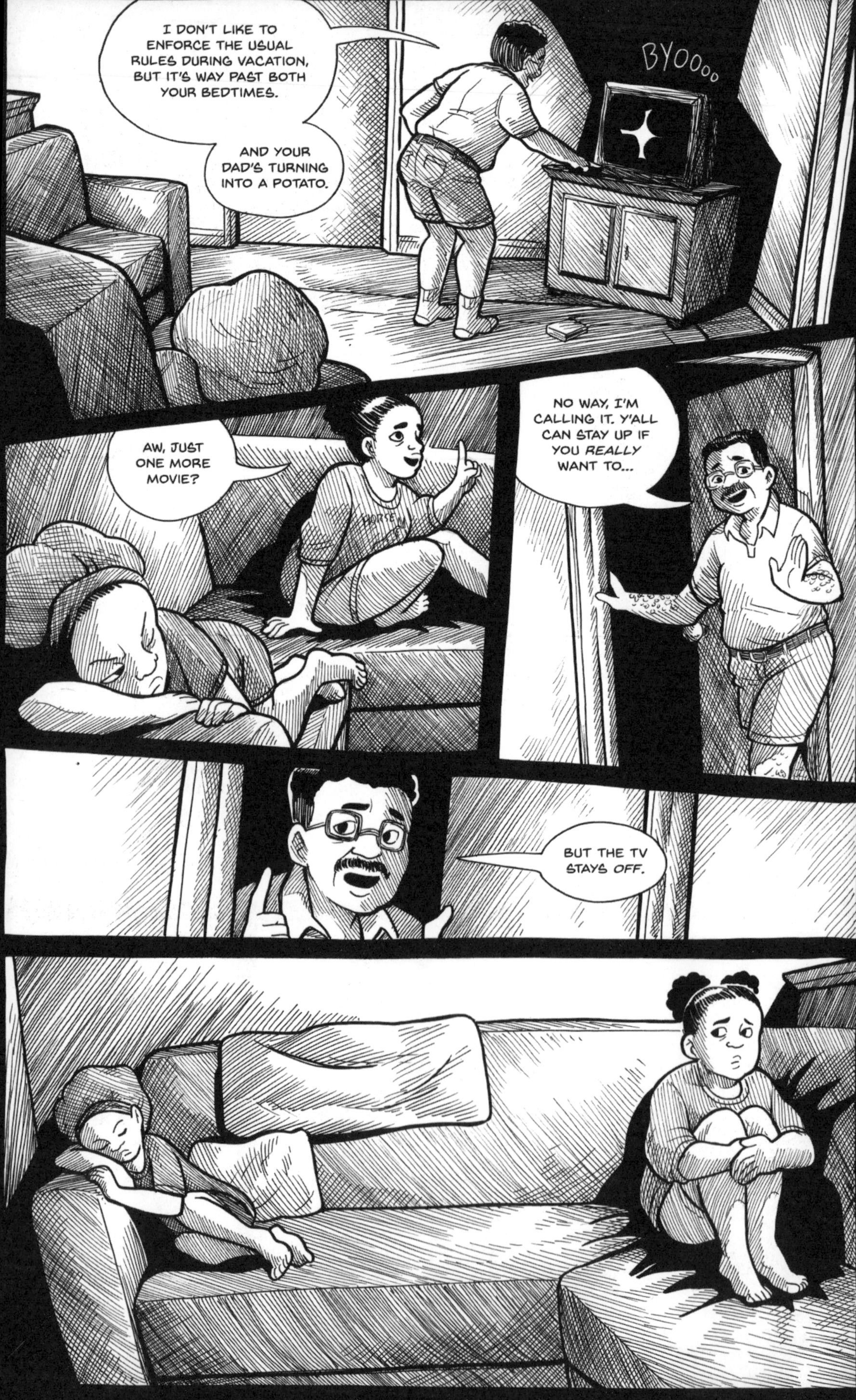

BYOOooo
I DON'T LIKE TO ENFORCE THE USUAL RULES DURING VACATION, BUT IT'S WAY PAST BOTH YOUR BEDTIMES.
AND YOUR DAD'S TURNING INTO A POTATO.
AW, JUST ONE MORE MOVIE?
NO WAY, I'M CALLING IT. Y'ALL CAN STAY UP IF YOU *REALLY* WANT TO...
BUT THE TV STAYS *OFF*.

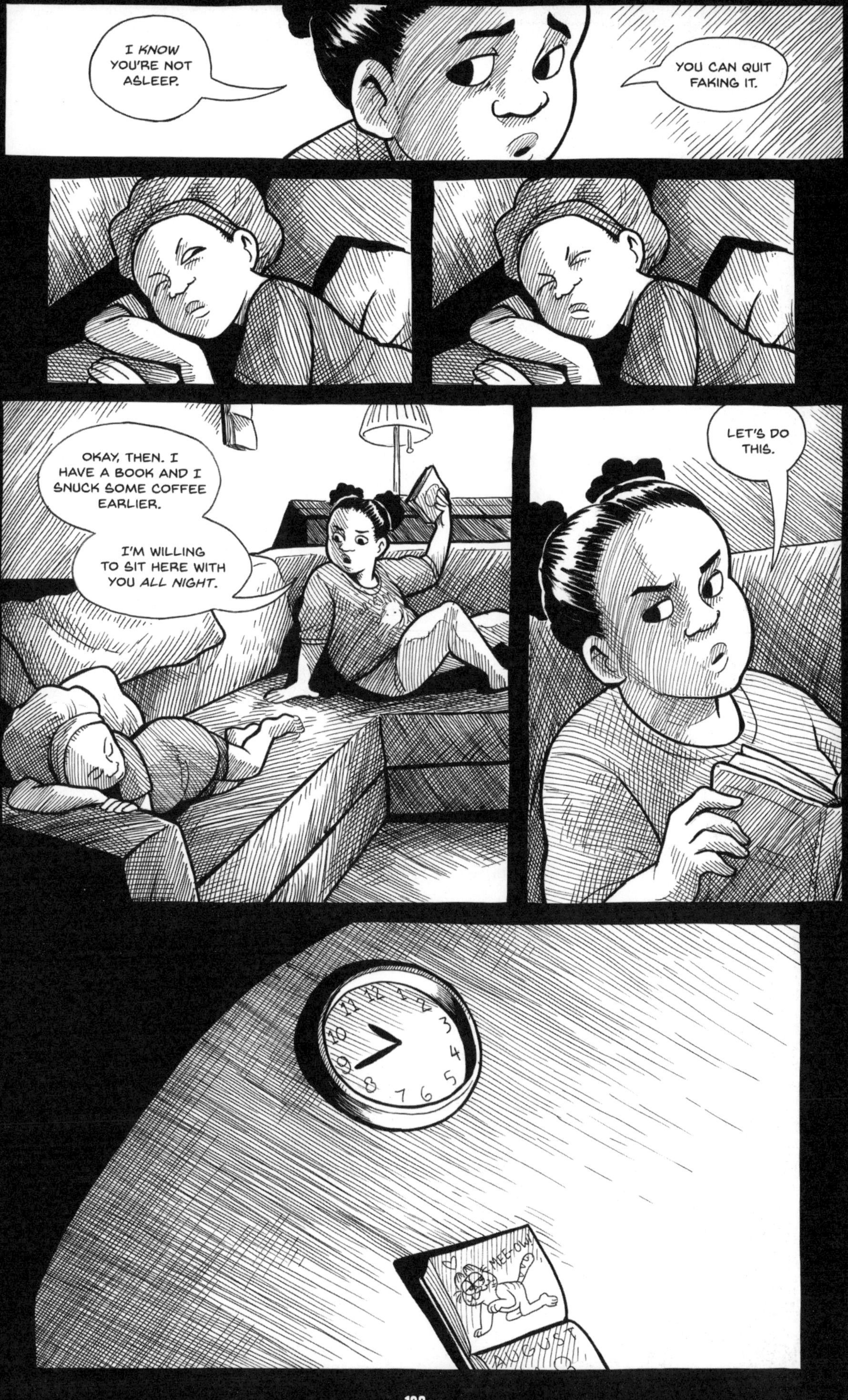
I KNOW YOU'RE NOT ASLEEP.
YOU CAN QUIT FAKING IT.
OKAY, THEN. I HAVE A BOOK AND I SNUCK SOME COFFEE EARLIER.
I'M WILLING TO SIT HERE WITH YOU ALL NIGHT.
LET'S DO THIS.

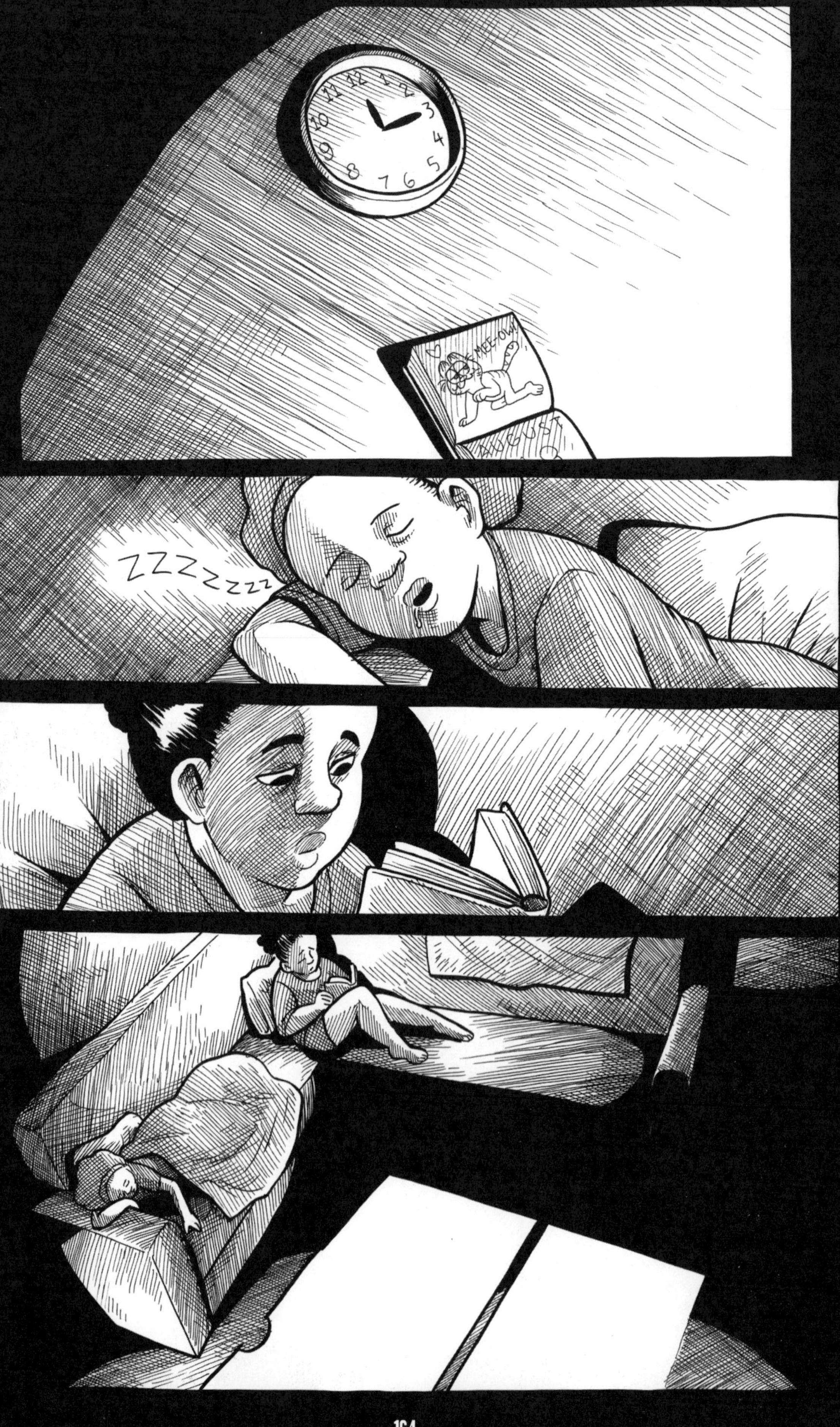
MEE-OW!
AUGUST
ZZZZzzzz

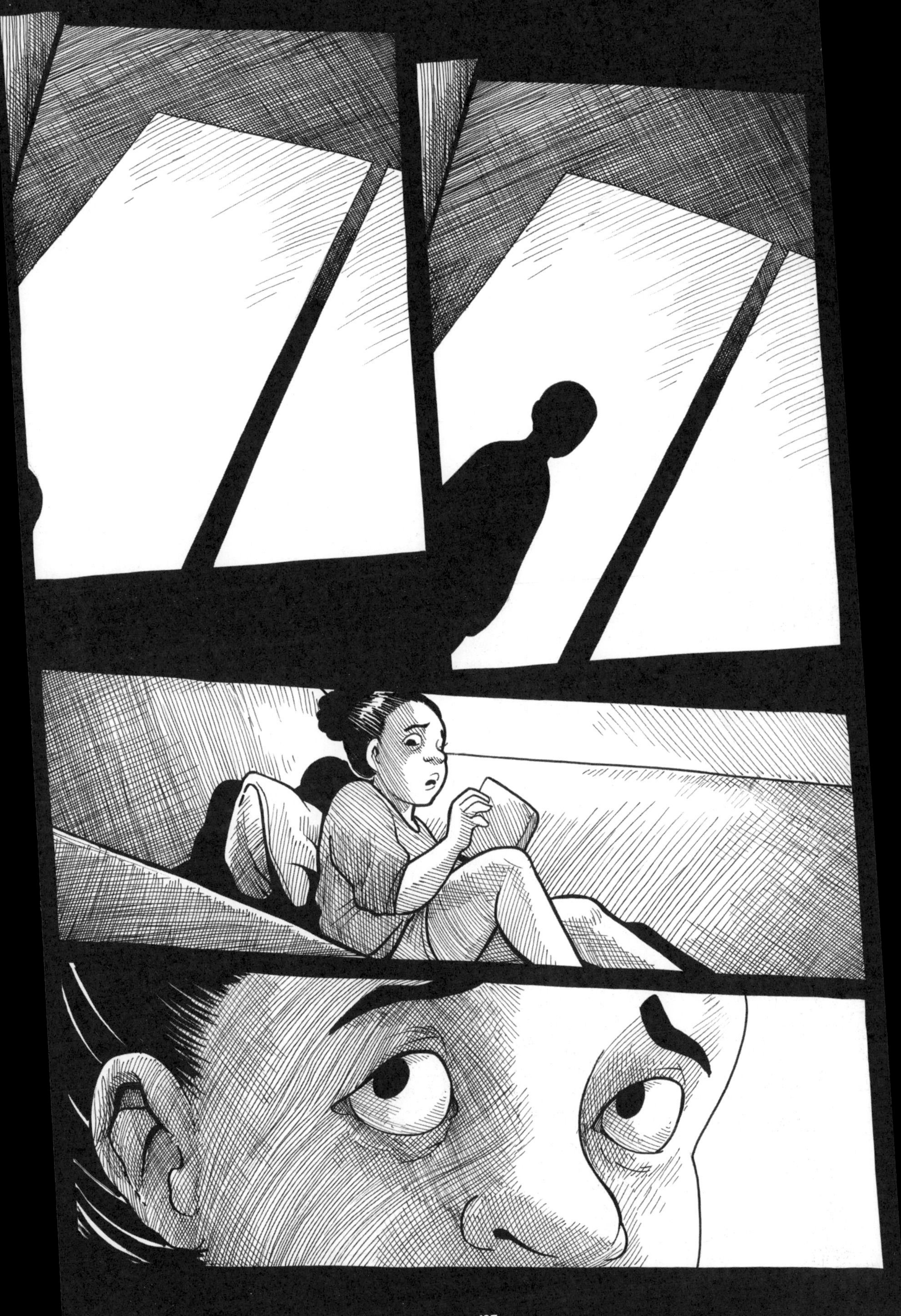

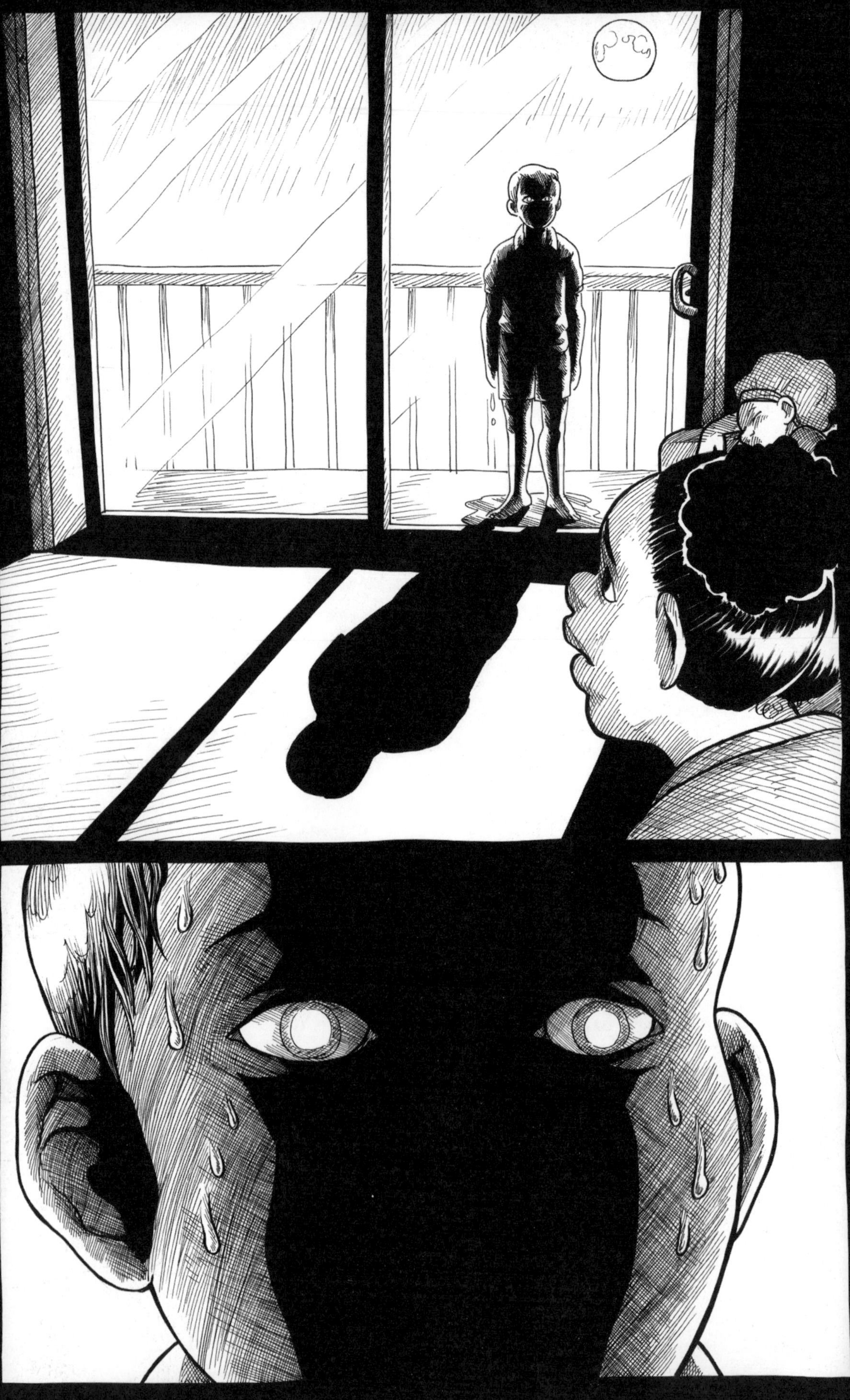

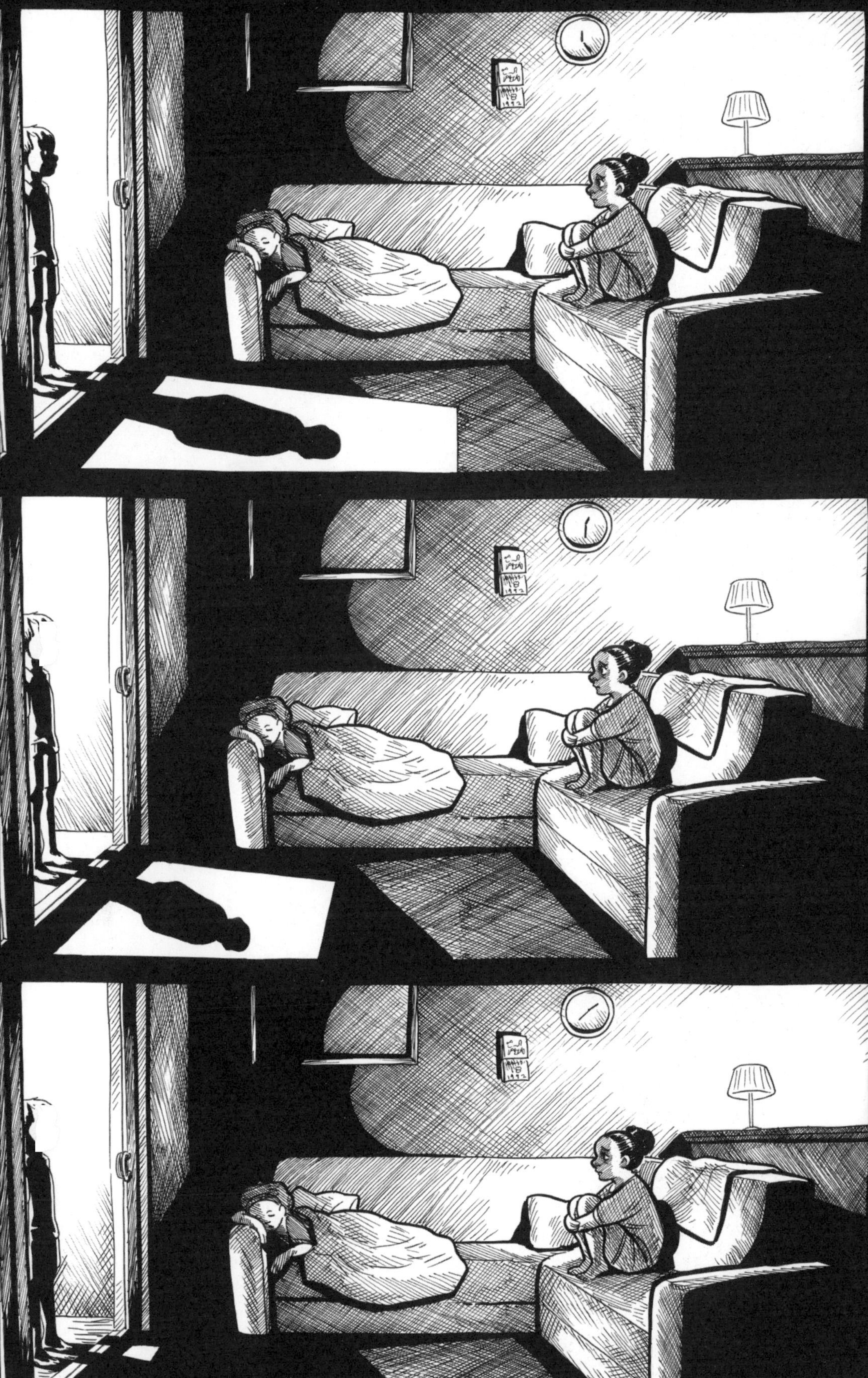

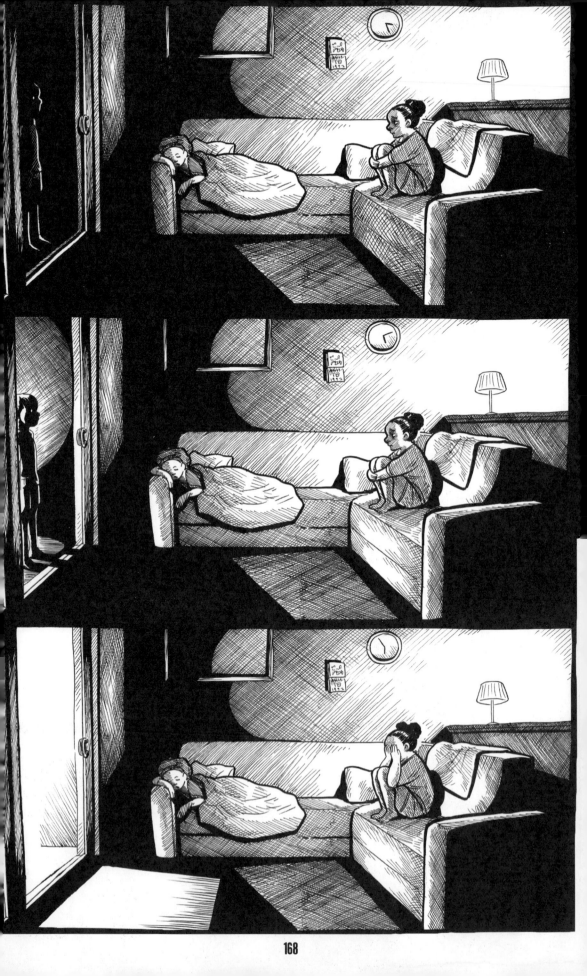

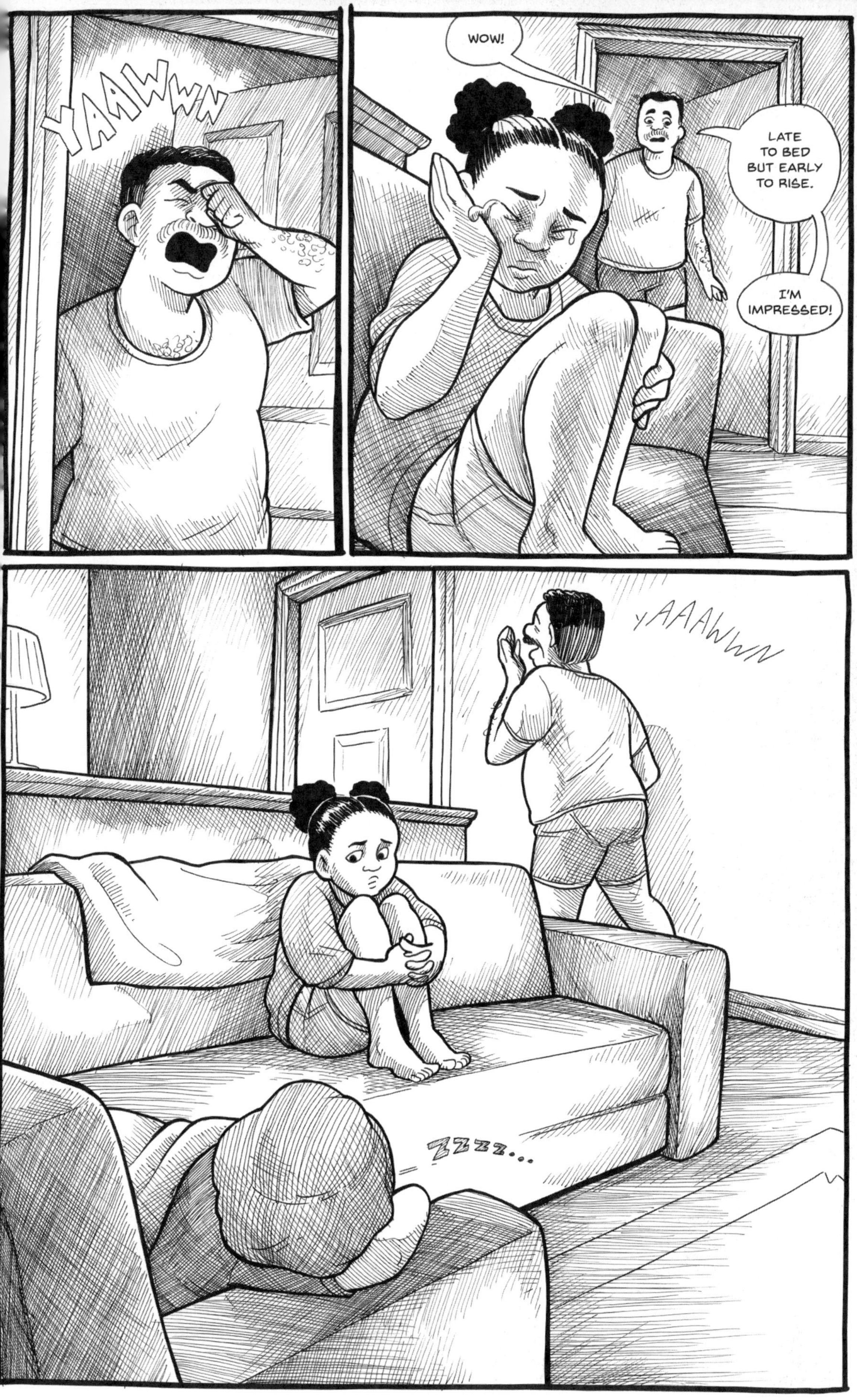
YAAWWN
WOW!
LATE TO BED BUT EARLY TO RISE.
I'M IMPRESSED!
YAAAWWN
ZZZZ...

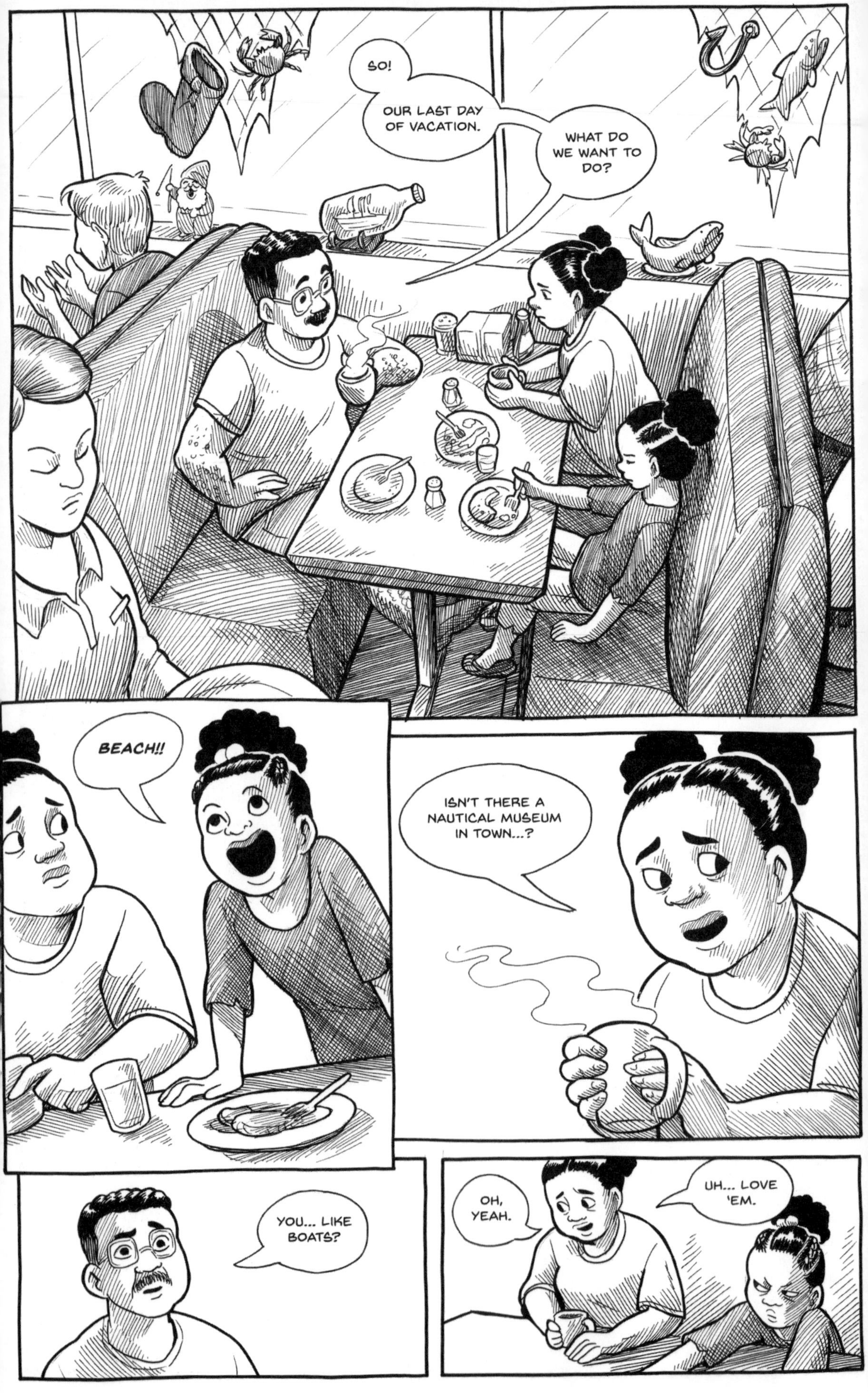
SO!
OUR LAST DAY OF VACATION.
WHAT DO WE WANT TO DO?
BEACH!!
ISN'T THERE A NAUTICAL MUSEUM IN TOWN...?
YOU... LIKE BOATS?
OH, YEAH.
UH... LOVE 'EM.

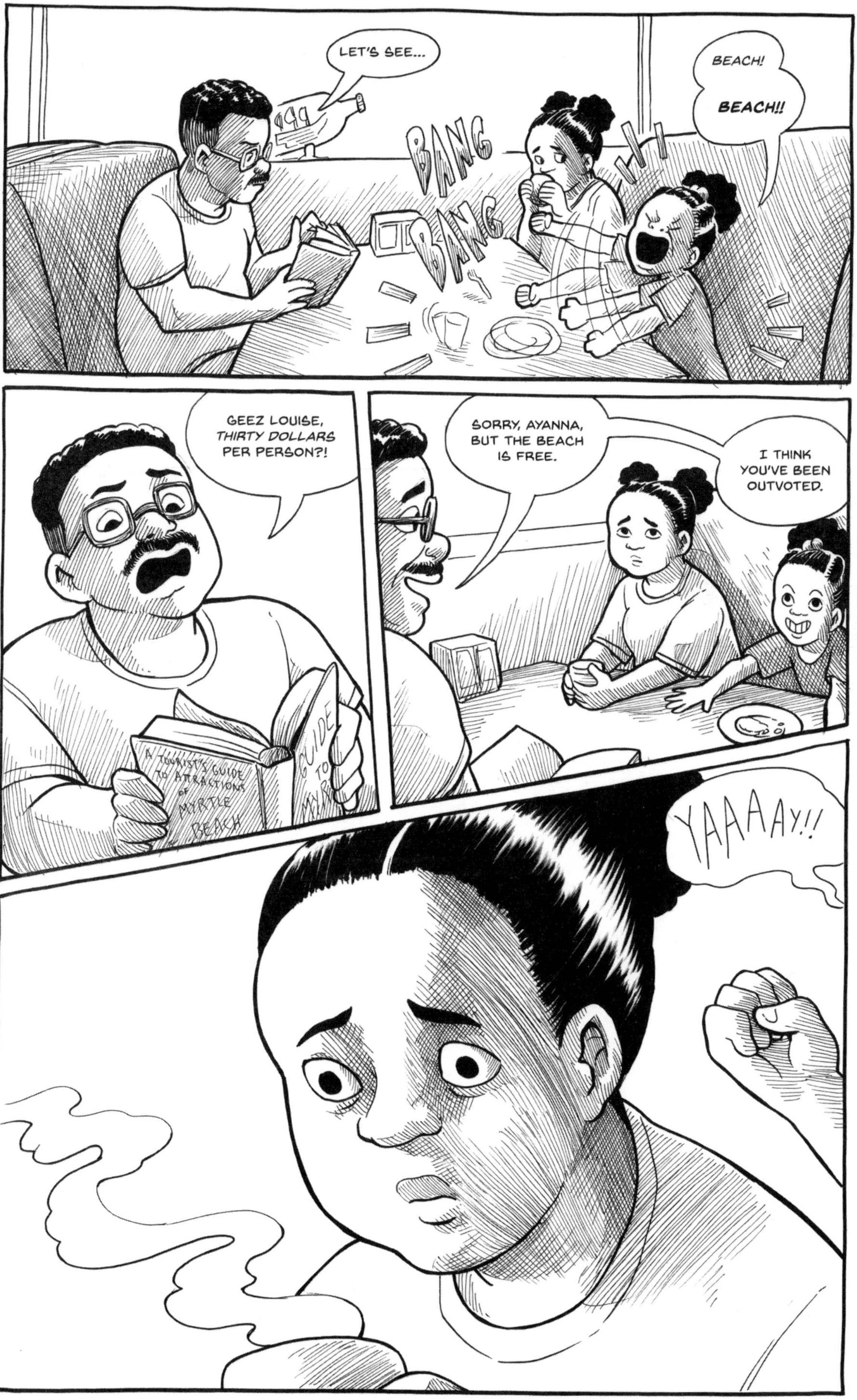
LET'S SEE...
BEACH!
BEACH!!
BANG
BANG
BANG
GEEZ LOUISE, *THIRTY DOLLARS* PER PERSON?!
A TOURIST'S GUIDE TO ATTRACTIONS OF MYRTLE BEACH
SORRY, AYANNA, BUT THE BEACH IS FREE.
I THINK YOU'VE BEEN OUTVOTED.
YAAAAY!!

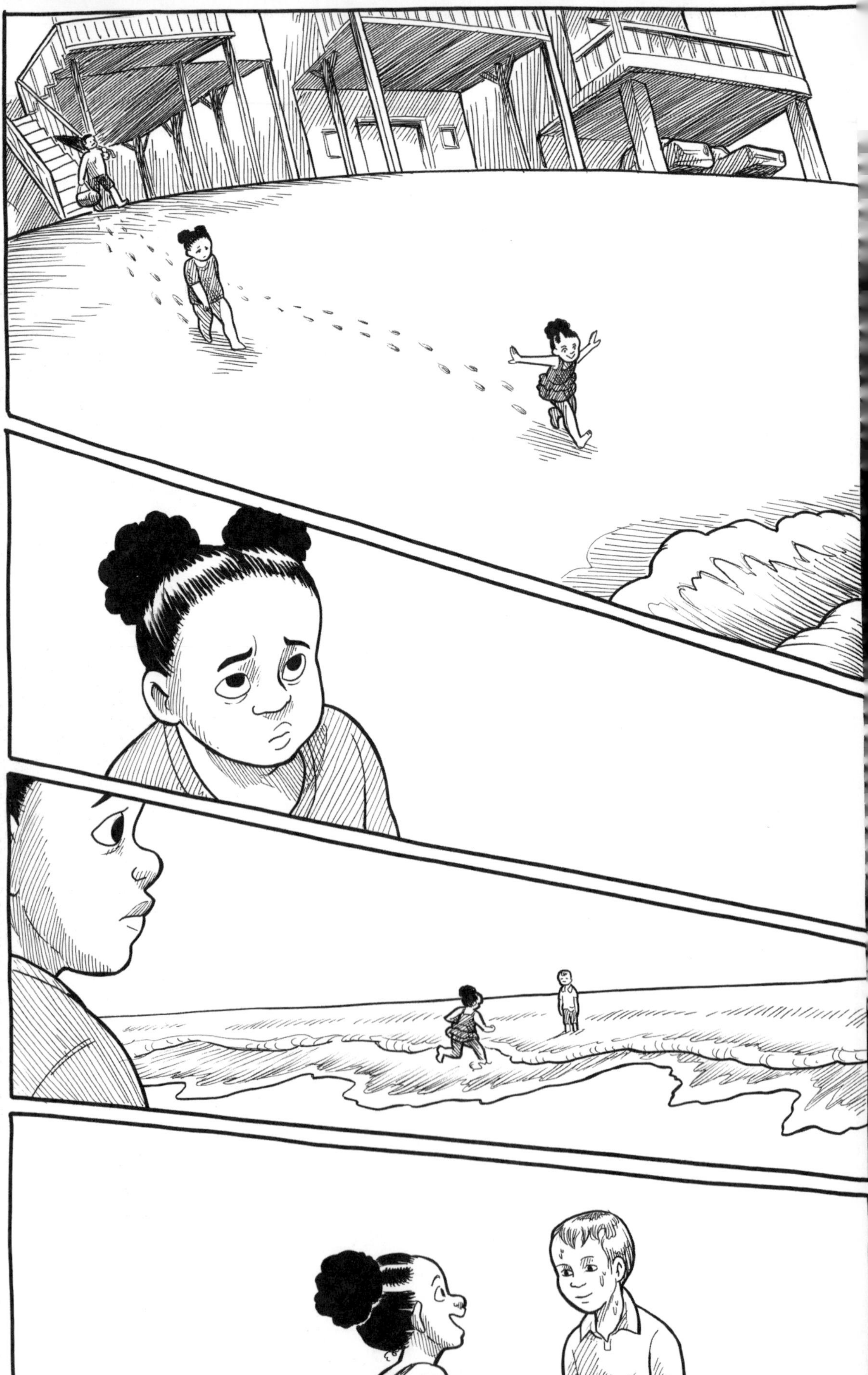

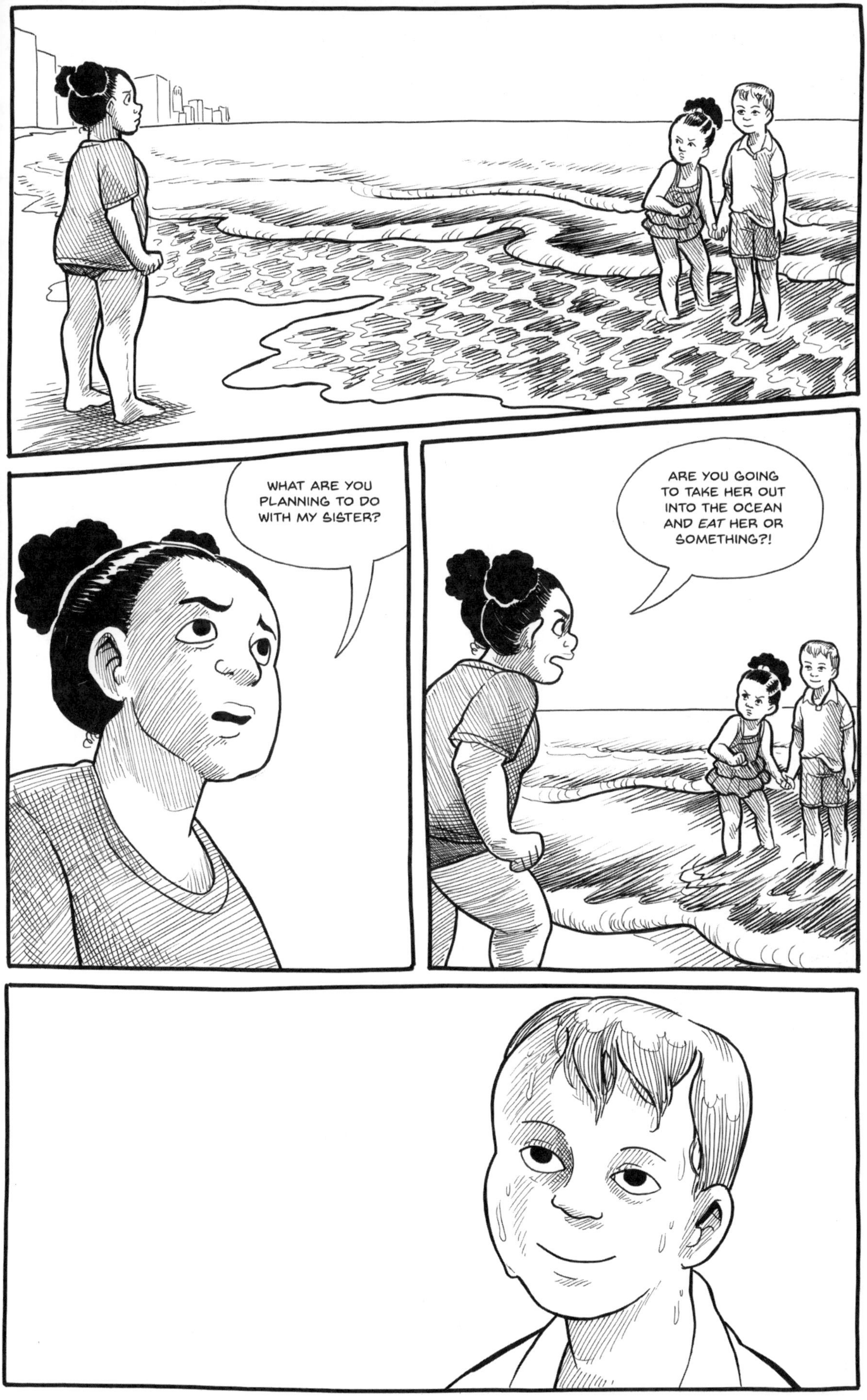
WHAT ARE YOU PLANNING TO DO WITH MY SISTER?
ARE YOU GOING TO TAKE HER OUT INTO THE OCEAN AND *EAT* HER OR SOMETHING?!

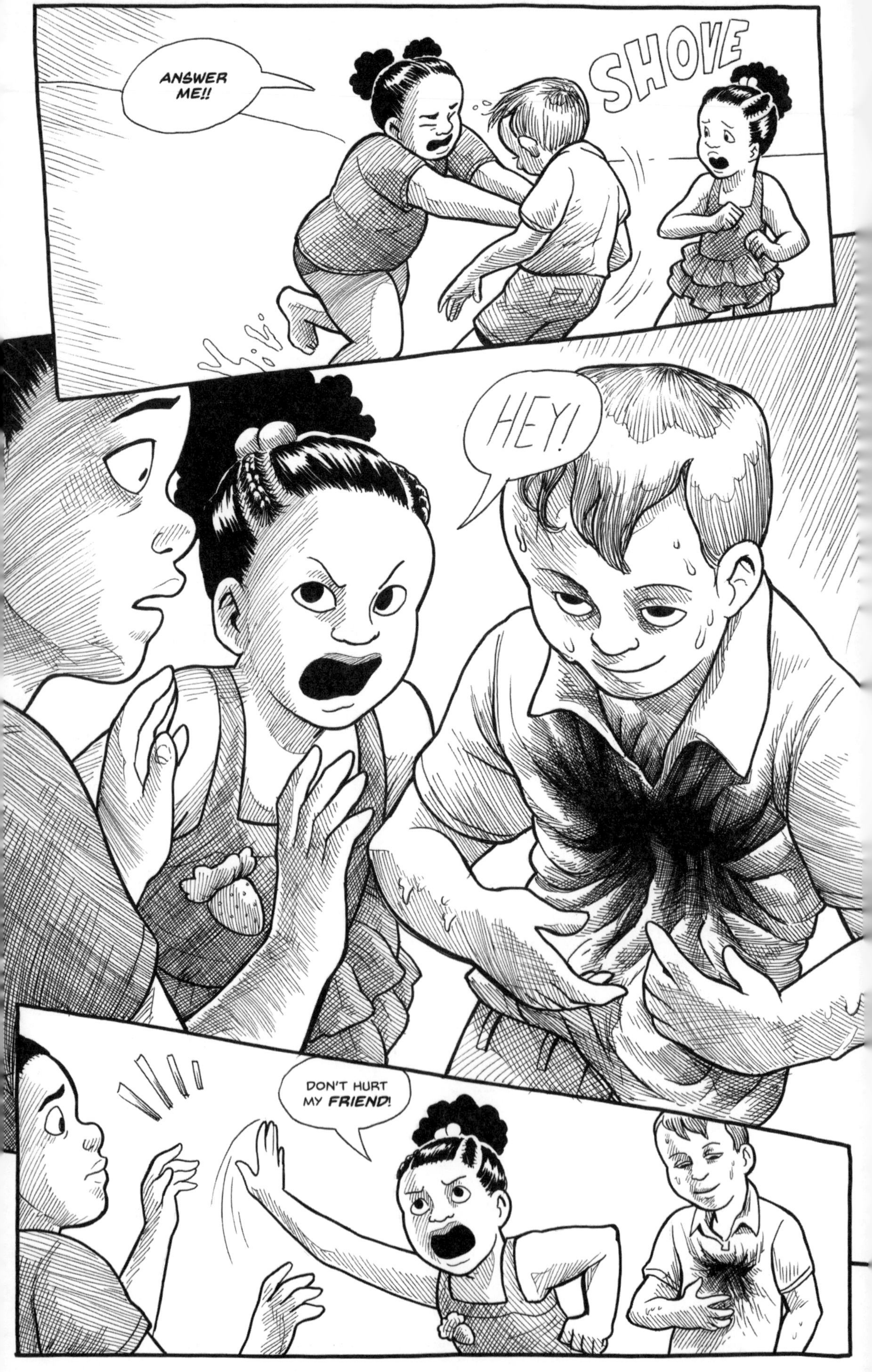
ANSWER ME!!
SHOVE
HEY!
DON'T HURT MY FRIEND!

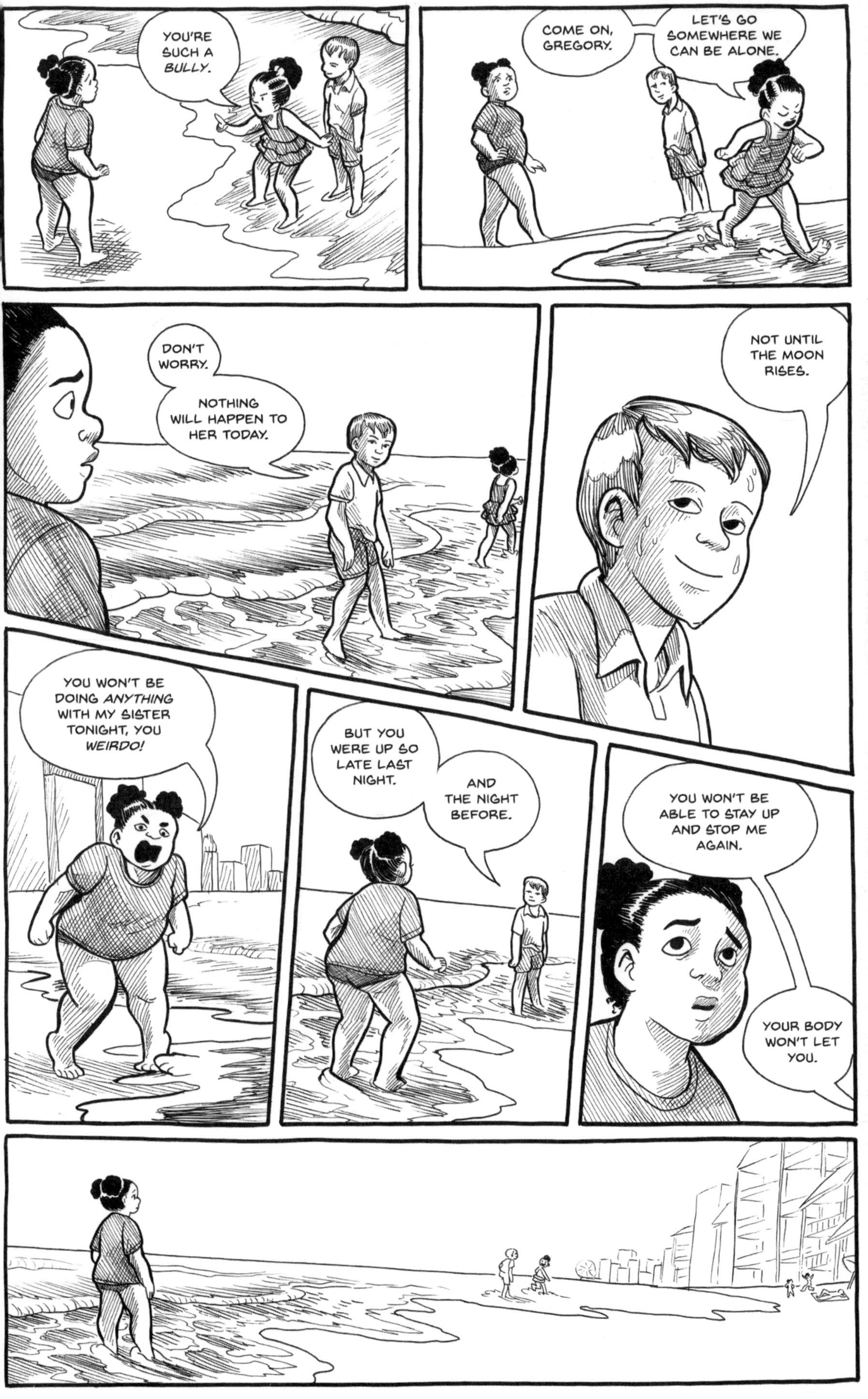
YOU'RE SUCH A *BULLY.*
COME ON, GREGORY.
LET'S GO SOMEWHERE WE CAN BE ALONE.
DON'T WORRY.
NOTHING WILL HAPPEN TO HER TODAY.
NOT UNTIL THE MOON RISES.
YOU WON'T BE DOING *ANYTHING* WITH MY SISTER TONIGHT, YOU *WEIRDO!*
BUT YOU WERE UP SO LATE LAST NIGHT.
AND THE NIGHT BEFORE.
YOU WON'T BE ABLE TO STAY UP AND STOP ME AGAIN.
YOUR BODY WON'T LET YOU.

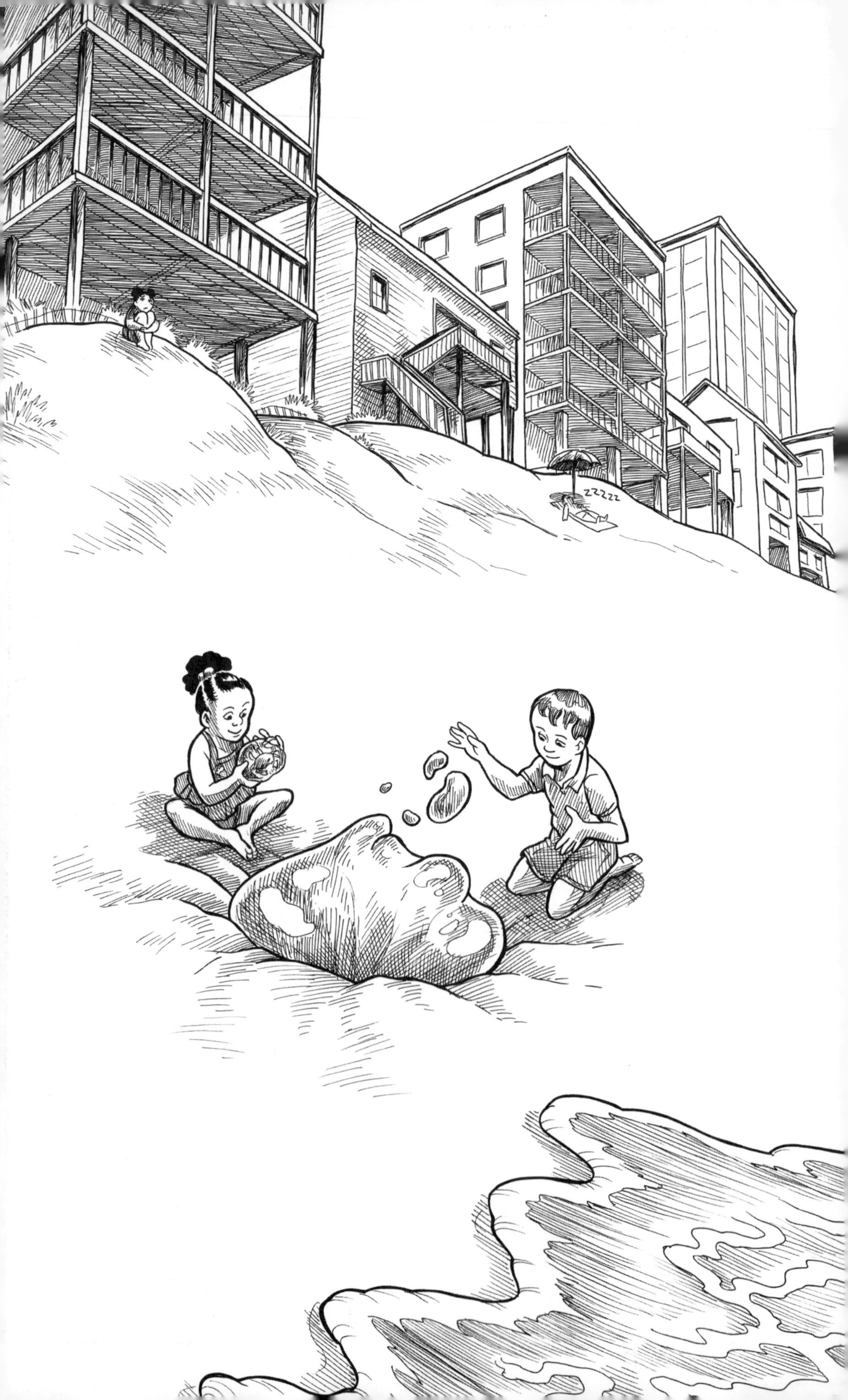
ZZZZZ

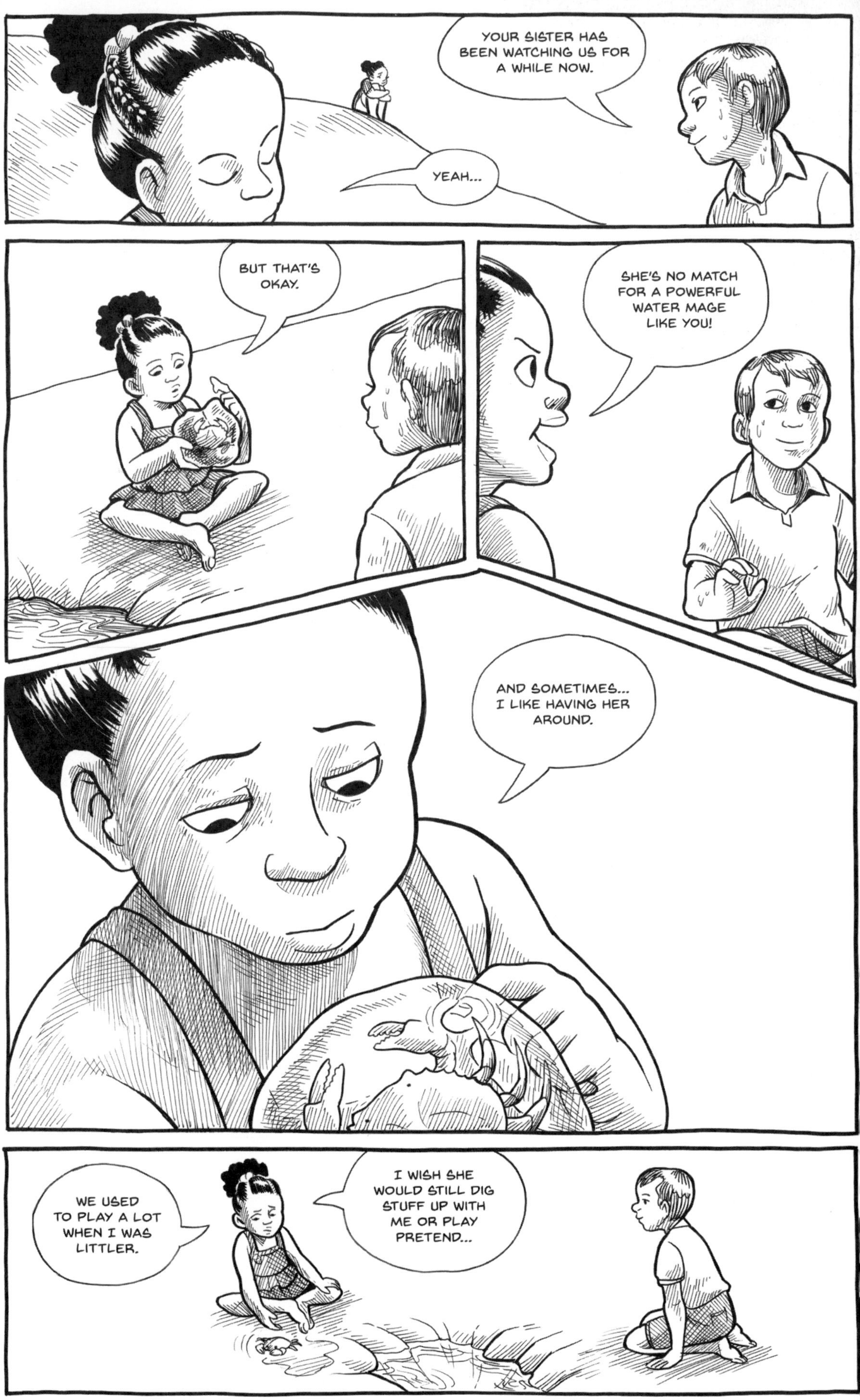
YOUR SISTER HAS BEEN WATCHING US FOR A WHILE NOW.
YEAH...
BUT THAT'S OKAY.
SHE'S NO MATCH FOR A POWERFUL WATER MAGE LIKE YOU!
AND SOMETIMES... I LIKE HAVING HER AROUND.
WE USED TO PLAY A LOT WHEN I WAS LITTLER.
I WISH SHE WOULD STILL DIG STUFF UP WITH ME OR PLAY PRETEND...

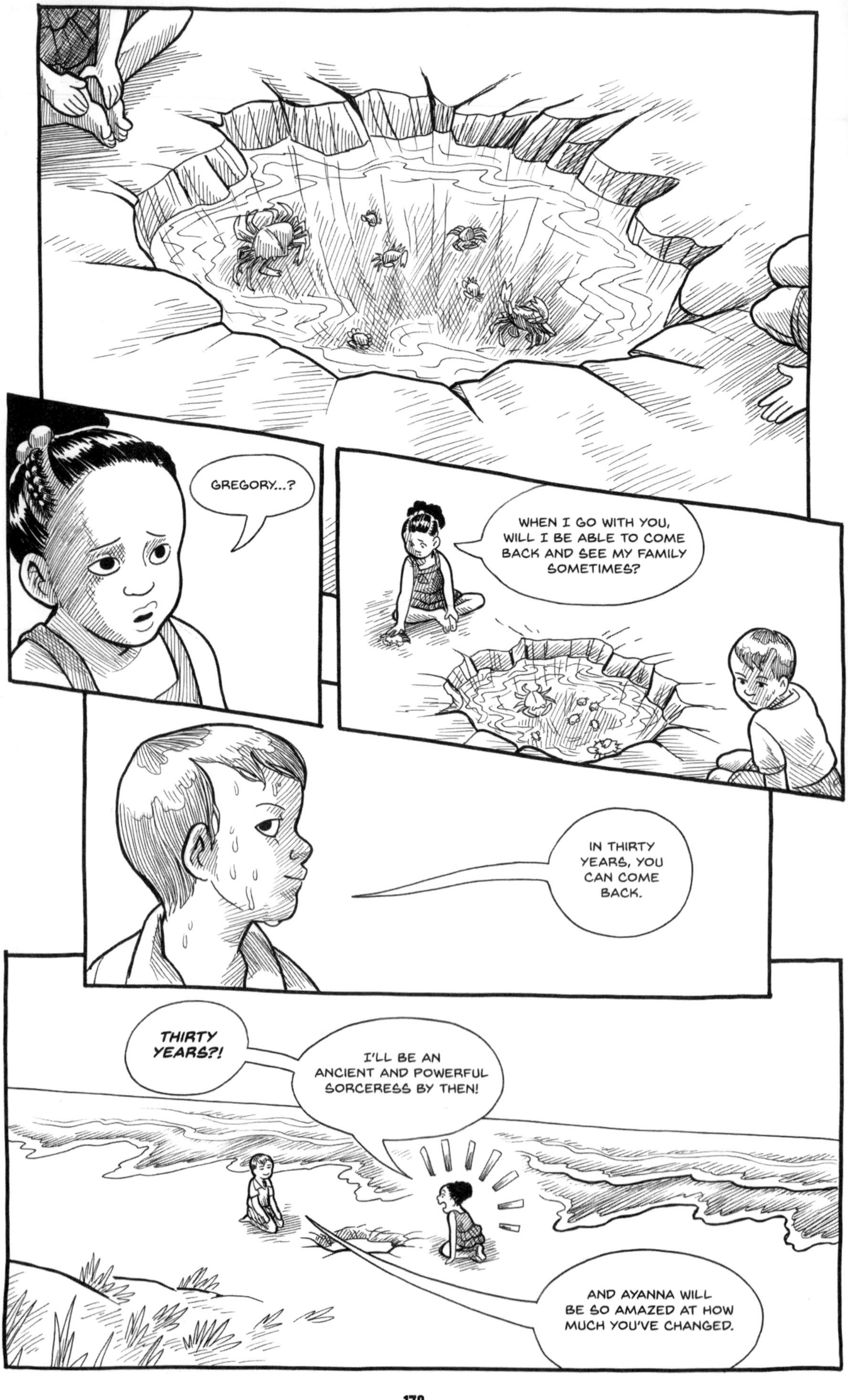
GREGORY...?
WHEN I GO WITH YOU, WILL I BE ABLE TO COME BACK AND SEE MY FAMILY SOMETIMES?
IN THIRTY YEARS, YOU CAN COME BACK.
THIRTY YEARS?!
I'LL BE AN ANCIENT AND POWERFUL SORCERESS BY THEN!
AND AYANNA WILL BE SO AMAZED AT HOW MUCH YOU'VE CHANGED.

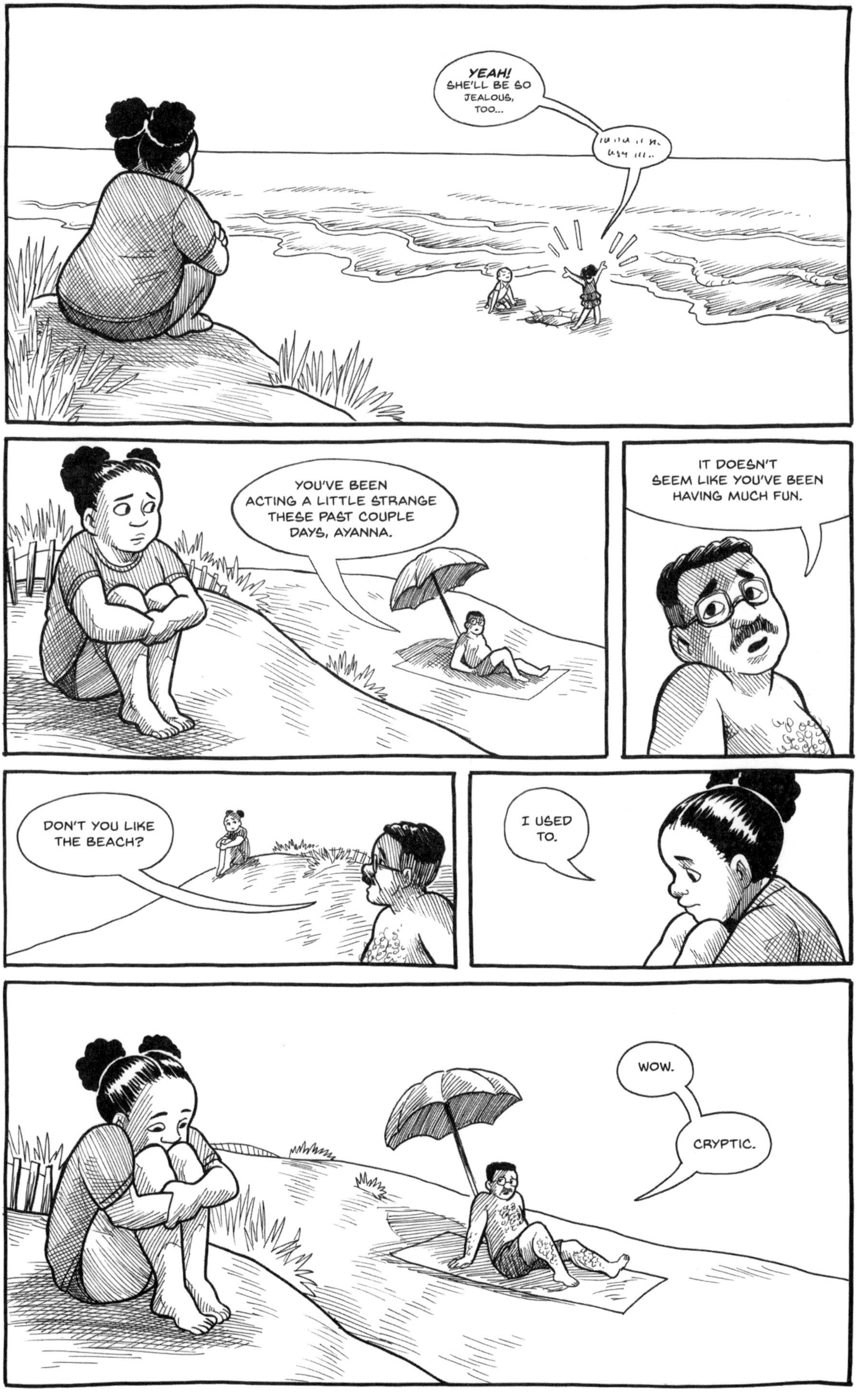
YEAH! SHE'LL BE SO JEALOUS, TOO...
YOU'VE BEEN ACTING A LITTLE STRANGE THESE PAST COUPLE DAYS, AYANNA.
IT DOESN'T SEEM LIKE YOU'VE BEEN HAVING MUCH FUN.
DON'T YOU LIKE THE BEACH?
I USED TO.
WOW.
CRYPTIC.

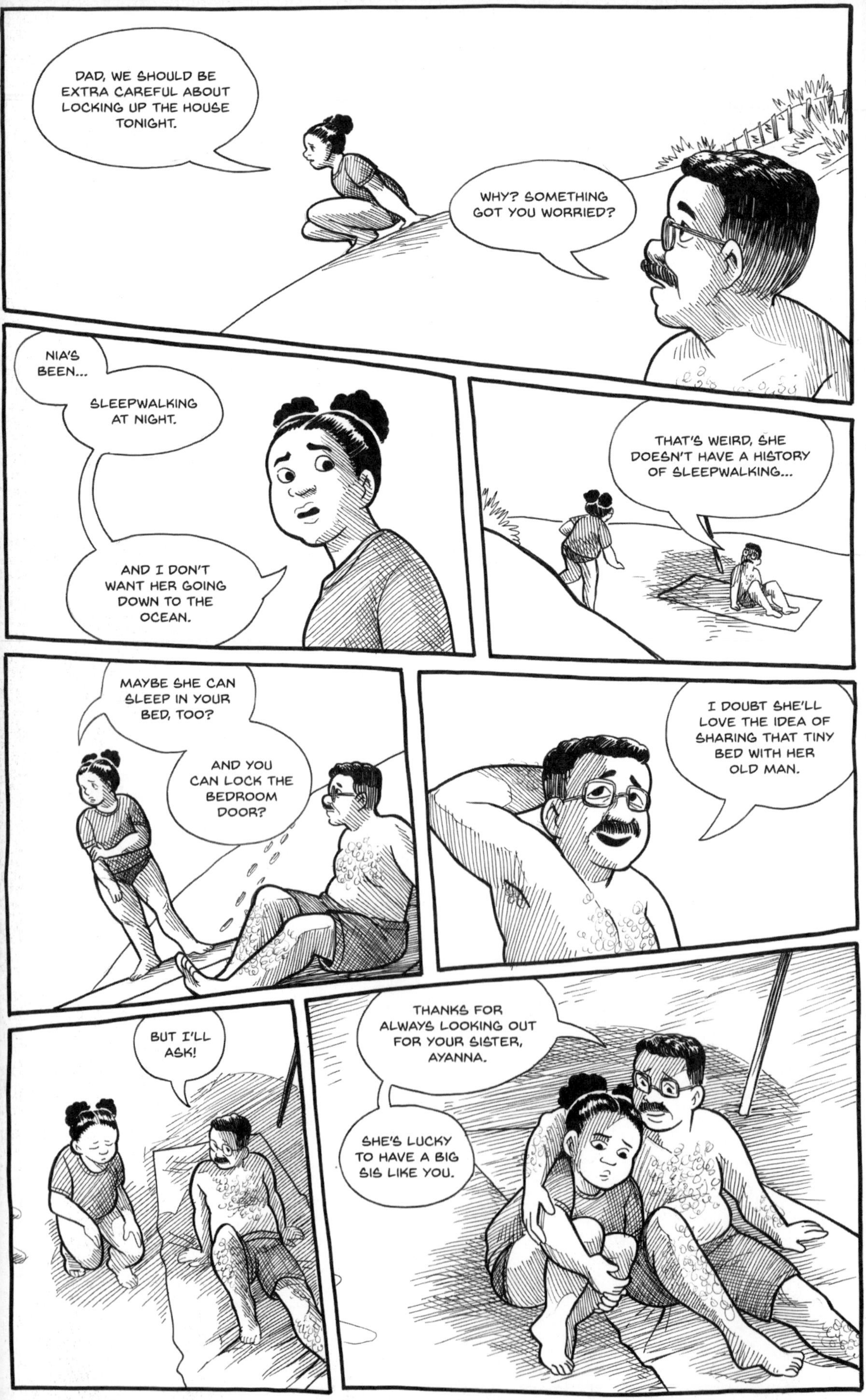
DAD, WE SHOULD BE EXTRA CAREFUL ABOUT LOCKING UP THE HOUSE TONIGHT.
WHY? SOMETHING GOT YOU WORRIED?
NIA'S BEEN...
SLEEPWALKING AT NIGHT.
AND I DON'T WANT HER GOING DOWN TO THE OCEAN.
THAT'S WEIRD, SHE DOESN'T HAVE A HISTORY OF SLEEPWALKING...
MAYBE SHE CAN SLEEP IN YOUR BED, TOO?
AND YOU CAN LOCK THE BEDROOM DOOR?
I DOUBT SHE'LL LOVE THE IDEA OF SHARING THAT TINY BED WITH HER OLD MAN.
BUT I'LL ASK!
THANKS FOR ALWAYS LOOKING OUT FOR YOUR SISTER, AYANNA.
SHE'S LUCKY TO HAVE A BIG SIS LIKE YOU.

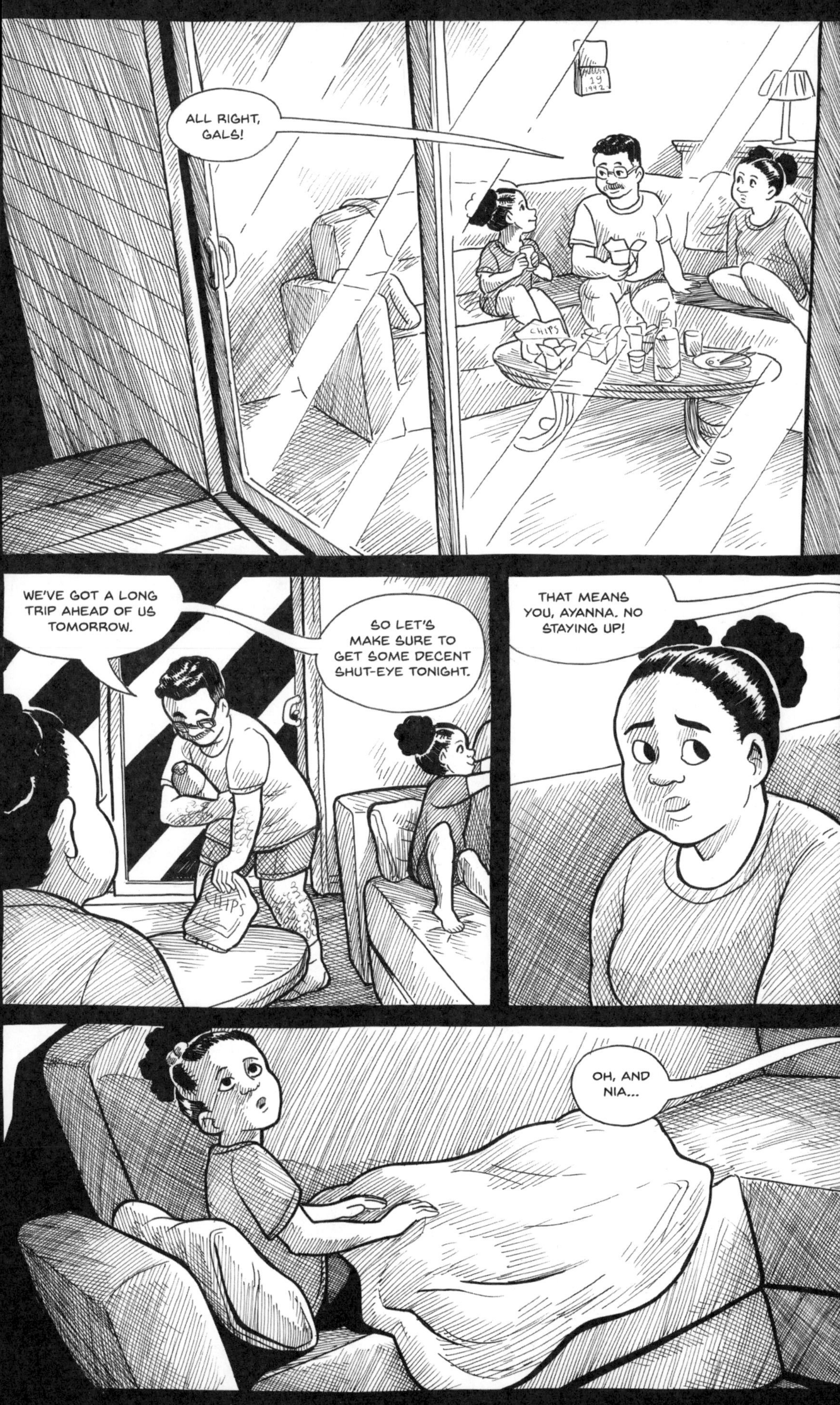
AUGUST 19 1992
ALL RIGHT, GALS!
CHIPS
WE'VE GOT A LONG TRIP AHEAD OF US TOMORROW.
SO LET'S MAKE SURE TO GET SOME DECENT SHUT-EYE TONIGHT.
CHIPS
THAT MEANS YOU, AYANNA. NO STAYING UP!
OH, AND NIA...

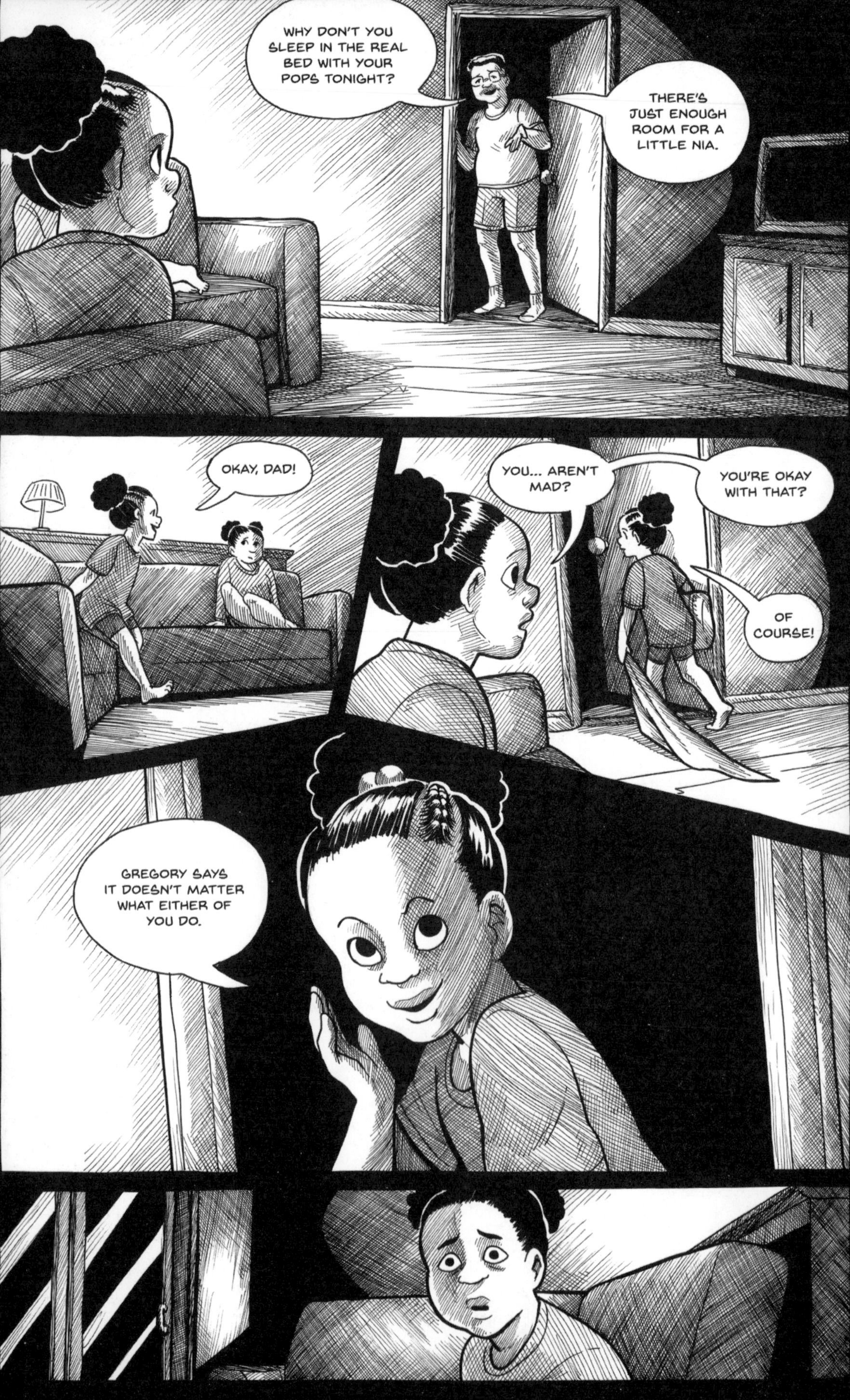
WHY DON'T YOU SLEEP IN THE REAL BED WITH YOUR POPS TONIGHT?
THERE'S JUST ENOUGH ROOM FOR A LITTLE NIA.
OKAY, DAD!
YOU... AREN'T MAD?
YOU'RE OKAY WITH THAT?
OF COURSE!
GREGORY SAYS IT DOESN'T MATTER WHAT EITHER OF YOU DO.

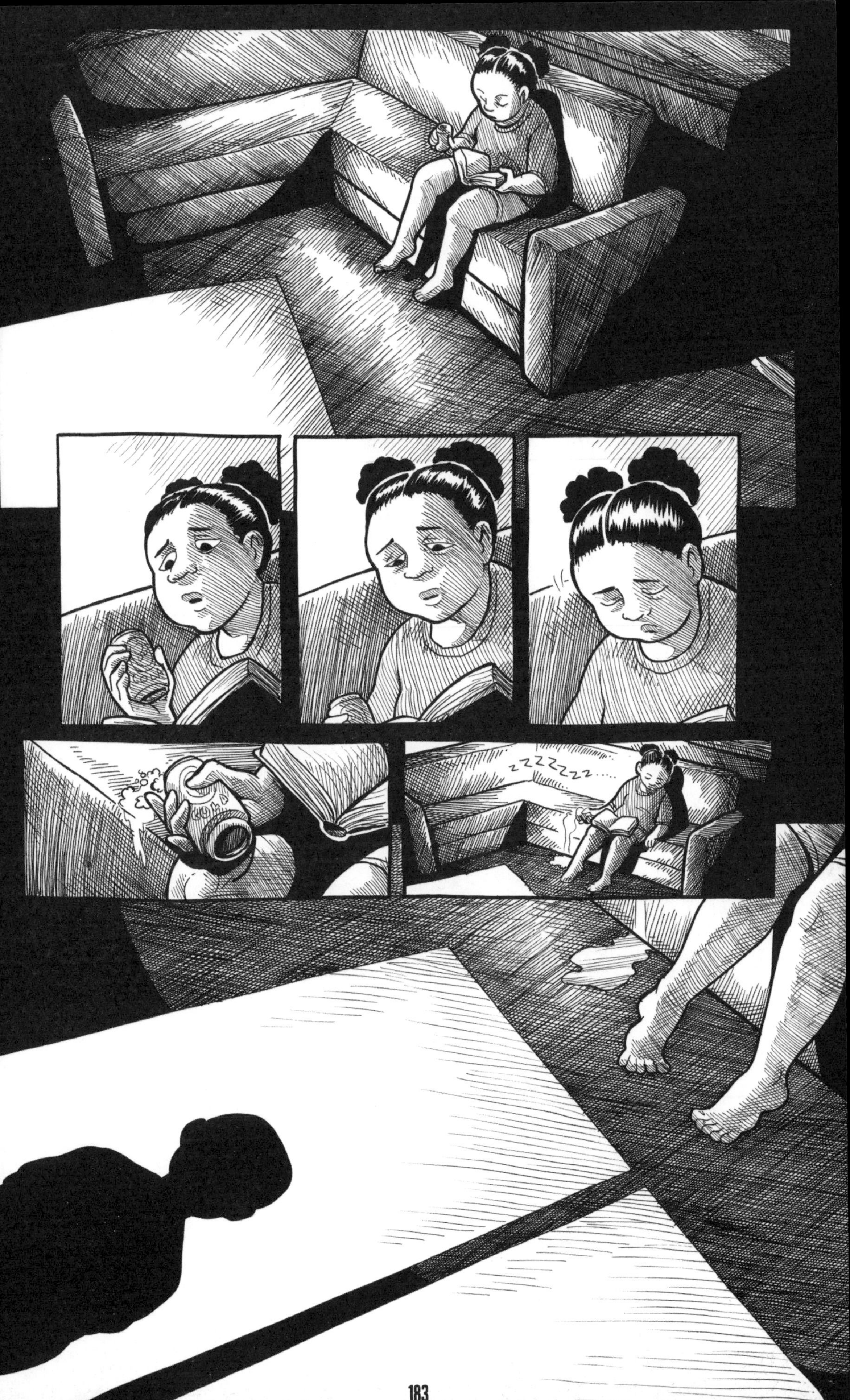
ZZZZZZZ.....

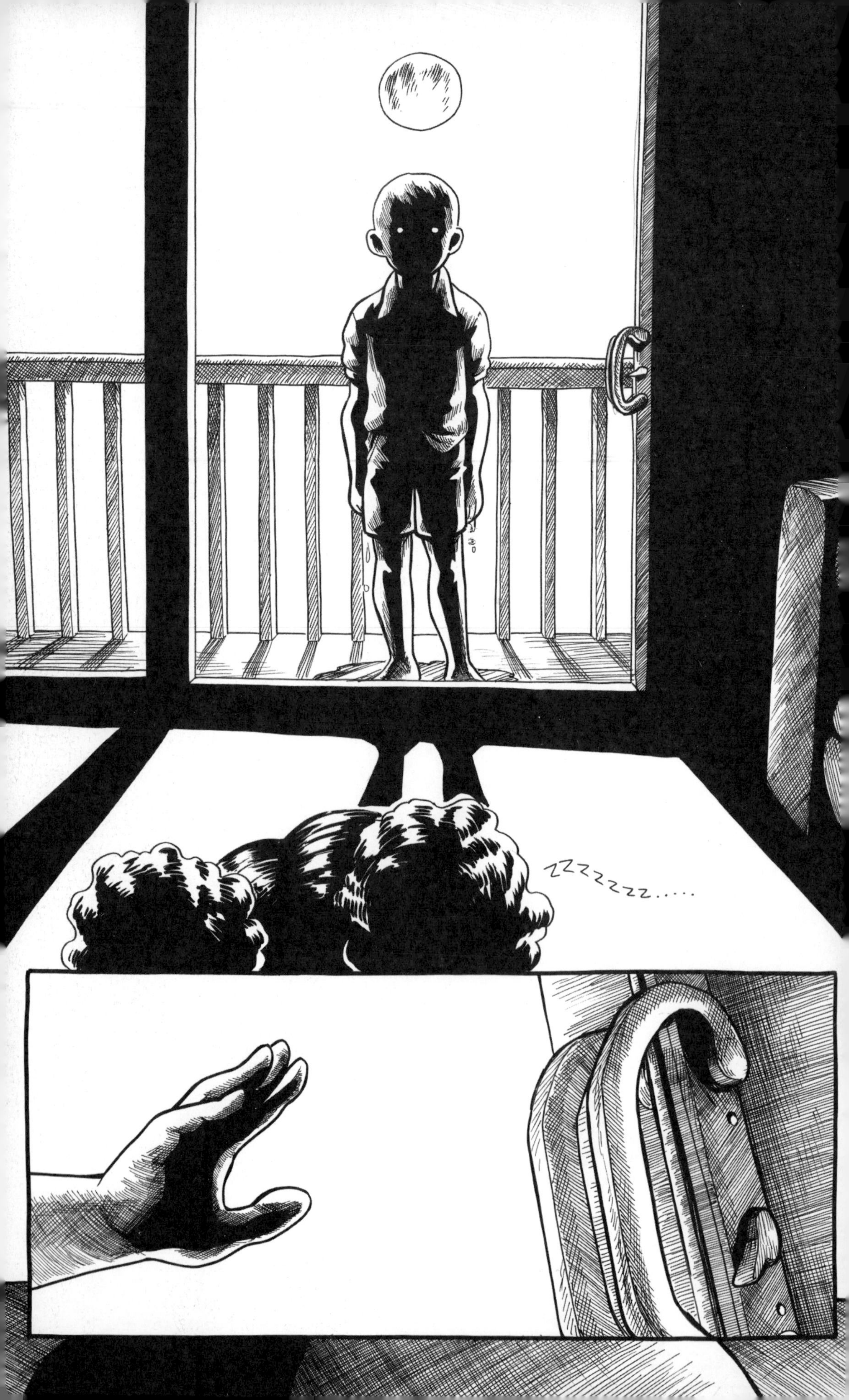
ZZZZZZZZ.....

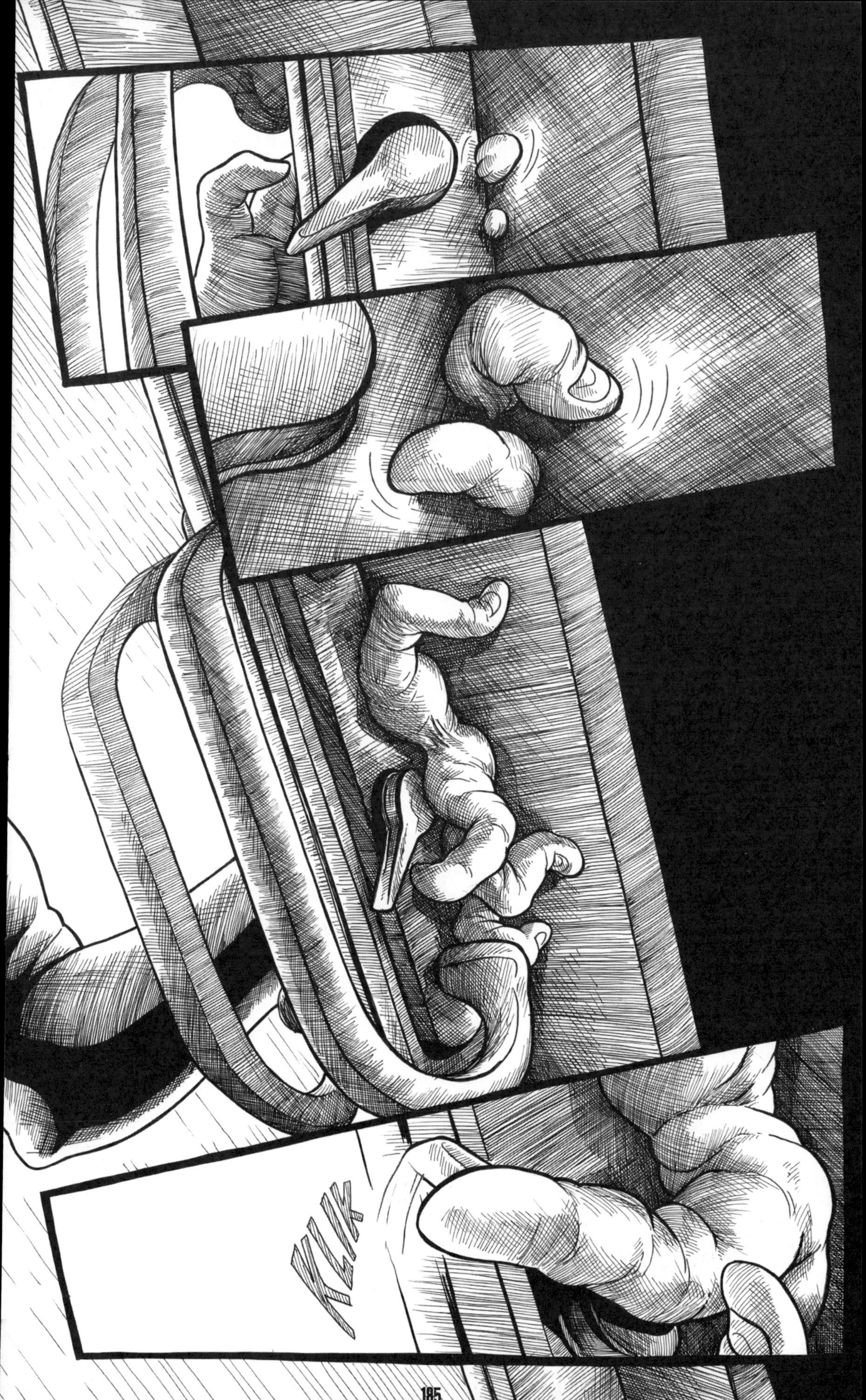
KLIK

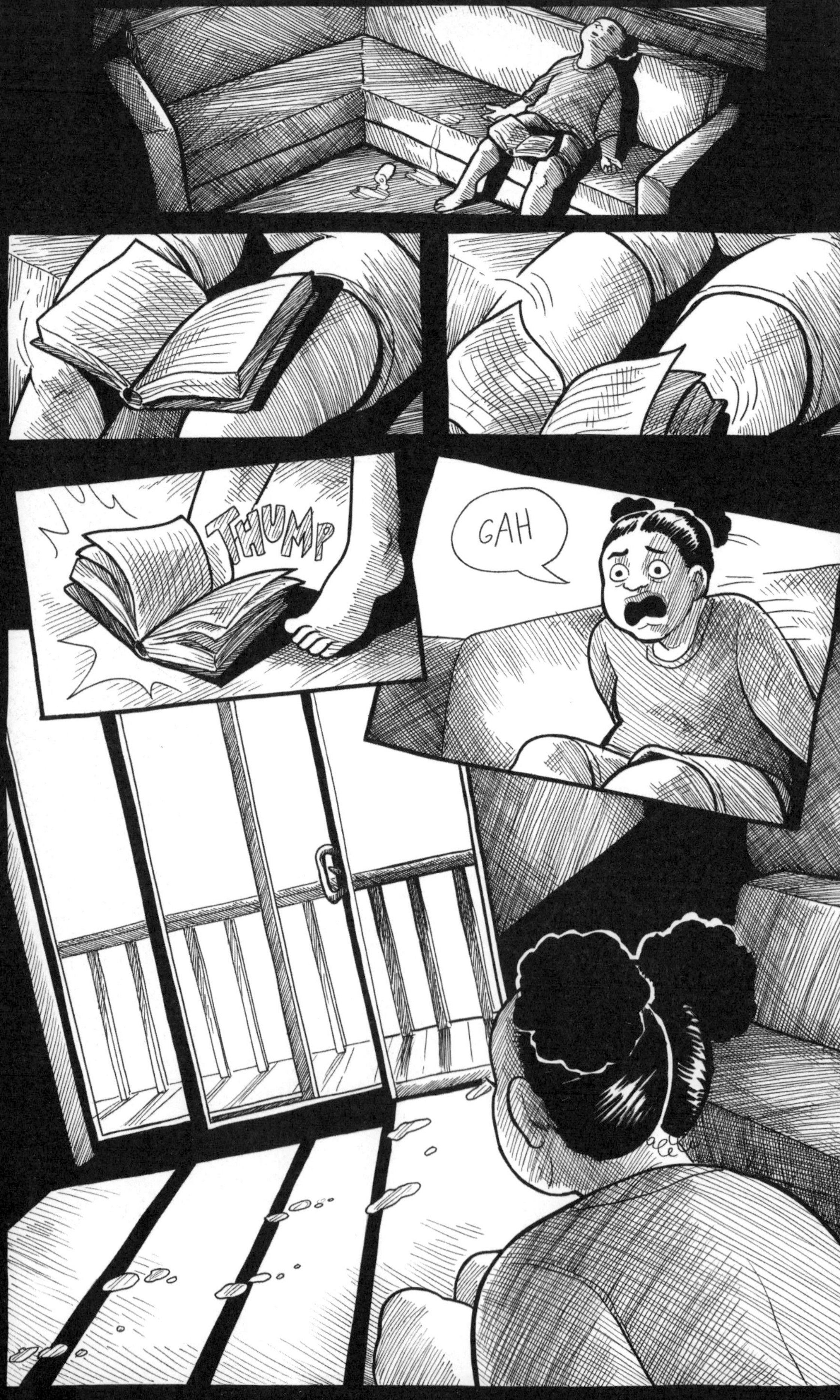
THUMP
GAH

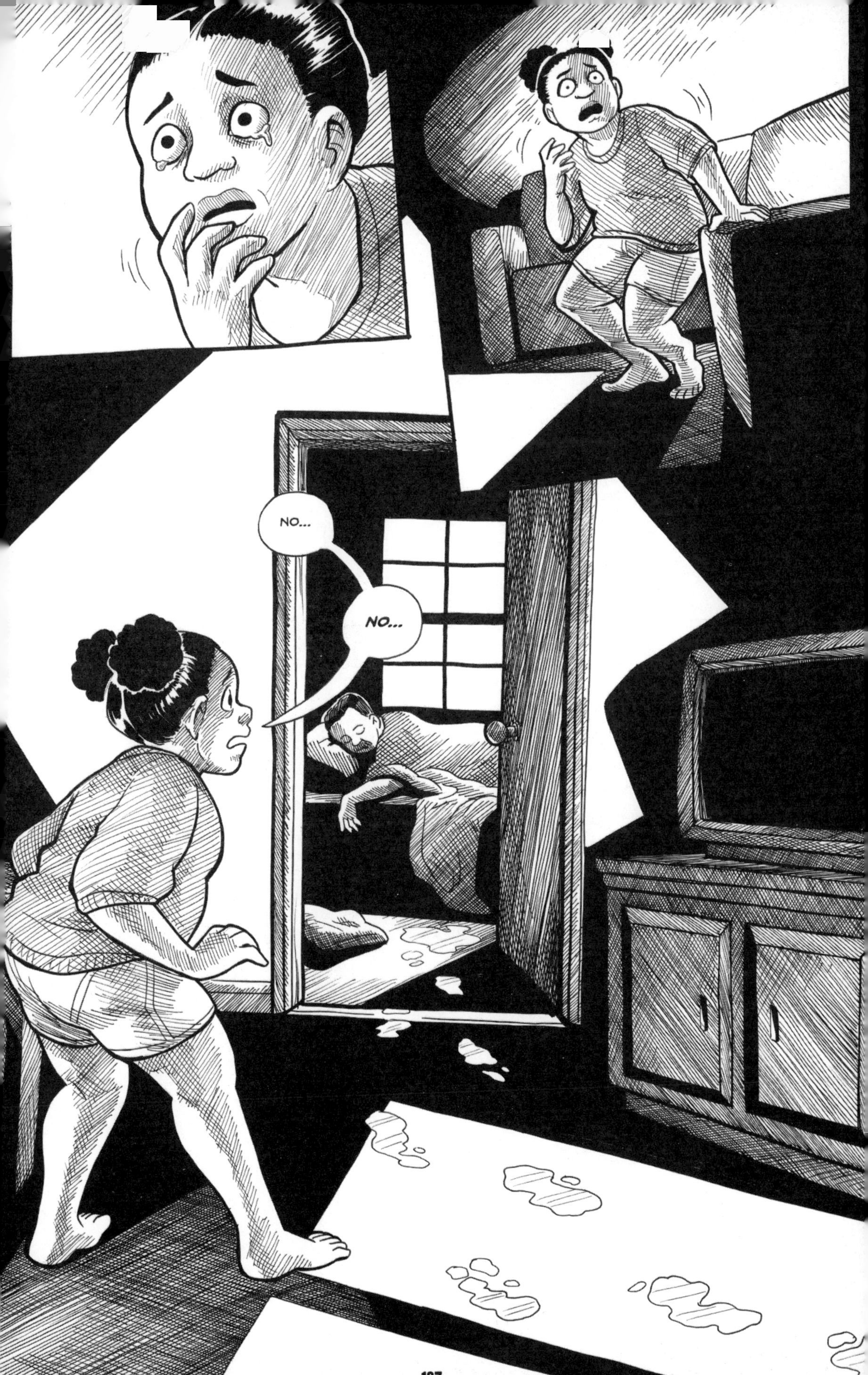
NO...
NO...

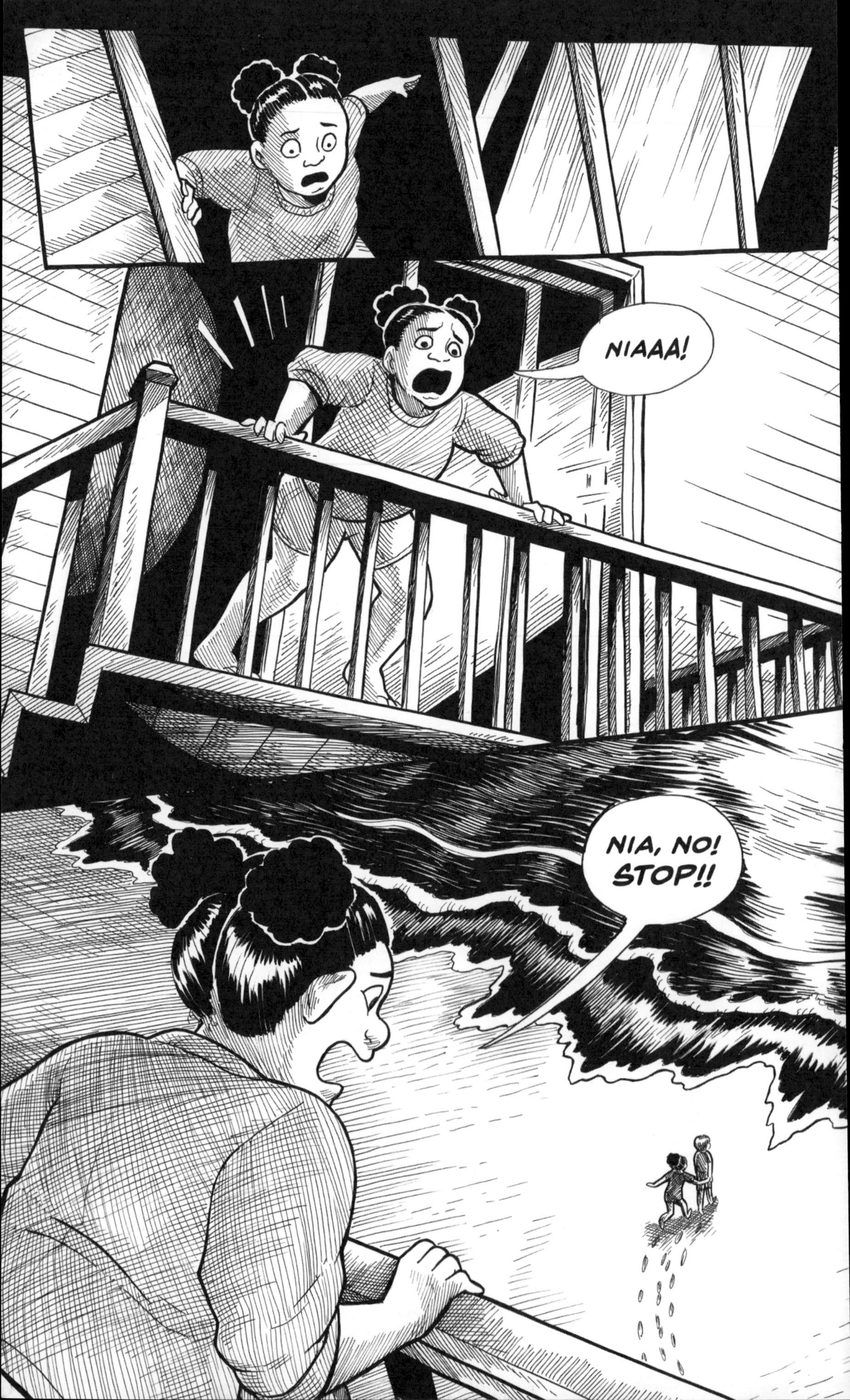
NIAAA!
NIA, NO! STOP!!

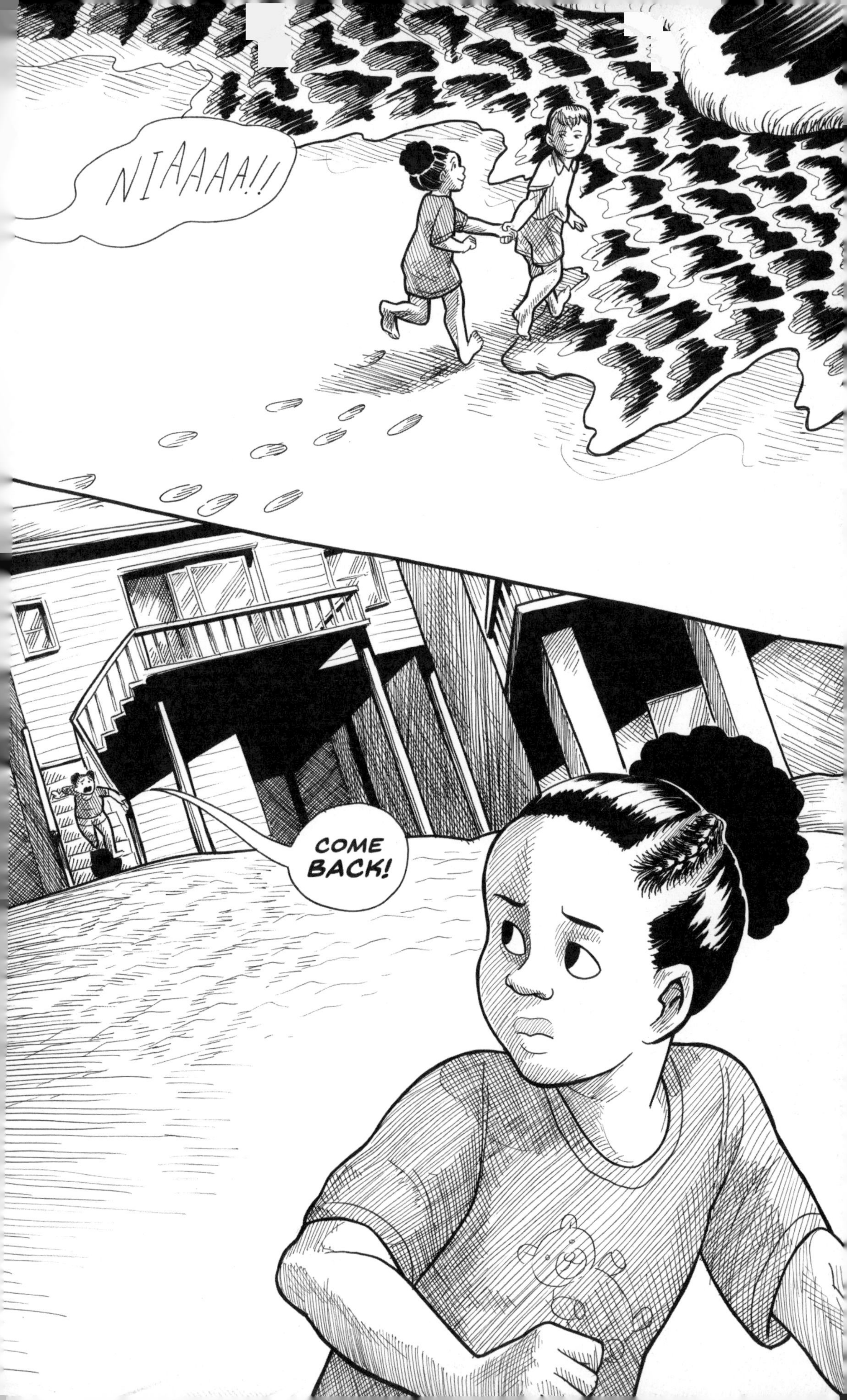
NIAAAA!!
COME BACK!

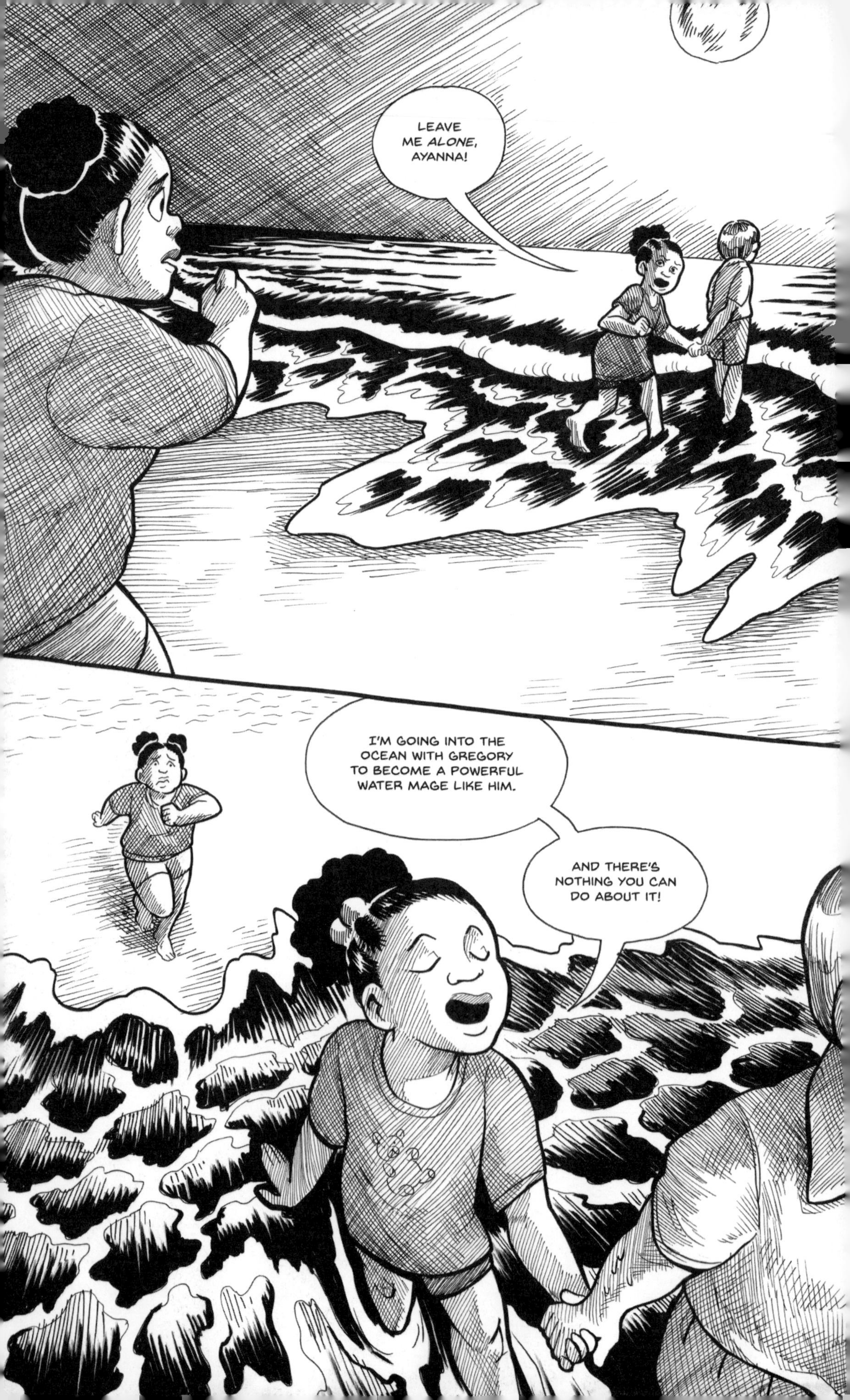
LEAVE ME *ALONE*, AYANNA!
I'M GOING INTO THE OCEAN WITH GREGORY TO BECOME A POWERFUL WATER MAGE LIKE HIM.
AND THERE'S NOTHING YOU CAN DO ABOUT IT!

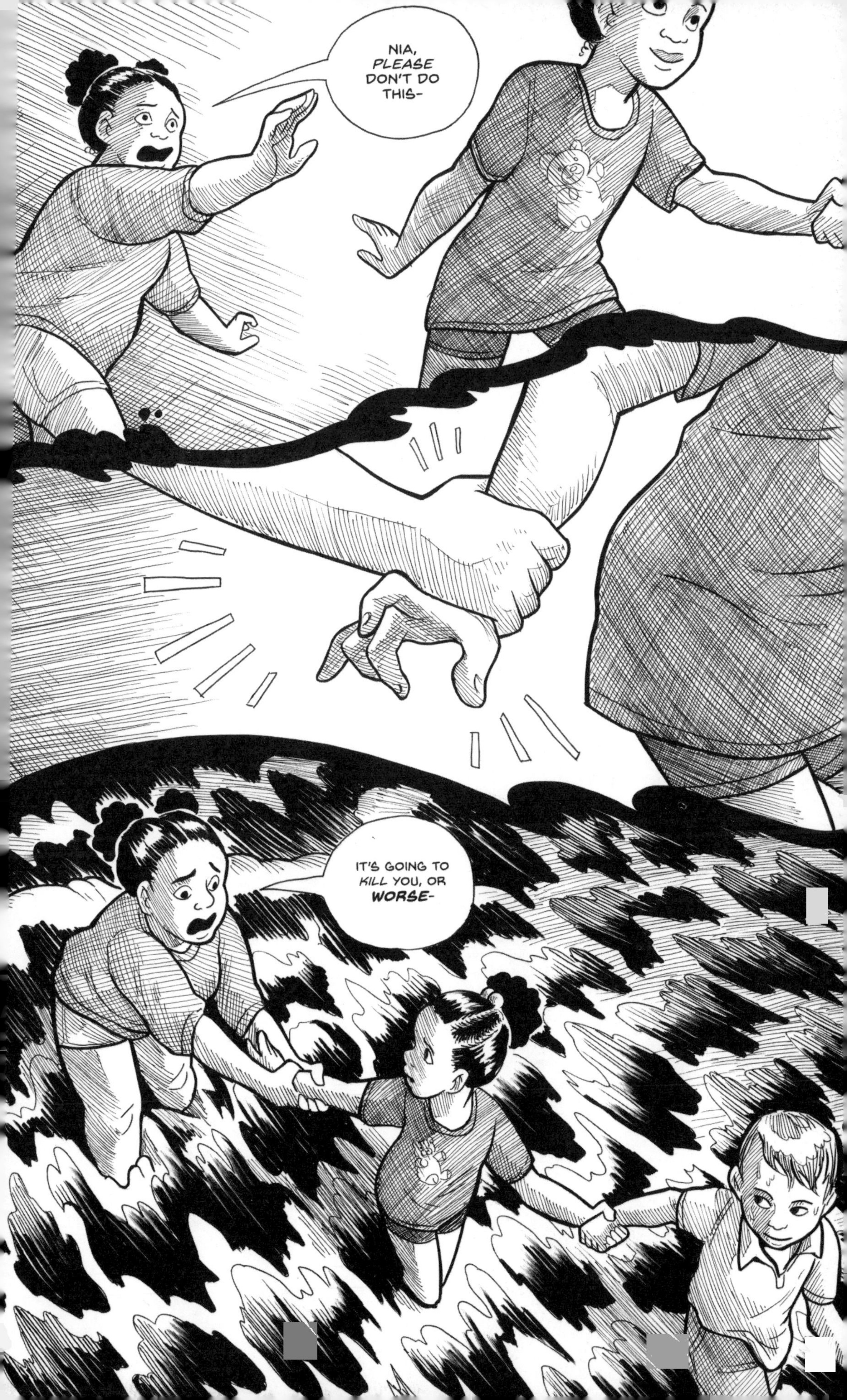
NIA, PLEASE DON'T DO THIS-
IT'S GOING TO KILL YOU, OR WORSE-

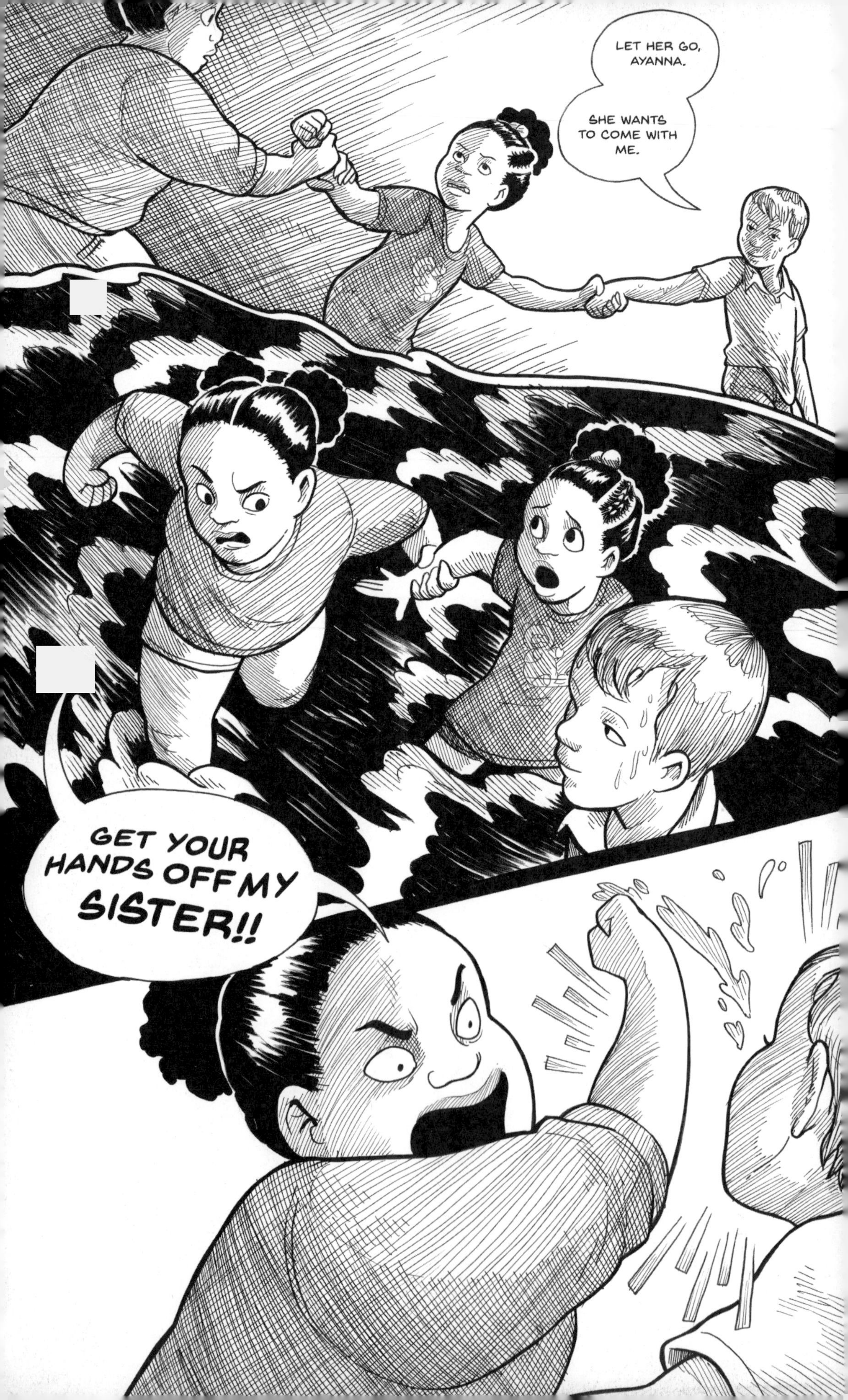
LET HER GO, AYANNA.
SHE WANTS TO COME WITH ME.
GET YOUR HANDS OFF MY SISTER!!

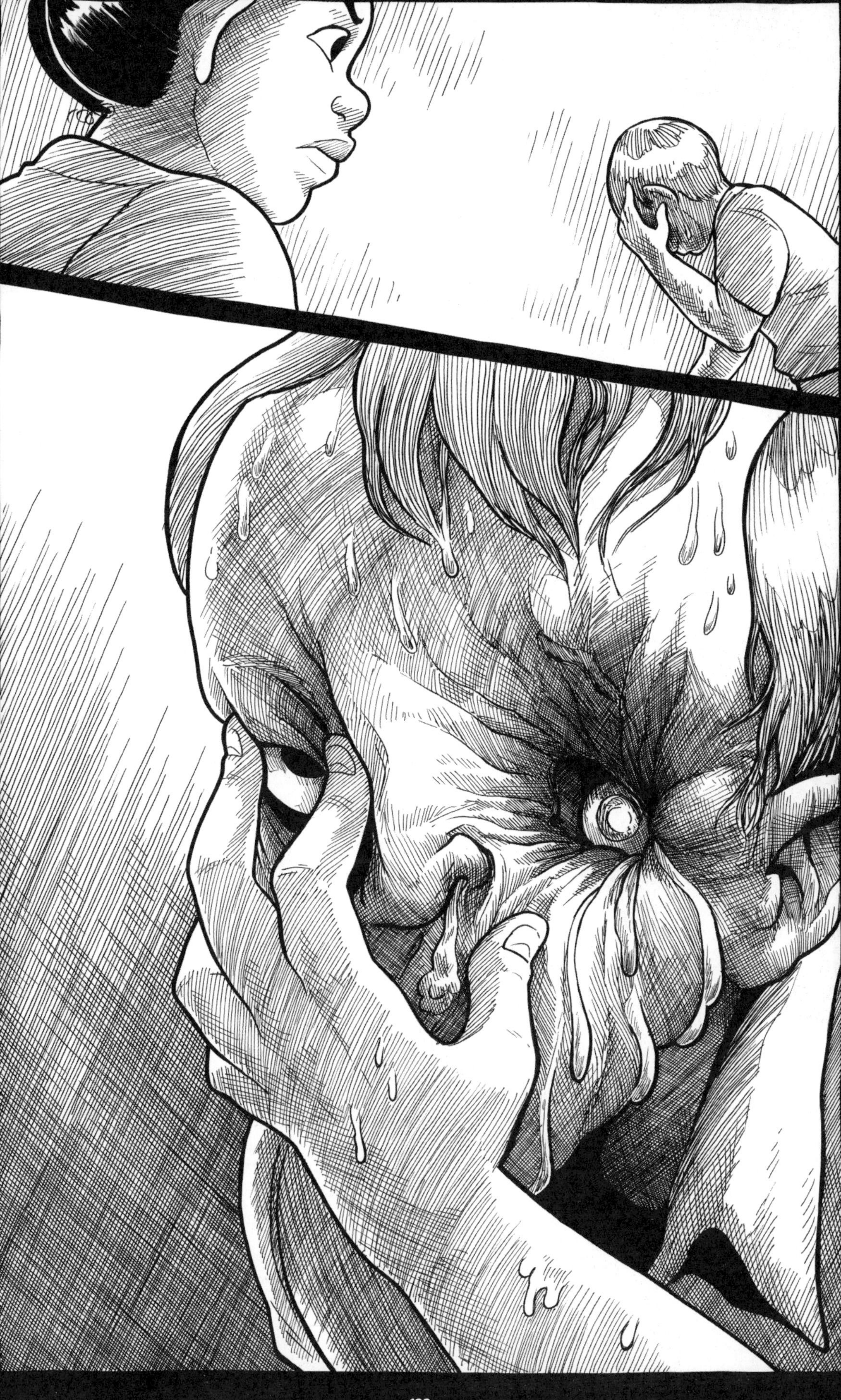

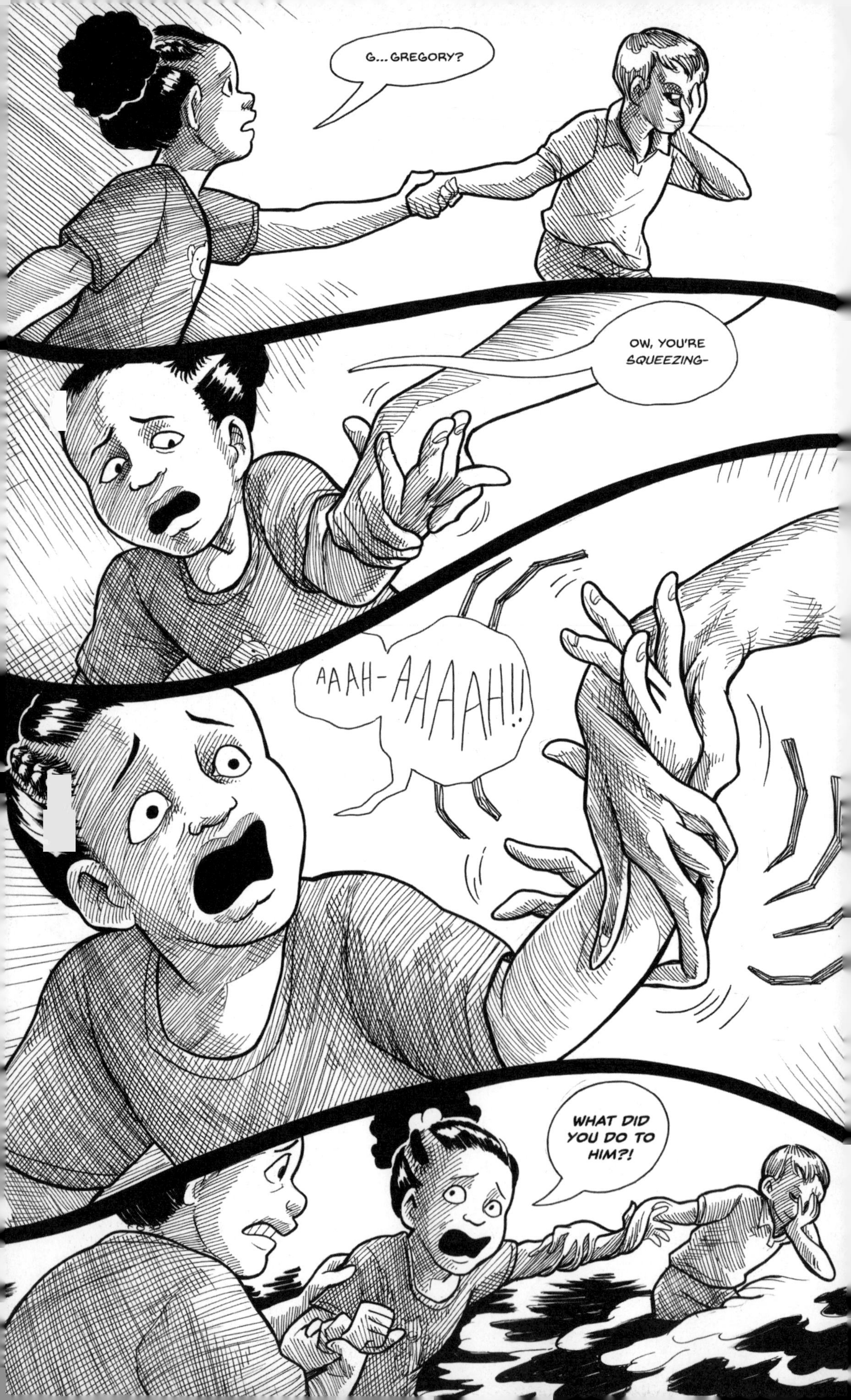
G... GREGORY?
OW, YOU'RE SQUEEZING-
AAAH-AAAAH!!
WHAT DID YOU DO TO HIM?!

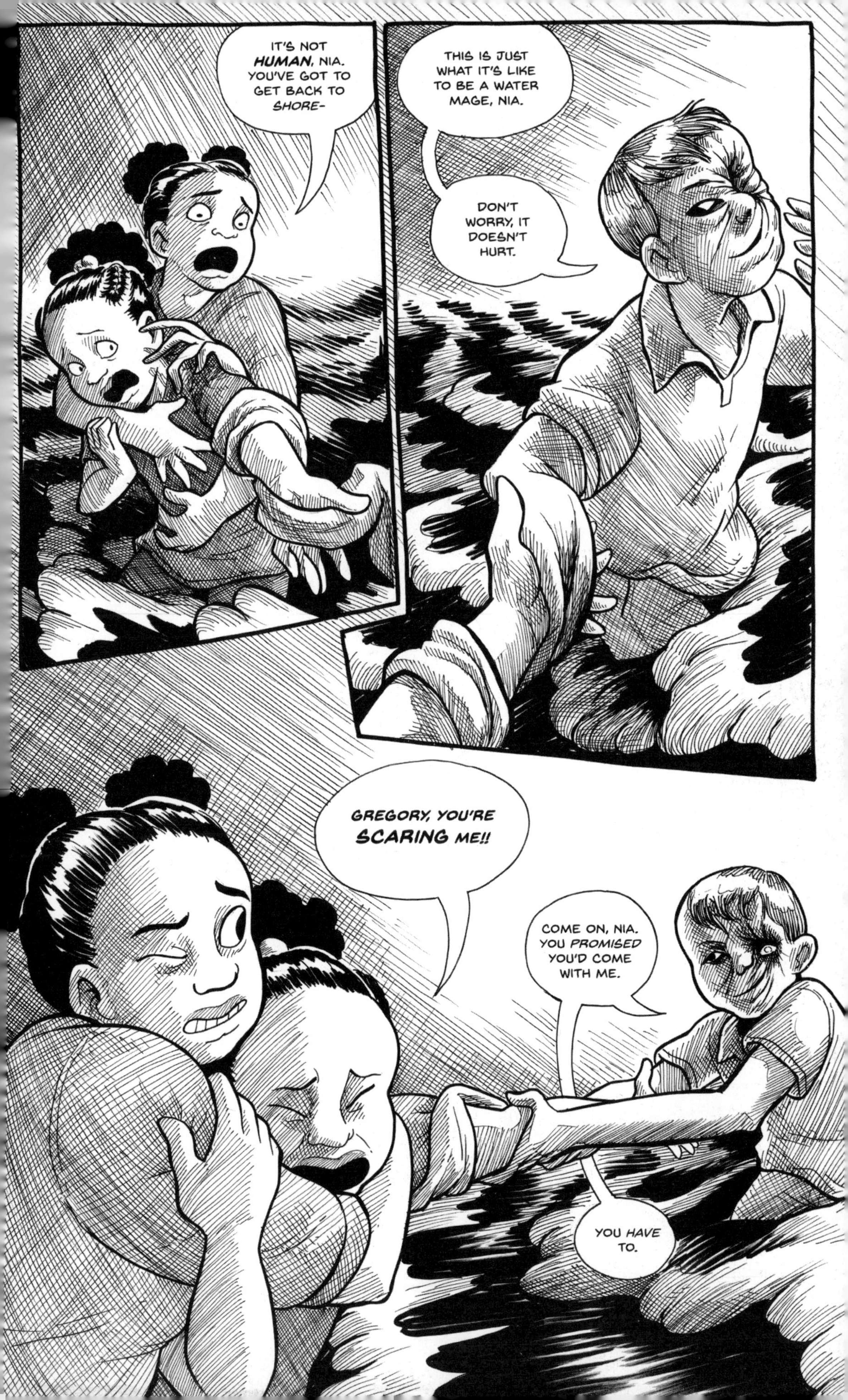
IT'S NOT *HUMAN*, NIA. YOU'VE GOT TO GET BACK TO *SHORE*-
THIS IS JUST WHAT IT'S LIKE TO BE A WATER MAGE, NIA.
DON'T WORRY, IT DOESN'T HURT.
GREGORY, YOU'RE SCARING ME!!
COME ON, NIA. YOU *PROMISED* YOU'D COME WITH ME.
YOU *HAVE* TO.

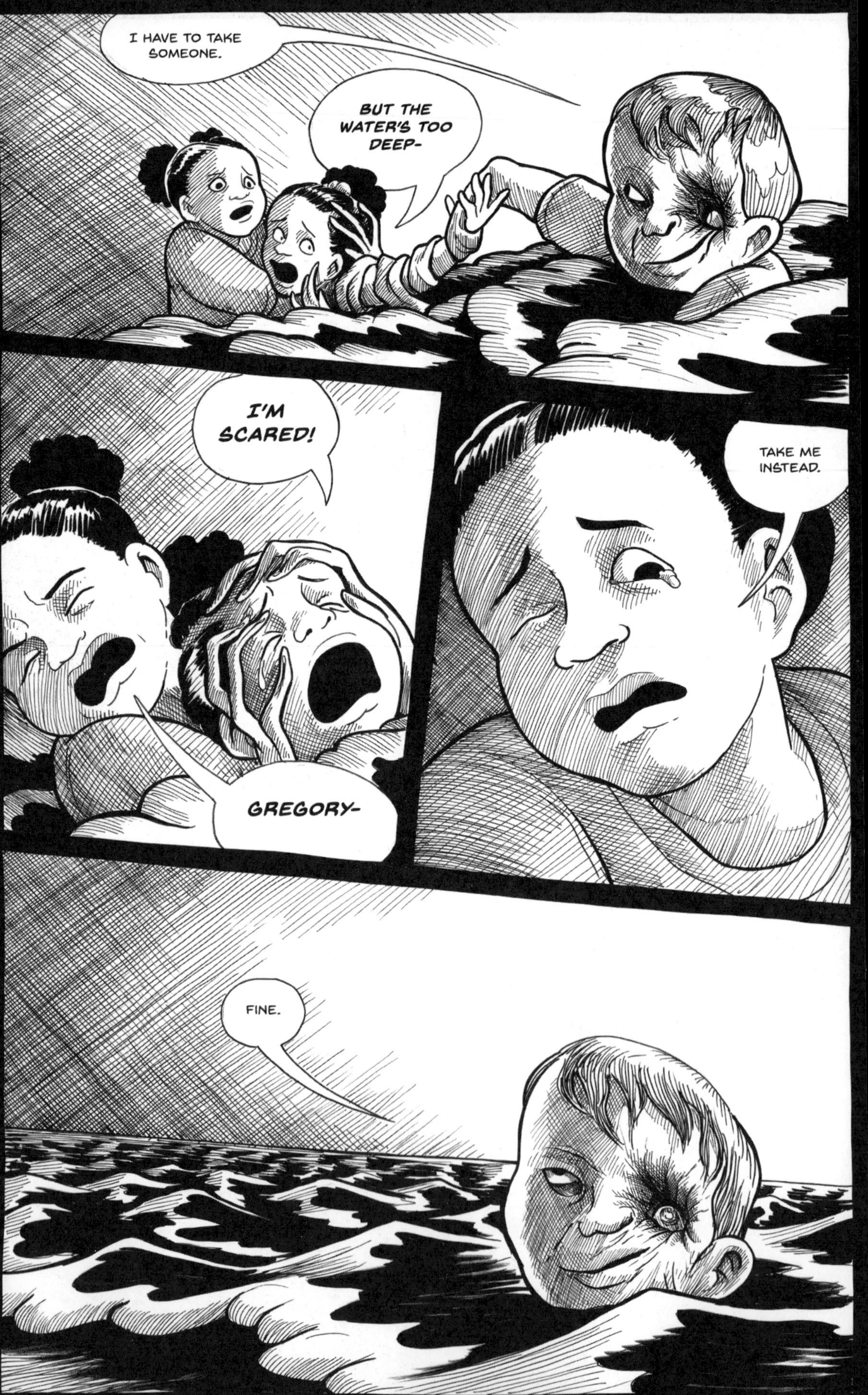
I HAVE TO TAKE SOMEONE.
BUT THE WATER'S TOO DEEP-
I'M SCARED!
GREGORY-
TAKE ME INSTEAD.
FINE.

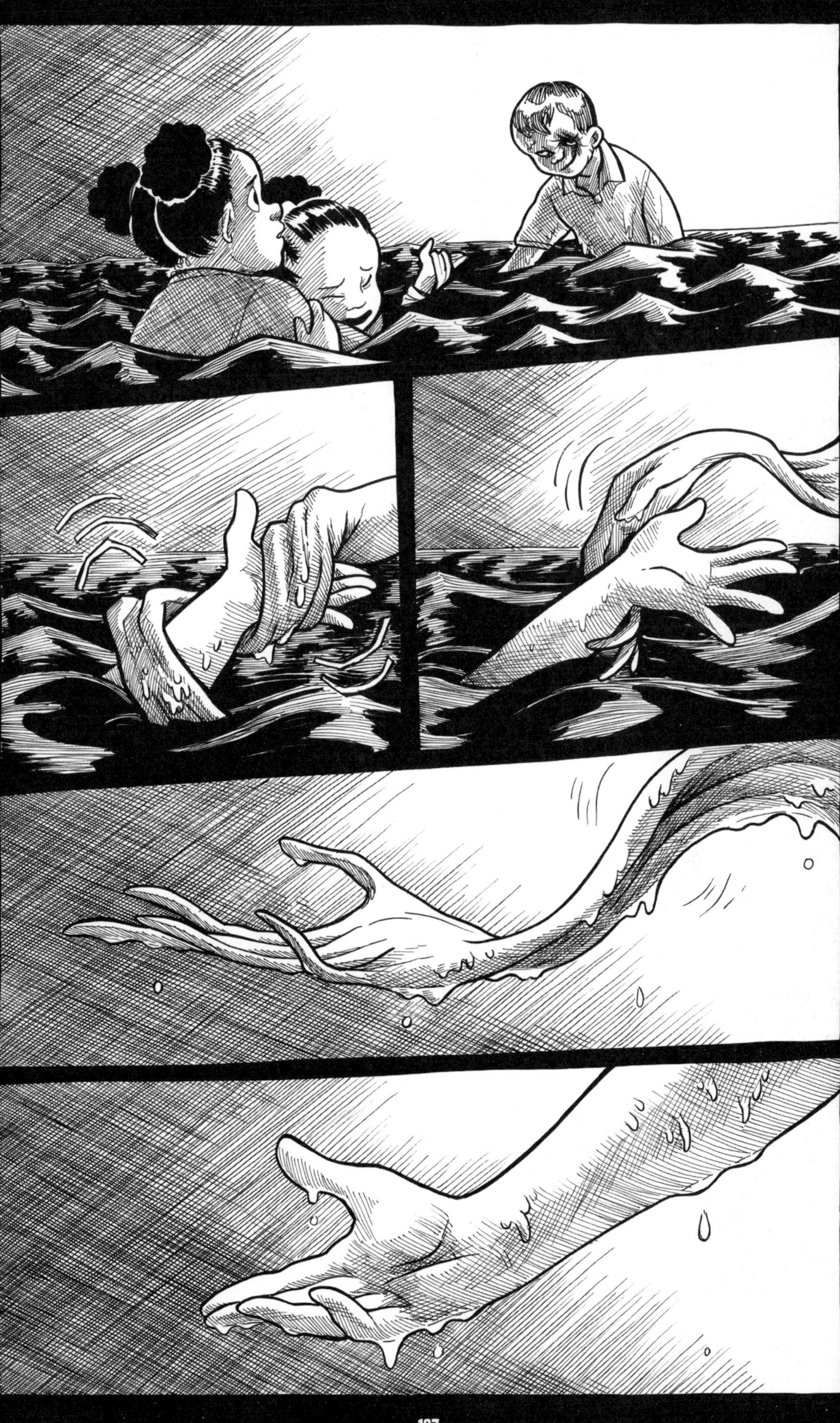

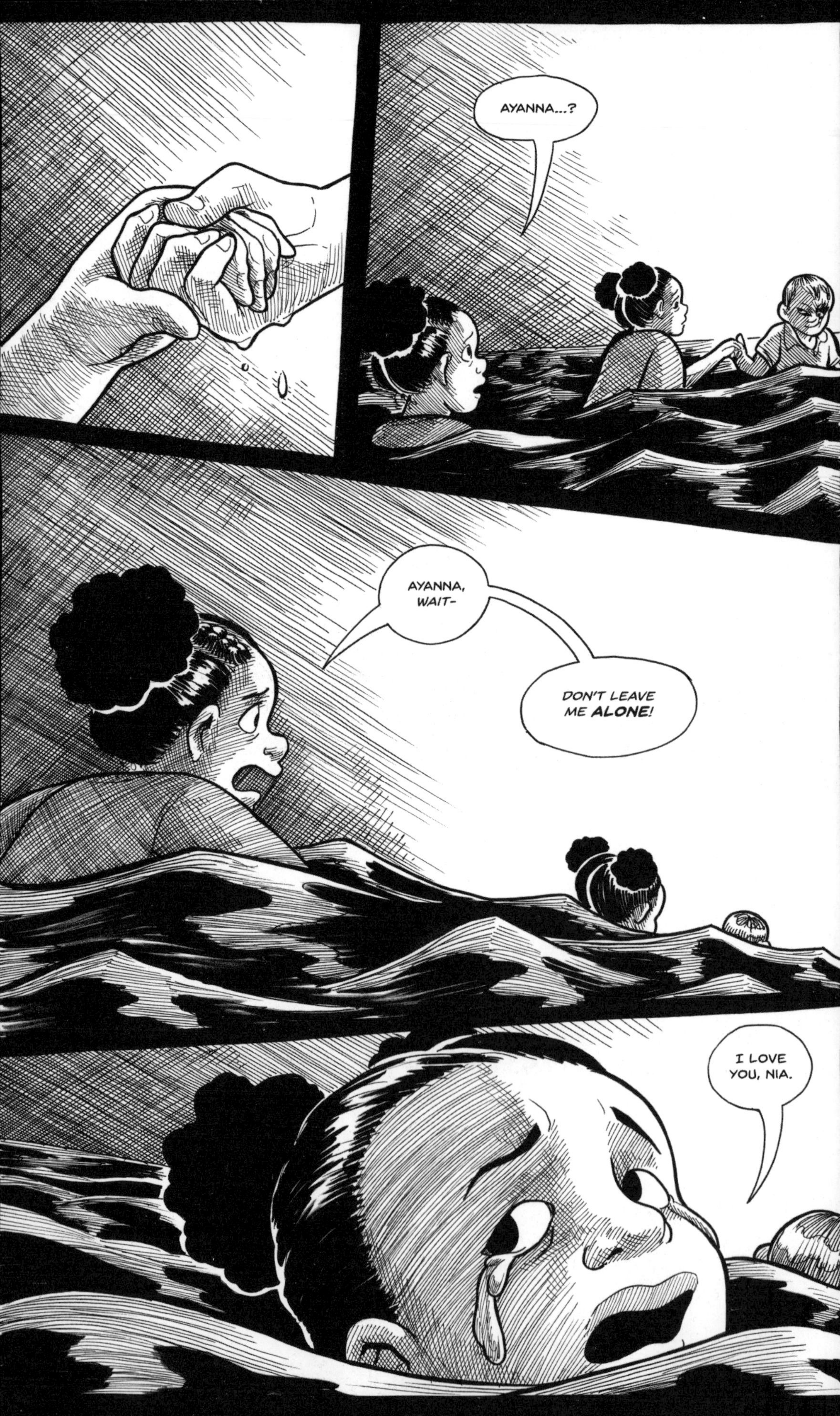
AYANNA...?
AYANNA, WAIT-
DON'T LEAVE ME ALONE!
I LOVE YOU, NIA.

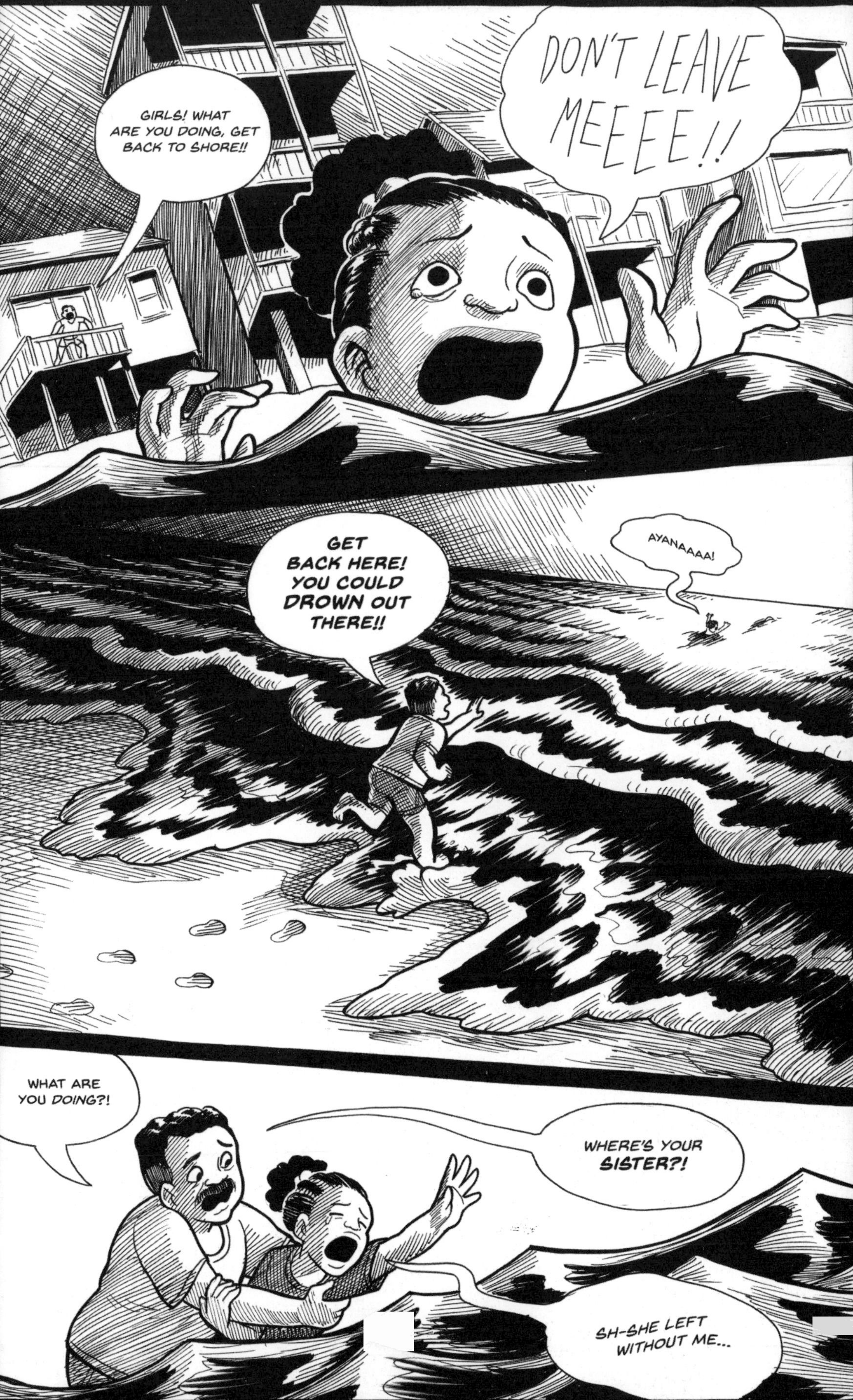
GIRLS! WHAT ARE YOU DOING, GET BACK TO SHORE!!
DON'T LEAVE MEEEEE!!
GET BACK HERE! YOU COULD DROWN OUT THERE!!
AYANAAAA!
WHAT ARE YOU DOING?!
WHERE'S YOUR SISTER?!
SH-SHE LEFT WITHOUT ME...

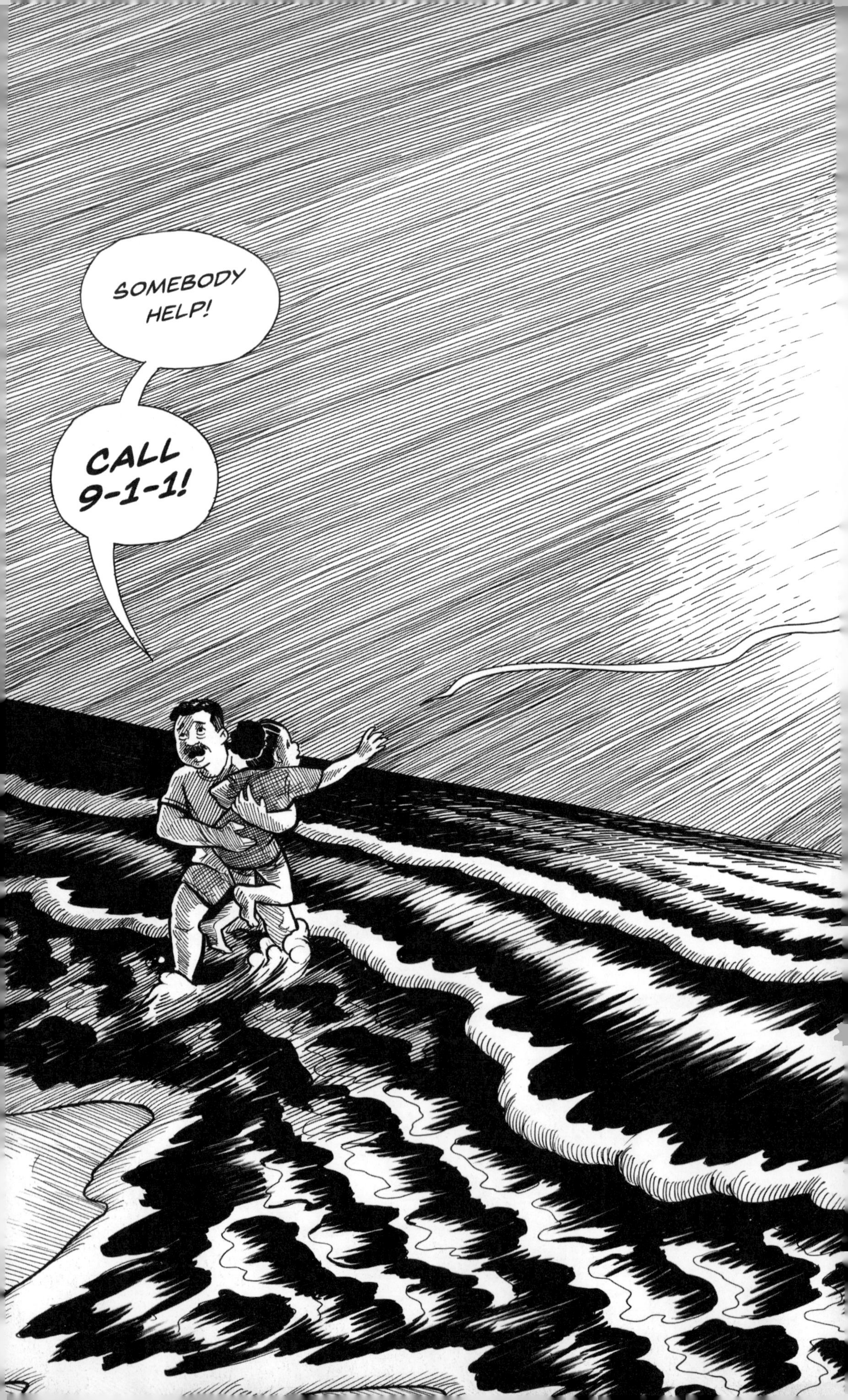
SOMEBODY HELP!
CALL 9-1-1!

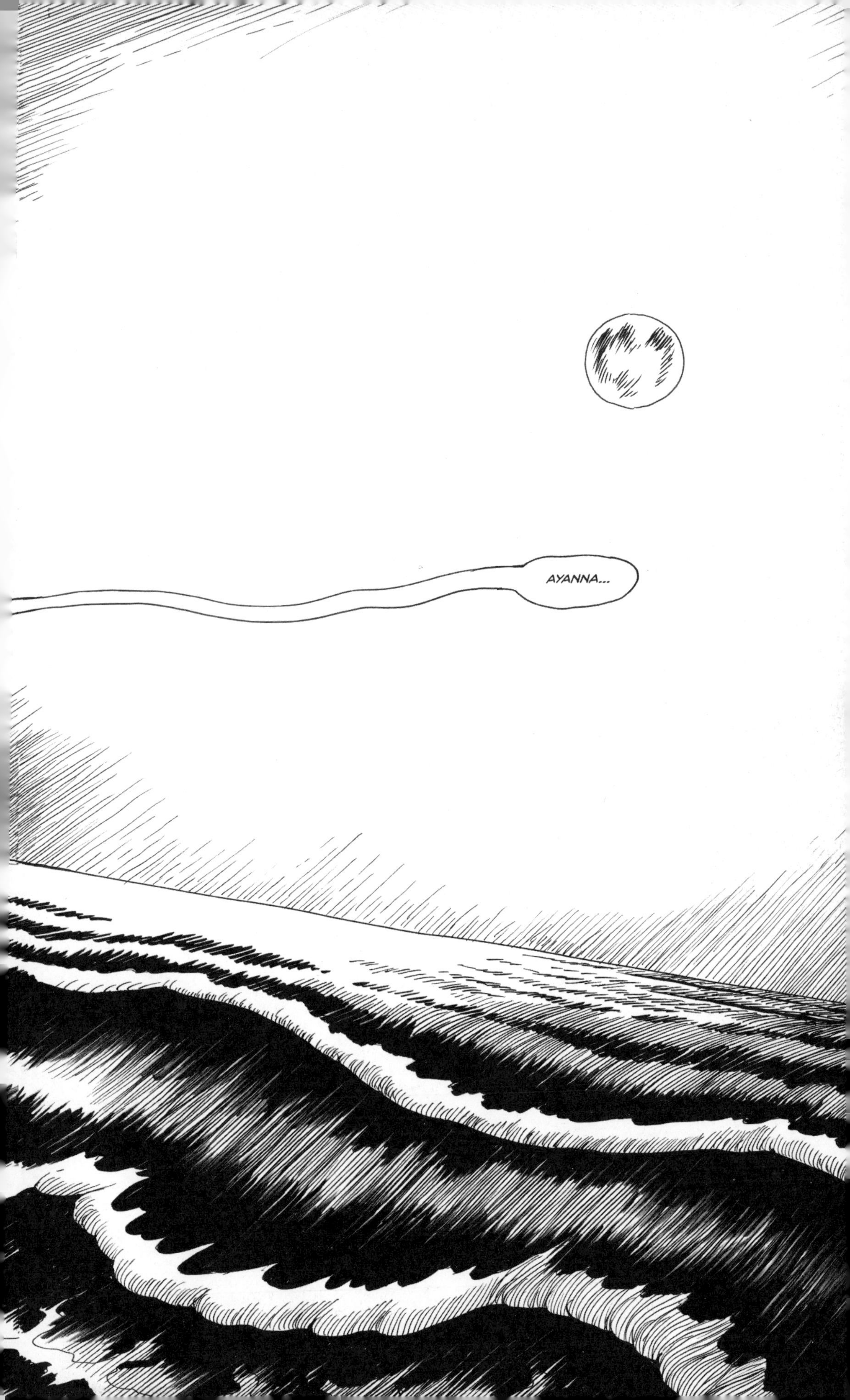
AYANNA...

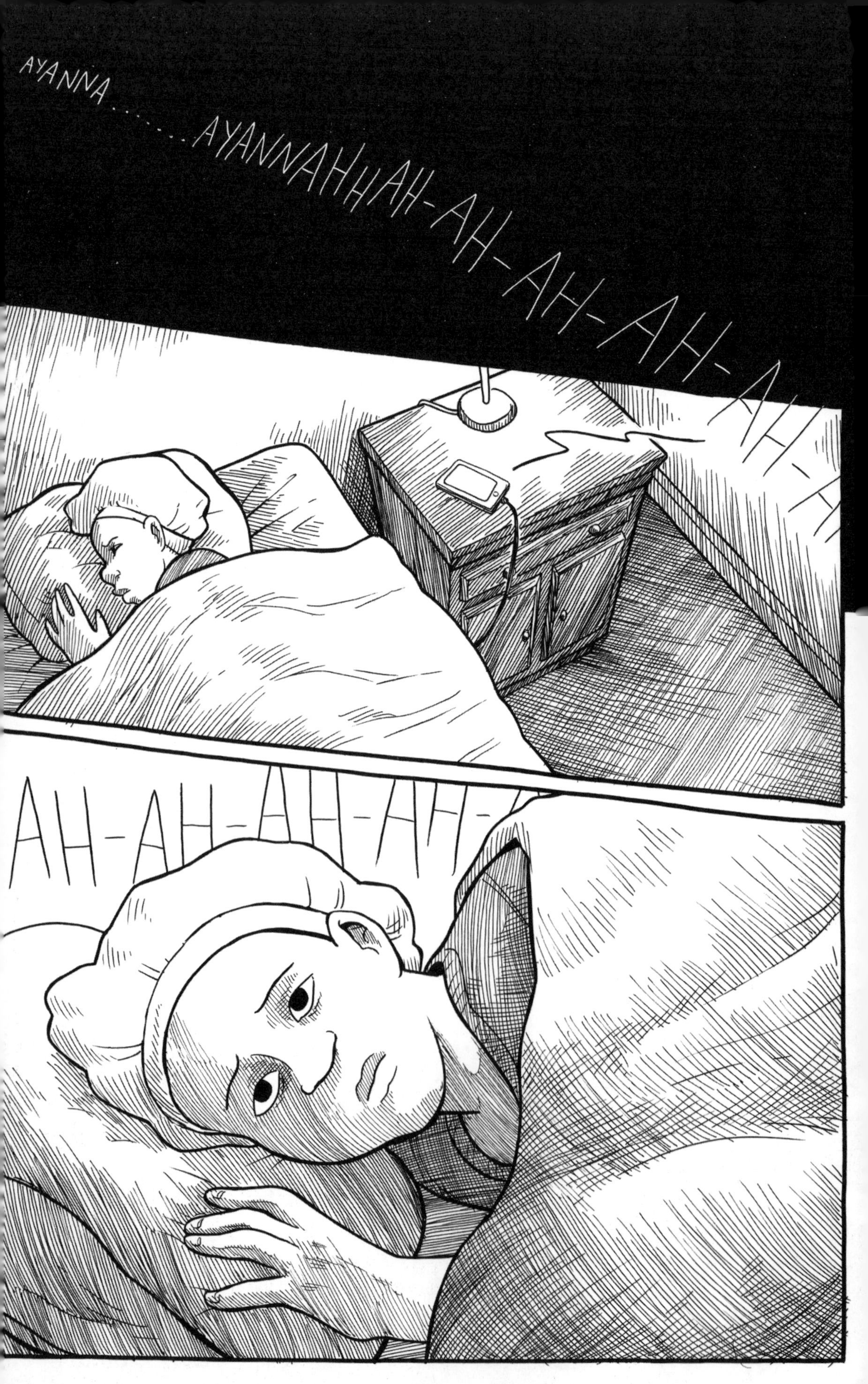
AYANNA..........AYANNAHHHAH-AH-AH-AH-AH-AH-A
AH-AH-AH-AH-

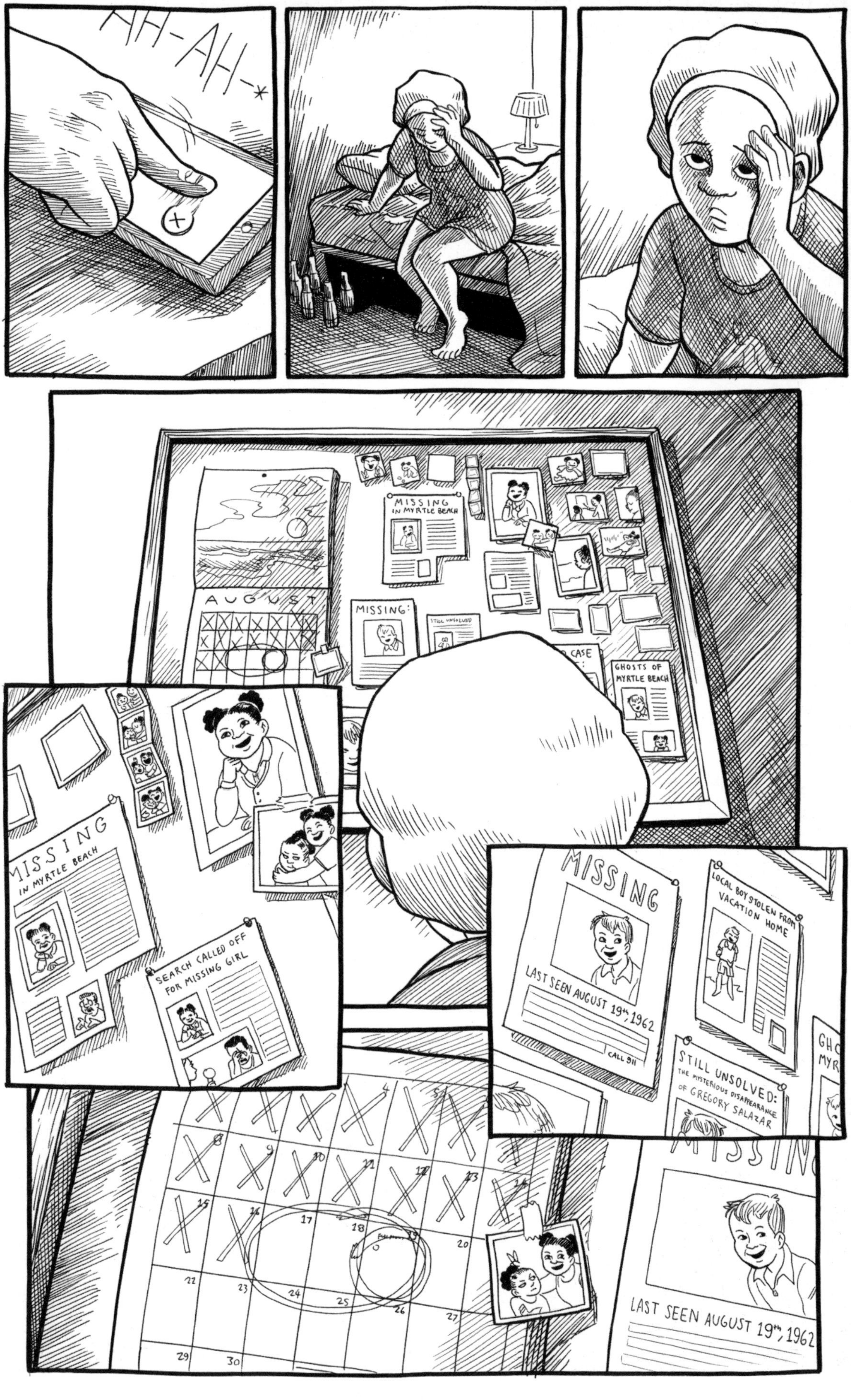
AH-AH-*
MISSING IN MYRTLE BEACH
AUGUST
MISSING:
STILL UNSOLVED
GHOSTS OF MYRTLE BEACH
MISSING IN MYRTLE BEACH
SEARCH CALLED OFF FOR MISSING GIRL
MISSING
LAST SEEN AUGUST 19th, 1962
CALL 911
LOCAL BOY STOLEN FROM VACATION HOME
STILL UNSOLVED: THE MYSTERIOUS DISAPPEARANCE OF GREGORY SALAZAR
LAST SEEN AUGUST 19th, 1962

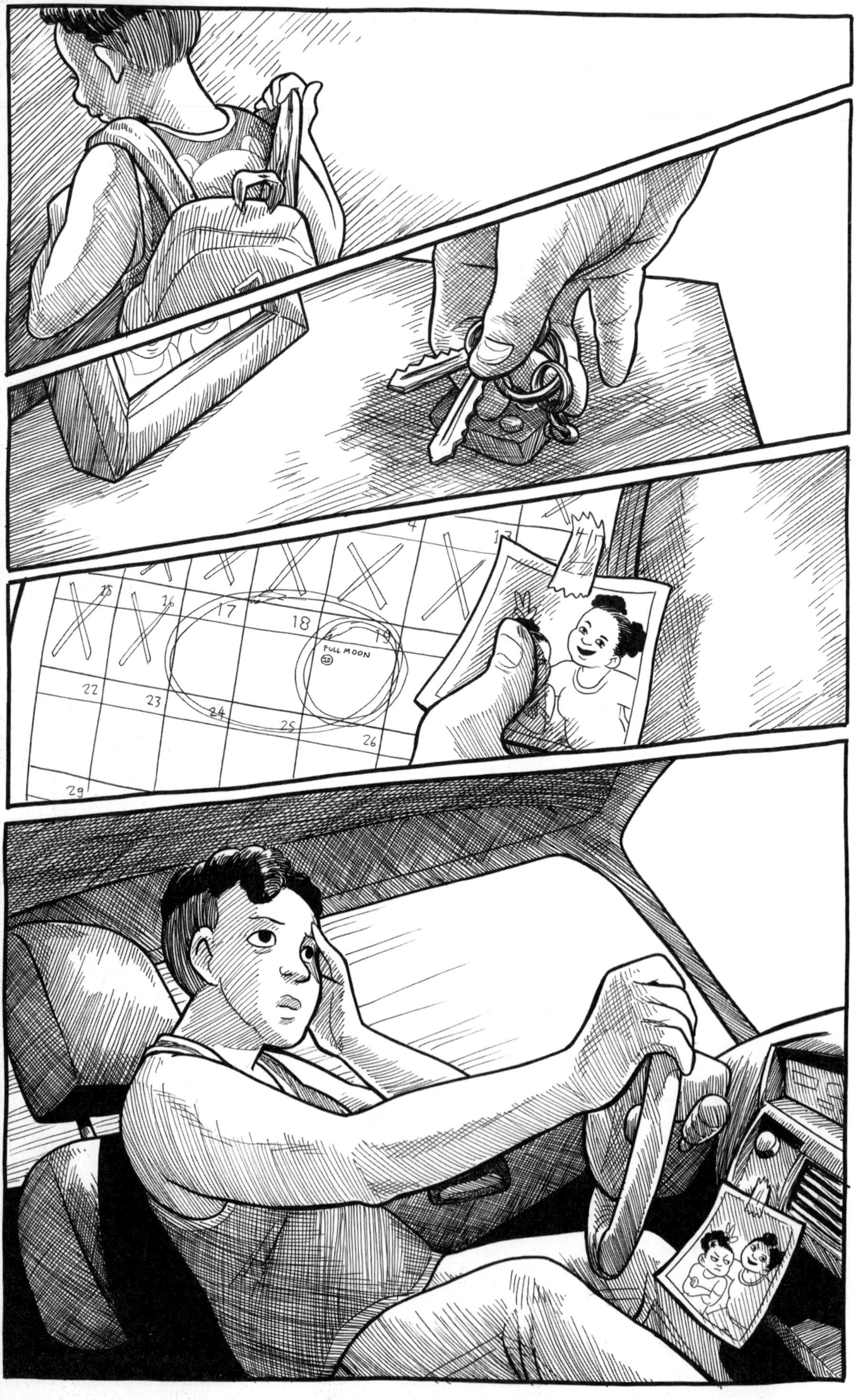
FULL MOON

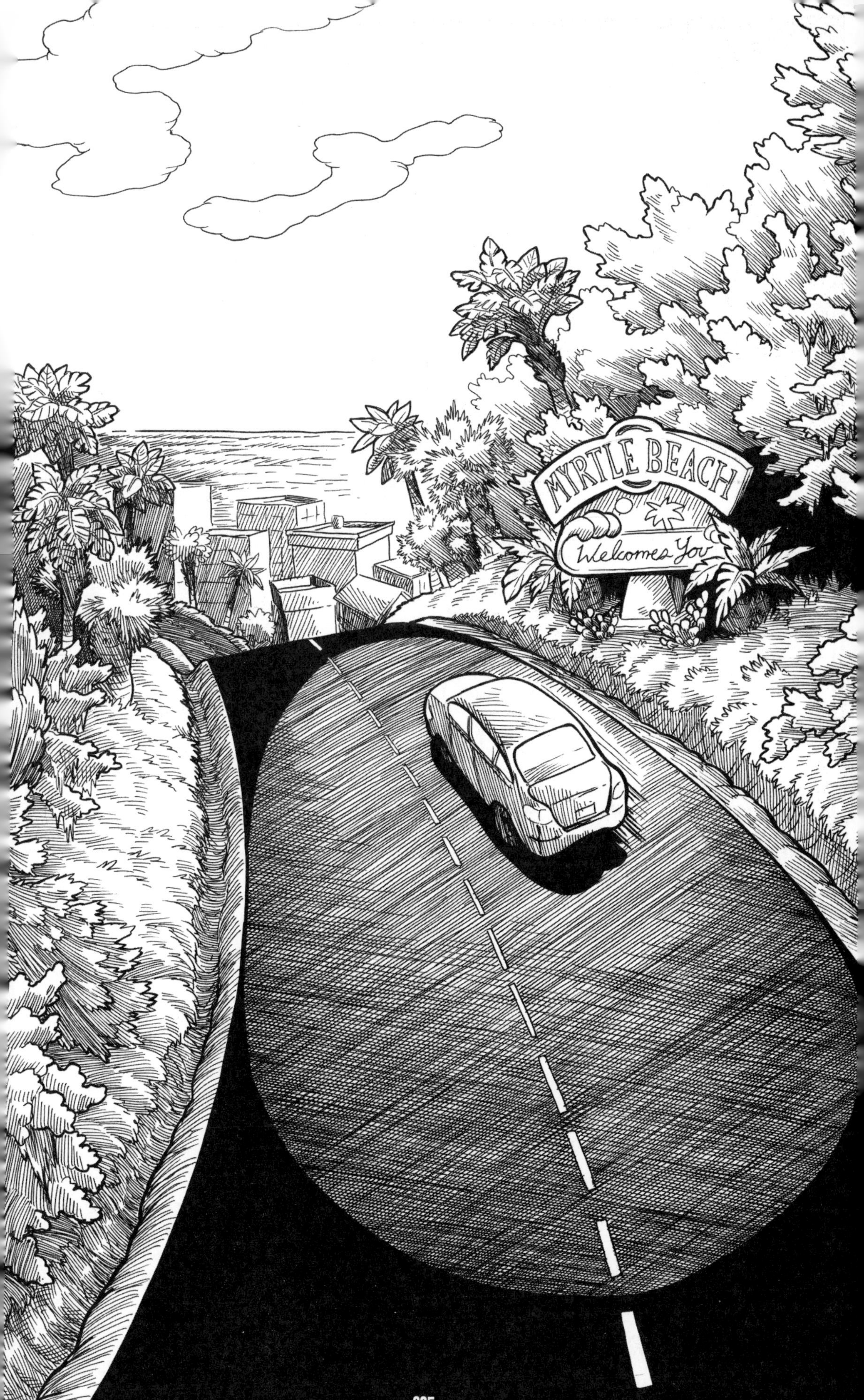
MYRTLE BEACH
Welcomes You

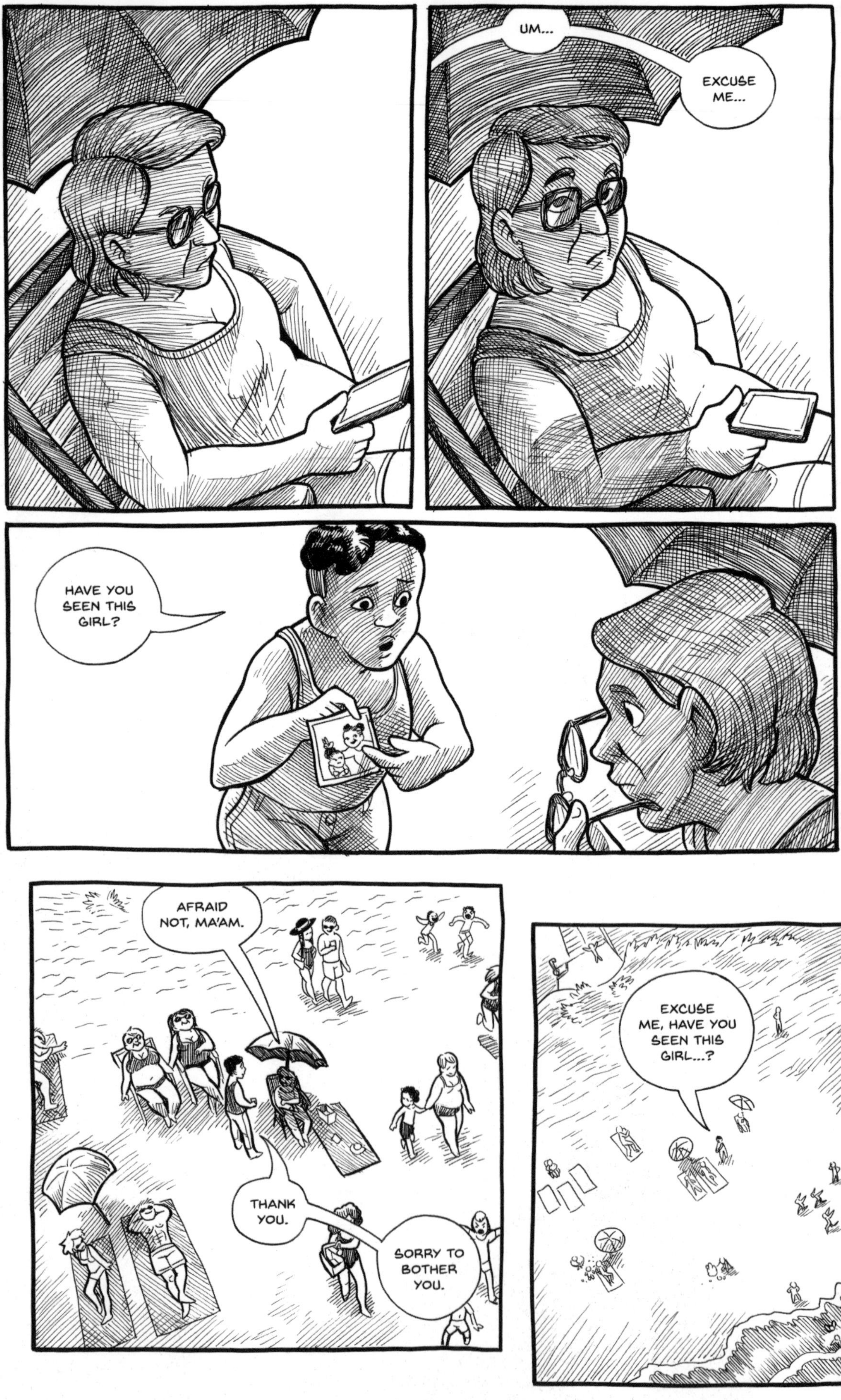
UM...
EXCUSE ME...
HAVE YOU SEEN THIS GIRL?
AFRAID NOT, MA'AM.
THANK YOU.
SORRY TO BOTHER YOU.
EXCUSE ME, HAVE YOU SEEN THIS GIRL...?

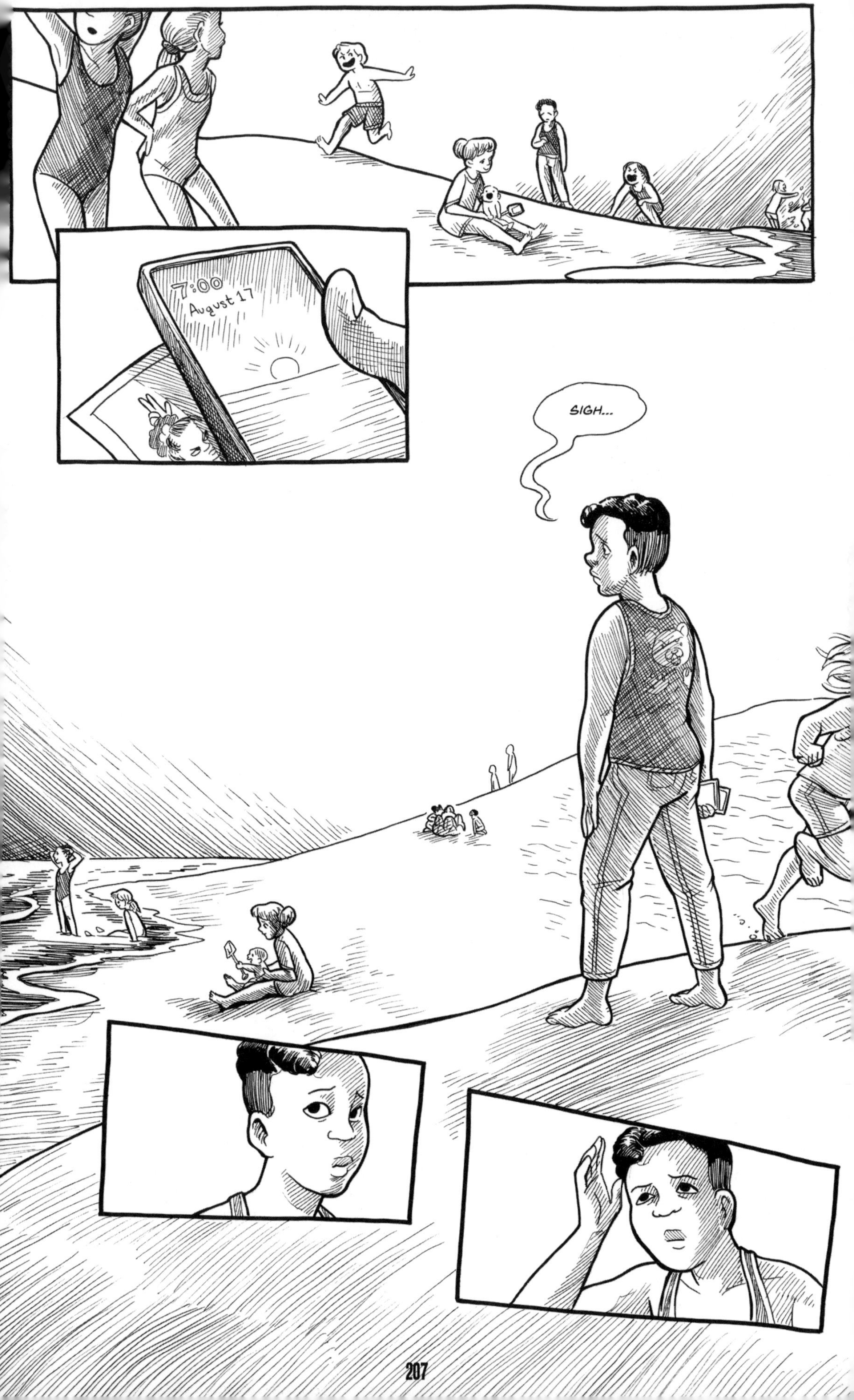
7:00
August 17
SIGH...

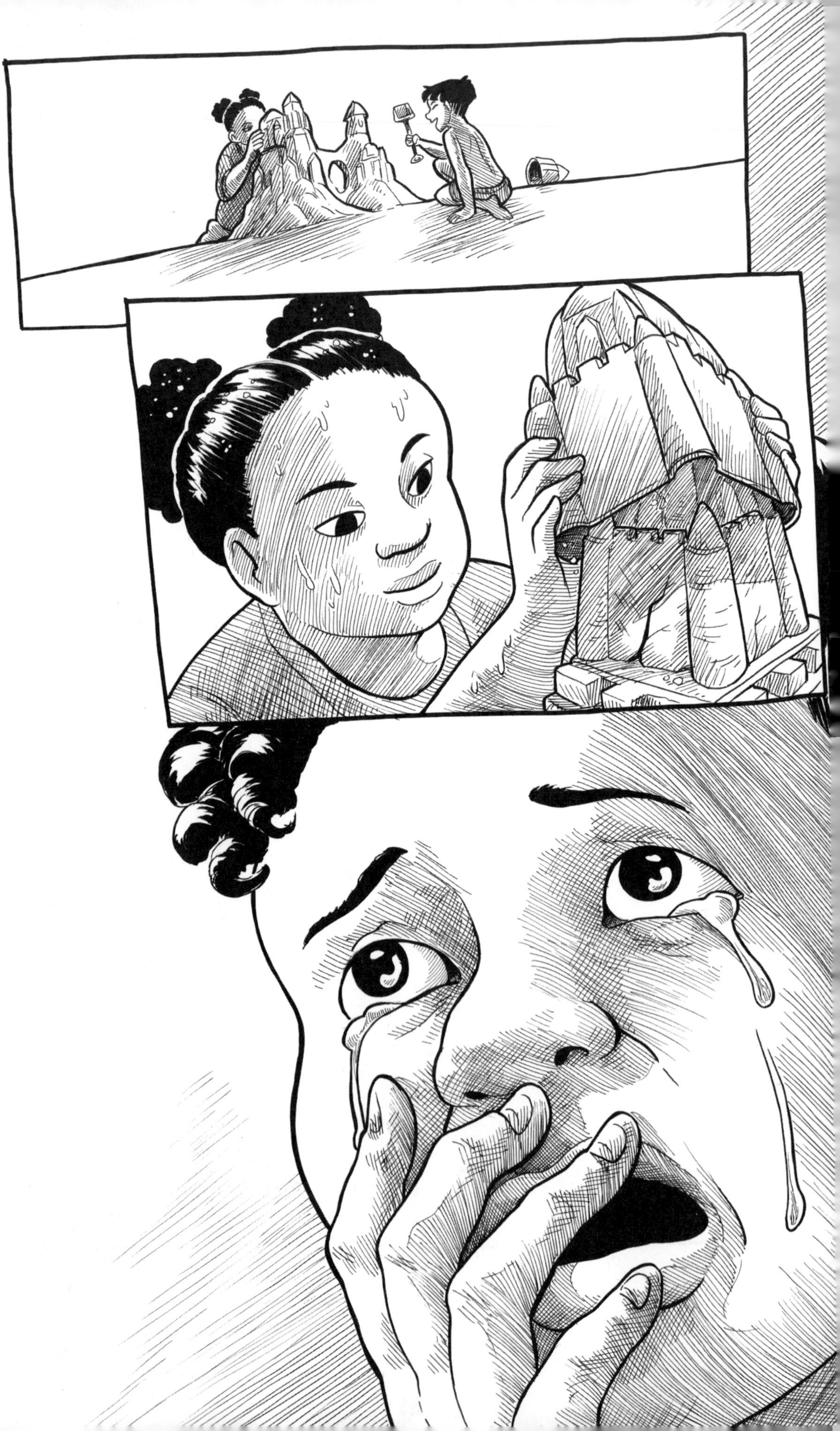

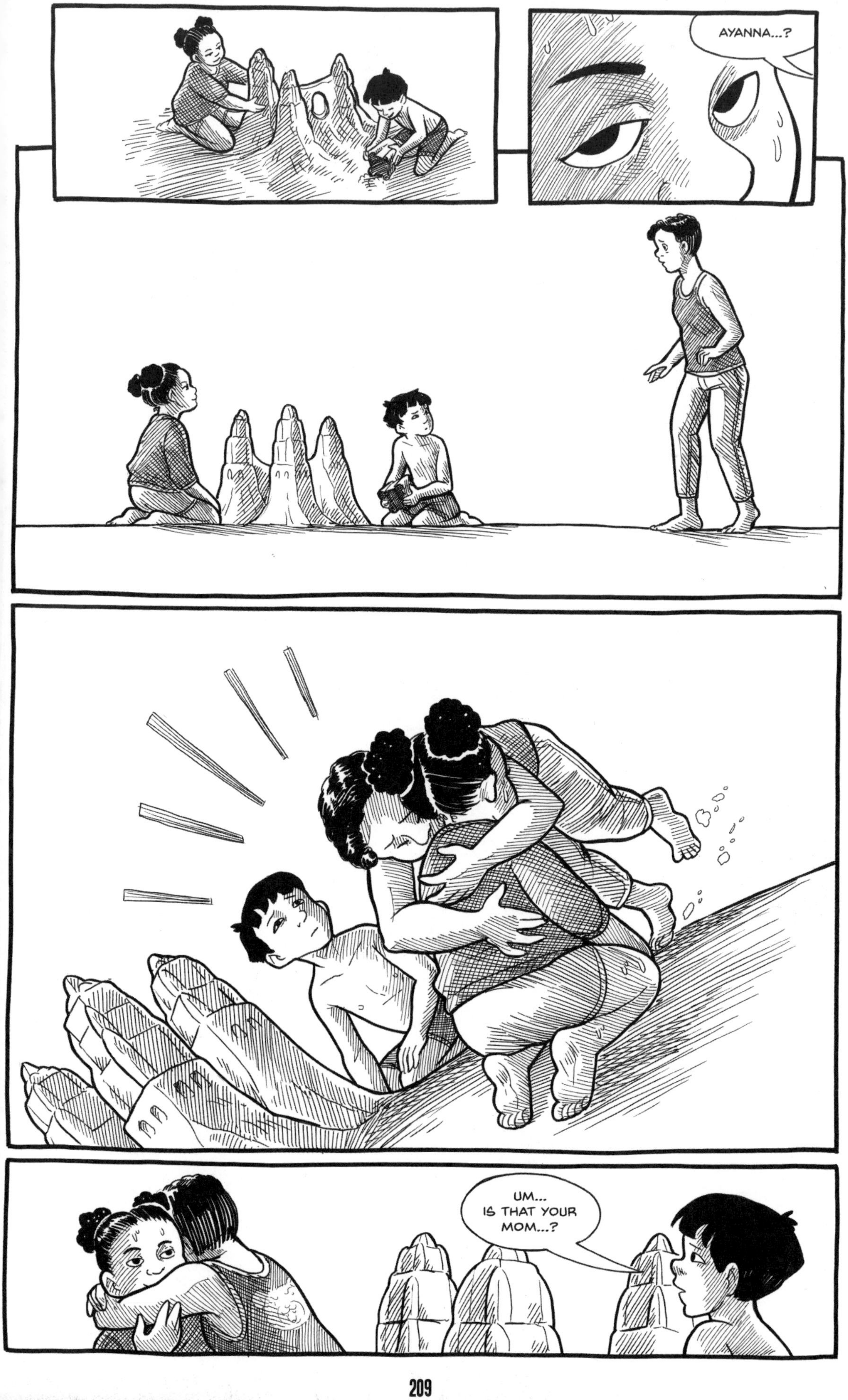
AYANNA...?
UM...
IS THAT YOUR
MOM...?

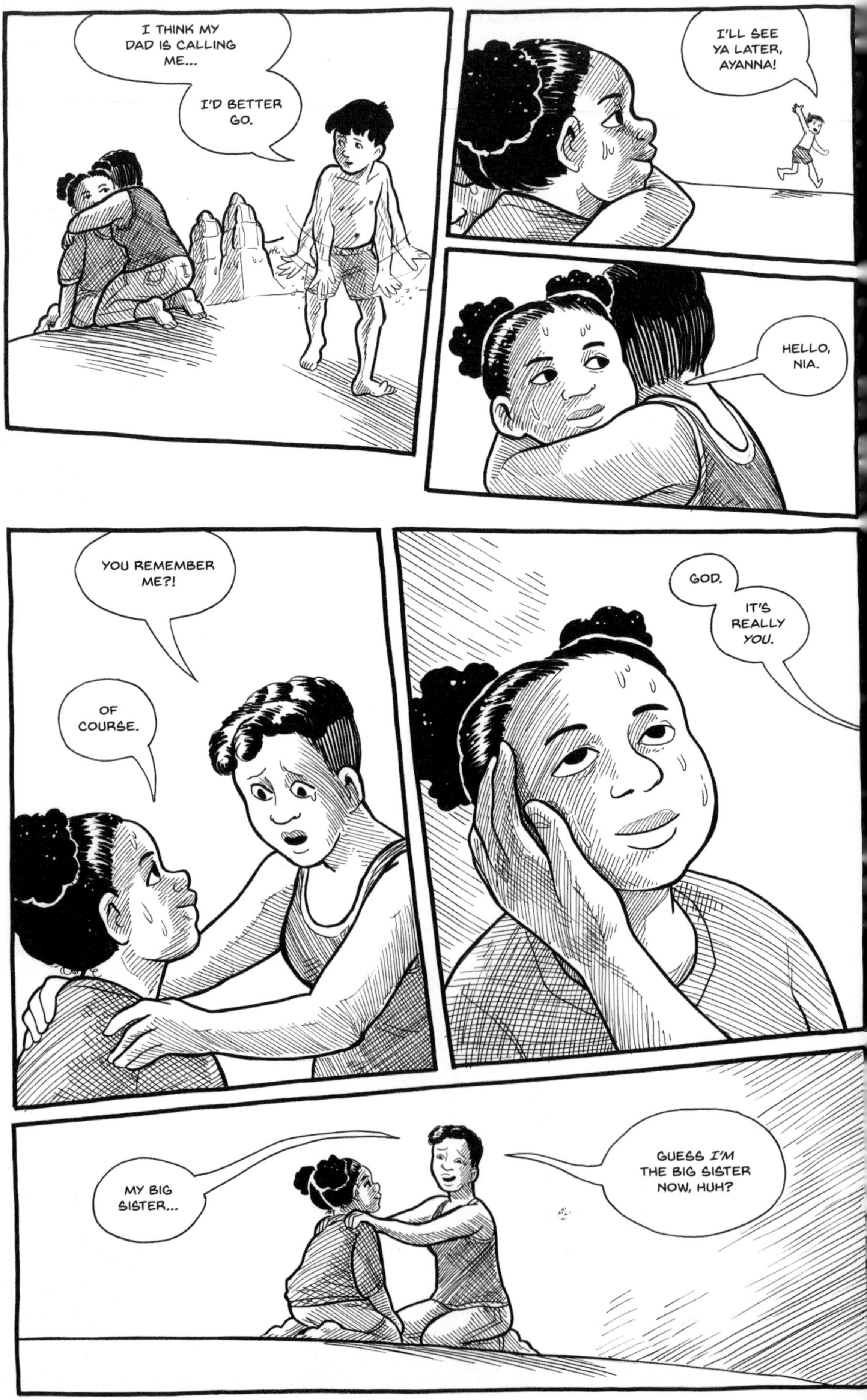
I THINK MY DAD IS CALLING ME...
I'D BETTER GO.
I'LL SEE YA LATER, AYANNA!
HELLO, NIA.
YOU REMEMBER ME?!
OF COURSE.
GOD.
IT'S REALLY *YOU*.
MY BIG SISTER...
GUESS *I'M* THE BIG SISTER NOW, HUH?

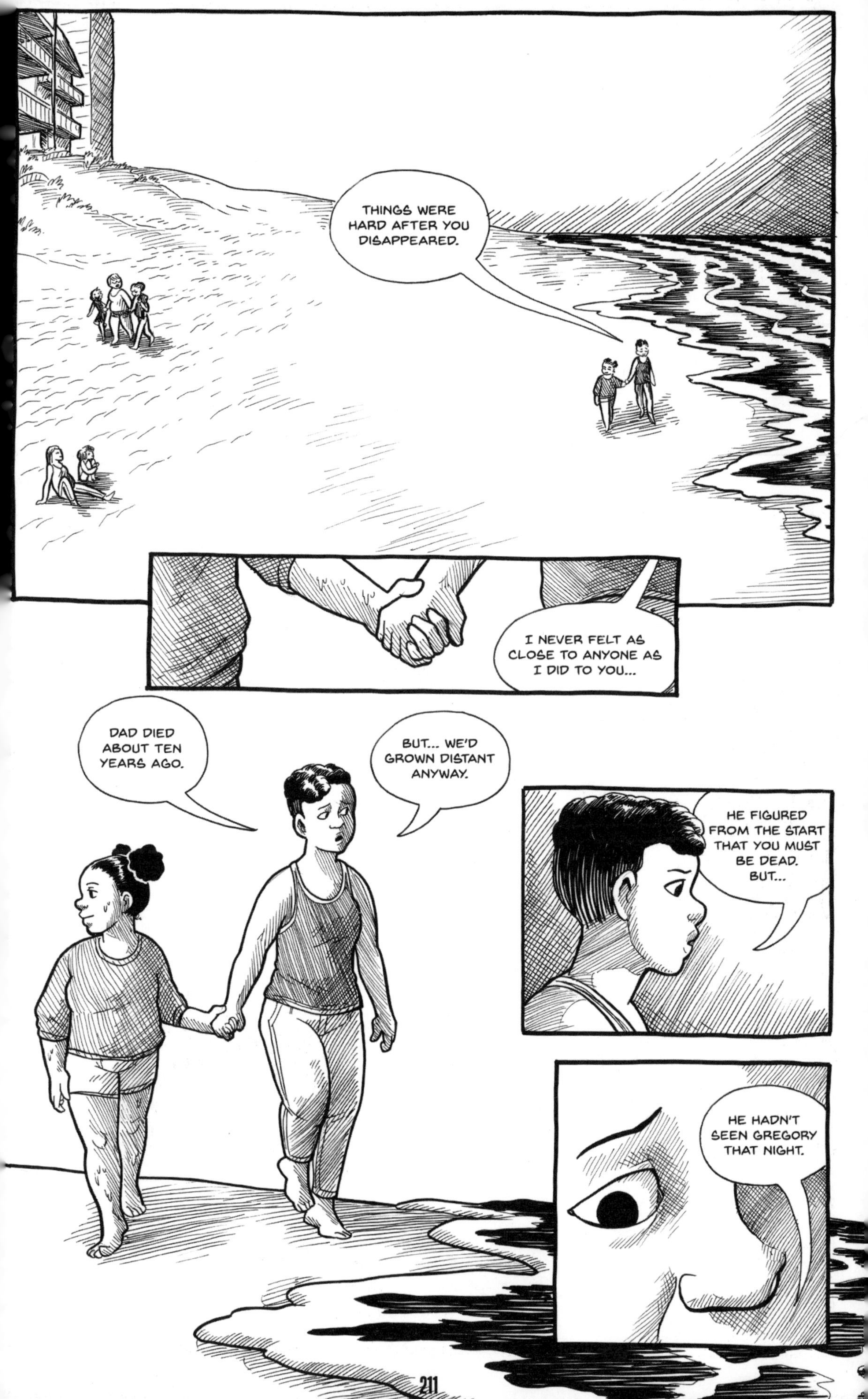
THINGS WERE HARD AFTER YOU DISAPPEARED.
I NEVER FELT AS CLOSE TO ANYONE AS I DID TO YOU...
DAD DIED ABOUT TEN YEARS AGO.
BUT... WE'D GROWN DISTANT ANYWAY.
HE FIGURED FROM THE START THAT YOU MUST BE DEAD. BUT...
HE HADN'T SEEN GREGORY THAT NIGHT.

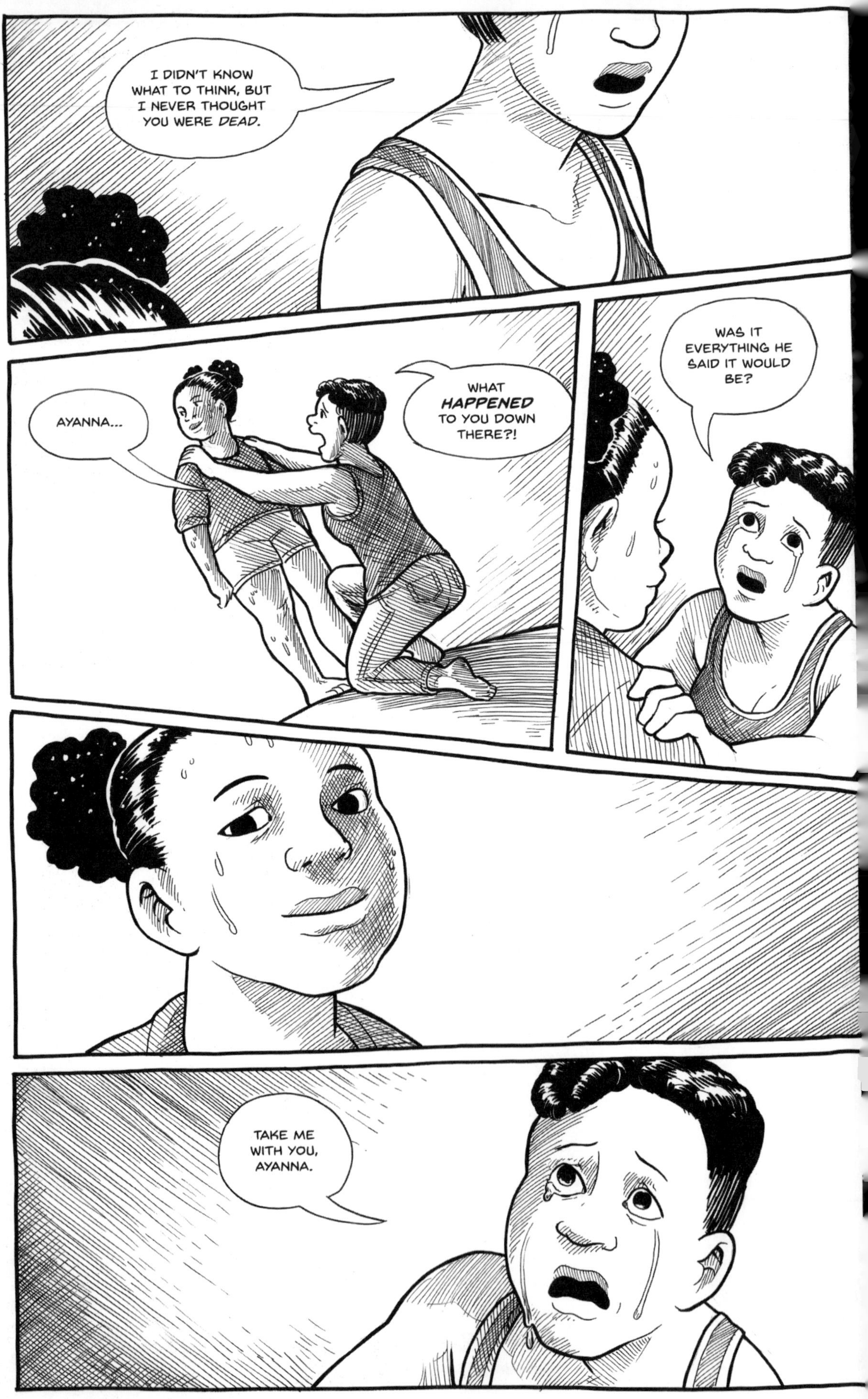
I DIDN'T KNOW WHAT TO THINK, BUT I NEVER THOUGHT YOU WERE *DEAD*.
AYANNA...
WHAT ***HAPPENED*** TO YOU DOWN THERE?!
WAS IT EVERYTHING HE SAID IT WOULD BE?
TAKE ME WITH YOU, AYANNA.

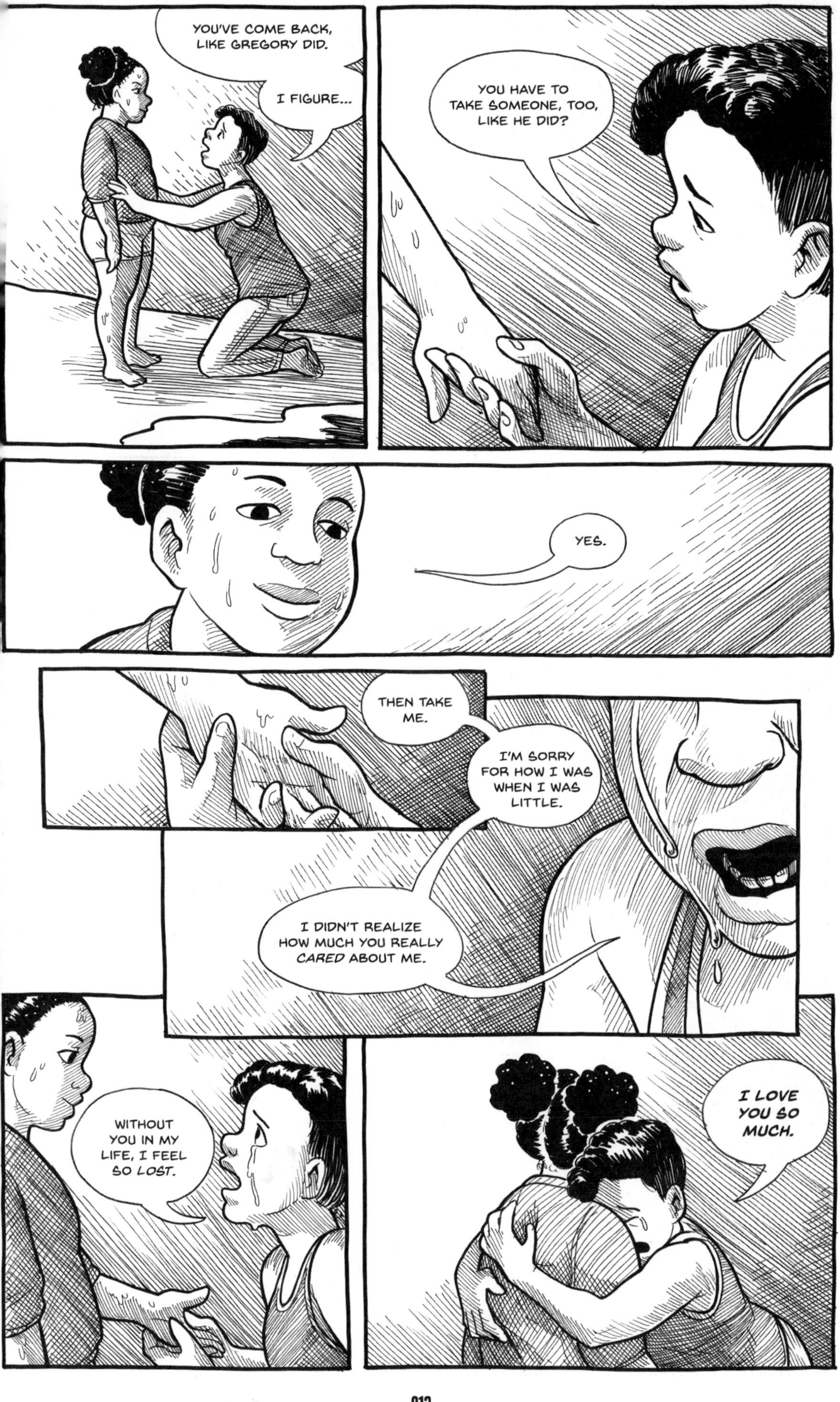
YOU'VE COME BACK, LIKE GREGORY DID.
I FIGURE...
YOU HAVE TO TAKE SOMEONE, TOO, LIKE HE DID?
YES.
THEN TAKE ME.
I'M SORRY FOR HOW I WAS WHEN I WAS LITTLE.
I DIDN'T REALIZE HOW MUCH YOU REALLY *CARED* ABOUT ME.
WITHOUT YOU IN MY LIFE, I FEEL SO *LOST*.
I LOVE YOU SO MUCH.

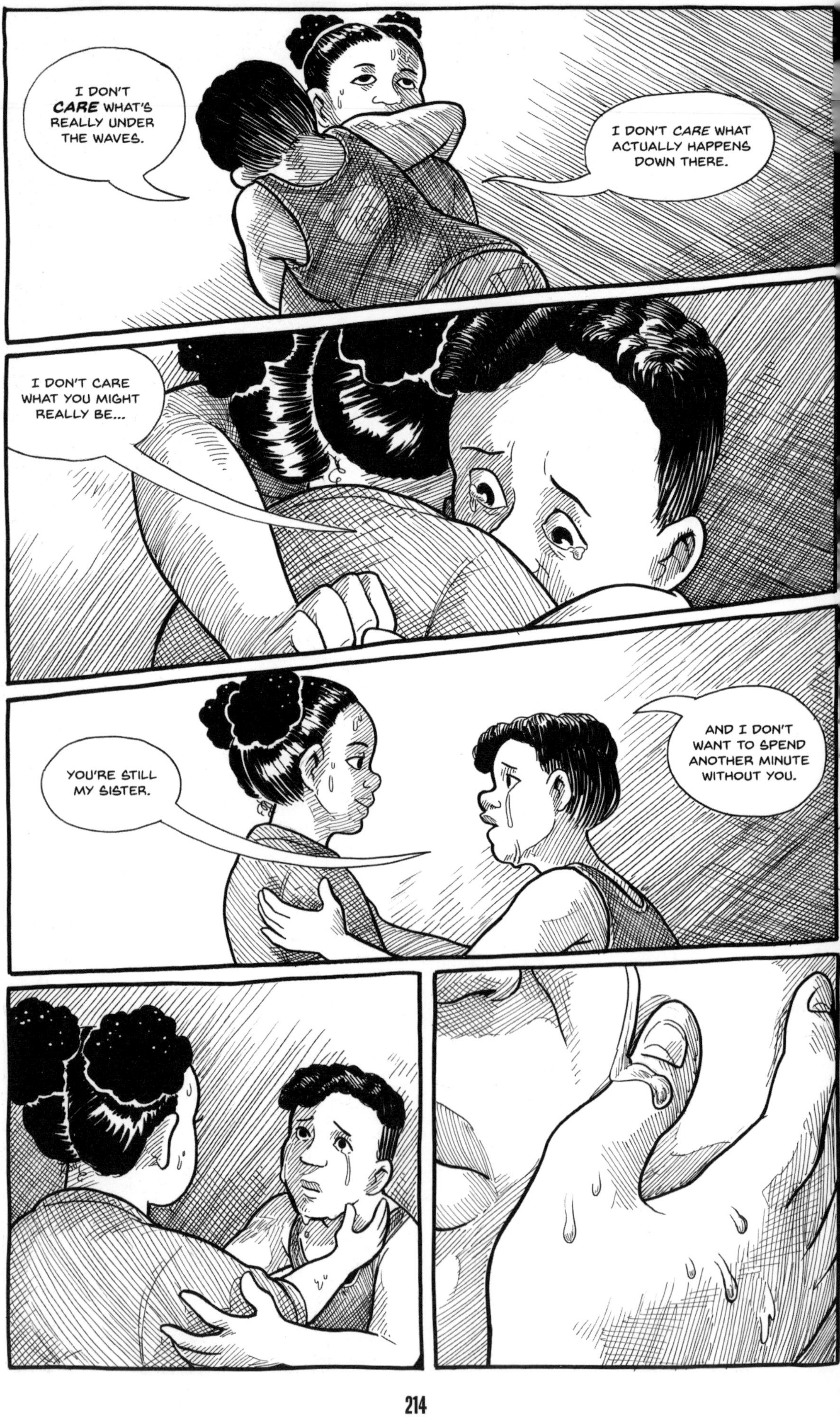
I DON'T CARE WHAT'S REALLY UNDER THE WAVES.
I DON'T CARE WHAT ACTUALLY HAPPENS DOWN THERE.
I DON'T CARE WHAT YOU MIGHT REALLY BE...
YOU'RE STILL MY SISTER.
AND I DON'T WANT TO SPEND ANOTHER MINUTE WITHOUT YOU.

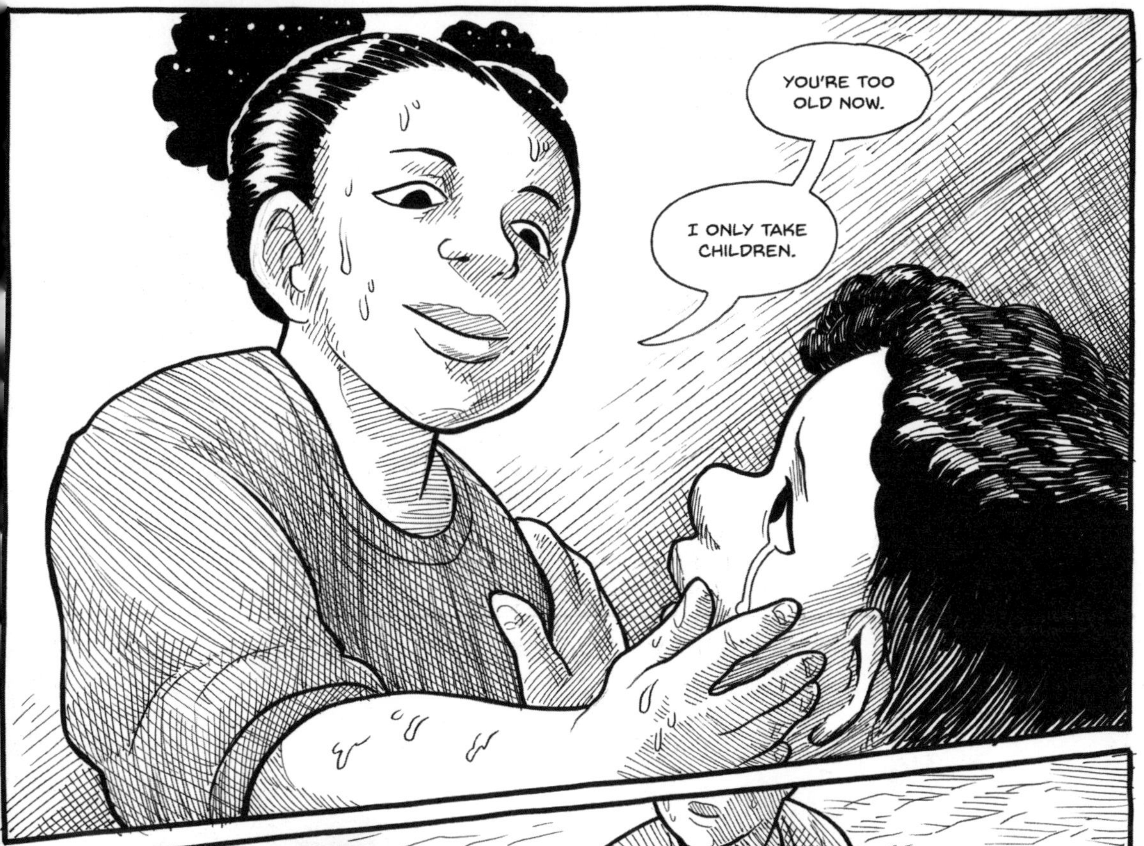
YOU'RE TOO OLD NOW.
I ONLY TAKE CHILDREN.

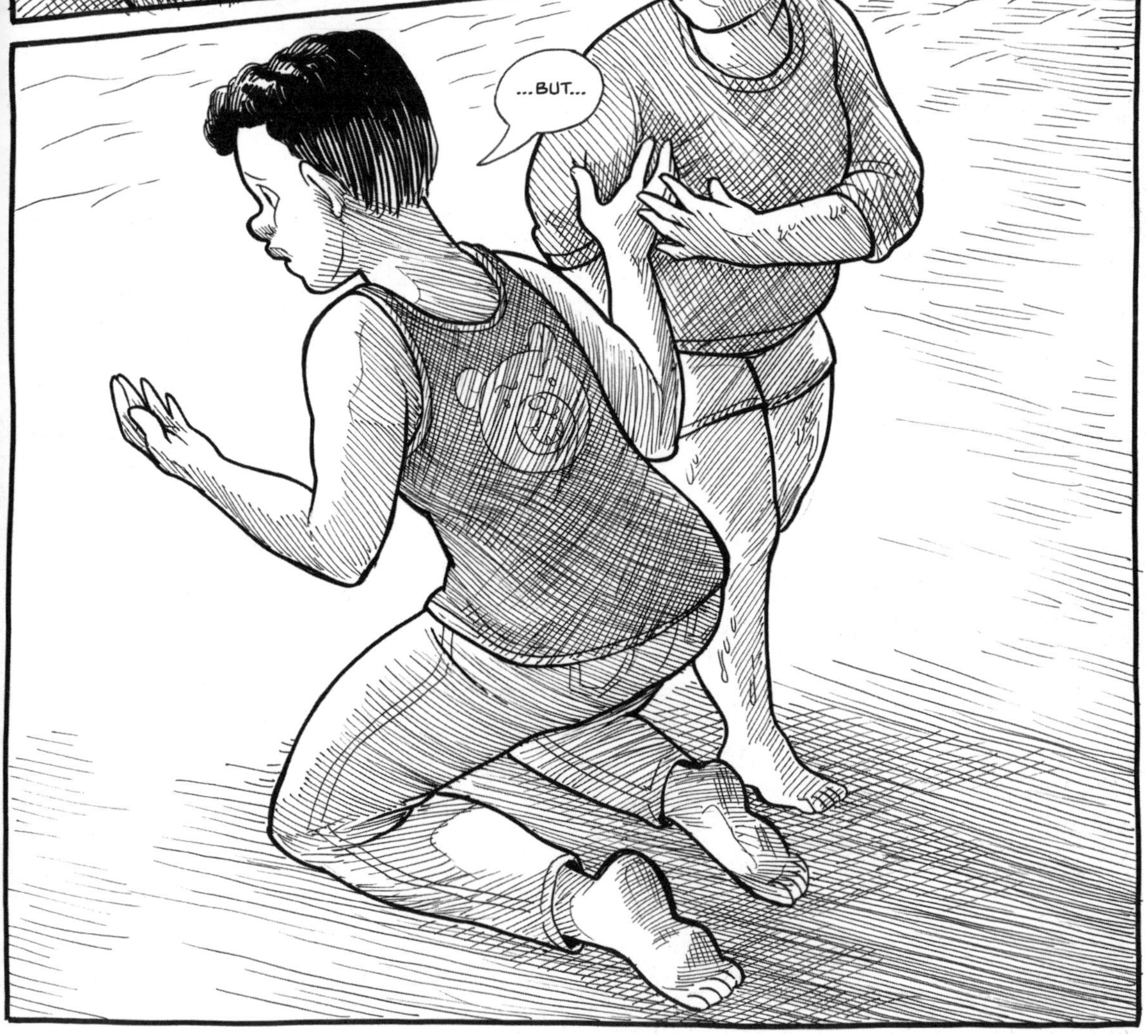
...BUT...

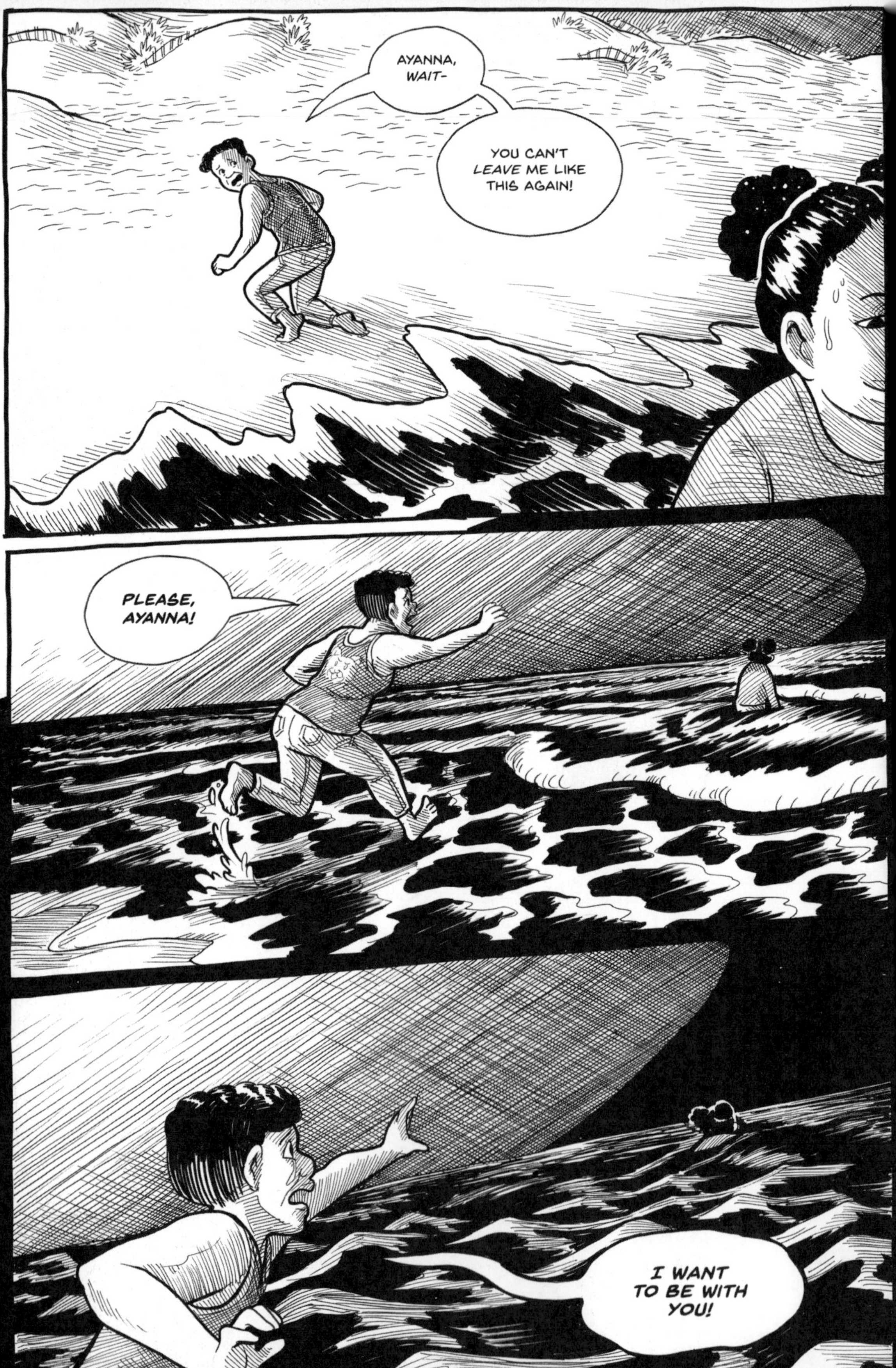
AYANNA, WAIT-
YOU CAN'T *LEAVE* ME LIKE THIS AGAIN!
PLEASE, AYANNA!
I WANT TO BE WITH YOU!

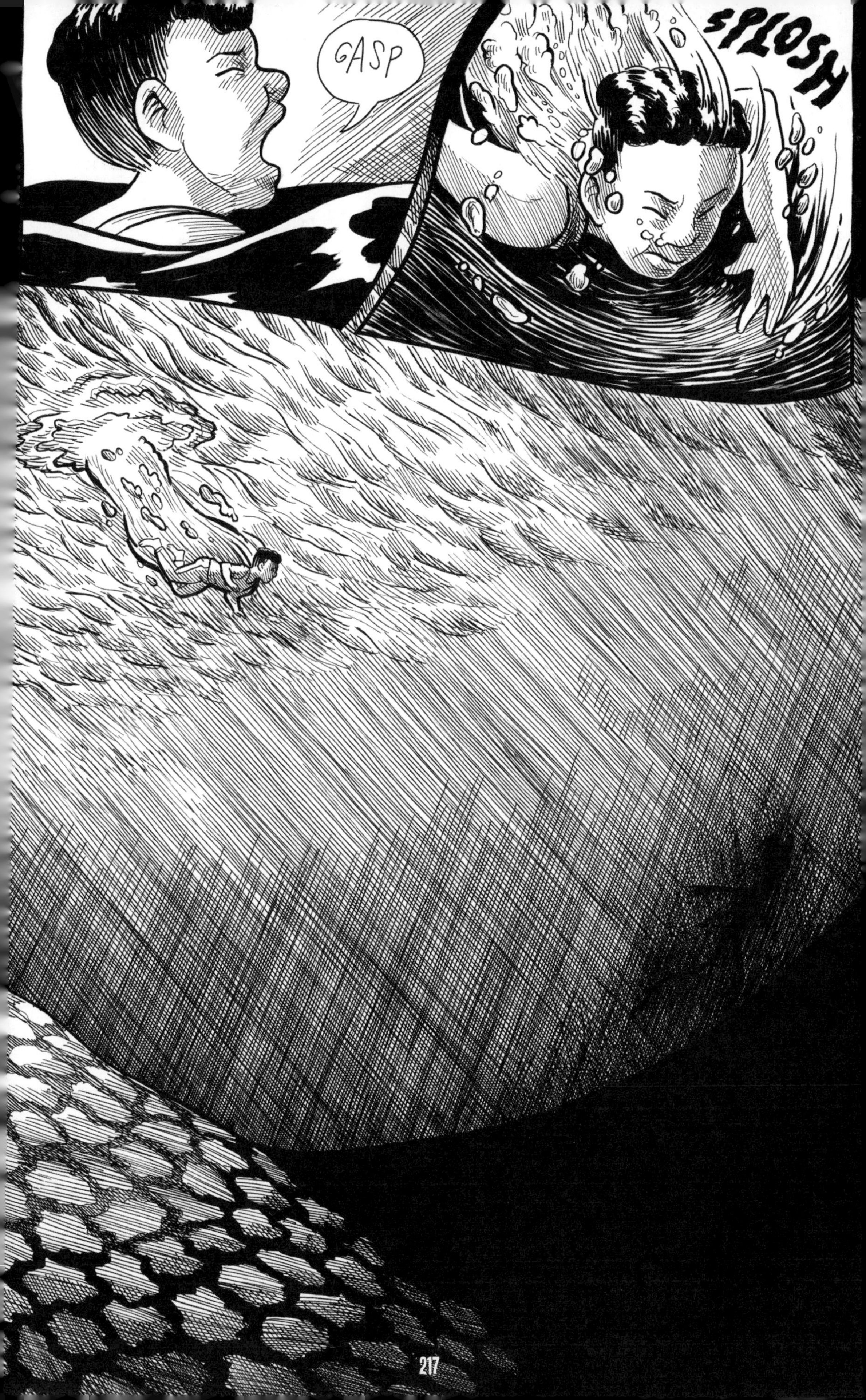
GASP
SPLOSH

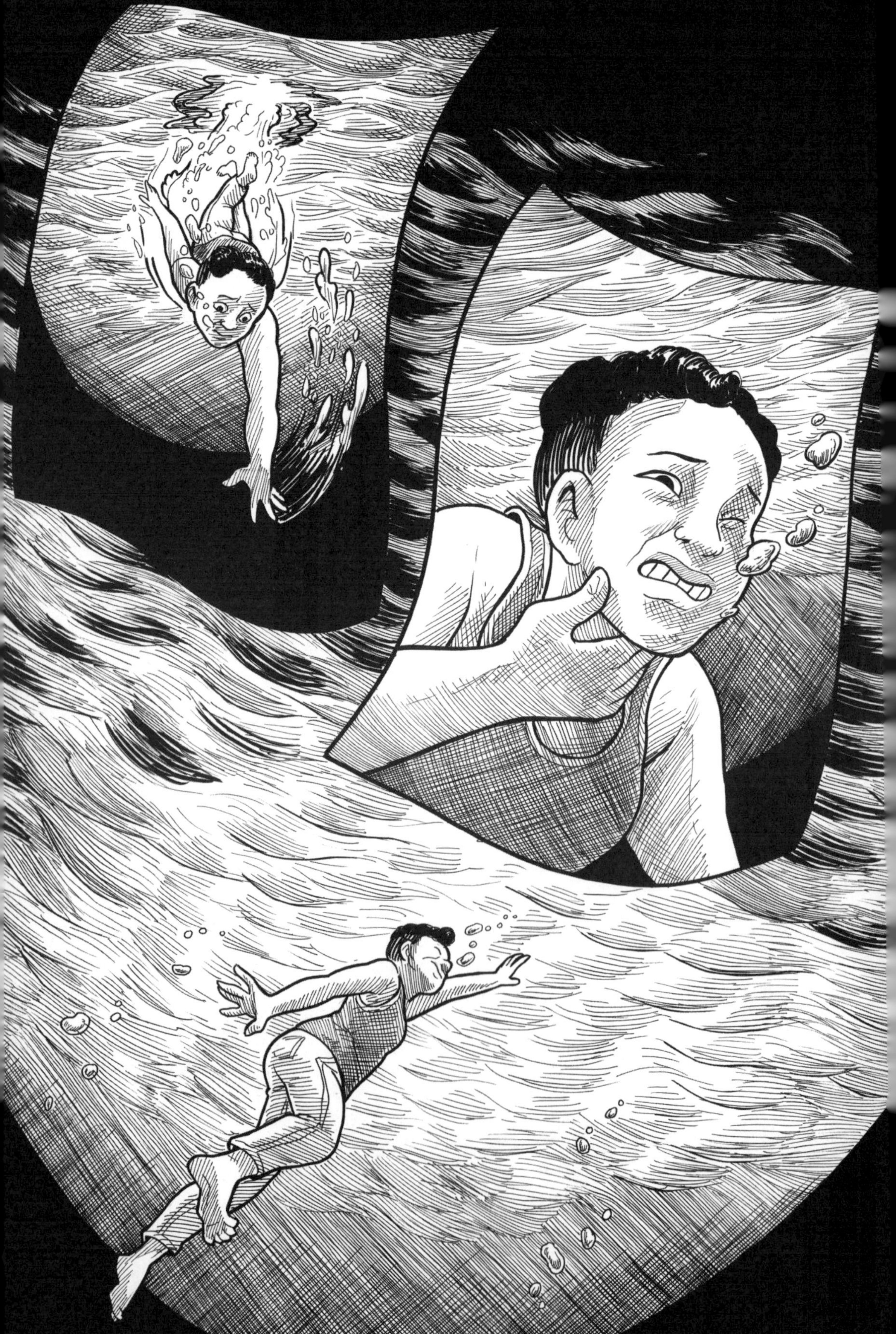

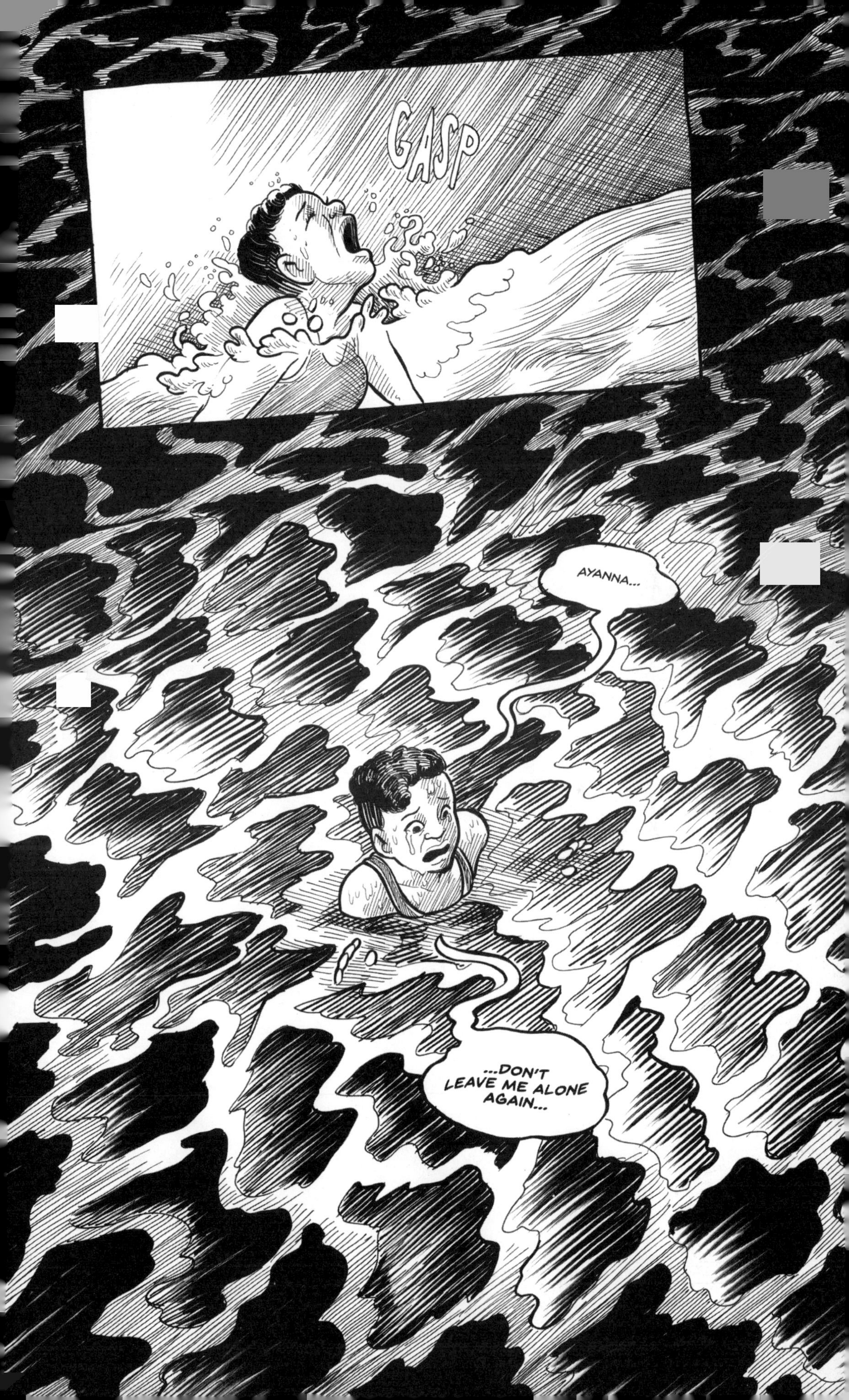
GASP
AYANNA...
...DON'T LEAVE ME ALONE AGAIN...

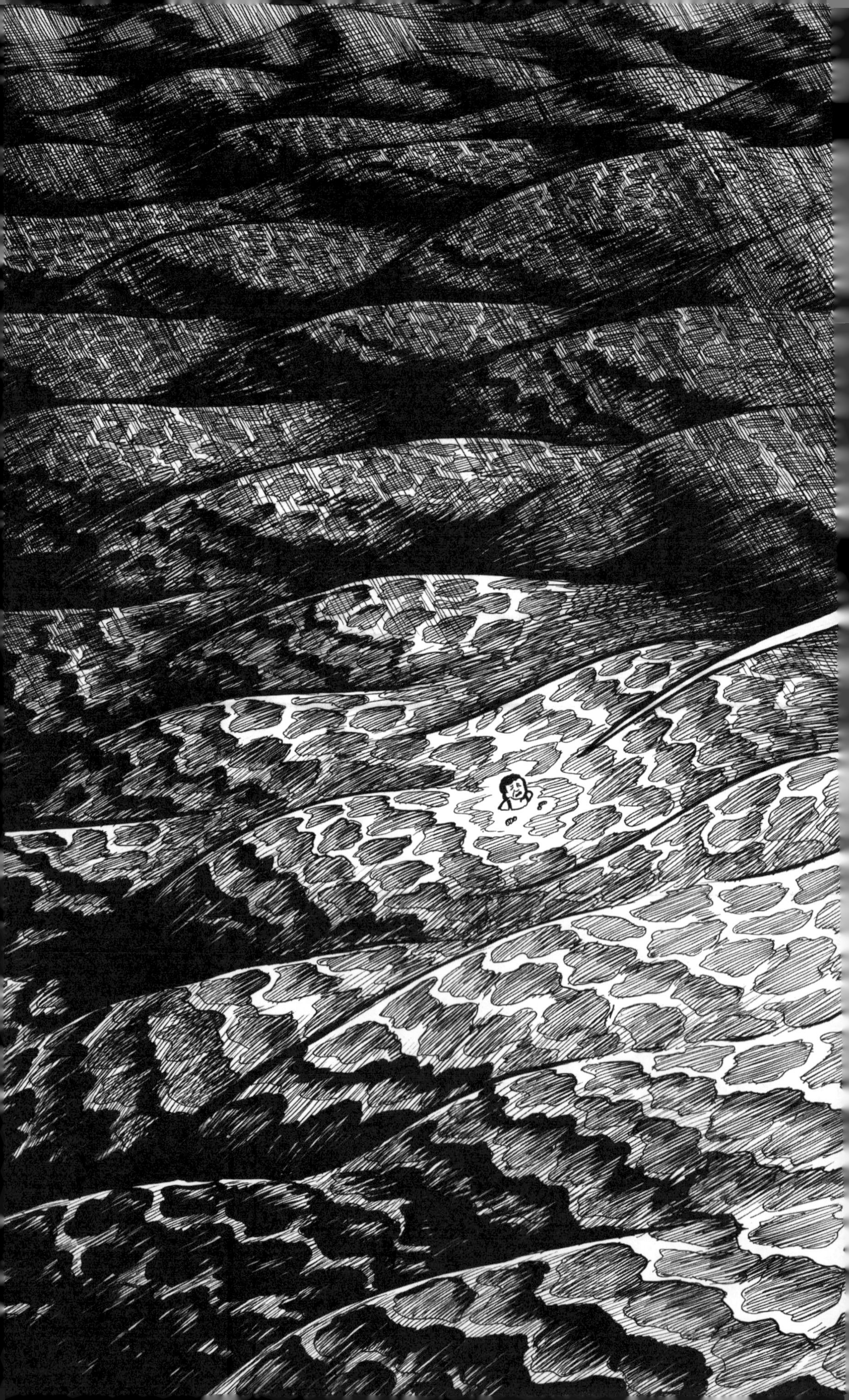

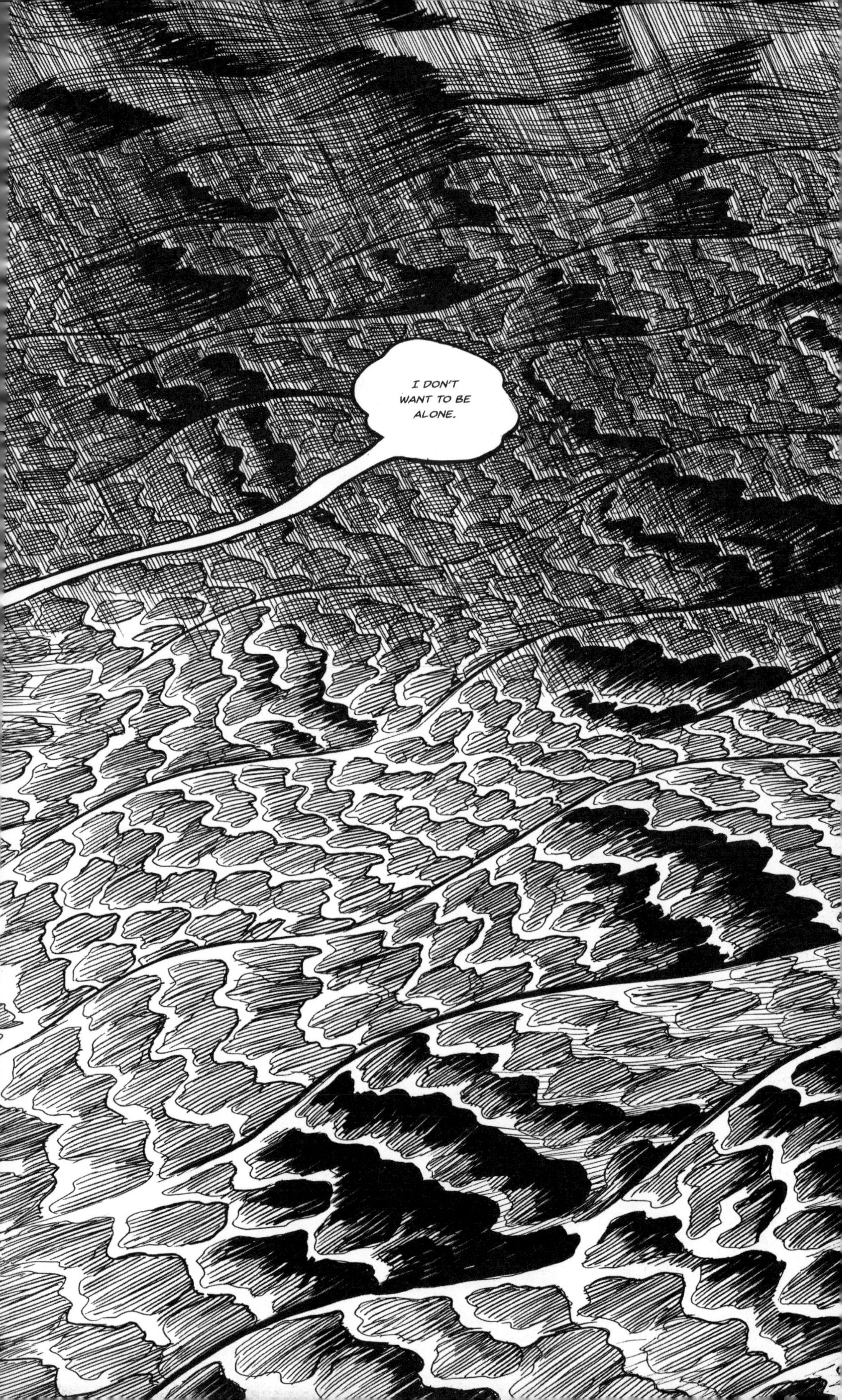
I DON'T WANT TO BE ALONE.

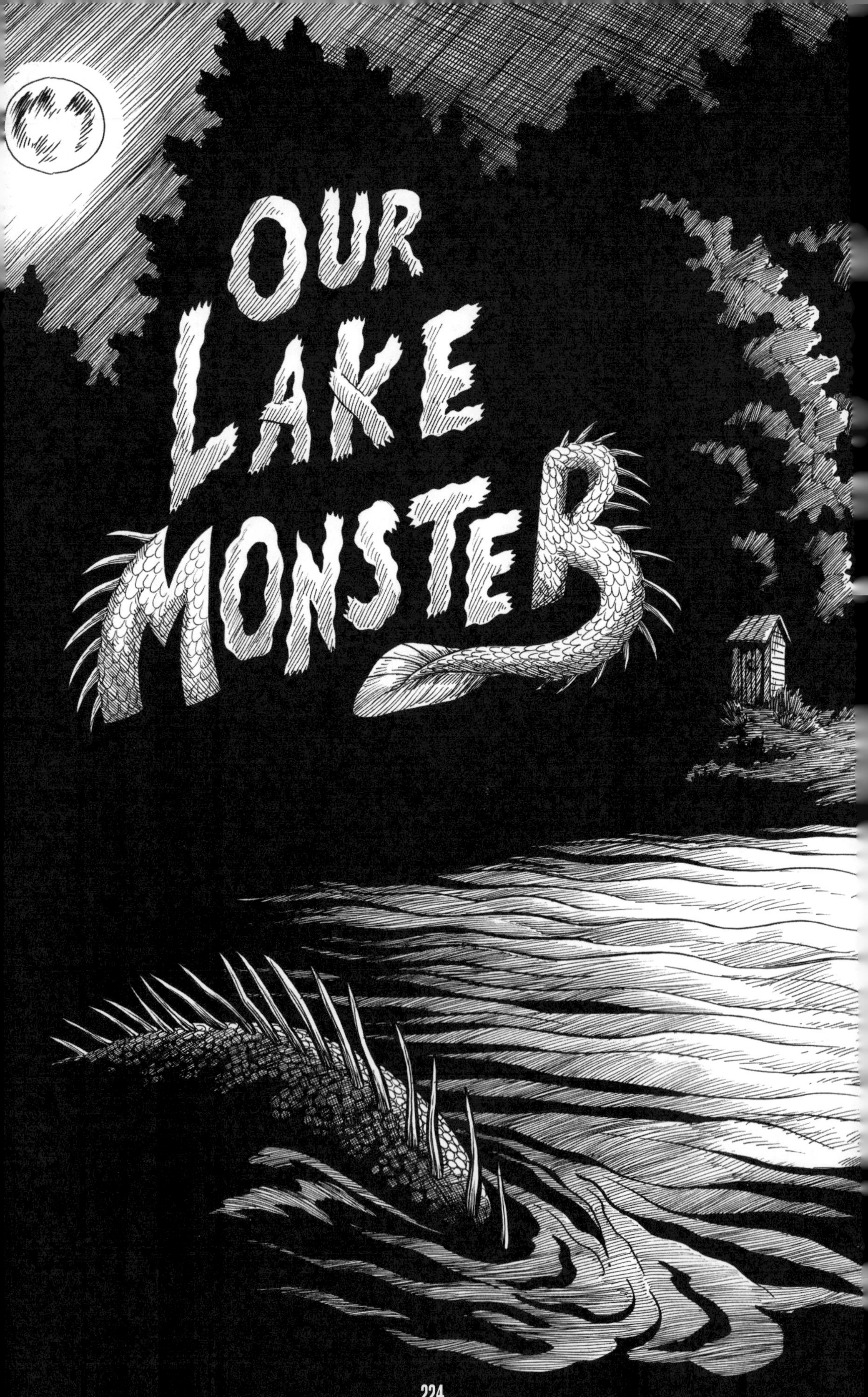
OUR
LAKE
MONSTER

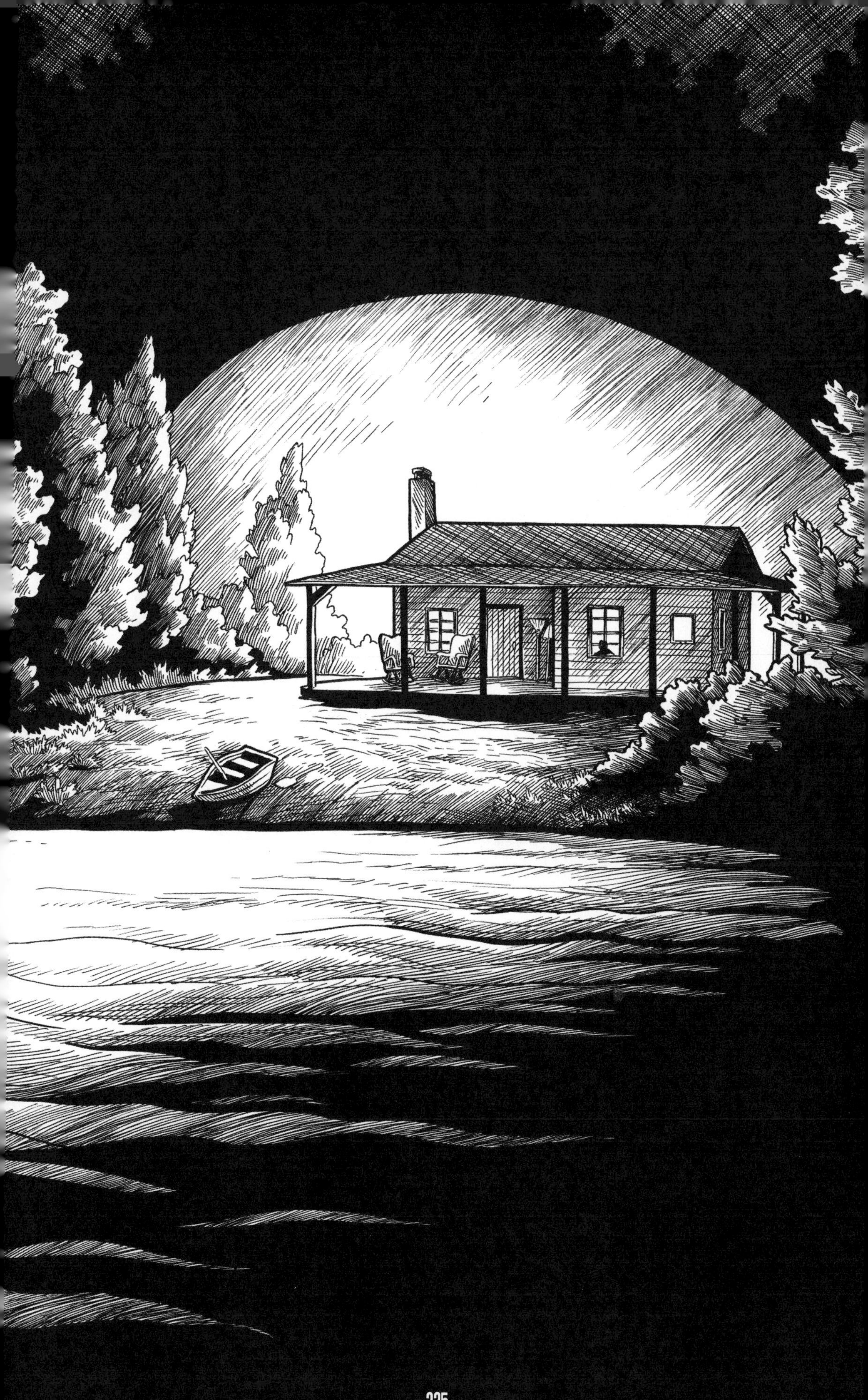

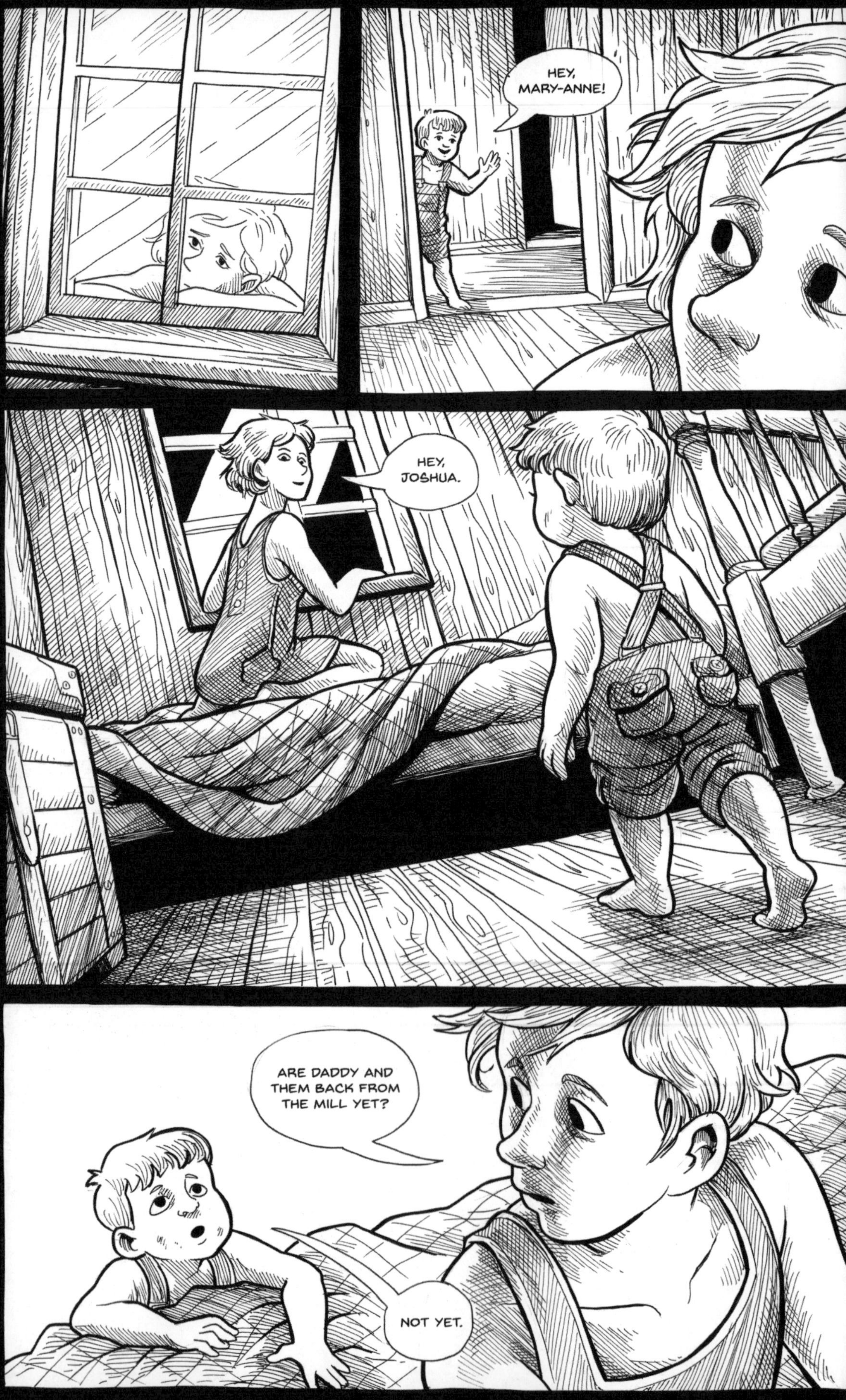
HEY, MARY-ANNE!
HEY, JOSHUA.
ARE DADDY AND THEM BACK FROM THE MILL YET?
NOT YET.

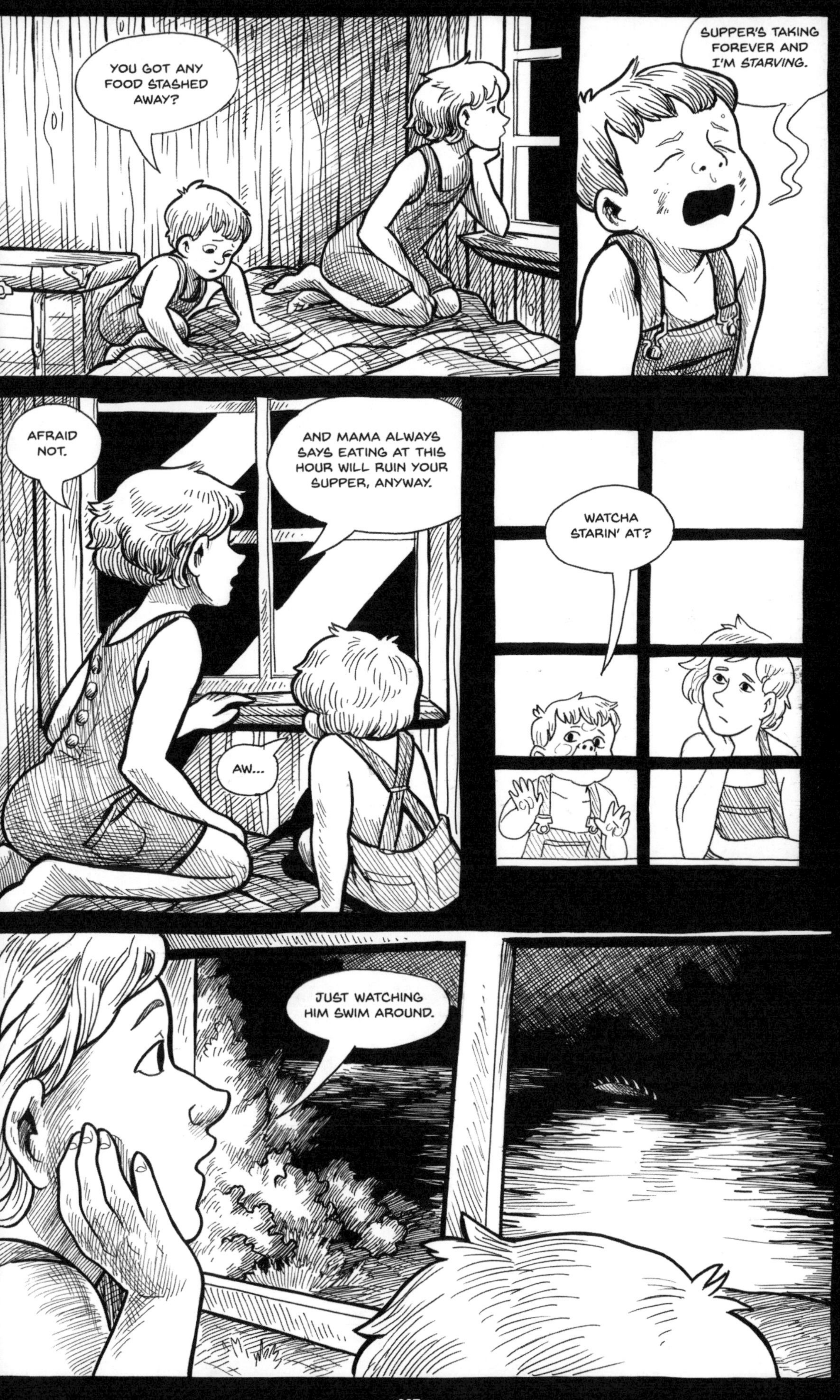
YOU GOT ANY FOOD STASHED AWAY?
SUPPER'S TAKING FOREVER AND I'M STARVING.
AFRAID NOT.
AND MAMA ALWAYS SAYS EATING AT THIS HOUR WILL RUIN YOUR SUPPER, ANYWAY.
AW...
WATCHA STARIN' AT?
JUST WATCHING HIM SWIM AROUND.

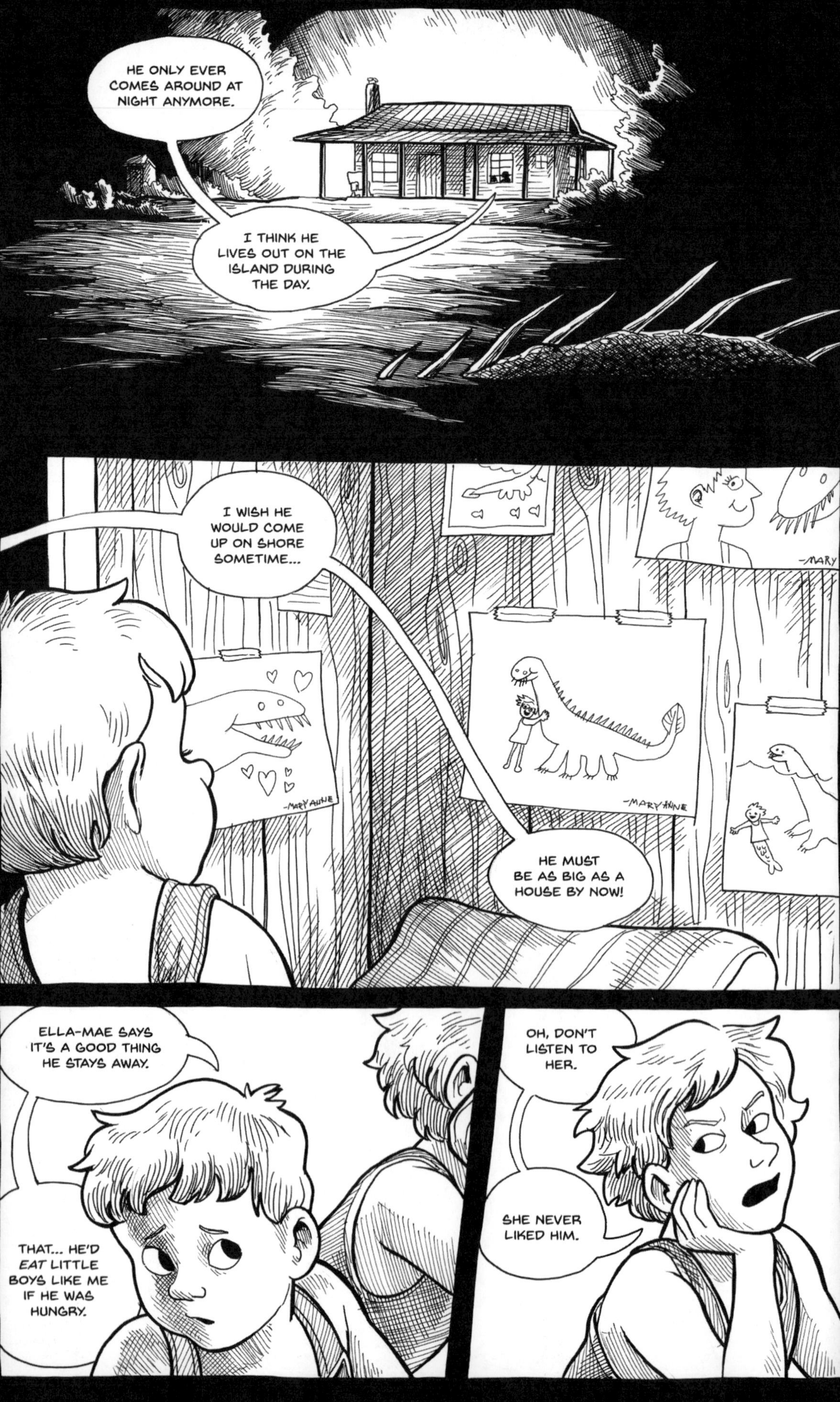

HE ONLY EVER COMES AROUND AT NIGHT ANYMORE.
I THINK HE LIVES OUT ON THE ISLAND DURING THE DAY.
I WISH HE WOULD COME UP ON SHORE SOMETIME...
-MARY ANNE
-MARY ANNE
-MARY
HE MUST BE AS BIG AS A HOUSE BY NOW!
ELLA-MAE SAYS IT'S A GOOD THING HE STAYS AWAY.
THAT... HE'D *EAT* LITTLE BOYS LIKE ME IF HE WAS HUNGRY.
OH, DON'T LISTEN TO HER.
SHE NEVER LIKED HIM.

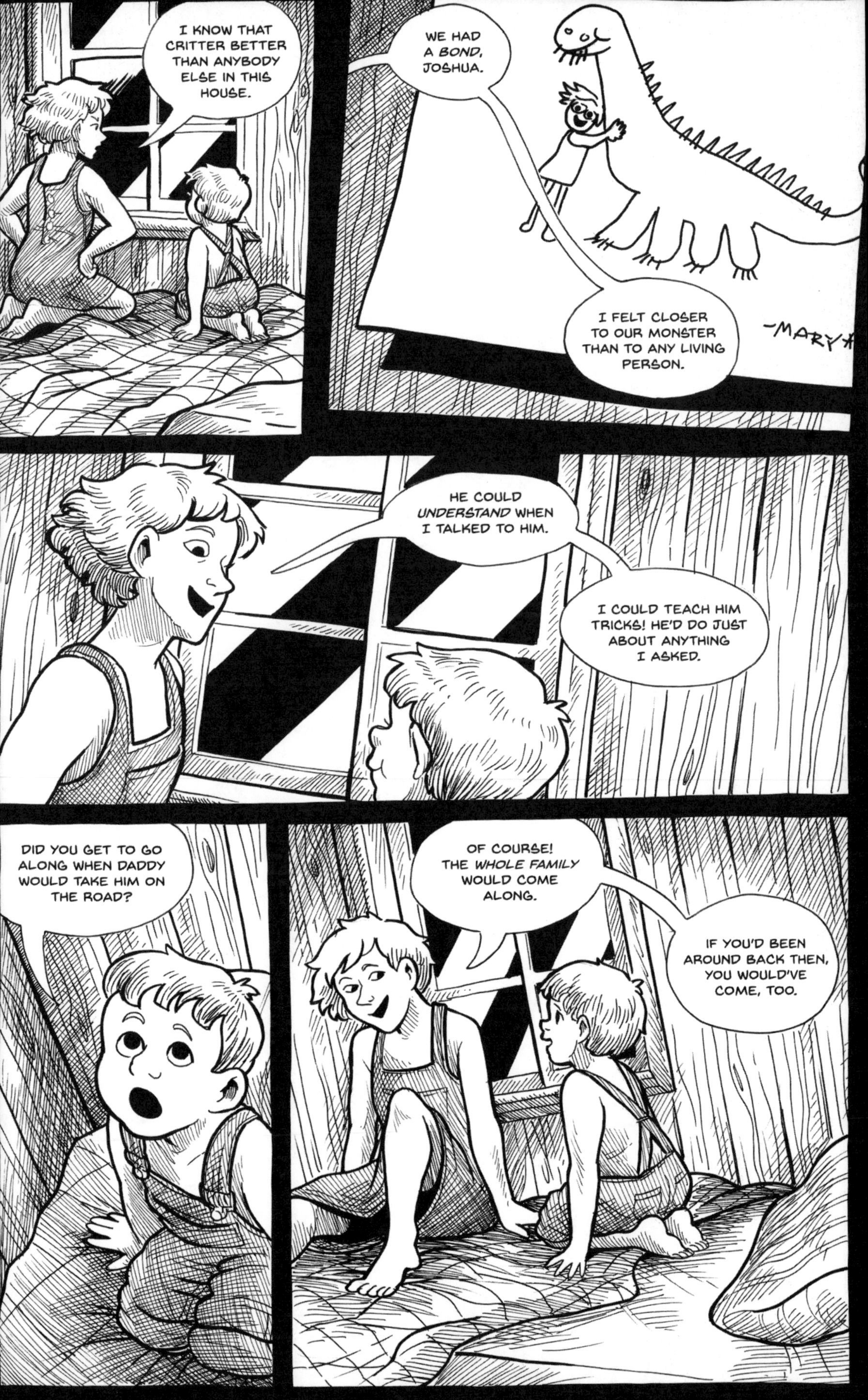
I KNOW THAT CRITTER BETTER THAN ANYBODY ELSE IN THIS HOUSE.
WE HAD A *BOND,* JOSHUA.
I FELT CLOSER TO OUR MONSTER THAN TO ANY LIVING PERSON.
-MARY
HE COULD *UNDERSTAND* WHEN I TALKED TO HIM.
I COULD TEACH HIM TRICKS! HE'D DO JUST ABOUT ANYTHING I ASKED.
DID YOU GET TO GO ALONG WHEN DADDY WOULD TAKE HIM ON THE ROAD?
OF COURSE! THE *WHOLE FAMILY* WOULD COME ALONG.
IF YOU'D BEEN AROUND BACK THEN, YOU WOULD'VE COME, TOO.

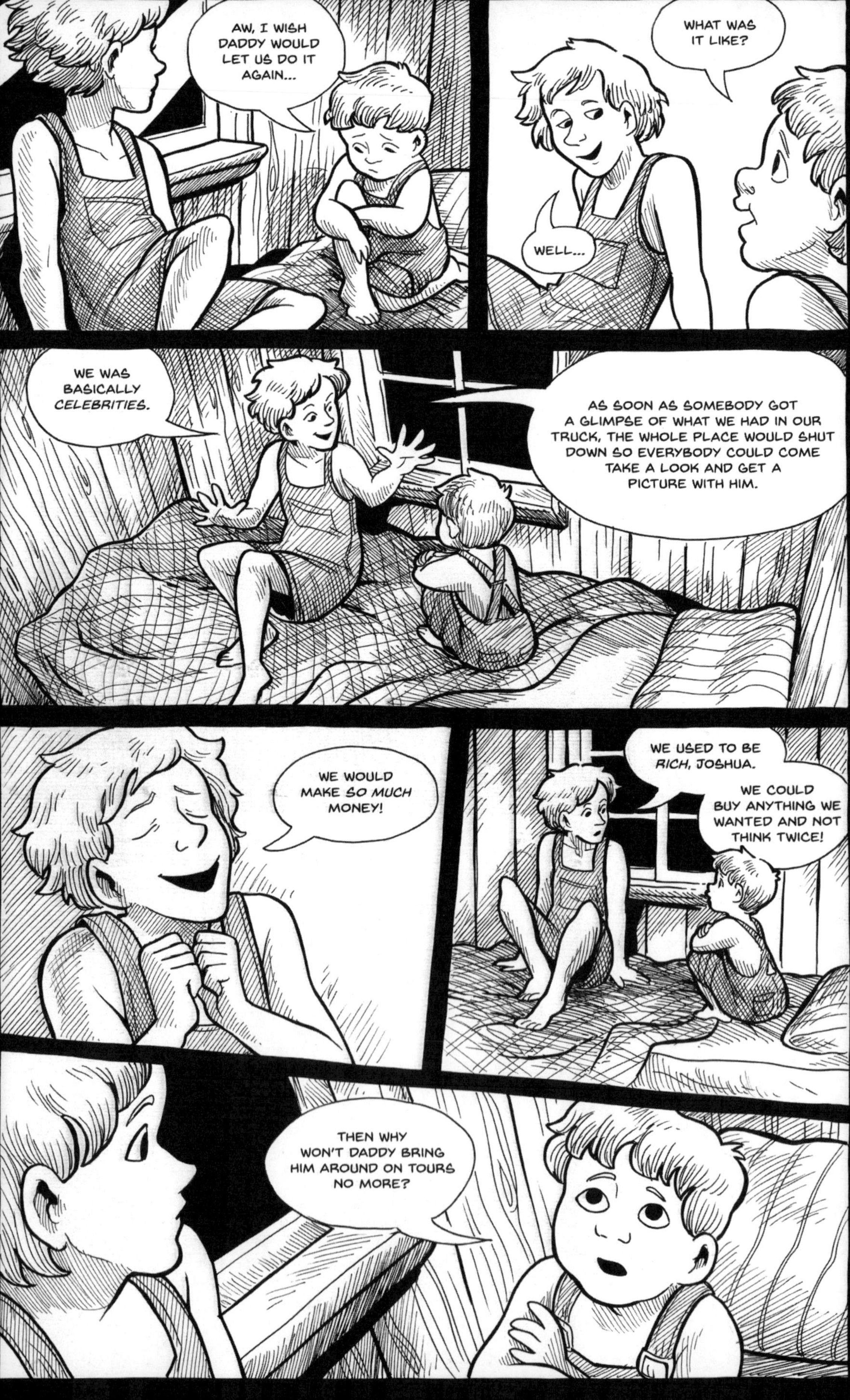

AW, I WISH DADDY WOULD LET US DO IT AGAIN...
WHAT WAS IT LIKE?
WELL...
WE WAS BASICALLY *CELEBRITIES.*
AS SOON AS SOMEBODY GOT A GLIMPSE OF WHAT WE HAD IN OUR TRUCK, THE WHOLE PLACE WOULD SHUT DOWN SO EVERYBODY COULD COME TAKE A LOOK AND GET A PICTURE WITH HIM.
WE WOULD MAKE *SO MUCH* MONEY!
WE USED TO BE *RICH*, JOSHUA.
WE COULD BUY ANYTHING WE WANTED AND NOT THINK TWICE!
THEN WHY WON'T DADDY BRING HIM AROUND ON TOURS NO MORE?

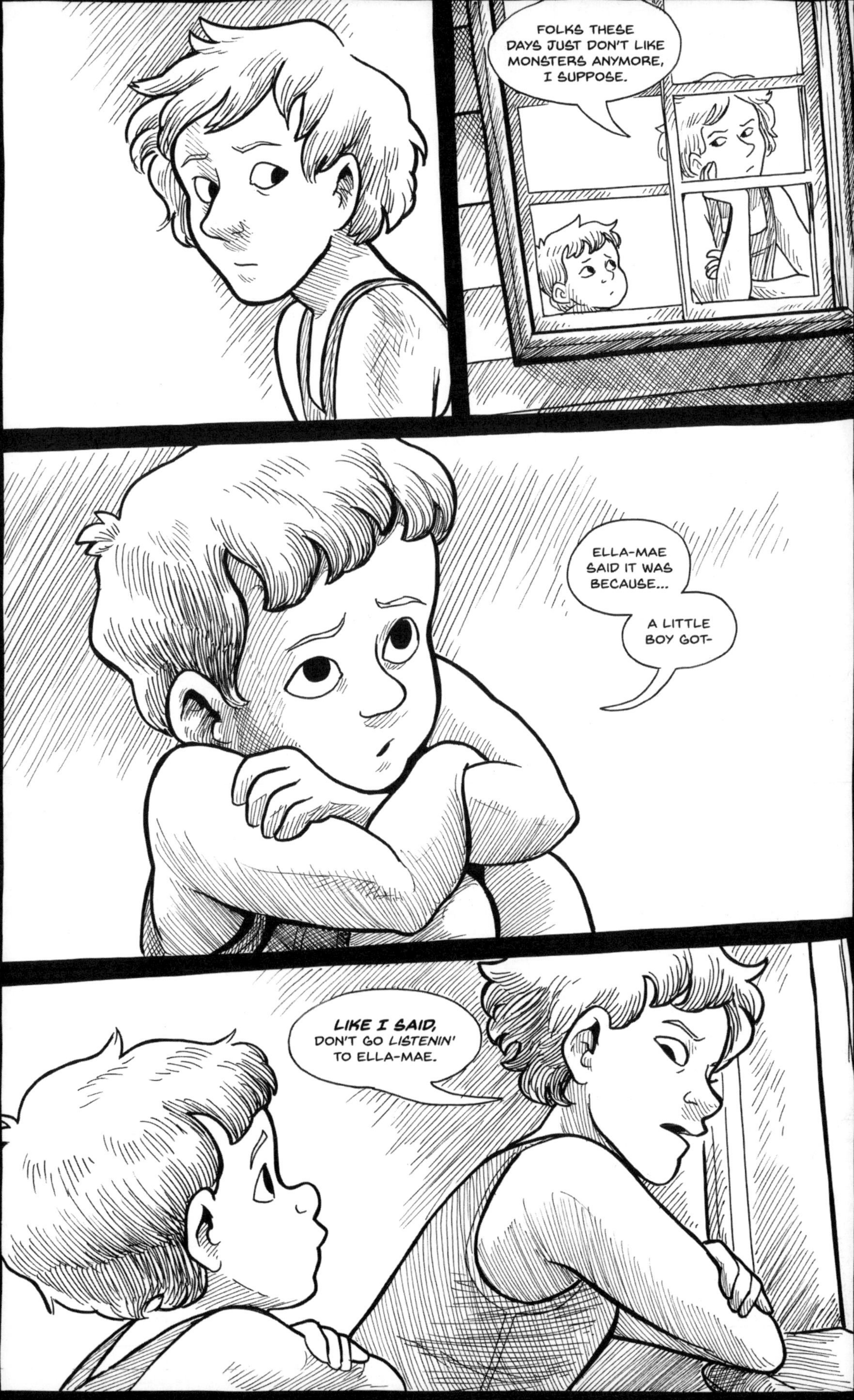
FOLKS THESE DAYS JUST DON'T LIKE MONSTERS ANYMORE, I SUPPOSE.
ELLA-MAE SAID IT WAS BECAUSE...
A LITTLE BOY GOT-
LIKE I SAID, DON'T GO *LISTENIN'* TO ELLA-MAE.

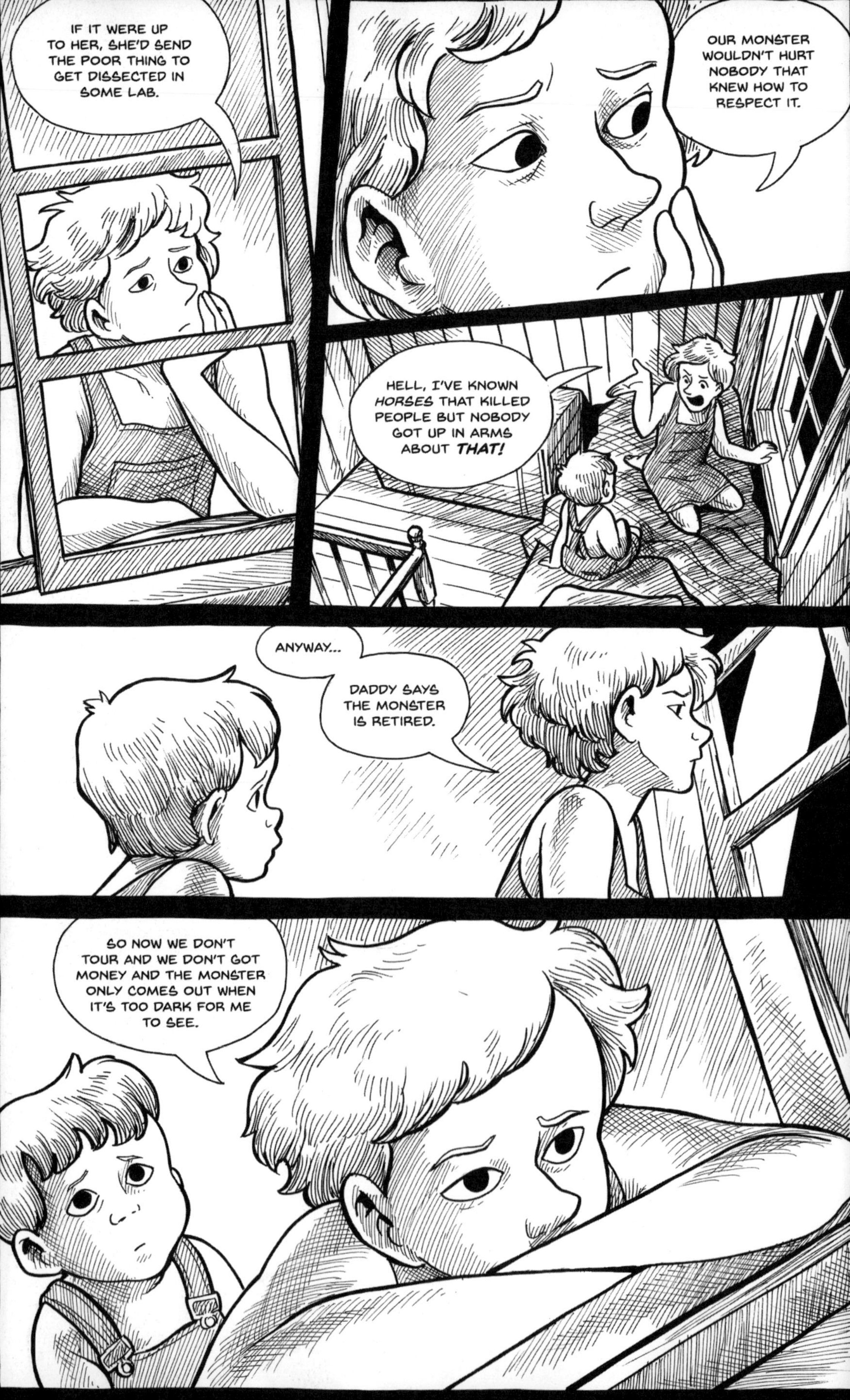
IF IT WERE UP TO HER, SHE'D SEND THE POOR THING TO GET DISSECTED IN SOME LAB.
OUR MONSTER WOULDN'T HURT NOBODY THAT KNEW HOW TO RESPECT IT.
HELL, I'VE KNOWN *HORSES* THAT KILLED PEOPLE BUT NOBODY GOT UP IN ARMS ABOUT ***THAT!***
ANYWAY...
DADDY SAYS THE MONSTER IS RETIRED.
SO NOW WE DON'T TOUR AND WE DON'T GOT MONEY AND THE MONSTER ONLY COMES OUT WHEN IT'S TOO DARK FOR ME TO SEE.

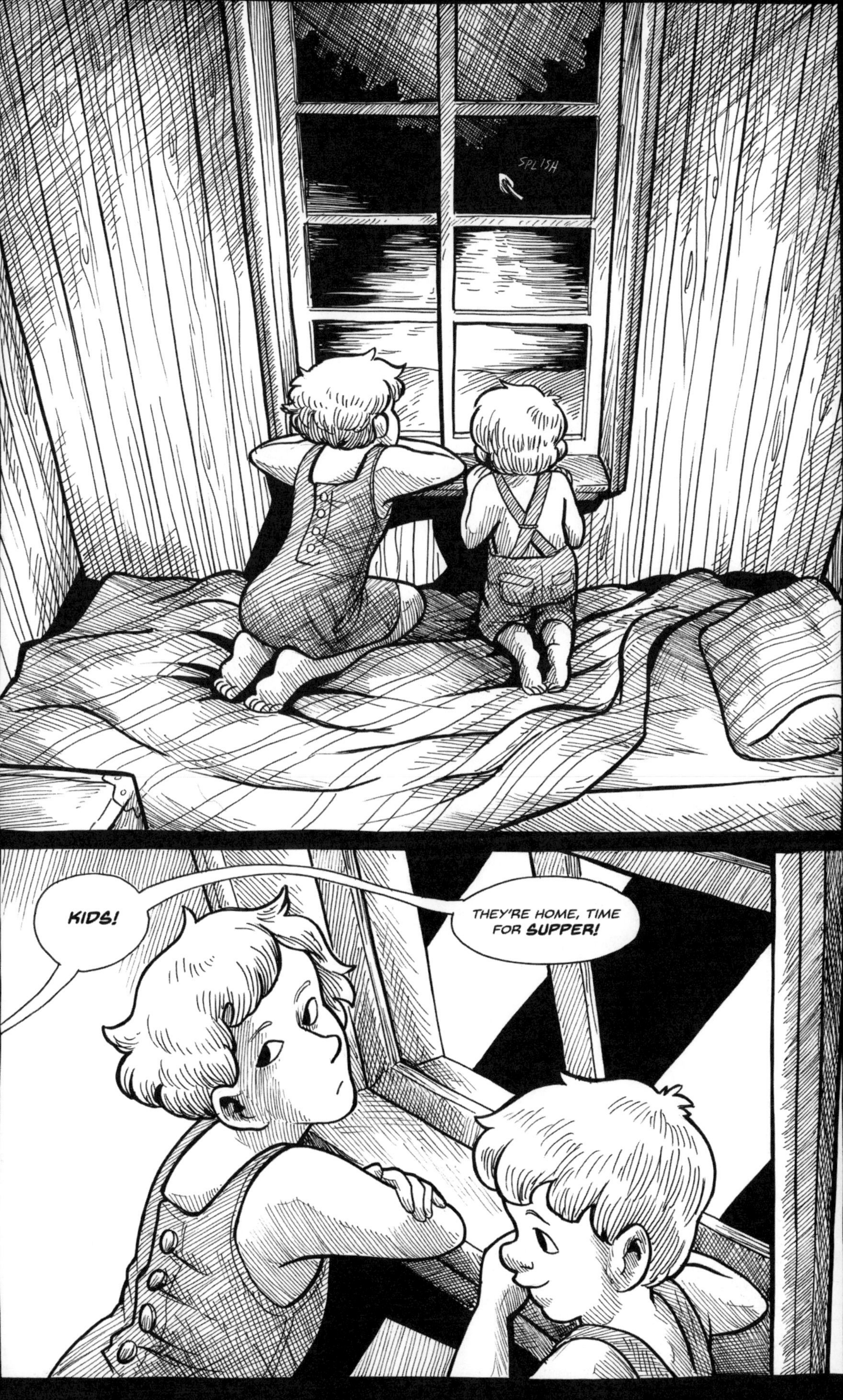
SPLISH
KIDS!
THEY'RE HOME, TIME FOR SUPPER!

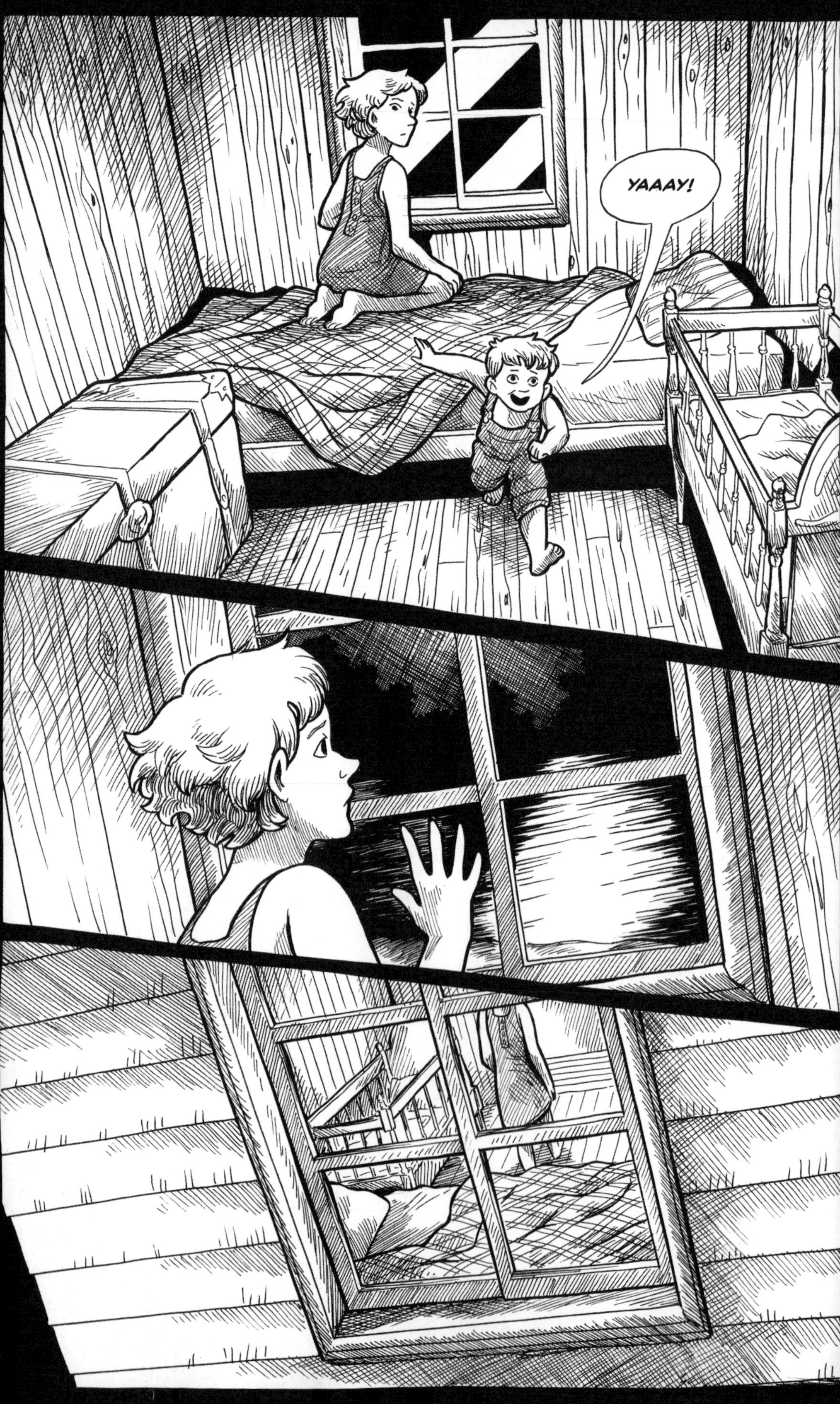
YAAAY!

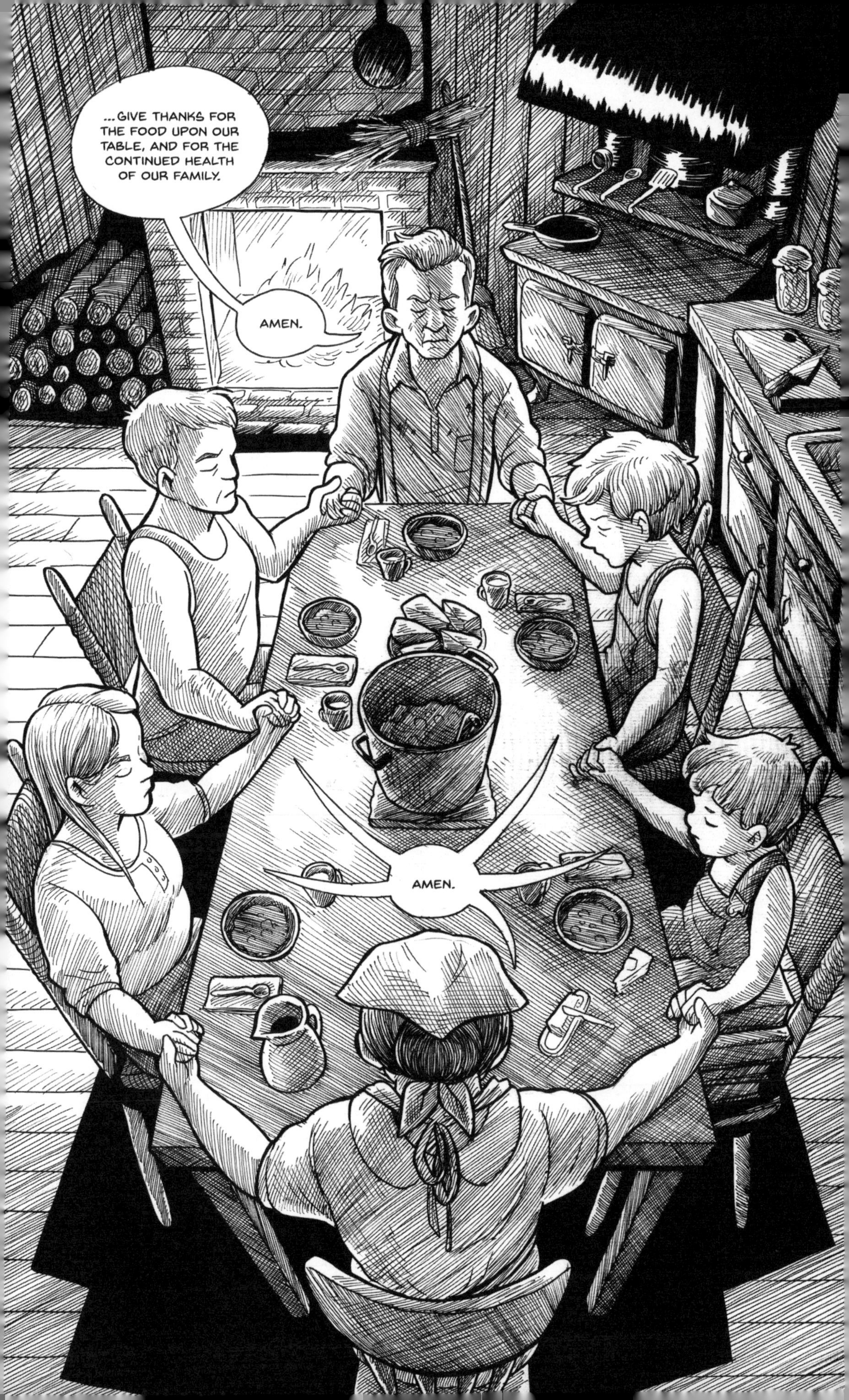
...GIVE THANKS FOR THE FOOD UPON OUR TABLE, AND FOR THE CONTINUED HEALTH OF OUR FAMILY.
AMEN.
AMEN.

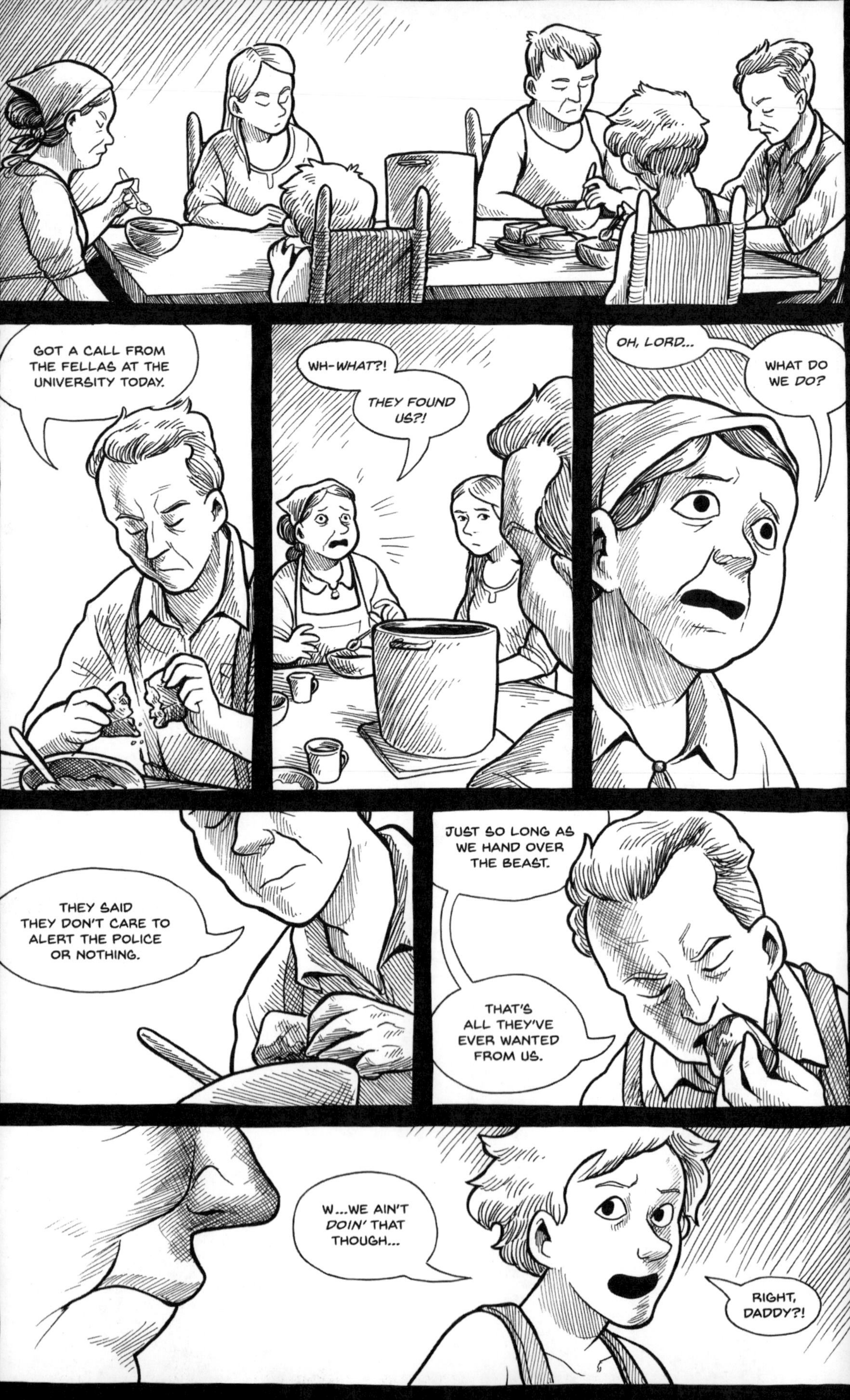

GOT A CALL FROM THE FELLAS AT THE UNIVERSITY TODAY.
WH-*WHAT?!*
THEY FOUND US?!
OH, LORD...
WHAT DO WE *DO?*
THEY SAID THEY DON'T CARE TO ALERT THE POLICE OR NOTHING.
JUST SO LONG AS WE HAND OVER THE BEAST.
THAT'S ALL THEY'VE EVER WANTED FROM US.
W...WE AIN'T *DOIN'* THAT THOUGH...
RIGHT, DADDY?!

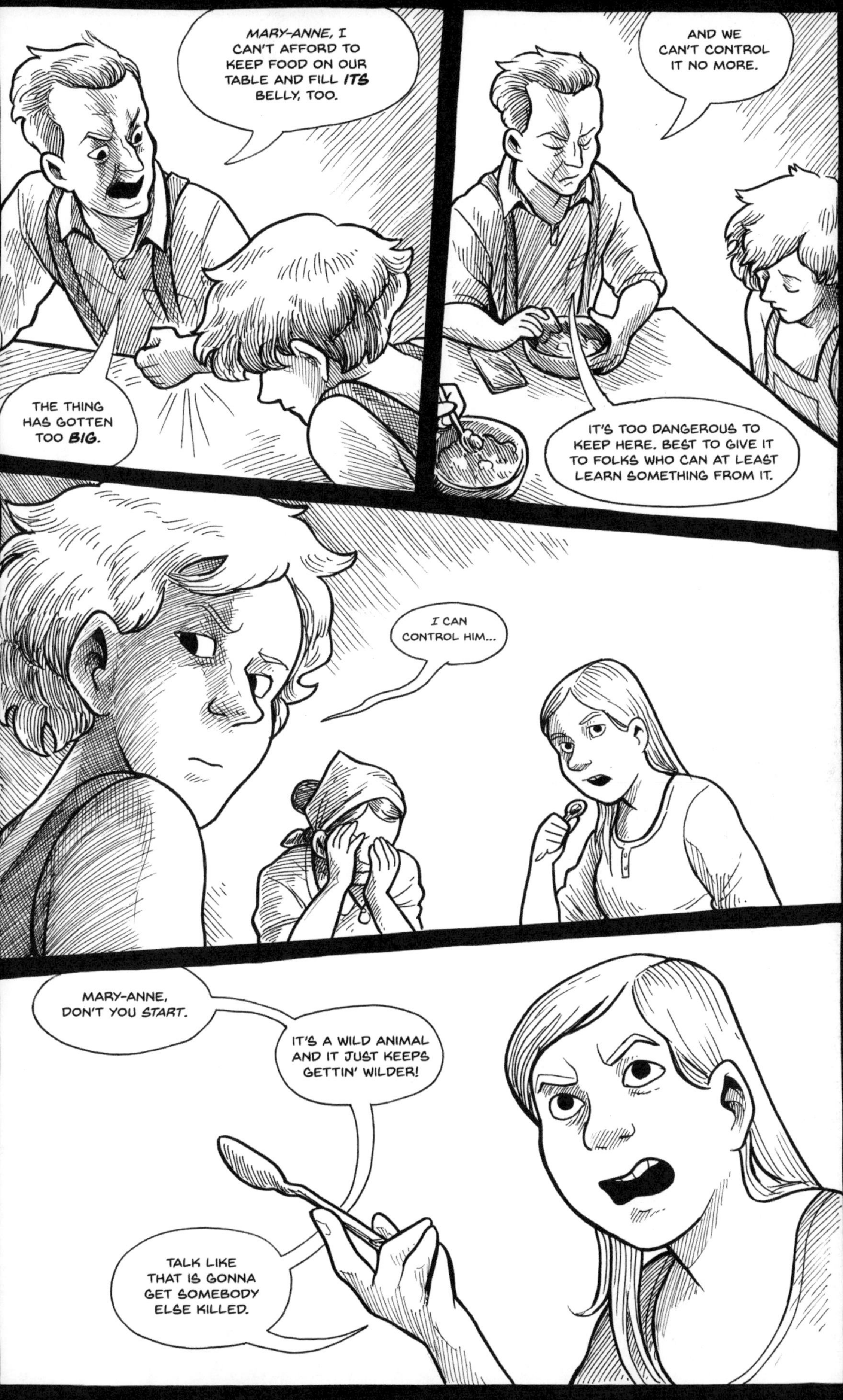
MARY-ANNE, I CAN'T AFFORD TO KEEP FOOD ON OUR TABLE AND FILL ITS BELLY, TOO.
THE THING HAS GOTTEN TOO BIG.
AND WE CAN'T CONTROL IT NO MORE.
IT'S TOO DANGEROUS TO KEEP HERE. BEST TO GIVE IT TO FOLKS WHO CAN AT LEAST LEARN SOMETHING FROM IT.
I CAN CONTROL HIM...
MARY-ANNE, DON'T YOU START.
IT'S A WILD ANIMAL AND IT JUST KEEPS GETTIN' WILDER!
TALK LIKE THAT IS GONNA GET SOMEBODY ELSE KILLED.

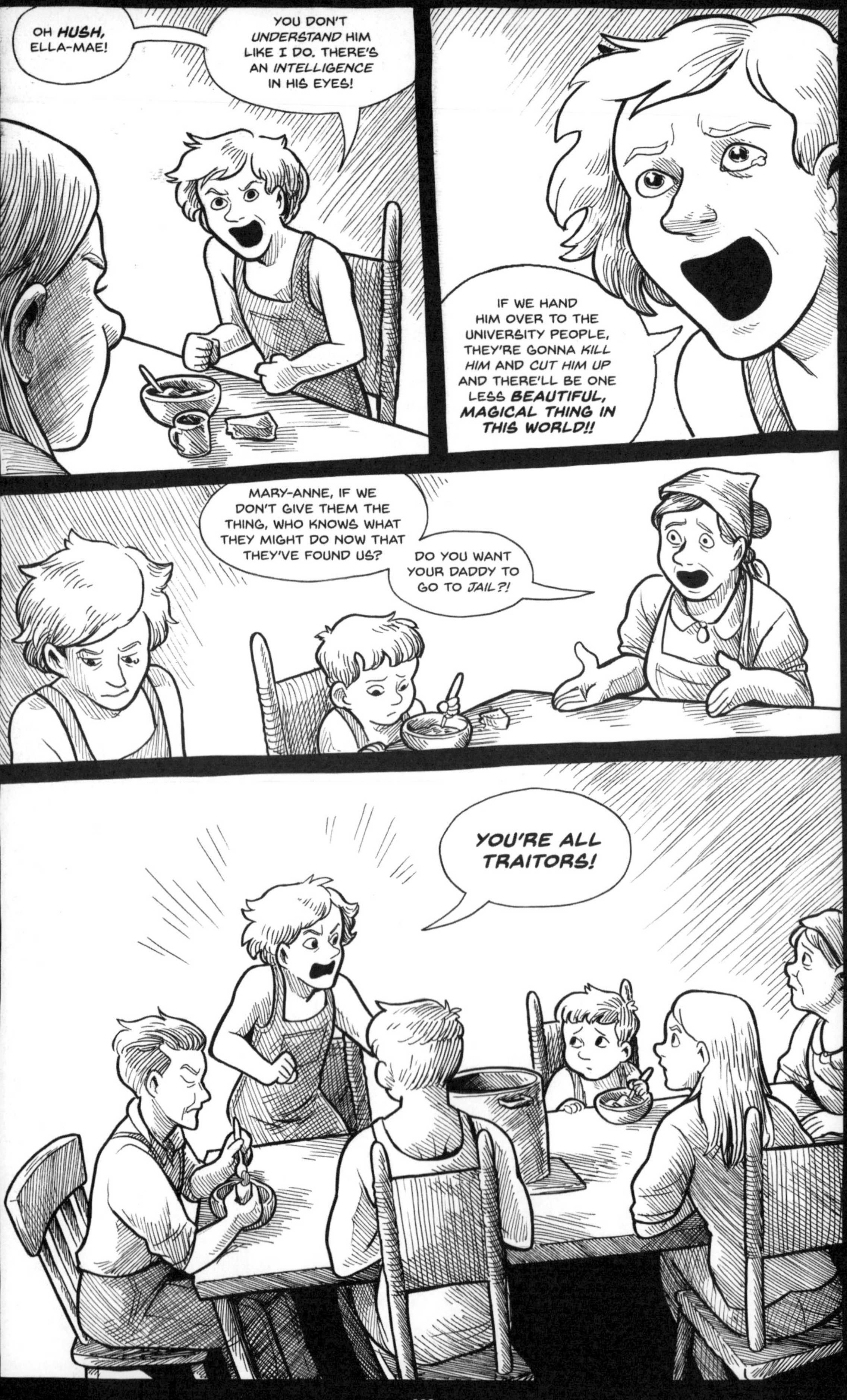
OH HUSH, ELLA-MAE!
YOU DON'T UNDERSTAND HIM LIKE I DO. THERE'S AN INTELLIGENCE IN HIS EYES!
IF WE HAND HIM OVER TO THE UNIVERSITY PEOPLE, THEY'RE GONNA KILL HIM AND CUT HIM UP AND THERE'LL BE ONE LESS BEAUTIFUL, MAGICAL THING IN THIS WORLD!!
MARY-ANNE, IF WE DON'T GIVE THEM THE THING, WHO KNOWS WHAT THEY MIGHT DO NOW THAT THEY'VE FOUND US?
DO YOU WANT YOUR DADDY TO GO TO JAIL?!
YOU'RE ALL TRAITORS!

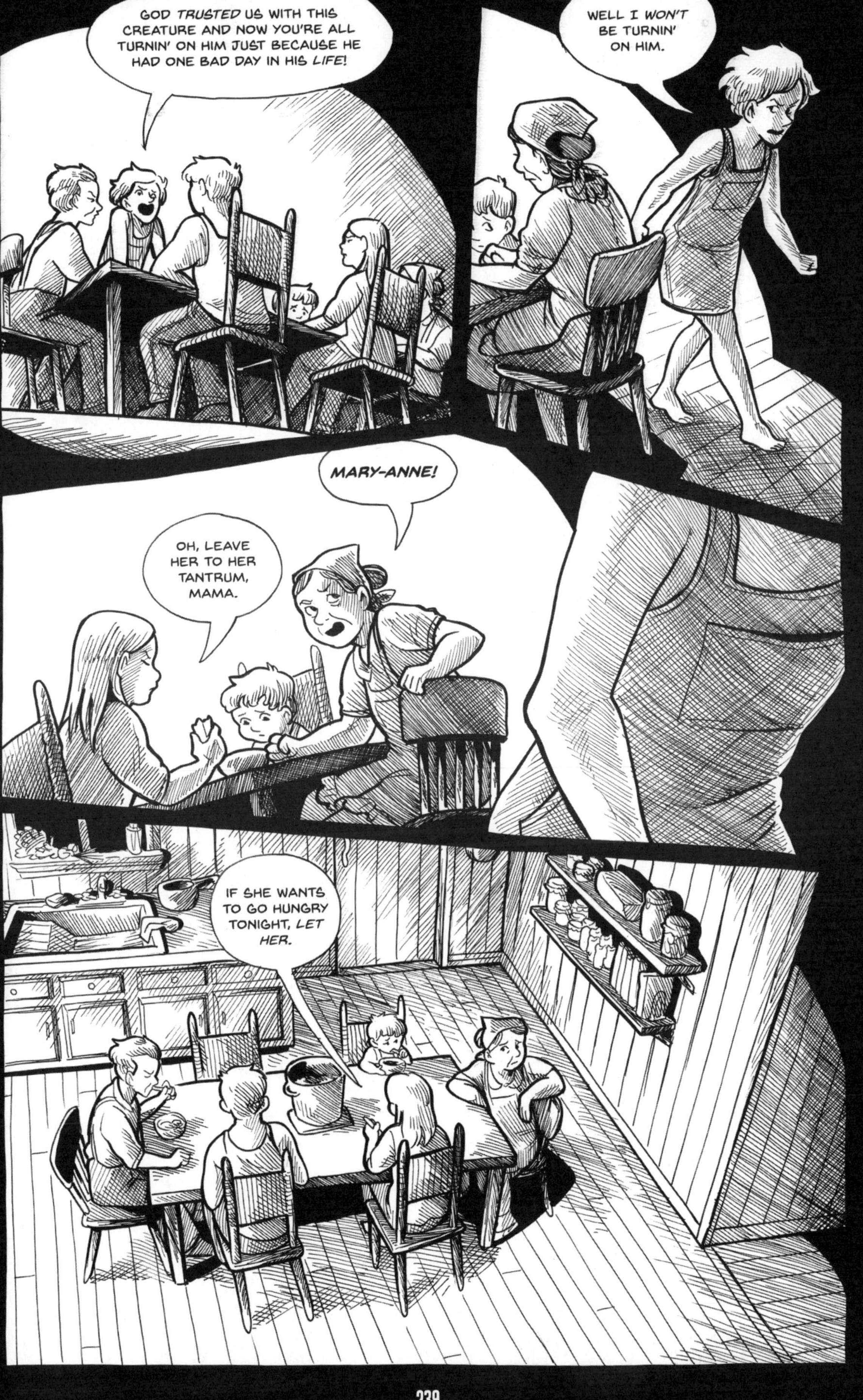
GOD *TRUSTED* US WITH THIS CREATURE AND NOW YOU'RE ALL TURNIN' ON HIM JUST BECAUSE HE HAD ONE BAD DAY IN HIS *LIFE*!
WELL I *WON'T* BE TURNIN' ON HIM.
MARY-ANNE!
OH, LEAVE HER TO HER TANTRUM, MAMA.
IF SHE WANTS TO GO HUNGRY TONIGHT, *LET HER*.

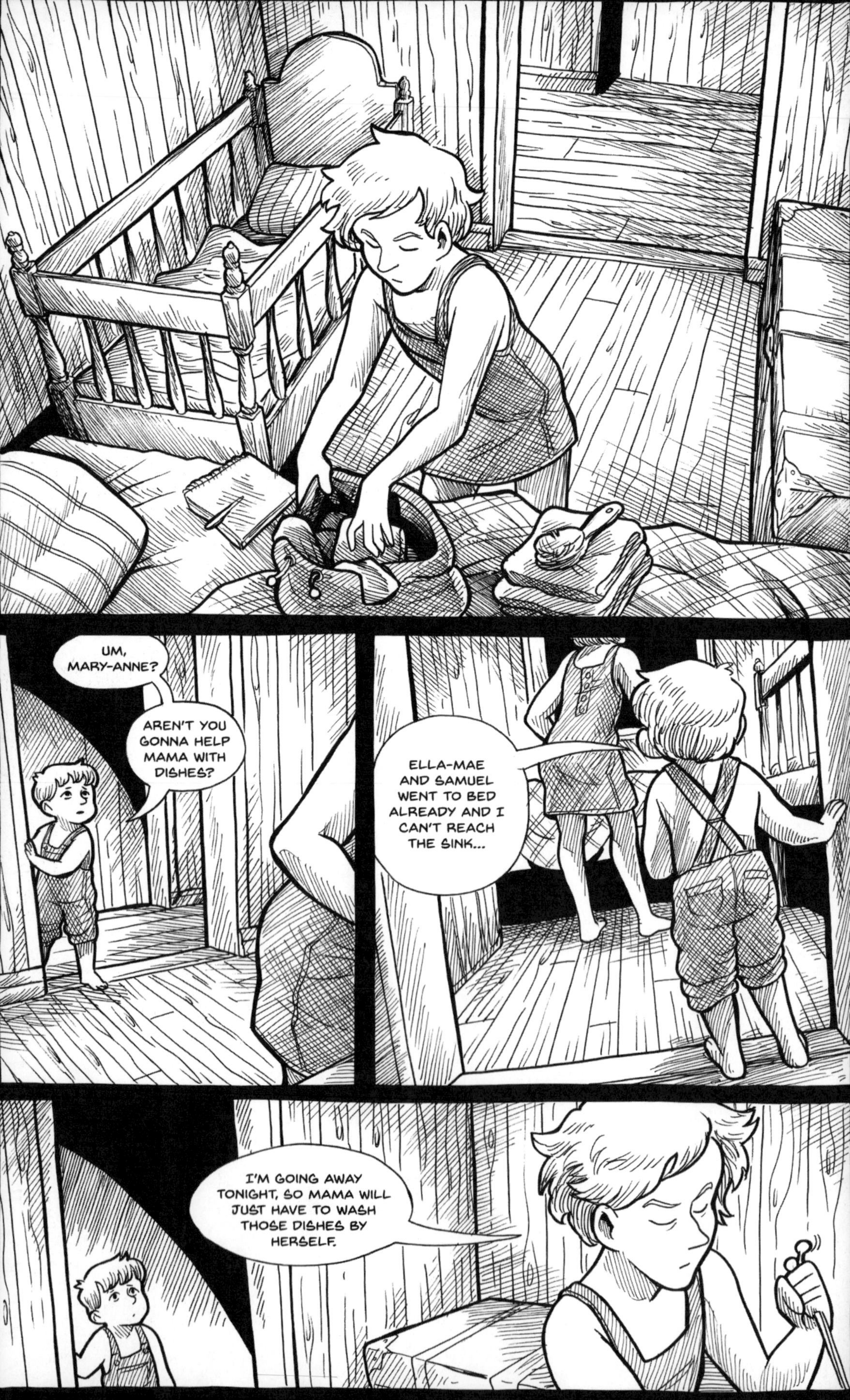
UM, MARY-ANNE?
AREN'T YOU GONNA HELP MAMA WITH DISHES?
ELLA-MAE AND SAMUEL WENT TO BED ALREADY AND I CAN'T REACH THE SINK...
I'M GOING AWAY TONIGHT, SO MAMA WILL JUST HAVE TO WASH THOSE DISHES BY HERSELF.

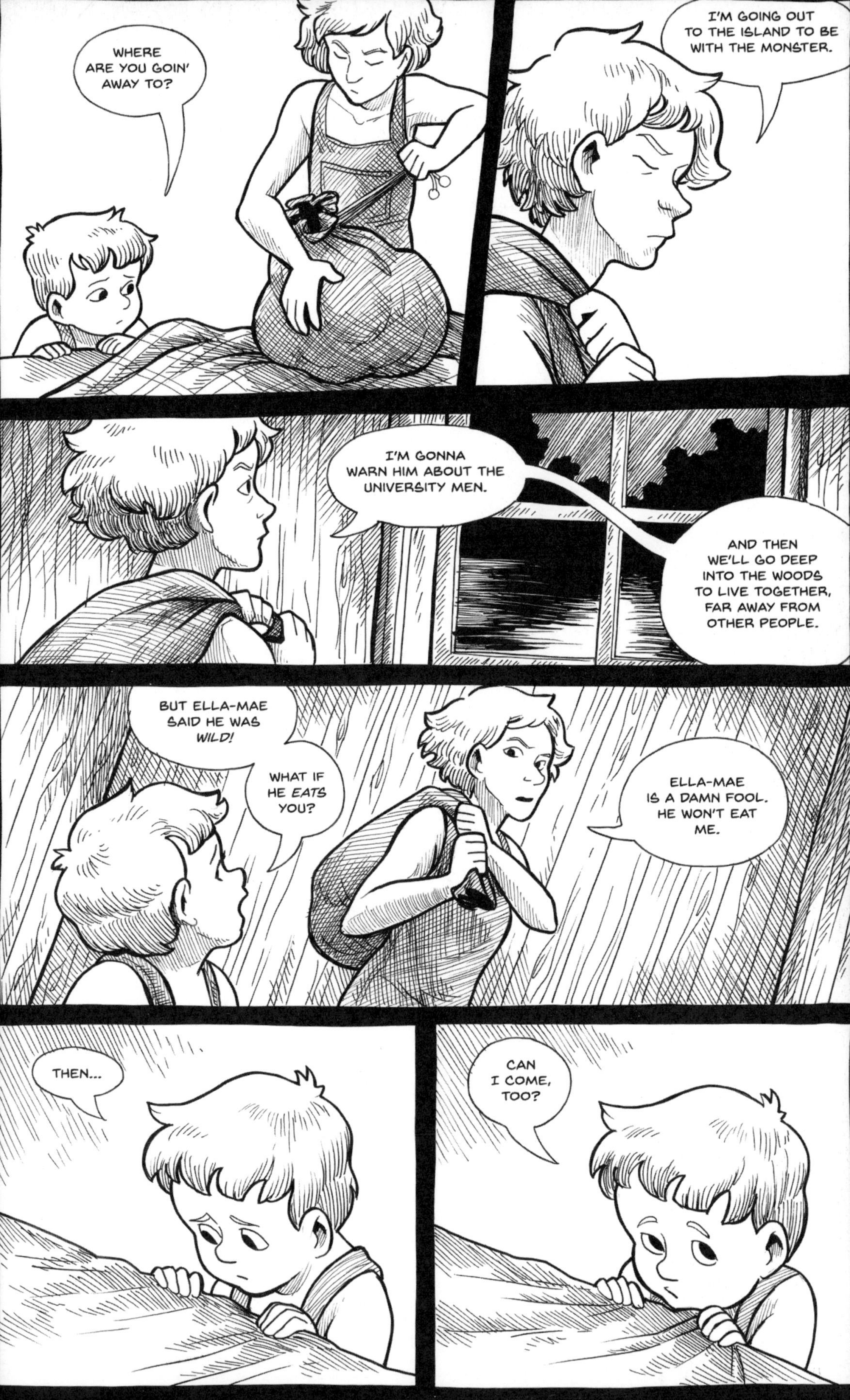
WHERE ARE YOU GOIN' AWAY TO?
I'M GOING OUT TO THE ISLAND TO BE WITH THE MONSTER.
I'M GONNA WARN HIM ABOUT THE UNIVERSITY MEN.
AND THEN WE'LL GO DEEP INTO THE WOODS TO LIVE TOGETHER, FAR AWAY FROM OTHER PEOPLE.
BUT ELLA-MAE SAID HE WAS *WILD!*
WHAT IF HE *EATS* YOU?
ELLA-MAE IS A DAMN FOOL. HE WON'T EAT ME.
THEN...
CAN I COME, TOO?

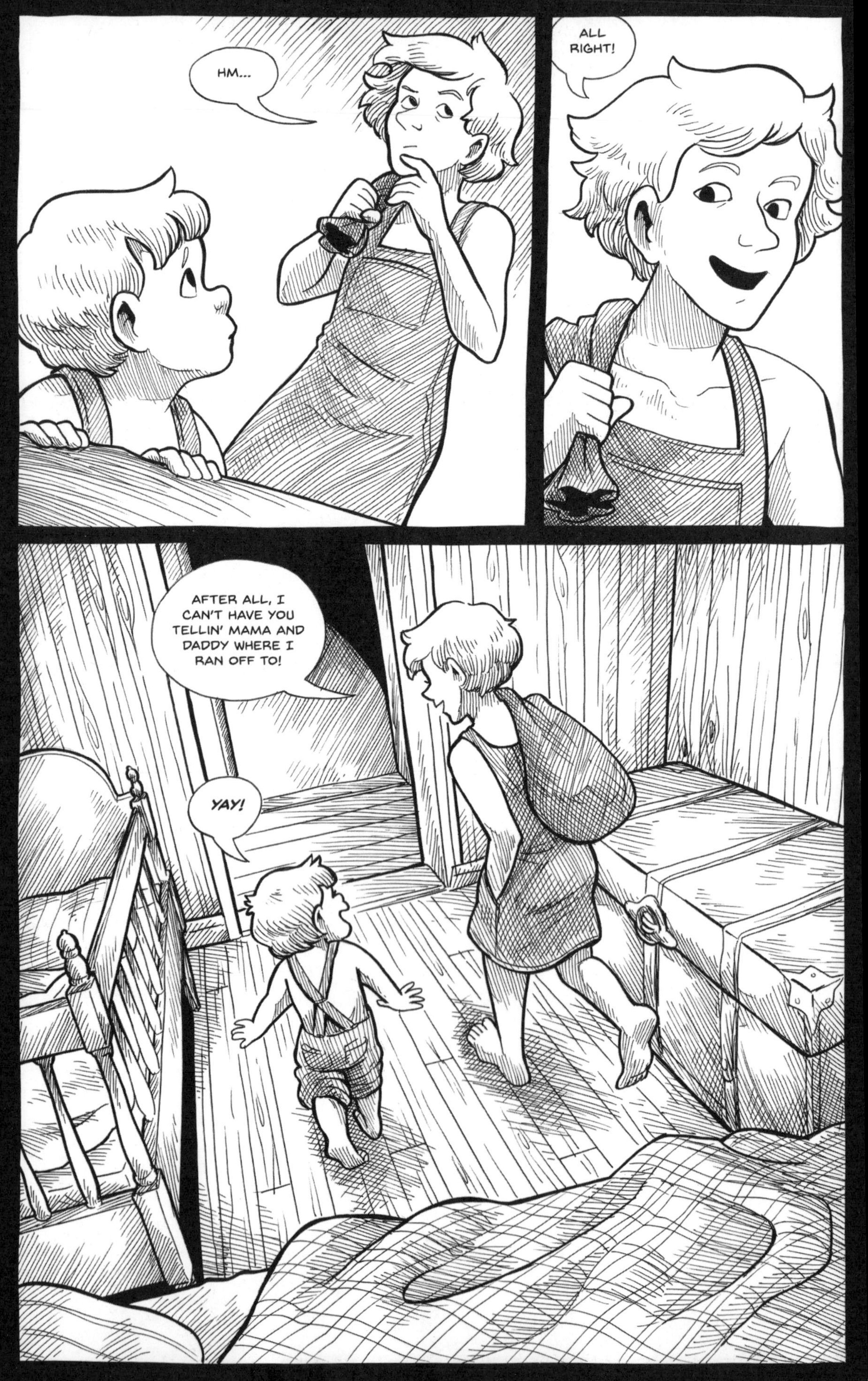
HM...
ALL RIGHT!
AFTER ALL, I CAN'T HAVE YOU TELLIN' MAMA AND DADDY WHERE I RAN OFF TO!
YAY!

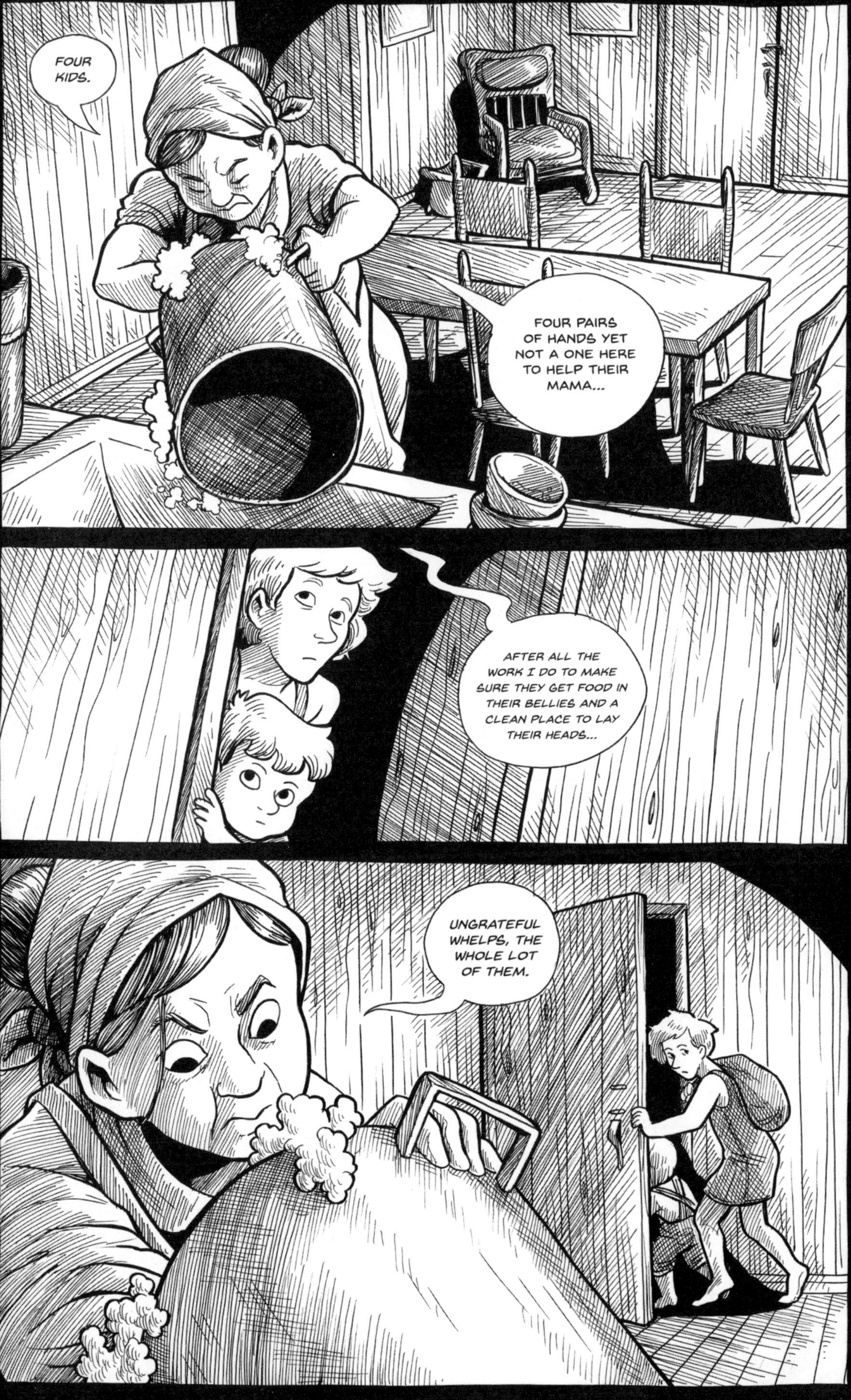
FOUR KIDS.
FOUR PAIRS OF HANDS YET NOT A ONE HERE TO HELP THEIR MAMA...
AFTER ALL THE WORK I DO TO MAKE SURE THEY GET FOOD IN THEIR BELLIES AND A CLEAN PLACE TO LAY THEIR HEADS...
UNGRATEFUL WHELPS, THE WHOLE LOT OF THEM.

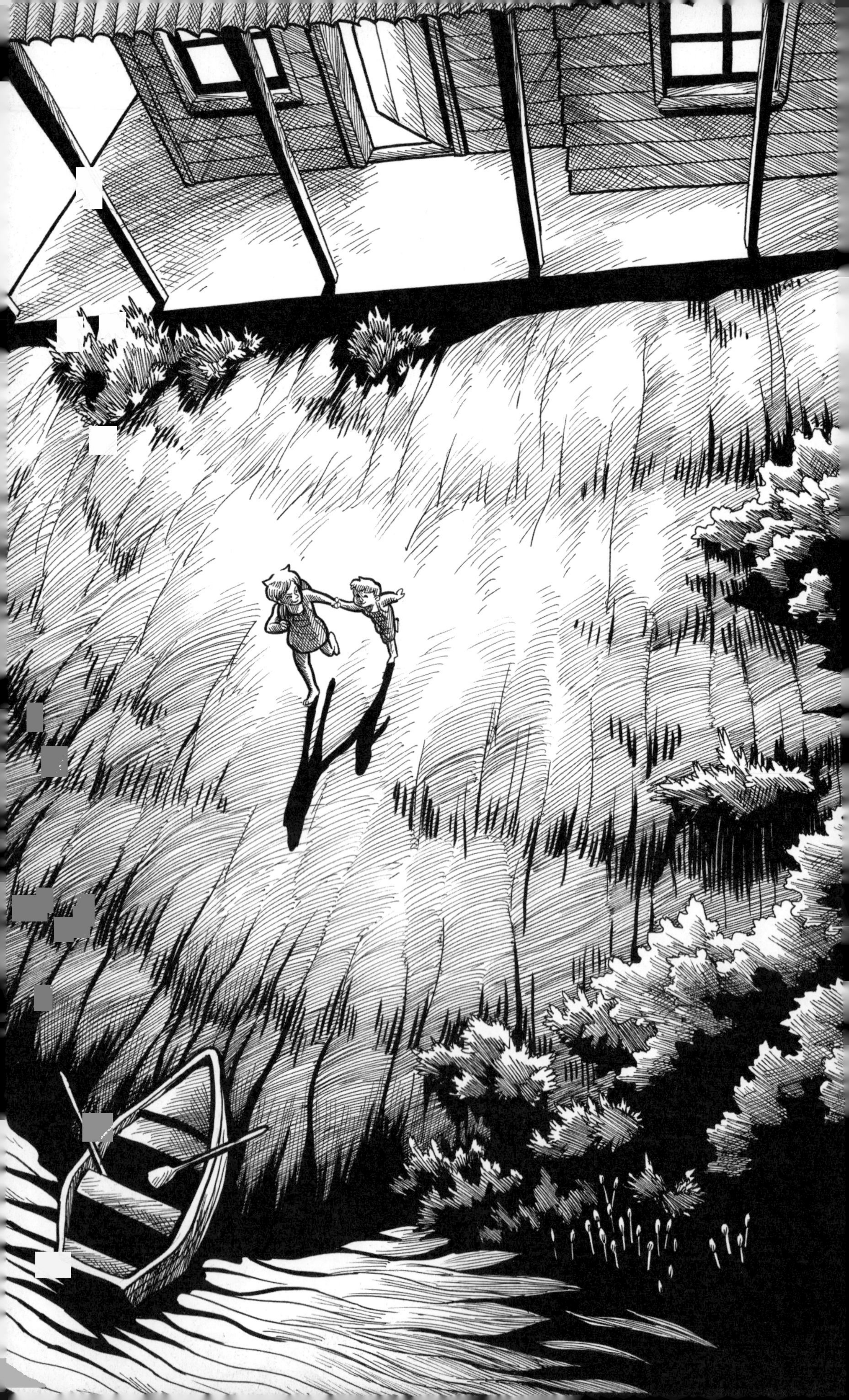

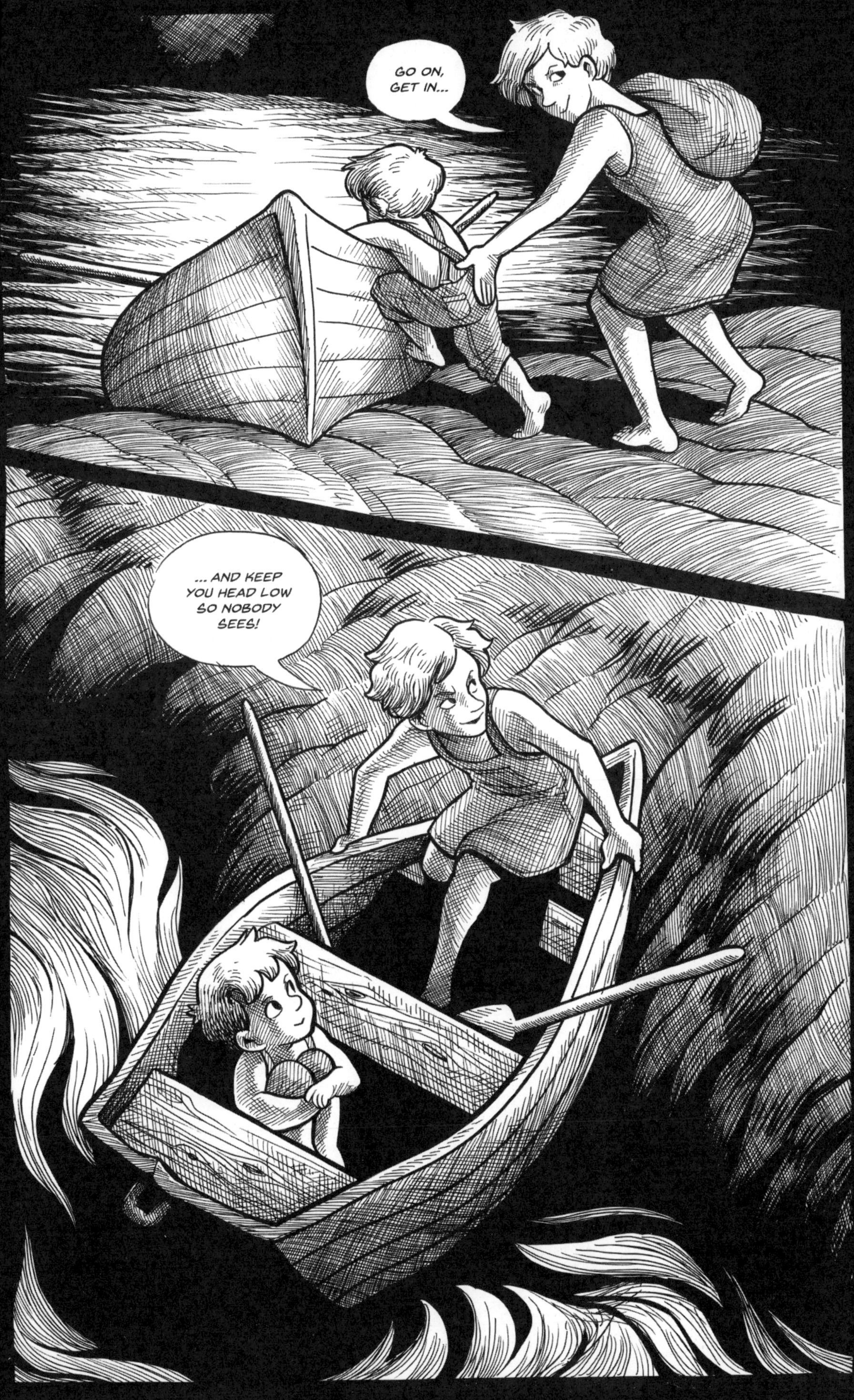
GO ON, GET IN...
... AND KEEP YOU HEAD LOW SO NOBODY SEES!

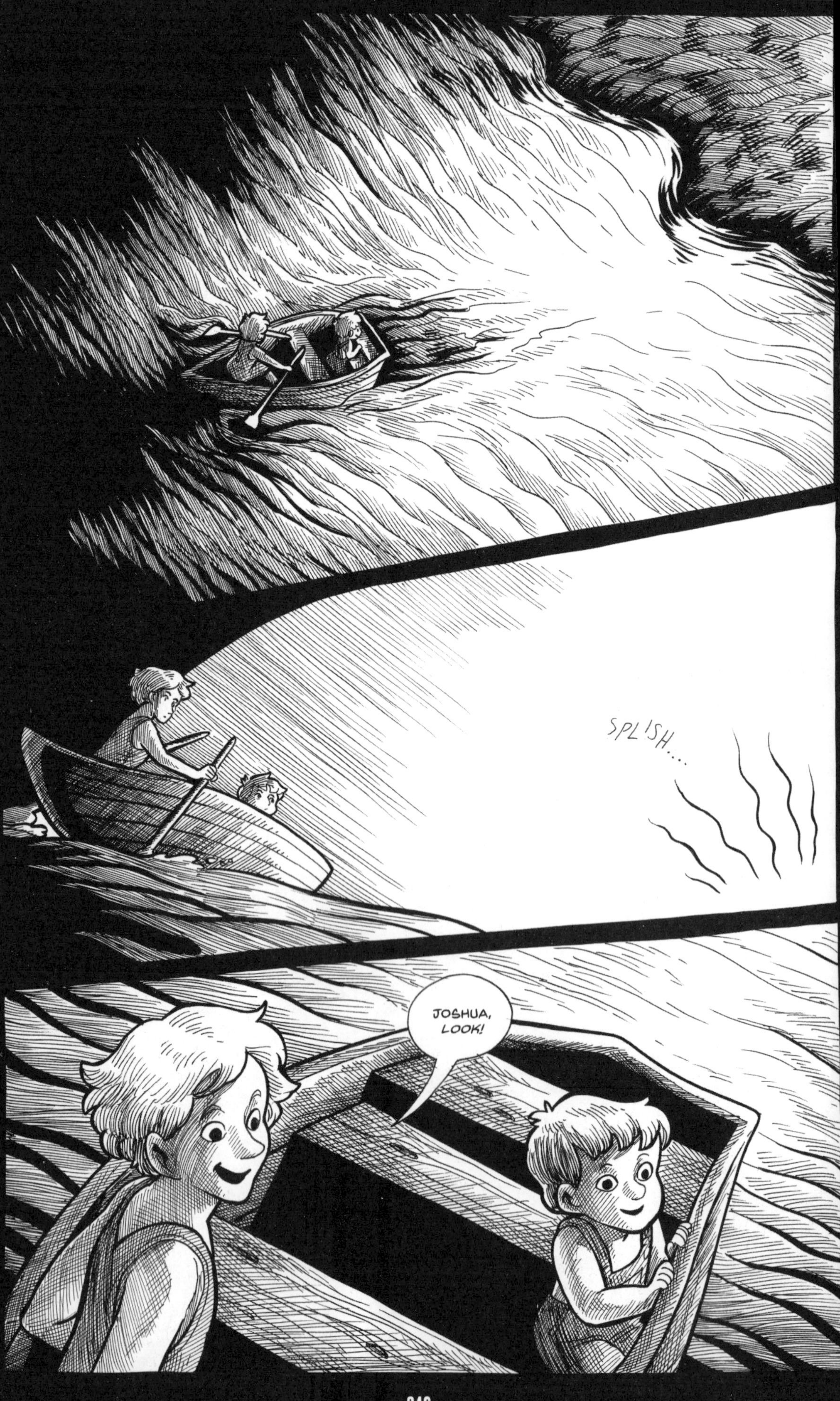
SPLISH....
JOSHUA, LOOK!

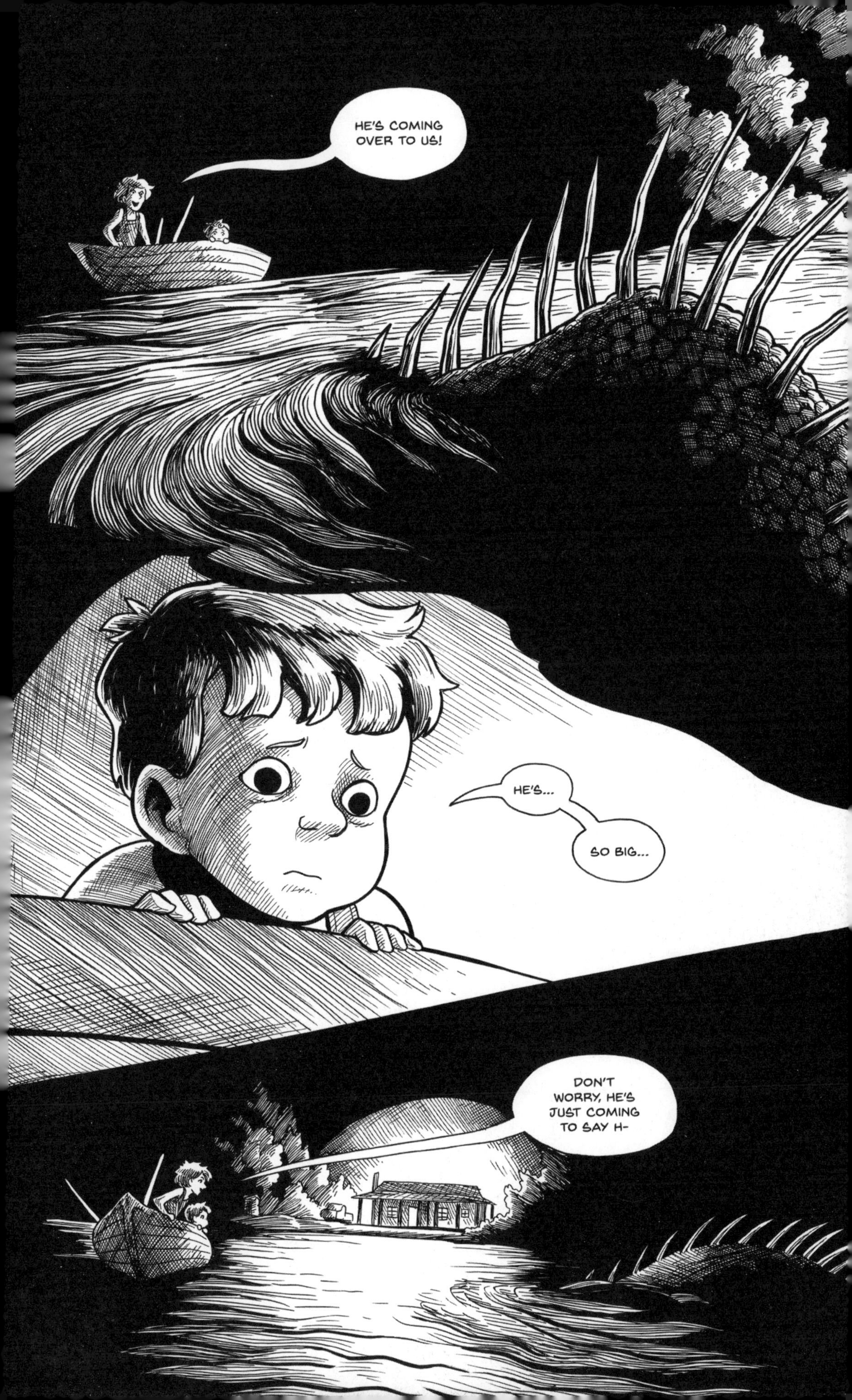
HE'S COMING OVER TO US!
HE'S...
SO BIG...
DON'T WORRY, HE'S JUST COMING TO SAY H-

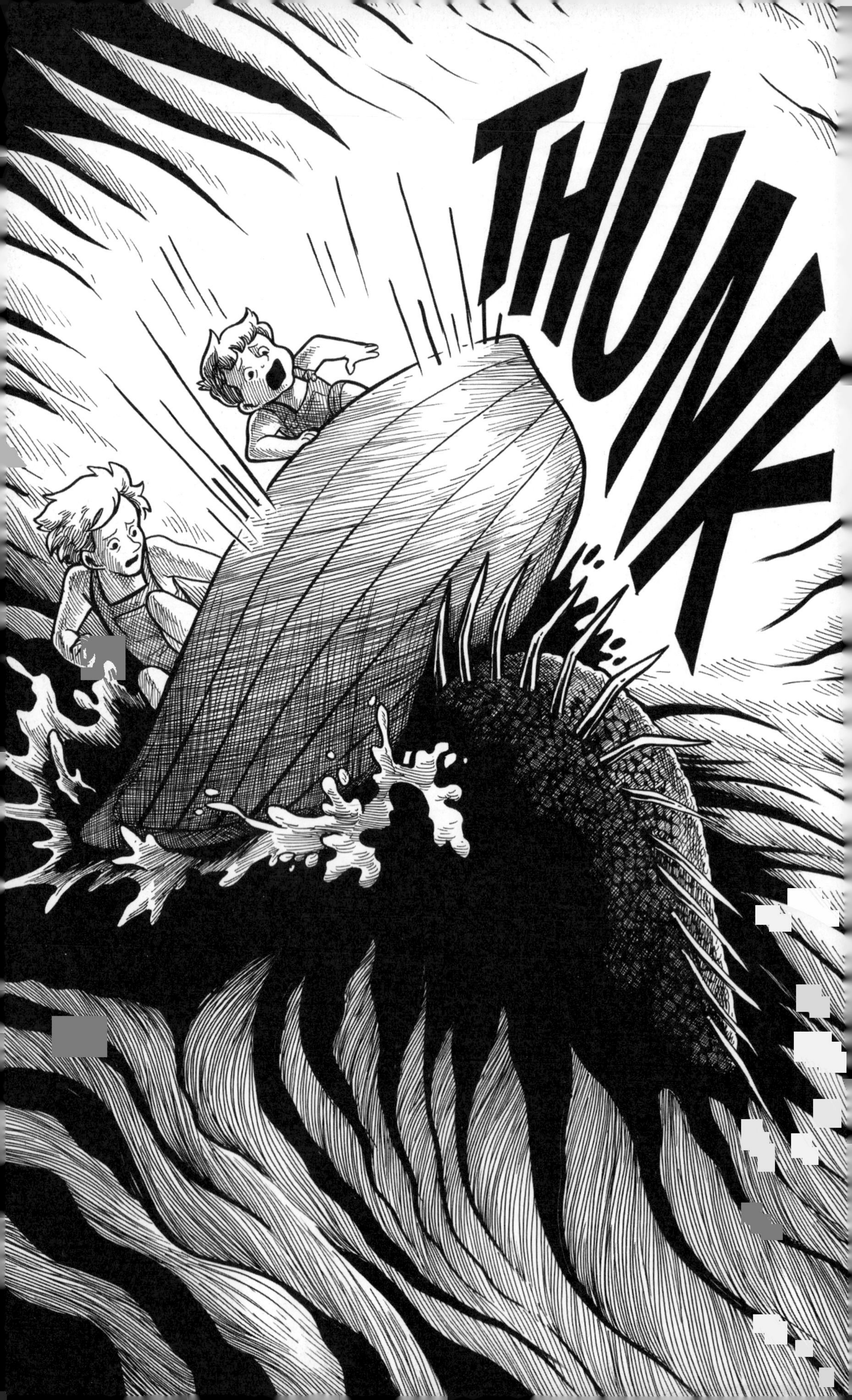
THUNK

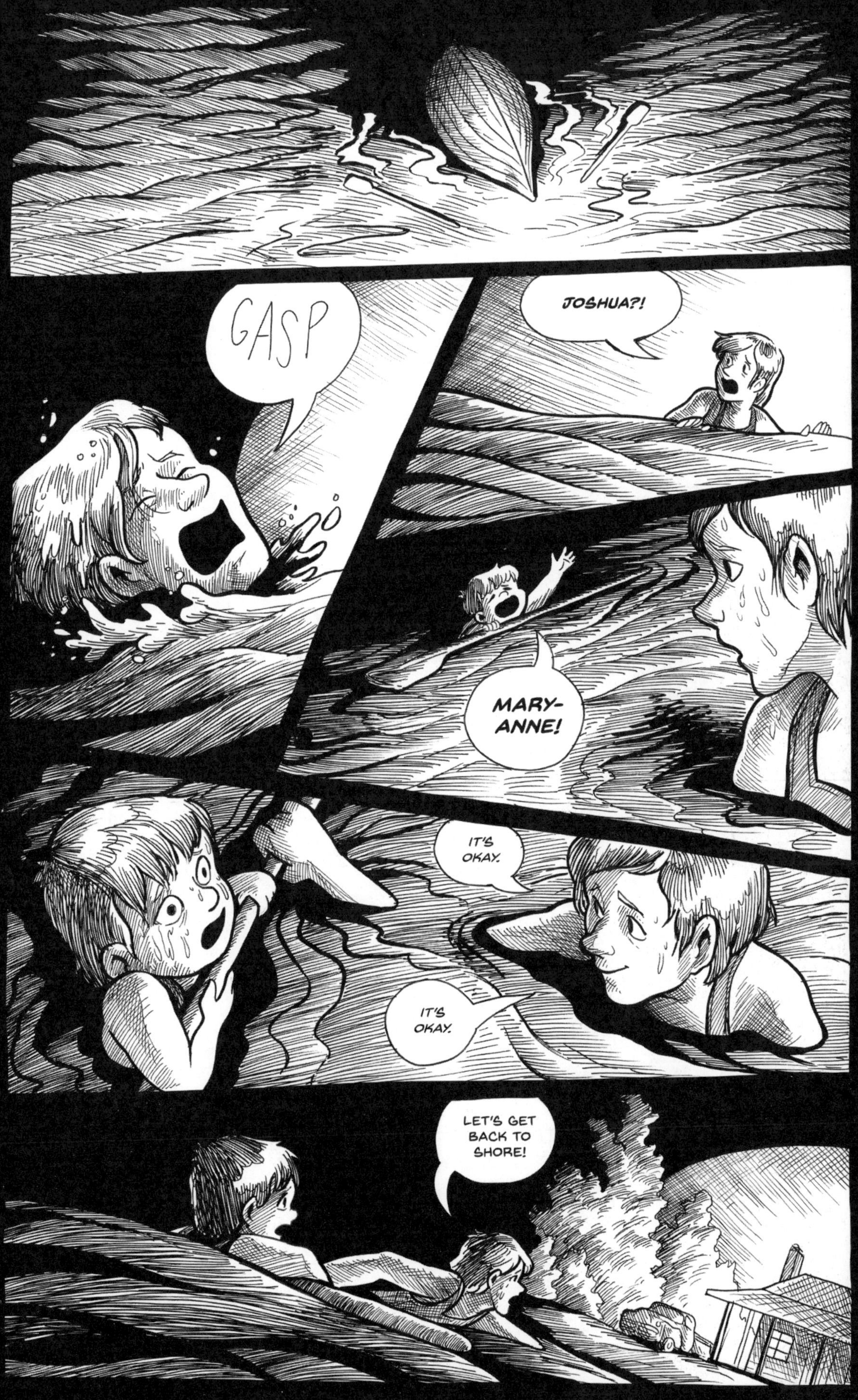
GASP
JOSHUA?!
MARY-ANNE!
IT'S OKAY.
IT'S OKAY.
LET'S GET BACK TO SHORE!

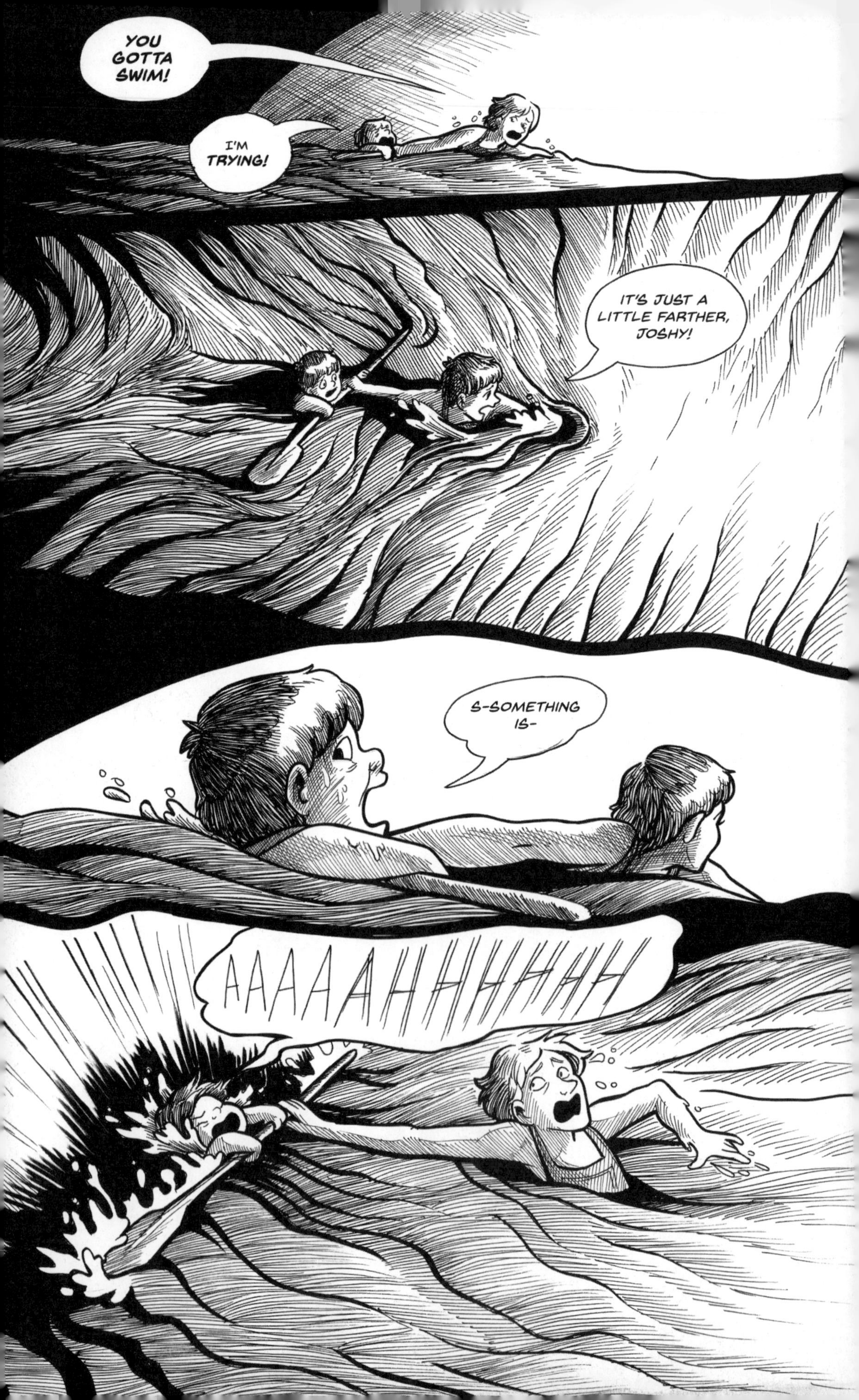
YOU GOTTA SWIM!
I'M TRYING!
IT'S JUST A LITTLE FARTHER, JOSHY!
S-SOMETHING IS-
AAAAAHHHHHHH

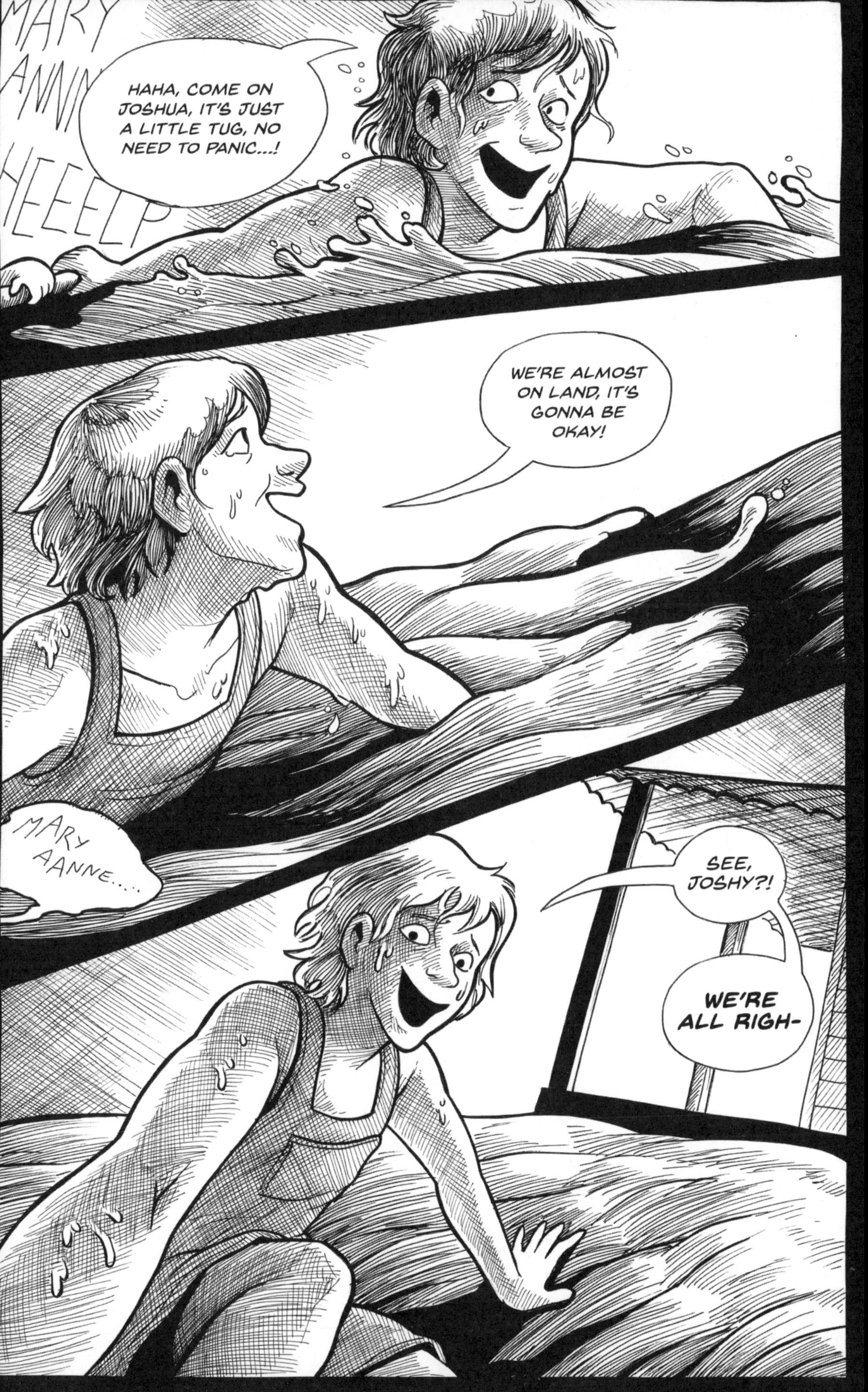
MARY ANNN HEEELP
HAHA, COME ON JOSHUA, IT'S JUST A LITTLE TUG, NO NEED TO PANIC...!
WE'RE ALMOST ON LAND, IT'S GONNA BE OKAY!
MARY AANNE.....
SEE, JOSHY?!
WE'RE ALL RIGH-

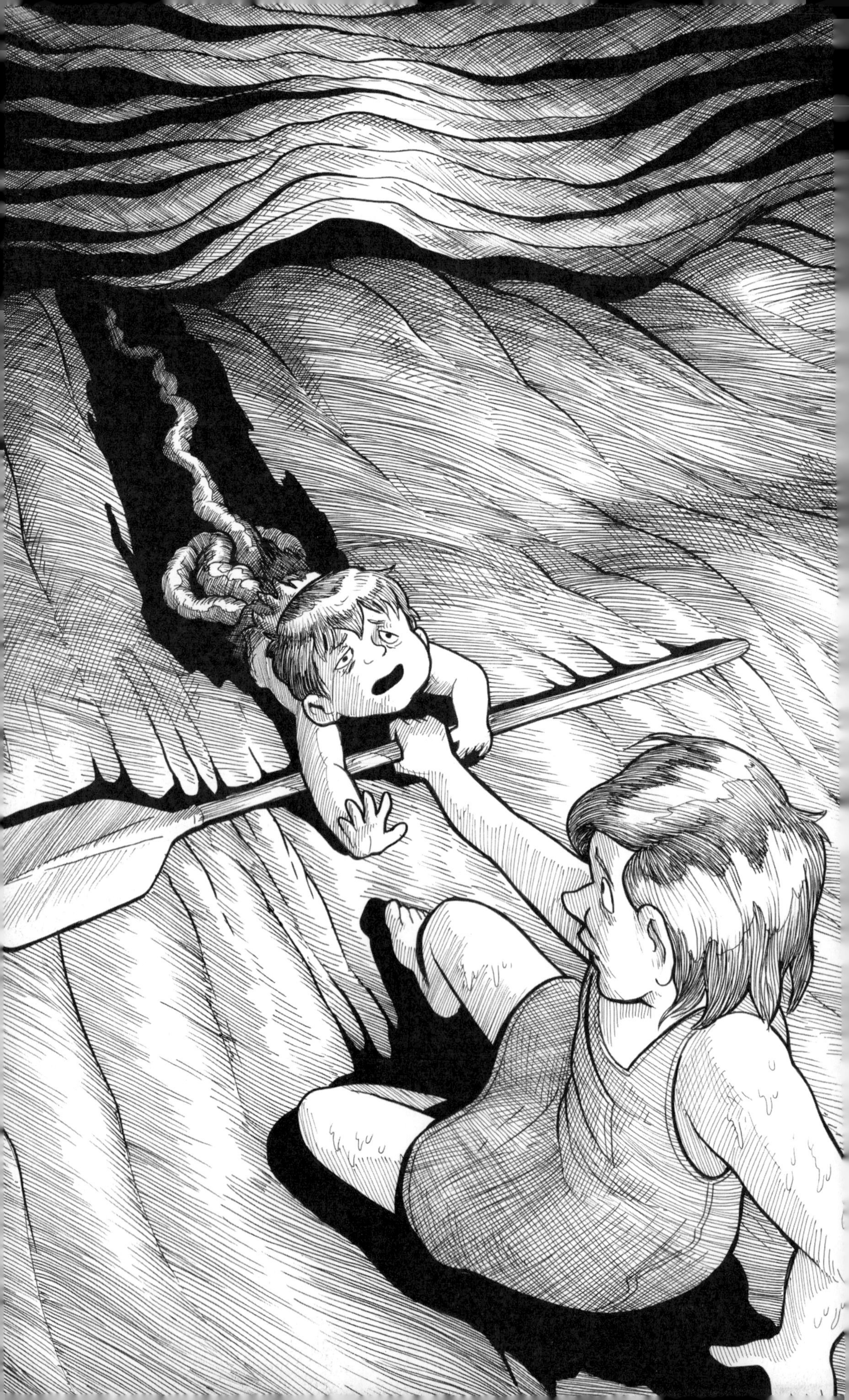

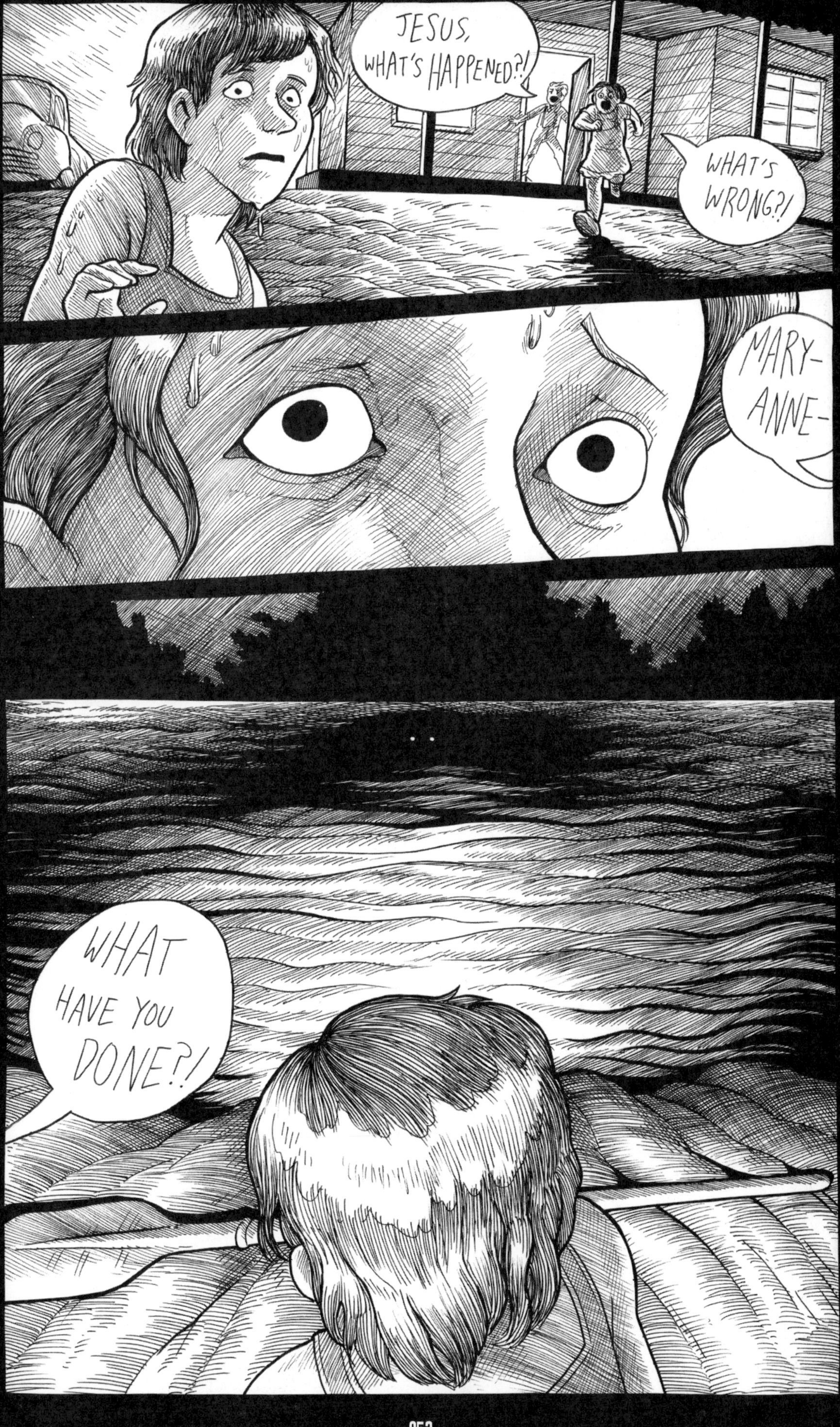
JESUS, WHAT'S HAPPENED?!
WHAT'S WRONG?!
MARY-ANNE-
WHAT HAVE YOU DONE?!

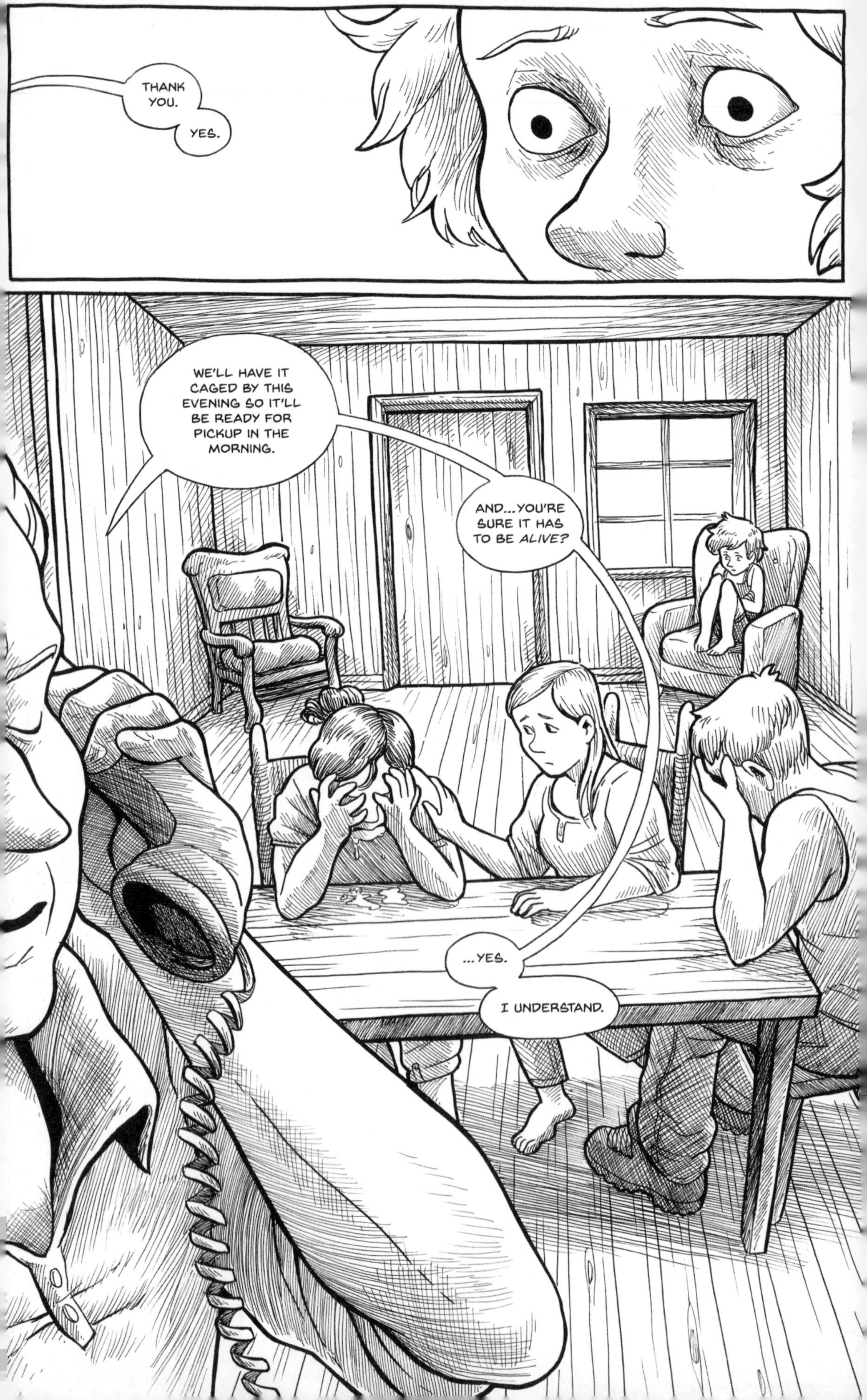
THANK YOU.
YES.
WE'LL HAVE IT CAGED BY THIS EVENING SO IT'LL BE READY FOR PICKUP IN THE MORNING.
AND...YOU'RE SURE IT HAS TO BE *ALIVE?*
...YES.
I UNDERSTAND.

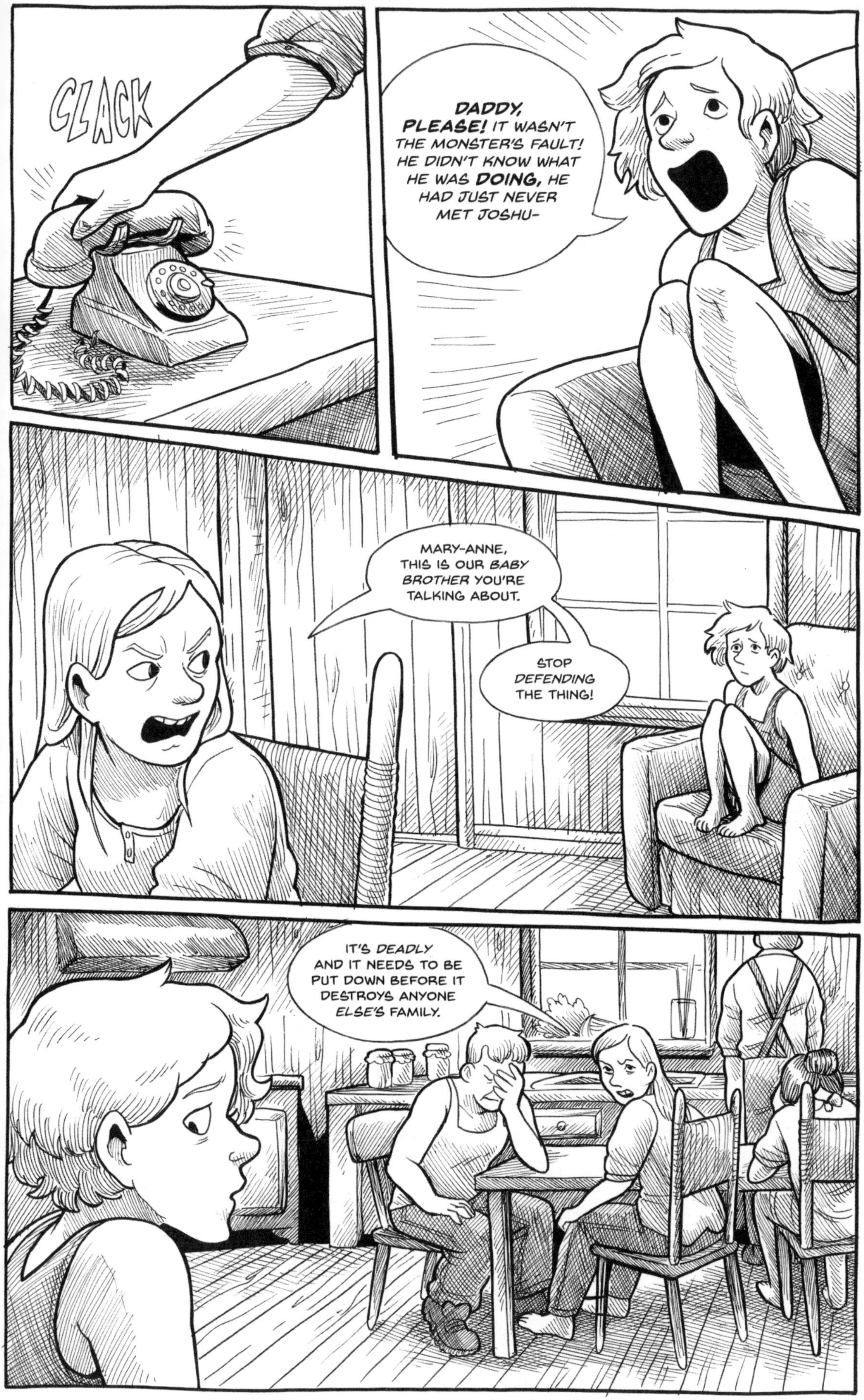
CLACK
DADDY, PLEASE! IT WASN'T THE MONSTER'S FAULT! HE DIDN'T KNOW WHAT HE WAS DOING, HE HAD JUST NEVER MET JOSHU-
MARY-ANNE, THIS IS OUR BABY BROTHER YOU'RE TALKING ABOUT.
STOP DEFENDING THE THING!
IT'S DEADLY AND IT NEEDS TO BE PUT DOWN BEFORE IT DESTROYS ANYONE ELSE'S FAMILY.

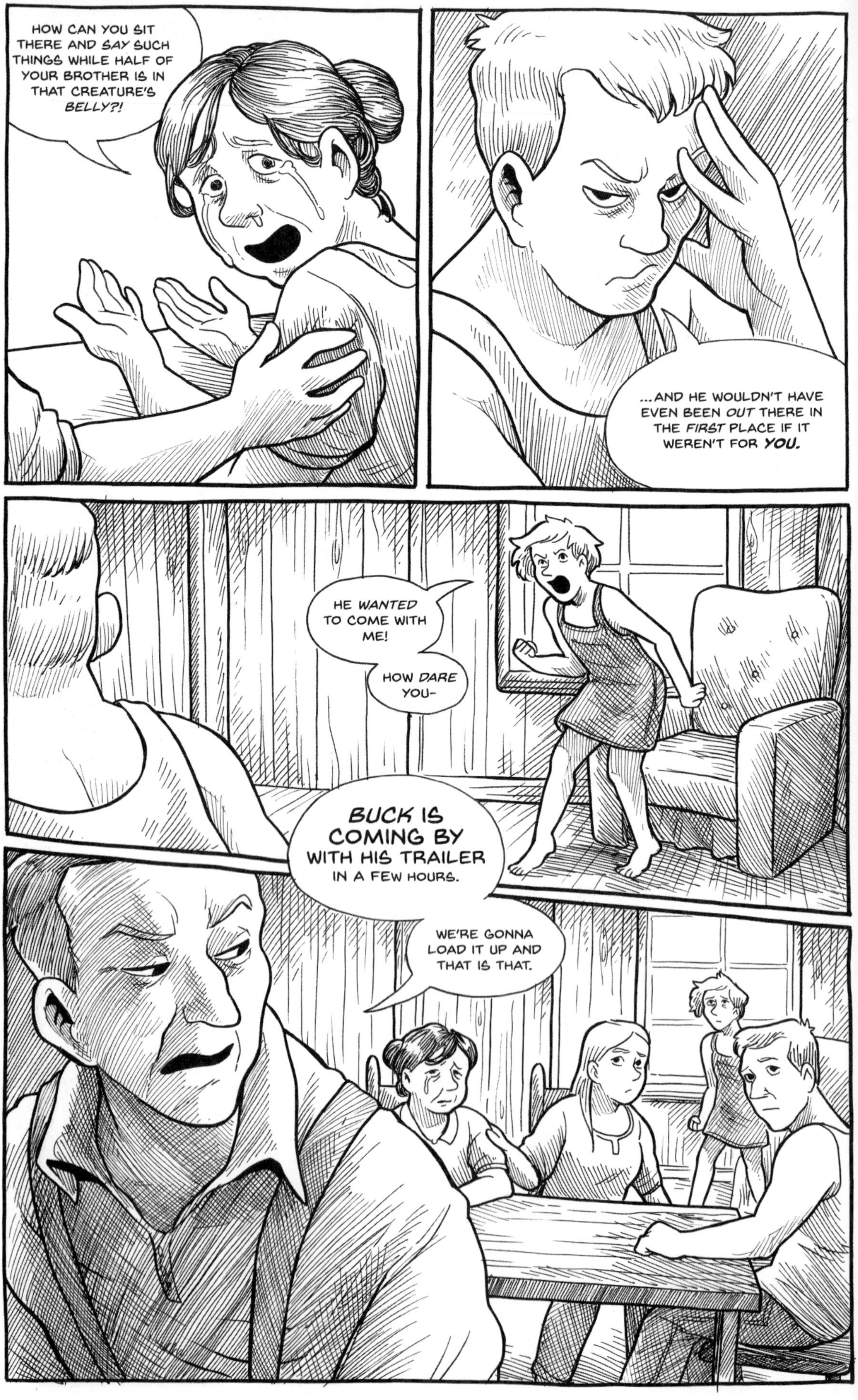
HOW CAN YOU SIT THERE AND SAY SUCH THINGS WHILE HALF OF YOUR BROTHER IS IN THAT CREATURE'S BELLY?!
...AND HE WOULDN'T HAVE EVEN BEEN OUT THERE IN THE FIRST PLACE IF IT WEREN'T FOR YOU.
HE WANTED TO COME WITH ME!
HOW DARE YOU-
BUCK IS COMING BY WITH HIS TRAILER IN A FEW HOURS.
WE'RE GONNA LOAD IT UP AND THAT IS THAT.

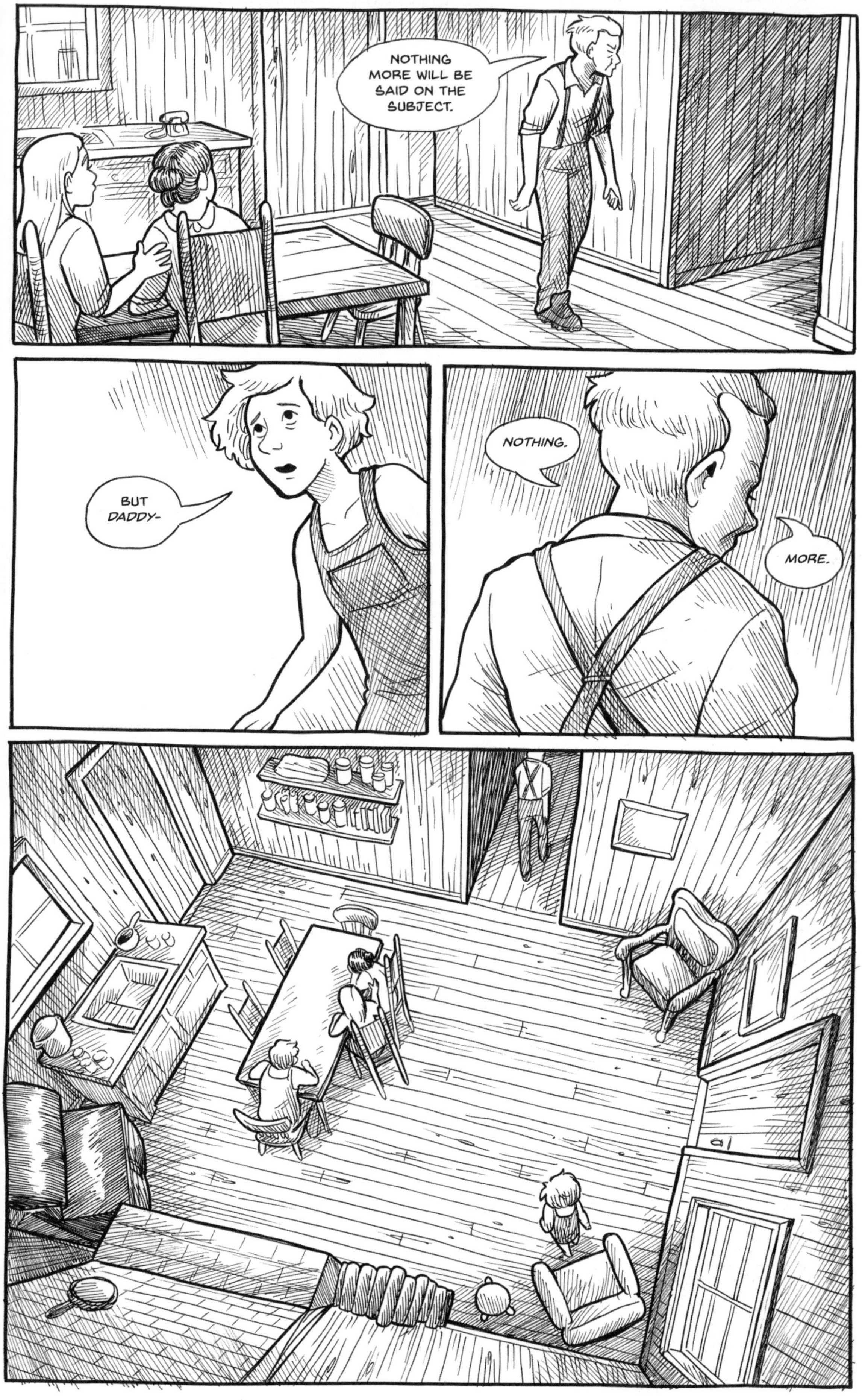
NOTHING MORE WILL BE SAID ON THE SUBJECT.
BUT DADDY-
NOTHING.
MORE.

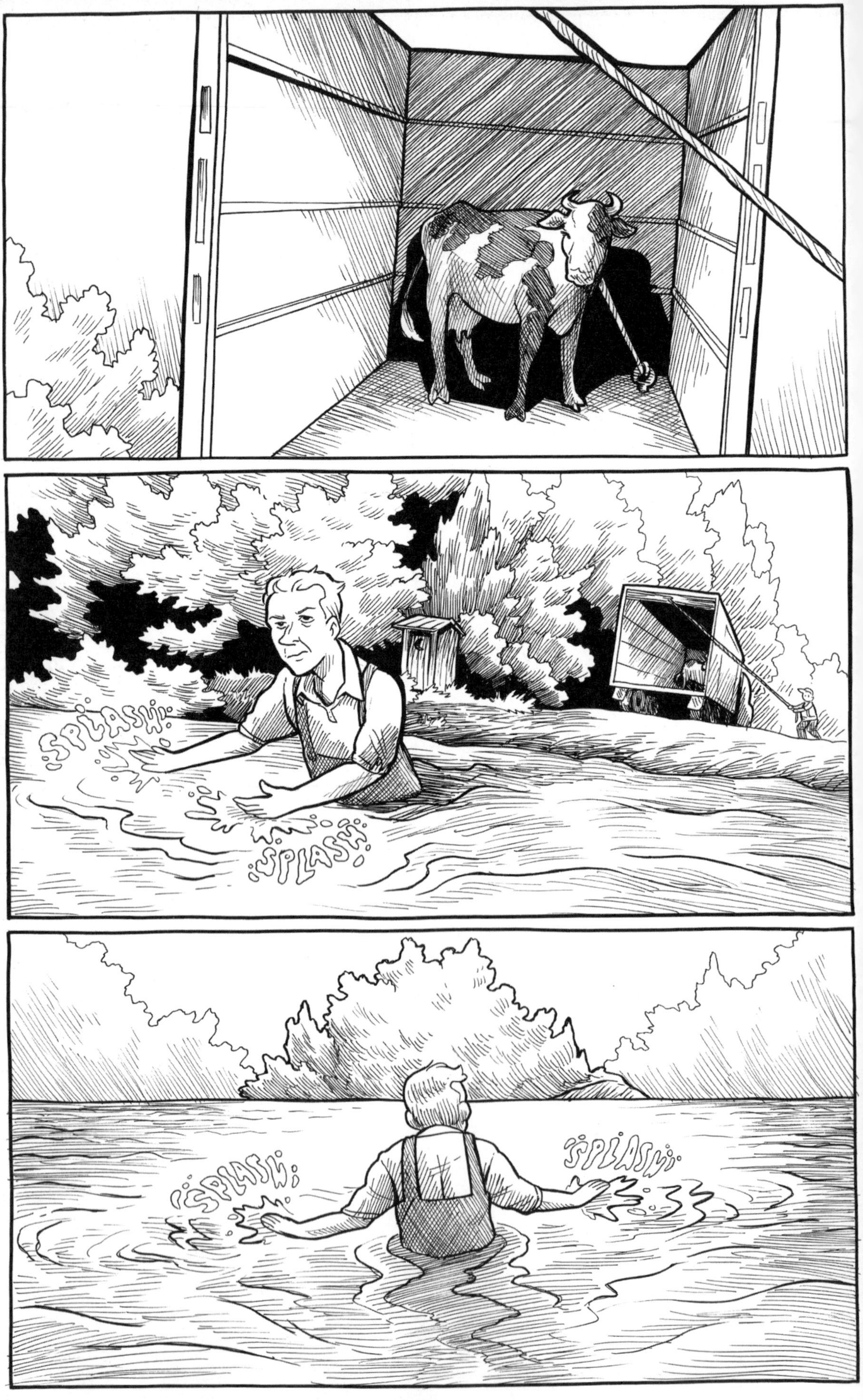
SPLASH!
SPLASH!
SPLASH!
SPLASH!

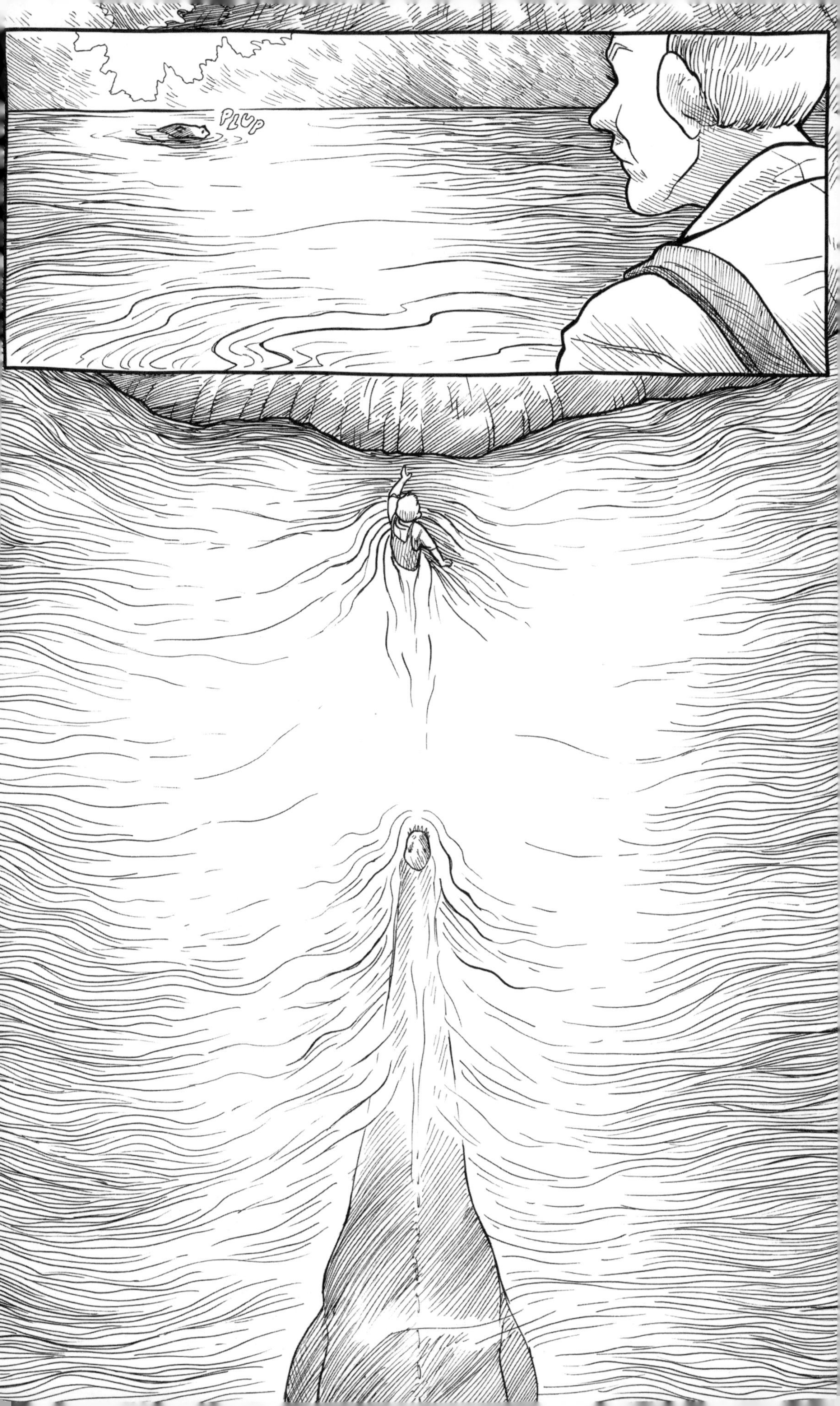
PLUP

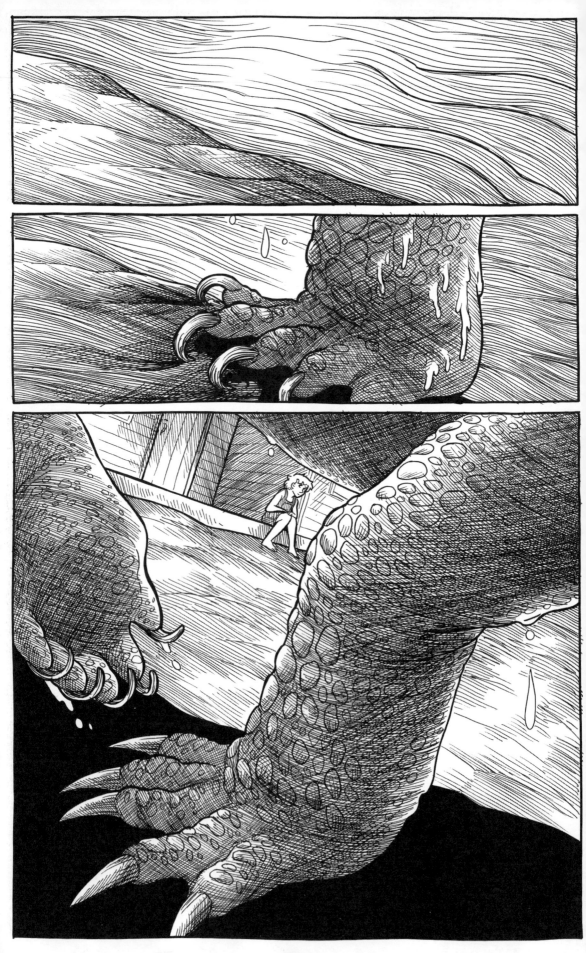

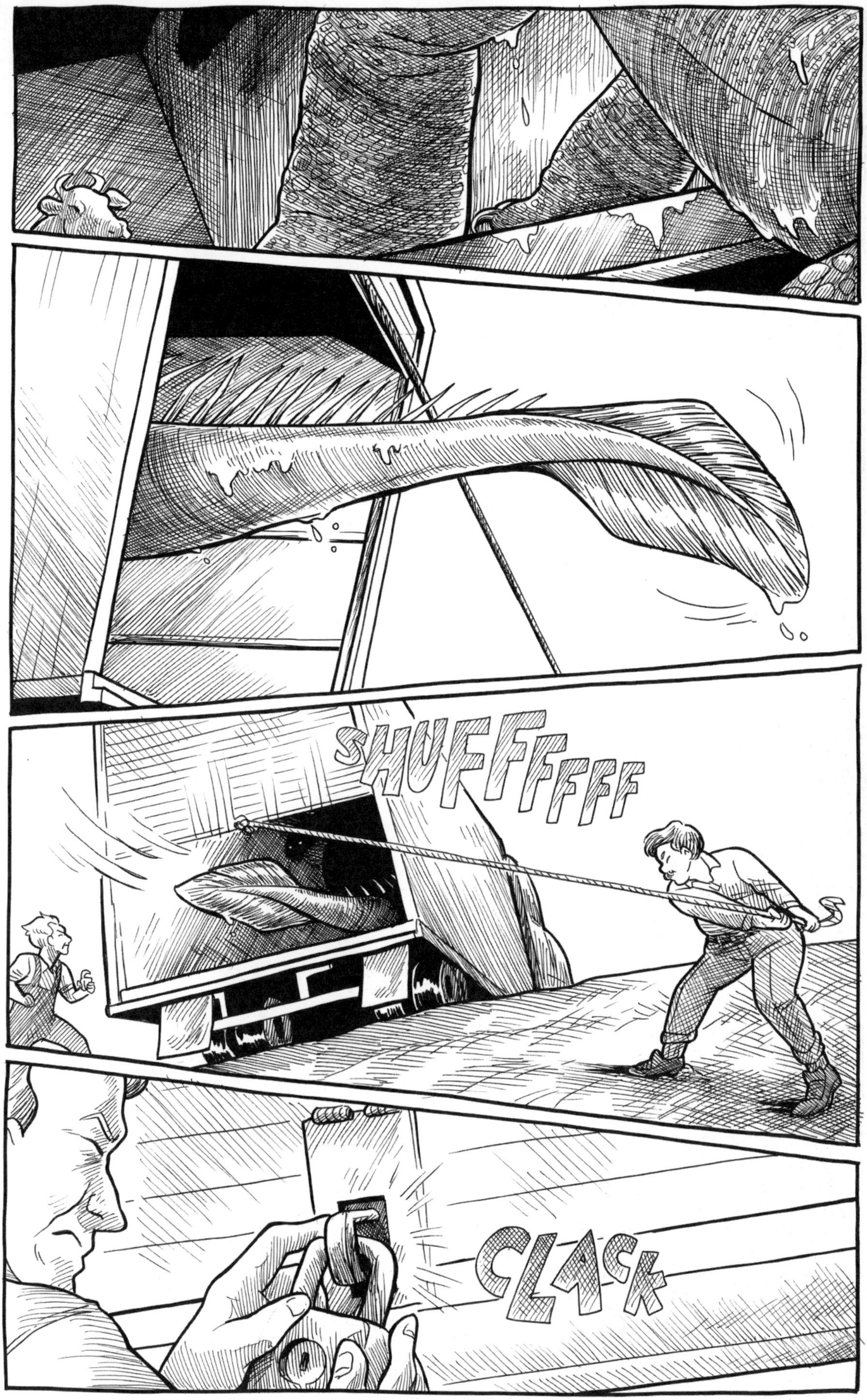
SHUFFFFFFF
CLACK

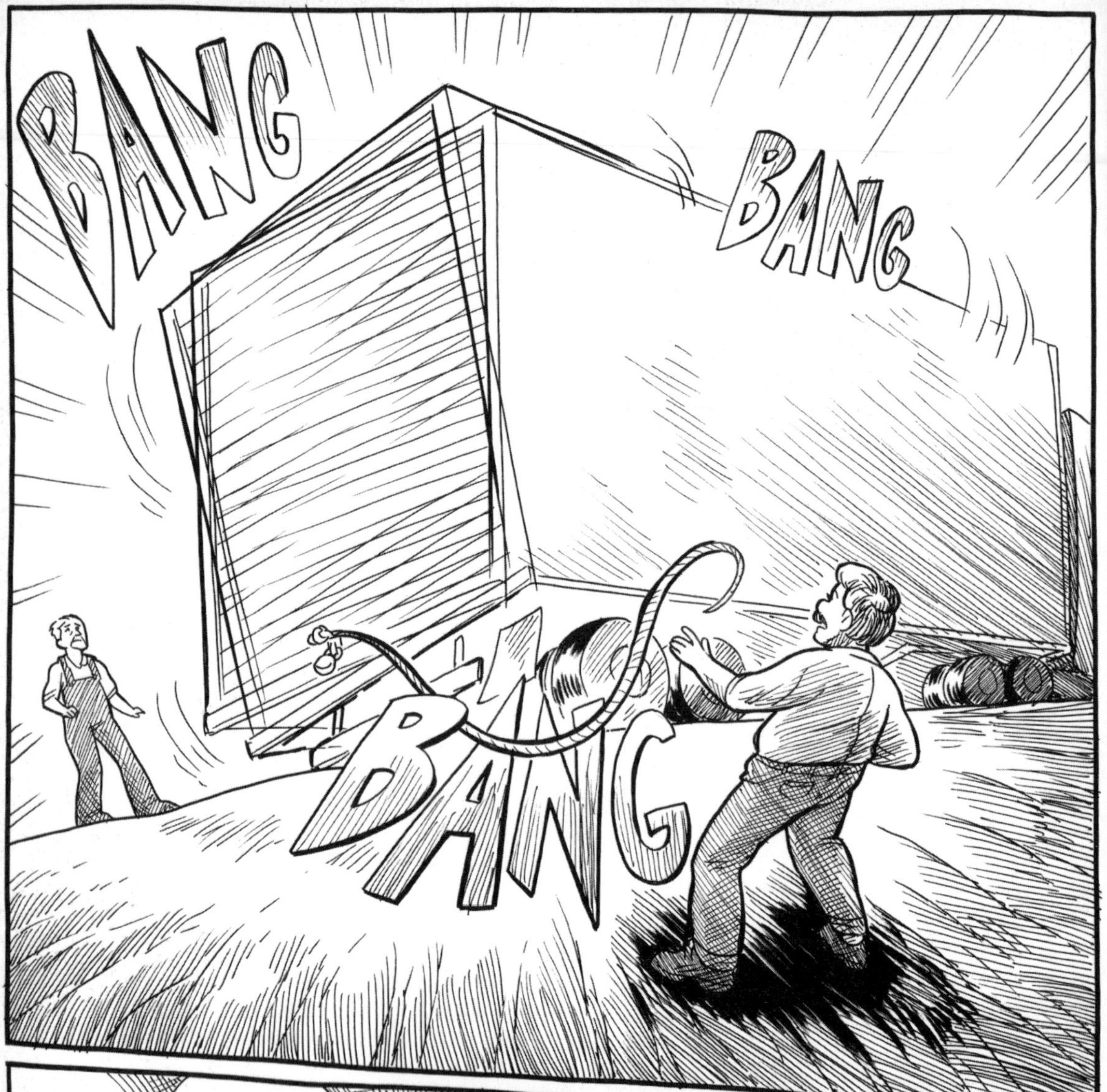
BANG
BANG
BANG

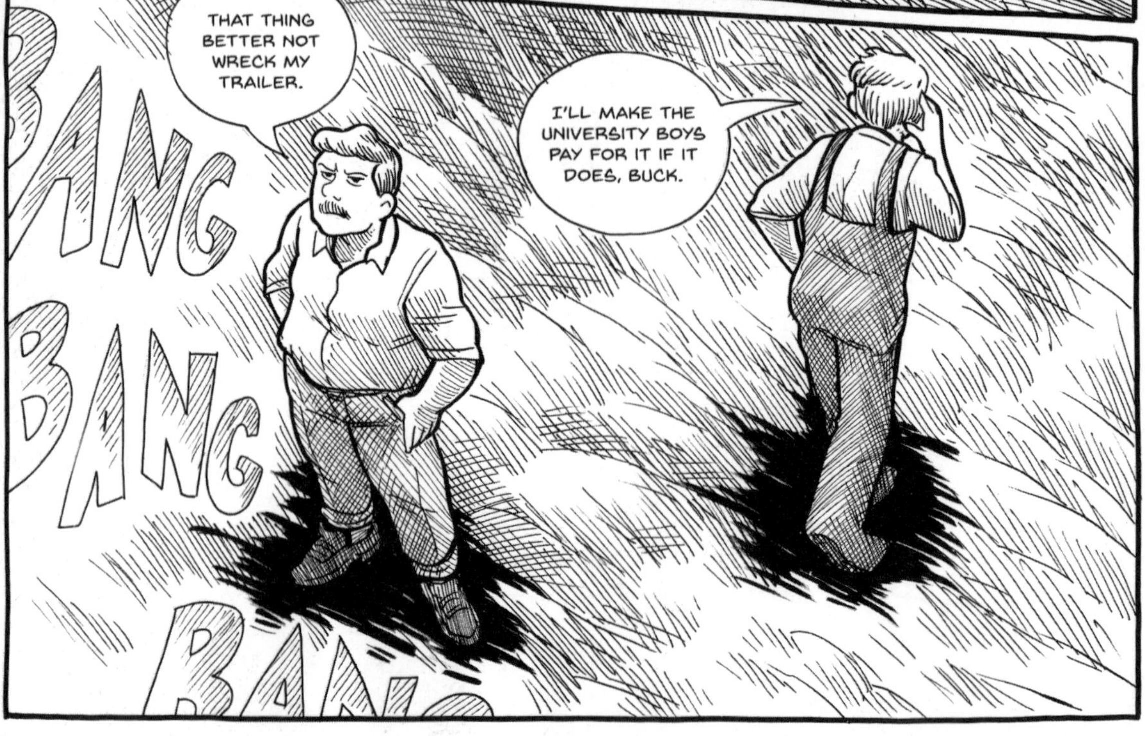
THAT THING BETTER NOT WRECK MY TRAILER.
I'LL MAKE THE UNIVERSITY BOYS PAY FOR IT IF IT DOES, BUCK.
BANG
BANG

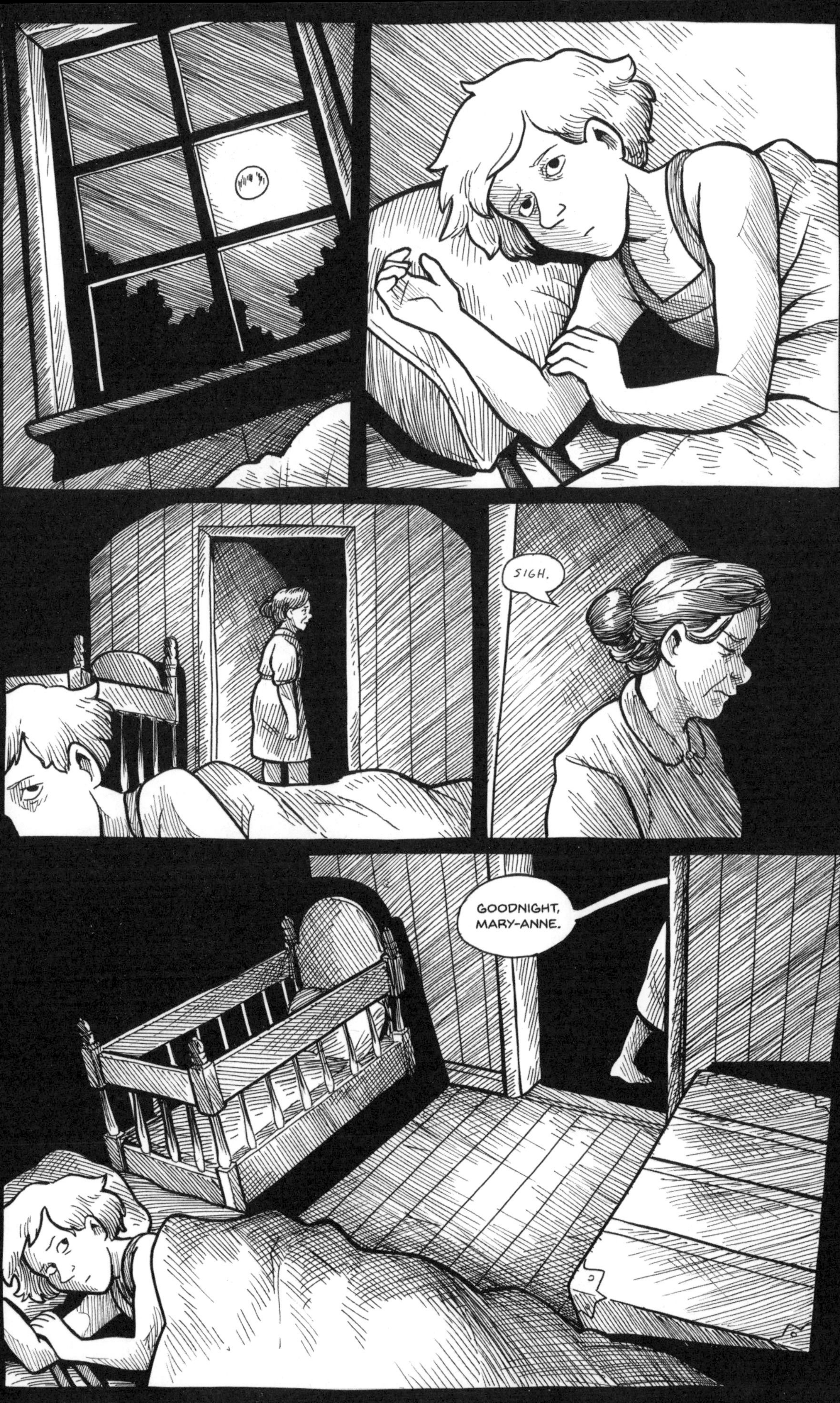
SIGH.
GOODNIGHT, MARY-ANNE.

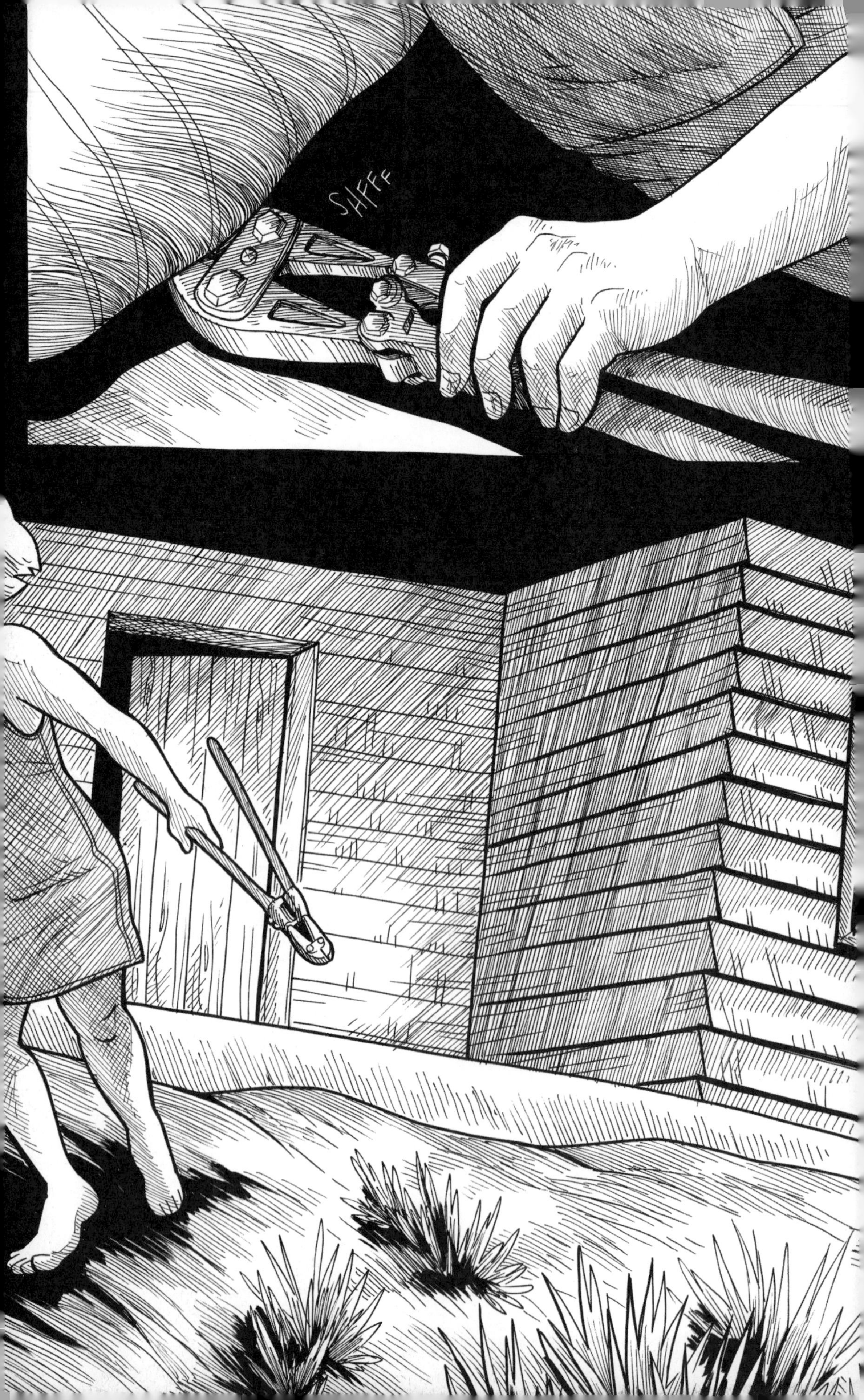
SHFFF

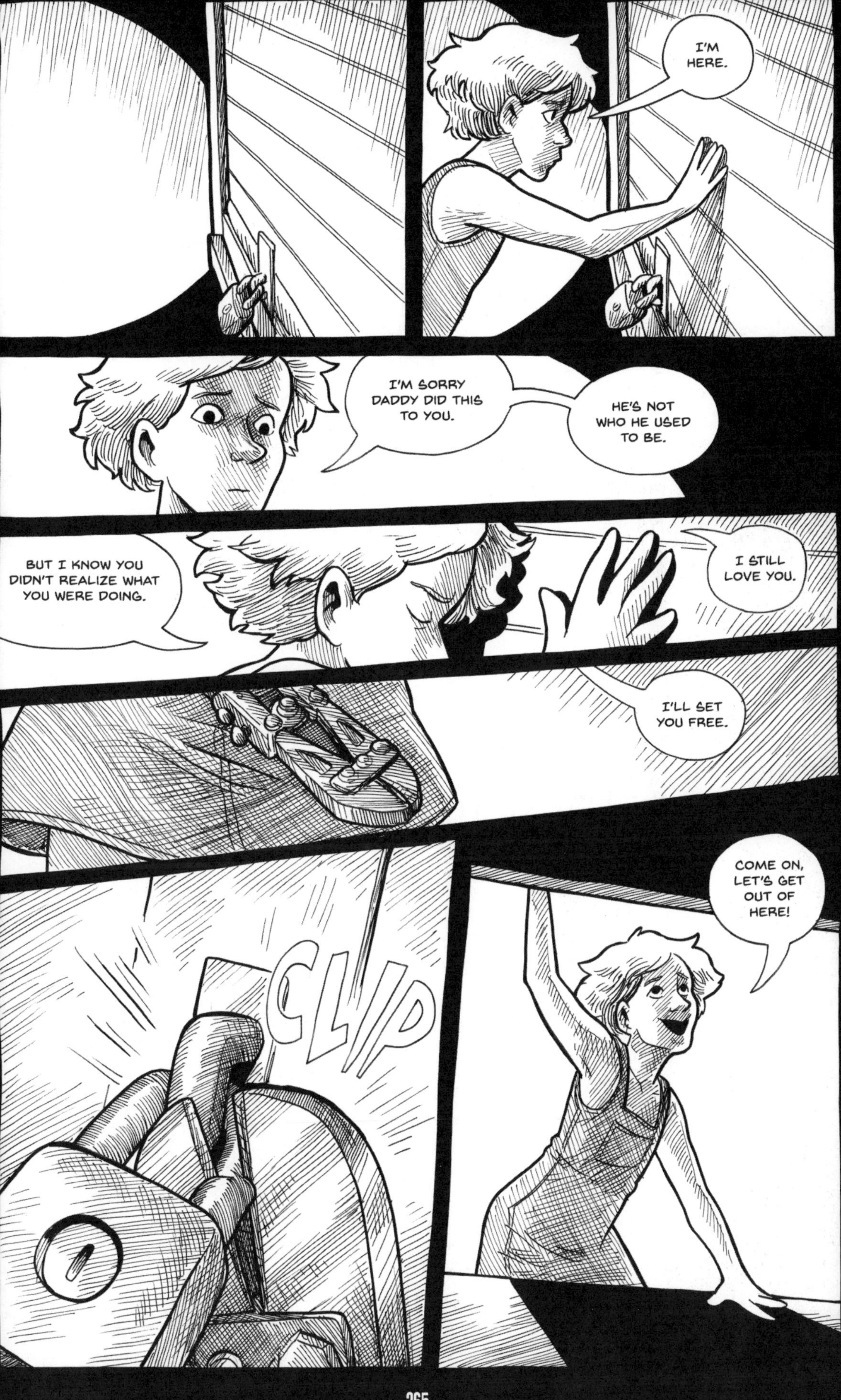
I'M HERE.
I'M SORRY DADDY DID THIS TO YOU.
HE'S NOT WHO HE USED TO BE.
BUT I KNOW YOU DIDN'T REALIZE WHAT YOU WERE DOING.
I STILL LOVE YOU.
I'LL SET YOU FREE.
CLIP
COME ON, LET'S GET OUT OF HERE!

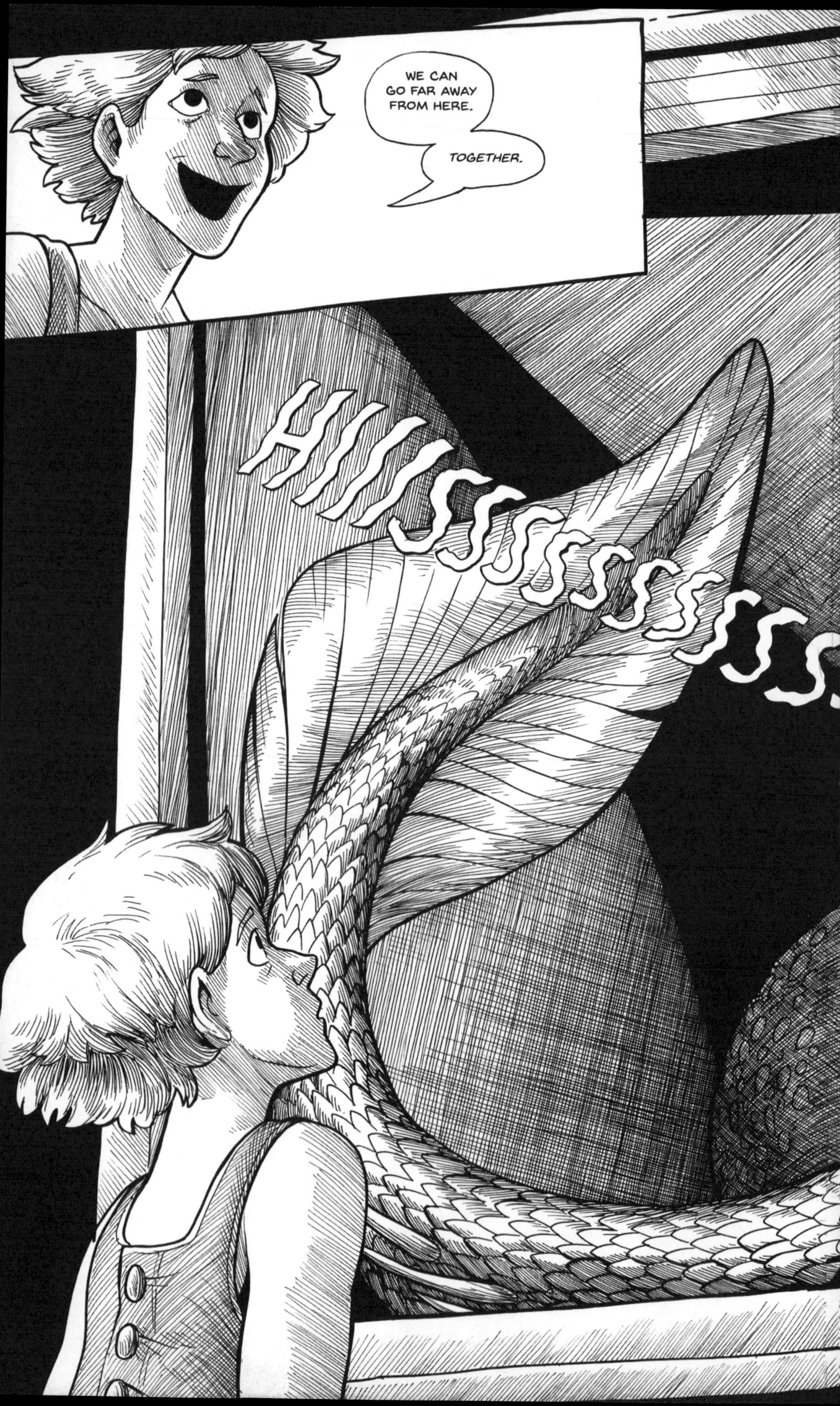
WE CAN GO FAR AWAY FROM HERE.
TOGETHER.
HIISSSSSSSSSSS

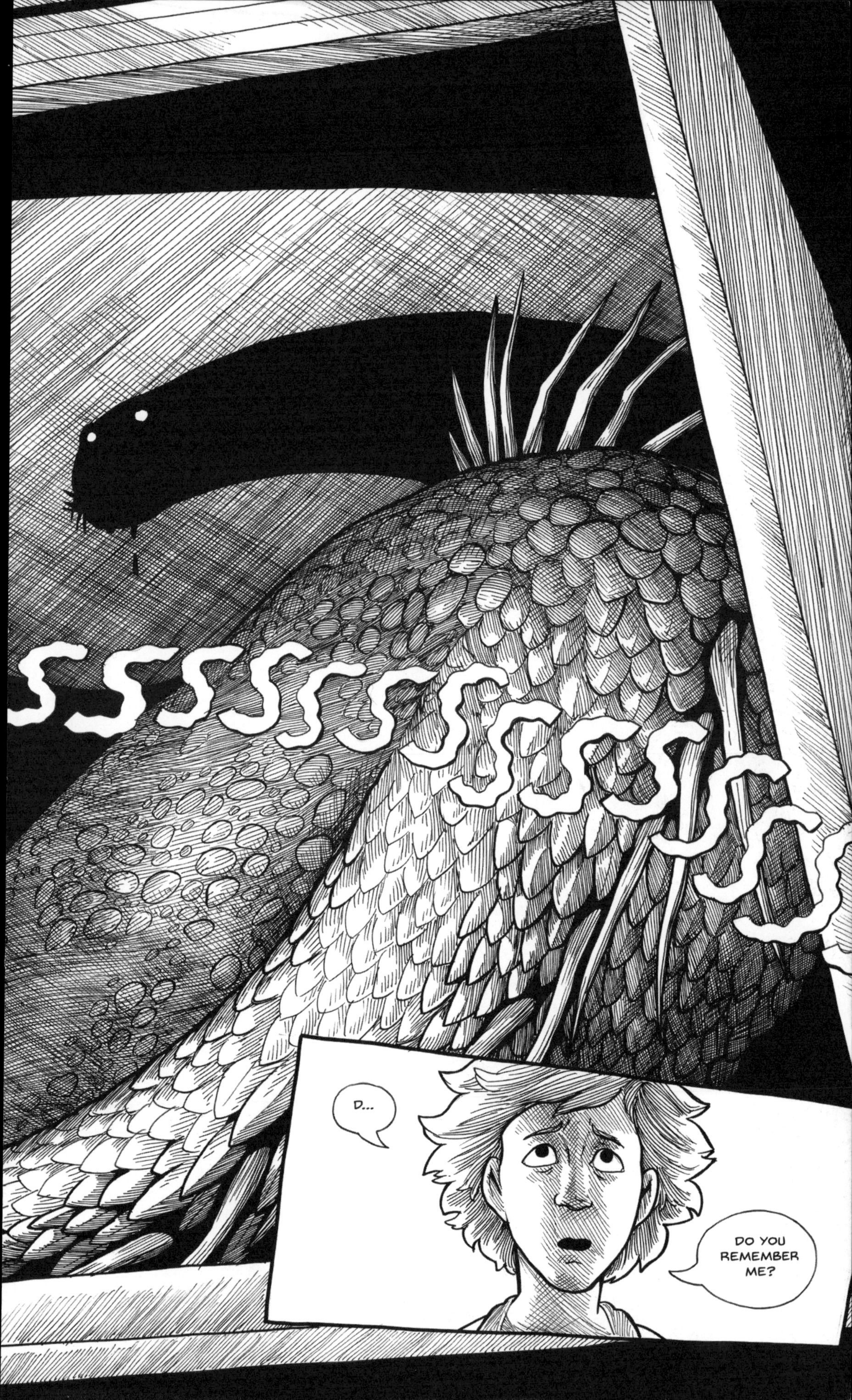
SSSSSSSSSSSSSS
D...
DO YOU REMEMBER ME?

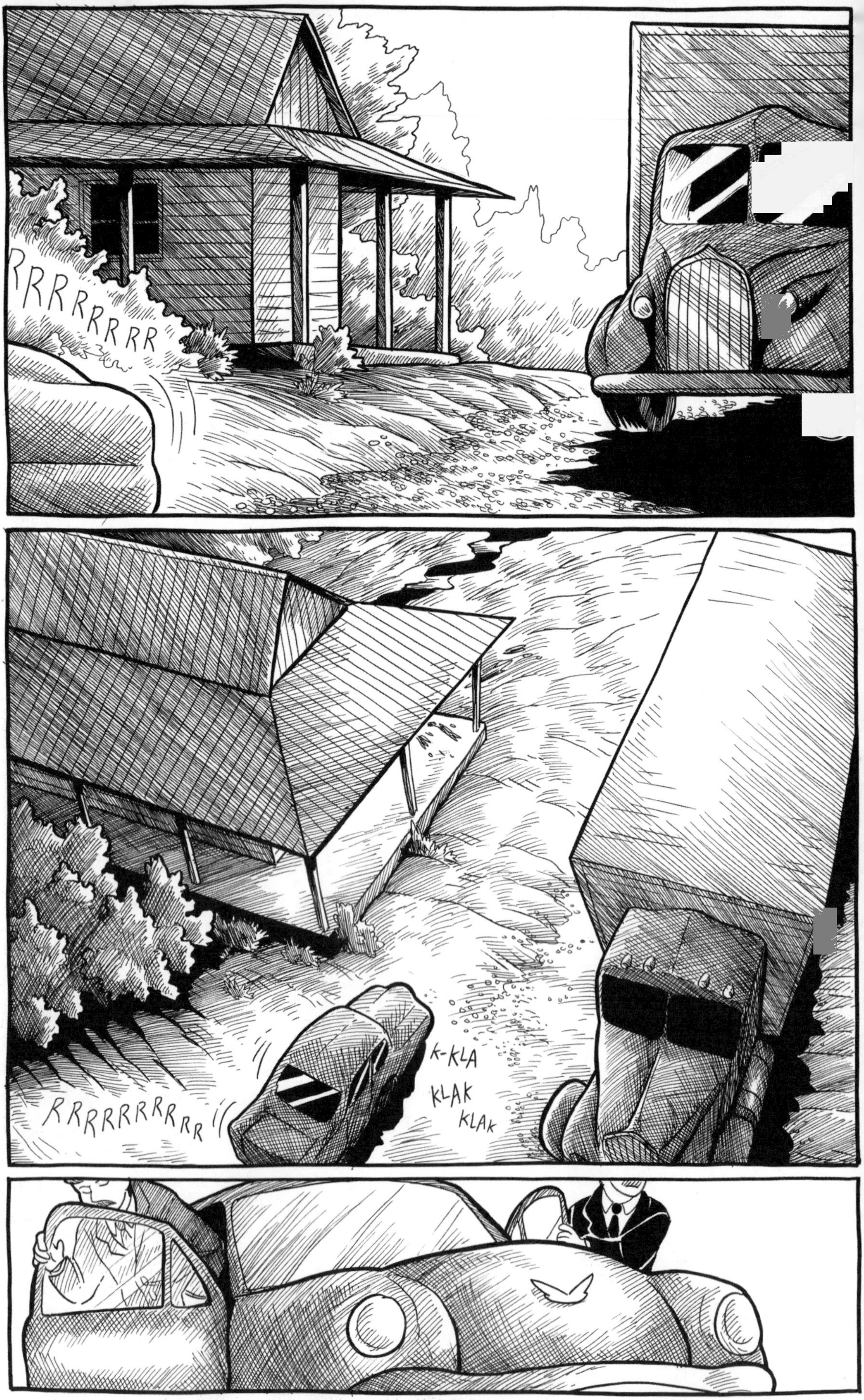
RRRRRRRR
K-KLA
KLAK
KLAK
RRRRRRRRRR

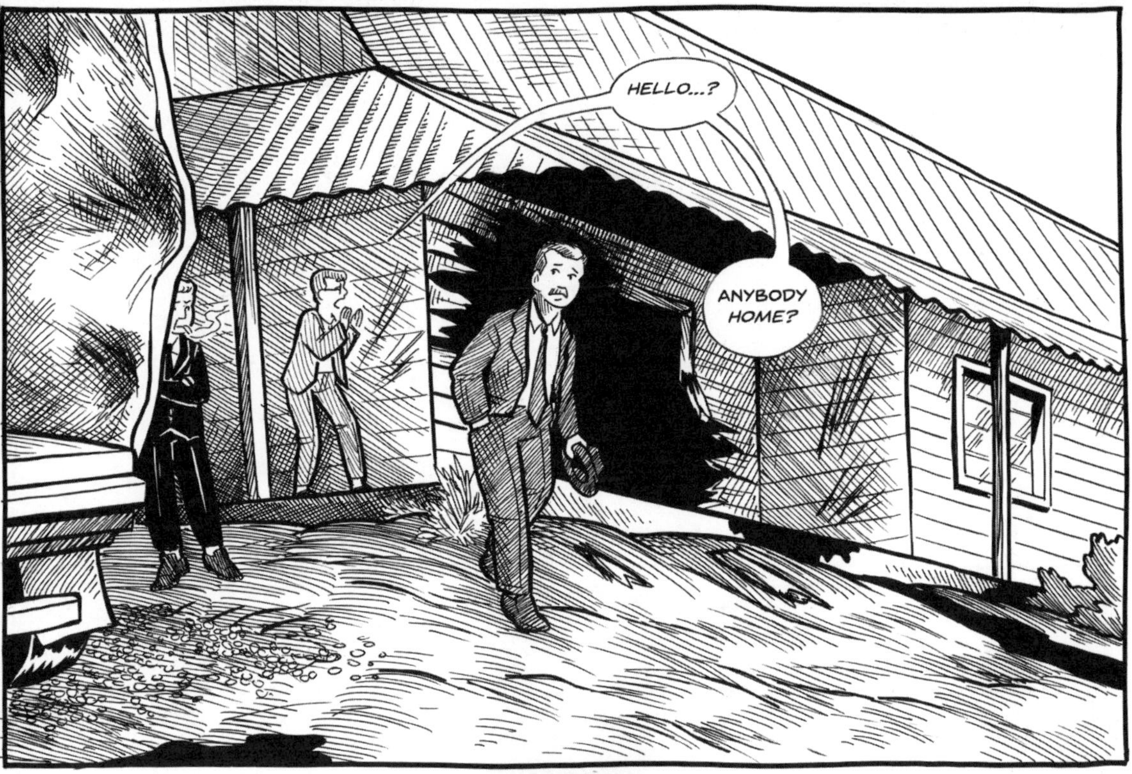
HELLO...?
ANYBODY HOME?

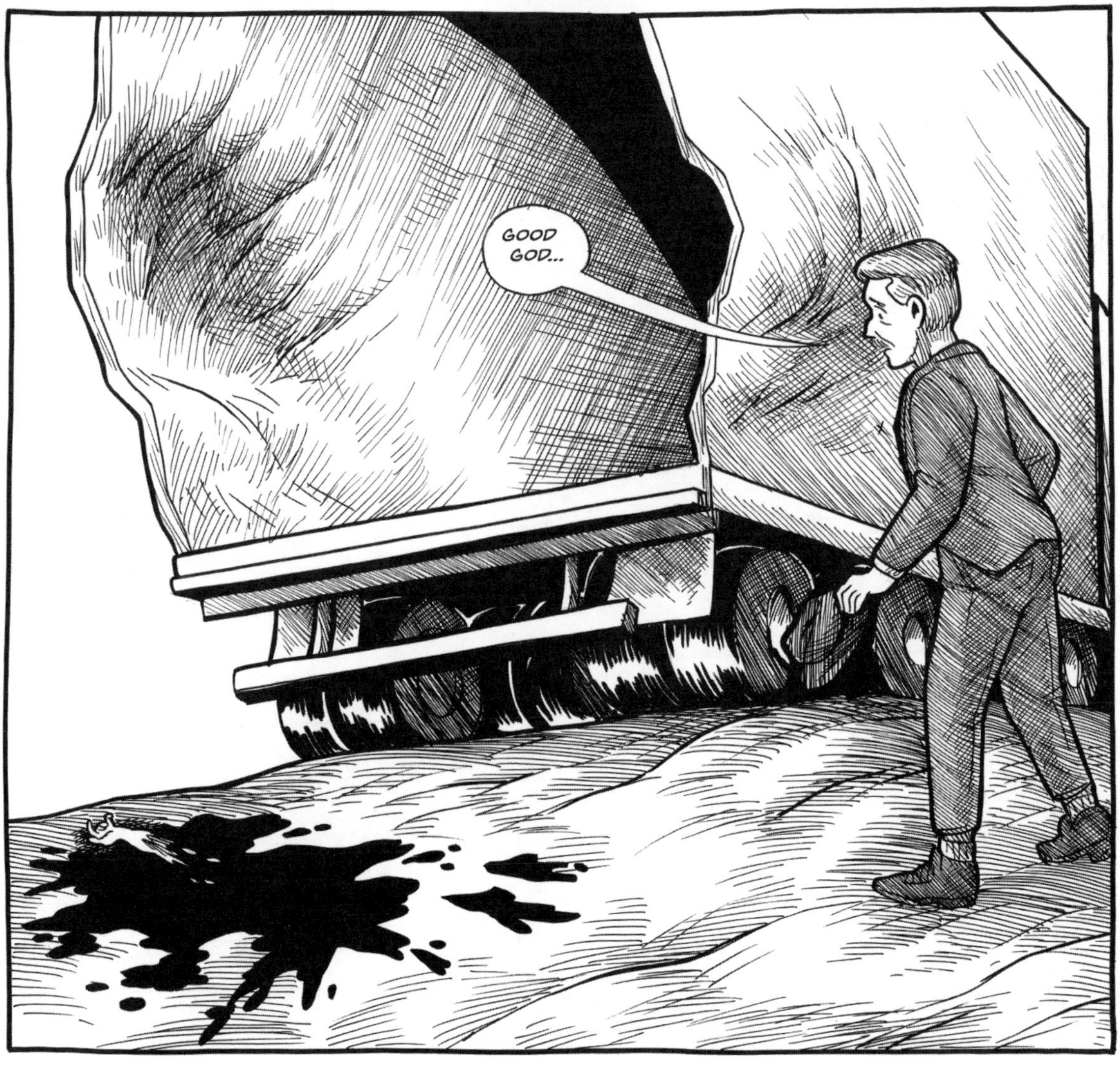
GOOD GOD...

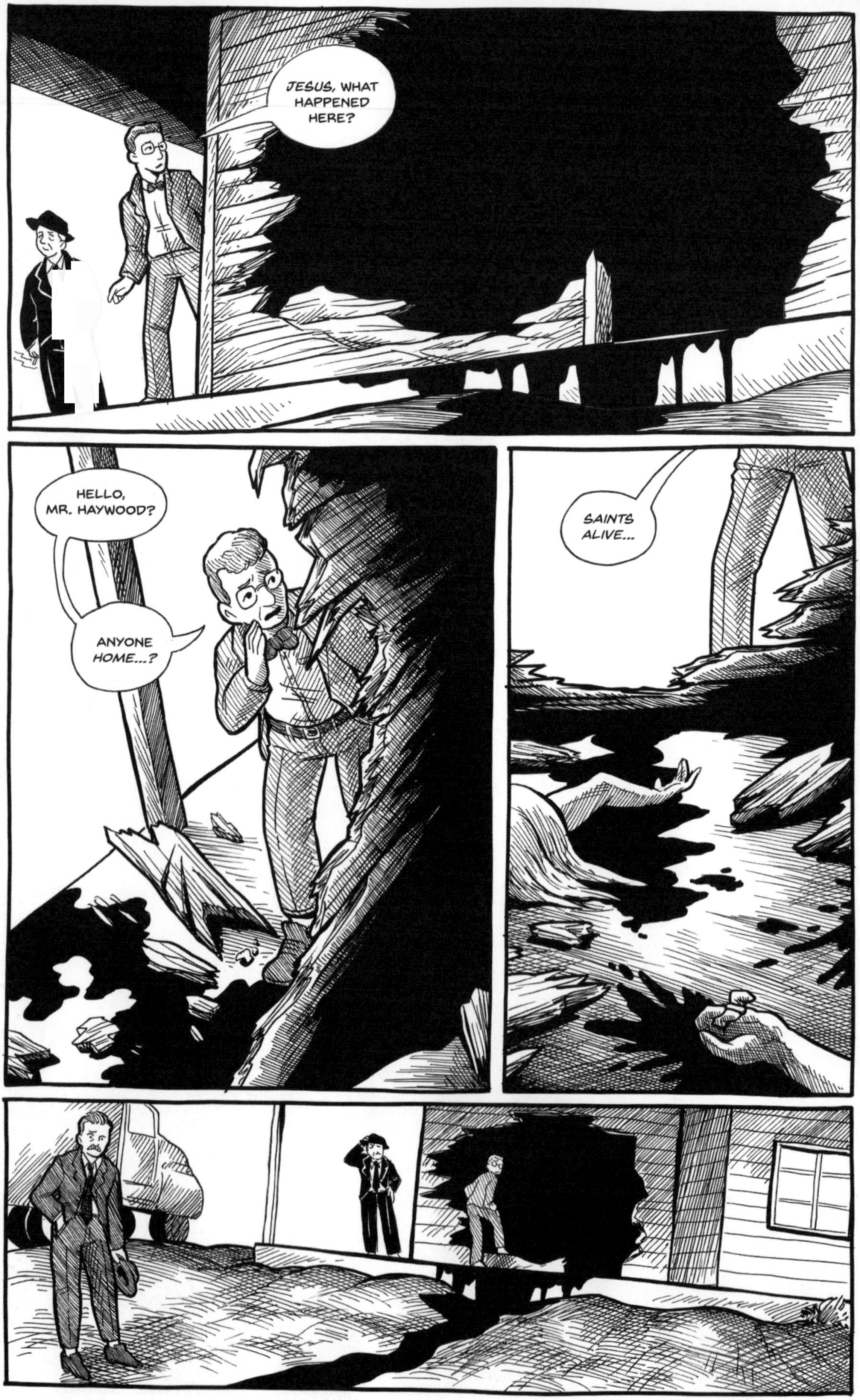
JESUS, WHAT HAPPENED HERE?
HELLO, MR. HAYWOOD?
ANYONE HOME...?
SAINTS ALIVE...

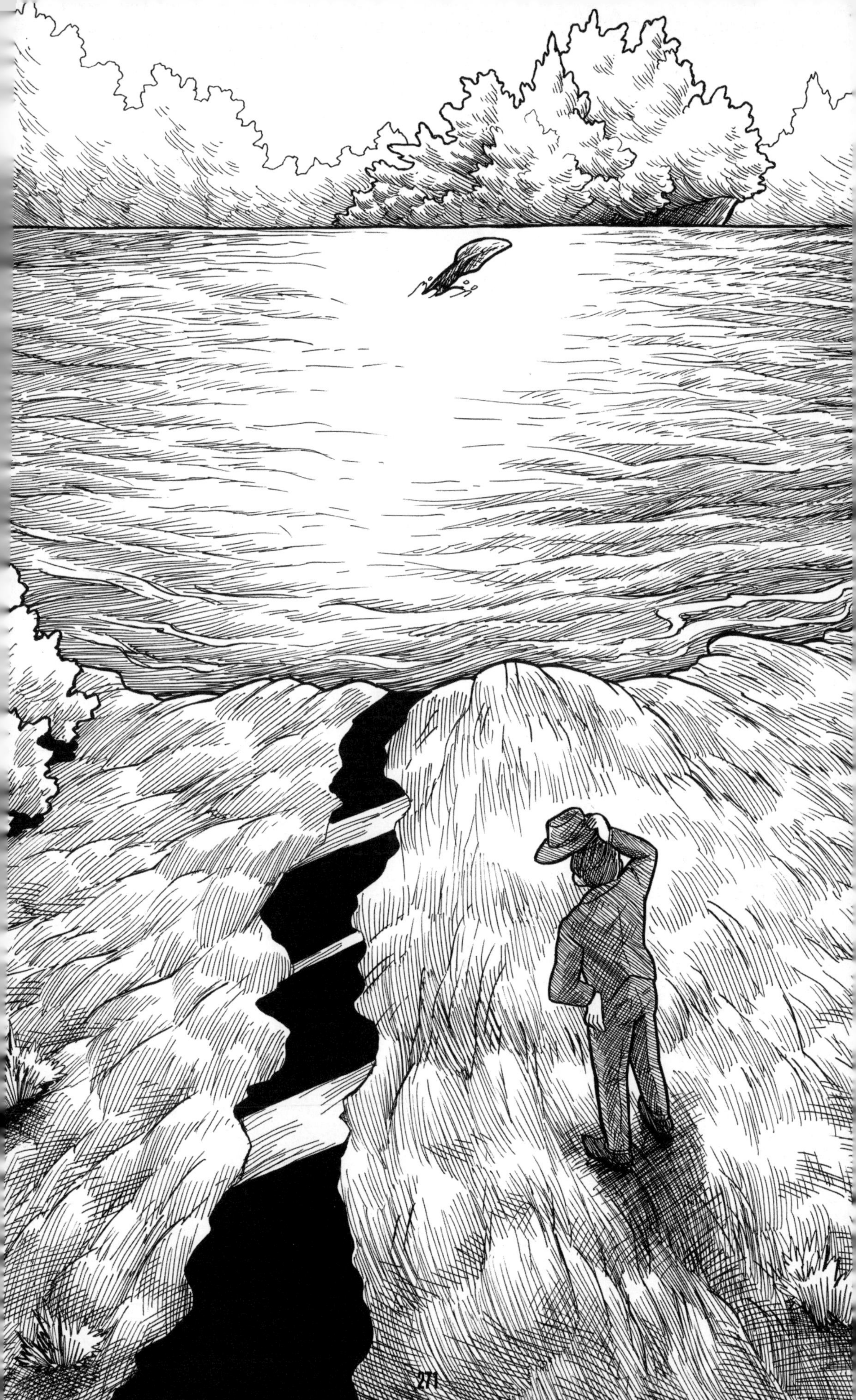

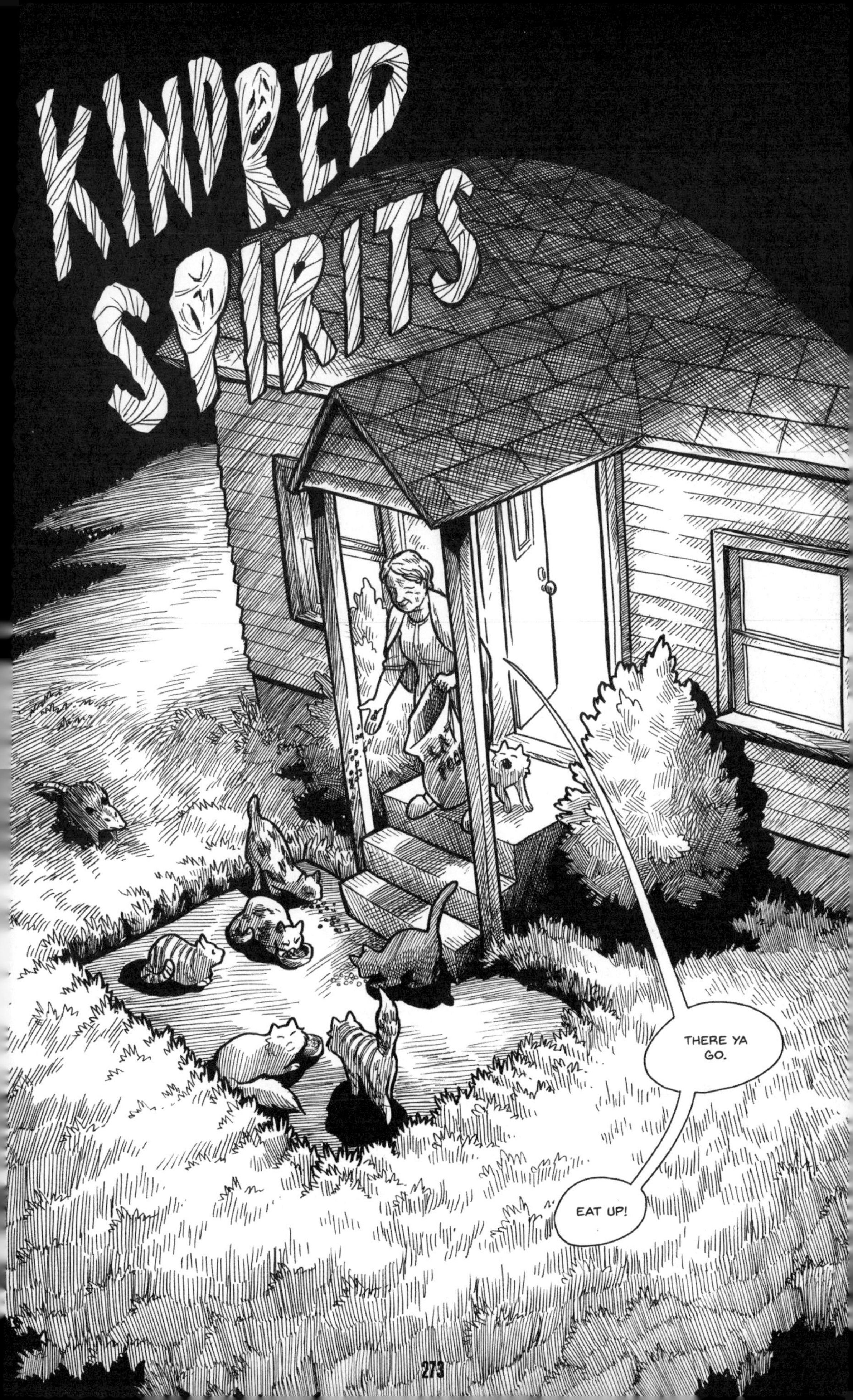
KINDRED SPIRITS
CAT FOOD
THERE YA GO.
EAT UP!

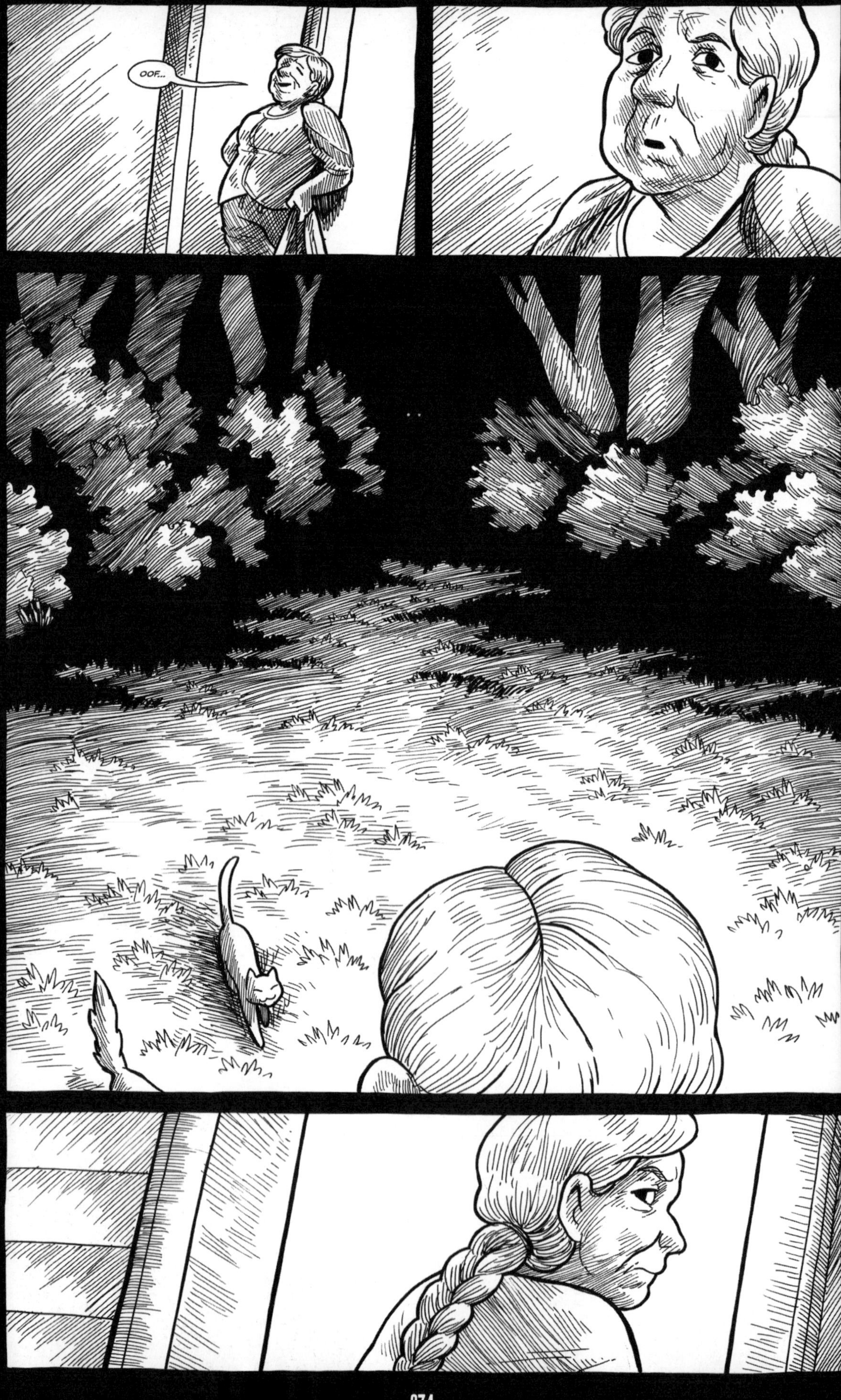
OOF...

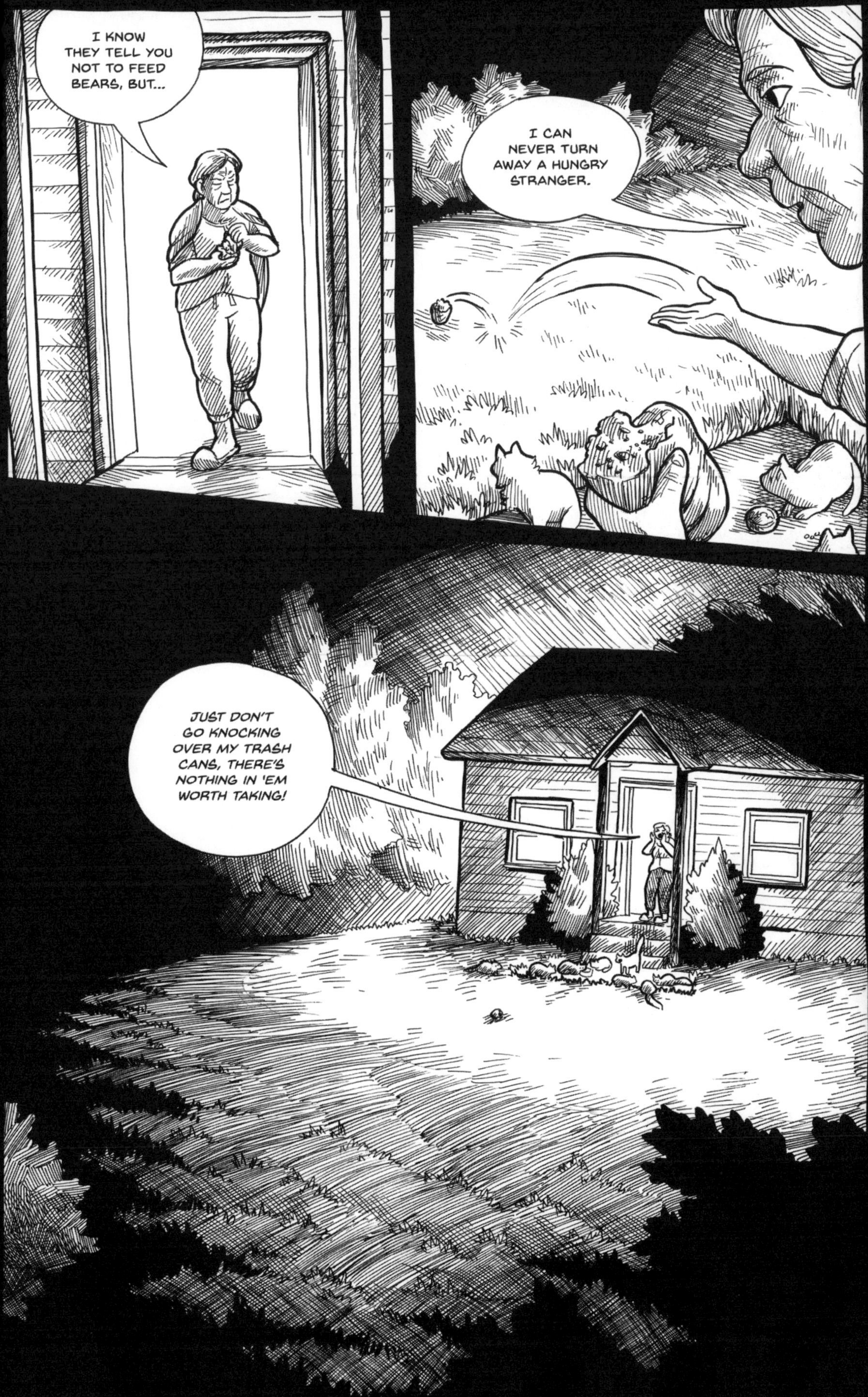
I KNOW THEY TELL YOU NOT TO FEED BEARS, BUT...
I CAN NEVER TURN AWAY A HUNGRY STRANGER.
JUST DON'T GO KNOCKING OVER MY TRASH CANS, THERE'S NOTHING IN 'EM WORTH TAKING!

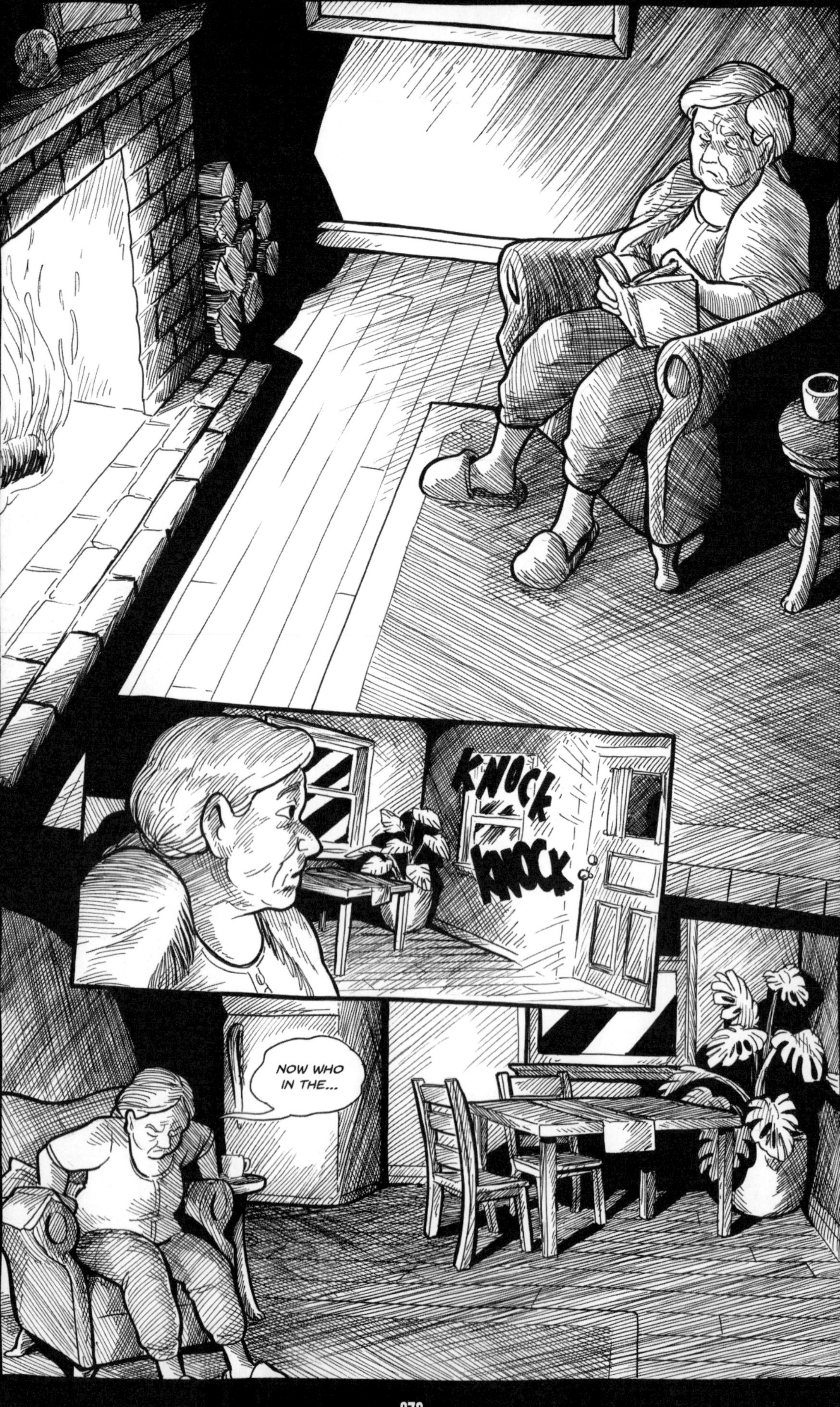
KNOCK
KNOCK
NOW WHO IN THE...

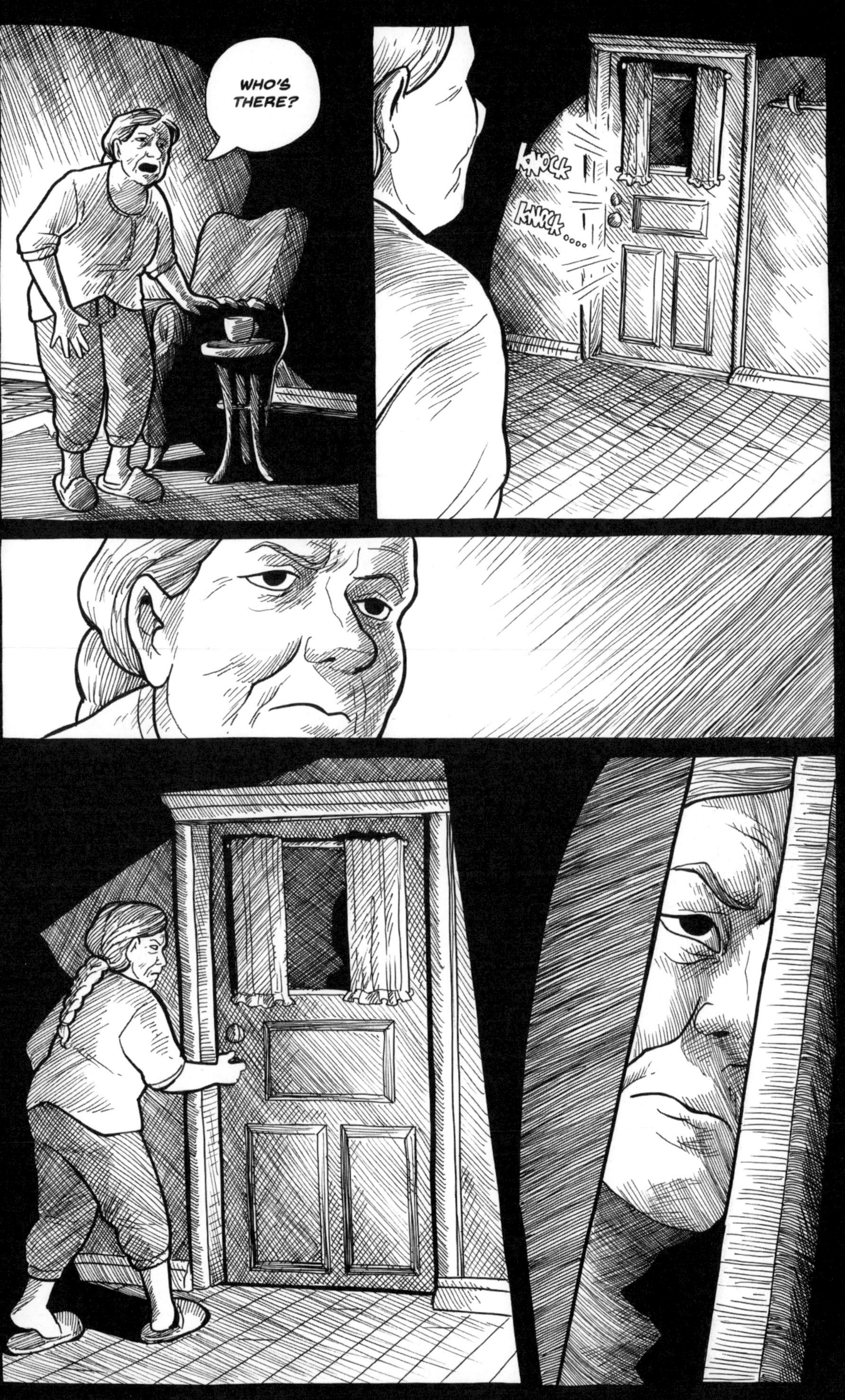
WHO'S THERE?
KNOCK
KNOCK....

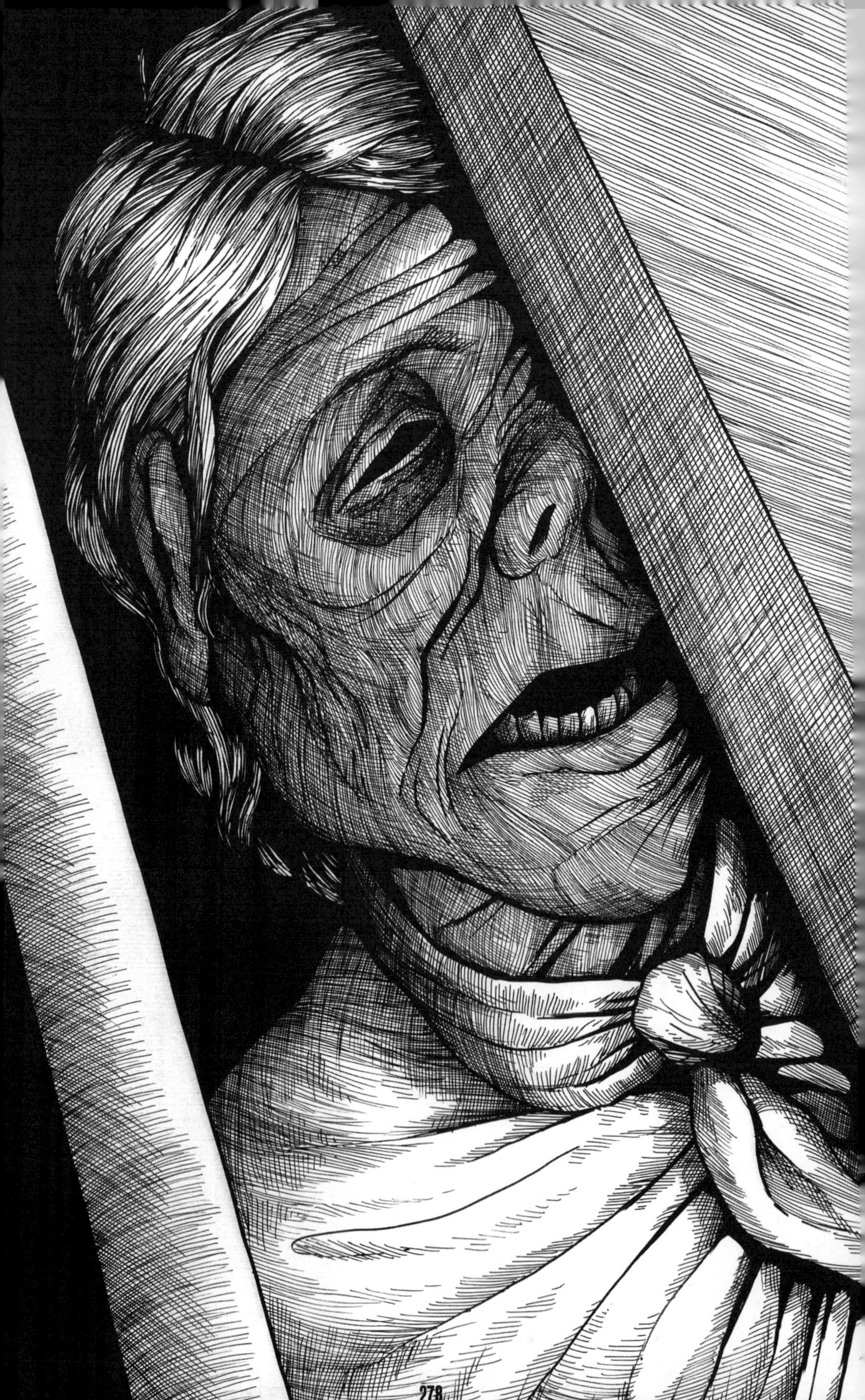

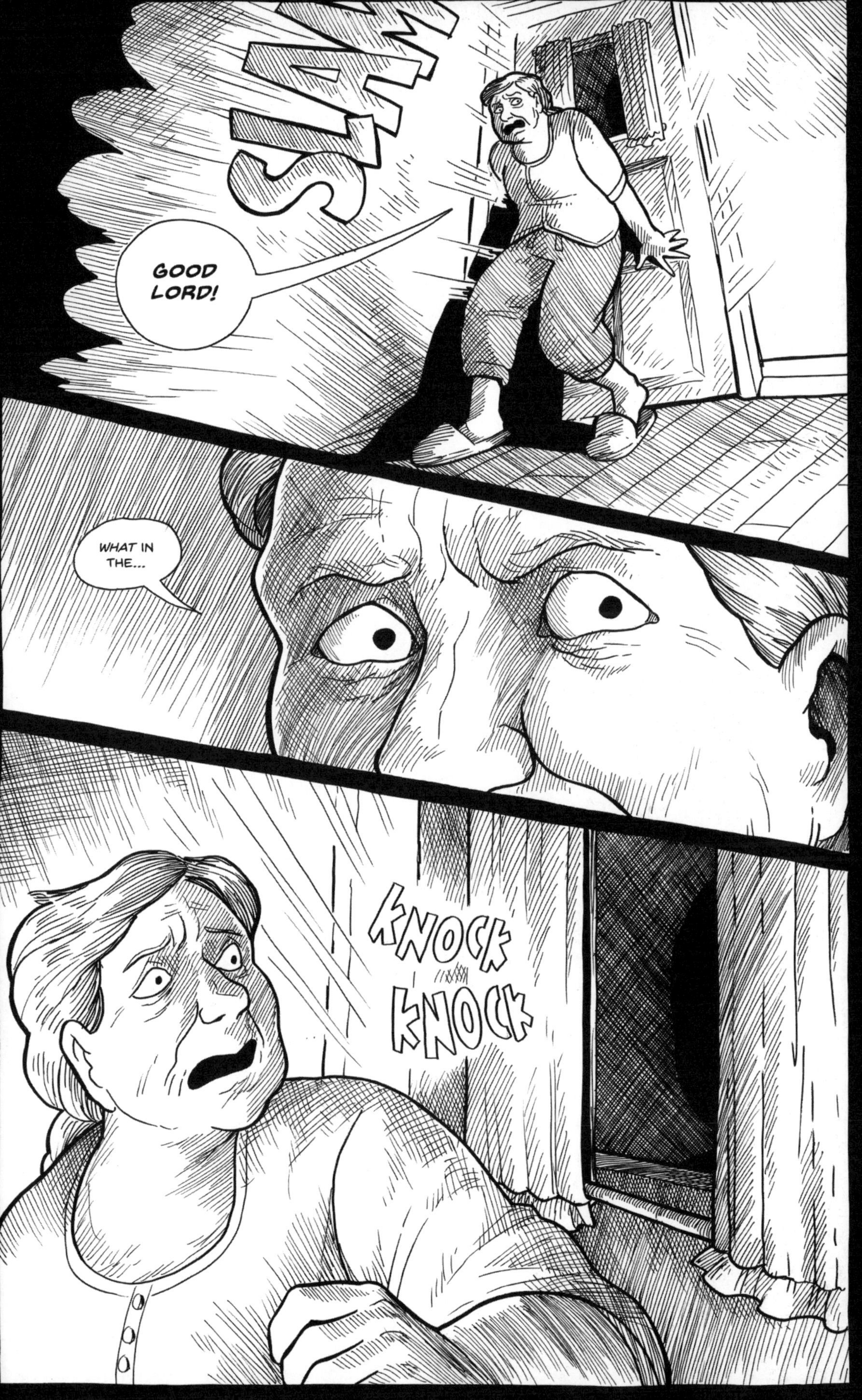
SLAM
GOOD LORD!
WHAT IN THE...
KNOCK KNOCK

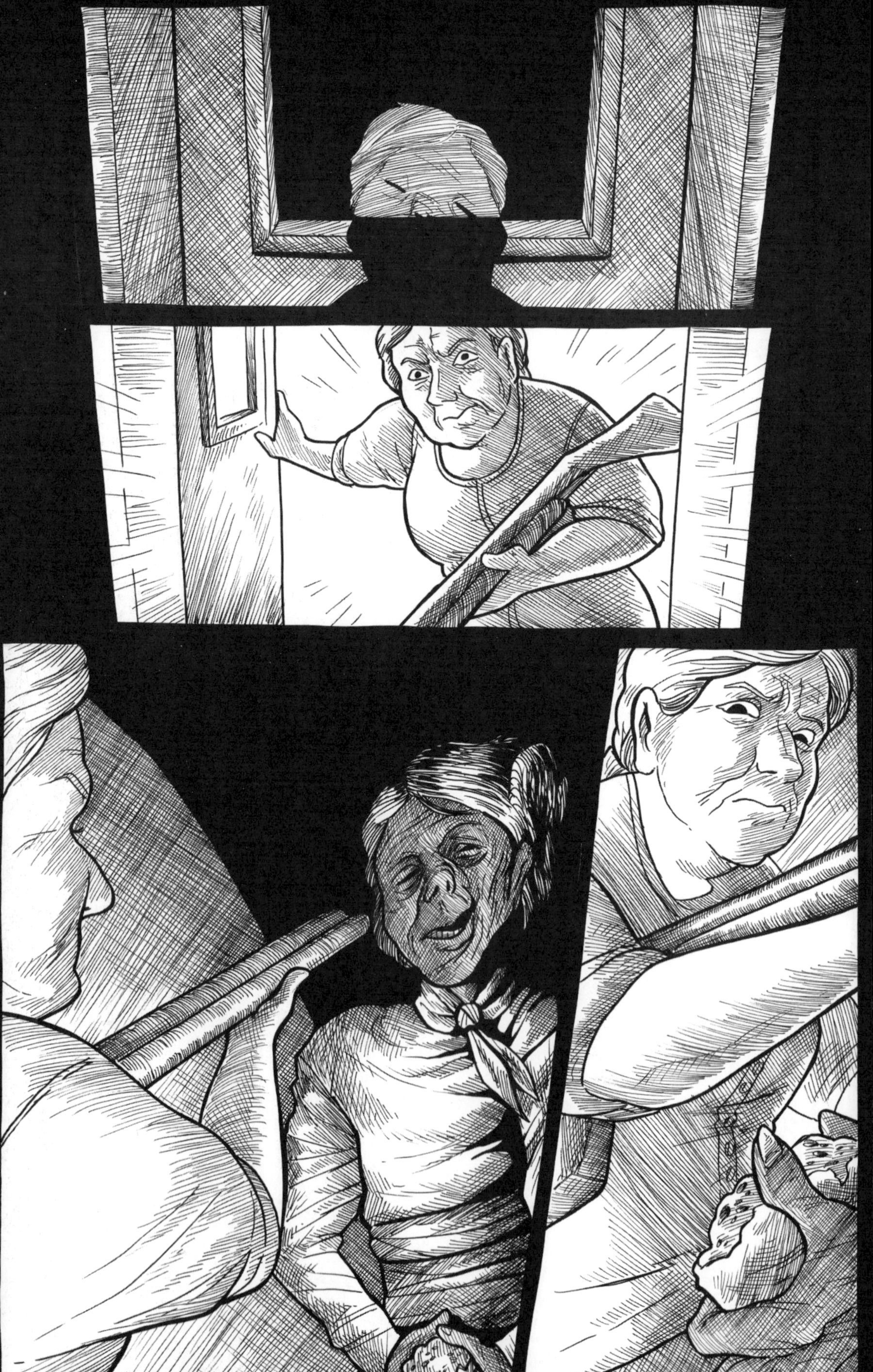

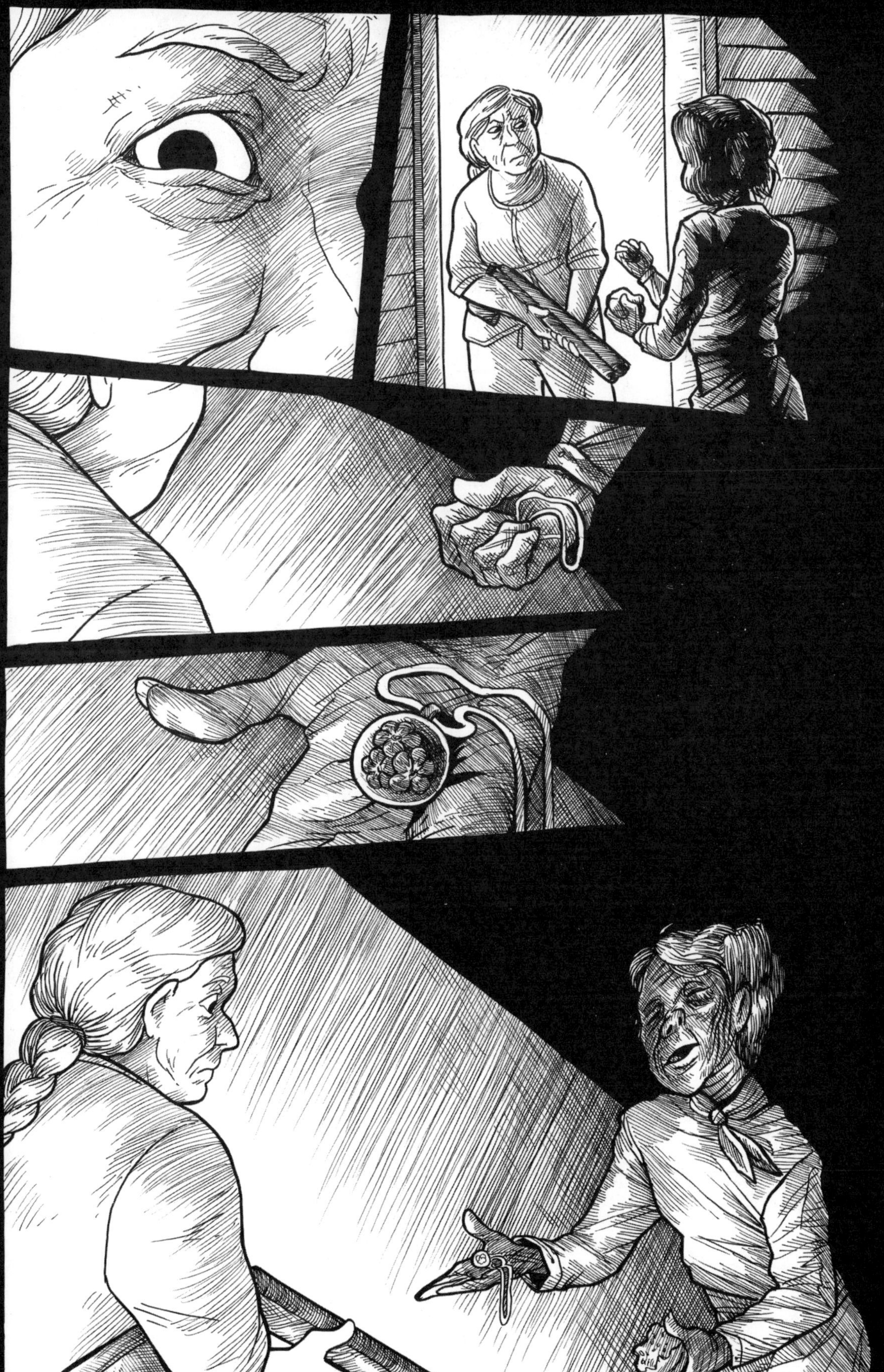

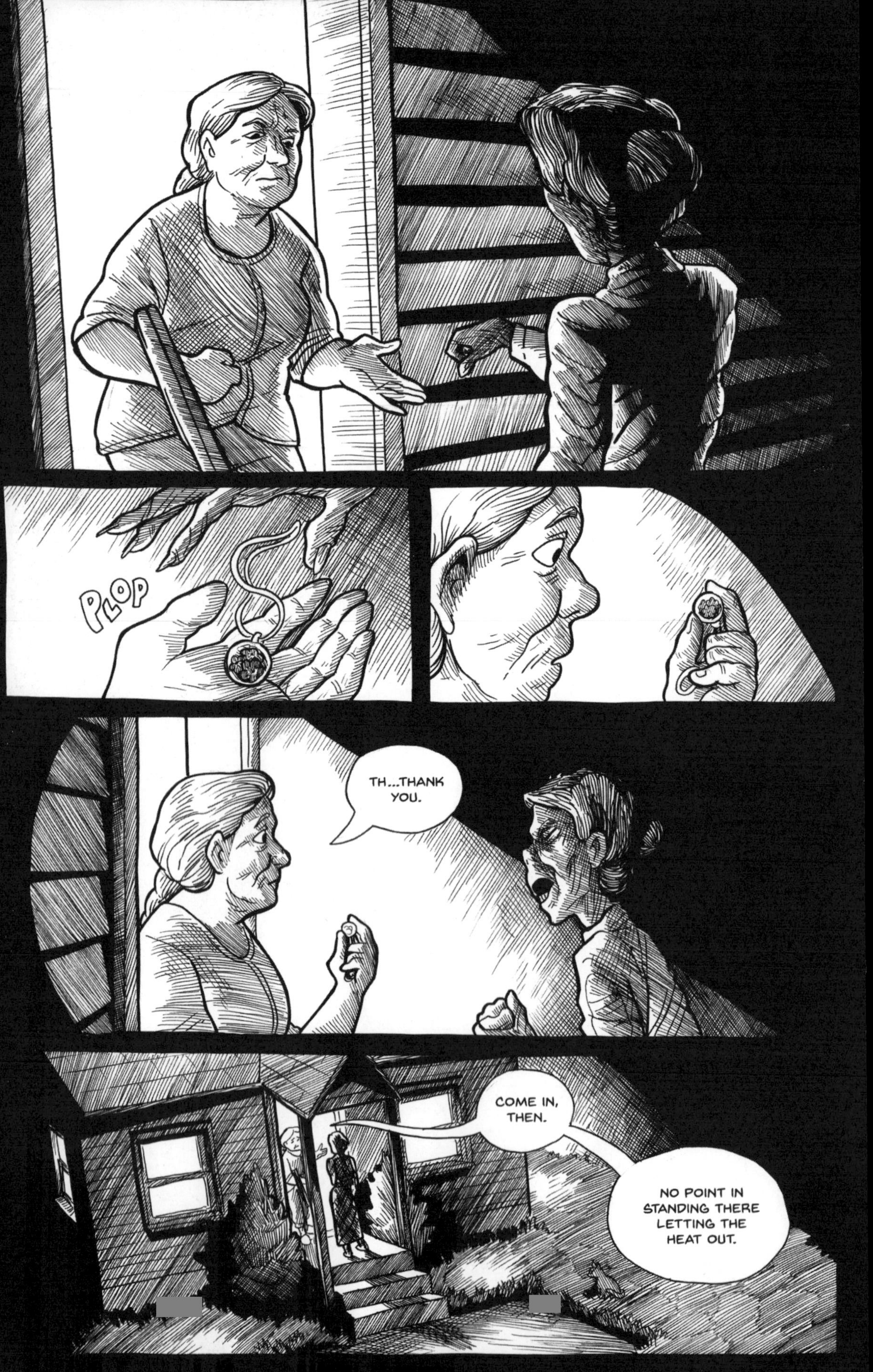
PLOP
TH...THANK YOU.
COME IN, THEN.
NO POINT IN STANDING THERE LETTING THE HEAT OUT.

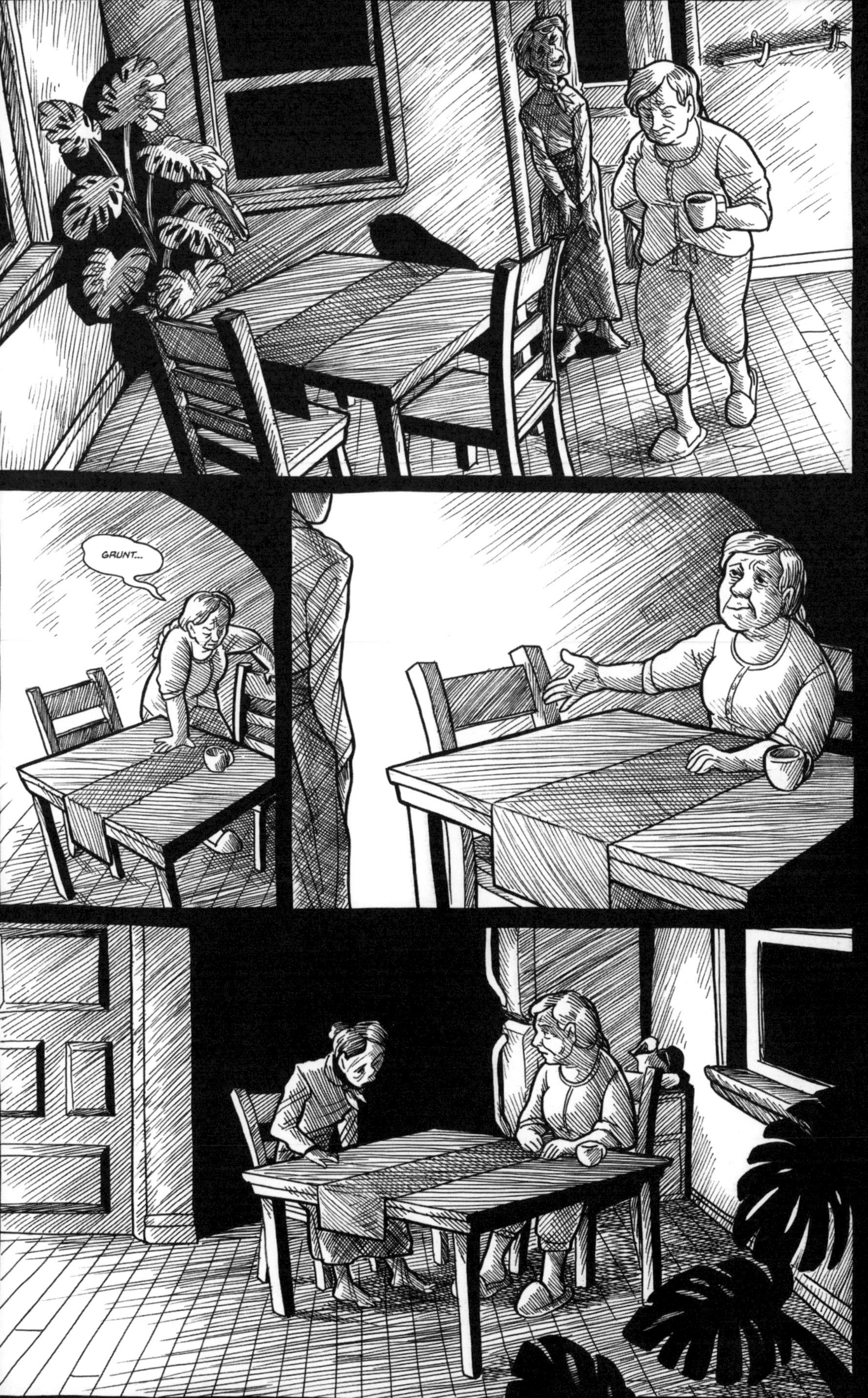
GRUNT...

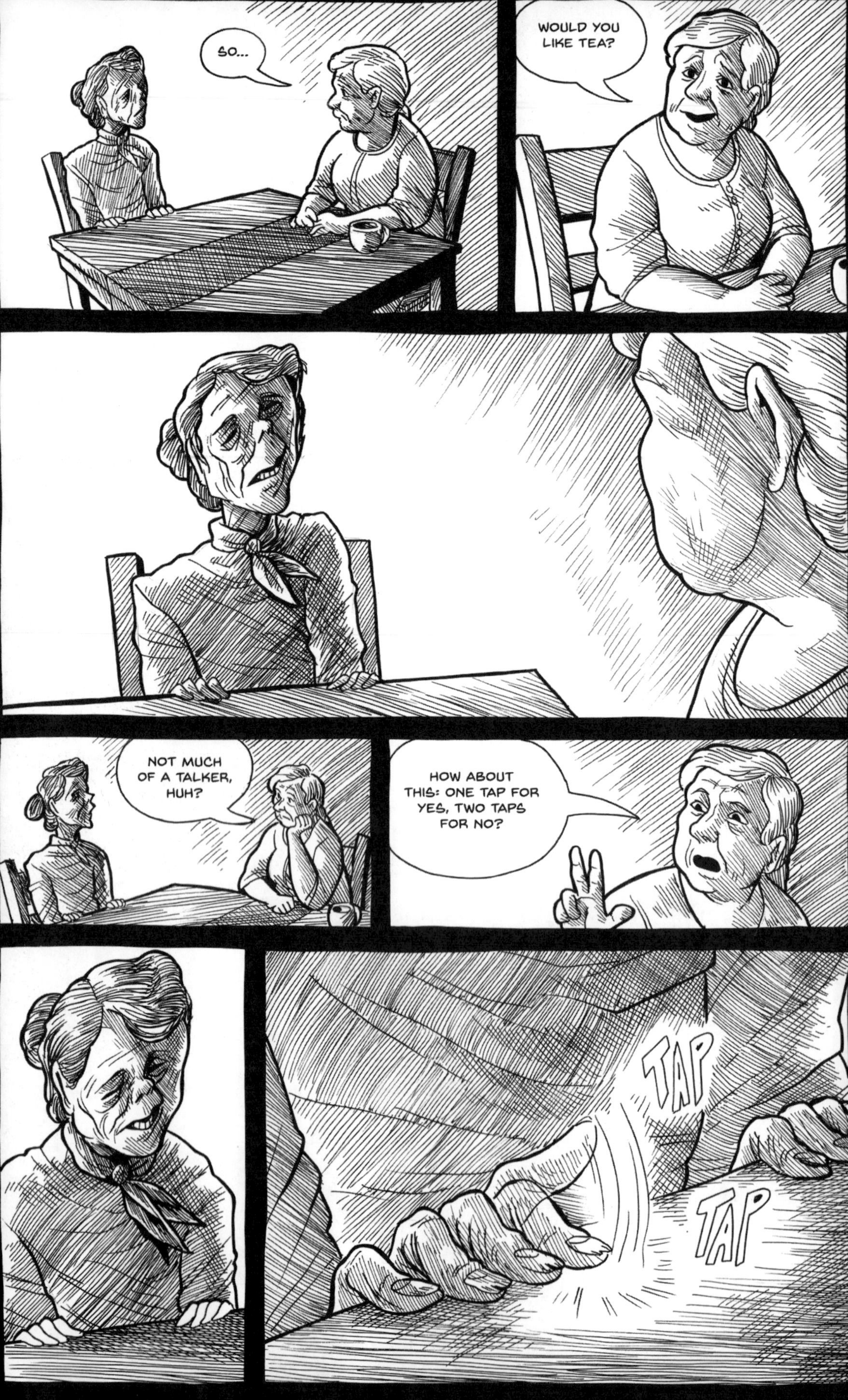
SO...
WOULD YOU LIKE TEA?
NOT MUCH OF A TALKER, HUH?
HOW ABOUT THIS: ONE TAP FOR YES, TWO TAPS FOR NO?
TAP
TAP

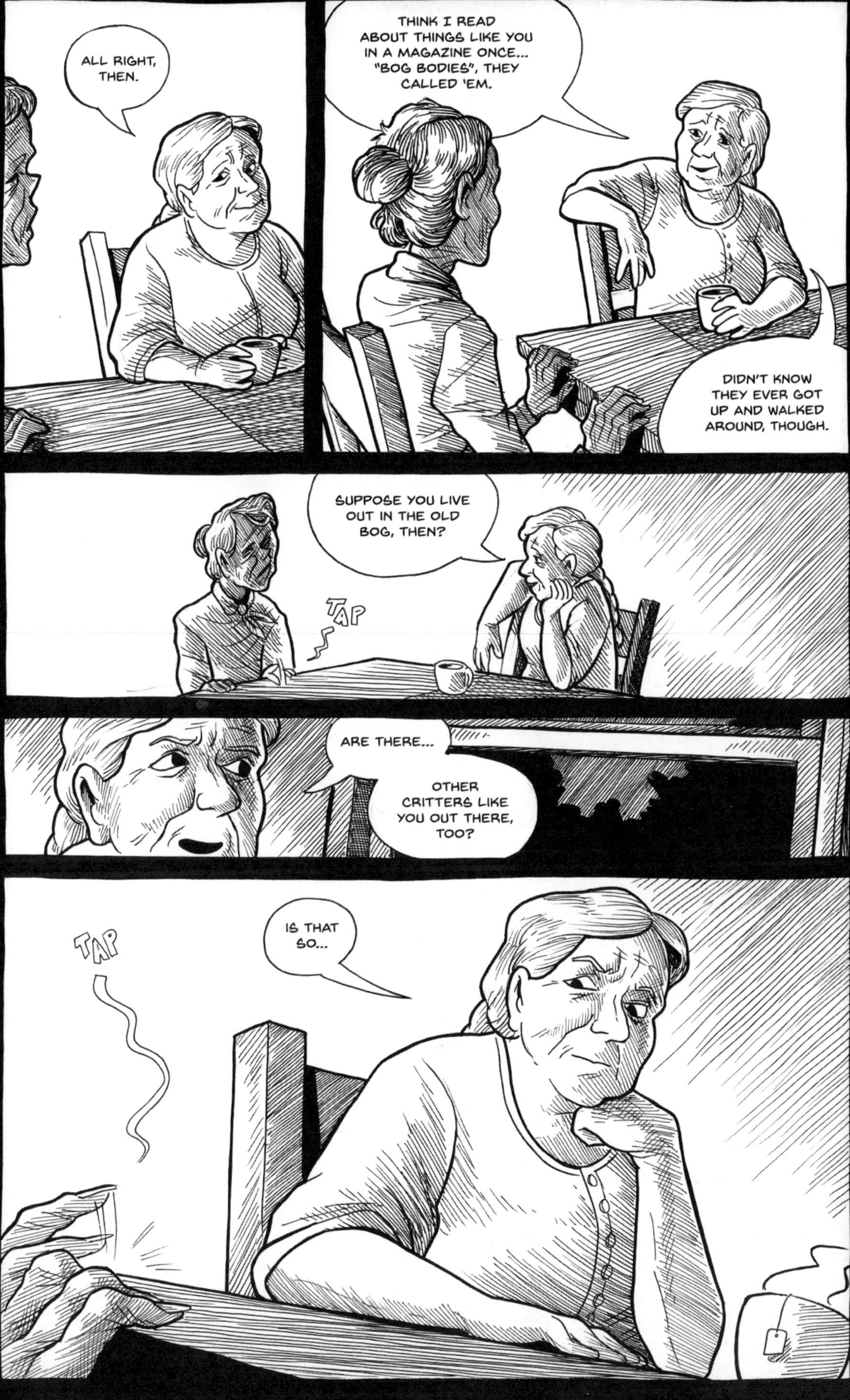
ALL RIGHT, THEN.
THINK I READ ABOUT THINGS LIKE YOU IN A MAGAZINE ONCE... "BOG BODIES", THEY CALLED 'EM.
DIDN'T KNOW THEY EVER GOT UP AND WALKED AROUND, THOUGH.
SUPPOSE YOU LIVE OUT IN THE OLD BOG, THEN?
TAP
ARE THERE...
OTHER CRITTERS LIKE YOU OUT THERE, TOO?
TAP
IS THAT SO...

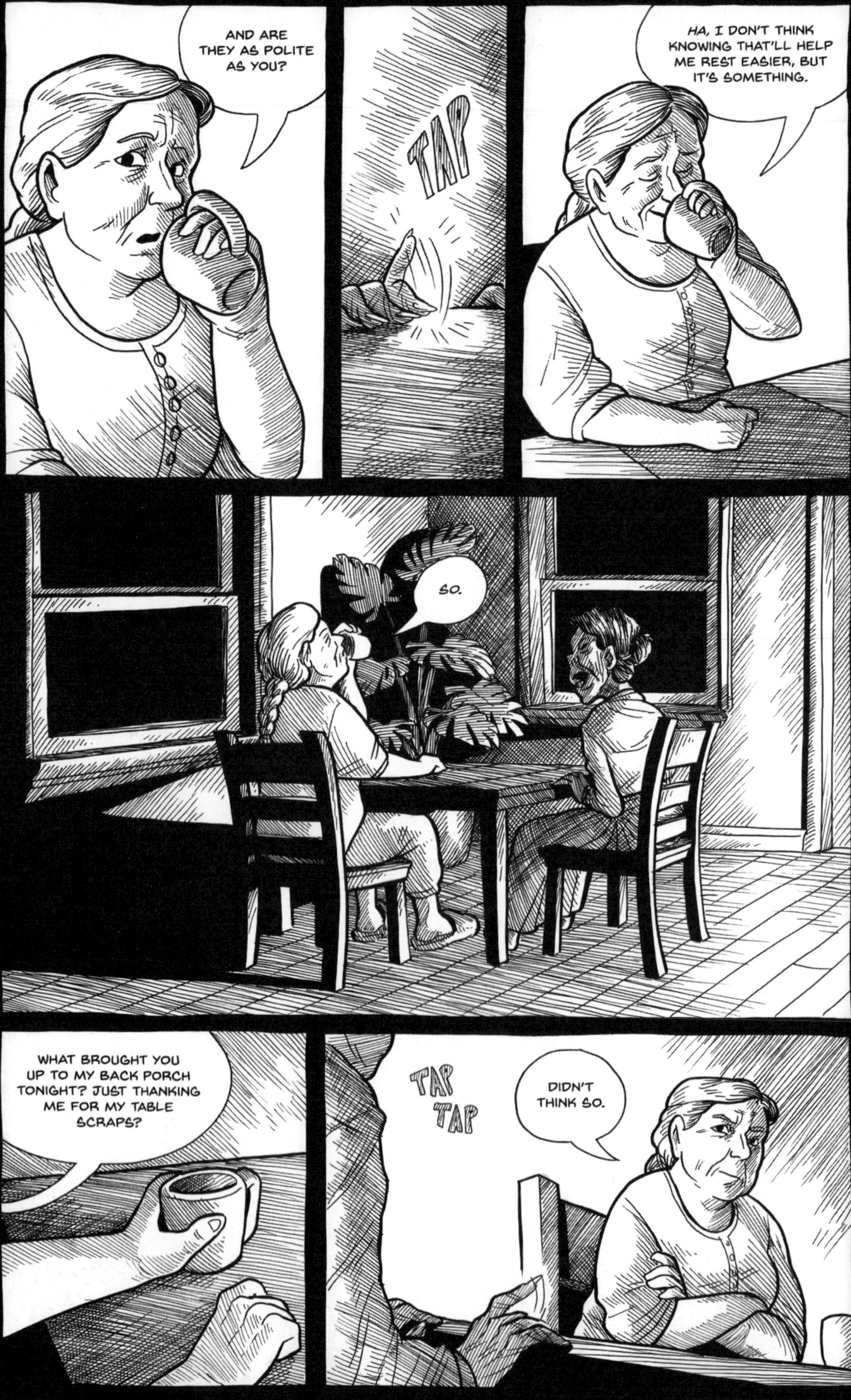
AND ARE THEY AS POLITE AS YOU?
TAP
HA, I DON'T THINK KNOWING THAT'LL HELP ME REST EASIER, BUT IT'S SOMETHING.
SO.
WHAT BROUGHT YOU UP TO MY BACK PORCH TONIGHT? JUST THANKING ME FOR MY TABLE SCRAPS?
TAP TAP
DIDN'T THINK SO.

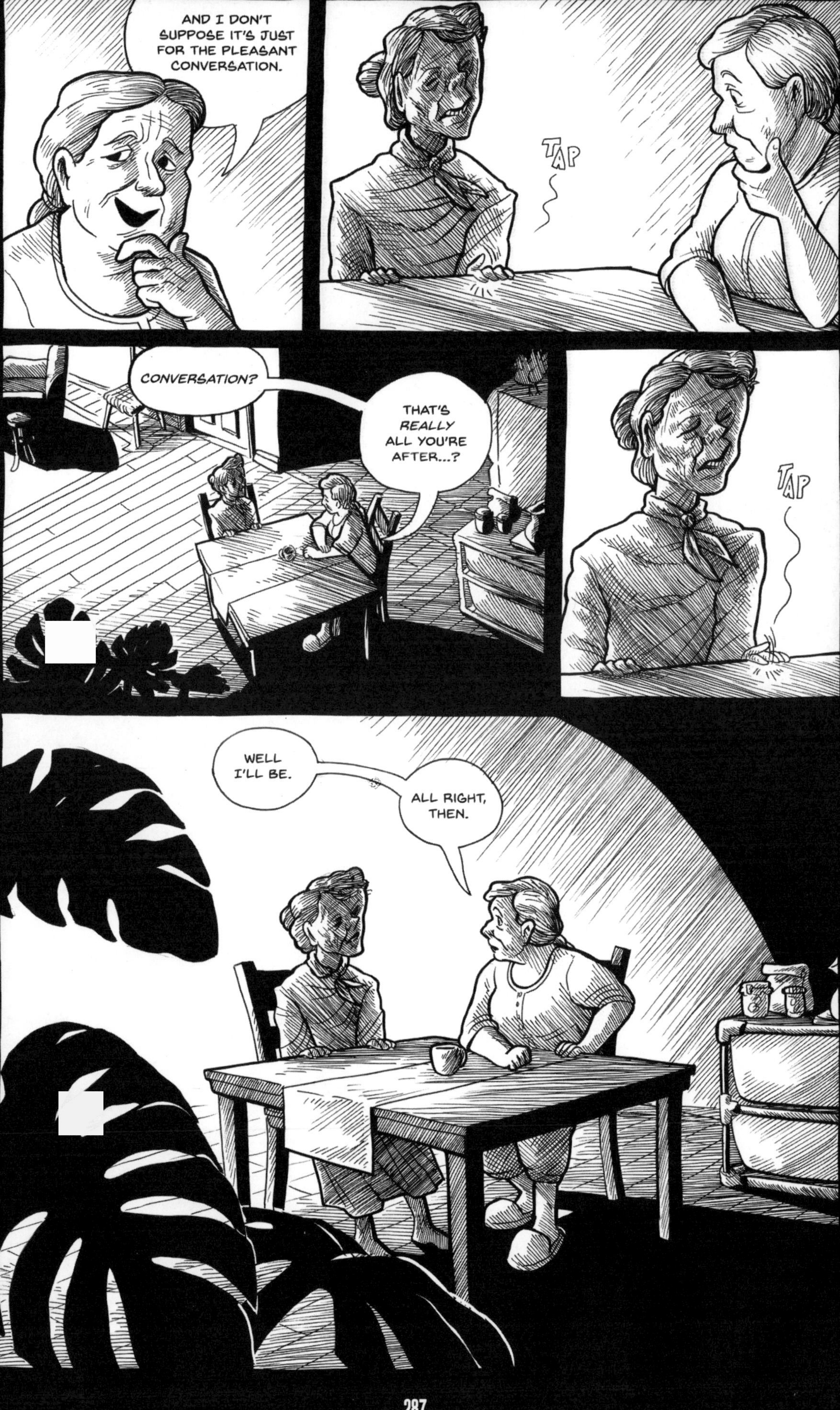
AND I DON'T SUPPOSE IT'S JUST FOR THE PLEASANT CONVERSATION.
TAP
CONVERSATION?
THAT'S REALLY ALL YOU'RE AFTER...?
TAP
WELL I'LL BE.
ALL RIGHT, THEN.

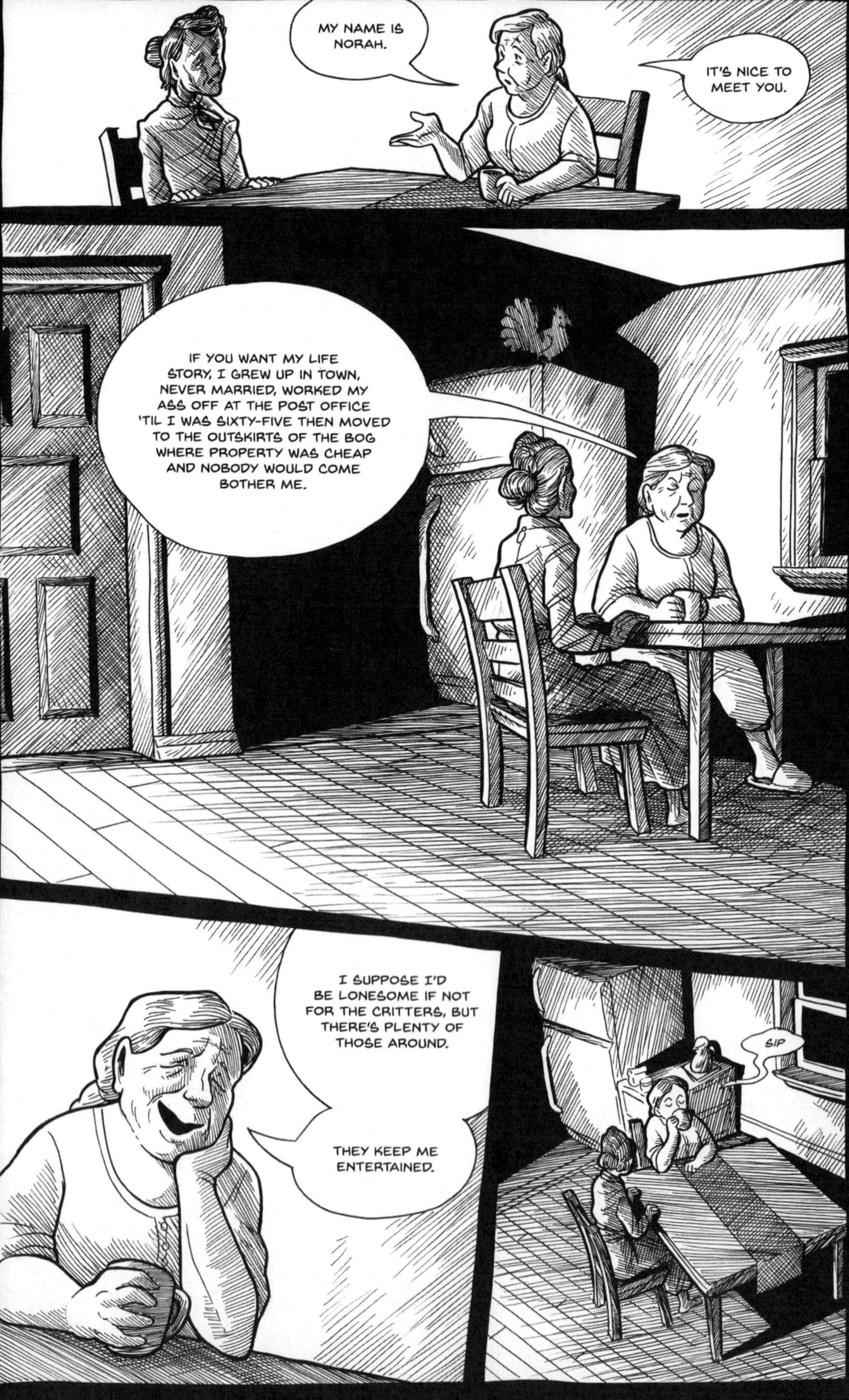
MY NAME IS NORAH.
IT'S NICE TO MEET YOU.
IF YOU WANT MY LIFE STORY, I GREW UP IN TOWN, NEVER MARRIED, WORKED MY ASS OFF AT THE POST OFFICE 'TIL I WAS SIXTY-FIVE THEN MOVED TO THE OUTSKIRTS OF THE BOG WHERE PROPERTY WAS CHEAP AND NOBODY WOULD COME BOTHER ME.
I SUPPOSE I'D BE LONESOME IF NOT FOR THE CRITTERS, BUT THERE'S PLENTY OF THOSE AROUND.
THEY KEEP ME ENTERTAINED.
SIP

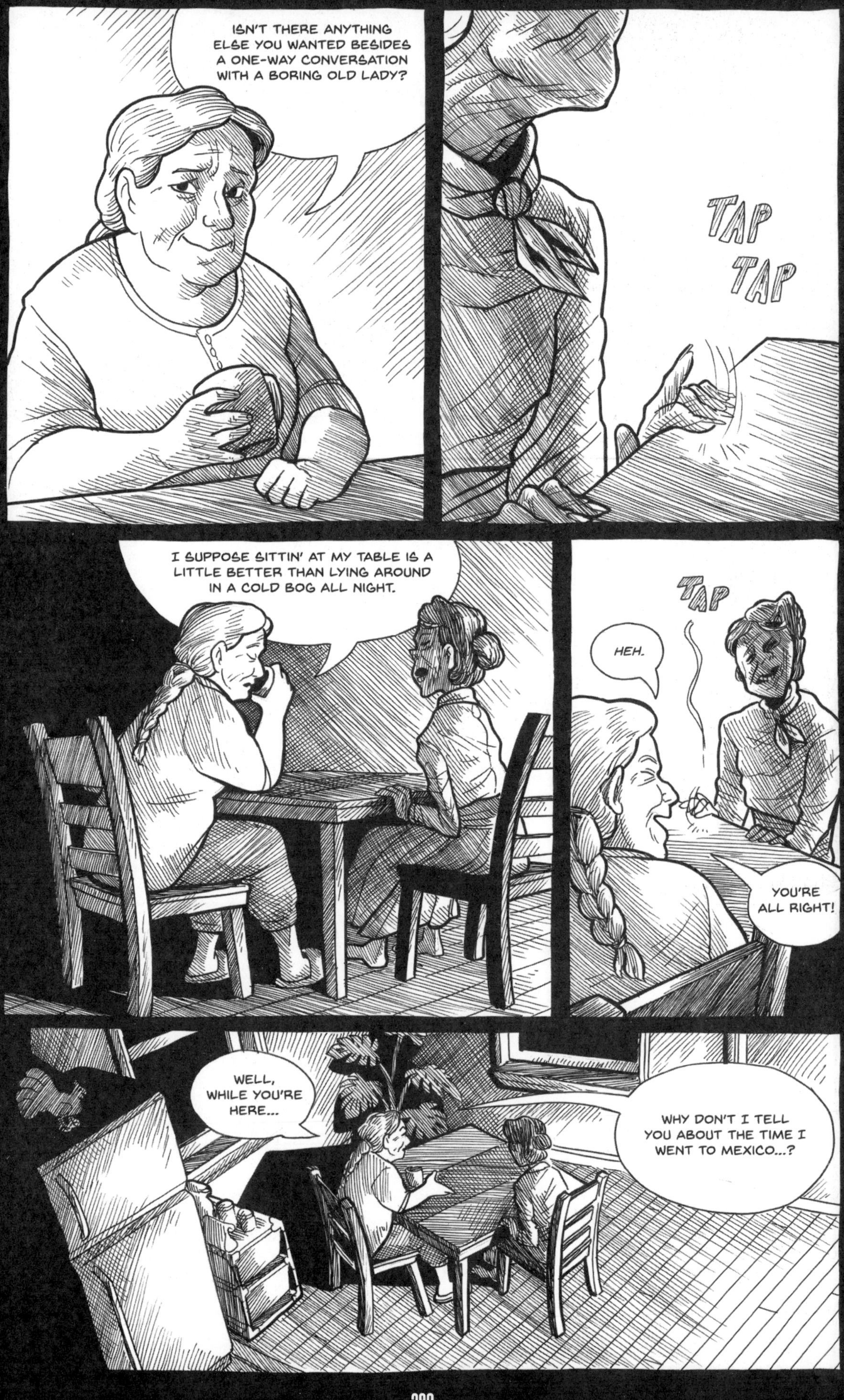
ISN'T THERE ANYTHING ELSE YOU WANTED BESIDES A ONE-WAY CONVERSATION WITH A BORING OLD LADY?
TAP TAP
I SUPPOSE SITTIN' AT MY TABLE IS A LITTLE BETTER THAN LYING AROUND IN A COLD BOG ALL NIGHT.
TAP
HEH.
YOU'RE ALL RIGHT!
WELL, WHILE YOU'RE HERE...
WHY DON'T I TELL YOU ABOUT THE TIME I WENT TO MEXICO...?

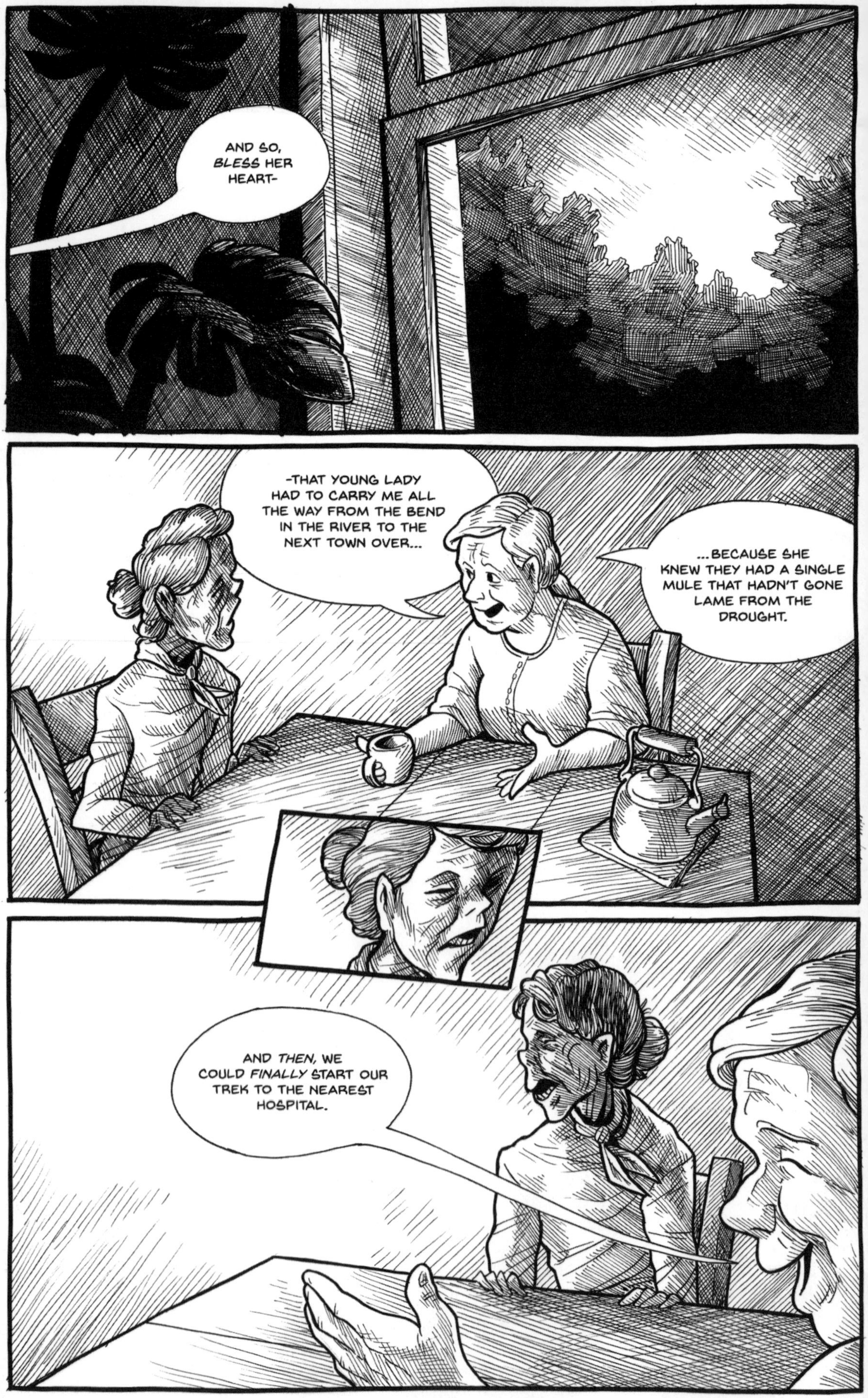
AND SO, *BLESS* HER HEART-
-THAT YOUNG LADY HAD TO CARRY ME ALL THE WAY FROM THE BEND IN THE RIVER TO THE NEXT TOWN OVER...
...BECAUSE SHE KNEW THEY HAD A SINGLE MULE THAT HADN'T GONE LAME FROM THE DROUGHT.
AND *THEN*, WE COULD *FINALLY* START OUR TREK TO THE NEAREST HOSPITAL.

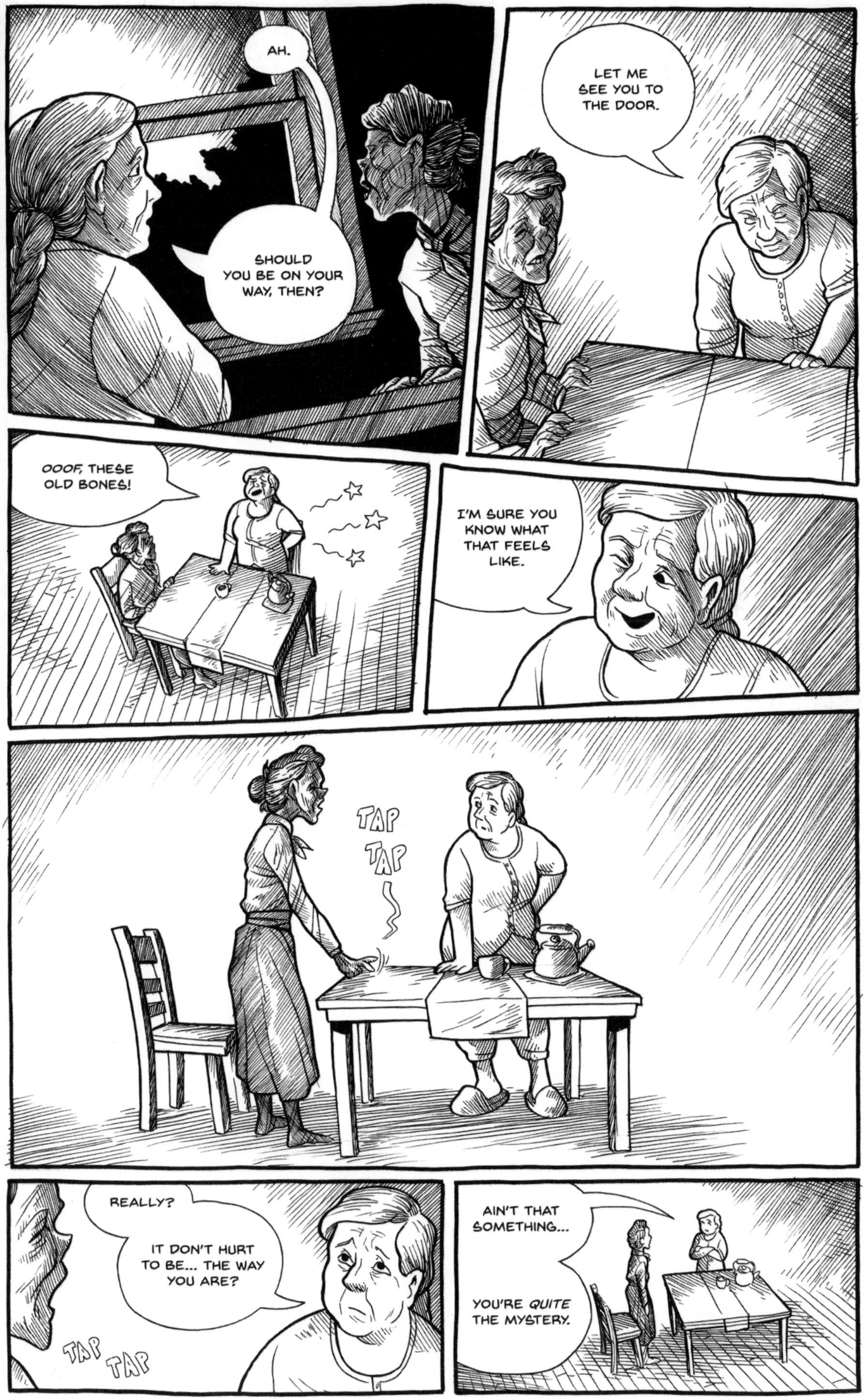
AH.
SHOULD YOU BE ON YOUR WAY, THEN?
LET ME SEE YOU TO THE DOOR.
OOOF, THESE OLD BONES!
I'M SURE YOU KNOW WHAT THAT FEELS LIKE.
TAP TAP
REALLY?
IT DON'T HURT TO BE... THE WAY YOU ARE?
TAP TAP
AIN'T THAT SOMETHING...
YOU'RE *QUITE* THE MYSTERY.

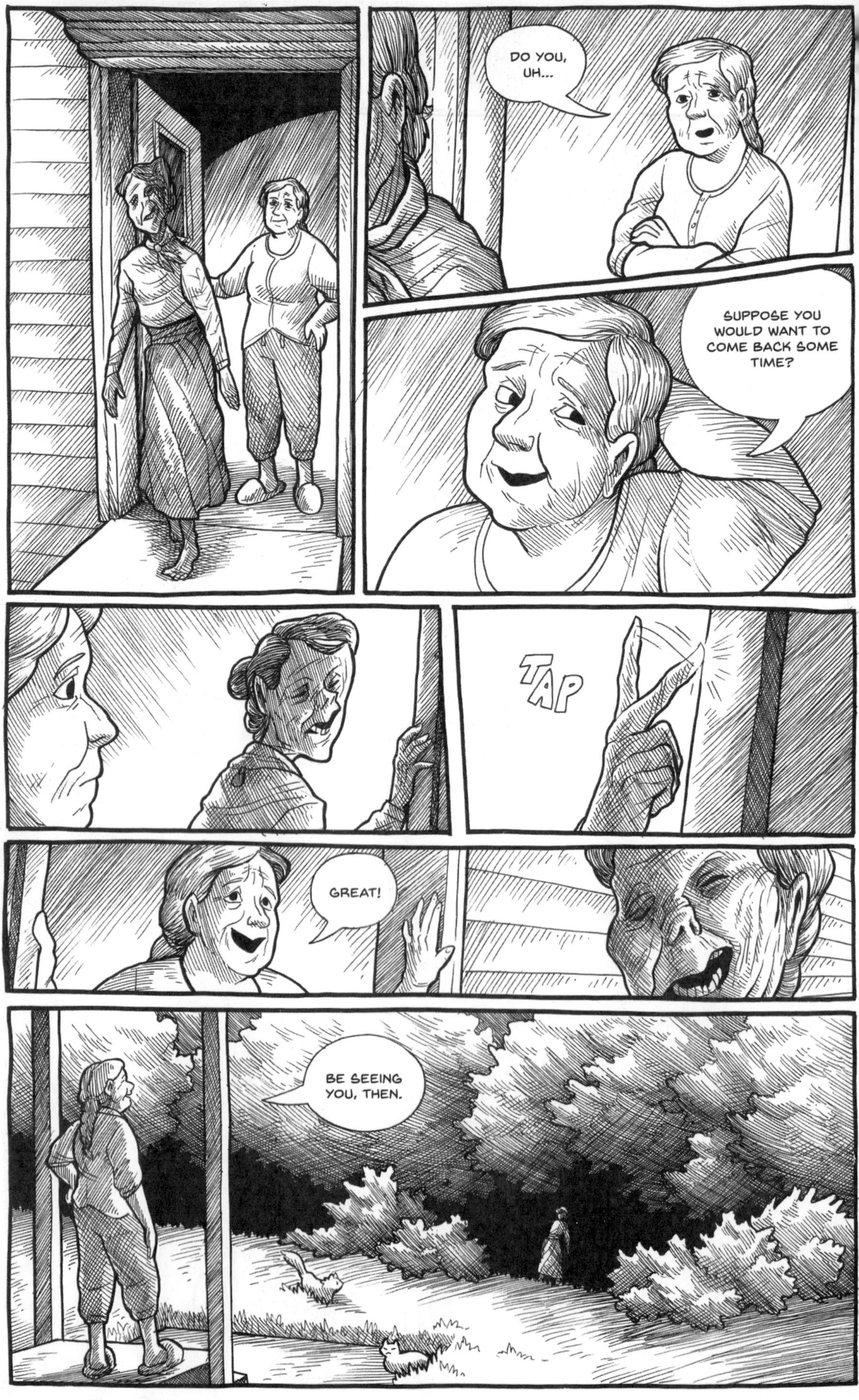
DO YOU, UH...
SUPPOSE YOU WOULD WANT TO COME BACK SOME TIME?
TAP
GREAT!
BE SEEING YOU, THEN.

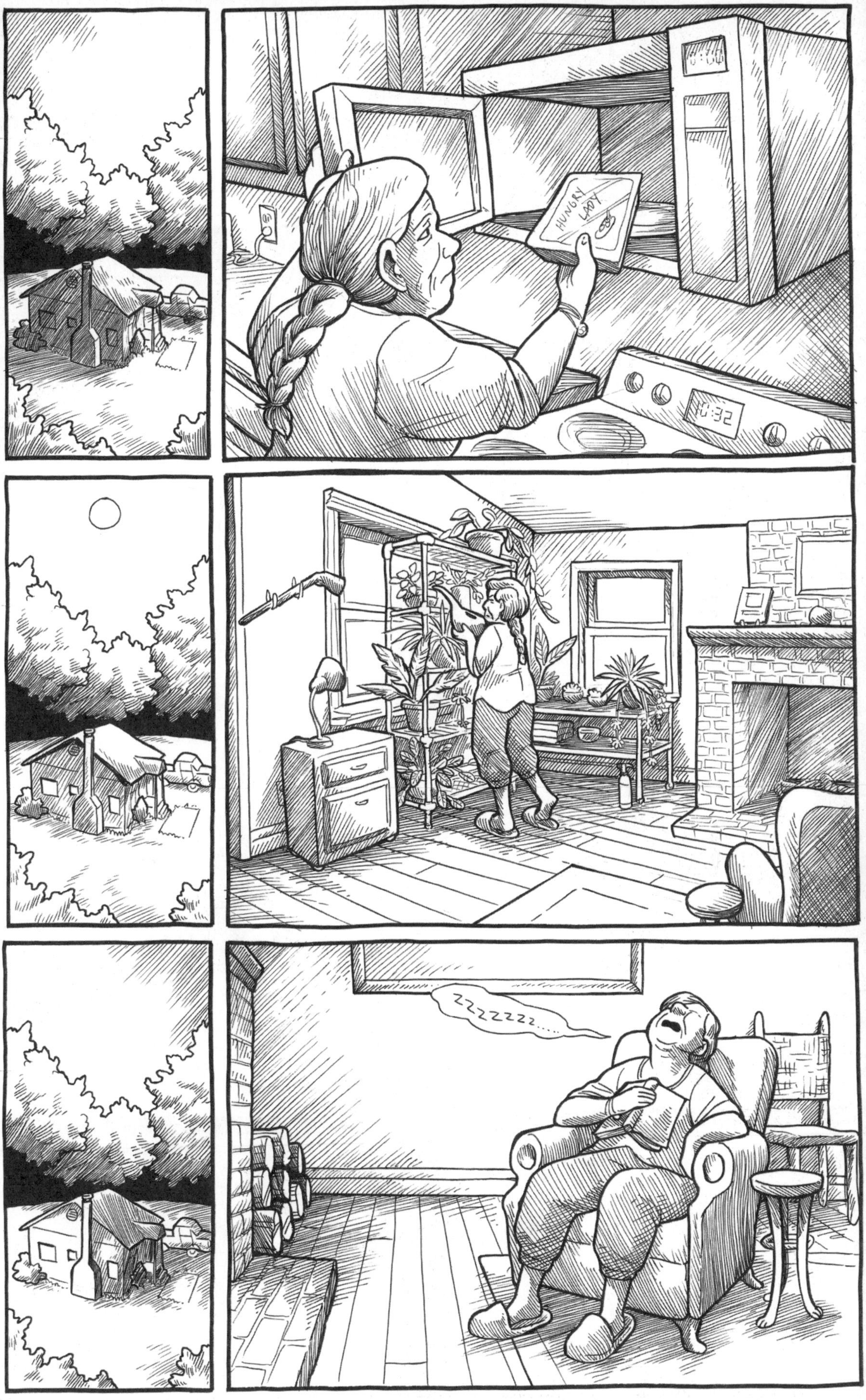
HUNGRY LADY
10:32
ZZZZZZZ.....

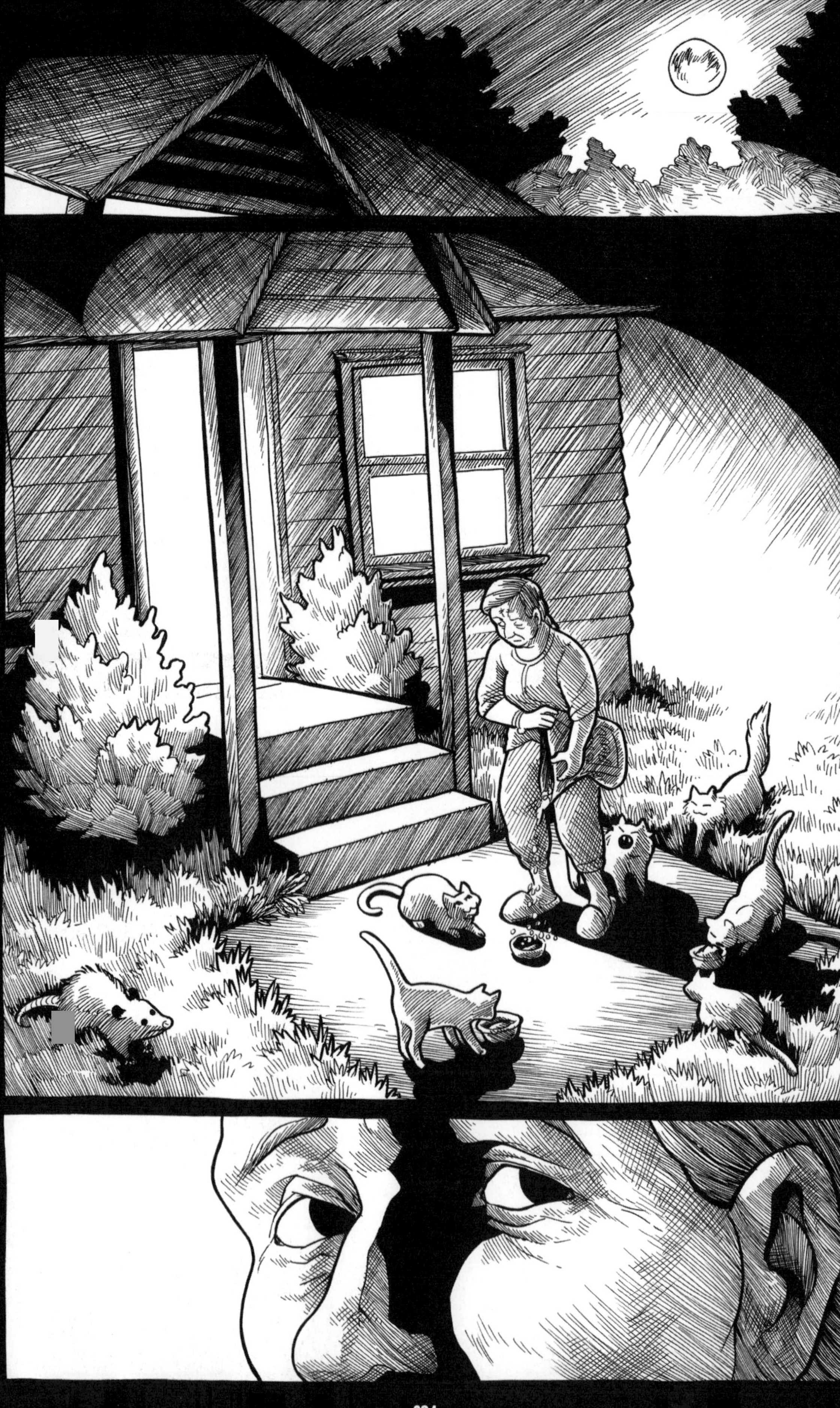

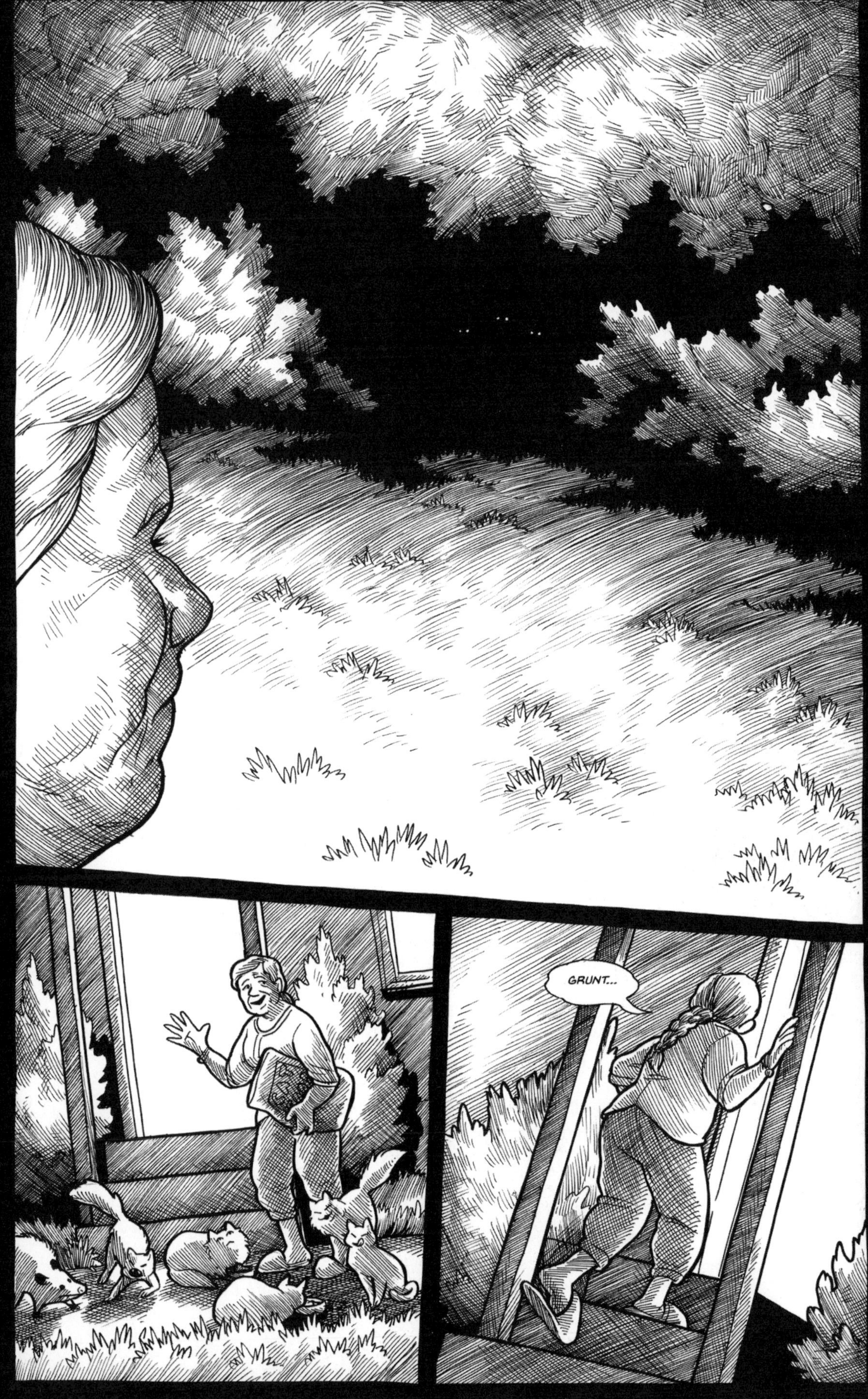
GRUNT...

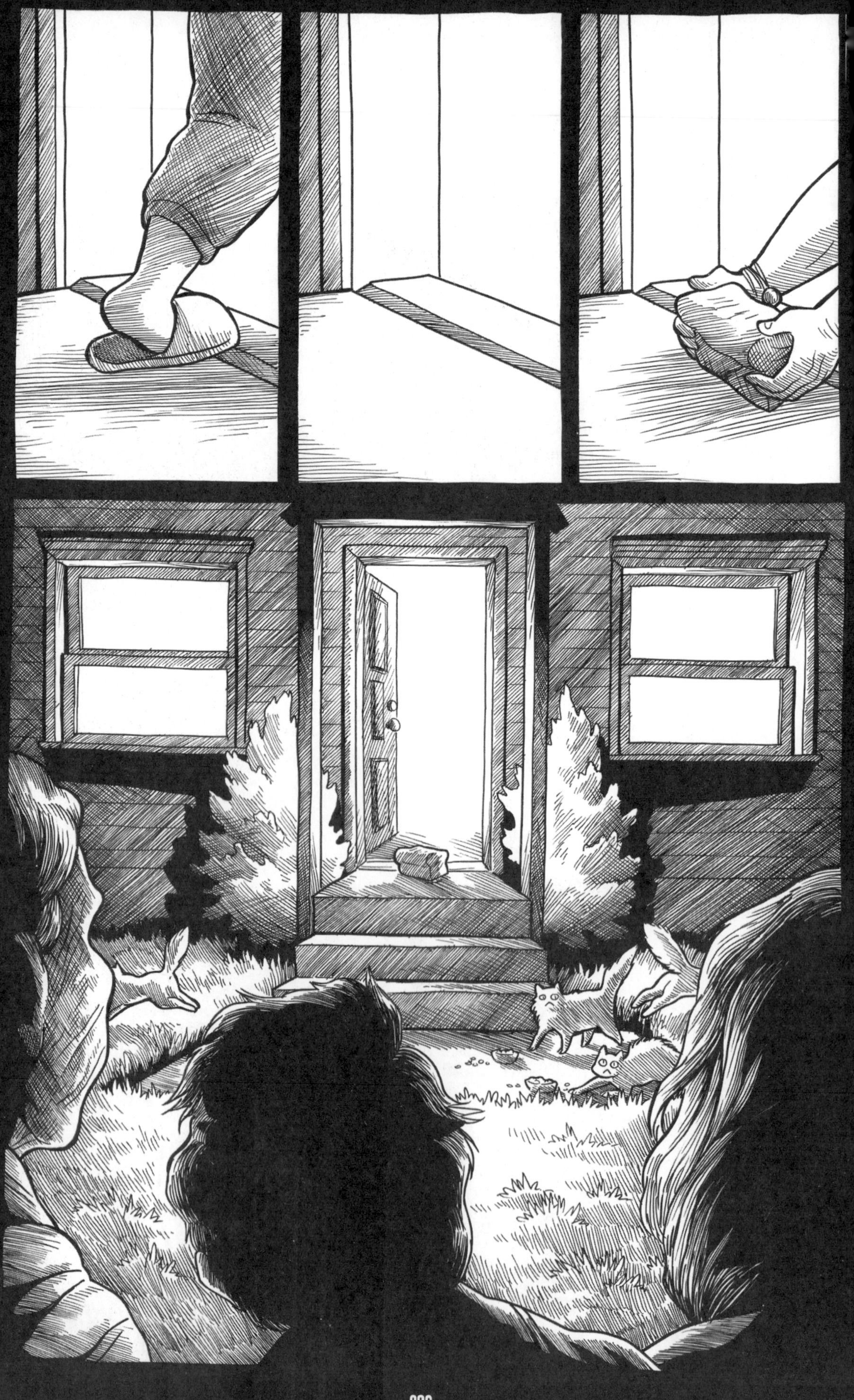

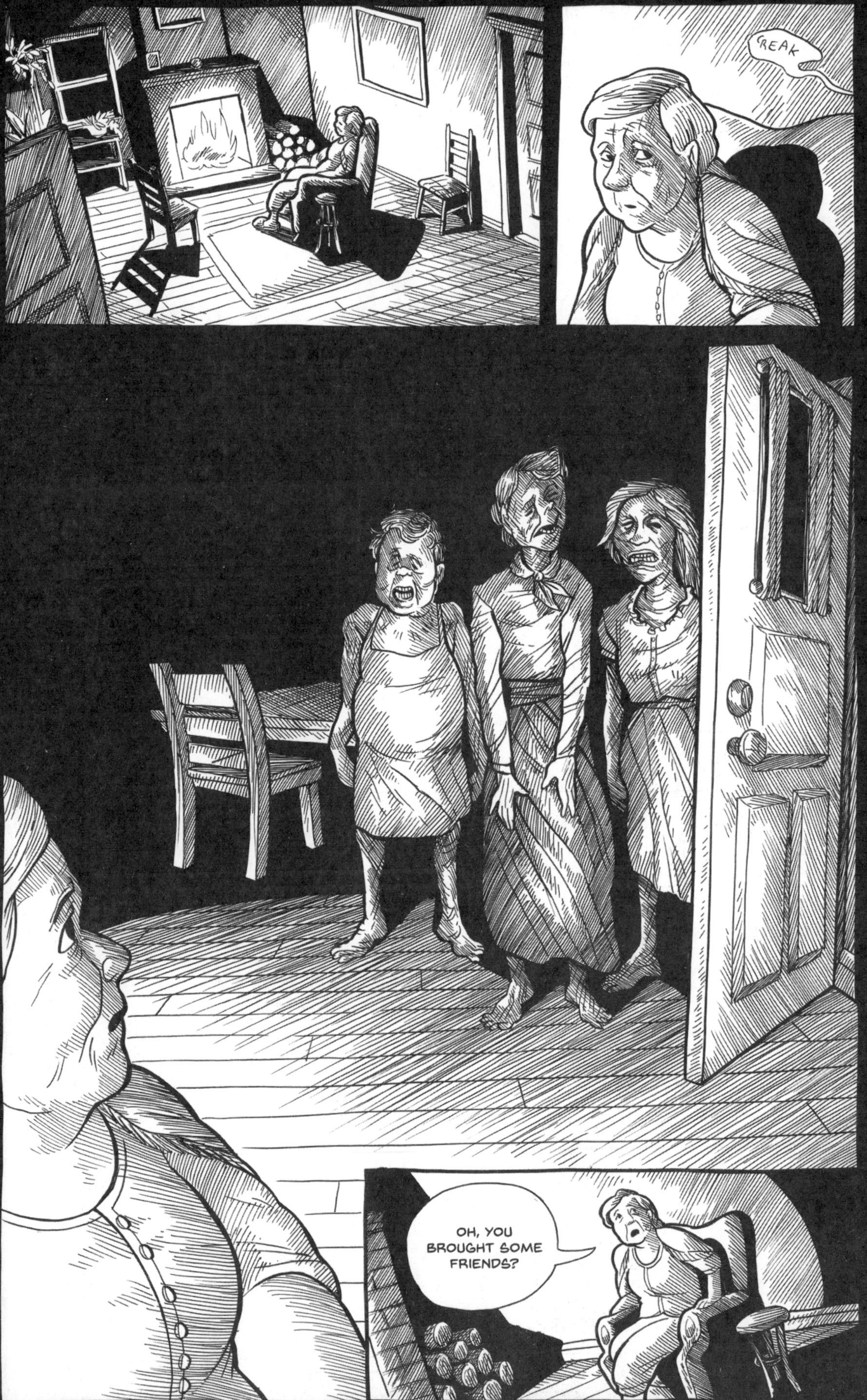
CREAK
OH, YOU BROUGHT SOME FRIENDS?

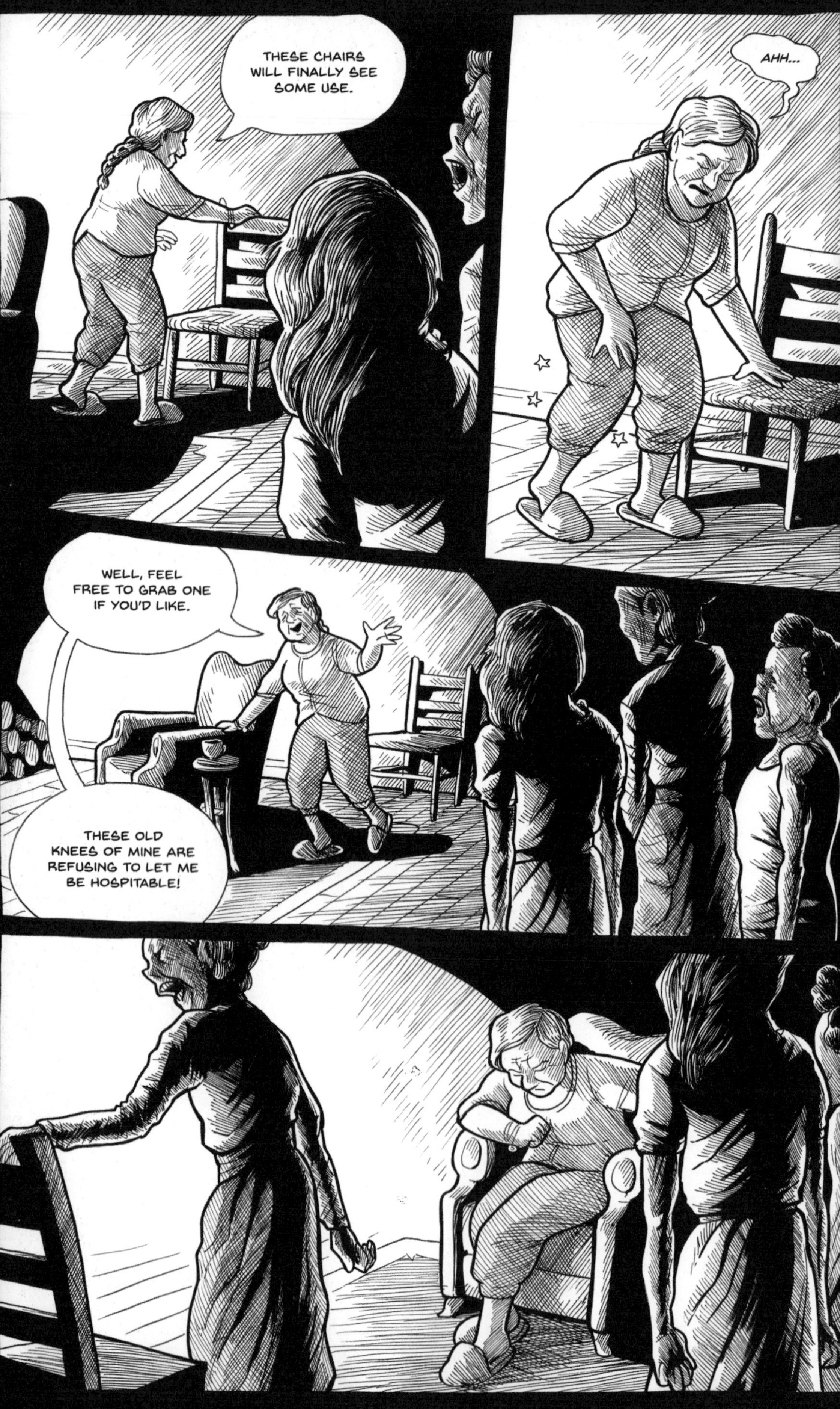
THESE CHAIRS WILL FINALLY SEE SOME USE.
AHH...
WELL, FEEL FREE TO GRAB ONE IF YOU'D LIKE.
THESE OLD KNEES OF MINE ARE REFUSING TO LET ME BE HOSPITABLE!

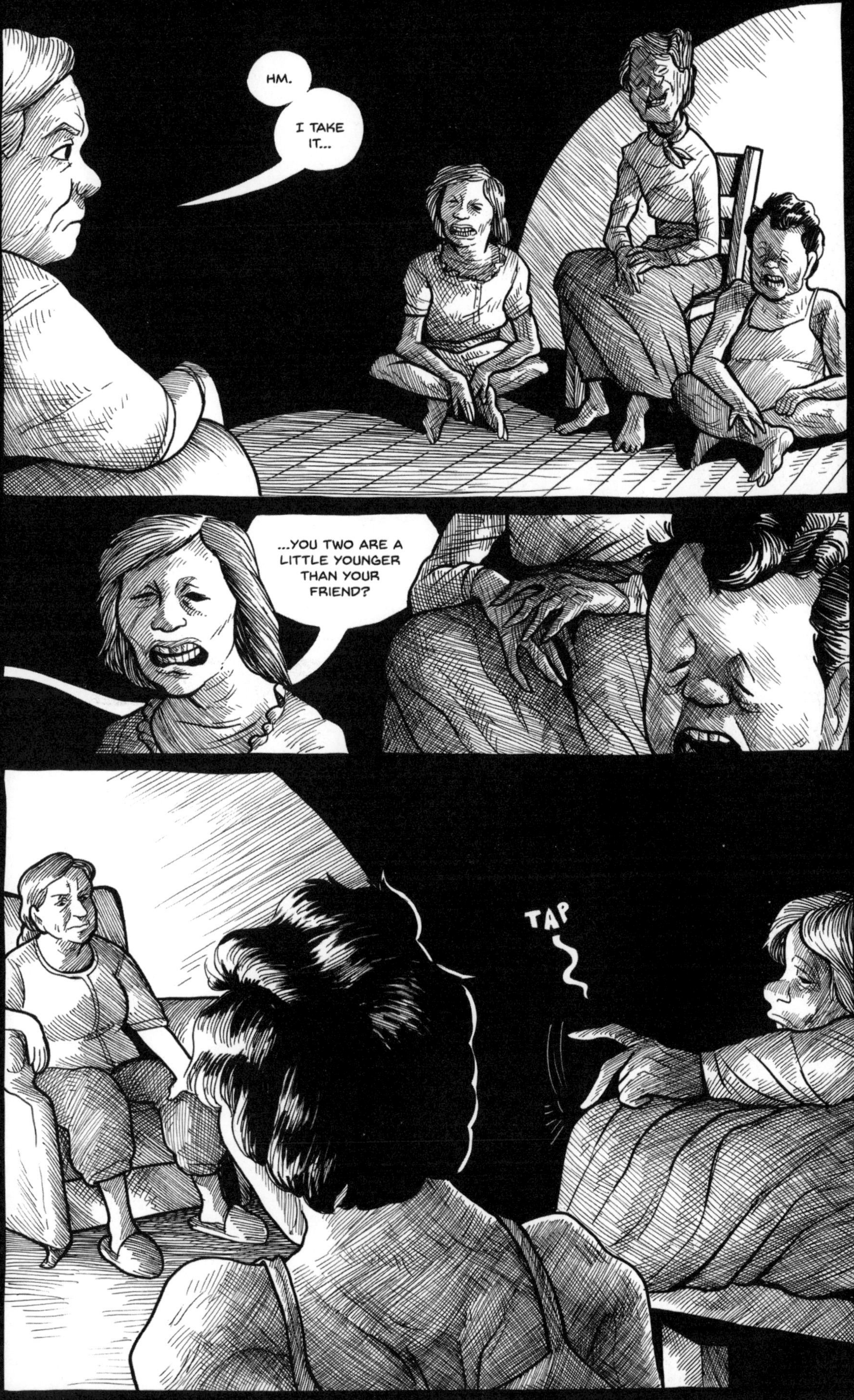
HM.
I TAKE IT...
...YOU TWO ARE A LITTLE YOUNGER THAN YOUR FRIEND?
TAP

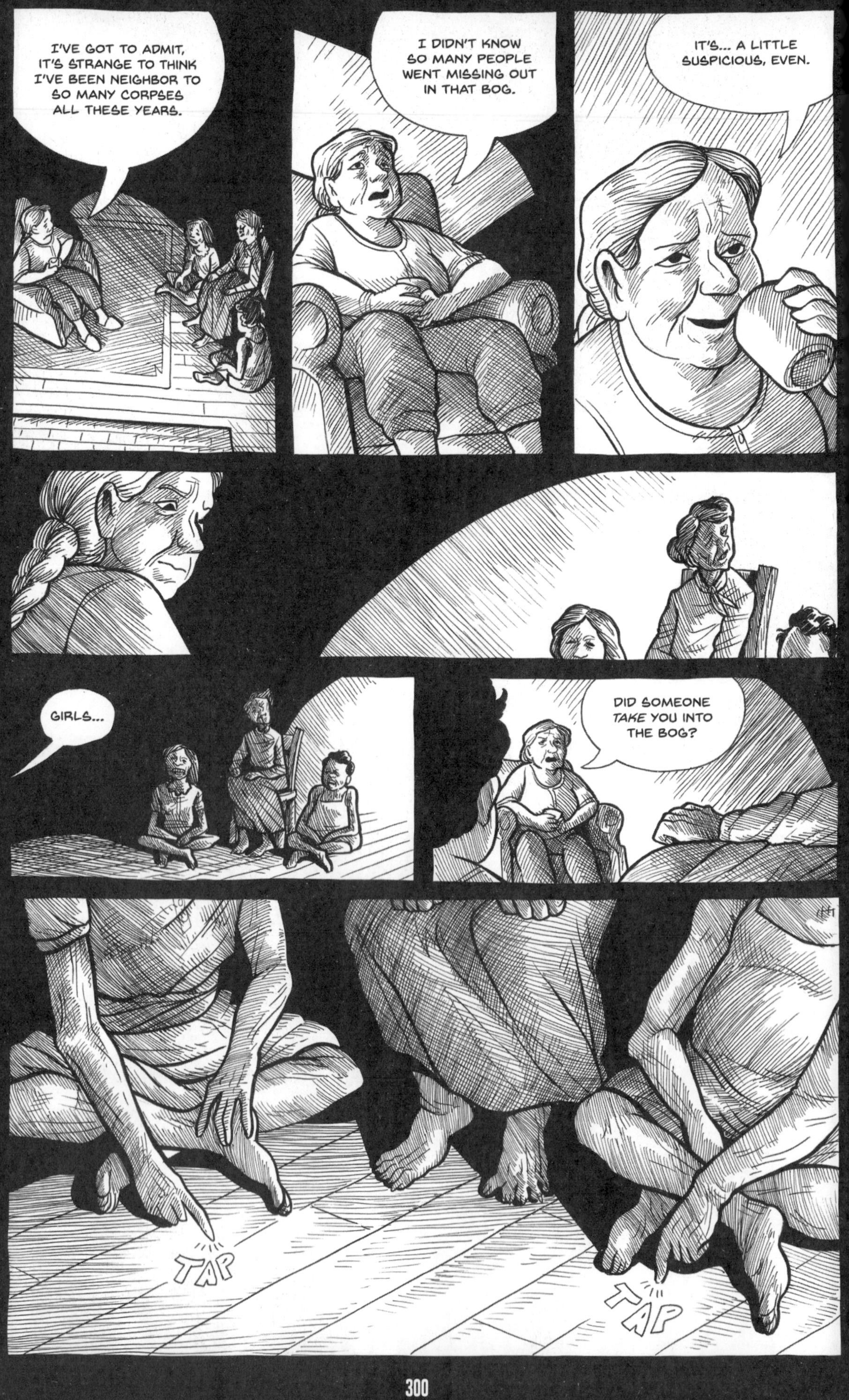

I'VE GOT TO ADMIT, IT'S STRANGE TO THINK I'VE BEEN NEIGHBOR TO SO MANY CORPSES ALL THESE YEARS.
I DIDN'T KNOW SO MANY PEOPLE WENT MISSING OUT IN THAT BOG.
IT'S... A LITTLE SUSPICIOUS, EVEN.
GIRLS...
DID SOMEONE *TAKE* YOU INTO THE BOG?
TAP
TAP

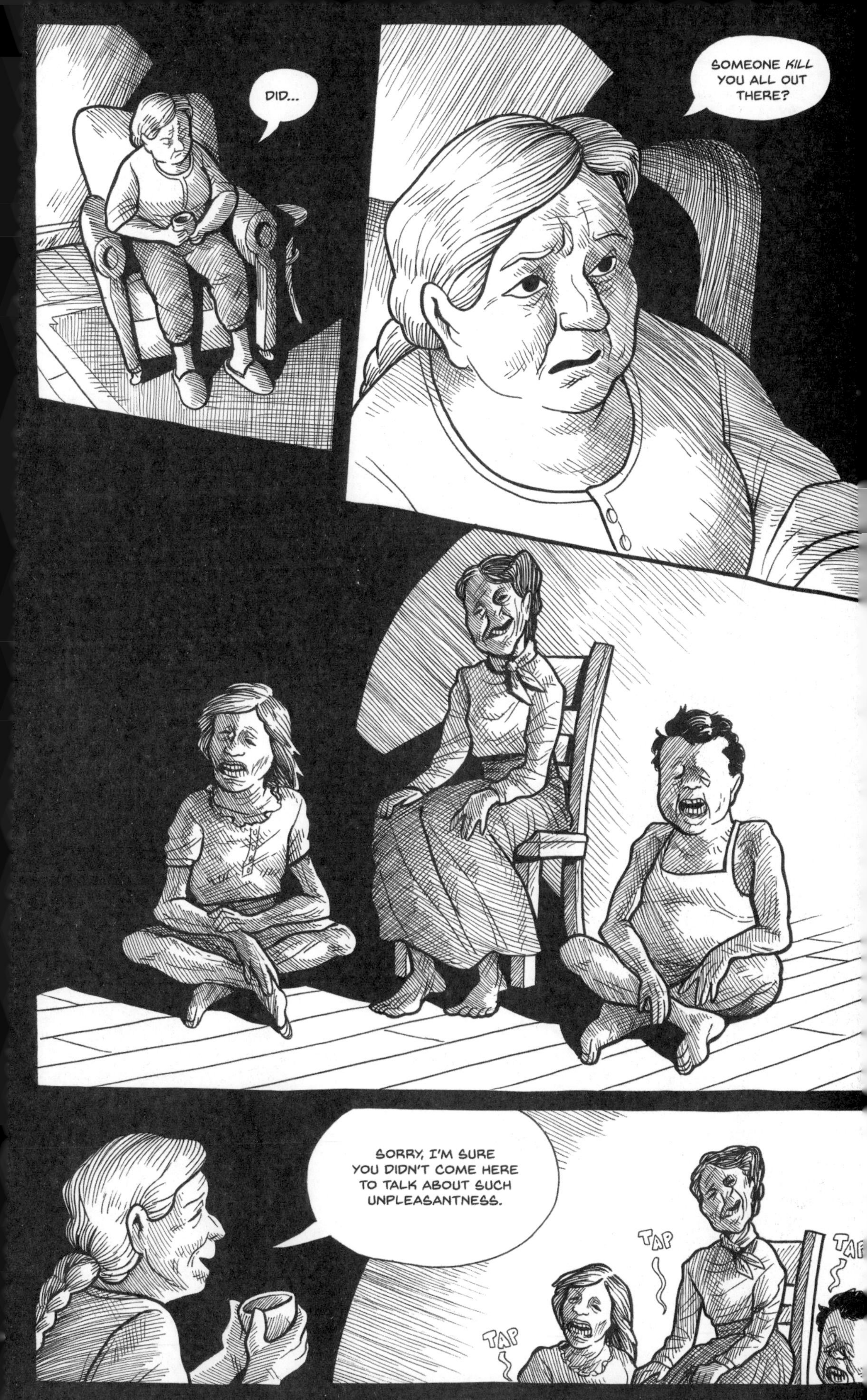
DID...
SOMEONE KILL YOU ALL OUT THERE?
SORRY, I'M SURE YOU DIDN'T COME HERE TO TALK ABOUT SUCH UNPLEASANTNESS.
TAP
TAP
TAP

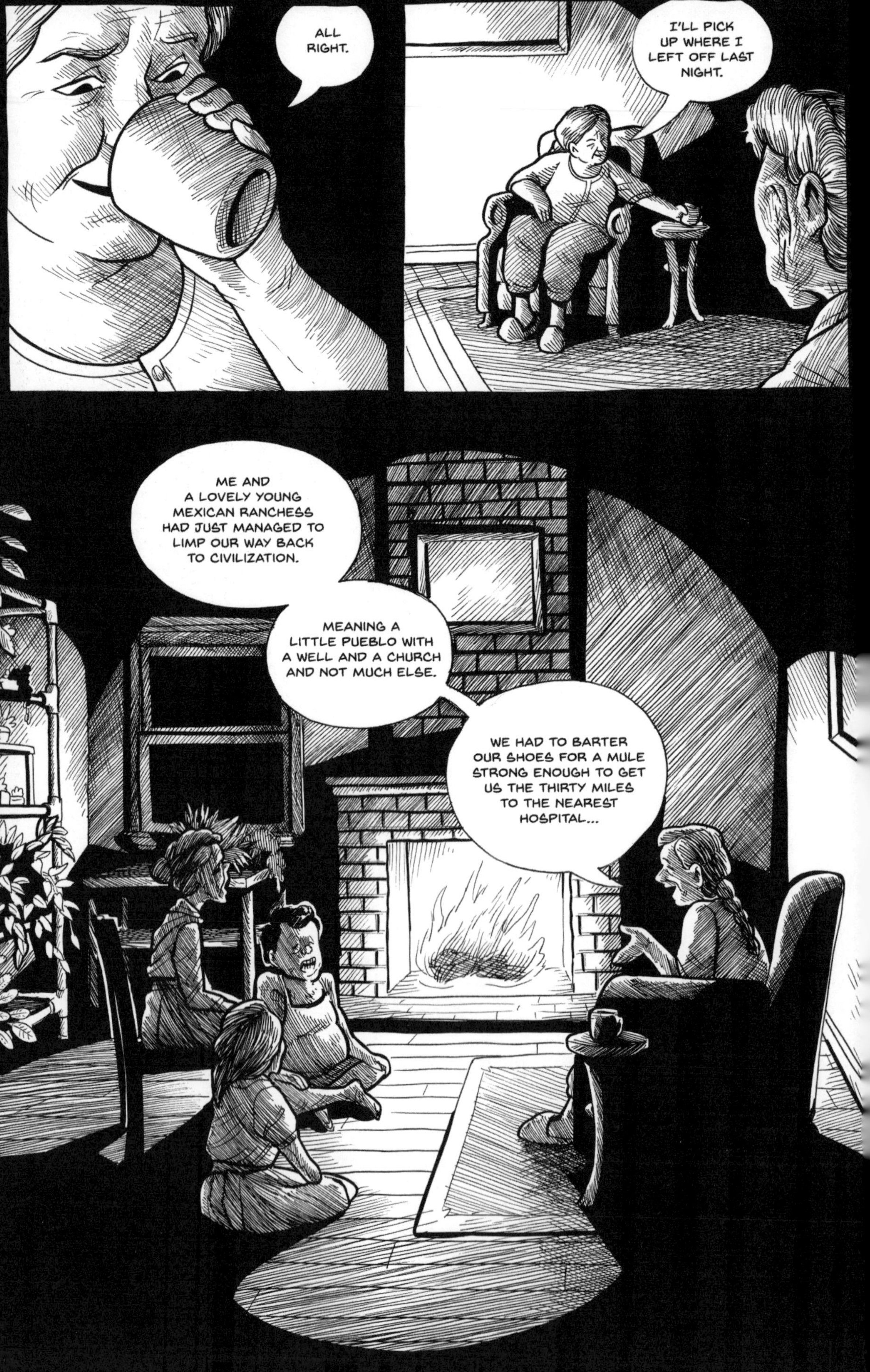
ALL RIGHT.
I'LL PICK UP WHERE I LEFT OFF LAST NIGHT.
ME AND A LOVELY YOUNG MEXICAN RANCHESS HAD JUST MANAGED TO LIMP OUR WAY BACK TO CIVILIZATION.
MEANING A LITTLE PUEBLO WITH A WELL AND A CHURCH AND NOT MUCH ELSE.
WE HAD TO BARTER OUR SHOES FOR A MULE STRONG ENOUGH TO GET US THE THIRTY MILES TO THE NEAREST HOSPITAL...

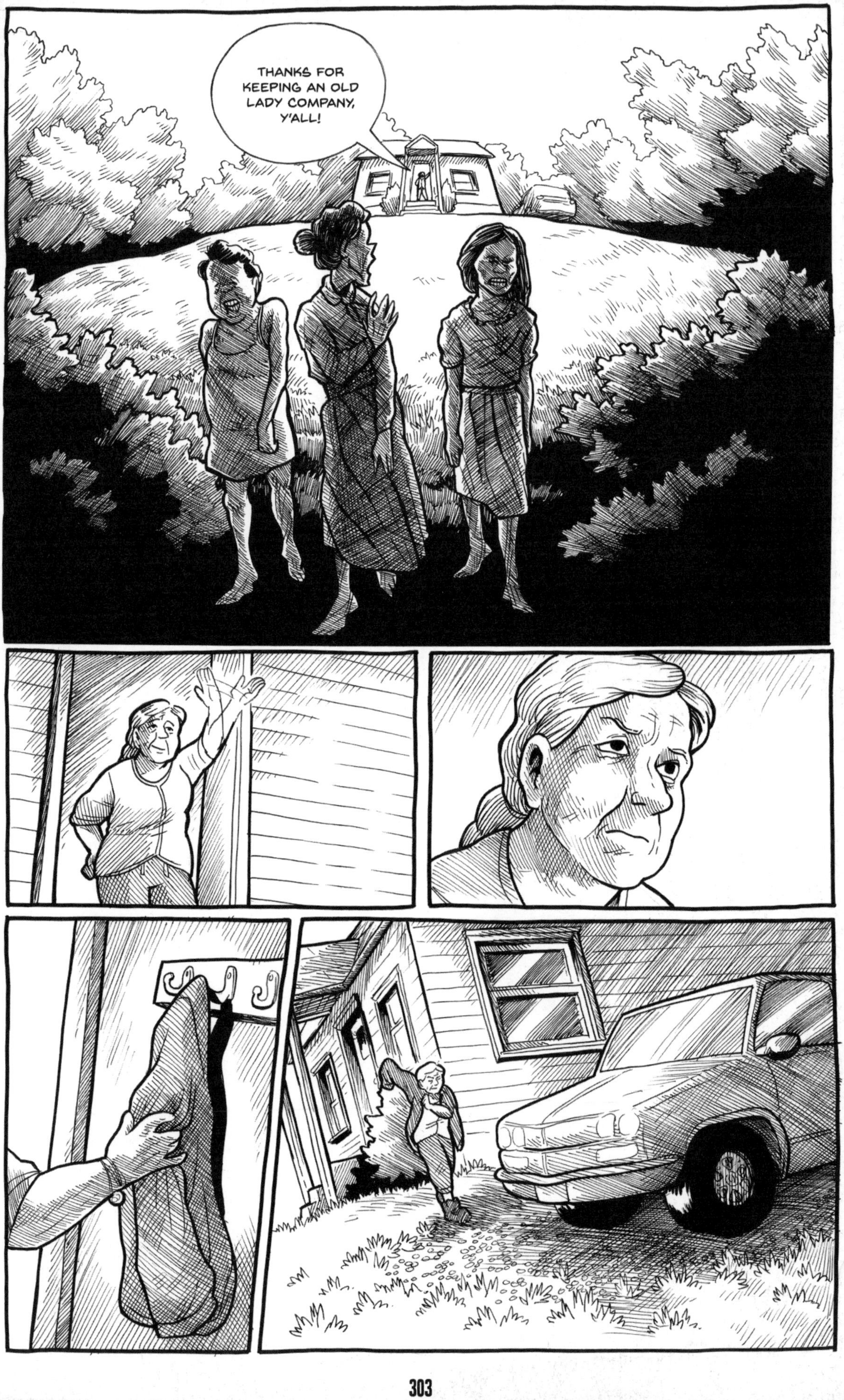
THANKS FOR KEEPING AN OLD LADY COMPANY, Y'ALL!

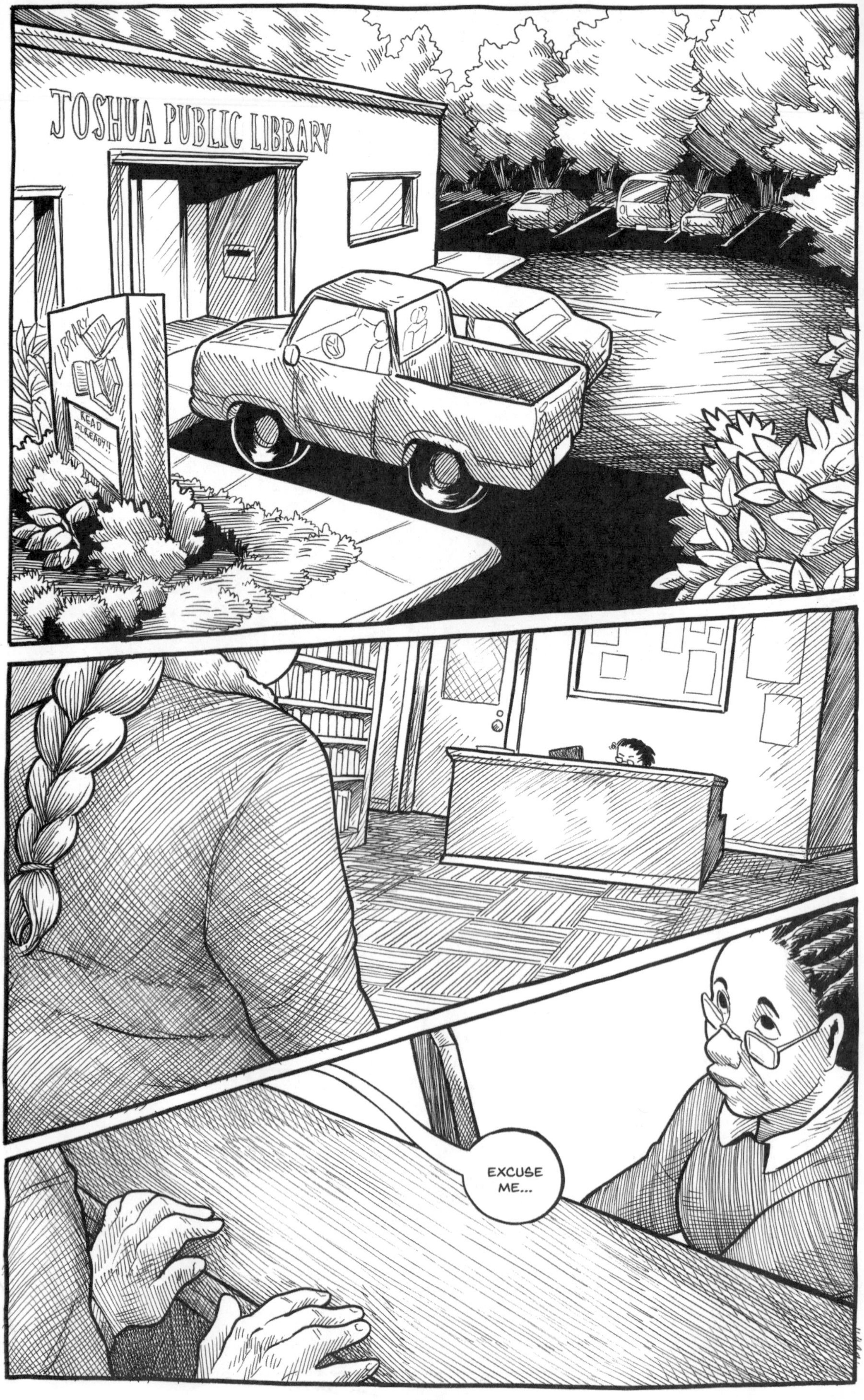
JOSHUA PUBLIC LIBRARY
LIBRARY
READ ALREADY!!
EXCUSE ME...

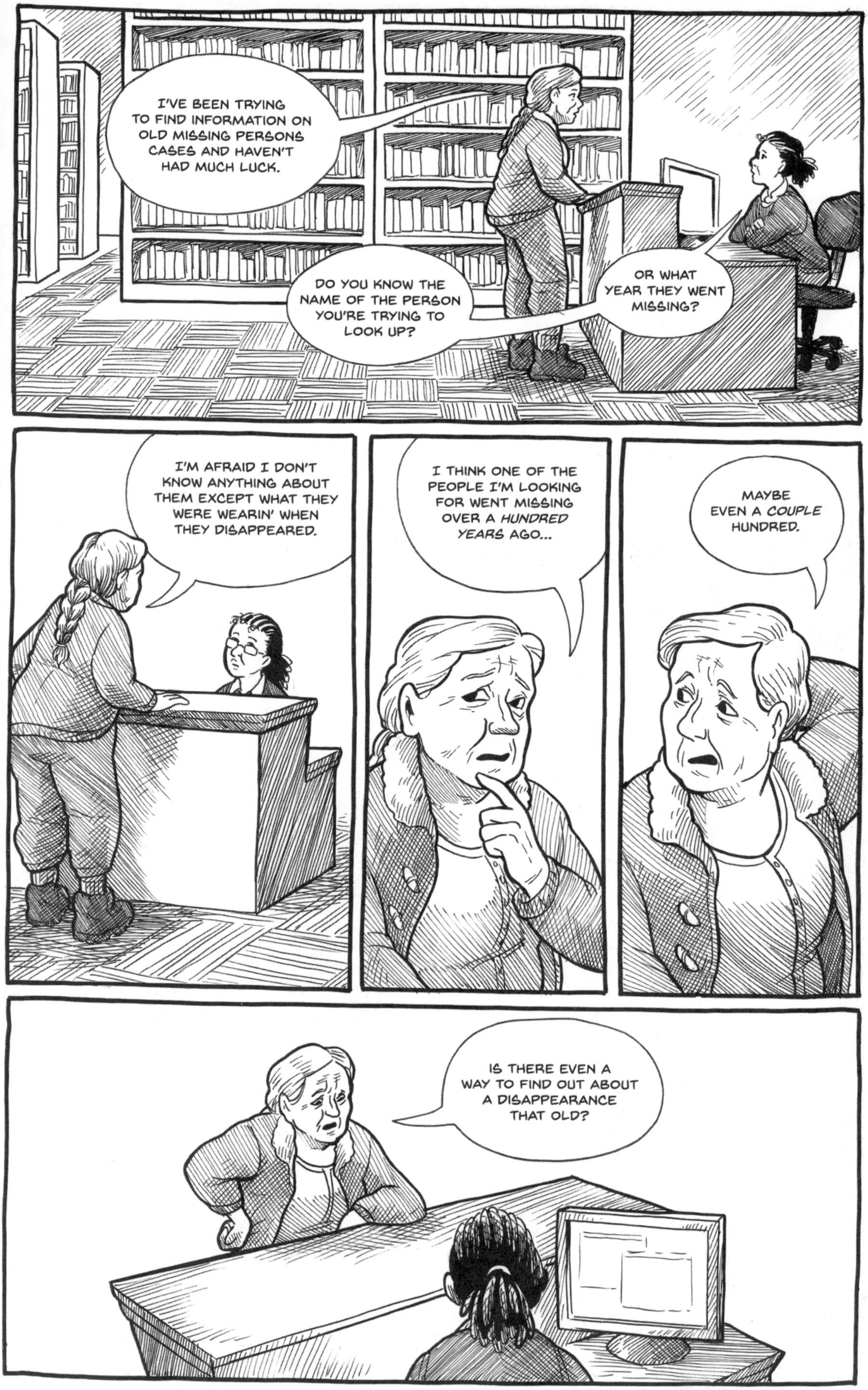
I'VE BEEN TRYING TO FIND INFORMATION ON OLD MISSING PERSONS CASES AND HAVEN'T HAD MUCH LUCK.
DO YOU KNOW THE NAME OF THE PERSON YOU'RE TRYING TO LOOK UP?
OR WHAT YEAR THEY WENT MISSING?
I'M AFRAID I DON'T KNOW ANYTHING ABOUT THEM EXCEPT WHAT THEY WERE WEARIN' WHEN THEY DISAPPEARED.
I THINK ONE OF THE PEOPLE I'M LOOKING FOR WENT MISSING OVER A *HUNDRED YEARS* AGO...
MAYBE EVEN A *COUPLE* HUNDRED.
IS THERE EVEN A WAY TO FIND OUT ABOUT A DISAPPEARANCE THAT OLD?

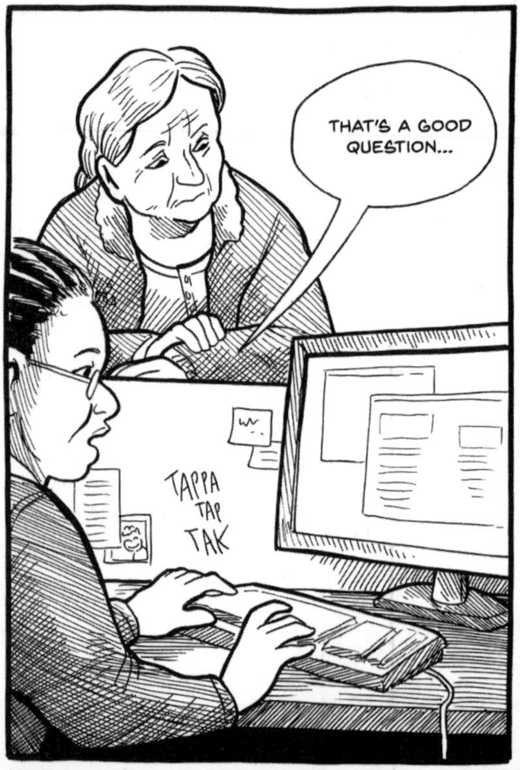
THAT'S A GOOD QUESTION...
TAPPA TAP TAK

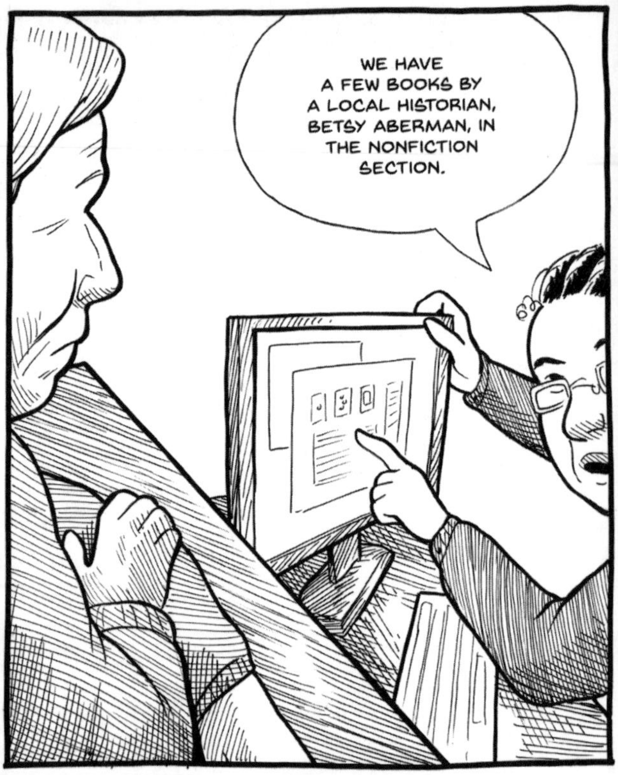
WE HAVE A FEW BOOKS BY A LOCAL HISTORIAN, BETSY ABERMAN, IN THE NONFICTION SECTION.

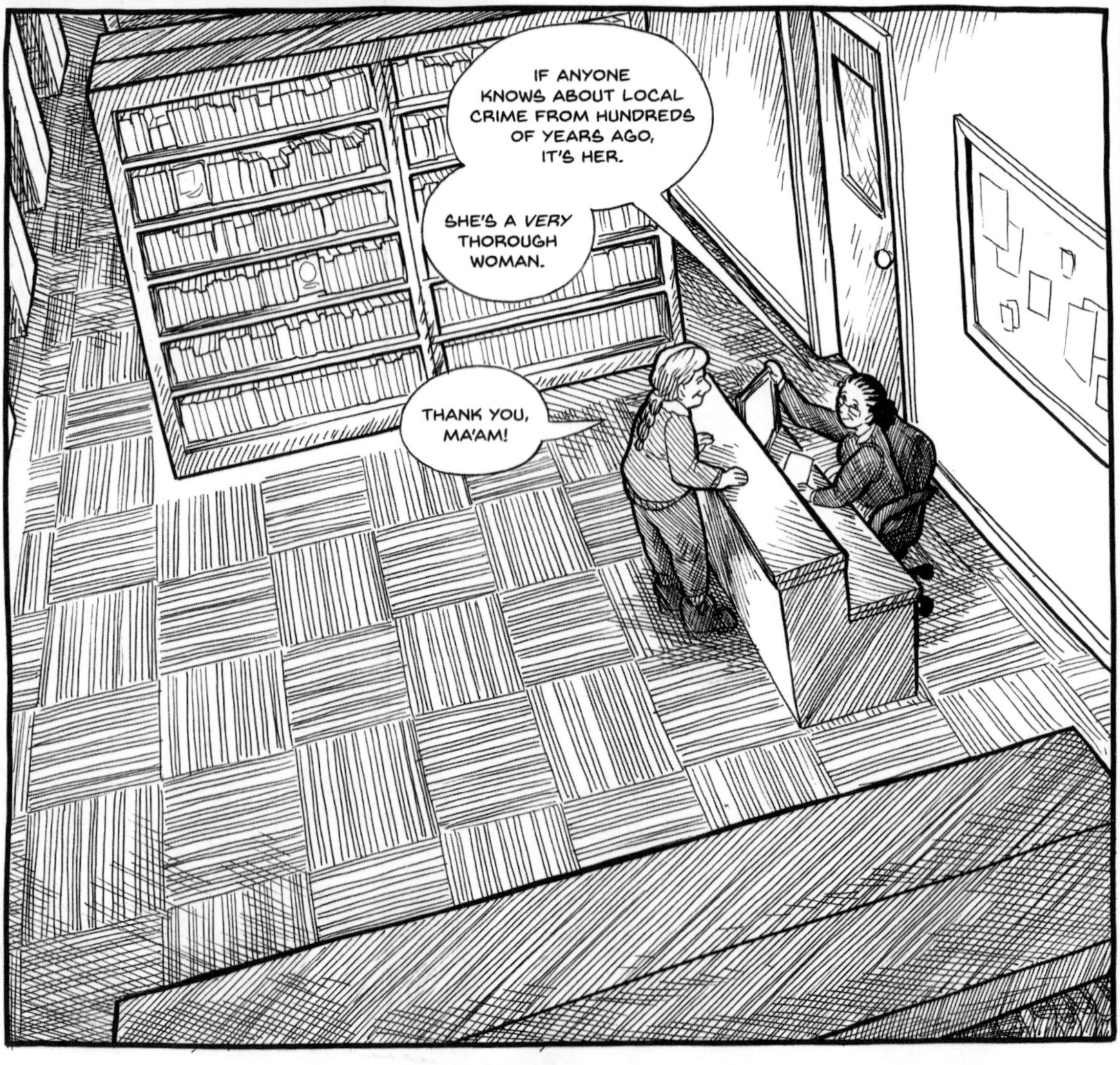
IF ANYONE KNOWS ABOUT LOCAL CRIME FROM HUNDREDS OF YEARS AGO, IT'S HER.
SHE'S A *VERY* THOROUGH WOMAN.
THANK YOU, MA'AM!

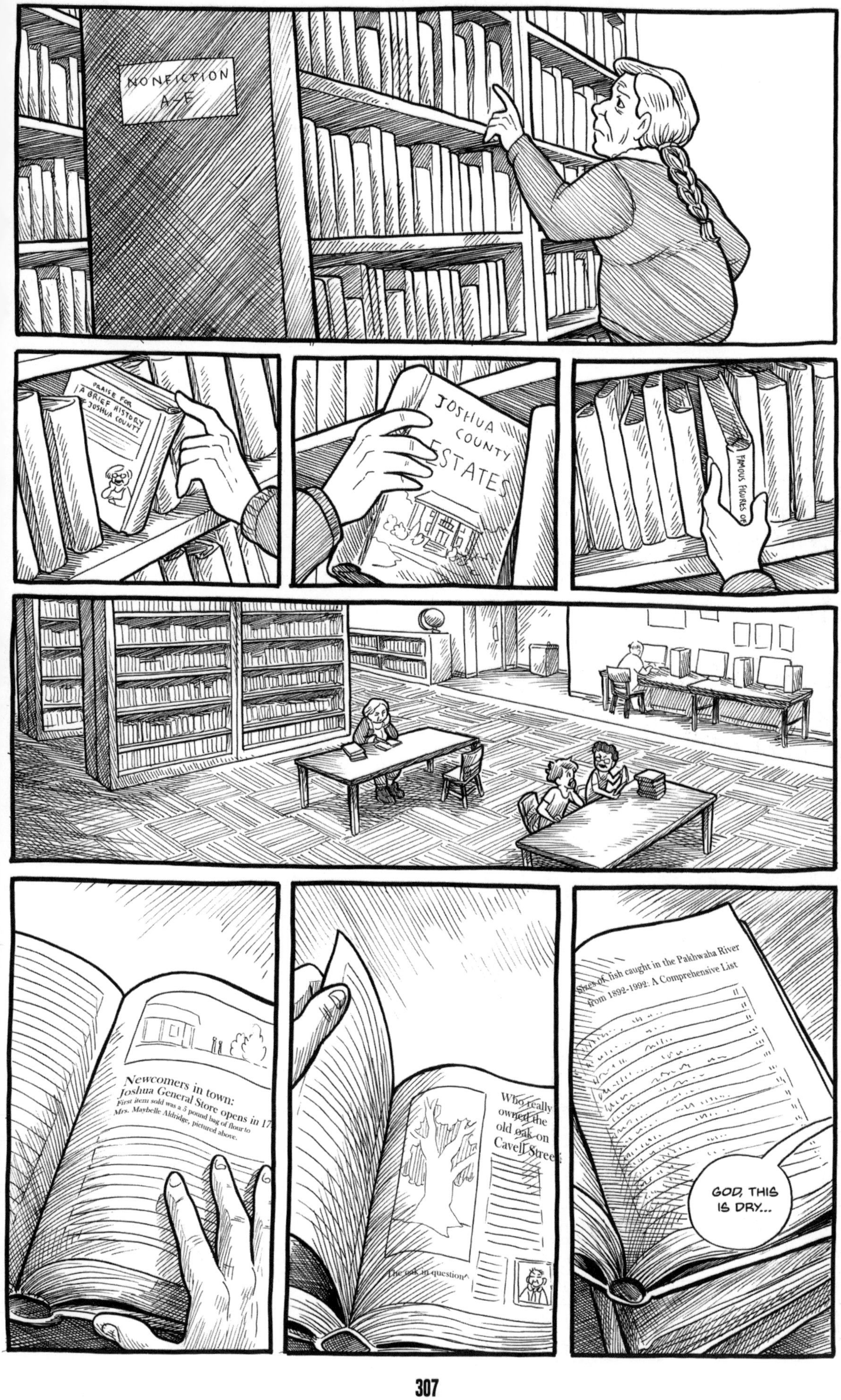
NONFICTION A–F
PRAISE FOR
A BRIEF HISTORY
JOSHUA COUNTY
JOSHUA COUNTY
STATES
FAMOUS FIGURES OF
Newcomers in town:
Joshua General Store opens in 17
First item sold was a 5 pound bag of flour to
Mrs. Maybelle Aldridge, pictured above.
Who really owned the old oak on Cavell Stree
The oak in question
Sizes of fish caught in the Pakhwaha River
from 1892-1992: A Comprehensive List
GOD, THIS IS DRY...

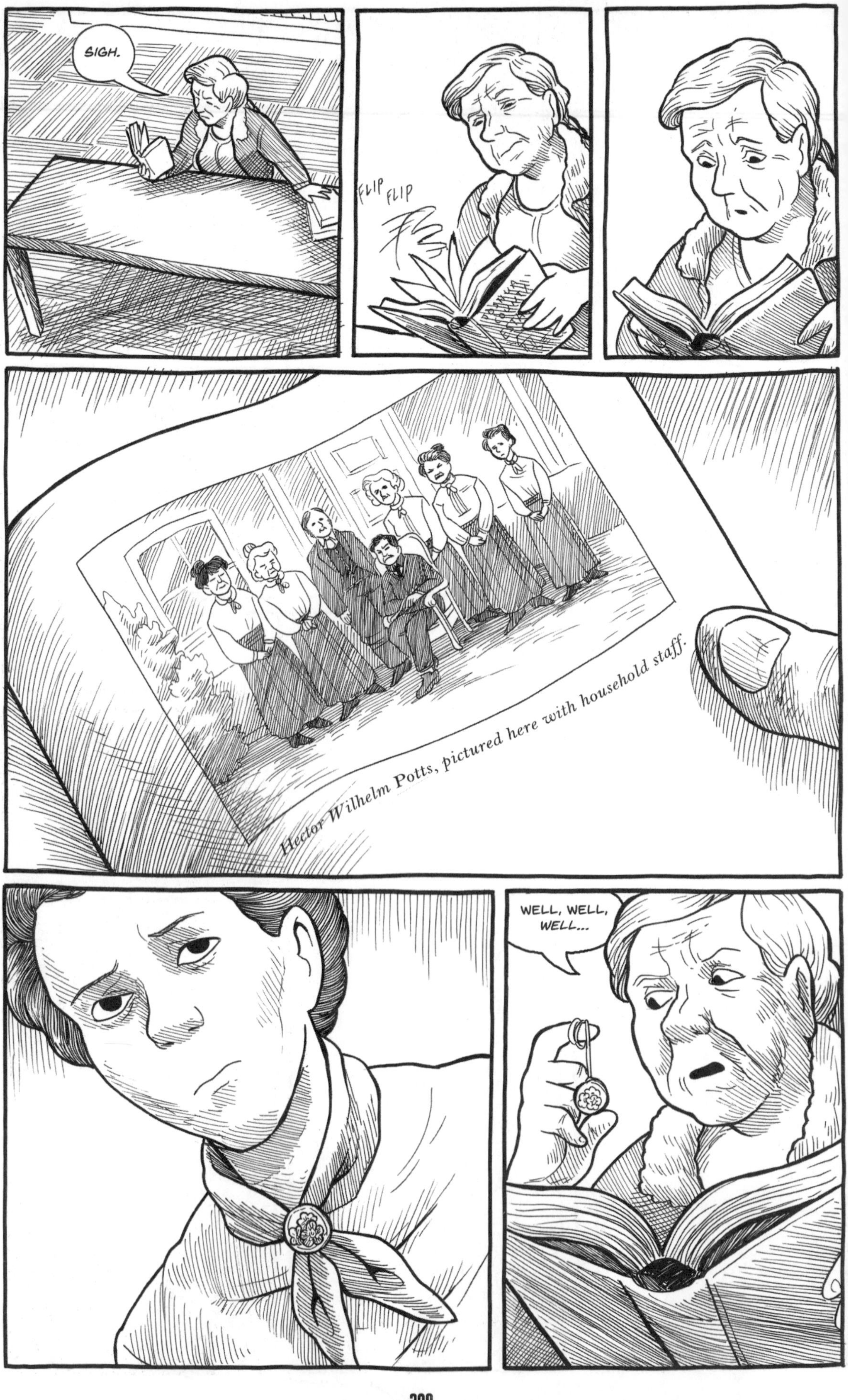
SIGH.
FLIP FLIP
Hector Wilhelm Potts, pictured here with household staff.
WELL, WELL, WELL...

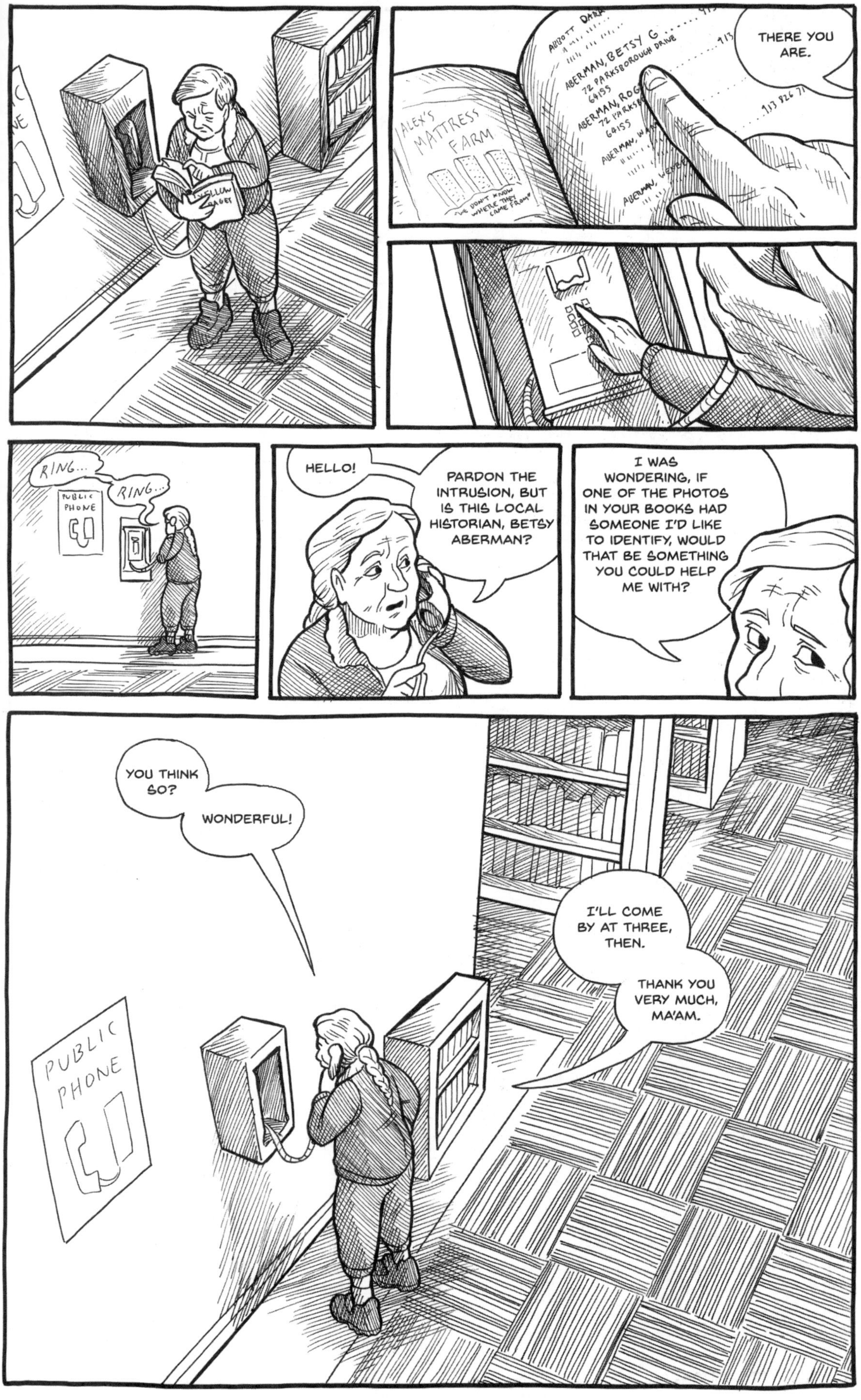

YELLOW PAGES
ABERMAN, BETSY G
72 PARKSBOROUGH DRIVE
64155
ALEX'S MATTRESS FARM
WE DON'T KNOW WHERE THEY CAME FROM!
THERE YOU ARE.
RING...
RING...
PUBLIC PHONE
HELLO!
PARDON THE INTRUSION, BUT IS THIS LOCAL HISTORIAN, BETSY ABERMAN?
I WAS WONDERING, IF ONE OF THE PHOTOS IN YOUR BOOKS HAD SOMEONE I'D LIKE TO IDENTIFY, WOULD THAT BE SOMETHING YOU COULD HELP ME WITH?
YOU THINK SO?
WONDERFUL!
I'LL COME BY AT THREE, THEN.
THANK YOU VERY MUCH, MA'AM.
PUBLIC PHONE

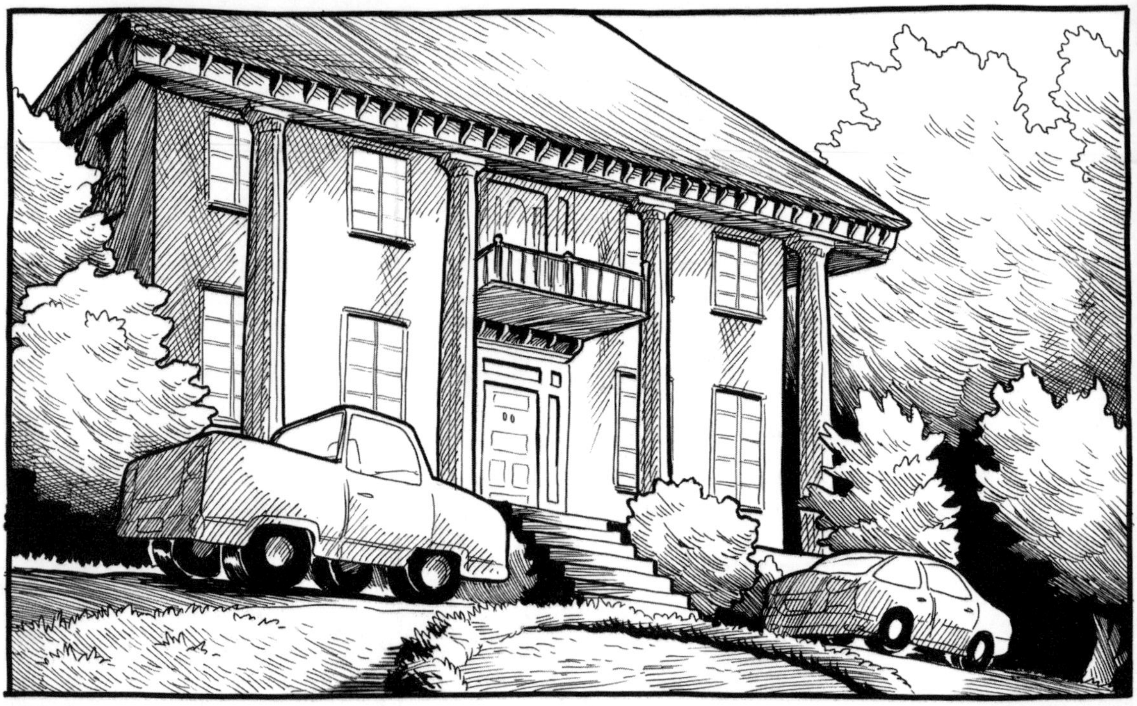

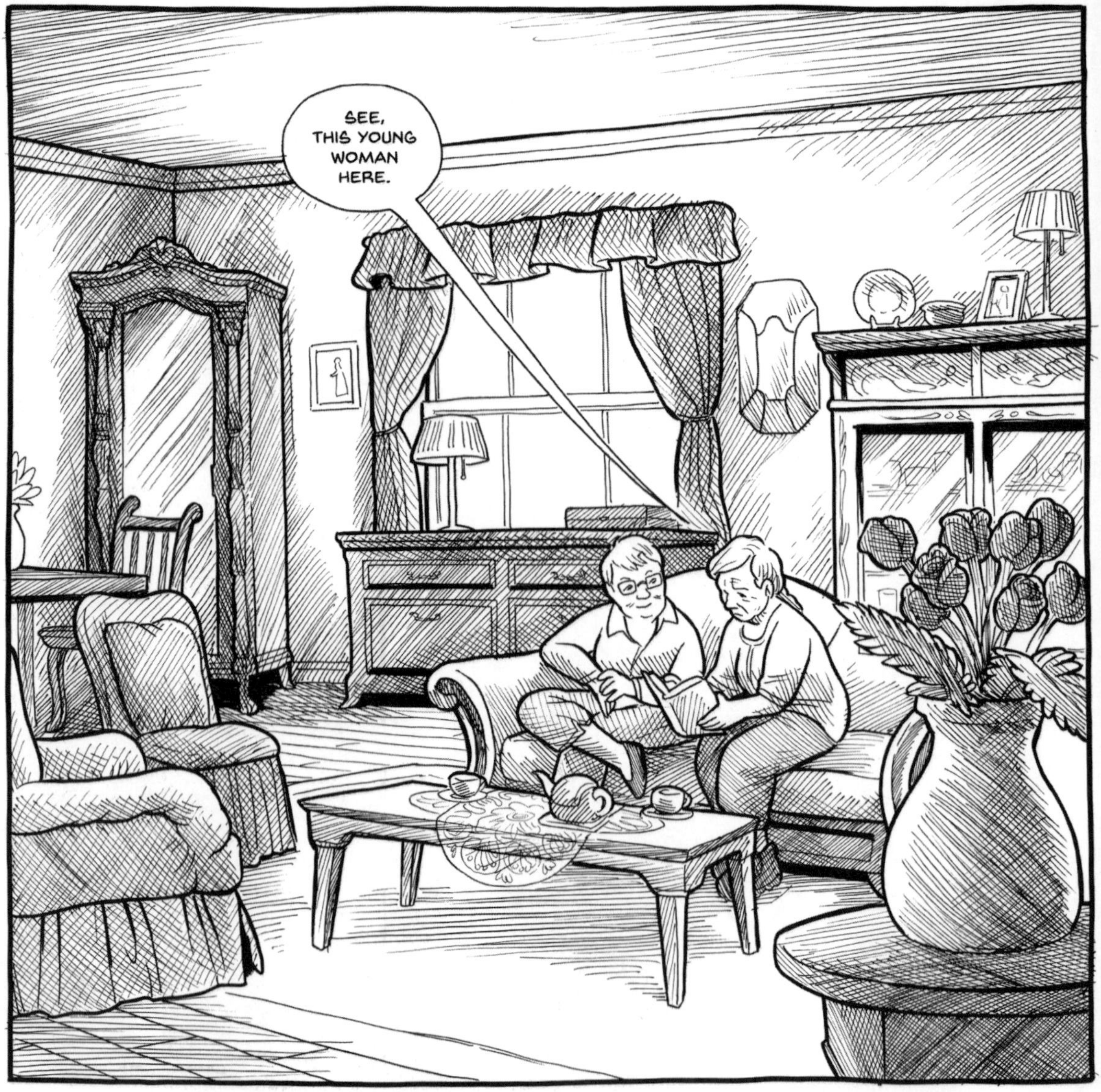
SEE, THIS YOUNG WOMAN HERE.

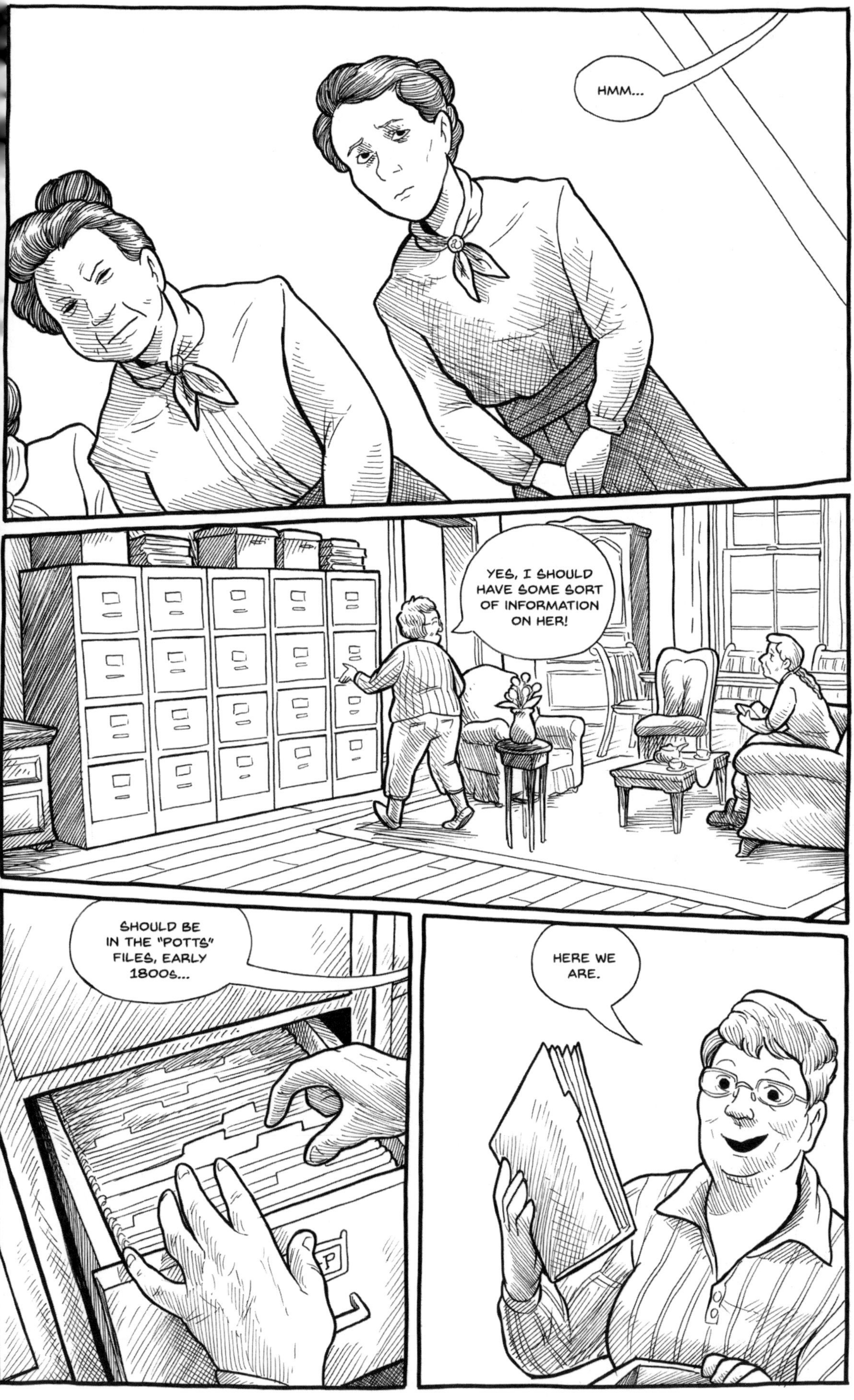
HMM...
YES, I SHOULD HAVE SOME SORT OF INFORMATION ON HER!
SHOULD BE IN THE "POTTS" FILES, EARLY 1800S...
HERE WE ARE.

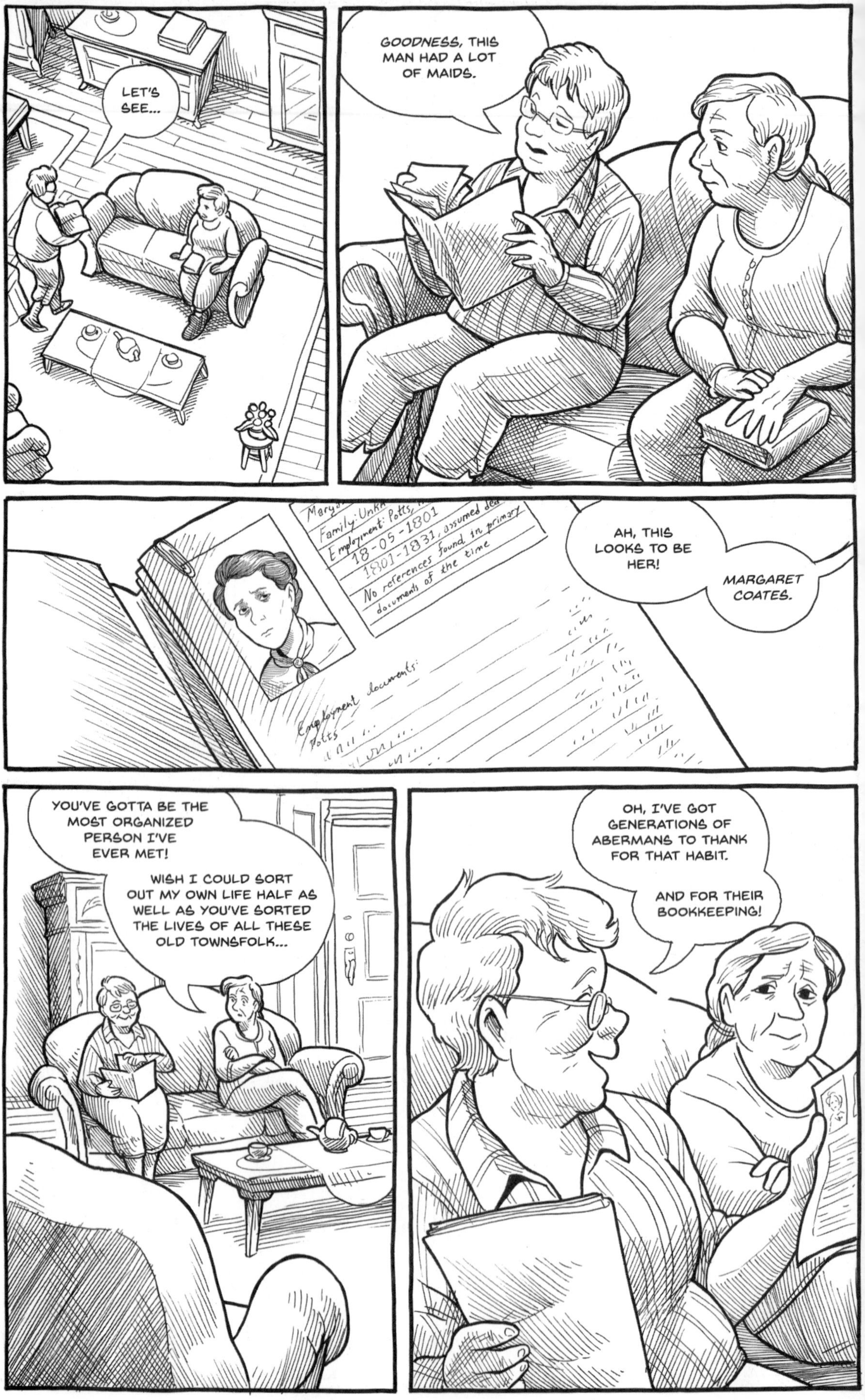
LET'S SEE...
GOODNESS, THIS MAN HAD A LOT OF MAIDS.
18-05-1801
No references found in primary
documents of the time
Employment documents:
Potts
AH, THIS LOOKS TO BE HER!
MARGARET COATES.
YOU'VE GOTTA BE THE MOST ORGANIZED PERSON I'VE EVER MET!
WISH I COULD SORT OUT MY OWN LIFE HALF AS WELL AS YOU'VE SORTED THE LIVES OF ALL THESE OLD TOWNSFOLK...
OH, I'VE GOT GENERATIONS OF ABERMANS TO THANK FOR THAT HABIT.
AND FOR THEIR BOOKKEEPING!

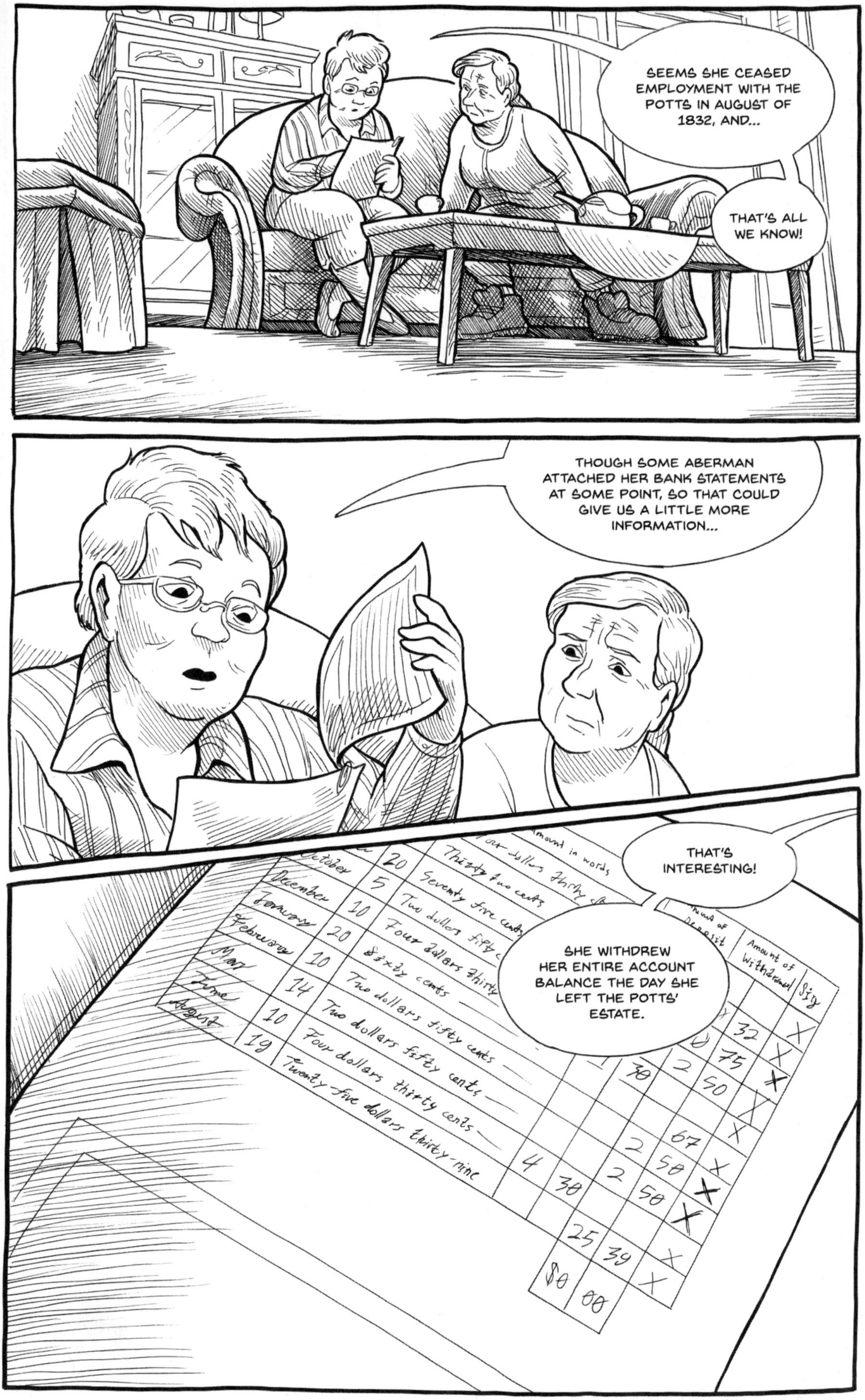
SEEMS SHE CEASED EMPLOYMENT WITH THE POTTS IN AUGUST OF 1832, AND...
THAT'S ALL WE KNOW!
THOUGH SOME ABERMAN ATTACHED HER BANK STATEMENTS AT SOME POINT, SO THAT COULD GIVE US A LITTLE MORE INFORMATION...
THAT'S INTERESTING!
SHE WITHDREW HER ENTIRE ACCOUNT BALANCE THE DAY SHE LEFT THE POTTS' ESTATE.

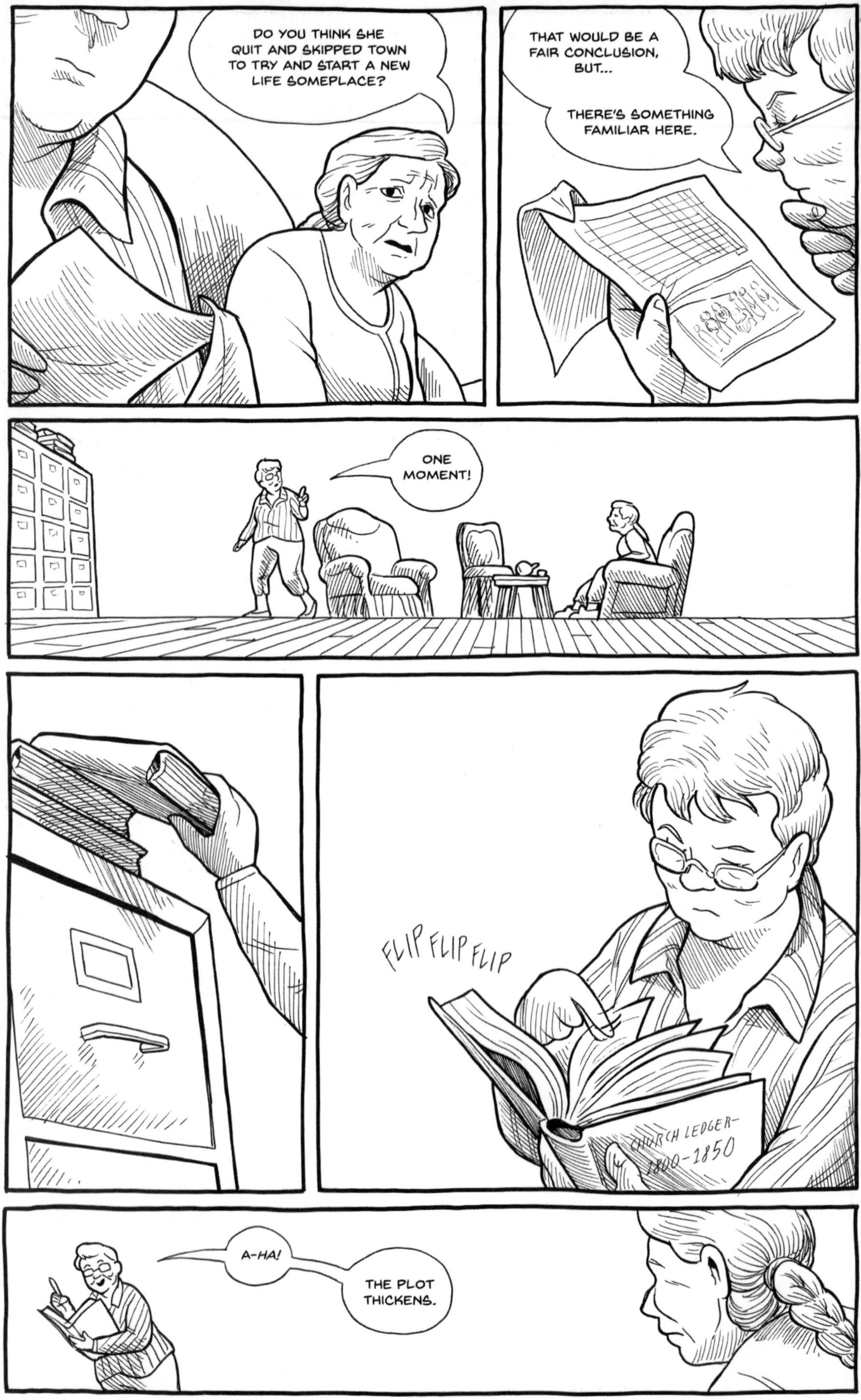
DO YOU THINK SHE QUIT AND SKIPPED TOWN TO TRY AND START A NEW LIFE SOMEPLACE?
THAT WOULD BE A FAIR CONCLUSION, BUT...
THERE'S SOMETHING FAMILIAR HERE.
ONE MOMENT!
FLIP FLIP FLIP
CHURCH LEDGER 1800-1850
A-HA!
THE PLOT THICKENS.

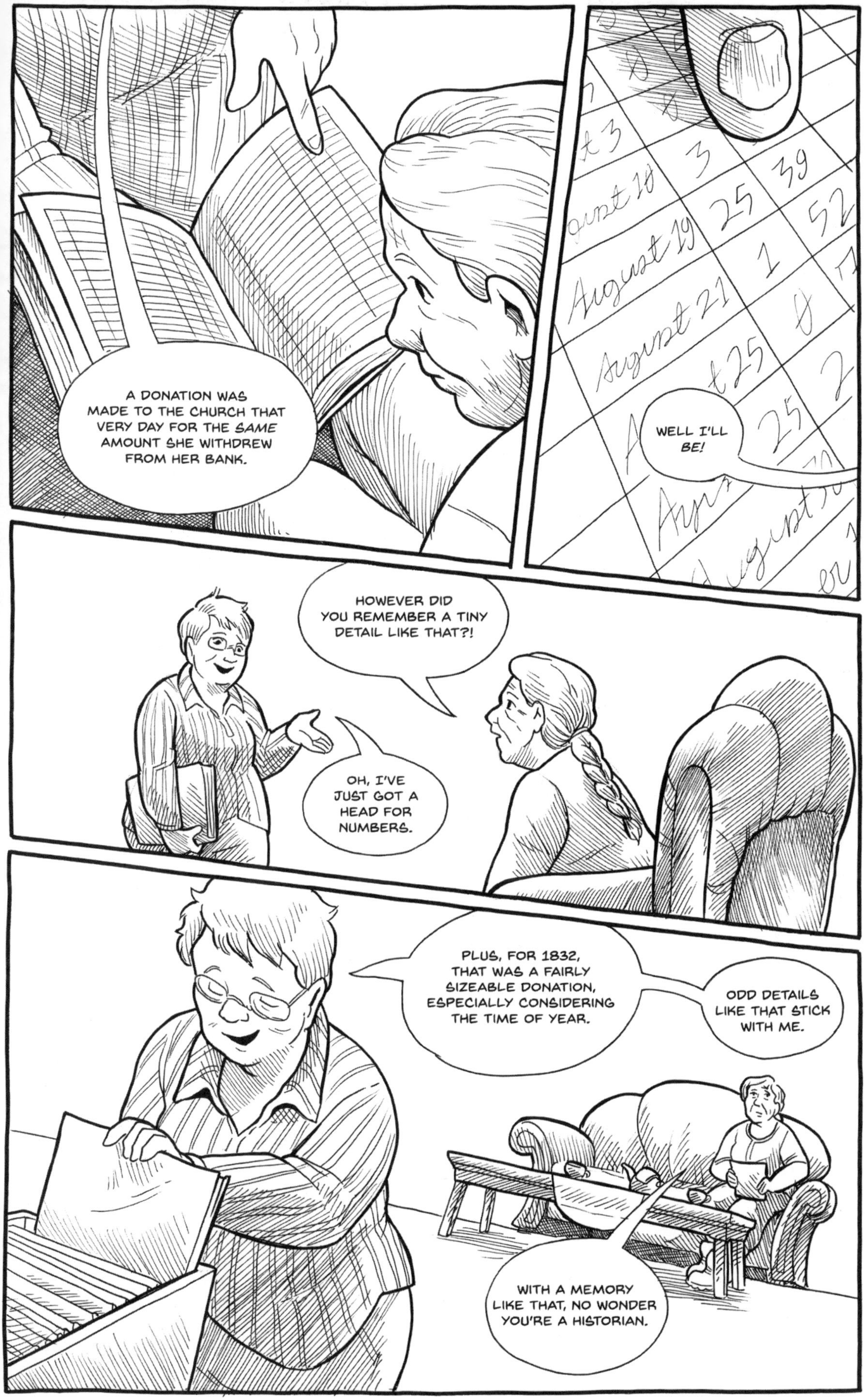
A DONATION WAS MADE TO THE CHURCH THAT VERY DAY FOR THE *SAME* AMOUNT SHE WITHDREW FROM HER BANK.
WELL I'LL *BE!*
HOWEVER DID YOU REMEMBER A TINY DETAIL LIKE THAT?!
OH, I'VE JUST GOT A HEAD FOR NUMBERS.
PLUS, FOR 1832, THAT WAS A FAIRLY SIZEABLE DONATION, ESPECIALLY CONSIDERING THE TIME OF YEAR.
ODD DETAILS LIKE THAT STICK WITH ME.
WITH A MEMORY LIKE THAT, NO WONDER YOU'RE A HISTORIAN.

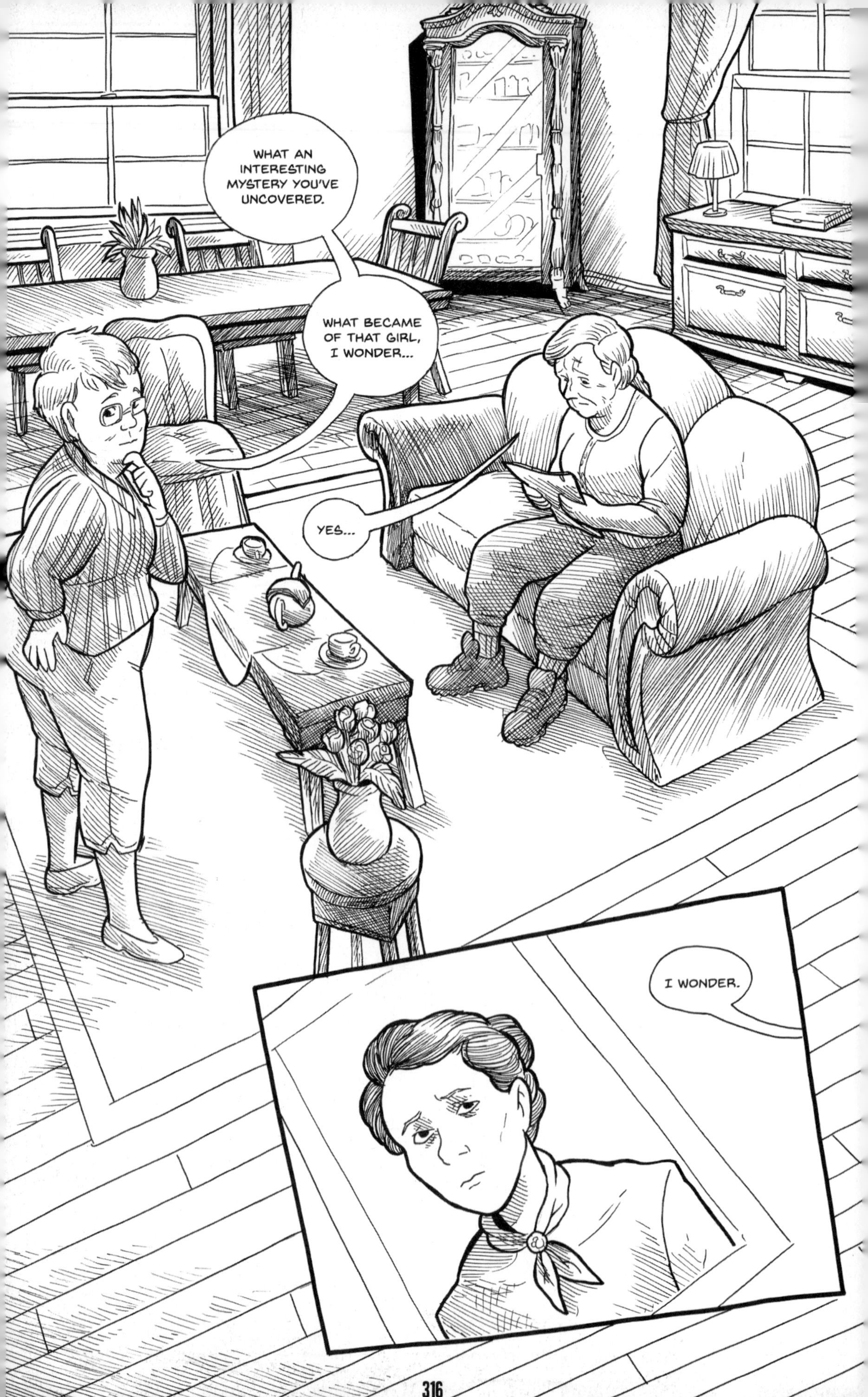
WHAT AN INTERESTING MYSTERY YOU'VE UNCOVERED.
WHAT BECAME OF THAT GIRL, I WONDER...
YES...
I WONDER.

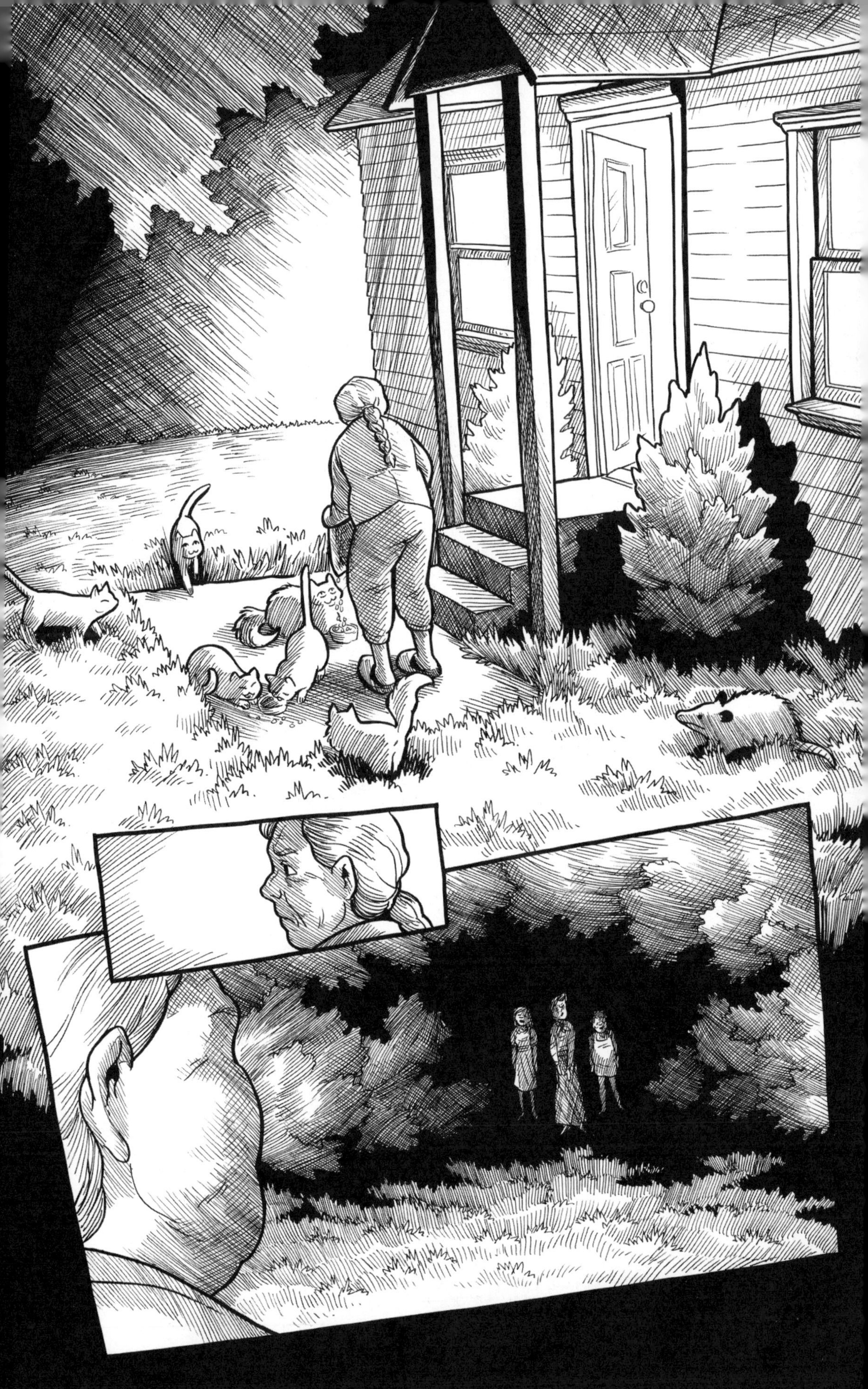

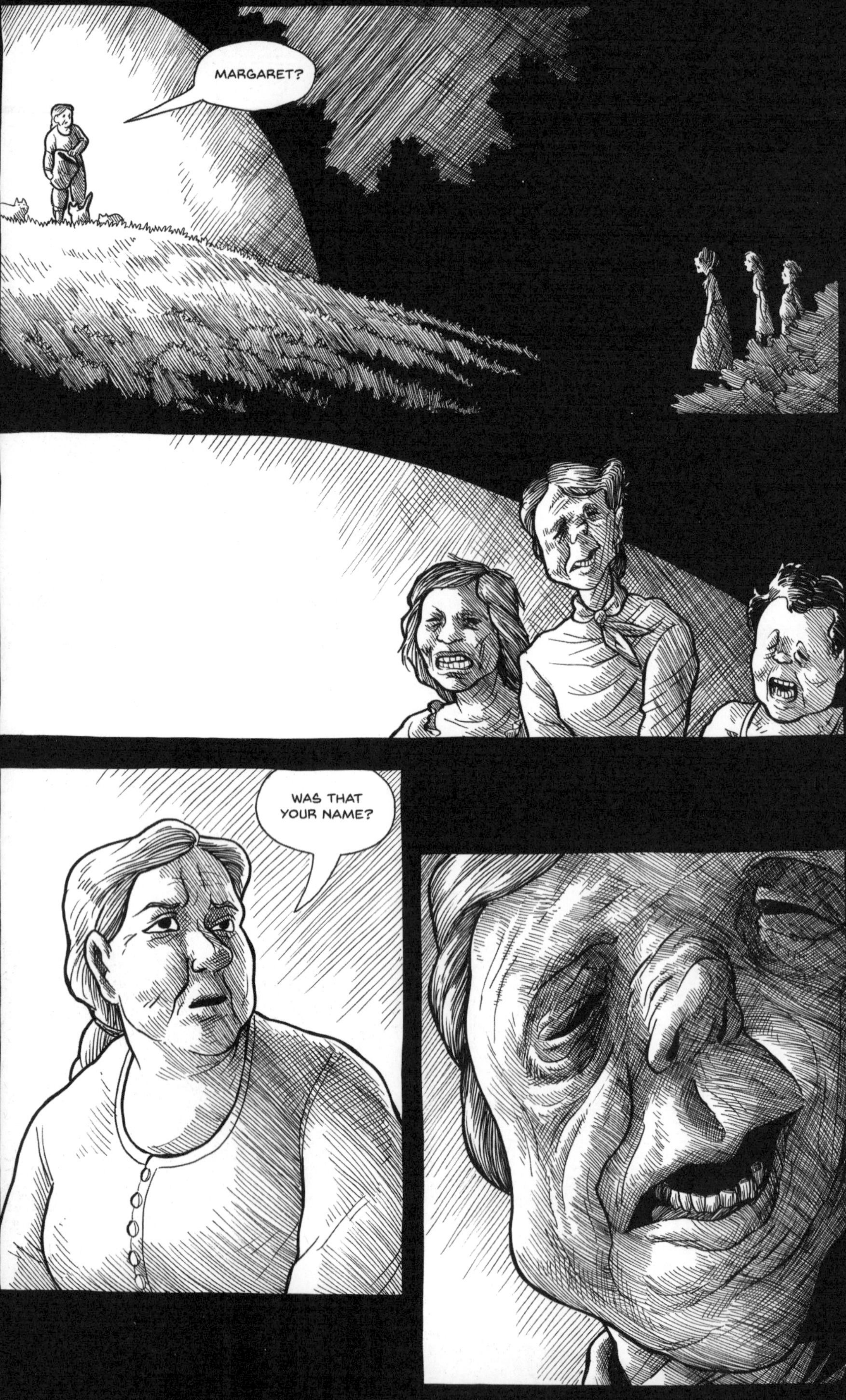
MARGARET?
WAS THAT YOUR NAME?

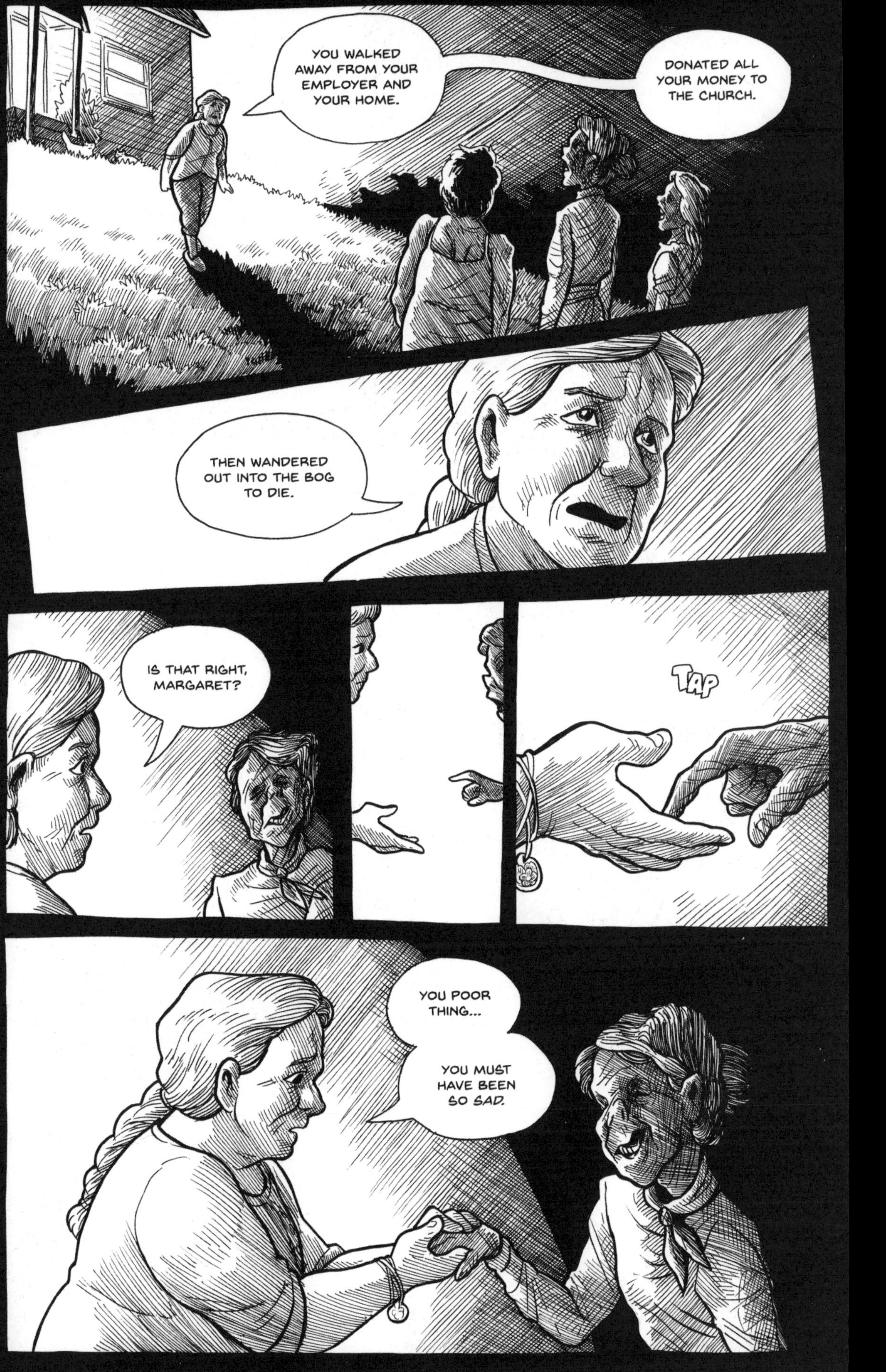
YOU WALKED AWAY FROM YOUR EMPLOYER AND YOUR HOME.
DONATED ALL YOUR MONEY TO THE CHURCH.
THEN WANDERED OUT INTO THE BOG TO DIE.
IS THAT RIGHT, MARGARET?
TAP
YOU POOR THING...
YOU MUST HAVE BEEN SO SAD.

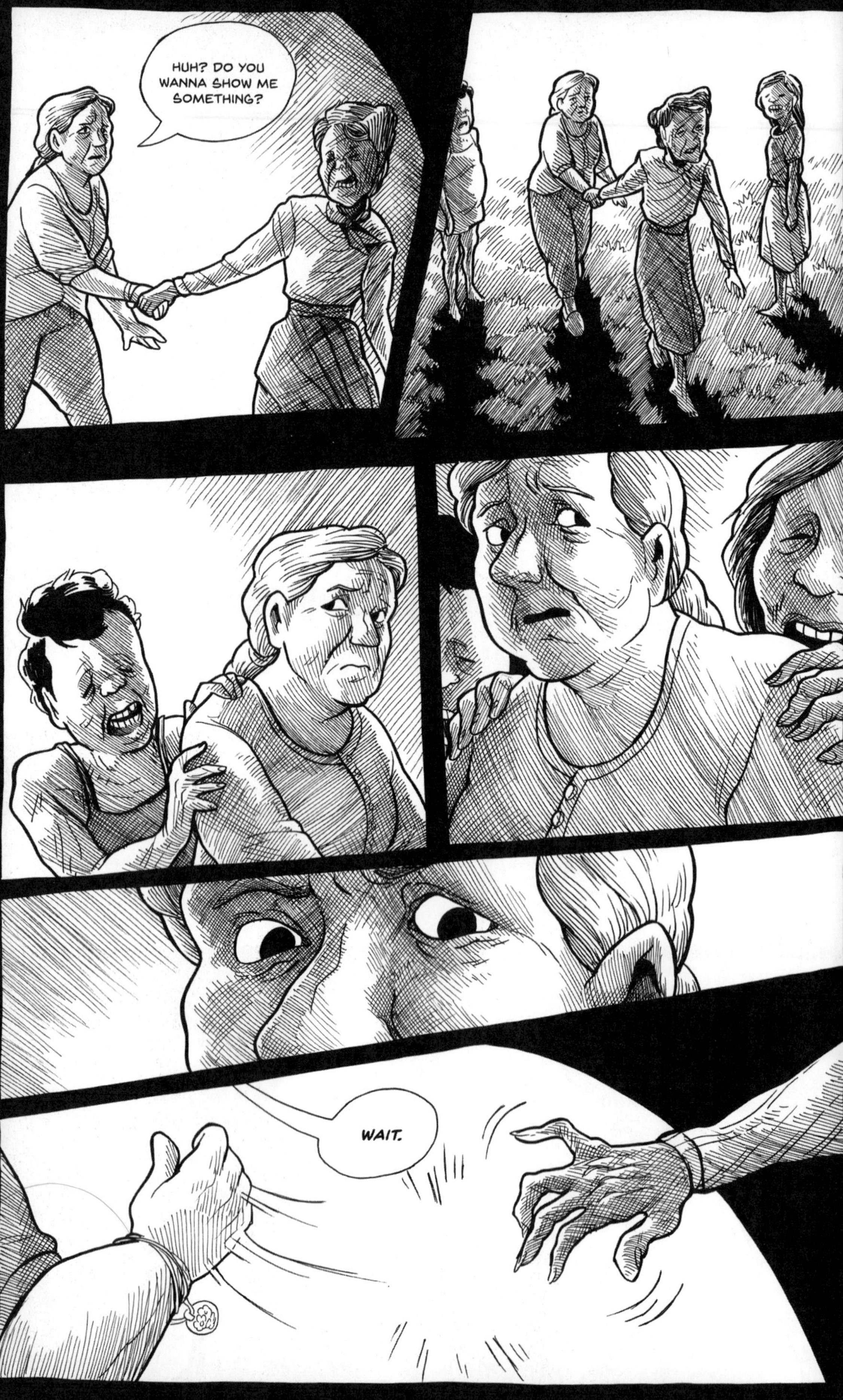
HUH? DO YOU WANNA SHOW ME SOMETHING?
WAIT.

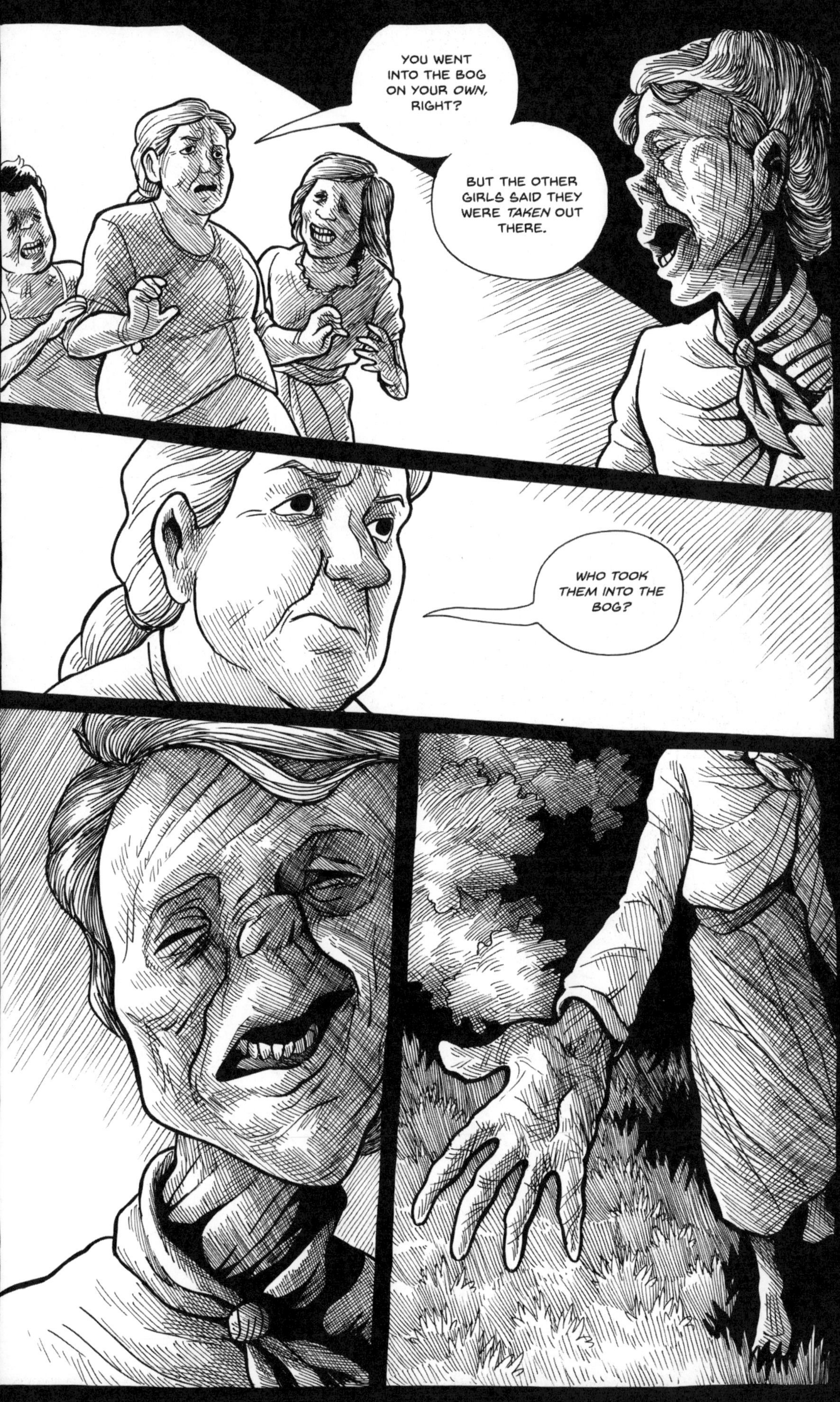
YOU WENT INTO THE BOG ON YOUR *OWN*, RIGHT?
BUT THE OTHER GIRLS SAID THEY WERE *TAKEN* OUT THERE.
WHO TOOK THEM INTO THE BOG?

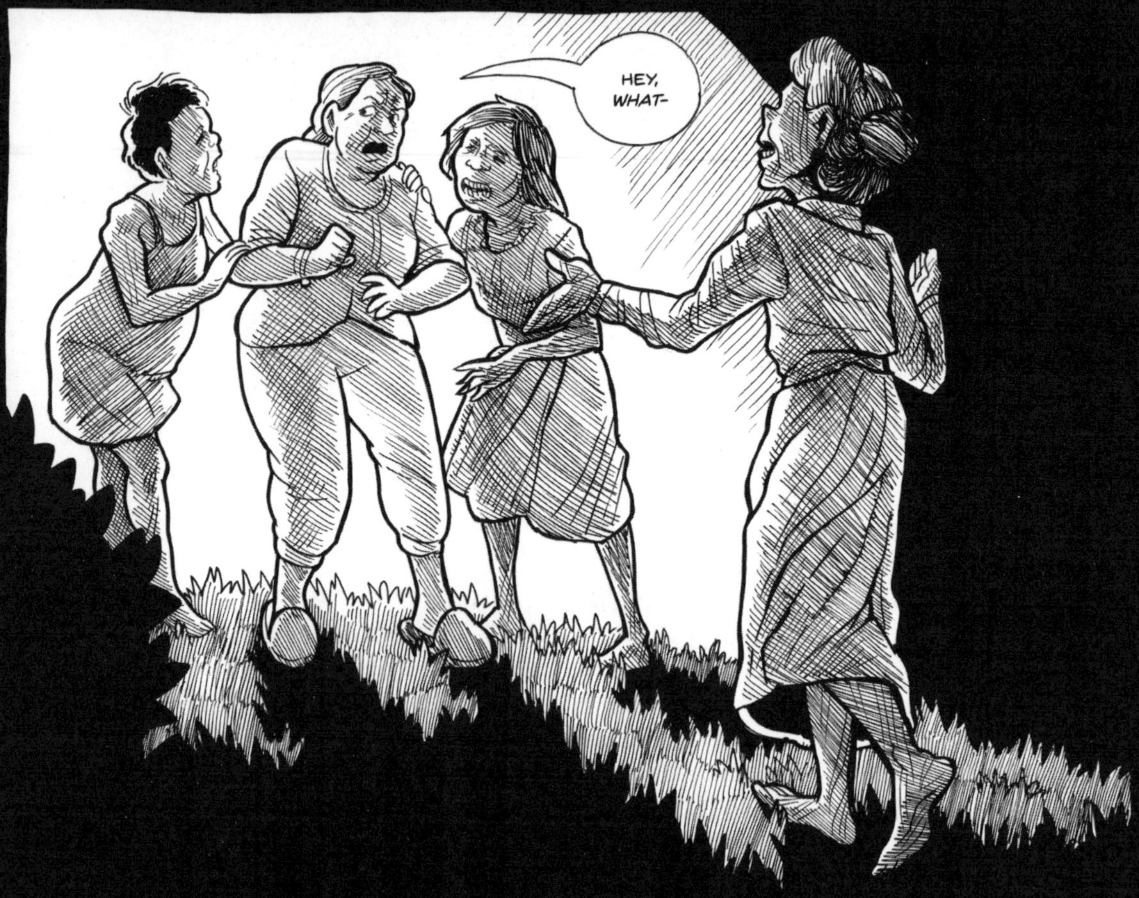
HEY, WHAT-

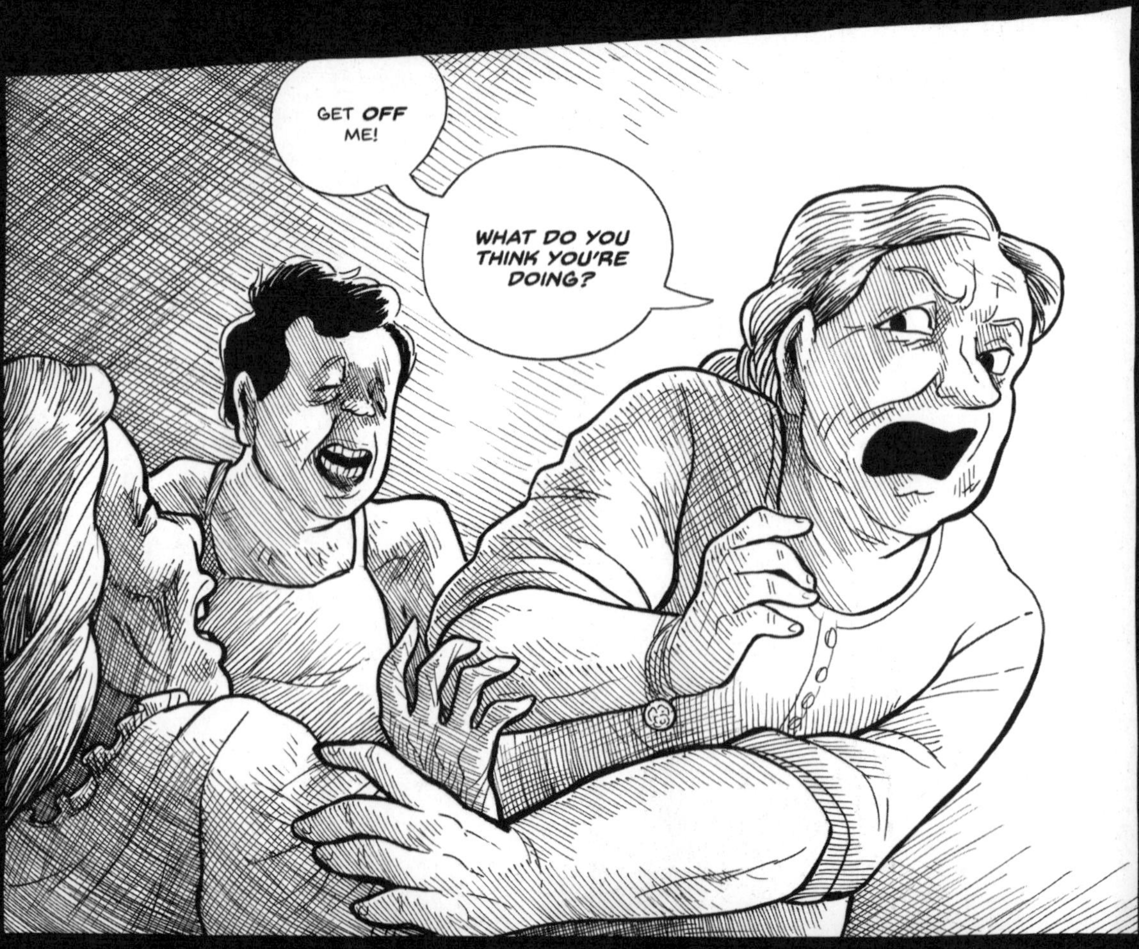
GET OFF ME!
WHAT DO YOU THINK YOU'RE DOING?

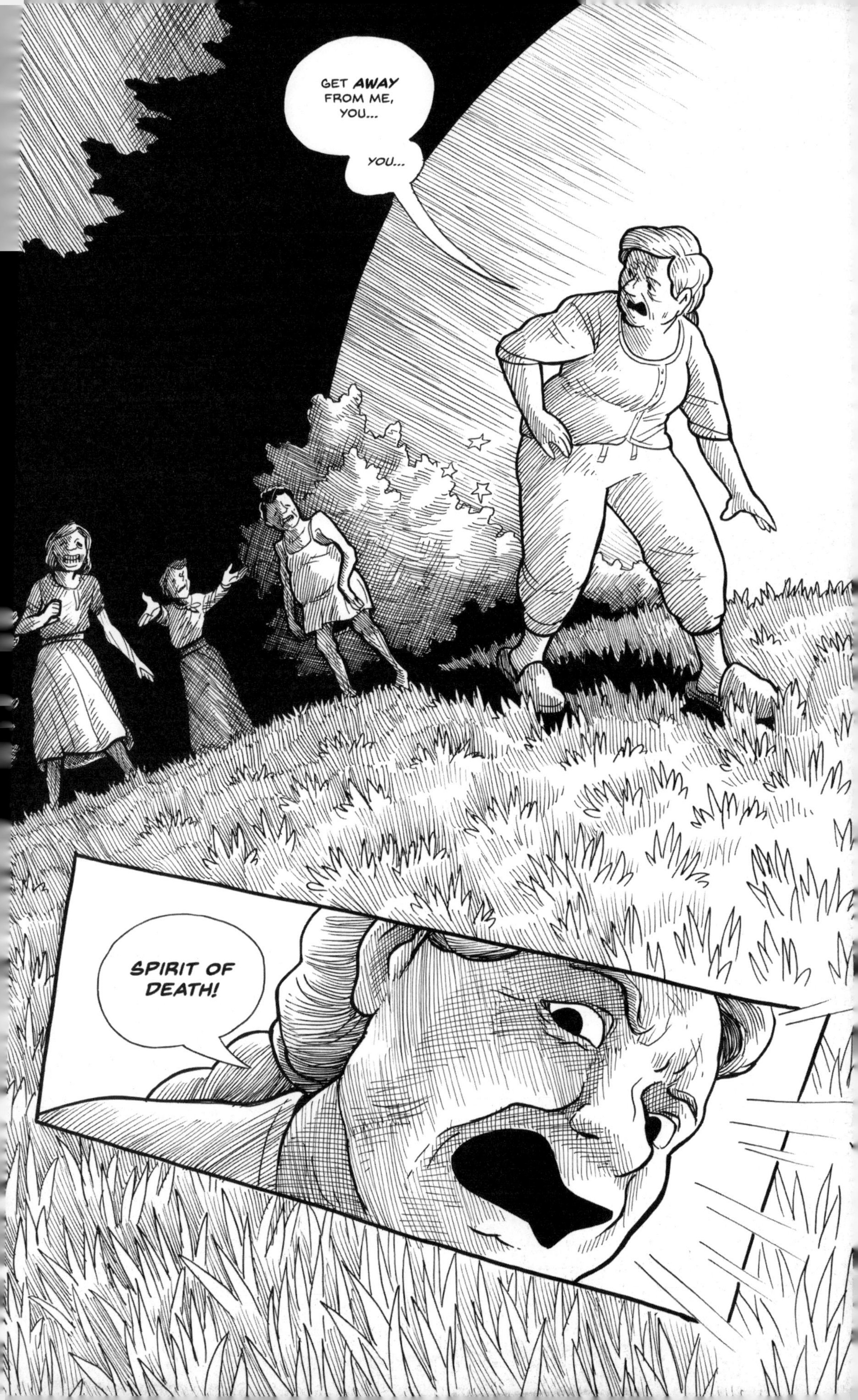
GET AWAY FROM ME, YOU...
YOU...
SPIRIT OF DEATH!

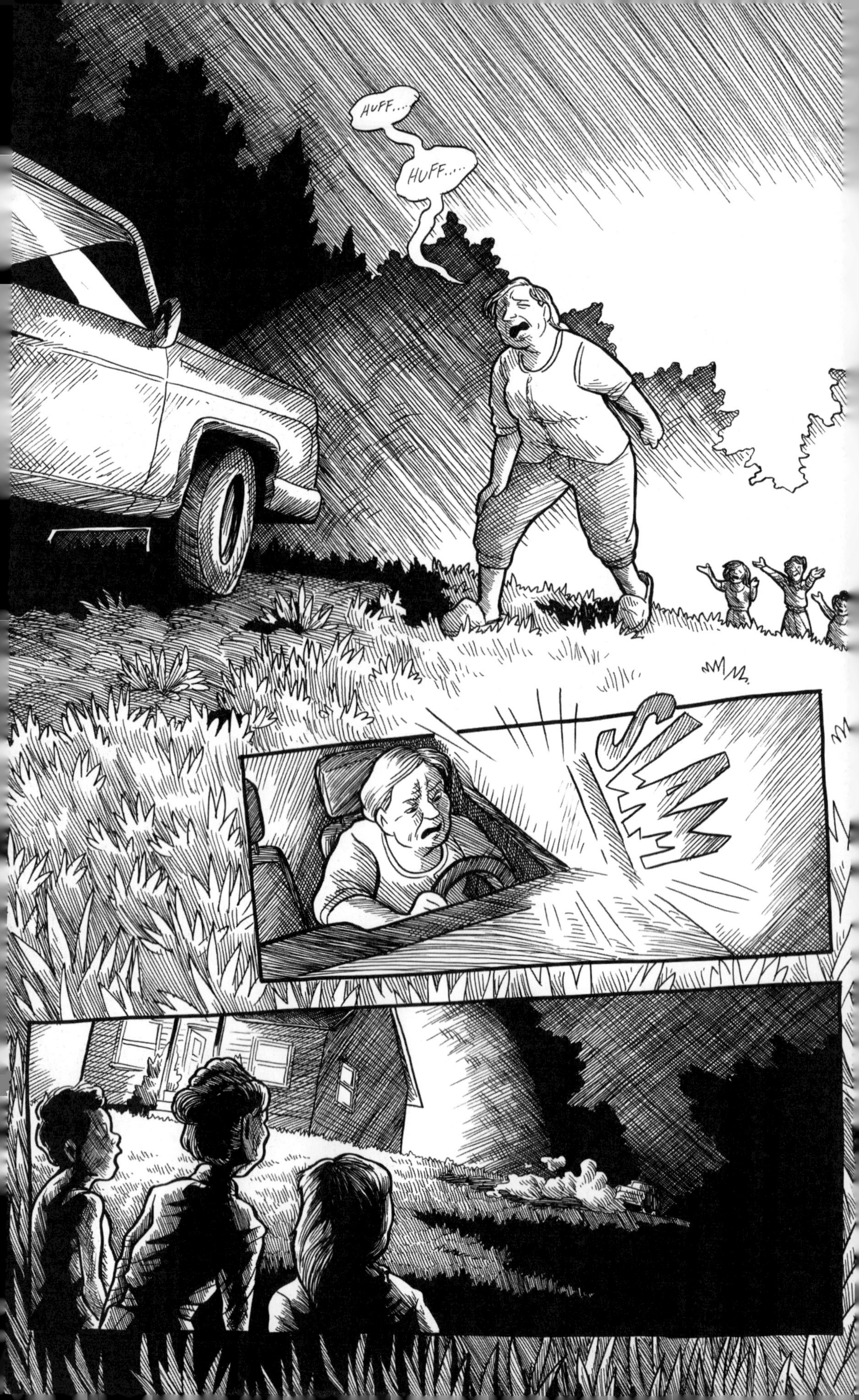
HUFF.....
HUFF.....
SLAM

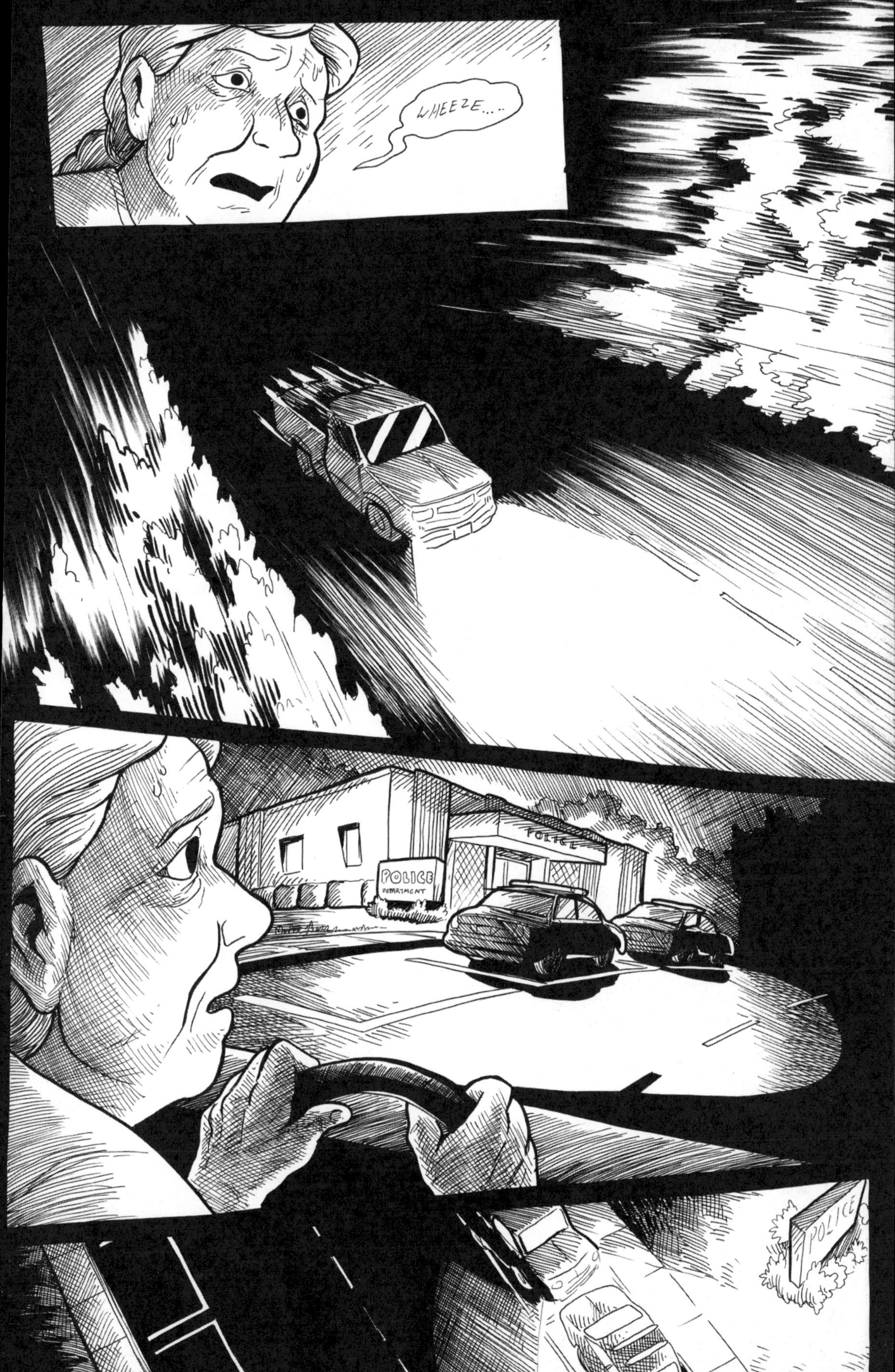
WHEEZE.....
POLICE
POLICE
DEPARTMENT
POLICE

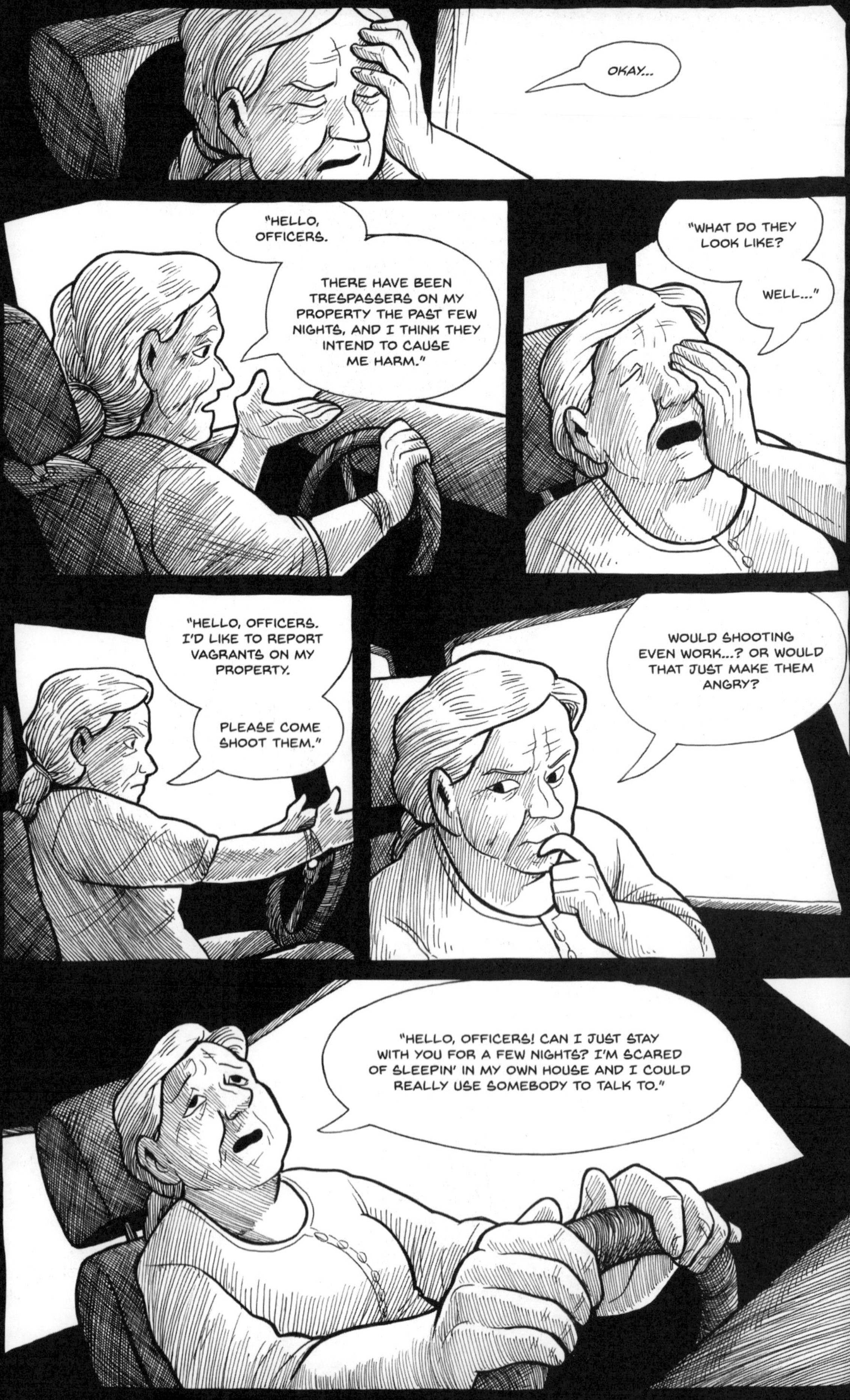
OKAY...
"HELLO, OFFICERS.
THERE HAVE BEEN TRESPASSERS ON MY PROPERTY THE PAST FEW NIGHTS, AND I THINK THEY INTEND TO CAUSE ME HARM."
"WHAT DO THEY LOOK LIKE?
WELL..."
"HELLO, OFFICERS. I'D LIKE TO REPORT VAGRANTS ON MY PROPERTY.
PLEASE COME SHOOT THEM."
WOULD SHOOTING EVEN WORK...? OR WOULD THAT JUST MAKE THEM ANGRY?
"HELLO, OFFICERS! CAN I JUST STAY WITH YOU FOR A FEW NIGHTS? I'M SCARED OF SLEEPIN' IN MY OWN HOUSE AND I COULD REALLY USE SOMEBODY TO TALK TO."

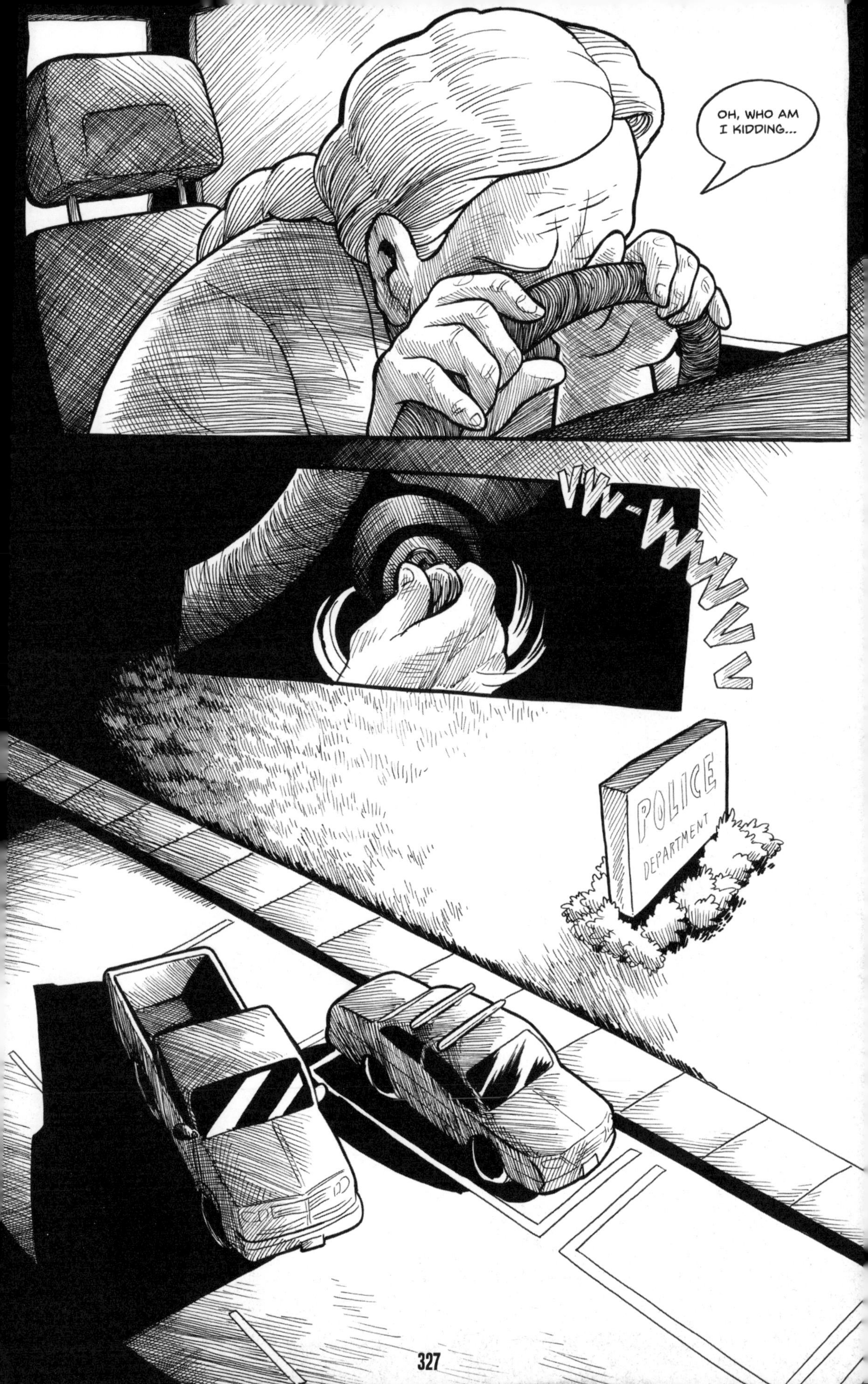
OH, WHO AM I KIDDING...
VW-WWWVV
POLICE
DEPARTMENT

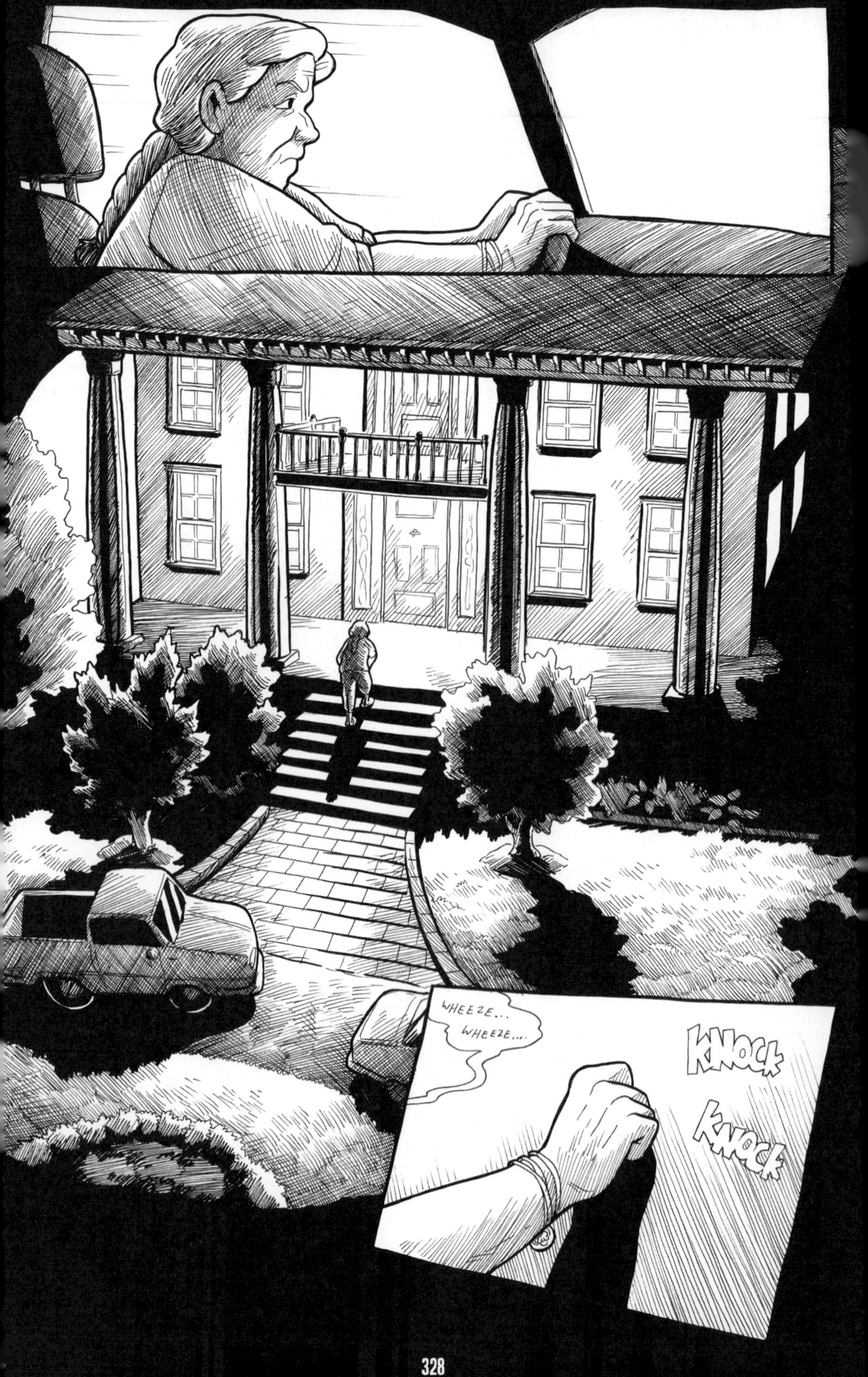
WHEEZE...
WHEEZE...
KNOCK
KNOCK

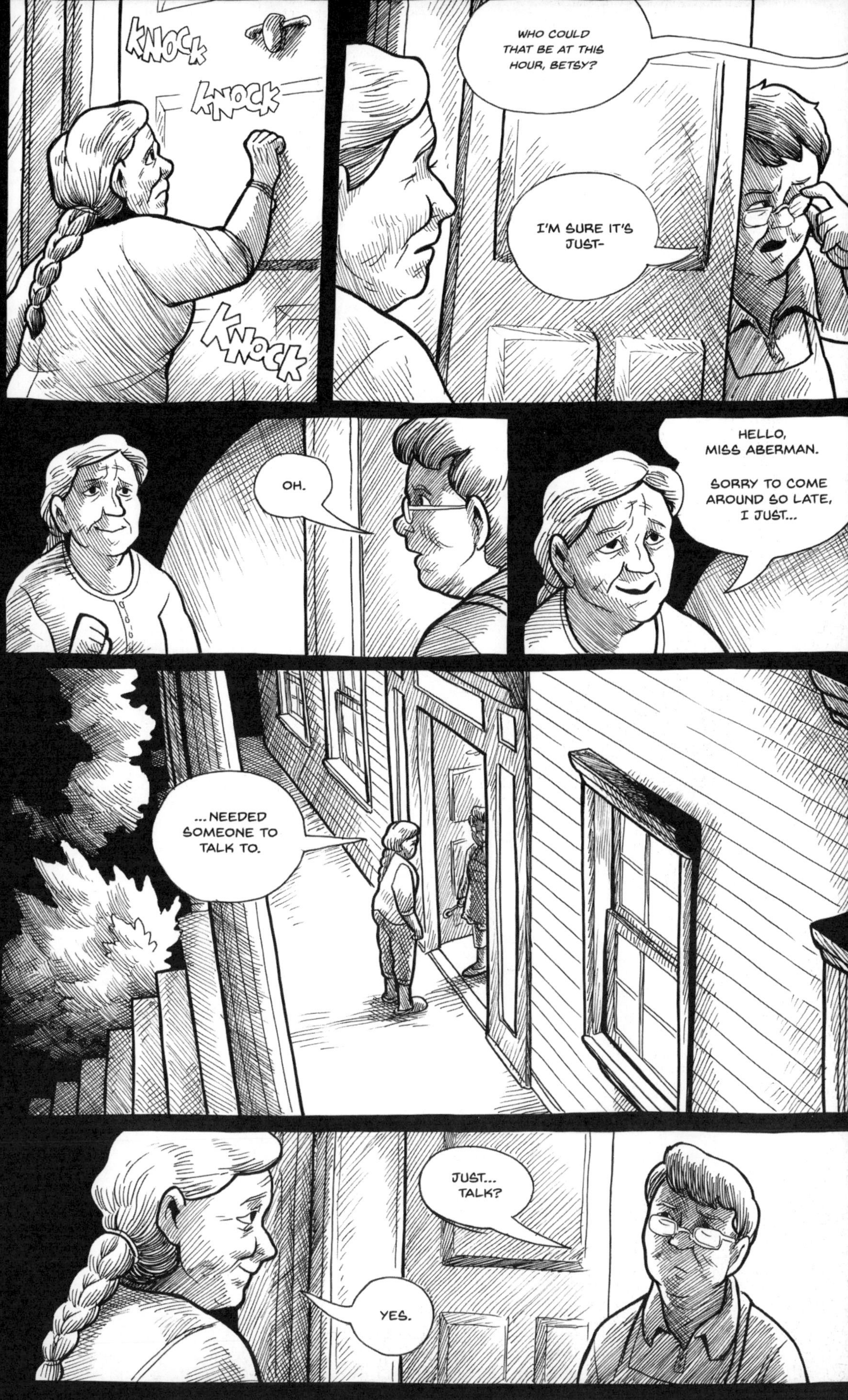
KNOCK
KNOCK
KNOCK
WHO COULD THAT BE AT THIS HOUR, BETSY?
I'M SURE IT'S JUST-
OH.
HELLO, MISS ABERMAN.
SORRY TO COME AROUND SO LATE, I JUST...
...NEEDED SOMEONE TO TALK TO.
JUST... TALK?
YES.

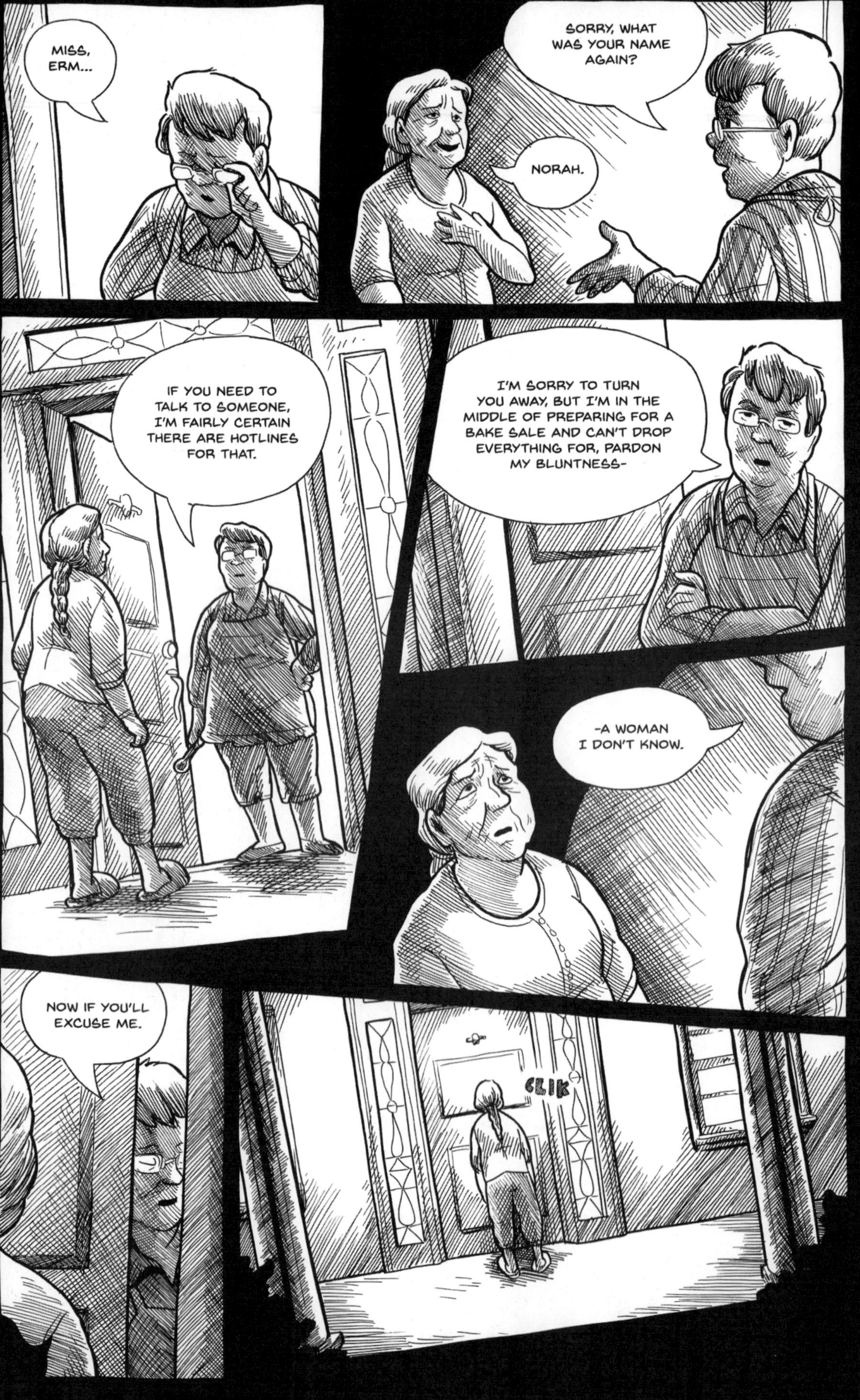
MISS, ERM...
SORRY, WHAT WAS YOUR NAME AGAIN?
NORAH.
IF YOU NEED TO TALK TO SOMEONE, I'M FAIRLY CERTAIN THERE ARE HOTLINES FOR THAT.
I'M SORRY TO TURN YOU AWAY, BUT I'M IN THE MIDDLE OF PREPARING FOR A BAKE SALE AND CAN'T DROP EVERYTHING FOR, PARDON MY BLUNTNESS-
-A WOMAN I DON'T KNOW.
NOW IF YOU'LL EXCUSE ME.
CLIK

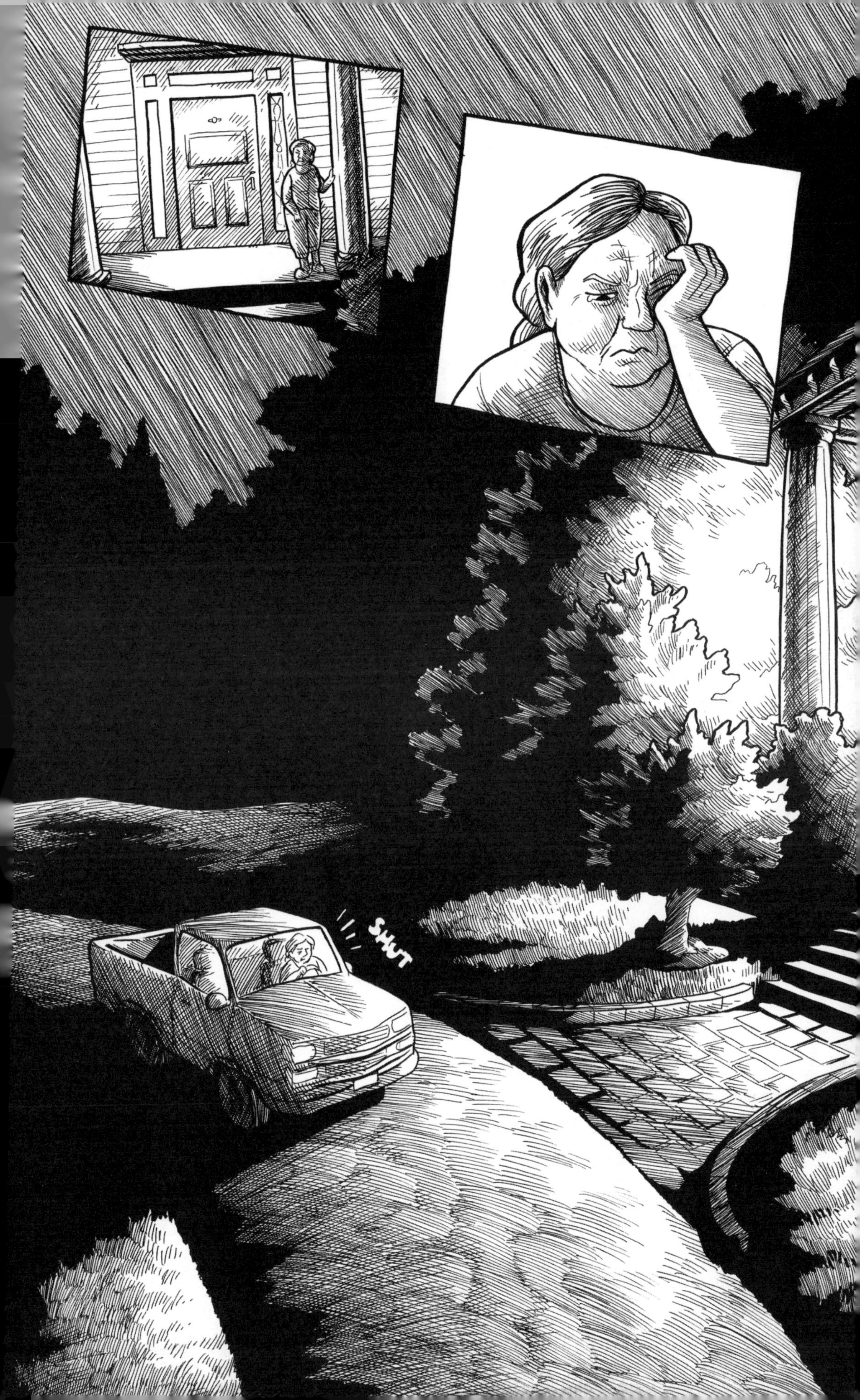
SHUT

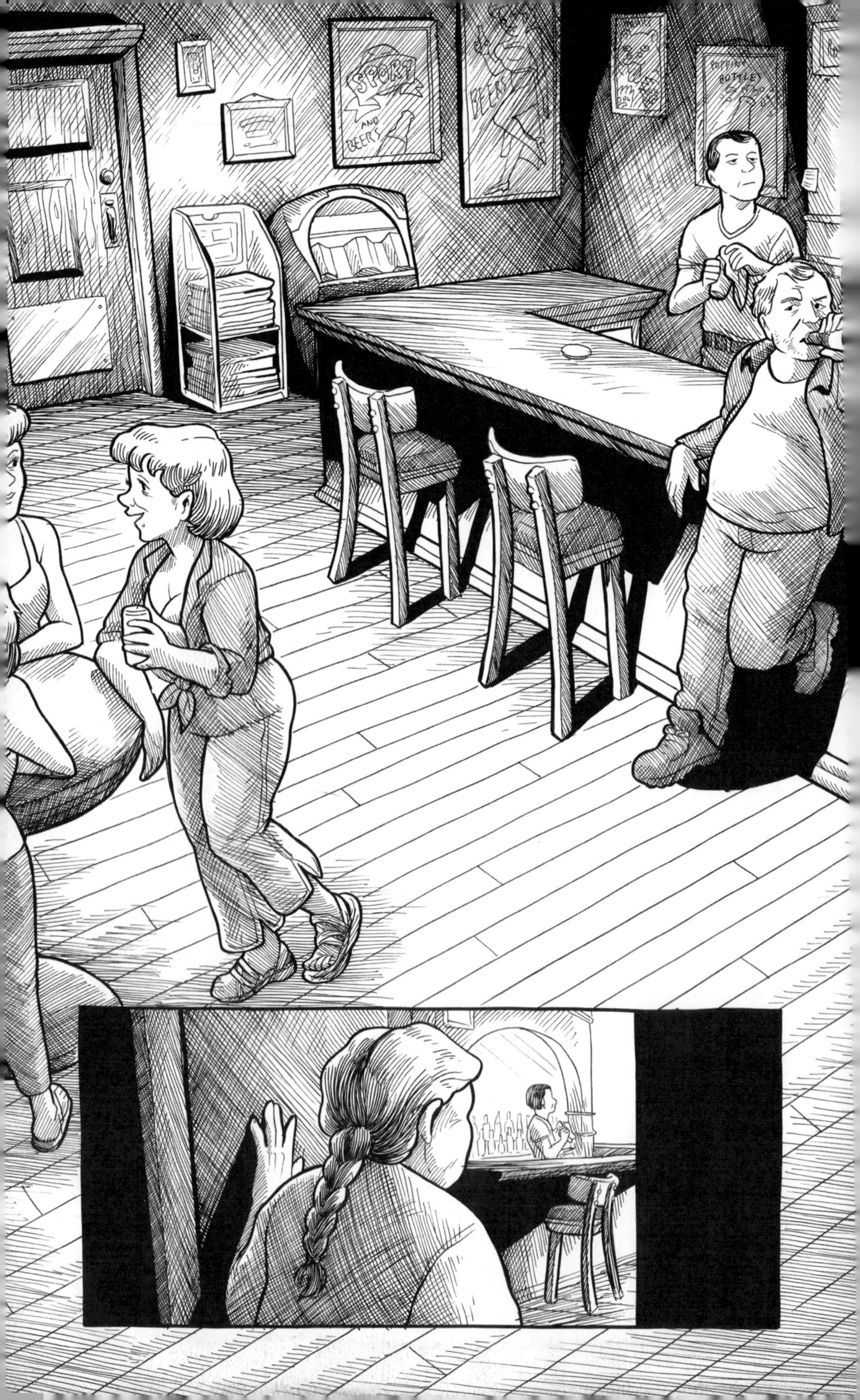
SPORT
AND
BEER'S
BEERS

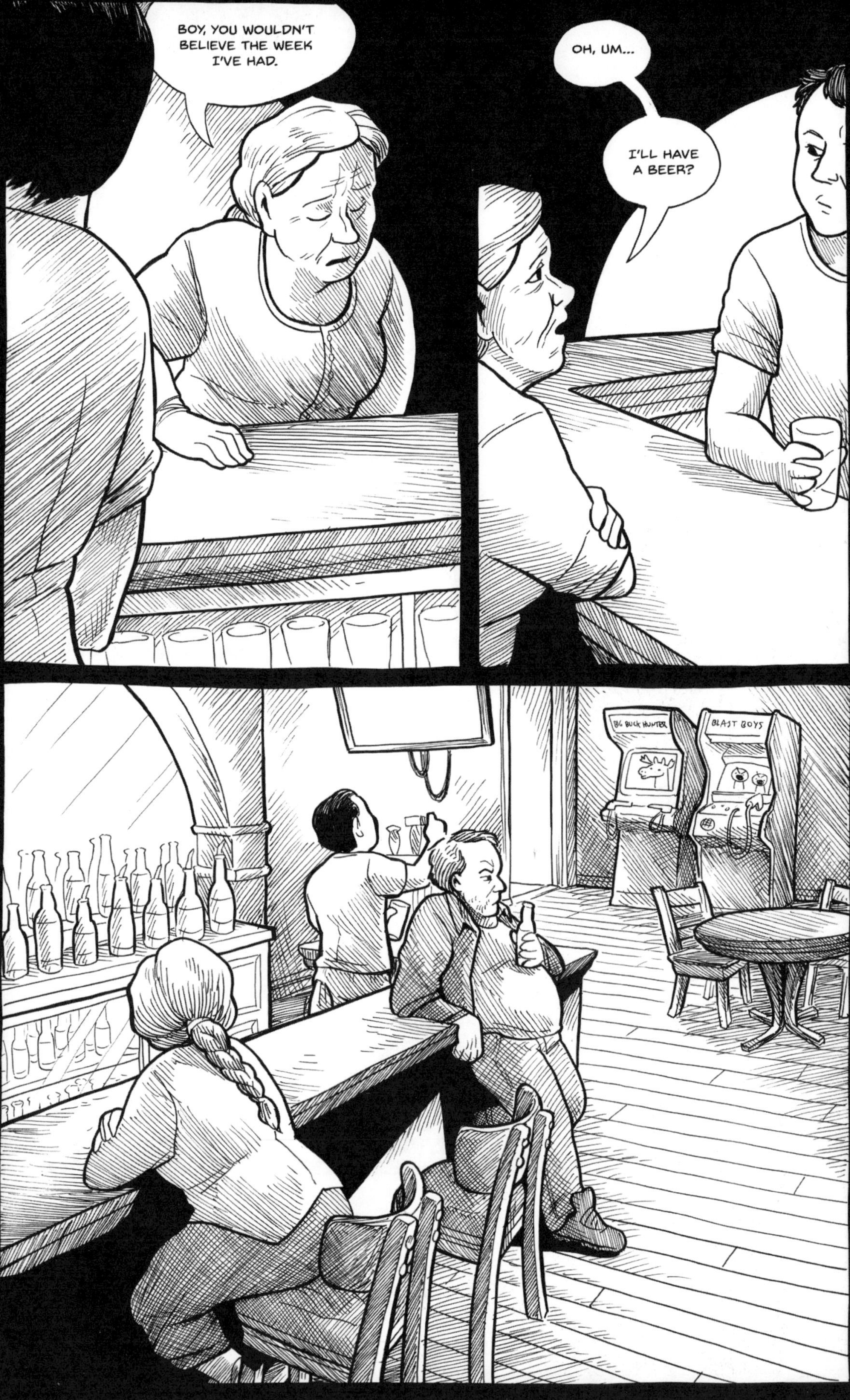
BOY, YOU WOULDN'T BELIEVE THE WEEK I'VE HAD.
OH, UM...
I'LL HAVE A BEER?
BIG BUCK HUNTER
BLAST BOYS

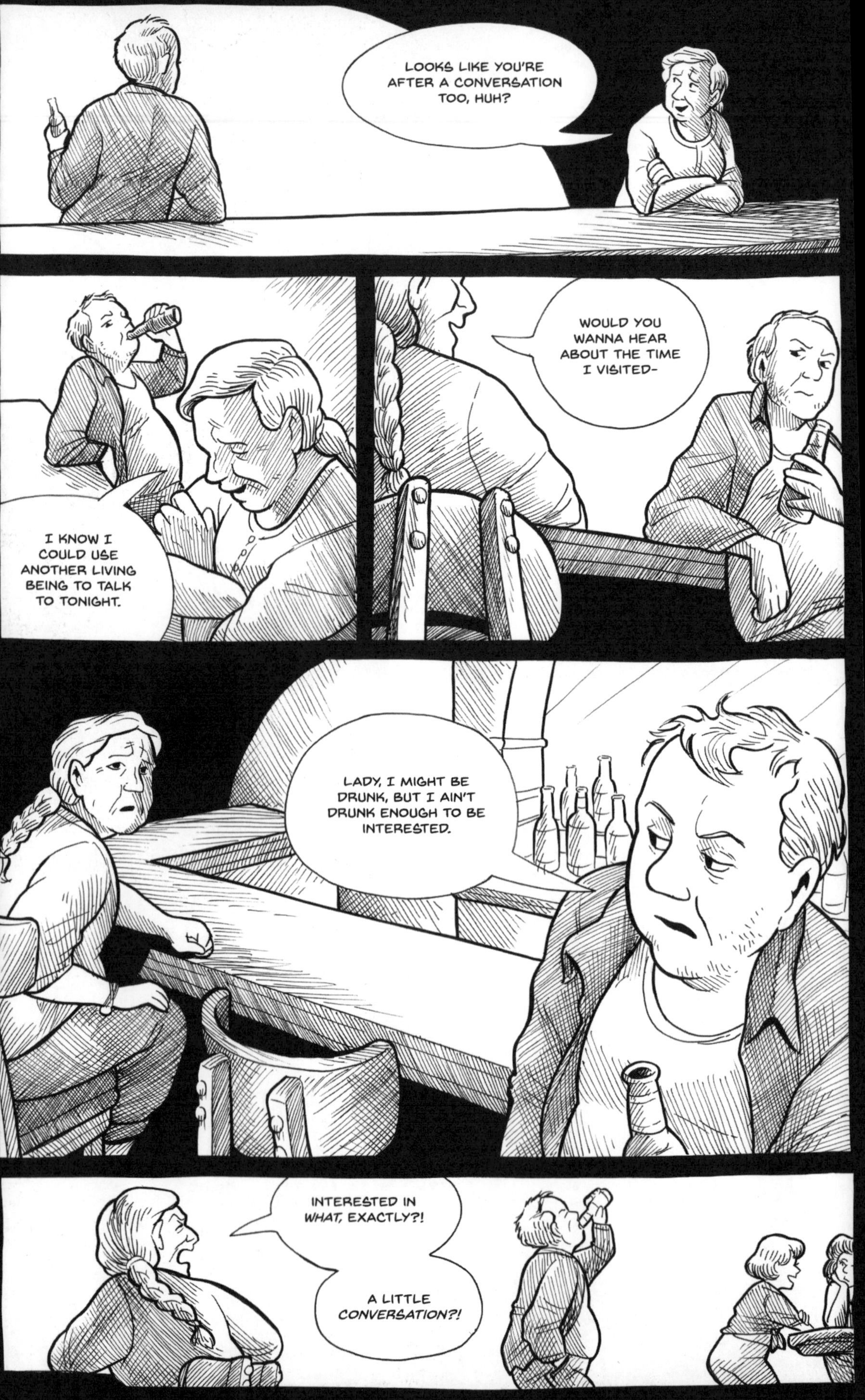
LOOKS LIKE YOU'RE AFTER A CONVERSATION TOO, HUH?
I KNOW I COULD USE ANOTHER LIVING BEING TO TALK TO TONIGHT.
WOULD YOU WANNA HEAR ABOUT THE TIME I VISITED-
LADY, I MIGHT BE DRUNK, BUT I AIN'T DRUNK ENOUGH TO BE INTERESTED.
INTERESTED IN *WHAT, EXACTLY?!*
A LITTLE *CONVERSATION?!*

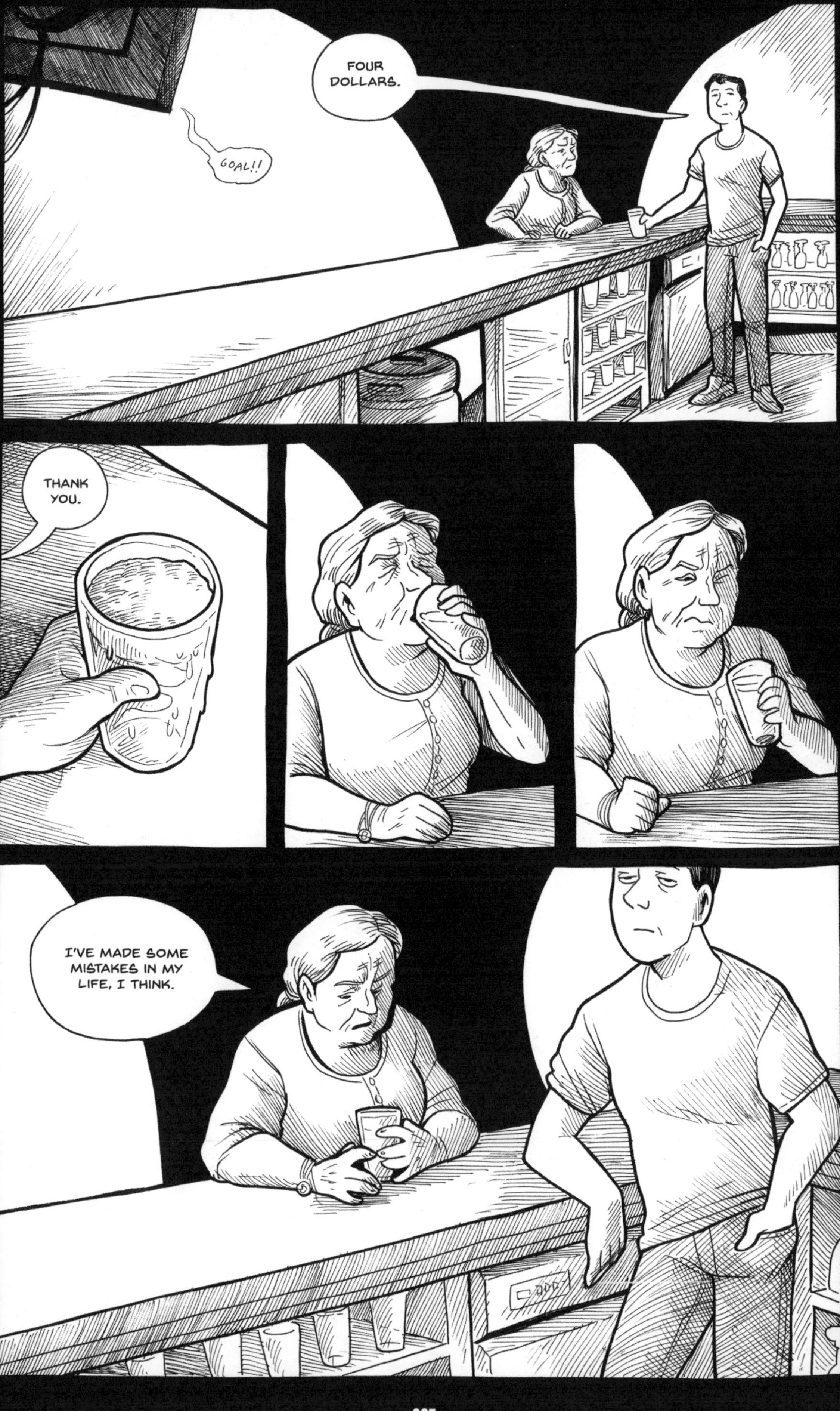
GOAL!!
FOUR DOLLARS.
THANK YOU.
I'VE MADE SOME MISTAKES IN MY LIFE, I THINK.

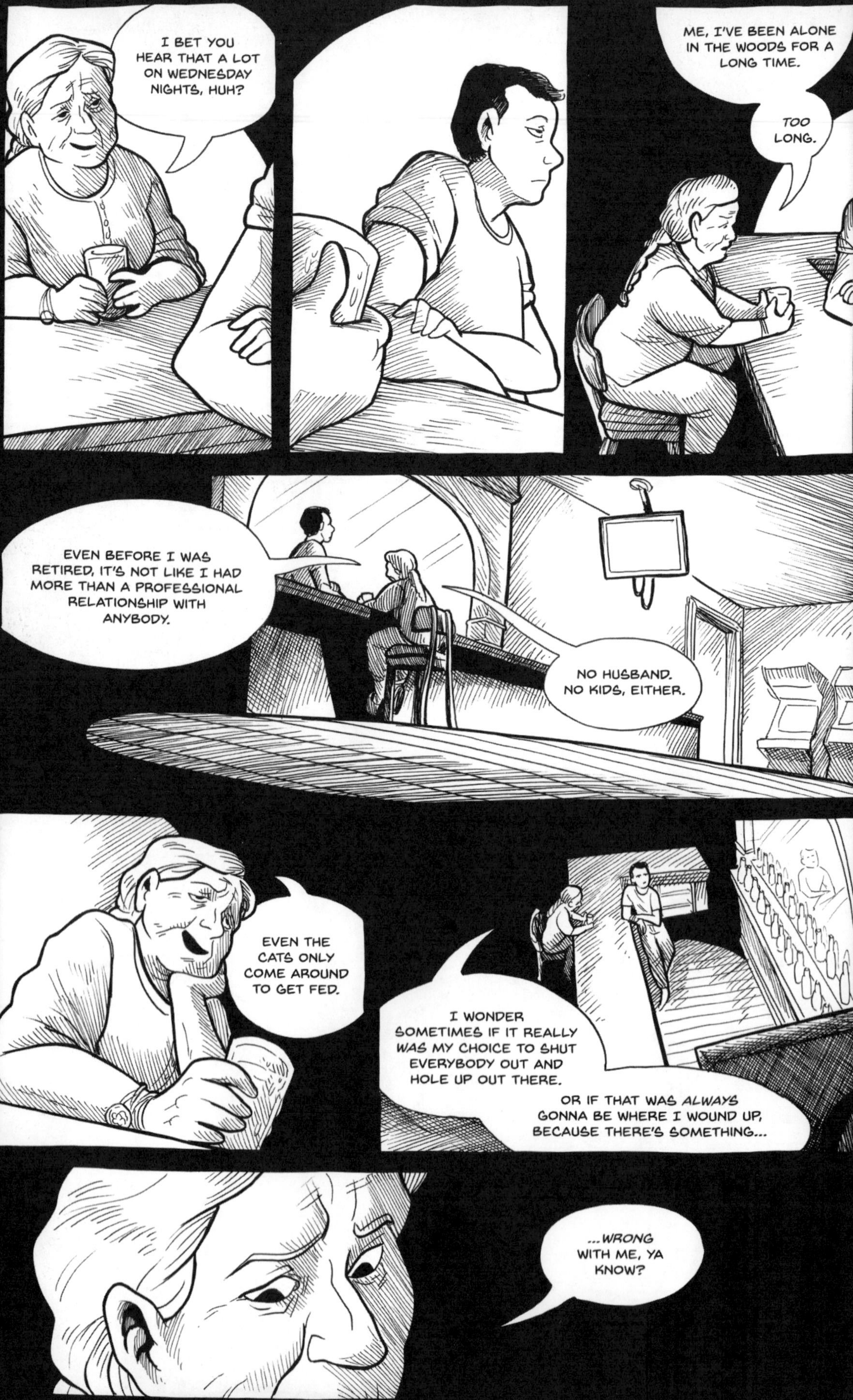
I BET YOU HEAR THAT A LOT ON WEDNESDAY NIGHTS, HUH?
ME, I'VE BEEN ALONE IN THE WOODS FOR A LONG TIME.
TOO LONG.
EVEN BEFORE I WAS RETIRED, IT'S NOT LIKE I HAD MORE THAN A PROFESSIONAL RELATIONSHIP WITH ANYBODY.
NO HUSBAND. NO KIDS, EITHER.
EVEN THE CATS ONLY COME AROUND TO GET FED.
I WONDER SOMETIMES IF IT REALLY WAS MY CHOICE TO SHUT EVERYBODY OUT AND HOLE UP OUT THERE.
OR IF THAT WAS ALWAYS GONNA BE WHERE I WOUND UP, BECAUSE THERE'S SOMETHING...
...WRONG WITH ME, YA KNOW?

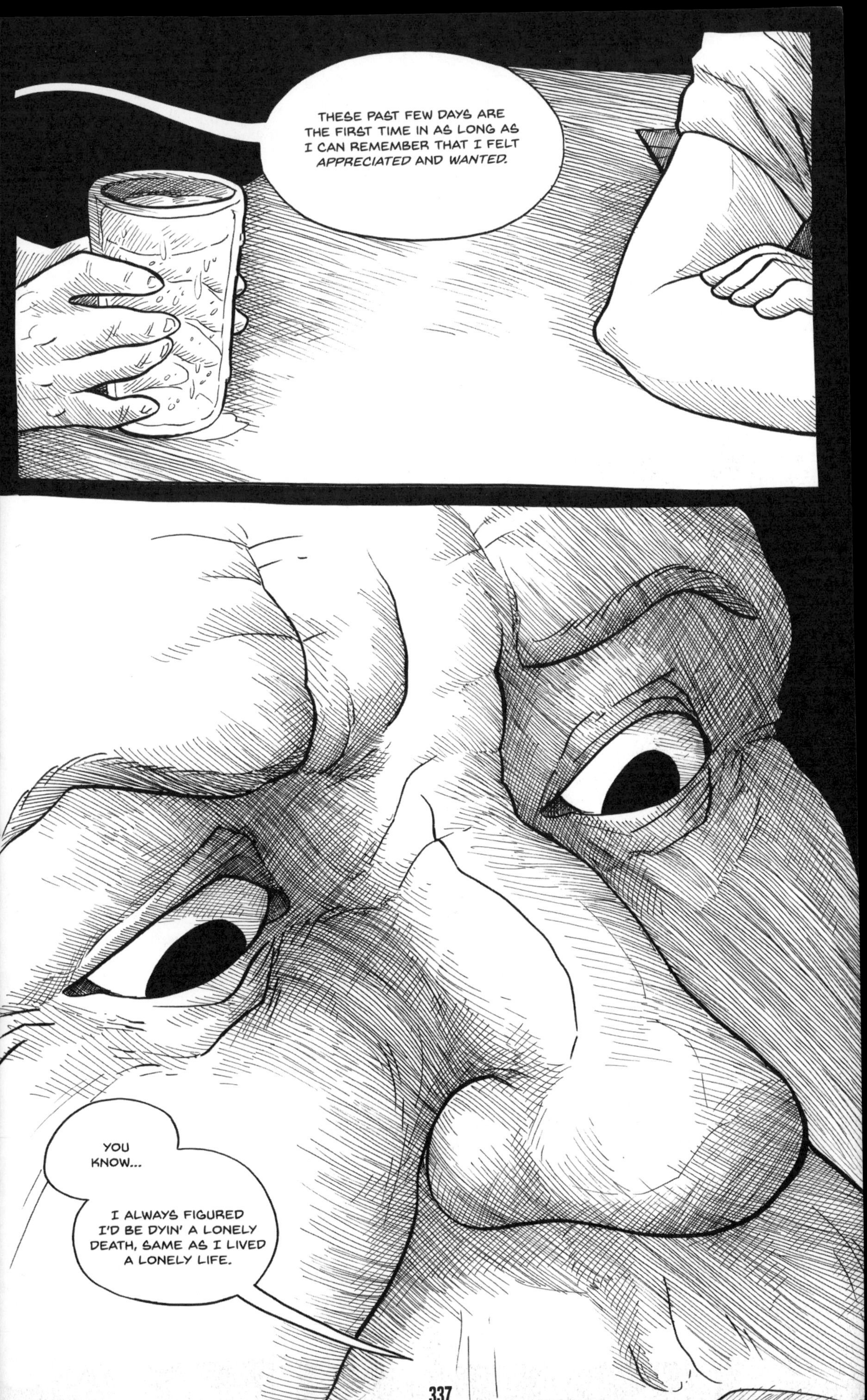
THESE PAST FEW DAYS ARE THE FIRST TIME IN AS LONG AS I CAN REMEMBER THAT I FELT *APPRECIATED* AND *WANTED*.
YOU KNOW...
I ALWAYS FIGURED I'D BE DYIN' A LONELY DEATH, SAME AS I LIVED A LONELY LIFE.

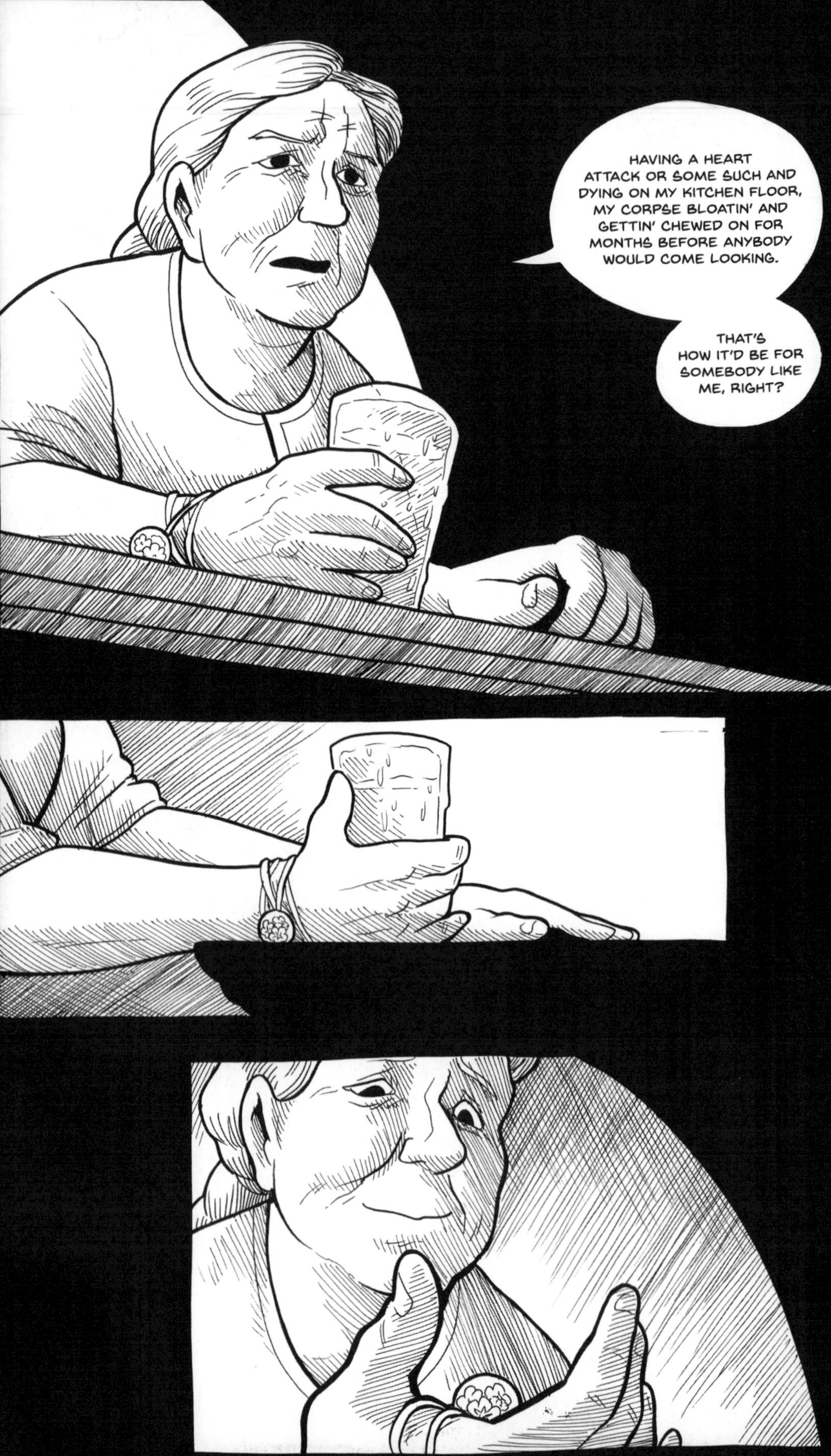
HAVING A HEART ATTACK OR SOME SUCH AND DYING ON MY KITCHEN FLOOR, MY CORPSE BLOATIN' AND GETTIN' CHEWED ON FOR MONTHS BEFORE ANYBODY WOULD COME LOOKING.
THAT'S HOW IT'D BE FOR SOMEBODY LIKE ME, RIGHT?

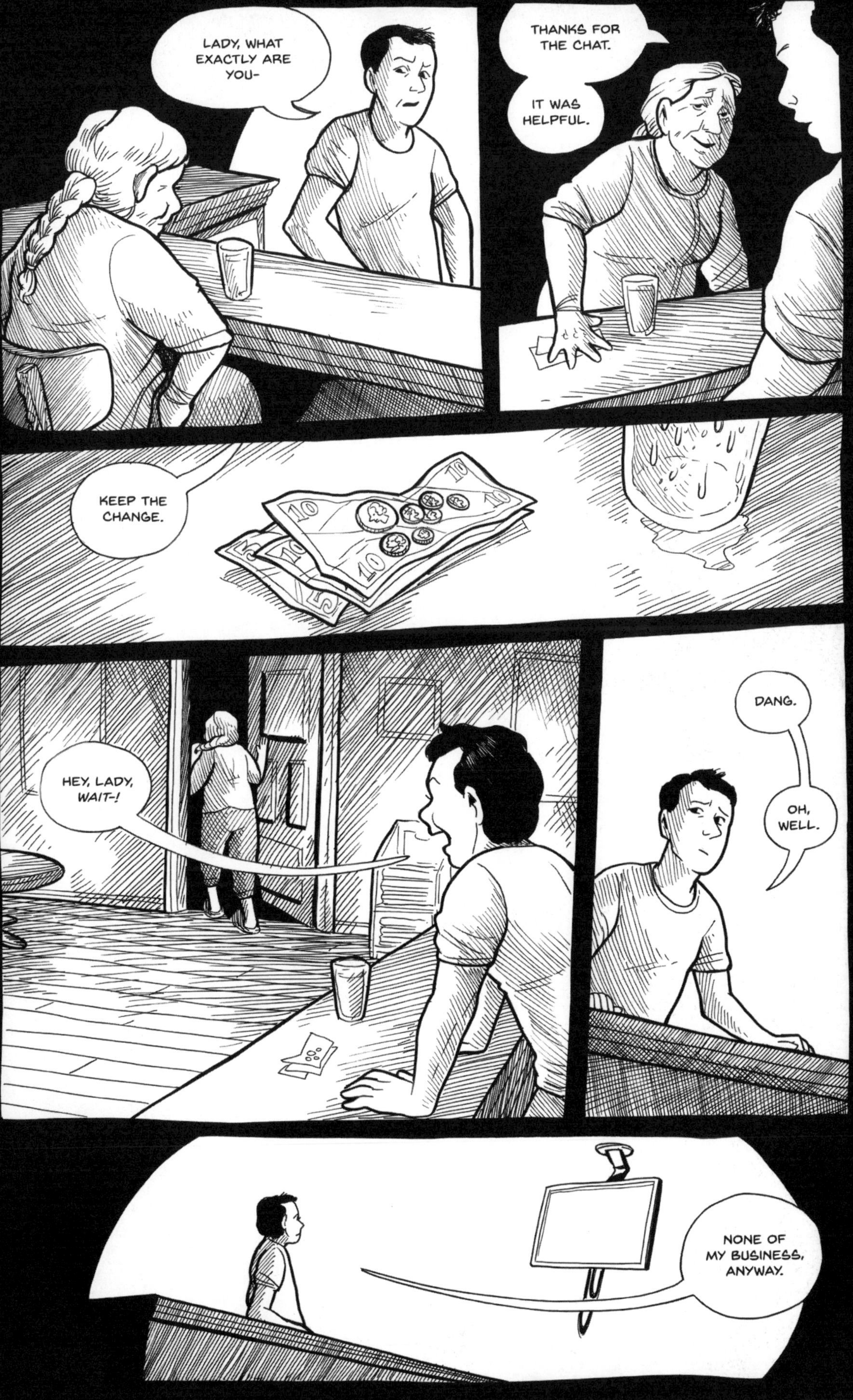
LADY, WHAT EXACTLY ARE YOU-
THANKS FOR THE CHAT.
IT WAS HELPFUL.
KEEP THE CHANGE.
HEY, LADY, WAIT-!
DANG.
OH, WELL.
NONE OF MY BUSINESS, ANYWAY.

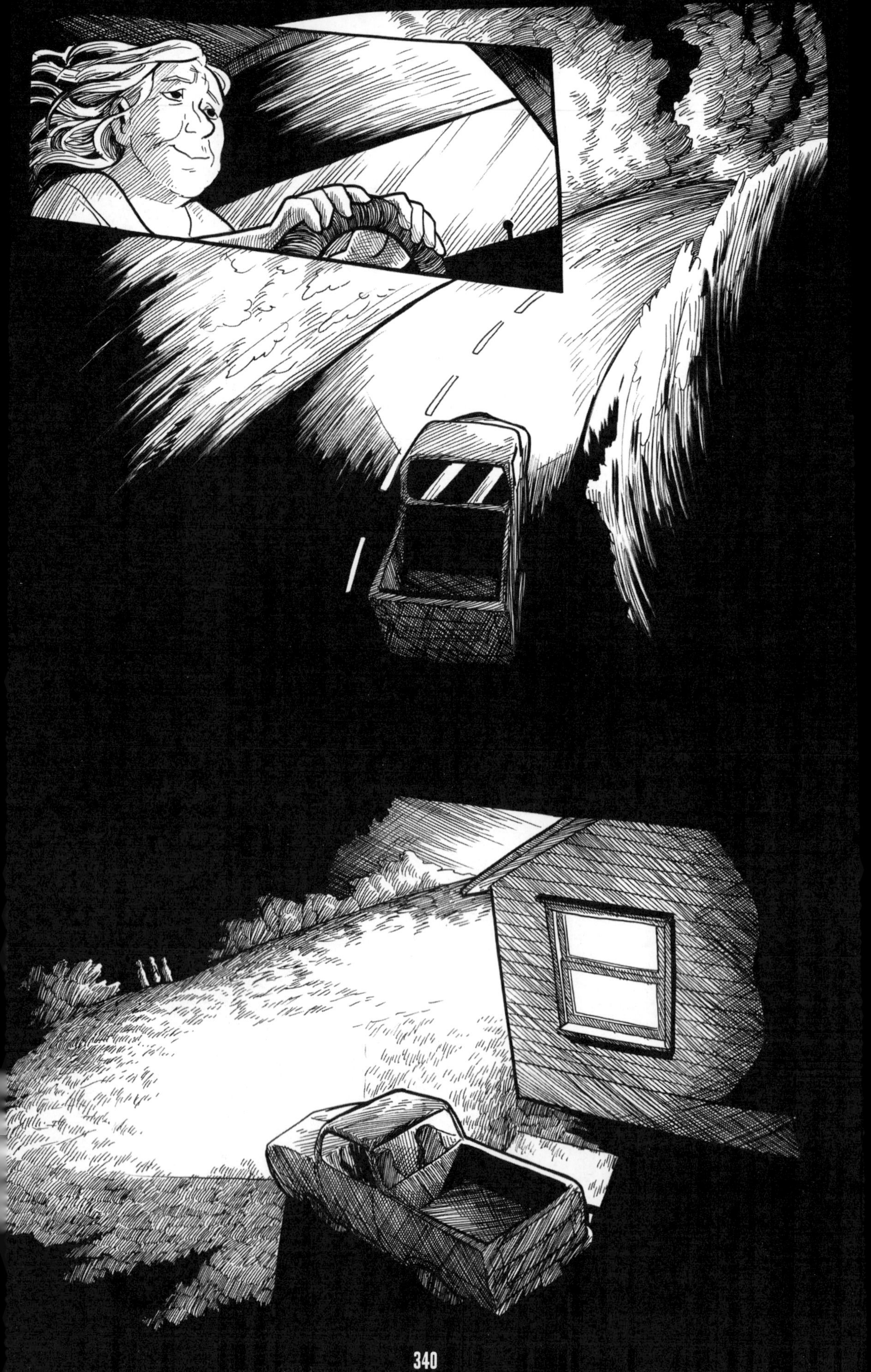

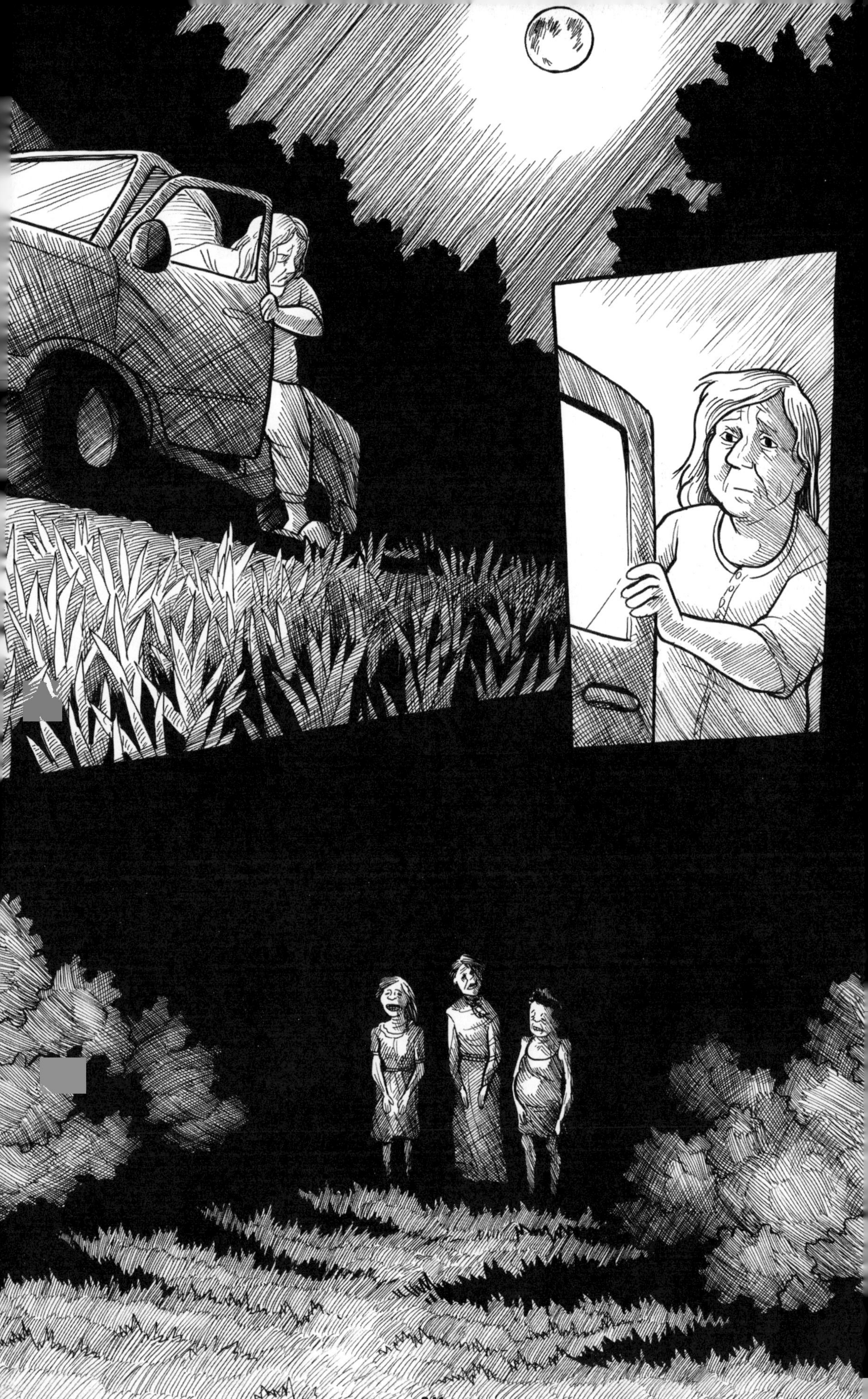

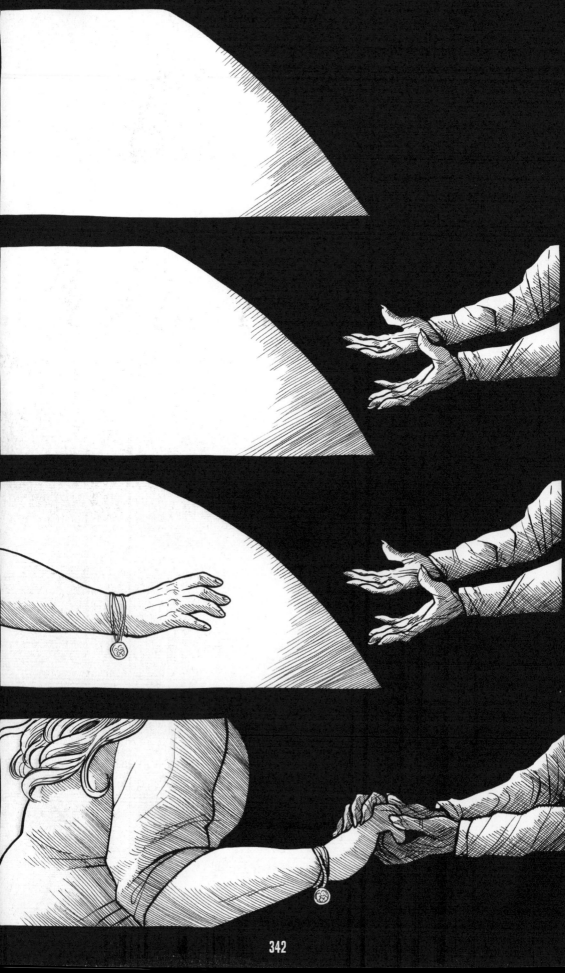

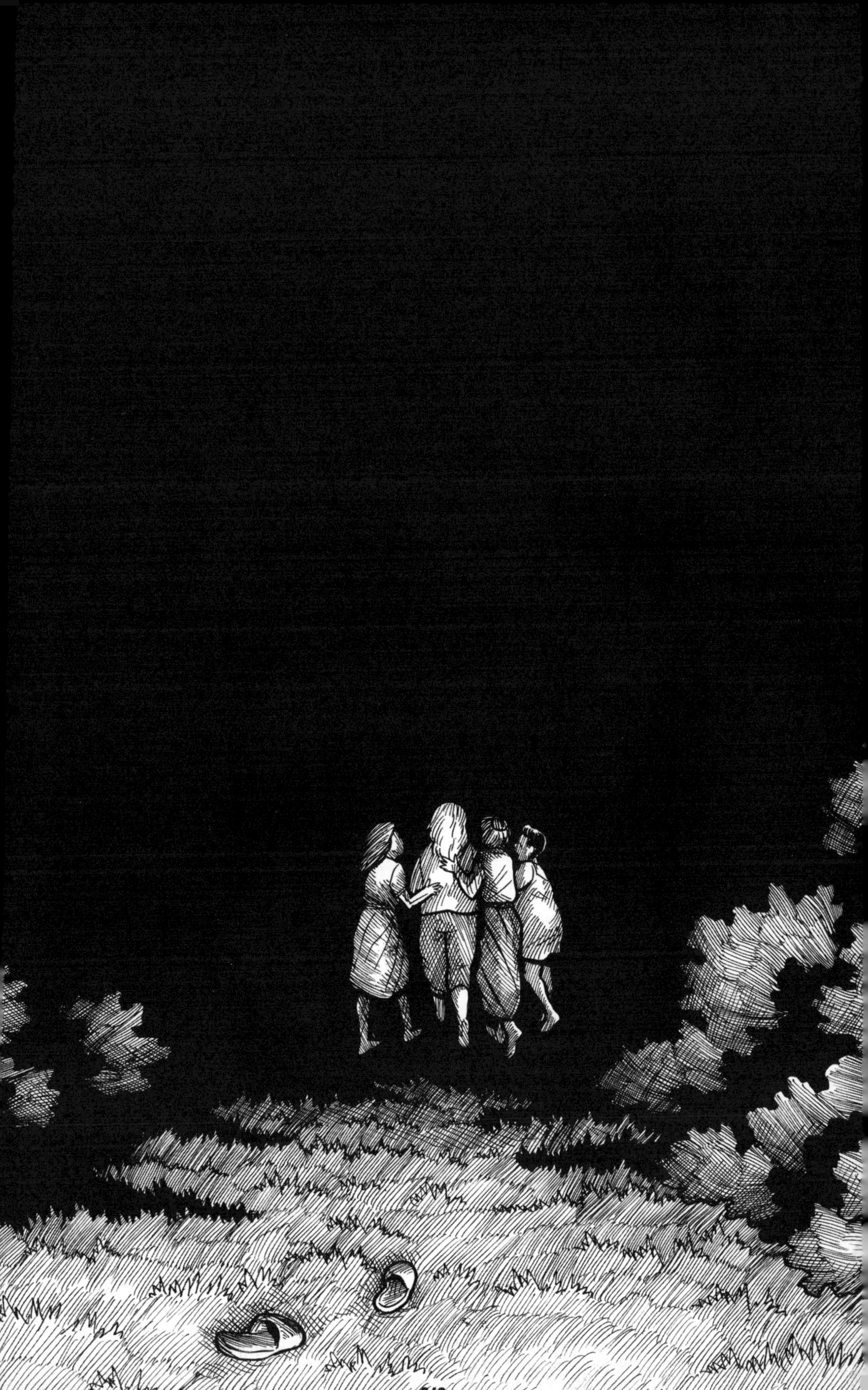

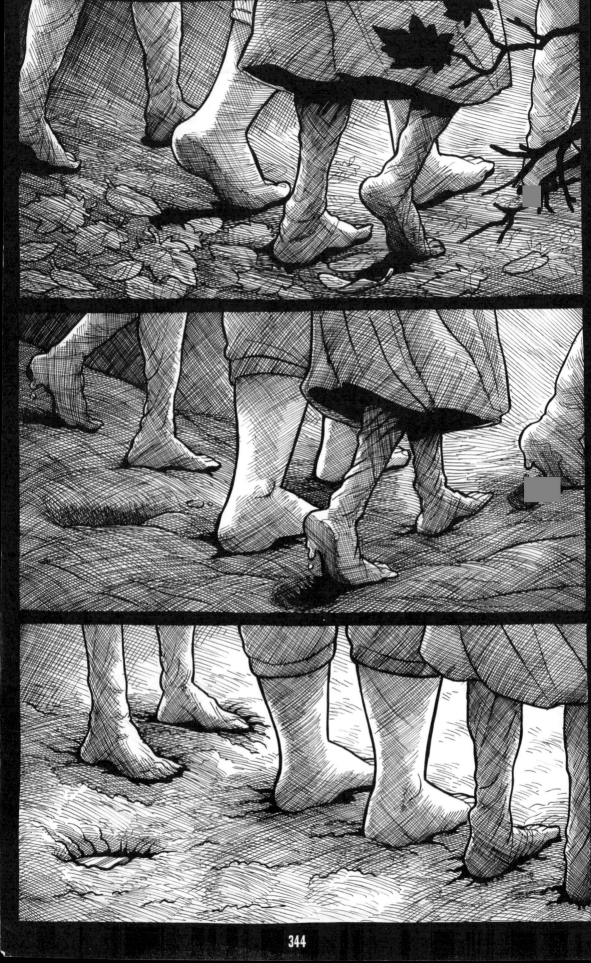

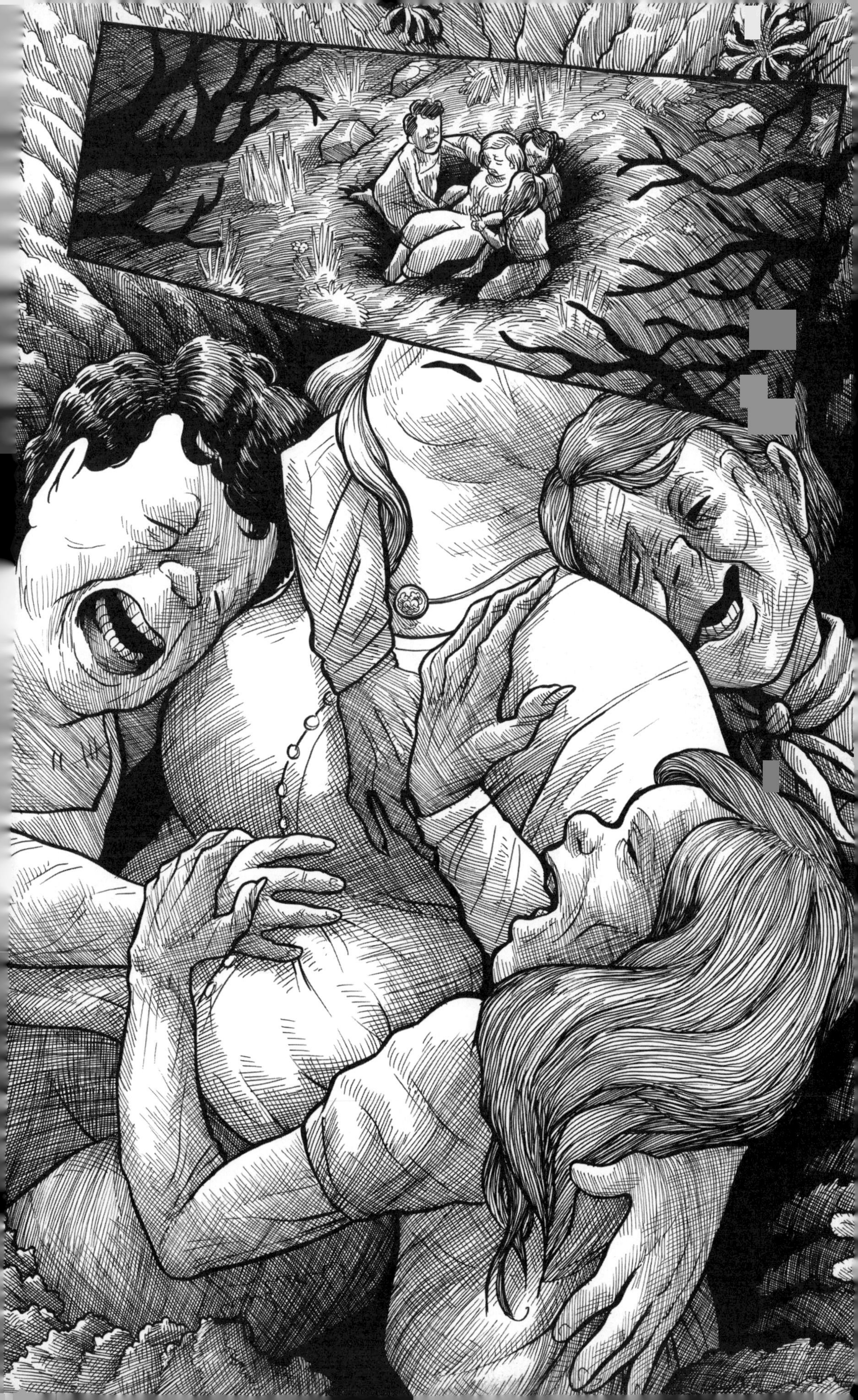

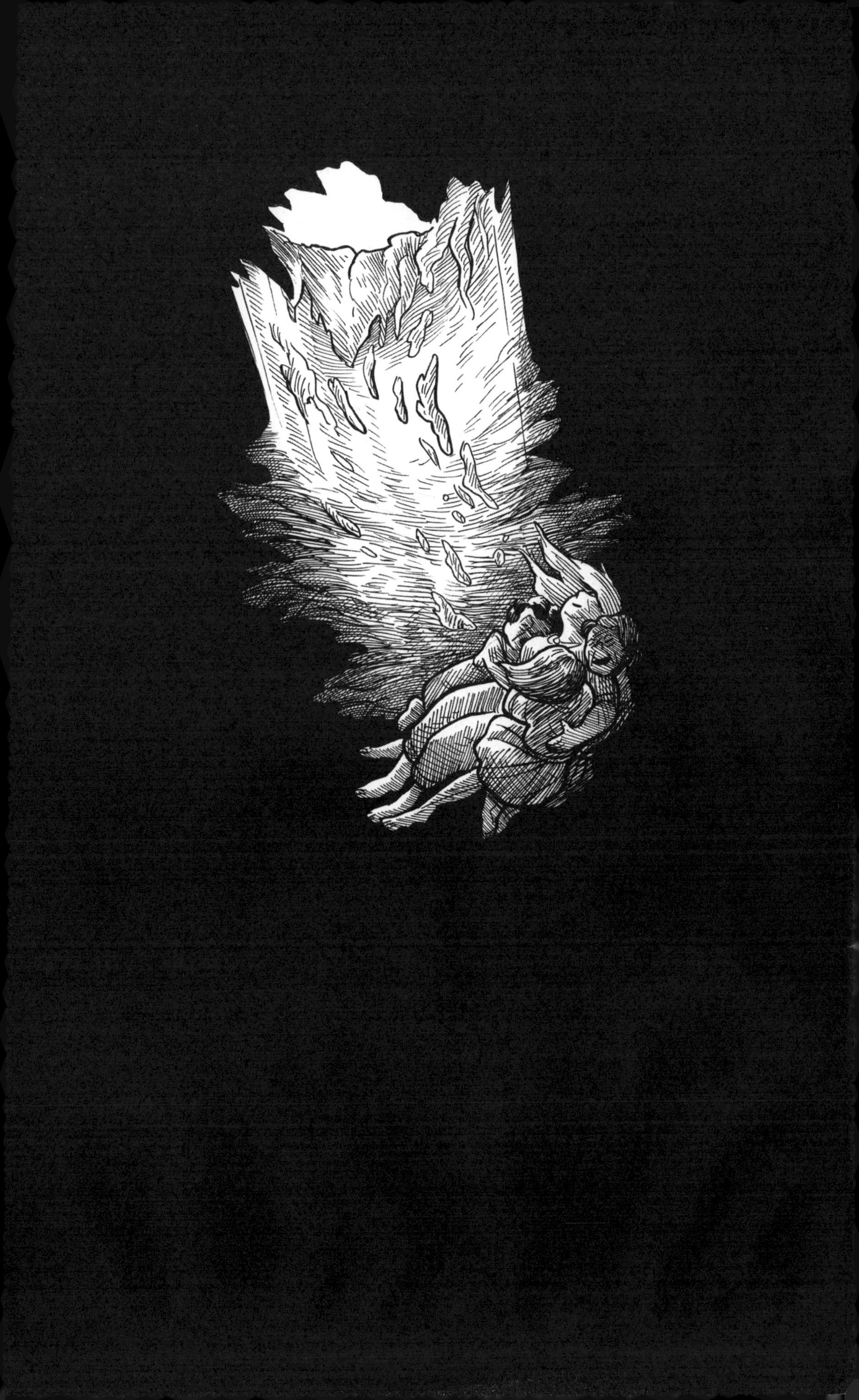

Concept Art

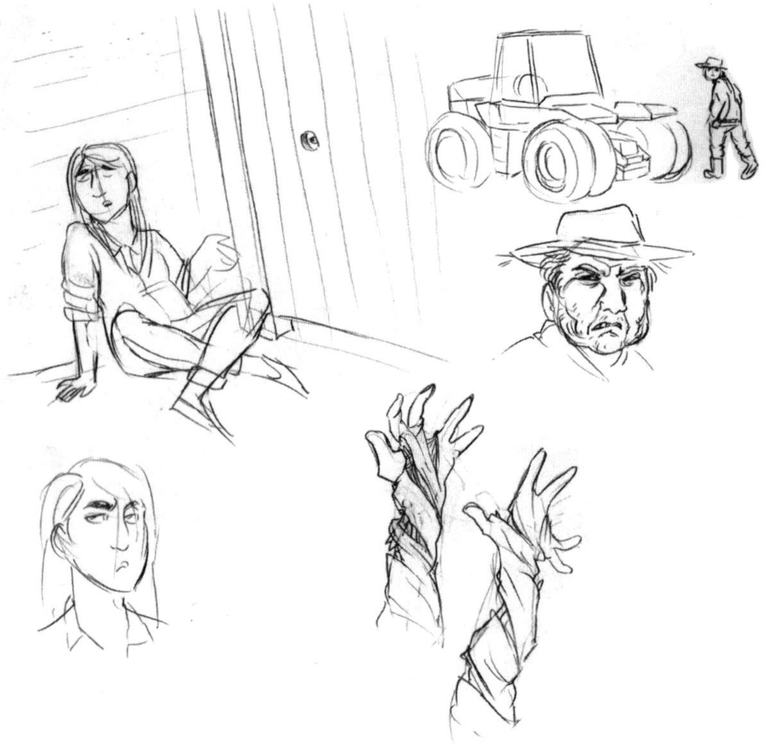

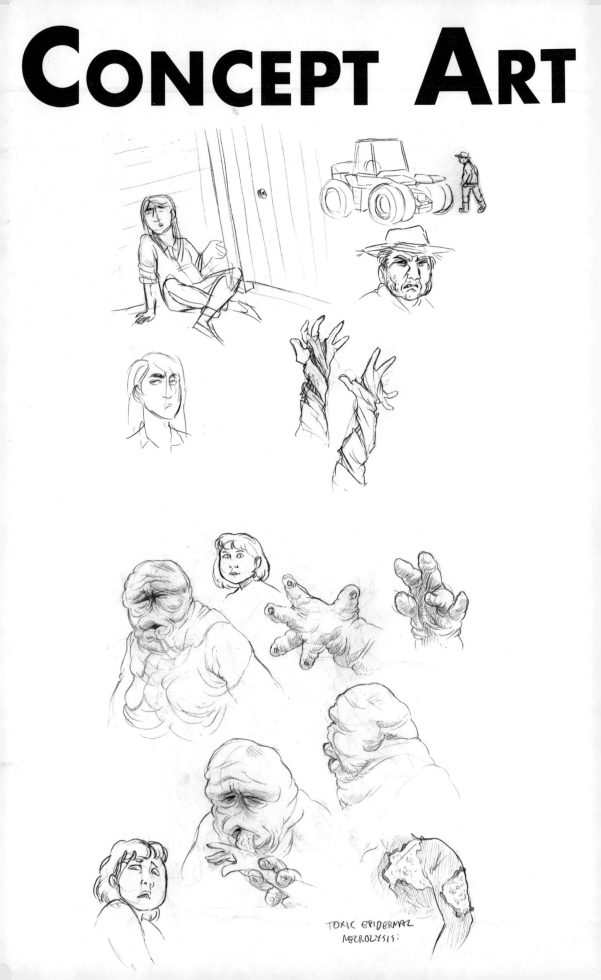

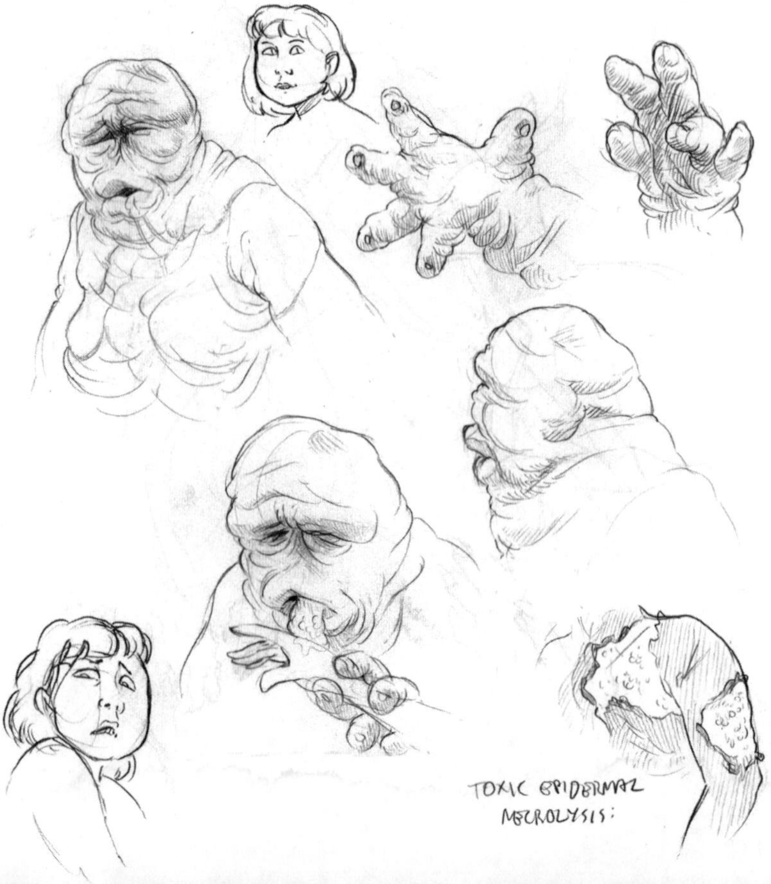
TOXIC EPIDERMAL NECROLYSIS:

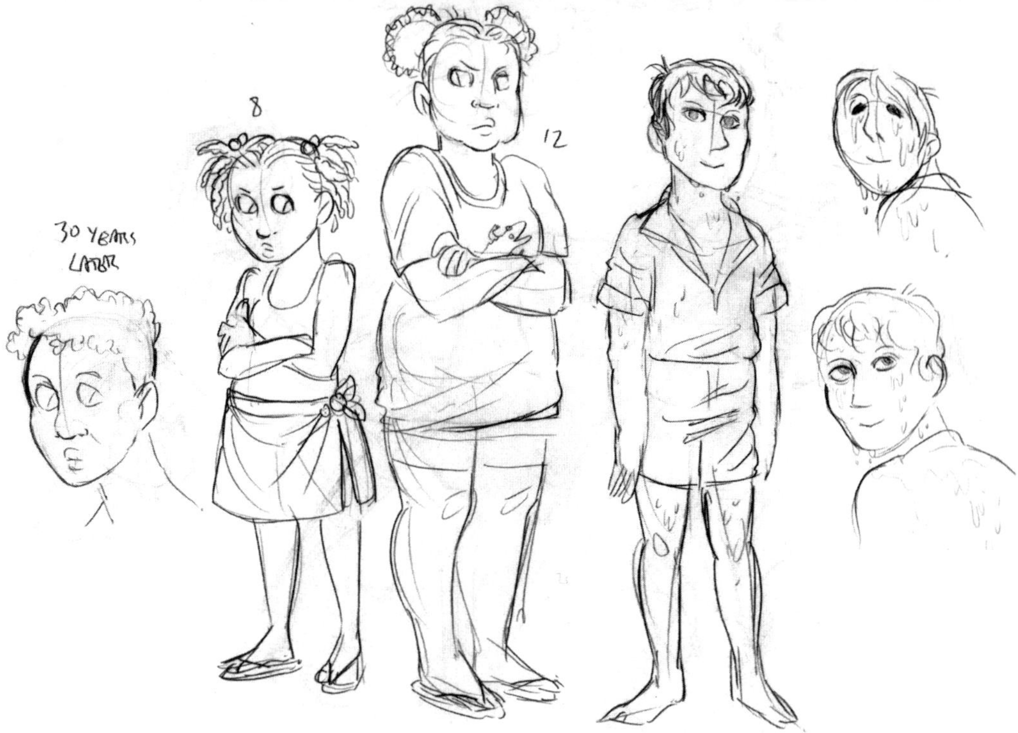
30 YEARS
LATER
8
12

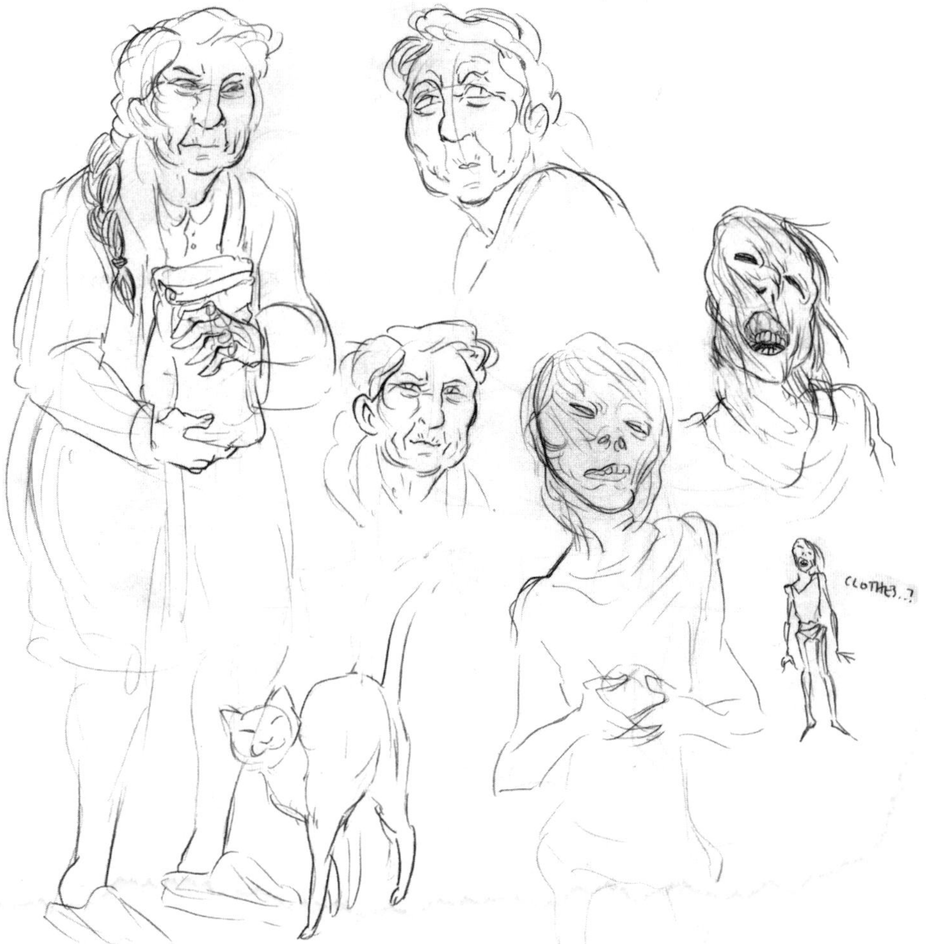
CLOTHES..?

Dedicated to my sister, for always watching out for me,
and to Tony, for being there to hold my hand when it gets dark.

And to my cat, Spoons.